Daughters of Fire

BARBARA ERSKINE

Daughters
of Fire

HarperCollins*Publishers*

HarperCollins*Publishers*
77–85 Fulham Palace Road,
Hammersmith, London W6 8JB

www.harpercollins.co.uk

Published by HarperCollins*Publishers* 2006
1

First published in Great Britain by
HarperCollins*Publishers* 2006

A catalogue record for this book
is available from the British Library

ISBN-13 978-0-00-717426-3
ISBN-10 0-00-717426-8 (hardback)
ISBN-13 978-0-00-721294-1
ISBN-10 0-00-721294-1 (trade paperback)

Set in PostScript Linotype Meridien with Photina display by
Rowland Phototypesetting Ltd, Bury St Edmunds, Suffolk

Printed and bound in Great Britain by
Clays Ltd, St Ives plc

For Diz, who started the hare.

The lamps now glitter down the street;
Faintly sound the falling feet;
And the blue even slowly falls
About the garden trees and walls.

Now in the falling of the gloom
The red fire paints the empty room:
And warmly on the roof it looks,
And flickers on the backs of books.

Armies march by tower and spire
Of cities blazing, in the fire;
Till as I gaze with staring eyes,
The armies fade, the lustre dies.

Then once again the glow returns;
Again the phantom city burns;
And down the red-hot valley, lo!
The phantom armies marching go!

Blinking embers, tell me true,
Where are those armies marching to,
And what the burning city is
That crumbles in your furnaces!

'Armies in the Fire'
A Child's Garden of Verses
           · Robert Louis Stevenson

'The evil that men do lives after them,
The good is oft interred with their bones . . .'

Julius Caesar
           William Shakespeare

Prologue

She had demanded initiation. Without it she could not be queen.

And now she was afraid. For the first time in her life she was really afraid.

Not of the ancestors amongst whose bones she sat in the dark, but of the others, the shadows, the voices, the faces from the future. Those, she had not expected.

As the last remnant of light disappeared she had crouched quite still, the only sound in the silence beyond the settling of the stones and earth with which they had blocked the entrance tunnel behind her, the thudding of her heart. She had imagined she would hear the Druid priests' footsteps as they withdrew, perhaps their whispered voices dying away in the distance, but there was nothing save an awareness of the weight of rocks and soil over her head and of the presence of the bones somewhere near her feet. Cautiously she stretched out her hands, feeling around her in the darkness. As her fingers at last met those of the woman with whom she shared the grave there was no sound but the rattle of dried bones.

Taking a deep breath she sat down, her back against the wall of limestone, and closed her eyes, waiting for something to happen. What. She didn't know.

Outside, the moors grew dark. There was no guard outside the living grave. There was no need. No one sane would stray there by day or night. It was the place of the ancestors. A place of the gods. When she was released, if she was alive and in her right mind, she would be an initiate. A member of the élite. A woman who could mediate the gods and rule the people. A woman fit to be queen. If she was dead her bones would join those around her and her spirit would roam the fells until it was called to the place of rest beyond the western seas, the land of the ever young, and thence once more to the world of men to live again.

At first the voices were indistinct – a mumbling out of the darkness. She clenched her fists in terror, straining her ears to make out the words. Slowly the meaning came and with the meaning, pictures. She saw men with war chariots forming up on the edge of the hills, their eyes cruel, their hard bodies cased in armour; she saw women weeping. She saw swords and fire and blood. She saw the landscape change – from forest to heather moor and back to forest again. She saw men plough the land, their ploughs pulled and pushed by men, and then pulled by oxen, then horses, and then strange chariots which smoked above their huge wheels. She saw flocks of gulls following the furrows age after age through famine and plenty; through war and peace. She saw her people live. She saw her people die. She saw them laugh and she saw them weep. And one voice above all others came to her clearly out of the shadows. It called her name, Cartimandua, Sleek Pony, with an accent strange to her ears. She shook her head, trying to see more clearly in the swirling mists and a woman's face swam into focus. A woman who held out her hands. Who stretched out across aeons to touch her mind. Who wanted to know who she was and what she had done. A woman who had chosen her above all others as a lesson and a story.

The tomb was growing colder. Outside, the sun was sinking into a bank of cloud. Soon it would be dark. She shivered suddenly and the mind that had reached out to touch hers drew back.

'Where are you?' Carta called out. 'Wait. Are you one of the gods?'

There was no reply.

Somewhere near her feet she heard something rustle and click amongst the bones and she gritted her teeth against a scream. For the first time she wondered if anyone would come back to release her, or would they leave her here to lie amongst the dead whilst another took up the mantle of leadership?

Another, more fitted for the role because he was a man.

1

I

'Have you any idea of what you have done to this department?'
Professor Hugh Graham threw the magazine down on the desk in
front of him. It was folded open at an article entitled, 'Cartimandua,
the First British Queen?' 'You've made us a laughing stock! And
me! You've made me a laughing stock in the academic community.'
He spoke with the soft lilt of the Scottish Borders, usually scarcely
noticeable but now emphasised by his anger.

Behind him the sun, shining in through the office window which
looked out onto Edinburgh's George Square, backlit his thick,
unruly pepper-and-salt hair and cast the planes of his weather-
beaten face into relief. 'I don't think you and I can go on working
together, Viv. Not when you clearly hold my views in such low
esteem.'

'Rubbish!' Viv Lloyd Rees was thirty-five years old, five foot four,
slightly plump and had short fiery red hair which had been cut to
stand out in a hedgehog frame around her face, emphasising her
bright green eyes. In spite of the Welsh name her accent was cut-
glass English, another fact that irritated intensely the nationalist
that resided deep in the professor's soul.

'Are you telling me that suddenly no one is allowed to have their
own opinions in this place?' she went on furiously. 'For goodness'
sake, Hugh! We study Celtic history. We are not a think tank for
some politburo!'

'No.' He leaned forward, his hands braced on the shambles of
papers and open books which lay strewn across the desk behind his
computer monitor. Somewhere under there, presumably, lurked a

1

keyboard and mouse. 'No, you are correct. We study. We examine facts. We spell them out –'

'That's all I've done, Hugh. I've spelled out some facts. Interpreted them . . .'

'Your own interpretation, not mine.'

The atmosphere crackled between them.

'Mine, as you say. It is my article, Hugh. Not yours.'

'Fictional twaddle!'

'No, Hugh. Not fictional.' Her temper was rising to match his. 'Intuitive interpretation.'

But there was more than that, wasn't there, if she was honest. He was right.

'Intuitive!' He spat out the word with utter disdain. 'Need I say more! And your book. Your much vaunted – hyped – book. Do I assume it will be along these same lines?' He gestured at the supplement lying on his desk.

'Obviously. Haven't you been sent a copy to review yet?' She met his eye in a direct challenge.

She had fought it. She had fought it so hard, that strange voice in her head, the voice she had conjured from her research. The voice that had wanted her to write the book, and now wanted her to write a play. The voice she could not tell anyone about. But its promptings had been too subtle, its information too specific to pretend it wasn't there. She hadn't managed to catch the information, to keep it out of the book, the book which was going to be published in exactly four weeks' time on 14th July. She had tried to sieve the facts, separate the known from the unknown. She had failed.

She waited miserably to see what he would say next, as she did so staring fixedly at the small box lying in a ray of sunlight in his in-tray. She did not want to meet his eye.

There was a long silence as Hugh tried, visibly, to calm himself. In his early fifties, of middle height and with deep-set, slightly slanted hazel eyes, he was a strikingly handsome man. Today he was also formidable as he glared at the woman who stood before him on the layered threadbare rugs which carpeted the floor of his small, overcrowded, first-floor study.

'Your by-line here,' he went on at last, ignoring her question, '"Viv Lloyd Rees of the Department of Pan-Celtic History and Culture at the University of Edinburgh",' – the last dozen words, normally abbreviated to DPCHC by its members and students, were

2

heavily emphasised – 'I trust that will not be appearing on this famous book of yours. I am withdrawing the funding for your research facilities. And your post here will not be renewed at the end of the year.'

Viv stared at him. 'You can't do that!' She was paralysed with shock.

'I am sure I can find a way.' He folded his arms. 'This department prides itself in scholarship, not guesswork. There is no room here for fantasists.' Leaning forward, he picked up the *Sunday Times* magazine by one corner and tossed it across the desk towards her. 'You may as well take this. I shall not be looking at it again.' He refolded his arms and sat watching her from beneath frowning sandy brows.

The knowledge that he was right in many of his criticisms, and that she was already in an agony of guilt about them, made her angrier than ever.

She had been overjoyed when he had asked her to come back to Edinburgh to work with him and accepted the lectureship and research post with eager optimism. It was a chance to put the past behind her, to start again and forward her career under the guidance of the man she most respected in their field.

The past was in Dublin. His name was Andrew Brennan and for four years she and he had had a passionate affair, an affair which she, in her perhaps deliberate naïveté, had assumed would lead if not to marriage, at least to a live-in relationship once he had obtained the divorce which he promised was only a matter of time. It never happened. Of course it never happened; had never even been on the cards. When she finally brought herself to accept the fact, she had broken it off and written to Hugh in response to a rumour that a lectureship might be coming up in his department. He had invited her to join him and she had bought a tiny flat in the Old Town with a monstrously large mortgage and put Andrew and his protestations behind her with sufficient alacrity for her to wonder just how much she had really loved him. Even so, at the beginning it was hard in many ways. Harder than she expected. She had friends in Edinburgh from her student days but the gap in her life was huge. She missed Andrew's close companionship, his unquestioned lien on her spare time, and it was this newly raw loneliness which led her to see more of Hugh Graham and his wife than perhaps she should.

Alison Graham became one of her closest friends. They confided in one another; she told Alison about Andrew; she told her about her sadness after her brother David, like their father a respected consultant paediatrician, had emigrated to Australia with his wife and their baby and she told her about her sense of utter bewildered loss after her parents had followed them five years later to Perth. Alison and Hugh had been there for her. They had supported her. They had all seen a great deal of one another and gradually she had begun to suspect that she was falling in love with Hugh. She drew back. Nothing would persuade her to threaten her friends' marriage. She went to see them less often and avoided Hugh where possible. Puzzled and hurt by her sudden rejection without suspecting its reason, Hugh had become angry. Then unbelievably, heart-breakingly, Alison had died.

His anger had not abated after she had gone, far from it, and his easy friendship with Viv had deteriorated into something like enmity in their professional relationship. She found that he had an unbearable, overweening ego. He refused to acknowledge that the study of history had changed its emphasis; that maybe scholasticism should nowadays allow itself a more popular, approachable face, and above all he refused to admit that anyone else could be good at it! The man who had been the youngest, most ambitious professor ever to head the department appeared to have sunk into staid orthodoxy.

He was returning her gaze steadily, studying her as though she were some kind of strange specimen he had found in a bell jar in a laboratory. Every line of his face was set with disapproval. The look stung.

Taking a deep breath she launched back into the fray. 'You are calling me a fantasist!' Her voice was shaking suddenly. 'May I remind you that you are the one who gave me a first-class honours degree, *Professor*.' She emphasised the word sarcastically. 'You thought my standard of work good then. You helped me get into Aberystwyth to get my Masters and then my doctorate from the University of Wales. You underwrote my application to go to Dublin and you helped me to get the position at UCLA. Then you, *you*,' she repeated, 'offered me a research grant and a lectureship here! You encouraged me to write the book!'

'And you were an excellent student. Otherwise I would never have offered you the job in my department.' He shrugged. 'And

4

you were a first-class historian when you first came back here. My friendship and my trust in you has obviously gone to your head. In your anxiety to gain recognition and self-publicity you have lost touch with reality. So you are no more use to me. I suggest you go and write romances somewhere where your claims to all this inside knowledge of Iron Age life can do no harm and leave the writing of serious history to those of us who know how to do it!'

Staring at him as he sat there Viv felt, for a moment, as she was surely supposed to, like a naughty school girl who had been caught cheating and knew it, and had then been called up before the head. She drew in a shaky breath to ward off the hurt, trying to keep her voice steady. 'So that's what this is all about. At last!' She was deliberately disingenuous. 'You're writing a book as well! Why didn't you tell me? Oh, I was supposed to guess, was I, that that is what you are doing?'

'Indeed you should, as this period is my speciality.' He threw himself back in his seat. 'It would have been a fairly easy assumption to make.' She was wearing a baggy magenta sweater and tracksuit bottoms. Just looking at her gave the professor a headache. Especially when she was angry.

'And you're writing about Cartimandua in spite of the fact that it was no secret that she is my subject!' Viv narrowed her eyes.

He shrugged. He did not mention the fact that his book was as yet barely more than a few files of notes, an outline and a chapter or two, and that it was unlikely that anyone at all beyond his editor at the university press knew about it as yet. 'No,' his tone was disdainful, 'as it happens I am not writing about Cartimandua. She would hardly merit a serious study. Whatever you claim, not enough is known about her. No, my book will be – is – a treatise on the British opposition to the Roman invasion with Venutios as its central figure.'

'Cartimandua's husband.'

'Indeed.'

She took a deep breath, trying to retrieve the situation. 'But surely that doesn't matter? There is room for both books.' She eyed him with a quizzical lift of the left eyebrow. 'And whatever you think of my article,' she glanced at the magazine lying on his desk, 'I can assure you that mine is a serious study.' That at least was true. More or less. She paused, looking at him thoughtfully. 'Can it be that you are afraid my sales will so eclipse yours that you will be embarrassed? Surely the great Professor Hugh Graham wouldn't worry about that?'

'No, strangely, I do not fear that.' He gave a grim smile. 'My book will be published by the university press. Yours, I understand, is being produced by a commercial publisher. That means you are bound to sell more copies than I do, I am sure. To an ignorant public who are not concerned with intellectual probity. No, I have given you my reason for my objections. Your research and writing are not of the standard I expect and require from someone in my department. Now, if you would excuse me, I have work to do.'

'I'm sure you do.' Viv tried and failed to keep the irony out of her voice. 'I won't keep you.' She turned to the door, still shaking with anger. Then she paused. God! She had completely forgotten why she had come to see him in the first place. Turning back, she forced herself to smile. 'Before I go, I need to ask you a favour.' Not an auspicious moment, but it was the purpose for which she had walked so unsuspectingly into the lion's den twenty minutes before. 'I wanted to ask you if I may borrow the Cartimandua Pin before you return it to the museum.' It had been a while before she had realised that was what was lying there in its box, in his in-tray. 'You won't grudge me that, at least. I am appearing on *History Discussion Night* on Channel 4 next month and I would like to show it when I talk about my book. It would interest the viewers to see a piece of jewellery contemporary with the period.'

Hugh folded his arms. 'Impossible.' It was an instant response. Unconsidered. Automatic.

'Why?' She held her temper in check with an effort.

'I've given an undertaking to the museum not to let it out of my sight.'

'But it's your property. You only loaned it to them in the first place. And it's already been out of your sight!'

'Exactly. It is a priceless artefact so I do not propose to lose track of it again.' He bristled. The pin had been presented to his archaeologist father by Sir Mortimer Wheeler in the 1950s after the excavation of the fortifications at Stanwick.

'So priceless in fact that rather than keep it in the department safe, you've chucked it in your in-tray next to your stapler.' Gesturing towards it, Viv took a deep breath. 'I'd take better care of it than that, Hugh! After all, I'm not contemplating melting it down.'

She reached over and picked up the transparent Perspex box in which the enamelled pin nestled in its protective packing.

'Put it down!' Hugh's voice was like acid. 'Don't touch it!' His father had hated the brooch. A scientist to his core, he had nevertheless had a superstitious horror of this beautiful object and refused to let anyone in his family handle, or even look at it.

'I'm not hurting it.' The naughty child in Viv had surfaced again in spite of her anger and she fought an absurd urge to stick out her tongue and dodge away from the desk out of his reach, waving the box under his nose. 'Do you think Venutios really gave it to Cartimandua?' Carefully removing the lid, she studied it closely. The light from the desklamp caught the coloured enamels and the exquisitely engraved gold as she turned it this way and that. It exuded an aura of richness and power.

'I doubt it.' Hugh's tone was repressive.

'It's very beautiful. And expensive. And the right date.'

'Put it down.' He was becoming more and more agitated.

'Think how it would capture the viewers' imagination on the telly.'

'No!'

'But you lent it to Hamish for his lecture tour.'

'That was a personal favour.'

'I only want it for one evening before you return it to the museum. It would be a personal favour to me.'

'No.'

'Because you don't like my style of writing?'

'Exactly.'

'That's childish!'

'No, it's an academic judgment. Put that box down, please.'

Her face flushed angrily. 'Do you know what – that's petty and vindictive!' Gently, almost reverently, she touched the brooch with the tip of her little finger. The enamels felt ice cold. Unnerved, she hastily fitted the lid back on and tossed the box onto his desk, where it skidded down a heap of papers and vanished into the scholarly detritus. For a second, as she touched it, she had felt an almost overwhelming sense of unease.

His visible relief when she put it down was replaced by a scowl. 'Please don't let me detain you.'

'You're being a bastard, Hugh.' She shuddered and without quite knowing why rubbed the palms of her hands on the seat of her

7

tracksuit as though to rid herself of the cloying feel of the brooch.

'Please go, Viv. I don't think we have anything else to say to each other.' Standing up angrily, he walked over to the window and stood with his back to her.

This was insane. Unbelievable! 'You can't sack me, Hugh, and you know it,' she said quietly.

'As I said, I'm sure I'll find a way.' He did not turn round.

Leaning forward, she picked up the discarded magazine supplement. Beneath it the gleam of gold and red and green caught her eye again. She glanced up at the taut shoulders of the man by the window and gave a small smile. It took a tenth of a second to slip the box into her bag.

'Goodbye, Hugh.'

He did not deign to reply. Nor did he turn round after he heard the door bang. When at last he sat down once more at his desk he did not look for the brooch; he didn't notice it had gone. He shivered. The room was suddenly very cold.

II

'I walked out at that point, Cathy. If I hadn't, I would have throttled him!'

Completely exhausted, Viv threw herself down on the sofa in the living room of Cathy French's shambolically elegant maisonette in Abercromby Place. She had not mentioned her last defiant action, the removal of a valuable artefact from the professor's study. She still could not believe that she had done it. She shook her head as she went on. 'He's turned into an utter total and complete bastard! And to think how long I've spent marking exam papers for him this last couple of weeks.' She reached out for the glass of wine Cathy had poured for her. 'What am I going to do?'

The two women sat in companionable silence for a couple of moments. Normally noisy and humorous, the dejection which had replaced Viv's fury was completely uncharacteristic.

Cathy was her complete opposite in looks. Tall and slim, her dark hair swinging just above shoulder length, dressed in a long skirt and cotton shirt, she sat facing her friend, wine glass in one hand, spectacles dangling from the other.

'Is this really irreconcilable? It sounds to me more as if he has had his nose put out of joint.'

Viv grimaced. 'Can the psychology, Cathy. I'm not one of your patients. Even if Hugh and I could agree on the history – any fragment of the history – we seem to have become incompatible personalities.' She took another sip from the glass. She loved this sprawling, two-floor flat with its beautiful large rooms, its views over Queen Street Gardens with their lovely trees in full summer leaf and its air of controlled chaotic creativity. It relaxed her. Normally. 'If he is serious my career is over. Kaput. Finished.'

'Right.' Cathy gave a rueful smile. 'I take it that's a "no" then? So,' she took a deep breath, 'you carry on to what, the end of term? The end of the academic year? Then what?'

'The semester is already over; the exams are finished. And to be honest, he can't actually sack me. Not without a specific and very good reason and he doesn't have one.' Viv sighed. 'But he can make my life impossible. He has already said he will withdraw funding for my research. Or at least make sure it's not renewed. He can do that. And he can change his mind about promoting me. I was hoping to be made Reader next year after Hamish Macleod retires. That would mean a hike in my salary which I badly need. Some of us have huge mortgages.'

Cathy leaned back and crossed her legs, ignoring the jibe. Her flat had been left to her by her father, a renowned Edinburgh doctor and former colleague of Viv's father, a bequest which made her, according to Viv, nothing more or less than a trust fund kid. 'If you give him his heart's desire and leave, what could you do instead? What has happened about the radio documentary you're writing?'

Viv let out another deep sigh. 'I've screwed that up as well. I showed my first draft to Maddie Corston at the BBC and she thinks it's rubbish.'

'Did she say that?'

'Not exactly, but she implied it. She thinks I need help getting it finished by the deadline.'

'Ah.' Cathy frowned. 'Help from who? Hugh?'

'Good God, no! He doesn't know about it. If he did it would be another nail in my coffin. No, she's suggested that I meet up with an experienced producer she knows who she thinks would help me write it.' Viv was defensive. 'Some stranger who knows nothing about Cartimandua. Who has probably never even heard of her. Someone who's going to waltz in and wave her wand and make it work even if she knows sod all about the subject.'

'If she knows about radio, Viv,' Cathy put in mildly, 'perhaps it's good advice.'

'Maybe.' Viv was still doubtful.

'Who is she? Would I know her through Pete?'

Pete was Cathy's partner and they had been together for four years. He was a travel writer and independent TV documentary producer and came with baggage: a daughter and an ex. Viv envied Cathy her easy relationship with this lovely, supportive man, but not the complications his family appeared to cause in her life. His former wife, as tall and thin as he was, compounded her many faults, apparently, by being exquisitely blonde, beautiful, elegant and clever. Her only advantage, according to Cathy, was that she had decided to live once again in her native Stockholm. Viv had never met her.

Being in the world of TV and film, Pete might well have come across the woman Maddie was suggesting. Viv rummaged in her bag for the piece of paper with the name on it.

'She's called Pat Hebden. She lives in London.'

Cathy let out a shout of laughter. 'Small world! I do know Pat. And your editor is probably right, she would be helpful. She's got a lot of experience. She's been in radio for years. She does a bit of writing and producing and she's an actress as well. She's even stayed here once or twice when she came up for the Festival.'

Viv took another sip of wine. 'It sounds like a conspiracy! So you think I should meet her? Would I like her?' She was still apprehensive.

Cathy hesitated for only a second. 'She's quite a character. I think you'd get on. And meeting would do no harm, Viv. Who knows? It might be a huge success. Why don't I ring her, or has Maddie done it already? Yes, the more I think about it, the more I think it would be a fantastic idea. OK, so writing this drama is one thing you can do to earn some money. What else?'

Viv thought. 'Well, there is the book of course, but that's not going to make me a fortune. Otherwise not much. I work in a small world, Cathy. Hugh could pretty much scupper me. All he needs to do is put the word round that I'm trouble or unreliable or a useless historian and no department would look at me.' Putting down her glass she slipped off the sofa onto the floor and reaching up for a cushion, wedged it behind her head. 'I can't believe this has happened, Cathy! I can't believe just reading an article can turn him into an enemy like this!' Purring, the large tabby cat which had been watching the proceedings from the arm of the sofa leaped heavily into her lap and settled down.

Cathy eyed him fondly. 'Pablo knows success when he sees it. He is giving you his seal of approval.'

'Soft old thing.' Viv scratched the cat's ears.

'Surely there's more to this than just an article.' Cathy raised an eyebrow. 'Are you sure you haven't antagonised Hugh in some other way?'

Viv shrugged. 'I suppose I might have, inadvertently.' She had been so pleased for her parents when they had left Britain. Envied them their new exciting life, had even been out to see them twice. That was the problem. They never stopped trying to persuade her to follow them down under, but how could she? Her career, her interests, and her obsessions were all tied to the world of the Ancient Celts. Hugh had understood. They had been close, then. It was her fault she had fallen in love with him; and it had been her decision to erect a barrier between them.

'We used to get on well,' she said wistfully, 'but if I'm honest we haven't for a while now.' She didn't elaborate. 'And the trouble is, I'm going to be so vulnerable. If Hugh reviews this book he will trash it. He and his cronies in the academic world will rubbish everything I've said. And if he doesn't review it everyone will want to know why. Either way I'm sunk.'

'Then you'll have to fight him.' Cathy grinned amiably. 'Come on, lady, where is that feisty female who stormed in here just now spitting nails? And you know as well as I do,' she added, 'being completely cynical about it, that the more controversial the book is, the more you two row in public, the better it will sell. When are you going to give me a copy, by the way?' With a rueful laugh she slipped down onto the floor to be on the same level as her guest and topped up both their glasses once more. Pablo stood up, stretched and stepped carefully across the table to sit instead on his mistress's knee. 'So, remind me. Why is this book so controversial?' she went on. 'What is so shocking about it that it has wound him up like this?'

11

Apart from the facts that weren't facts, you mean. The details I have tried so hard to weed out which shouldn't be there because they are not part of the historical record. The 'fictional twaddle' which Hugh had spotted at once! Viv didn't say it. Instead she shook her head adamantly. 'The only shocking thing is that I have had the temerity to finish it ahead of the book Hugh is writing himself!'

'Yours is about Cartimandua and the Celtic tribe called the Brigantes, right?'

'And it turns out that Hugh's is about Venutios. Her husband!' Viv scowled. 'Two different views on Iron Age Britain around the time of the Roman invasion in AD 43.'

'But surely,' Cathy took a sip of wine thoughtfully, 'that shouldn't matter, should it? Won't people be interested in the two different stories?'

'You'd think so.' Viv sniffed. 'And they are very different.' That much at least she would admit. 'I'm coming from a woman's point of view, writing about a controversial queen. The antithesis of Boudica. A gutsy, clever Celtic queen, yes, but she cosied up to the Romans and because of that she is – was – regarded by many, including her husband, as a traitor. A quisling.'

'Ah.' Cathy eased the purring cat into a more comfortable position on her knees. 'And Hugh takes the opposite position to you.'

'In everything. He is writing about a man who is regarded as a patriot because he opposed Rome, and about war and military tactics and stuff like that.'

'I still don't see why that should matter. Surely both points of view are valid?'

'In a rational world, yes.' Viv grabbed the bottle of wine and poured herself a refill. She stood up and walked over to the window. 'I've blown it. He used to respect me. He was impressed by my research. He encouraged me to do my first TV show. We used to get on so well.' She heard the wistful note in her own voice and frowned, despising herself for it. He used to like me. That was what she had been going to say. And I used to like him. A lot. Why was she so angry that he had seen through her? Had she really expected him not to react to that article? And when – or if – he read the book, had she really thought he would give it his seal of approval? She took another swig from the glass. 'He's jealous, of course.'

12

'Of your success?'

'Yes. Of my success. He hates it that I've appeared on TV more than he has. And that they've profiled me in the *Sunday Times* magazine with the article based on my book. And that I'm going to be in another programme – a discussion programme on Channel 4 –' She broke off abruptly and glanced at her bag, lying on the coffee table. The box with the two-thousand-year-old brooch inside it was in there, lying in the bottom somewhere amongst the litter of her possessions. She hadn't taken it out since she had thrown it into the bag; hadn't been able to believe what she had done.

'You have to stand up to him, Viv.' Cathy was quietly insistent as she sat stroking the sleeping cat. 'You can't go on letting him get to you like this.'

'No.' Viv turned back to the window. 'No, I know I can't. I'm just not sure what I'm going to do about it. I have a copy of the book for you, Cathy, of course I have. Signed and everything. You must read it and tell me what you think.'

III

Pat Hebden was sitting slumped on the arm of the sofa in the living room of her small Victorian house in Battersea, staring into space, her mobile still in her hand. David Roach, her agent, had called her with the news as soon as he heard it. 'I'm so sorry, Pat. I thought it was in the bag. It was so you, darling.'

The woman who had got the TV part was fifteen years her junior. 'But I'm the right age, David. I have the experience. The part was *me*.'

'I know, darling. I can't believe it either.' He had a slight American intonation. Fake. She knew he hailed from the East End of London. 'But we'll find the right part for you. It's out there somewhere. It will just take a little bit longer.' Ever pragmatic – and anodyne. She could hear the shrug. And the unspoken words: very few parts for women your age, darling. Unless you're a character actress and the public know you. You've spread yourself too thin, that's the problem. Too many irons in the fire.

She was still sitting staring into space five minutes later, disappointment washing through every fibre of her body. With a groan she stood up at last. Damn it, she wasn't that old. Mid-fifties. Could pass for forty. Or less. With make-up. A lot of make-up. She chuckled wryly. Who was she kidding? They were right. She'd have been lousy in the part.

As she reached for her mobile again her eye fell on the notepad on the table, half hidden under yesterday's *Guardian*. Pulling it out, she stared down at it. ***Cartimandua,*** it said. **Queen. Romans. Celts. Viv Lloyd Rees. Play? Docu-drama? <u>Ring Maddie Corston</u>!!!**

The way Maddie had described the story there was melodrama. Romance. War. A strong story. Commissioned. Overdue. A writer with huge talent but who had never written for radio before and was in need of a strong guiding hand. And maybe a female lead.

Glancing up, she caught sight of herself in the mirror and frowned. Fantastic voice. Good face. Golden hair. Well, greyish with expert highlights! Just the right height – five foot five – well, perhaps five foot four if she forgot to stand up straight. Excellent cheekbones. Unconsciously she tilted her head slightly. She used reading glasses now, she had to admit, but that didn't matter for in her head she had ceased to see herself as an actress. Now she was an academic. A mentor. The calm, skilled hand on the rudder which would bring a play first to the radio, then, who knows, to the TV. Big Screen? Stage? Maddie had hinted at an inexperienced and vulnerable author and a background of academic rancour. War behind the scenes. Perfect publicity. In the mirror the face she was scanning smiled. Ever optimistic, the defeat was forgotten. Ahead was a new scheme. A scheme she could get her teeth into. And one that involved a trip to Edinburgh.

Outside it was a glorious summer day, though you wouldn't guess it from here. The cherry trees which lined the narrow road were in full leaf and the air had a faint trace of freshness in it; a strong breeze from Battersea Park and the river beyond it, cutting through traffic fumes and the blankets of diesel which spewed down from the low-flying aircraft shaking the house every couple of minutes on their way to Heathrow. She glanced round the small narrow rectangular room which comprised virtually the whole of the ground floor area of her tiny house. Light seeped fitfully through the heavy lace curtains she kept constantly drawn across the front window to keep prying eyes out. The room looked tired and dusty. She ran a finger over the table ruefully and examined the ensuing faint line with a sigh. She was between cleaning ladies at the moment. She was always between cleaning ladies. She had caught the last one shooting up in her kitchen. Shame. She had been a nice, bright girl. Trustworthy, or so she had thought. On the slippery slope, so it turned out, from the third year of a degree course in modern languages to, no doubt, a horrible death under a bridge somewhere. Two days after the girl had gone the house had been done over. Pat sighed. She knew it was Sarah because of the things taken. Not the treasures which would have hurt so much. Not even her grandmother's gold bracelet which she had left so carelessly on the table in her bedroom. Just the electronic stuff which could be replaced. The cash from the kitchen cupboard and the silver candlesticks which she and Sarah had agreed were really rather vulgar.

She had changed the locks now, finally made up her mind to install security bars over the front windows, and acknowledged a huge reluctance to become involved with yet another personality who would bring their problems to her door while vaguely pushing her vacuum up and down and flicking the dust from one surface to watch it settle on another. What she really wanted was to leave London for a bit.

'Maddie?' She had picked up the phone, almost without being aware of the fact. 'I've given your suggestion some thought and I'd love to come and discuss it.'

2

I

Next morning, Viv found herself pacing up and down her living room thinking about the brooch. She had hidden it in the back of a drawer in her desk when she came in the night before, tucking it well out of sight.

She had to give it back. She couldn't keep it. She shivered. She didn't want to keep it. But how was she to return it without admitting what she had done?

The overnight rain had blown away and watery sunlight pooled across the rugs on the floor warming her as she came to a halt, arms folded, staring out of the window across the rooftops. She loved this view; being part of the historic heart of the City, so near the castle. It was for this that she tolerated the narrow twisting flights of stairs, the stone landings, the need to park her car so far away, the walk back up the steep hill in the evenings to the small alleyway off the Lawnmarket, her arms full of books, her shoulder weighted by the strap of her computer case. She had set up her desk on the far side of the room, knowing that if she sat in front of the window she would do no work, lost in dreams amongst the grey slates, the chimneys, the odd spot of colour from a flower pot on a window sill or rooftop oasis, the torn rags of smoke, the wheeling birds settling, sleeping, rising again into the air.

Behind her, her desk was neat. Tidy. The rejected manuscript of the play stacked carefully. The textbooks back on their shelves. The box files neatly lined up on the floor. In front of her the sky was the colour of a Canaletto lagoon.

The book itself was finished. Edited. Printed. Jacketed. There was a box full of copies on the floor beside the bentwood rocker near the door into the kitchen. She ought to be feeling content. Excited. Satisfied. One project complete, another on the drawing board. Instead she was on edge, worried. And guilty. Guilty about her research methods and guilty about the pin and worried about having to collaborate on the play. Collaboration was not something she was eager to contemplate. Especially not if it involved confessing her research methods to someone else.

But then the play was not going to work without help.

She gave a deep sigh. She had a thousand things to do, all the things which had been put on hold as she coped with lecturing, tutoring her students and writing a 231-page book – plus ten pages of notes and bibliography followed by two major articles, one for the *Sunday Times* and one for the *History Magazine*, to say nothing of marking the end of year papers for her first-and second-year students. She needed to buy some shoes; she needed to have her hair cut – she ran her fingers through the wild untidy red mop. She needed to sort out her finances, and now on top of all that she needed to start this bloody rewrite, so why was she standing, almost paralysed with uncertainty, staring out of the window?

The answer came as a whisper in the corner of her mind. The voice, the increasingly powerful voice she had been fighting for the last few months had come back, echoing to her over unimaginable distances. She felt an uneasy shiver tiptoe down her spine. She had been so sure it would go away once the book was finished. But it hadn't. If anything it was more insistent than ever. And now it was beginning to frighten her.

The sound of her doorbell distracted her from her thoughts. There was one good thing about living on the top floor of a six-storey tenement house. No one was going to arrive without a good reason for being there.

Opening the door she found herself face to face with Steve Steadman, one of her post-graduate students. Calm, reliable, and universally popular in the department he was, she had to admit, at the moment, also one of her favourite people. He was a good-looking man in his early thirties, tall and sturdy, with a thatch of fair hair and a weathered, ruddy skin liberally sprinkled with freckles. He was also one of the very few people of her acquaintance who wasn't completely out of breath after climbing the stairs to her front door.

17

'Hi, Viv.' He was holding a copy of *Cartimandua, Queen of the North.* 'I hope you don't mind me dropping by, but I wondered if you'd sign it for me.'

She stared at it, frozen to the spot. 'Where did you get that?' Then she relented. 'Sorry. Of course I'll sign it. Come in. It's just that it's not in the shops yet.' She grabbed his arm and drew him inside the room. 'I've got a bone to pick with you, Steve.'

Before he had a chance to reply she had gestured him towards the rocking chair as she went to hunt for a pen on her desk. 'Why didn't you tell me that Hugh was writing about Venutios?'

Steve frowned. 'I had no idea that he was.'

She turned to face him, pen in hand. 'Are you sure?'

He nodded. 'I'm surprised he hasn't told me.' His voice wavered slightly as he caught sight of her face. 'You didn't know either, I take it?'

She sighed. 'No. So, where did you get the book?'

'Hugh gave it to me.' He sat down on the edge of the rocking chair, balancing easily as he stuck his long legs out in front of him.

'So, it's a review copy.' She gave a wry smile.

It was rapidly dawning on Steve that he was tiptoeing around a minefield. 'I suppose he is sent so many . . .' The comment trailed away as he began to see only too clearly that he had fallen into the Professor's trap. 'Go and ask her to sign it for you,' he had said, with a gleam in his eye which Steve now suspected had been purely malicious. 'She's probably going to resign some time during the summer so you won't be seeing much more of her, and I'm sure she would like to think she has a fan.'

Viv was riffling through the book. Had it been read? She was almost afraid she would find red lines striking out paragraph after paragraph – a phenomenon his students grew used to as the terms progressed. There were no marks that she could see. She breathed a sigh of relief and turning back to the title page, signed it with a flourish.

Steve took the book as she handed it back and tucked it into the tatty canvas bag he had dropped beside his chair. 'The Prof hinted that you were thinking of resigning. It's not true, is it? We'd miss you tremendously if you did.' The remark was warm; totally genuine.

'No, I'm not leaving, Steve, however much the Professor might wish it,' she said firmly. 'That was his little joke.'

Steve shook his head. 'I'm glad! I must have misunderstood him!'

'No, you didn't misunderstand, Steve. Don't worry about it. I'll still be here next year.' She paused as a thought occurred to her. Hugh had passed the book on unread because he was not going to review it. He didn't think it was worth the bother. He probably hadn't even glanced at it. She stood for a moment chewing her lip. Was she angry or relieved? It was going to be an insult, either now or more publicly later. But then, what had she expected? Had she really thought she would get away with it? Had she expected him to act as anything other than a curmudgeonly, narrow-minded, devious chauvinist? She grinned broadly. Even silently thinking the invective made her feel better. 'I hope you enjoy the book, Steve.' Once he had read it he would know, of course, why Hugh didn't rate it. But then everyone was going to know soon.

Steve was smiling. 'I've read it already. I thought it was excellent.' He showed no sign of moving from the rocking chair. 'I read it last night after he gave it to me. It's brilliant. Really brilliant. It would complement the Professor's book perfectly if he's writing about Venutios. You make him out to be quite a bastard.' He chuckled. 'You mention Ingleborough a lot in the book, Viv. You did know I'm from there, didn't you? My parents' farm is just below the hill fort. Actually on the slopes, more or less. You say that was where Cartimandua was born and brought up.' He didn't notice the way Viv clenched her fists, the stress in her face. 'I didn't know that was a fact. It's local legend, of course, but I've never seen it acknowledged in a history book before. Tacitus and the other historians wouldn't have known or cared where she came from of course, and they never referred to the smaller sub-sects of the Brigantian tribes, did they? It's strange, because of living there I feel I have always known Cartimandua really well. I was brought up with her ghost.'

Looking up at last, he noted Viv's white face, her raised eyebrows, and he shook his head hastily. 'Not literally, of course. At least, I don't think so. Though my mother could tell you a thing or two about ghostly noises in the night. The clash of swords. Horses galloping by. That sort of stuff.' He grinned. 'Not the kind of thing I would tell the Prof!'

'Indeed, not.' Viv grimaced. 'I went there, of course, but only for a couple of hours. I didn't hear any ghosts.'

Liar! Of course she had. She had heard more than ghostly hooves. She had heard a voice.

Steve was shaking his head. 'I wish I'd known. You could have stayed with us while you were visiting the area. My mother's been doing B&B since the foot and mouth epidemic.' He sighed. 'You can't leave the department, Viv. You mustn't.'

'I don't intend to if I can help it.' Viv met his gaze. He would know all about the row soon enough. The grapevine was pretty good and it was a small department and she doubted if Hugh was going to be even slightly discreet about his dislike of her book. She sighed, and realised suddenly that it was partly with relief. The moment had passed. Steve wasn't going to ask her where all her information had come from. He was content that it was legend. For him at least that was good enough. He was picking up his bag and standing up.

'Stay and have a coffee,' she found herself saying. She didn't want to be alone. Not at the moment, not with the voice still clamouring in her ear. 'I want to hear about your mother's ghosts. I'm intrigued. I can't think why we've never talked about this before.'

He slid his bag off his shoulder and, clearly pleased with the invitation, dropped it on the floor before following her into her small kitchen. The sky outside the mansard window was a bright duck-egg blue now as the sunlight poured in, spotlighting the cupboards, the shelves, the jars and bottles, as she reached for the kettle. 'I had some strange experiences myself while I was visiting the sites I've written about.' Keep the tone casual. Humorous. Don't let him see how much it all worried her. 'The trouble is I was always on my own so I had no one to compare notes with.' She gave a self-deprecating laugh. She mustn't let him think she took this seriously.

Steve was leaning against a cupboard, arms folded, watching as she scooped coffee into the pot. He seemed to be considering what she had said. 'My dad has lived there all his life.' He had a soft Yorkshire accent which she had always found rather attractive. 'The farm has been in the family for hundreds of years. I know there are all sorts of stories – there always are, aren't there, in the country?' He paused. 'But you know farmers,' he added, shrugging. 'They see things, all sorts of things, but they won't admit it.' He glanced at her from under his eyelashes and she saw a strange mixture of emotions flash across his face. Caution. Suspicion. Maybe he was testing her reaction? But the moment had passed and he was his usual relaxed self again at once. 'My mother is a local girl. From the dale. She loved the farm from the first day Dad took her up there to visit,' he went on. 'It's so beautiful and remote and wild. She was all romantic then. And young.' He paused. 'It's a hard life being a farmer's wife.'

She looked up again, hearing the change in his tone. 'It must have been awful when you got foot and mouth.'

He nodded. 'The worst. My dad nearly gave up. Then she came up with this idea of doing B&B – advertising on the Internet and all that. At first we hated the thought of having strangers in the house – she more than anyone – but it's not so bad.' He shrugged.

'I don't suppose she has time to hear ghosts now.' Viv plunged the coffee and poured it into two scarlet mugs.

'She doesn't go up on the hill much.' He shrugged a second time, his face wistful. 'She's changed a lot. But she does still hear things. Sometimes I think she's always been too sensitive. Dad's far more down to earth. The visitors love it up there, of course.' Again the quiet chuckle. 'They come back some evenings with some cracking stories.'

Viv handed him a mug, then faced him, leaning against the cooker, her hands cupped around her own. 'What sort of stories?'

He raised an eyebrow. 'Are you really interested? Well, there's the boggart holes, of course.' He smiled. 'And sometimes they think they've heard the barguest, shrieking in the night! They talk about horses, too. Galloping hooves. Sometimes they get quite spooked. There was one woman, she said she had "feelings".' He rolled his eyes. 'She was a bit freaky, but I saw Mum's face and I reckoned she knew what the woman was talking about.' Again the quick glance at Viv. 'That woman wanted to hold a séance, but Mum wasn't having that. Not in our house. Dad wouldn't stand for it and she thought it was wrong. Disrespectful.'

'I'd like to meet your mum.' Viv sipped her coffee thoughtfully. 'Maybe I will book myself in some time. I need to do some more research –' She stopped herself abruptly but Steve picked up on the word at once.

'Are you going to write more about Cartimandua? You've found some new sources, haven't you?'

Oh God, so he had spotted all the extra stuff. Well, so he should have done. He was after all one of their best students and if he hadn't noticed she would have been very surprised. She had let so many details slip in. Cartimandua's tribe, her birthplace, were obvious traps; facts no one knew. Facts, if they were indeed facts, which she had no business to know.

Steve was nodding. 'It's frustrating, isn't it, working just over the pre-history border; only having the Roman texts to go on. If only the Celts had written down stuff themselves.'

21

'But they did.'

Viv was becoming more and more uncomfortable at the turn the conversation was taking. She wagged her finger at him in mock reproof. 'Remember that where necessary they wrote in Greek and Latin as well as Celtic using Latin script. We know the Celts had an oral culture but remember their phenomenal feats of memory did not mean they were illiterate. We can't be certain they didn't write history too.' She paused. 'Maybe they even wrote down the sacred stuff and it was destroyed. We just don't know.'

Steve shook his head. 'We'd have found something by now if they had. I've been doing exhaustive research on this, you know I have, for my thesis. Their traditions were broken. The memories lost. The Romans and the Christians utterly determined to root out their culture. So it is only the Roman and Christian sources left.' He paused. 'Unless . . . ?' He was looking at her hard. 'Is that what's happened? Viv? They wrote something down after all and you've found it?'

There was a moment of silence. Oh yes, she had found something. But it was not a scrap of old parchment. It was in her head. An echo out of time.

He was still gazing at her, taking her silence for acquiescence. 'My God, how exciting! And Hugh is jealous because you found something he doesn't know about? Wow!'

'No, Steve –'

But he was already convinced. 'No, don't worry. I shan't say a word to anyone. I promise. Where did you find it? You're sure it's not been faked like Iolo?'

Viv shook her head, taking a deep swig of coffee. Iolo Morganwg, the eighteenth/early-nineteenth century Welsh Celticist had faked and/or created, depending on which way you looked at it, numerous so-called Druidic and Celtic manuscripts which had convinced the academic world for a long time. This was getting far too close for comfort to something she did not want to face at the moment. She glanced at her watch. 'Sorry, Steve, but I'm going to have to go. I have to be somewhere.' She smiled ruefully. 'We'll talk some more about this, I promise. But please, please, don't say anything to Hugh. It is nothing that would interest him or be remotely important for his area of research, honestly.' She hesitated. 'And maybe I will go and stay with your parents. I would like to go back to Ingleborough. It was enormously atmospheric.'

Closing the door behind him she paused, looking down at the card he had pressed into her hands:

Peggy and Gordon Steadman

Winter Gill Farm
High Fell
Ingleborough
N. Yorks

High Fell, Ingleborough. The name resonated in her head. Suddenly she was shivering with excitement.

II

It was focussing so closely and so constantly on Cartimandua that had first brought the woman closer. It must have been. It was as though she was there at the end of a phone line and it had begun soon after Viv had actually started writing the book following two years of intense research, two years of studying Roman texts, of following up the latest archaeological, anthropological and social studies. She had interviewed archaeological conservators, forensic archaeologists, philologists. She had, she used to say to herself, learned to extract blood from stones.

Then one day, out of nowhere, as she sat staring at her computer screen she had heard the voice. Not clearly at first. No words. Just a strange resonance deep inside her brain. It had worried her. She wondered if she was going potty; she took a couple of days off. Then it happened again and this time she had heard the one word clearly.

Vivienne.

A strange, foreign-sounding version of her own name and one she never, ever, used herself.

She worked harder every time it happened, fighting it; ignoring it. So the voice used another approach. In her dreams. And in her dreams she could do nothing to stop it.

She grew confused. Cartimandua was emerging from the shadows of archaeology as a flesh and blood personality. She had grey-green eyes with dark flecks in them, red-blonde hair which was thick and long, she had strong broad cheek bones and a generous mouth. A forceful character. She was clever. Sometimes amusing. Often troubled. Sometimes hard to understand.

It had been so difficult to ignore her. To stick to the facts. The facts as far as they are known through a few Roman historians and Cartimandua's place within the historical context of first-century Britain.

Each time it happened she had fought it tooth and nail. Thrown down her pen. Another whole passage of the book to be erased. Romantic, imaginative rubbish. Her book was to be factual.

She had spoken to a colleague in the modern history department, cautiously, casually, not giving too much away, about getting too close to the subject of one's biography.

'Oh God, yes!' he had said, roaring with laughter. 'It's spooky. You become so intimate with someone you get right under their skin. You feel you know them better than they know themselves. Don't worry, old thing. We read too many letters and diaries in our job, that's the problem.'

Viv had nodded and grinned and walked away. Too many letters and diaries?

No. Not in the Iron Age.

If only.

If Cartimandua had written letters and diaries they had long ago dissolved into the sodden mires of northern England where she had lived and loved and died, and academics are not supposed to know how the subjects of their biographies feel and think without those indispensable written sources.

Hugh was right. She was probably a novelist at heart. Someone who could write good convincing historical fiction.

'But I'm not!' The words exploded out of her, heard only by the pot plants on her window sill. 'I am an academic, damn it! I have studied Celtic history for fifteen years. That's why this has all come so easily. It's not because of –' She paused. 'It's not because of *her*.'

Viv's editor had loved it. So had the publishers' readers; the publicity department; the sales team. Parts of it which she had cut, her editor insisted on reinstating – the best bits – the most 'imaginative'! And the first person to look at it who knew what he was talking about, Professor Hugh Graham, had spotted it immediately. Cartimandua's voice was there. It shouldn't have been.

And now Viv was hearing it again, more insistently than ever. The book was finished. The voice should have gone away. Instead it was louder and now there was no reason – no academic reason – not to listen. After all, there were so many pieces of the jigsaw still missing. So much she still wanted to know.

Walking slowly back into her living room, so empty after Steve's departure, Viv was lost in thought. Where was the voice coming from? Was it from her imagination? Was it a memory? An echo? A ghost? Why did she have this strange feeling suddenly that on top of all the other reasons not to listen to the voice that called itself Cartimandua, there might be one overriding factor. That it was dangerous?

She stood staring at the phone thoughtfully. Perhaps she should tell Cathy what was happening. Cathy would know what to do. She was after all the psychologist; the expert. But then, supposing Cathy said it was stupid and potentially harmful and that she should stop?

The words of the first scene of her play resonated in her mind again suddenly. Once written, she had not been able to erase them. Most of them hadn't gone into the book, but they were still there. In her computer. In her notes. In her head. They were the bit of the play that Maddie Corston had praised. They were the words that had first brought Cartimandua alive.

III

For as long as she could remember she had known that she would be a queen some day. It wasn't a dream, or a memory of past existences or a knowledge of a destiny which was the result of birth or fortune. It was a certainty. A knowing in her blood. Besides, the goddess had told her. The first time she had heard the voice clearly she had been standing quite alone amongst the trees near the river in the lush valley below her hilltop home. She had left her pony to graze and was staring down into the glittering churning sweep of the brown waters, her mind a blank, mesmerised by the movement of the ripples.

Cartimandua

The voice seemed to echo off the stones beneath her feet, resound from the boulders, rustle in the leaves above her head. *Cartimandua, Queen of the North.*

Awed, she stared round. This valley was full of gods; it was a sacred place and this was a sacred river and a goddess had spoken her name. A goddess called Vivienne. She knew what she looked like, her goddess. She had glimpsed her green eyes in the reflections of the water, seen her hair, the russet of oak leaves in autumn, in weed streaming amongst the rocks. And it was there that, cautiously, shyly, for the first time, she answered the call of the goddess who called her queen.

Her brothers had laughed. Good-natured, tolerant, fond of their small sister, they encouraged her fantasy. They taught her all day, every day, to run, to throw a spear, to wield her small razor-sharp sword and to ride. To ride as though she were part of the horse itself. It was they who had given her her special name – Cartimandua, which meant Sleek Pony – teasing her as, soaked to the skin in the rain and the mist of her native Pennine Hills she leaned forward against the neck of her pale cream garron, her own long fair hair hanging in ropes about its neck, blending with its mane as they tore across the heather-clad fells and the dales and into the forest. It was her brothers and their friends who set her up to stand on an upturned box to address her troops, the children and young men and women of the hilltop fort on the high northern moors where they had been born, and who led the cheering as she rallied her followers to their next adventure.

She did not enjoy weaving.

Or sewing.

Or playing with other girls save those who, tomboys like herself, dreamed of being warriors alongside their menfolk.

It didn't matter what she did. She was the apple of her father, the tribal chieftain's eye, her uncle's darling, and if she was the despair of her ambitious mother she didn't care. She romped unchecked through the small township, her clothes peat-stained, her

26

fingernails split and dirty, her straw-coloured hair unkempt. Until the autumn of her twelfth year. The year her world was to change forever.

Her own special hound, Catia, had whelped in the night. She was a small bitch and the sire had been huge. The birth had torn the dog badly. Gentle and strong as she always was with her animals Carta had done her best to help, her small fingers easing out the last of the pups, tearing apart the membranes the bitch was too weak to break with her teeth, plugging the baby to the teat even as she knew the mother was dying. Three of the pups were already dead. Her eyes full of tears, she was sitting in the watery dawn sunlight, her hand on the bitch's head as it lay in the shelter of the log-shed outside the great round house, when a shadow fell across her and she looked up blindly. 'She won't live,' she wailed. She did not ask for help. It never occurred to her to ask help from an adult. Already she was self-sufficient.

It was a stranger who stood over her. A tall lean man of some forty summers wrapped in a mantle of green and blue dyed wool. She had heard with some part of her the watchman's horn and knew someone must be approaching the gates of the township, but had taken no notice, too preoccupied to care. He bent towards the dog, laying down his staff and the leather bag he carried and, going down on one knee he put a gentle hand on the dog's flank.

'She can still be saved.' His voice was deep. 'Take the surviving pups from her. She has no strength to feed them. Is there another bitch here to adopt them? If not I'll twist their necks.'

'No!' Her eyes flashing fury Carta pushed at him, trying to place herself between him and the dog. 'I will not have the pups killed. She has plenty of milk. They can feed till she dies. Then I will feed them myself with goat's milk. And maybe she'll be all right.' Her certainty faded. 'I will ask the goddess to bless her.' She looked doubtfully down at the dog who lay, eyes closed, without moving.

The man studied Carta's face briefly, then he reached forward and taking her hand examined her blunt, dirty little fingers covered in dried blood. 'Is she your bitch?'

Carta nodded.

'And you are willing to nurse her? And the pups if necessary?'

The girl nodded. She wiped her eyes defiantly with the back of her hand and set her jaw in determination.

27

'Then we will try to heal her. The goddess needs our help in this, child. Or she will take the dog to herself where it will play forever in the summer lands. Do you want to help her?' He glanced up and saw the eager nod, the sudden frown, the inclination of the head as though she was trying to recall some forgotten memory. He studied her face. 'What is it, child?'

She shook her head as if irritated at some unknown failure. 'The goddess does not want Catia. Not yet.' The goddess whose voice she heard in the wind on the fells. The goddess who had spoken to her from the river. Vivienne.

He held her gaze for a moment, then he nodded as though satisfied at some conclusion he had arrived at in his own mind. 'Go and fetch a pot of boiling water, and – wait!' He had hardly raised his voice as she jumped to her feet but the authority in it turned her to stone. 'Wash your hands before you come back.'

When she returned it was to find he had opened his bag and extracted packages of dried herbs and mosses, small glass phials, and a set of sharp bladed knives and scalpels. 'You are a healer?' Her eyes were round with relief. 'Why didn't you say?' She was carefully carrying a pitcher of hot water drawn from a cauldron hanging over one of the cooking fires.

He was sliding moss between the bitch's back legs.

'I am here to settle matters of dispute, child. But I retain an interest in healing, certainly. Here, put these to steep in the water till it cools.' He handed her a small wooden pot of herbs and dried berries. 'Now, whatever you say, we must remove these puppies. They will drain her life force. They can come back to her later when she is stronger.'

Her eyes had widened. He was a Druid, then. She had not noticed his robes under the warm mantle. A wise man come to settle the legal disputes within the huge hill fort compound formed by the hilltop ramparts. Her father, king of the Setantii, had his own Druids, of course. They ran a school and a college in the forest near the river in the valley below the fort and two of their most senior members were his advisers at the tribal councils. This man must be very special and very senior to have been summoned specially. She was dimly aware of there having been quarrels amongst her father's followers; the reason for them did not interest her. She reached out for the puppies, detaching them with much whimpering and squealing from their mother's teats and snuggled them into her

28

arms. 'I can put them with my brother's hound. She is so stupid she won't notice the extra.'

'Take them.' He smiled at her, reading perhaps more into her comment than she had intended. This bright, wilful girl obviously had little respect for the sibling whose dog she described so dismissively. 'Then come and watch what I do. Your hands are strong and gentle. You have the makings of a healer.'

As she had suspected, the pups settled to their foster mother at once with no sign of surprise or hesitation on either side as she lay in the shade of the wool store with her own litter. Carta watched for a moment, making sure the week-old pups did not push the newcomers aside, but there seemed space for all and with one or two indignant squeaks and a gentle inspection and lick from the new mother all was peaceful. Threading her way through the dozen or so houses with their attendant granaries, barns, stores, workshops and stables which comprised the settlement where she had grown up, she found a small respectful circle of spectators had formed around the visitor and the sick dog in the beaten-earth courtyard in front of her father's house.

She pushed between them impatiently only to find her father standing in the way as he addressed their visitor. 'Welcome, friend. I am sorry this child has waylaid you. She had no business bothering you with such trifles.' Her father was a tall well-built man, handsome and much respected within the tribe. He was, she noticed, wearing his best mantle with the silver circlet denoting his kingship around his shaggy mane of reddish hair.

Their visitor looked up. 'The life of a dog is not a trifle, Bellacos. On the contrary,' he smiled gravely. 'Matters of law can wait. Let us see what we can do for this creature, then I shall come to your fireside later.'

That evening, certain that Catia was sleeping soundly on the rug on her own heather bed and that the puppies were content and replete with their new mother, Carta crept back at last into the great feasting hall of the Setantii. Built several years ago beside her father's house, this hall, slightly larger than her family home and without smaller rooms around the circular walls, formed a great ceremonial space, kept for tribal gatherings and entertainments and for communal meals. Richly decorated with colourful woven wall hangings, elaborately carved support pillars, and everywhere riots of colour and design, it was lit by dozens of lamps. As the population of the settlements crowded in, the great hall was smoky from the central fire and the lamps and smelling strongly of the food which was even now being carried in on great heavy trays. Carta arrived in time to see her father passing their guest a horn of the best mead. She wriggled onto the bench between the two men, almost deafened by the noise of shouting and laughter as the whole community crowded in to see their visitor and to share the evening meal. By the flickering light of the flaring lamps, meat from the firepits and ovens in the kitchens was being passed round on platters swimming in rich blood gravy together with bowls of stew and baskets of bread and hunks of fine rich cheese. By the wall Enocios, the harper, was strumming a gentle background music all but inaudible in the hubbub around him.

Bellacos and his visitor, engaged in serious talk, had not seemed to notice the small girl who had forced her way onto the cushioned bench between them, but now the newcomer glanced down. He laid his knife beside his platter and wiped his fingers on the napkin before patting her unruly head. 'So, is the bitch comfortable?'

Carta nodded. 'She's asleep on my bed.'

He smiled gravely. 'And where will you sleep, little one?'

'Anywhere. I don't care.' She was immediately on the defensive. She was aware that her father's attention had already wandered. He was scanning the company for someone. Her uncle was there, on the other side of their visitor, so it must be her eldest brother, Triganos, he sought. She scowled, hoping fervently that Triganos would as always be somewhere else, lurking in the stables or the arms hall with his friend and foster brother, Venutios. If they came over she would be chased away to sit with the other children or sent to sit at her mother's side at the far side of the fire and forgotten. She hadn't stirred beneath the stranger's hand. It was light. Gentle. Warm. Normally she would have wriggled away, ducked aside and fled but he fascinated her and he had won her trust as easily as he had won that of her dog.

'So, child. What do they call you?' His voice was deep and melodious. He took his hand away and she felt for a moment bereft.

'My birth name was Áine. Radiance. But my brothers call me Sleek Pony.' She shrugged in acceptance. 'Cartimandua.'

'And does it suit you, this new name?' He was smiling.

Her father answered for her. 'Indeed it does.' He gave a roar of laughter. 'Carta is a child of Epona and no mistake.' A huge muscly arm encircled her bony shoulders and he gave her a bear hug.

'And what does your mother plan for you?' The stranger was looking down at her thoughtfully.

'Nothing. Or if she does, there is no point.' Carta looked up at him and fixed him with large eyes which were in some lights blue-grey and in others the green of the mountain lakes. 'I am going to be a queen.'

Her father's shout of laughter was echoed by the men and women around them who had overheard the exchange. It was warm, loving laughter. She was popular, their leader's small daughter, much loved and much admired for her courage and her wild beauty.

The stranger didn't laugh. He was looking at her thoughtfully. 'Who told you this, child? Your mother?'

She shook her head.

'Then who?'

'The Lady.'

She saw his pupils dilate as he held her gaze and she felt a moment of fear. 'She speaks to me when I'm by myself sometimes,' she said defiantly. 'She is called Vivienne.'

A hush had fallen on the hall. The stranger was nodding wisely. 'Remind me, Bellacos. This child is a daughter of Brigantia. Through your blood a daughter of the Setantii. But also of the Trinovantes through her mother, is that not so?'

Carta's father sobered rapidly. He shot a quick glance across his daughter's head towards their guest. 'Indeed. The bards tell us that her mother's mother's mother was the daughter of Mandubraccios of the Trinovantes. After his death, his wife, also a princess of Brigantia, of the Corionototae, brought her home to her people here in the north. It was not safe to remain in the south. Cassevellaunus's heirs were hunting for anyone of his blood. To wipe them out.'

'And your mother's line?'

'The daughter of the king of the Textoverdi.'

'So. This little one has many lines of royal blood in her veins. A bloodline which makes you the most likely choice as next high king of the Brigantes in your turn.' The Druid stroked his chin for a moment. 'And she has no sisters? Only brothers?' When Bellacos nodded he thought for several more moments, then abruptly he made to stand up. 'I will retire to consult with the gods. Her destiny is written, Bellacos, and she knows it.'

31

Bellacos's mouth dropped open. 'But she is only a child.'

'Children grow up, my friend.' The Druid had climbed to his feet. He rested his hand on the other man's shoulder. 'And the time may come when there is no one else of the royal blood to lead your people. When you and your sons and your brothers' sons have gone to join the gods she may be the only one left of the family.' In the silence that followed everyone held their breath. He was foretelling not only Carta's future, but the death of the king and of his sons. His eyes held those of his host calmly. What the gods ordained would come to pass whatever attempts were made to circumvent their plans. 'If it is her destiny,' he went on into the silence, 'if she is to be chosen as queen, then she will need to be trained for her life to come and no longer allowed to run wild with the ponies.' He touched Carta lightly on the forehead with his index finger. 'I will look into the future for her tonight. Tomorrow we will speak further.'

IV

Hugh Graham was sitting at his desk at home in his grey stone Gothic house behind its tall hedges of laurels in the pretty village of Aberlady. The story of Venutios was ringing in his head. Cursing, he tried once again to banish it. The notes on his desk were about the Roman invasion; legionary dispersements; the south of England. He had not yet reached the part of his book where he would concentrate on the Brigantes, let alone the story of Venutios. He was wishing profoundly that he hadn't mentioned the book to Viv. He had implied that it was to be about the Brigantian king, and it wasn't. Oh yes, Venutios would feature in it, indeed play an important part, but not to the exclusion of all else, so why was the man's story suddenly obsessing him like this?

He glared at the piles of books around him. It was the third time he had sat down. He had been walking restlessly up and down the floor, unable to settle at anything since his interview with Viv. He frowned in irritation. He should be in the department this morning; had had two important appointments this afternoon which now he had been forced to ask the departmental secretary to reschedule. Why?

Why had he left in such a hurry after Viv had stormed out yesterday? Too much of a hurry to check where the brooch was in the litter of his desk and lock it up for safe-keeping. That worried him. He was treating it with almost deliberate carelessness and he wasn't sure why. He shivered. He hadn't wanted Viv to touch it for a very good reason. It felt poisonous. When, cautiously, with his fingertips because he had no special gloves on, he had touched it himself, he had almost dropped it, appalled by the cold sense of evil the thing exuded.

So, why had he left it on his desk at all? Because for some insane reason he had wanted it to sit, if only for a few moments, in a ray of clean, hot sunshine. For a few seconds he contemplated the irrationality of the thought.

The atmosphere in the room had been Viv's fault of course, not the brooch's. The anger she had left behind her had been tangible. No one could settle down to work after that. He sighed, even more irritated with himself to find he was thinking about her again, especially considering the annual review upon which he was supposed to be working. He dragged his attention to the backlog of papers on his desk.

The exams had gone well this year. There would be fewer resits over all, and none in the second year and that was largely down to Viv. She was a good teacher, he had to admit it. He frowned. She was also an infuriating woman, wasting her life with this popular – and there was no doubt it would be popular – claptrap !

He pushed his chair back again and went to stare out of the window at his garden. It was a mess. Alison used to adore the garden. Perhaps it had taken the place of the children they had never had. She had had green fingers. Everything she touched flourished. It was as if all her life force had seeped away into the flowers, leaving her with nothing of her own to fight the vicious cancer that had taken her in only seven short months.

'Look after my plants, Hughie.' She had reached out to take his hand only a day or two before she died. 'I know you. You'll stick your head in your books and forget them.'

She had indeed known him so well.

He cleared his throat loudly and walked back to his desk, staring down at the letter lying there on top of all the other papers. It was about the funding of research projects in his department. With an angry exclamation he noticed Viv's name was still there. Snatching up his pen he scratched through it three times. The odd thing was he could picture Viv's hurt and anger so clearly he could almost see her standing there in the room with him, with her unruly red hair and vivid eyes, a vision which recurred strangely often. In the silence of the house he could imagine Viv's voice. Her peels of laughter; her irreverence. Even the thought of her anger made the place seem less lonely. He scowled and drew the pen through her name a fourth time before throwing the letter down on the blotter.

Alison had liked Viv. 'She's a natural historian, Hugh.' She had giggled at the unintended ambiguity of the phrase. 'Instinctive. Women can make leaps of deduction which turn out to be right, you know.' She would have loved Viv's article in the *Sunday Times* and the profile of Viv herself, devoured every word and rung Viv to enthuse about it for hours on the phone.

One of Alison's favourite excursions had been to drive out to Traprain Law with its Iron Age fort; to stand, staring out at the view from the top, or to go on perhaps towards the Lammermuirs or down to the Eildon Hills, where he had scattered her ashes, the magical, Celtic hills where Thomas the Rymer met the faery queen, and where King Arthur sleeps with his knights. He shook his head in exasperation. No wonder she had liked Viv. They had both been wrapped up in all this myth and magic, legends and pseudo Celticism, fun in its own way, but not real. Never real. He had tried so hard to put her right, explained that the population densities around these great hill forts would have been high, probably far higher than today if aerial photography and archaeology were anything to go by. A crowded landscape of farms and round houses, walls and tracks, centred on a central township, which would probably have been a settlement already for some two thousand years at least before the Iron Age. A real, busy, populated place, not some misty magical other-worldly fairy land. And even if Alison had not been able to get her head around the reality beyond the myth, Viv should be able to. Viv of all people should understand the realities of history.

Picking up his keys he abandoned the desk and the departmental review, left the house and headed for his car. He always found solace in the bracing air of the hills. There he could clear his head and concentrate on a new and strangely persistent backdrop to the lonely song of the skylark. The voice of Venutios.

V

Cathy had invited Viv to supper the following Sunday. Her partner, Pete Maxwell opened the door. He was tall, painfully thin, with skimpy hair and the deeply tanned complexion of a man who has spent most of his life in the sun.

'Sorry, I'm early.' She handed him two bottles of wine she had picked up at the nearest off-licence and reached up to kiss his cheek.

'Always good to see you, Viv, you know that.' He glanced warily out onto the landing. 'I'm expecting my ex with my daughter. Once she's dropped her off I can relax,' he said, by way of explanation.

Viv grimaced in sympathy. Over the years she had heard a lot about Pete's marriage from Cathy. The current point of contention was the daughter of the marriage, Tasha. Until now she had been no problem. She went to school in Edinburgh and had lived with her mother in Cramond. Holidays had been divided between Sweden and Scotland but now Greta wanted her to go to school in Sweden. Pete, dear laid-back Pete, hadn't really thought about it at all. Problem? What problem? Tasha wanted to live with them in the term time and stay at school in Scotland. Something that ought to be OK in theory but of course it wouldn't be. Greta, she gathered from Cathy, would see to that.

'Cathy's in the kitchen. Come through.' Pete turned and led the way down the corridor.

Cathy was peeling potatoes. 'Hi, Viv. Grab yourself a glass. Did Pete tell you, Tasha is joining us.'

'He did.' Viv poured herself some wine as Pete disappeared into the depths of the flat to answer the phone in his study.

'Let me do those.' Viv perched on the bar stool at the worktop.

As Cathy handed over the peeler she glanced at Viv's face. 'You look a bit peaky. Are you OK?'

'Sure.' Viv gouged a potato viciously. 'Well, sort of.' She gave a wry grin. 'Call me paranoid!' She took a gulp from the glass. 'But I think I'm being haunted.' She hadn't meant to say it; but the words were out before she could call them back.

'Haunted?' Cathy frowned. 'By whom? Or what? I hope you don't mind bangers and mash. That's the one thing I can be sure Tasha will eat.'

'Sounds great.' Viv grinned. 'You know me. I love my nosh.' She reached for another spud. 'By Cartimandua, I suppose. By the book.' Now that it was out she couldn't stop herself. She gave a small shudder. 'I suppose I'm suffering from withdrawal symptoms.'

Cathy glanced up at her as she laid the sausages out in a grill pan. 'It sounds very likely. So, what exactly are the symptoms?'

Viv shrugged. 'An inability to separate myself from the story, I suppose.' She kept the description deliberately vague.

'I think you should start a new book as soon as you've got this play sorted.' Cathy put the sausages under the grill. 'Start incubating the next child.'

Viv gave wry nod. 'I thought it would be to do with umbilical cords. It's all a bit physical, isn't it.'

'Yes, it is.' Cathy picked up her own glass. She stood for a moment, thoughtful. 'Yes, it really is. After all, you've been living with that book for, what, two years? It was bound to be a shock to your system to stop writing suddenly. I bet you were longing to finish and get it over and another part of you was dreading it. In fact, I know that's how you feel . You've more or less said so.'

'Have I?' Viv looked surprised. 'Well, I was right, I suppose. And I wanted Hugh to be supportive. I thought he would be. I suppose I thought the book would make him acknowledge the fact that I am an authority on my subject.'

'And it's done the opposite.' Cathy was watching her over the rim of the glass.

'Quite the opposite. It's stupid, but you, know, I feel really disappointed now that the anger has worn off a bit.'

Behind her the doorbell rang. Moments later they heard voices in the hall.

Viv watched amused as a tall, blonde woman appeared in the doorway followed by her daughter, a small, slim child with her mother's pale hair and delicate features. There was no sign of Pete. 'Cathy, you will have to take Tasha to the orthodontist after school tomorrow, and she wants new sandals for the summer. I won't have time at the end of term before I take her to Sweden, so you must do it. I have written down the makes that are acceptable.' The woman put a piece of paper down on the worktop.

'Greta, I don't think you've met my friend, Viv.' Cathy ignored the paper.

Greta glanced at Viv briefly and nodded. She didn't smile. 'I have to go. Don't let Tasha stay up late as you did last weekend.' Her accent was very faint, her words precise.

'I thought you might stay and have supper with us, Greta.' Cathy's expression was eager. Too eager. Viv suppressed a smile.

'Thank you, but no.' The glance Greta threw around the kitchen implied incipient botulism at the very best. In a moment she had gone, without goodbyes to her daughter or Pete who were hovering in the hallway, leaving only a faint whiff of expensive scent behind her.

As the door closed, Cathy and Viv subsided into giggles. 'What would you have done if she had said yes?' asked Viv weakly.

'Died of shock.' Cathy sobered with an effort.

'Does she always behave like that?'

'Always.'

'Wow.' Viv took another deep swig from her glass. 'And what is the daughter like?' It seemed incredible that she had never met Cathy's almost-stepdaughter and her mother before, but Cathy was usually careful to keep Pete's family at arm's length from her friends.

'I'm very fond of her, but she can be a handful, I have to admit.'

As Viv was about to find out.

'I have become a vegetarian! How could you eat poor dead animals!' Tasha had taken one look at the table and the pan of sizzling brown sausages and assumed an expression of extreme disgust, so like the one her mother had displayed only minutes before.

'No probs.' Cathy was unfazed. 'Eat the mash and vegetables and tomorrow we'll go and buy some special stuff at Sainsbury's on the way to the orthodontist. I think you're quite right, you know. It's much more healthy to be a veggie.' She put three sausages on Viv's plate. 'Help yourself to onion gravy, Viv. No, sorry, Tash. It's non-vegetarian.'

The child was staring at her plate. 'Mummy thinks potatoes make you fat,' she said stubbornly.

'Mummy is probably right.' Cathy shrugged. 'So, just peas, then?'

37

Pete was sitting in silence, watching the scene. Viv thought there was a twinkle in his eye. 'There are some tomatoes in the fridge, Tash.'

'Dad! You know I hate tomatoes.' The child was almost in tears.

'You know . . .' Viv thought it was time she said something helpful. 'As those are free-range sausages, and organic – organic, Cathy?'

'Definitely.' Cathy nodded firmly.

'They come from happy, healthy animals. It is tremendously important to support organic and free-range husbandry. Unless we do, farm animals will go on being treated badly.'

Tasha frowned. 'But my friend Susie says –'

'Viv is a university lecturer, Tasha,' Cathy said quietly. 'She knows about these things.'

'Have one sausage, Tasha, for the sake of the poor animals.' Viv caught Cathy's eye. 'And you can eat the gravy too. For the same reason.'

'This puts an interesting spin on the range of Celtic history.' Cathy grinned. 'You being an expert on free-range and organics and stuff. But then they did do human sacrifice, didn't they. Were they cannibals, too? If they ate their victims they would obviously have been organic so I'm sure a few pork sausages wouldn't have been a problem.'

'What?' Tasha threw down her knife and fork.

'Joke.' Cathy held up her hands. 'Got you!'

'Oh yuck!' Tasha made a face. For a moment, as the plate was put down in front of her she hesitated and Viv watched in amusement to see if Cathy had mishandled the situation fatally. She needn't have worried. Within seconds the child was tucking into her supper.

They had all been eating for several minutes, enjoying the food and wine, when Viv noticed that Tasha had thrown several quick curious glances in her direction. Viv, still considering the concept of the organic Celts, met them with a grin but as Tasha stared at her more and more intensely she began to feel uncomfortable. 'What is it, Tasha. Have I got a bird's nest in my hair?' she asked at last.

Tasha frowned. She looked scared. 'Who is that woman behind you?'

Viv froze.

Cathy and Pete were staring in the direction of the child's pointing finger.

'What do you mean? What woman?' Cathy said, puzzled.

Tasha scowled. 'There! Behind her.'

Viv put down her knife and fork. She felt a trickle of icy fear between her shoulder blades.

'There's no one behind her, Tash, don't be silly,' Cathy said sternly.

'There is.' The child looked confused. 'I saw!'

'Get on with your food, Tasha,' Pete put in. 'Stop making things up. It's boring.'

'No!' Viv leaned forward. 'Tell me. What did you see?' She put her hand on Tasha's wrist.

Tasha pulled her hand away. 'Nothing!' She had gone scarlet.

'Please, Tasha.' Viv said anxiously. 'Tell me!'

'I didn't see anything! It was a joke!' Tasha stood up and ran out of the room.

'Take no notice, Viv,' Pete said. 'Don't let her upset you.'

'No.' Viv gave an uncomfortable smile.

'She was winding you up. You know she was.'

'Was she?' Viv glanced at Cathy. Suddenly she was pushing back her chair and, leaping to her feet she headed for the bathroom. Slamming the door behind her, her heart pounding with fear, she stared hard at the mirror.

VI

'That dog will never be good for anything again. Why not have it knocked on the head. It would save a deal of trouble!'

The arrogant young voice behind her made Carta spin round. She had been encouraging Catia to walk slowly round the compound in the gentle sunshine.

'Mind your own business, Venutios!' Her cheeks flared with anger at the sight of her brother's friend lounging against the wheel of a wagon drawn up at the side of the kitchens. He was chewing the end of a piece of straw.

He laughed. 'Sorry. I forgot your new game. Still playing at healers, are we – instead of warrior queens? Your mother must be pleased to see her little girl doing that!'

The taunt was expertly aimed. Carta's anger was instantaneous and violent. Forgetting the dog, who sat down wearily where she was, Carta flew at the boy, more than a head taller as he was, her fingers clawed ready to scratch his eyes out. With a shout of laughter he dodged easily out of reach, dancing backwards away from her, jeering until he collided with the two carters emerging from the fragrant darkness of the baking rooms to collect two more sacks from the wagon.

One of them grabbed Venutios by the back of his tunic. 'Prince or no prince, you watch where you're going young man or I'll tan your backside for you!'

Venutios's strangled expletives were drowned by Carta's crow of laughter as her tormentor was held helpless within her reach.

Before her small fists connected, however, the angry voice of her mother from the doorway of the house behind her froze her in her tracks.

'Cartimandua! Come here now!'

The two waggoners dropped their captive and stood back as Venutios regained his feet and scrambled out of sight.

Carta scowled. For a second she contemplated running after him, but one look at the queen's face changed her mind. Meekly she followed her mother indoors.

Sighing, Fidelma surveyed her daughter. Of the queen's twelve children only four had lived beyond babyhood. Triganos, Fintan and Bran, the three boys and this the only surviving girl. The child had torn her gown yet again. Her face was grimy, her hair a bird's nest and the vivid grey-green eyes were blazing with anger.

'I want you to send Venutios back to his father. I hate him!'

Fidelma sat down on a stool beside the fire and drew her cloak around her shoulders. She sighed. 'The king of the Carvetii has sent his son here to learn how to be a warrior and a prince. We can't send him away,' she said patiently. 'His presence here, as you should know, seals the friendship and brotherhood between our two tribes.' It was hard to believe that at this moment her husband and their Druid guest were continuing to discuss this girl's destiny as a matter of the highest importance for the tribe, or that it was more than likely that she and not Venutios would be the one to be sent away. Fidelma, usually at her husband's side at all the important meetings with his advisers, had left them to it not long since, curious to find out what the young woman in question was actually doing with her time. Carta was too often, she had ruefully realised, out of sight and out of mind. 'Have you completed your tasks for the day, child?' She noted without comment that the dog had followed her daughter in and was now leaning trustingly against Carta's legs.

Carta shrugged. 'Mellia said she would do them for me.'

Fidelma bit back an angry retort. The child wasn't even remotely repentant that her convenient arrangement should be discovered. Somehow she managed to smile. 'Mellia is far too kind for her own good, Carta. It is you who needs to practise your skills with the needle and spindle.' She glanced across the room where Carta's companion, the daughter of one of Bellacos's senior warriors and almost the same age as Carta, had appeared. Neat, tidy, nimble-fingered and biddable the child was everything that Carta was not. Nor was she strictly speaking Carta's friend. Fidelma knew perfectly well that her daughter preferred the company of her brothers and their companions – barring Venutios – to that of this gentle child. She suffered her, no more, and, it appeared, exploited her as well. Fidelma shook her head wearily. Secretly she admired her daughter's spirit and her ambition if not her endless rebellion. As Bellacos's daughter she could look for a rich and powerful husband – almost certainly the heir to one of the neighbouring tribal kings – but she would need a modicum of education and restraint.

Eyeing her daughter's mutinous face, Fidelma gave a wry smile. The husband would need the blessing of the gods and the strength and determination of a bear to manage Cartimandua – but then the gods, their decisions interpreted by the Druids of the tribe, were going to choose her husband and so would presumably send her somewhere she would meet her master!

3

I

'Viv! Let me in. Are you OK?' Cathy was banging on the bathroom door.

Viv clenched her hands on the edge of the basin, her face sheened with icy sweat. Narrowing her eyes, she leaned forward trying to see past her own profile, past the wild hair, the pale, strained face. What had Tasha seen? She had described her as a lady. Not a child; not the young girl of those first deleted chapters Viv had seen just now in the depths of the cloudy mirror. No, Tasha had seen the shadow of the queen herself. 'She's real!' Viv whispered to herself shakily, her eyes wild. 'Somehow she's escaped from my dreams. She's appeared to someone else. I've created her!'

Her sense of dislocation was absolute. She was shaking, feeling intensely cold. Dear God in heaven, what had happened to her? She was standing surrounded by large unforgiving mirrors shrouded with Cathy's amazing tropical plants, but she had been there, at Carta's side. Seen the jeering waggoners, smelled the strange musky scent worn by the woman who was the child's mother, noted Carta's muddy shoes, seen how neat and docile Mellia seemed beside her.

The smell of brewing coffee drifted slowly through the flat as she stood paralysed with fear, staring at her own reflection. Only when Cathy rattled the handle and shouted again did she turn slowly and, unlocking the door pull it open.

'What happened?' Cathy passed her a mug of black coffee. Tasha had been sent to watch TV in the next room.

Viv shrugged. 'Sorry. Tired and emotional, I believe is how it's described.' She looked down at her hands, refusing to meet their eyes.

'Tasha didn't really see anything,' Cathy said gently. She reached forward and put her hand over Viv's.

'Didn't she?' Viv looked up. She shrugged. 'Perhaps not.' How could she tell them what had happened? She didn't know herself. There was nothing she could say.

It was a relief when at last Pete offered to drive her home.

The flat was very still. Standing in the doorway she looked round the living room uncomfortably. The desk drawers were open. She frowned. Surely she hadn't left them like that? Pulling open the top drawer with trembling hands she rifled through its contents. The pin. What had she done with the pin? It wasn't there. With a small cry of distress she turned her bag upside down and emptied it onto the floor, scattering the contents across the rug. Notebooks, pens, comb, diary, purse, wallet, shopping lists, receipts, car keys – but no Perspex box. Where was it? She picked up the bag and shook it hard. It was empty.

Wildly she glanced round the room. She couldn't have lost it. The thing was irreplaceable. Running next door, she searched her bedroom. Going down on her hands and knees she lifted the valance and peered under the bed. Nothing. Nothing under the pillows, on the bedside table, the bookshelves.

She had put it in the desk drawer. She knew she had. 'Perhaps it was another drawer.' She was talking to herself – another sign of madness! 'Dear God, what have I done?' Going back into the living room she pulled all the drawers out one by one and emptied them onto the floor, scattering papers and pens and pencils over the carpet. There was no sign.

In the street below Pete climbed thoughtfully back into the car and put the key into the ignition. With a glance up at her window at the top of the house he pulled away from the kerb.

Viv sat down on the sofa, her head in her hands. The flat was totally silent. The script of the play with its forest of red stickers courtesy of Maddie Corston lay on her desk in mute reproach. On top of it sat a small box. She stared at it for several seconds, her mouth dry, then leaping to her feet she pounced on it.

The enamelled pin shone in the lamplight as she opened the lid. It was exquisitely crafted. Shaped like the head of a crane, with an elegant elongated beak and curved neck, the gold was engraved and moulded into intricate designs, and set with scarlet and green enamels. For a long time she stared at it, then almost reluctantly she stroked it with her fingertip. A slight haze appeared on the surface of the gold from the contact with her skin and she pulled her finger away, with a shiver, biting her lip. The brooch was so cold. She glanced over her shoulder almost guiltily, sensing accusing eyes watching her from the corners of the room. She should not have touched it.

She should not have taken it at all. Why had she? Had someone else prompted her; guided her hand?

Outside the window the luminous night had settled over the city and slowly it was growing more silent. In the distance she heard a shout, then another and a short burst of music as somewhere down the Lawnmarket a door opened and then closed again.

The shadowy woman standing in the lamplight near the desk was staring at the brooch with intensity, her eyes the only part of her that seemed alive. As Viv picked up the lid of the box and carefully fitted it back into place, the figure reached out a hand as if in protest, then slowly faded into the darkness.

II

The ponies were kept at the far side of the compound. They were stamping impatiently, waiting for Carta and Triganos to appear from their mother's house.

Silently, careful not to be seen, a figure was creeping along in the shadow of the great wall, climbing over the rubble where it had fallen, coming closer to the horses every second. First one, then another cocked their ears watching and Carta's pony shifted restlessly, backing away as far as its halter would allow.

The boy glanced left and right, then ran sure-footed in between the animals. There was something in his hand, half-concealed behind his back. Ducking under the rope he approached Carta's pony and thrust something under the saddle cloth. The horses all moved restlessly now as he turned and ran out of sight, chuckling.

When the king's children appeared a few moments later the

horses had settled again. Triganos was laughing. 'Come on. I'll race you! To the forest and back before sundown.' He vaulted onto his own pony, leaning forward to pull the rein free, and turned it already galloping as he headed for the gates. Carta was not far behind him. As she leaped for her pony, bareback as his was, but for the backcloth, the animal let out a scream of pain and reared up. Carta flew over the horse's back and landed on the ground on the far side, winded. For a moment she didn't move.

From the shadows Venutios appeared. He stooped to help her climb to her feet. 'Are you all right? What happened.' His face was bland. Then concerned. Kindly. Behind him two men working at the bellows outside the smith's house dropped the great wooden handles and ran to her aid, as did another of Carta's companions, Mairghread, a tall dark-haired girl with buck teeth, who was just emerging from the house. Shaken and with her dignity wounded Carta scrambled to her feet and shook off Venutios's arm. 'I'm all right! I'm fine. How is Olwen?'

Venutios was beside the pony already, soothing it and gentling its trembling skin. The bunch of holly leaves had gone, tossed into the sunshadows out of sight beyond the other horses.

To his delight Carta was taken away, back to her mother to be cleaned and soothed and reprimanded for not checking the pony's saddle cloth was firmly fixed, for not approaching quietly, for not mounting carefully, and long before she was allowed once more to emerge into the sunshine Venutios had climbed onto his own pony and ridden in pursuit of Triganos, followed by some of the other boys and leaving Carta at home to sulk. It was a long time before she managed to slip away at last from her mother's eagle eye, but when she did she hurried straightaway over to the horse lines and whispering to the pony, fed it handfuls of titbits. Then carefully she ducked under the rope and began to search the ground.

From the top of the wall she could see far into the distance, beyond the forest, the scarlet gleam as the sun began to set into the sea. Pushing her hair out of her eyes she stood for a long time, listening for the voice. It wasn't there. All she could hear was the gentle moaning of the wind. Silently she watched as the colours changed to deeper richer red, then to orange, then slowly they dulled into night. Behind her the coming darkness was already thick on the fells. There was no trace of Triganos and his friends.

There was a rattle of stones behind her and she turned. Mellia had scrambled up beside her. For a moment she too stared at the sunset, then she shrugged. 'It'll be dark soon. Is there any sign of them?'

Carta shook her head.

'You think they'll spend the night in the forest?'

'I'm sure of it.'

'And you wanted to go with them.'

'You know I did.' Carta pursed her lips. 'Someone had put some holly under my saddle cloth.'

Mellia's eyes rounded. 'Are you sure?'

'I found it. And then the scratches on poor Olwen's back.'

'But who would do such a thing?'

'Venutios. He didn't want me to go with them. If I'm there Triganos looks after me and does what I say. If I'm not, then the boys can do what they like.' She gave an elaborate shrug.

Mellia studied the other girl's profile with misgiving. She recognised the set of the jaw. 'What are you going to do?'

'I haven't decided yet. I'll think of something.'

When the boys finally returned they brought with them a fine haul of game and had clearly enjoyed themselves enormously. Carta was not there to greet them. She had decided unaccountably to sit in the sunshine and watch Mellia's attempts at mending some of the tears in her friends' gowns; a thankless task, but one she seemed happy enough to try. Triganos brought his sister the gift of a pair of soft leather slippers which he had wheedled from the shoemaker near the entrance gates in an attempt to console her for leaving her behind. She smiled and accepted the gift with a gracious smile which filled him with foreboding.

Two days later Venutios was taken violently ill after the evening meal. Crouching behind the feasting hall as he vomited again and again into a latrine pit he glanced up at last, wiping his sweating face, to see Carta watching him. She was wearing her best gown and new slippers. And she was smiling. 'Poor Venutios . . . Aren't you well?'

'Obviously not.' He groaned and leaned down towards the stinking mess again.

'No one else has been ill.' She did not come any closer, wrinkling her nose fastidiously. 'The gods must be punishing you for something. I wonder why.'

'I can't imagine.' He looked up at her. 'I hope you haven't poisoned me, you little bitch!'

Carta frowned. 'Why would I want to do that?'

He was incapable of answering. With another groan he bent double again. By the time he had recovered enough to straighten and look round she had gone.

III

'Pete didn't tell you I'd rung him, did he!'

Pat took one look at Cathy's astonished face and read the situation correctly. 'Admittedly, I didn't give him much notice before I jumped on the Shuttle, but I didn't think he could forget that easily. Shit, I'm sorry. He said I could scrounge a bed after I'd been down to see Maddie. No worry.' She had dropped a large scarlet canvas bag and her computer case on the floor at her feet. 'I can stay with some mates of mine down in Leith. I'm sure they won't mind, if there is no room here.'

Cathy shrugged helplessly. Bugger Pete. 'It's not that I'm not glad to see you, Pat.' She kissed her visitor. 'It's just that we've got Tasha for a couple of nights.'

'Say no more. I remember the child from hell!' Pat chortled.

'Tasha adores you, Pat, you know she does.' Cathy didn't sound too convinced. 'And we've got room.'

'Somewhere I can lie late abed without screaming children or for that matter cats jumping on my diaphragm?' Pat peered over Cathy's shoulder. 'Is it safe to come in now?'

'Of course it is.' Cathy gestured her towards the living room. 'I'd love you to stay. In fact I'd be furious if you didn't. You can have the box room upstairs. It's a bit crowded with junk and stuff, but it's quiet and it's got a nice bed. You'll be safe up there! Come on. I'll show you.'

*

Cathy arranged their first meeting the next day and as the one o'clock gun resounded across the city, the three women seated themselves at a corner table in a small restaurant in a narrow street off the Grassmarket. It was a place Viv knew well, and one where she would almost certainly not run into any other members of the department.

After Cathy had introduced the two women to one another she raised her wine glass. 'Right, ladies, let's drink to your alliance, to the play and perdition to reactionary male academics.'

Viv grinned. 'You don't know how the thought of this meeting cheered me up this morning. Especially after I had opened my bank statement. That concentrates the mind.' She took a gulp of wine. She was looking strained and pale. She didn't mention the abrupt end to the supper party on Sunday night and neither did Cathy. 'Has Cathy told you my predicament?' she addressed Pat. 'If my boss, Hugh, is not going to promote me to Reader when Hamish Macleod goes, and if he succeeds in cutting the funding for my research I am going to have to find some other gainful employment and soon.'

'Isn't writing a successful biography gainful employment?' Pat asked curiously. She sat back in her seat and surveyed the woman sitting opposite her. Her initial reaction was to be slightly wary of this obviously highly intelligent redhead.

There was a shout of laughter at the next table as a late arrival tried to squeeze in amongst the other diners. The room was very hot.

'If it's successful, yes, then it might be employment of a sort.' Viv grimaced. 'If the book is slated by the critics and blackballed by my ex boss, probably no.'

'That hasn't happened yet, Viv,' Cathy put in calmly.

'To be honest, it won't matter if it is. The more controversy the better.' Pat accepted a menu from the waiter with an absent-minded smile. Maddie was right. Viv's slightly aggressive demeanour probably hid a lot of hurt and insecurity. 'It would bring us good publicity. Always a plus. More listeners for our play. More readers for your book. You wouldn't mind that, would you?'

Viv shrugged. 'Yes, to be honest. Not the more readers part, but the criticism. I'm an academic. That matters. It will put my scholarship in question.' She reached for a bread roll from the basket which had been set down on the table between them. Tearing it to shreds, she piled the crumbs into a heap on her table mat.

'Well, one of the first things you have to learn, Viv,' Pat said firmly, 'is that you need a thick skin in this business. And that's what I'm here to help you achieve!'

Cathy glanced from one to the other. 'If you don't mind my saying so, I think you two will make a good team. You're the academic, Viv. And Pat has lots of experience in this field, and has had some success with her script writing. So listen to her! She knows her stuff. And she can help you.'

'When is your book being published, Viv?' Pat asked after a pause.

'Just under a month. July 14th.'

'Great. And we have a deadline for the play, right? So we need to get down to it as fast as possible.'

Nodding, Viv met her eye with a determined smile. 'Your name would be a huge asset. No one's heard of me, after all.'

There was a moment's silence.

'I thought you were a TV pundit?' Pat raised an eyebrow.

'Only late-night programmes.' Viv shrugged. Pat's comments had unsettled her. The woman was too worldly, too confident, too knowledgeable about the nuts and bolts of this project without knowing anything about the subject itself. She was feeling threatened and uneasy. Yet it had to happen. Without Pat this play was not going to get off the ground.

Pat was frowning. 'I have a feeling you're being a bit disingenuous there. No matter. If you're not famous yet, you will be, darling! One way or another! History is a very sexy subject these days, so hopefully we can incorporate a bit of my know how and knowledge to make the play appeal widely, while keeping the academic integrity of the book as a serious study. Quite a challenge!'

There was a pause as Viv gave a wry smile. 'My serious academic approach.' Oh God, what had she got herself into? 'Ah, but that's maybe the trouble. Perhaps I'd better let you read it before you commit yourself to that opinion. The thing is,' she hesitated. 'I have a confession to make. Some of my sources are a bit suspect.' She paused again. 'That is the reason for Hugh's antagonism. And my crossed wires with Maddie. The book does not perhaps come over as quite as academically based as you expect and the play has gone a bit off track for that reason. I kept trying to rein it in and it hasn't worked.'

Pat looked puzzled. 'You mean it is fiction?'

'No, it's not fiction.' There was another momentary pause. 'Well, perhaps it is. Read it, Pat. Please. The book and my attempts at the script. Then let's talk again.'

4

I

'You've got to give it back.' Cathy stared at the brooch, awed. 'Think of its value. The insurance. What if you lost it!'

They had gone back with her to collect a pre-publication copy of her book each, duly signed by the author, and the draft of the play. As Viv moved the box backwards and forwards in the sunlight to reflect its colours, Pat reached for it with a gasp of delight. For a few seconds she gazed at it, then she took off the box's lid.

'Don't touch –' Viv was too late. It was already lying in Pat's palm.

'Why not?' Pat looked up curiously.

'One should wear gloves.' Viv shrugged. Who was she to talk? She shuddered.

Pat was staring down at it, frowning, studying it intently. After a moment she shivered and tipped it back into its box. 'You know, that's got a really nasty vibe,' she said. 'Isn't that odd, for something so lovely.' She handed it back to Viv with a grimace. 'Cathy's right, you should give it back to the horrid professor.'

And now they had gone and the brooch was back in its drawer and Viv was alone.

The voice was there, just outside her range of hearing. She found herself whispering out loud again. 'This way madness lies.'

Schizophrenia. Spiritualism. Necromancy? In spite of herself she glanced round the room. Was Carta there, lurking in the shadows? She grimaced. The voice had told her everything which had made her work come alive. Those were the bits her publisher had liked;

the bits Maddie liked. Those were the bits they all wanted more of. Natural. Lively. Real.

Too real.

Viv groaned out loud as a sudden wave of total terror flooded through her. 'Carta?' Her mouth was dry. 'Are you there?' The room was silent. She glanced up at the mirror which hung above her desk but the only reflection there was hers.

Then she heard it, the voice from the past, echoing in her head. *Vivienne?*

She couldn't ignore it. She wanted to know what it had to tell her. What Cartimandua had to tell her. Surely just to listen once more would not be dangerous?

The path to the cave was wet, the limestone steps slippery with moss. Carta walked slowly down it, the heavy wool of her skirt soaked as she brushed through the overhanging ferns. The roar of water in her ears was deafening. Here, where the river tumbled over the cliff the water dissipated into rainbows before plunging into the dark pool at the foot of the rocks. She often came here. It was a sacred place, a place where the goddess of the hill spoke to her. Where she brought her hopes and fears. And her dreams.

The gods were everywhere, but here in this dark place between earth and water, hidden from the sky, she felt close to them. So close she could communicate especially with her own tutelary spirit, Vivienne. She had been puzzled by the name. Ninian was a name she knew, but this female daughter of the gods was a stranger. Perhaps a goddess who had come with the Roman or Gaulish merchants who from time to time travelled the trade routes up the River Humbte from the coast, or perhaps one who had arrived from the west with the trading ships from Erin. Hers was a voice which reached Carta from beyond the mists which separated the world of the spirits from the world of men and women.

Pulling her cloak more tightly round her shoulders, she ducked through the curtain of ferns and grasses into the darkness. The offerings she had left before the small carved figurine had gone. The lamp had long ago blown out. Reaching into her bag she brought out fresh offerings to the spirits that dwelt in the cave. Be they gods or little people, animals or birds, it was right that they be rewarded and thanked for allowing her to use this place.

The small hollow horn in her bag, carefully stoppered with a plug of wax, contained oil for the lamp. She lit it quickly and easily, sparking dried moss and holding it to the lamp's wick, and then she sat down silently, eyes closed, to wait for the clear thoughts she sought.

The sound of running water faded as the silence deepened and at last she began to speak. There was much to tell. Much to ask of the goddess of the hill.

The decision had at last been made. She was to be sent as fosterling to the house of the king of the Votadini. Such arrangements were usual. Her brothers too would leave the house they knew to live with other family groups or tribes. Thus were alliances made; friendships between boys which hardened as they grew into warriors, and matches between girls and young men which would be sealed by marriage as a man or his father or mother chose the wives who would expand and ensure a dynasty. She was happy with this. It was part of her destiny. Companions would go with her on the journey north : Mellia and Mairghread, the daughter of her mother's best friend, who was the same age as she was and with them two slaves, Pacata and Éabha, who had looked after her since she was a baby and with whom she had formed a close friendship. Best of all her youngest brother, Bran, was part of the group as, with horses and carts and wagons full of possessions and gifts the procession left her father's dun at dawn, winding its way down the great hill on a spring morning, blessed and escorted by the Druid, Eochaid, who in a moment of gentleness had saved her bitch Catia. The bitch and both pups, already grown, followed at her pony's heels. Behind her, her mother and father and the people of the whole community had turned out to wave them farewell. Her mother, normally so strong, so determined, was crying softly. She had given her daughter a string of sacred beads to wear around her neck and keep her safe. Her father had pressed a lucky charm into her hand. Her only worry was that Venutios, alone of the children, was to remain, foster son to her father, to be trained by him as a warrior without her or her brothers there to keep an eye on him. The thought did not trouble her for long. There was too much to think about in the new exciting days ahead.

Spring had thrown a gentle mantle of green across the bleak hills and stark winter trees. Lulled by the rattle of the carts, the squeak and creak of harness and the warm familiar smell of oxen and horses she looked around her eagerly, exhilarated by the idea of the coming adventure.

Beside her Mellia was sobbing quietly as she rode. Carta glanced across at her companion with a flash of irritation, her own momentary sadness already forgotten. 'You'll see your mother again, Mellia. Do cheer yourself up. Look what a glorious day we have to start our journey. And think where we are going. It will all be new and wonderful.' She had not realised until almost that moment how much the thought of change excited her. New faces. New places. Perhaps she was about to meet the man she would marry and with whom she would have children. At that thought, her face reflected a wave of distaste, perhaps a frisson of fear. Her small fingers clenched on the soft leather reins as her mouth turned down at the corners and her pony, feeling the tension on its jointed snaffle bit, shook its head indignantly. At once she was back from the lurking shadows of that particular thought and at one with her horse, gentling, reassuring, her eyes on the track ahead where even as she watched, the lead wagon lurched to a standstill, its wheels mired in the mud.

Descending at last from the fells onto the plains the track joined the wider road of one of the main trade routes which led from the south through the rich lands of the Brigantian tribes, north towards their capital, the sprawling settlement of Dinas Dwr, seat of the high king. From there they journeyed on following a well-used network of roads and tracks, ridgeways and carefully constructed and maintained causeways where the track led across low-lying and marshy ground. They were passing homesteads and farms, townships, villages and trading posts, communities of workshops and mining areas where lead and silver were extracted from the living heart of the land. In places they were travelling through forests and over open moors and in others along the cliffs which to Carta's great delight, bordered the great Northern Ocean.

They were expected. Lookouts had alerted their hosts as their party forded the broad river which separated the territories of the Brigantes from those of the Votadini. Their escorts were waiting on its far bank. Carta eyed their warriors critically. The men rode sturdy horses and they rode them well. The war chariots of the warriors were well made and elegantly decorated, drawn by fine ponies.

The leader of the band jumped from his chariot and came forward to greet them. To greet her. Ignoring everyone else he came towards her, a girl of some twelve summers only, his hands outstretched to clasp hers. 'Greetings, cousin! I am Riach. I trust your journey has not been too long and arduous?' He was young too. Not as young as she was but still unbearded. His smile was huge, infectious in a broad-browed, tanned face, his eyes a piercing blue, the swirling tattoos decorating his forehead and temples expertly executed. From the golden ornaments at his neck and on his arms she guessed he must be a son or foster son of the royal house and she was suddenly very conscious of her own shabbiness. She was covered in splashes of mud from the journey. Her hair was uncombed and matted. The overnight stays they had made at farms and forts along the way and the two nights camping on the moors had not provided ideal conditions for primping and preening. She had not unpacked clothes or combs or her mirror, although doubtless her mother's slaves had put them in her bundles, and never before had she bothered about what the small animated face which looked out from beneath her frowsty hair looked like. Or cared about jewellery beyond the simple silver bracelet on her wrist and the string of protective amber beads about her neck. She frowned. A queen would care. A woman who was going to be a queen should care.

The young man into whose eyes she stared for two whole heart-beats before turning away, embarrassed, would care.

Snatching her hands from him, her face scarlet, she ran to climb back on the wagon she shared with the other women when too tired to ride another mile. Not a queenly mode of transport. Not at all. Under her breath she made a vow that day. Never again would she travel with slaves. She would demand her own light-cart, a war chariot of her own, and her own two matched horses to pull it and they would one day be the best in the whole of the Pretannic Isles.

Watching her, the boy laughed. He could see her discomfort and her shame, sense her pride; in fact he suspected he could read her very thoughts. But nothing about her displeased him. On the contrary. He admired her already for her courage and for her looks which under all the dirt were striking and would one day be spec-tacular. Which was just as well as his father had informed him that this child, as soon as she reached womanhood, would be his wife.

Viv started out of her reverie, shocked, her heart thudding as she stared round disorientated. She could still feel the heat and the cold. Sense the mud and the dirt, smell the sharp tang of the pine needles beneath the horses' feet, the earthy mist which hung low and cold over the bogs as the ox-carts and wagons rattled through the dales between the ranges of windswept fells, across the causeways and for a moment she was aware, just as the child Carta became aware, of the dirt beneath her fingernails and the strong smell of horse on her skin.

The detail. She must not forget the detail. Overwhelmed with excitement she pulled open a drawer in her desk with shaking hands and she extricated a pack of microcassettes. Slamming one into her little recorder she plugged in the mike, then as an afterthought she reached for a scribbling pad and ballpoint pen. She had to go back again. At once.

A bolt of fear hit her. She took a deep breath. There would be no danger now, surely. Now Carta knew she was listening.

'OK, lady. I'm ready this time.' She sat down at her desk and reaching forward she pressed the record button and picked up her pen.

Carta gazed at the hill fort in front of them in open-mouthed amazement as it rose out of the trees in the distance. Even from here she could see it was at least twice the size of Dun Righ, her home. They were travelling through rich farmland here, passing homesteads much like those they had passed continuously on their journey, but this fort was like nothing she had seen before: buildings clustered all over the top of the steep hillside of what had once been a volcanic crag, and as they moved closer she saw how truly enormous the fort was with its triple ramparts topped by a sharp, pointed palisade and huge gateways. The young man was riding beside the wagon now. 'Dun Pelder.' He grinned as he waved towards the settlement. 'Fortress of Spears. We're nearly there.'

The track led in between two gatehouses in the encircling walls, then climbed steeply, winding up the terraced sides of the hill between huge round houses, some built out onto the terraces themselves, with other buildings clustered near them. The Brigantian visitors were led to the guest house beside the largest round house of all, clearly that of the king himself. Noisy crowds were gathering about them already and she could smell woodsmoke and cooking as, suddenly shy, she edged closer to her companions.

Riach leaped from his chariot and came to the side of the wagon. With a bow he reached up to help Carta down. 'You will be anxious to rest and change your clothes,' he said, solemnly looking down at her. 'Later my father will greet you and we will all eat together this evening. A huge feast is being prepared to welcome the lady of the Brigantes and her brother.' He grinned at Bran, who had reined in his pony beside them and beckoned him closer. Bran and his companions would lodge in the house of the warriors, where the unmarried aristocratic young men of the tribe and leaders of visiting war bands slept.

The guest house was larger than her father's feasting hall. She stared round in awe. The hearth was piled high with logs and crackled merrily and the interior of the building was lit with dozens of lamps. The central area was well provided with benches and sumptuous cushions and behind them the small sleeping chambers around the walls were furnished with bed boxes piled high with heather mattresses, woollen blankets and soft silky furs. Carta continued to stare open-mouthed as slaves carried in her belongings before moving the wagon-load of gifts sent by her father further up the hill to the king's house.

'Look, Carta.' Mellia was standing in front of the table in the largest of the small chambers, much more cheerful now the long journey was over. 'This must be where you are to sleep. Look at the things they have put here for you.' Her voice was full of awe. There was a delicately worked bronze wash basin, exquisitely carved bone combs, a bronze mirror inlaid with coloured enamels. Already slaves were bringing jugs of hot water for her from the cauldron hanging over the central fire.

Carta was impressed and for once struck dumb. Meekly she allowed Pacata and Éabha to strip off her mud-caked clothes and wash her body with the sweet-scented soapwort solution they found waiting in a jug beside the basin. Then they dressed her in a clean linen gown and a plaid woollen mantle quickly dug from one of the packs and threaded pretty glass beads through her hair. They slipped on her best soft leather shoes and stood back to admire their handiwork. She looked almost respectable.

Lugaid, King of the Votadini, was a short, thick-set man of nearly forty summers, his long dark hair, bleached and stiffened with lye, caught back behind his head and tied with a leather thong. His face was scarred from a long-ago battle encounter which had made his eyebrow twist into a permanent quizzical loop and it said much for his strength and regal manner that this had not disqualified him from sacred kingship. He was terrifying. From his four wives he had fifteen children. Riach was the youngest of four sons by his senior and favourite wife, Brigit.

Brigit greeted Carta with a hug. 'So, my new foster daughter, you are welcome here.' Her arms clanked with silver bangles that caught the firelight in the great feasting hall.

Glancing up shyly, Carta noticed that the hall boasted a huge gallery, screened with wattle and hung with woven curtains. Brigit followed the girl's glance.

'That is the women's chamber. We will withdraw there after the feast, but meanwhile you will sit with me and Riach.' Taking her hand, Brigit drew Carta close beside her and led her to a bench, where she sat down amongst the warriors and the nobles and their wives and the dozens of strangers who all seemed to be casting covert glances in their direction.

From the shadows a harper began to play as the doors were flung wide and a succession of huge trays of food were carried in.

She had not expected she would have lessons. King Lugaid insisted that his children, foster children and those of his warriors who wished it, learn to speak and write the language of Rome.

'Why?' Her hands on her hips, her eyes flashing, her small feet planted firmly apart, Cartimandua of the Brigantes faced the king of the Votadini in fury. She was no longer afraid of him.

He hid a smile. He had a soft spot for the little wild cat he had imported for his favourite son.

'Because it is sensible.' He folded his arms, settling back onto his cushioned bench. She was the only one of all of them to question his decision. 'Our trading links with the Empire are good. It is a language which is beginning to be spoken all over the trading world.

Your great-grandfather visited Rome, did he not? Did he not leave stories of its marvels to his bards so that all might hear about them?'

Besides, his Druids had advised him that it was expedient. Rome was restless. Its conquests and trade routes spread ever towards the setting sun. One day the eagle of Rome would fly once more across the seas, plump with greed and aggression, and then those that understood the invader and spoke their language would be at an advantage.

She was bright. She learned to read and to carve her letters on the wax tablets, smooth them over and write again. She learned to write with liquid soot on fine leaves of wood, drawing and forming her letters and exchanging notes with the other students with ease both in her native Celtic language and in the lingua Latina. And she learned to count and calculate. The Druid teachers at the college on the eastern side of the great hill were pleased with her. From the bards she learned ever more stories and songs – she already had a fund of these from her father's fireside, and she learned to play the harp. She would never play well, she was too impatient, but she had a good singing voice and would sing to her companions as the women sat sewing in their gallery or out in the sun sheltered from the wind by the great stone walls. She still did not sew. She preferred to work with the horses.

Her intelligent questions and gentle hands were welcomed in the stables. She was quick to learn which herbs to add to a horse's feed to calm it down or increase its strength. She could soothe the most fretful stallion with her small hands and pull sharp stones from a huge and shaggy hoof without need for twitch or whip.

Viv stirred. Unconsciously she stretched her cramped fingers, but the story was racing on. Picking up her pen again she wrote on, the pages filling quickly under her uneven, untidy scribbled notes. When her doorbell rang once, echoing through her silent flat, she did not hear it.

Cartimandua was universally liked. One pair of eyes alone watched her balefully from the shadows and as she grew, so the resentment behind those eyes deepened. Their owner was careful, hiding her dislike and jealousy, but as the Brigantian girl blossomed into a beautiful young woman so dislike deepened into hatred.

It started with small things. Carta's favourite pottery bowl was found broken. Then a string of freshwater pearls disappeared. Her best shoes were found thrown into a latrine pit behind the house and the smooth surface of her precious mirror was viciously scratched. Sadly she surveyed the faces of the women around her, wondering, but as yet not angry enough to go to the king.

'Take care, Carta.' Mellia had brought her own small mirror as a replacement. 'Someone is jealous of you.'

'Who?' Carta sat down on the stool near her lamp stand. The fluttering wick needed tending and automatically Mellia moved across to see to it, the light reflecting on the girl's pale hair.

Mellia shrugged. 'None of the women in this house. They all love you.' She was speaking softly, while glancing quickly over her shoulder towards the screened doorway into the central chamber where Pacata was singing to the others. The slave girl had a pure gentle voice and was often excused her other duties so she could sing them the sad beautiful songs of her native Erin.

'I haven't done anything to make people jealous of me.' Carta was genuinely bewildered.

Mellia sat down beside her and fondled Catia's head as the dog lay next to her young mistress. The two pups had gone. One, Carta had shyly presented to Riach, the other had returned to Dun Righ with her brother, Bran, a link between them as they made their tearful farewells.

In her loneliness after his departure she had turned more and more to Mellia as a friend and confidante and the two girls had grown close in their time at Dun Pelder, often whispering their hopes and dreams to one another. 'You're too pretty!' Mellia smiled. 'And you're going to marry Prince Riach, everyone knows that. That would make most women jealous.'

'I don't know I'm going to marry him!' Carta protested, colouring slightly. 'No one has ever said anything. Not officially.' The thought made her feel tingly and embarrassed, scared and excited, all at the same time. 'If I did, you wouldn't be jealous?'

'No. I'd be happy for you. If it was what you wanted.'

'Because you're in love with someone else!' Carta raised an eyebrow. 'Don't tell me you haven't been flirting with Conaire.'

Conaire had accompanied them from her father's hall as a young and inexperienced musician and had been studying hard at the bardic school which nestled on the northern flank of Dun Pelder, between the stonemasons and the goldsmith's workshop, and he had done well. He was nearly halfway through his seven years' course and had already learned a vast stock of songs and poems as well as being an acknowledged master in composing his own.

Mellia blushed scarlet. 'That's not true!'

'It is!' Carta teased. 'And why not. He's going to be a great bard one day. He will need a very special wife.'

Mellia looked down at her feet. 'He wouldn't look at me.'

Carta stared at her. 'Why not?'

'I'm not good enough.'

For once Carta was speechless. She stared for several moments at Mellia then she shook her head. 'How can you be so silly! You are beautiful. Far more beautiful than me.' She was surveying the other girl critically. 'Your hair is gorgeous. Much nicer than mine. Your eyes are prettier. You can sew and stuff like that.' Carta was being scrupulously honest. As Catia sat up and rested her head trustingly on Carta's knee, she leaned forward and hugged the dog and kissed her forehead. 'Next to Catia you're my best friend, Mellia. I couldn't have lived here without you. And I want you to marry someone really special. If Conaire becomes my head bard he will travel everywhere with me, and that means you can too. We'll be together forever. I'd like that.'

Behind them a shadow crossed the doorway and vanished. As Pacata's pure voice soared to the roof, whoever had been standing there tiptoed across the central chamber behind the silent women spinning and sewing beside the fire and disappeared out into the night.

Two days later Carta found her beloved dog, Catia, lying dead in the passage between the feasting hall and the kitchens, a dirty froth of vomit around her mouth, the remains of a meat sauce in a bowl nearby.

She knelt there on the cold stones beside the dog, her hand on the cold matted fur, tears pouring down her face. For a long time she would not let anyone touch Catia. Her despair and her misery were too raw. Even Mellia could not come near her. When at last she stood up, it was to go straight to Lugaid, interrupting his consultation with his Druid advisers.

'You have to do something!' Her eyes were bright with tears still

61

but somehow she held her anguish back, concentrating only on her anger. 'Someone is trying to chase me away. A woman. It is a woman's trick to resort to poison.' She looked from one solemn face to another. Did these men understand? Did they even care?

Truthac, one of the oldest and most senior Druids in the community held up his hand to forestall her passionate accusations. 'I don't think we would disagree with you, Cartimandua. However, what is needed is subtlety and study to find out who is doing this to you.'

'And why,' his colleague Vivios put in. 'Have you angered someone, child?'

They were taking her seriously. She was not going to have to convince them of her accusations.

'I am not aware of angering anyone. The people here are my friends.' She was speaking to the king, her eyes clear of tears now and focussed on his.

She had her suspicions. She had had them for a while now, but without proof, as the Druid said, there was little she could do.

Truthac was watching her shrewdly and she found herself looking away quickly. He can read my thoughts, she realised. He knows I suspect someone.

As if answering her unspoken statement, he gave her a grave smile. 'Suspicions are not enough, child. There must be proof. Have you consulted the gods?'

She bit her lip. The gods were a part of her life, of course they were, as they were a part of everybody's, but in this matter she preferred to rely on her native wit.

He was watching her again. As was the king, who leaned back on his bench with his arms folded. 'Go and make offerings, child, and search for omens to see what they say to you,' the king put in. 'And ask someone to help you to the temple with the dog's body. She was your friend and companion. It is right to offer her to the gods so she may live again, is that not true, Truthac?'

The Druid nodded. 'Go, child. Be steadfast in your prayers and your actions and remember,' he held up his hand as she turned away. 'Tears are the offerings we give to our departed friends and loved ones, and rightly so. Never be ashamed to cry. But tears dry and disappear. Justice is what will serve best here. Be canny.' He tapped his nose with a gnarled finger.

Dun Pelder was a sacred hill. Upon it there were temples and offering pits and a healing centre as well as an open space, surrounded by a high hedge of yew, where the gods came to the sacred lochan beneath an ancient oak tree.

She wrapped Catia's body herself in a softly woven sheet and sprinkled it with flowers. Then a servant lifted it for her and carried it to the place of offerings where it was lowered down the deep shaft to the otherworld of Annwn from where the animal would find her way into the land of everlasting summer. After the body went her leash and collar, her food bowl and her mistress's best comb. Then Carta went to the shrine of the goddess.

At home she had prayed at the sacred spring near the waterfalls. It was her nemeton, her special shrine, deep in the woods on the edge of the fells and very near the gods. It felt strange, here, amongst so many people, to seek for the other world, but there was a complex of temples sacred to the gods of the Votadini and she found her way to the shrine to Brigantia, the goddess of her own people and their land, known to her hosts and her new family as Brigit, after whom the king's wife was named.

Slipping into the darkness, she sat quietly watching a Druidess sprinkling herbs as she tended the sacred flame. The smoke from the vervain and juniper made her cough and she saw the Druidess glance at her, frowning. She sat there for a long time, without a sound, then at last, standing up, she crept into one of the two tiny sleeping chambers off the main temple. It was here that people came to pray, to ask for healing, and to seek solutions to their problems. Lying down on the couch, she closed her eyes and tried to empty her mind as she had been taught by the Druids. 'Sweet goddess hear me. Help me.'

Eventually she slept. The answer of the goddess would come in her dreams.

III

Viv sat up with a start. She could still smell the smoky incense in her nostrils, still hear the intense miserable young voice in her ears.

It was nearly dark in the room and she was extremely cold. She focussed on the table in front of her, confused, and then slowly she reached for the switch of the table lamp and throwing down her pen, stared at the notebook. Switching off the Dictaphone she wound it back a little way and pressed the play button. Silence. Then she made out a slight scratching sound. The sound of her writing. 'Damn.' She had so hoped she would speak out loud. Had tried to tell herself to speak out loud, to describe what was happening in her dream.

Or trance.

Or imagination, at last given free rein.

Or whatever it was.

It hadn't worked. She wound back the tape a whole lot further. Still silence. Just the endless automatic scribbling. With a groan she turned back in her notebook to the beginning and pulling the lamp closer, she tried to read what she had said.

Frustratingly she found there were long passages where she appeared to have been writing so fast the words had turned into long undecipherable lines and were lost forever, but in others, for instance as Carta lay silently waiting for the goddess to speak to her, the script was clear and unambiguous:

Carta beware.

Who had said that?

She wants to kill you. She does not want you to marry. She does not want you to bear children. She does not want her own seed usurped.

And who was she?

Medb of the White Hands, the king's youngest wife.

'Oh God!' Viv bit her lip, totally engrossed. 'Does she know? Did I warn her?'

It didn't matter of course. Nothing she did or said mattered. She couldn't change the course of history.

Could she?

5

I

Pat turned over in bed with a groan and glanced at the small alarm clock near the lamp on the table beside her. It was ten past three and she was still reading. With a sigh she laid down the book and sat up. She couldn't stop now. Padding down the stairs in her royal-blue pyjamas, she made her way through the silent flat to the kitchen. Turning on the light she reached for a glass and went across to the sink for some water.

She frowned. There was no mention of Medb in the book. None at all. She took a sip from her glass.

Medb.

Where had that name come from?

It had swum up from her subconscious while she was reading. Or had she dozed off without realising it and dreamed it?

'Pat? Are you OK?' Cathy appeared in the doorway behind her. She was wearing a dark red nightshirt.

'Yes, sorry. Did I wake you?' Pat leaned against the worktop, sipping from the glass. 'I was reading Viv's book. I didn't realise it was so late.'

'Is it any good?' Cathy went over to the kettle. 'I haven't started it yet. No, I was awake anyway, worrying about Tasha.'

Pat glanced at Cathy across her glass. 'Is she a problem? I thought you liked her.'

'I do. It's her mother I'm not so keen on. It's such an issue each time she comes over. Pete's got a meeting next time she brings Tasha so I've got to entertain the woman.'

'Can't you just grab the kid and shut the door in her face?'

Cathy gave a throaty laugh. 'I wish! No, I'll serve tea and cake and look all domesticated and try to outshine her at her own game as usual.'

'That's crazy. Pete lives with you. He didn't like domesticated, remember?'

'I know.' Cathy sighed. 'I may be a psychologist, Pat, but I'm still as insecure as the next woman.' Cathy reached for a jar of teabags. 'So, is Viv's book any good? I must confess I haven't read it yet.'

'Yes, it is.' Pat rubbed her eyes wearily. 'But it's really strange. She's an academic, right? And she's making a huge issue of the fact, but whatever she says it does read like fiction, she's right. It's almost lyrical. Even I can see it's full of stuff she could not possibly know for a fact and her professor is probably justified in his remarks. It is not kosher research. It can't be. I don't pretend to know anything about the subject, but I would have expected lots of other detail, social history, Roman background to the period, that sort of thing. Stuff which would be hard to convey in a drama documentary with no visual cues and not much time to spare, but this . . .' She paused, sipping from her glass. 'It doesn't matter. From my point of view it's brilliant! We can do a lot with it!'

Cathy shrugged. 'She's been translating old Celtic manuscripts and things and reading oghams, which are some sort of ancient Celtic sign writing, and running her hands over stones and stuff. She let on that much. She was really embarrassed about it!' She grinned. 'So, do I gather it is readable? After all, that is the important thing, isn't it?'

'Indeed, yes. It is readable. Very. And great material for a play, so I think we're in business, and,' Pat headed for the door, 'I'm going back to bed to finish it. As far as I remember from looking her up before I came, no one knows about Cartimandua's later life. I shall be intrigued to see what Viv has to say on the subject.'

The answer was, she didn't. She described the final confrontation between the Brigantian forces and Rome and the story stopped abruptly.

No more is heard of the Queen of the Brigantes.
She disappears from history every bit as enigmatically, if with less drama, than did her sister queen, Boudica. Did she live to grow old? Did she leave heirs? Did she meet her husband again? We do not know.

66

Pat closed the book and let it fall on the sheet. She felt absurdly cheated. The story had been exciting. Engrossing. Brilliant. Surely there must be more to the ending than that?

But of course even she, who was no historian, knew there wasn't. History is not interested in happy endings. It is not indeed interested in endings at all. It moves on with the current of events, ever following the path to the future. And Cartimandua was not even a part of history as such. She belonged to pre-history, her name only known because of her interest to Roman historians who recorded what they knew of her, or guessed, or invented, and then moved on to talk of different things.

Putting the book on the table with a sigh she reached over to turn out the light. It would make a brilliant play.

II

Sixteen miles away and some two hours later, in Aberlady, Hugh woke up and lay staring up at the ceiling. Outside the dawn chorus was in full swing, the birds so loud the glory of their song was an almost discordant force, pouring through the open window into his bedroom, drowning the silence.

He closed his eyes with a groan. It had been a long time since Alison had come to him in a dream. 'Hugh!' Her voice had been so clear. 'Hugh! Be careful.' Dropping his hand, she had moved away, turning towards the skyline. He remembered what would happen next and he reached out towards her desperately. 'Don't go. Please, don't go.'

She had paused and turned back. 'Speak to Meryn, Hugh,' she said softly. 'Speak to Meryn.' And then she had gone.

He frowned as the words came back to him.

As his car bumped over the mountain track towards the white painted stone cottage, Hugh gave a wry grin. Where else would his old friend, Meryn Jones, have come to rest in his peripatetic life when he needed to be near the National Library of Scotland for his research, than this remote glen in the Pentland hills? Any nearer the city would have been an anathema.

The two men had first met at Jesus College, Oxford over thirty years before, their point of contact their intense interest in the Celtic world in which both were working on post-graduate research, prior to setting off in very different directions, Hugh to Trinity College, Dublin, Meryn to his native Wales where he was to centre his life around his study of Druidism.

Parking near the door Hugh climbed out and looked round appreciatively. The cottage, nestling beneath a glorious great mountain, and within earshot of a swiftly running rocky burn was surrounded by a small garden where vegetables and herbs – always herbs, wherever Meryn lived, herbs for healing, and for magic and for divination – vied with flowers for the space within the tumbled grey stone garden walls.

As the two men shook hands and then turned to walk inside, Hugh grinned. He could smell coffee. Most of his friend's eccentricities he could tolerate, but herb tea morning noon and night was not one of them.

Tall, with dark hair greying at the temples, Meryn was in his mid-fifties, though his confident stride and upright posture had not changed at all from that of the young man who had gone from Oxford to live and work and study in the mountains of mid-Wales.

He led Hugh into the cottage where a large work table stood in the centre of the book-lined living room; its stone walls were nearly completely hidden by the shelves, the deep window recesses bright with scarlet geraniums, the fire in the hearth lit even though it was June.

He gestured Hugh towards one of the two deep armchairs and fetched their drinks.

'You look troubled, my friend,' Meryn said as he set down a cup beside Hugh.

Hugh sighed. There were never any preambles with Meryn. Straight to the point.

'I'm tired. Getting old and grouchy.'

Meryn smiled. 'You've always been grouchy, Hugh. As for old, you're younger than me. Prime of life! The target of many a beautiful undergraduate's lustful fantasies if rumours are true.' He smiled as he glanced across at the other man, as always acute in his summing up of the situation. 'Time for a sabbatical, perhaps?'

'In two years' time.' Hugh reached for his coffee and sniffed it appreciatively before taking a gulp. His host had a cup of something green steaming away beside him. He had not touched it, Hugh noticed. 'I dreamed about Alison,' he went on abruptly. 'I thought I was moving on, like we're told to, you know, getting on with my life,' he shrugged, 'and it's getting easier. Then suddenly, this.'

Meryn was studying his face. His silence led Hugh to continue.

'She told me to come and see you.' He gave an embarrassed laugh.

'She is a wise lady.'

Hugh nodded. Is. Not was. That was typical of Meryn. He and Meryn had re-established their close friendship thanks to Alison. She had adored Meryn's books, written to him without realising that he and her husband had once been so close, met him at last the year before she died, then on discovering the length and depth of their former friendship, insisted that Hugh and he get in touch again. They had kept in contact over the years, but their approach to their studies was very different and had in a sense driven them apart, Hugh's academic and based in the empirical record, Meryn's spiritual and psychological. His approach to Druidry was rooted not only in study, but in memory and meditation – in experience – something Hugh found hard to understand.

Meryn didn't deny being a Druid nowadays. In fact it was what he called himself. Not a member of any organisation. Nothing formal. Just a deep, passionate philosophy. A way of living. A way of believing and of remembering which came from the distant Celtic past of his country and his ancestors and his finely tuned intuition which was undoubtedly psychic. He frowned as he sat studying his visitor. His intuition was telling him now that something was very wrong.

Hugh put down his cup. He respected Meryn's learning, and his natural wisdom if not his academic purity, and lately he had begun to regard his friend as something of a mentor and guru. Meryn seemed to possess a knowledge and assurance which he himself lacked. It was something he envied.

Meryn reached for his drink at last. 'You must let her go, Hugh.'

'Who?' Hugh started almost guiltily.

'Alison, of course.' Meryn was watching him closely. 'Who did you think I meant?'

Hugh shook his head. He leaned back in the chair and took a deep breath. Then he plunged into his story, coming straight to the point. 'Did you ever meet Dr Lloyd Rees when you came up to the DPCHC?'

Meryn shook his head. 'One of your adoring disciples?'

Hugh gave a bitter smile. 'I used to think so.'

After a pause Meryn asked, 'So, what has Dr Lloyd Rees done to displease you?'

'She's written a damn stupid book. Made a complete ass of herself. It's going to show up the whole department, and she's –' He paused abruptly. 'She's done something else unutterably stupid as well, and I don't know what to do about it.'

'What sort of thing?'

'She's stolen something, Meryn. Something of inestimable value.' Hugh glanced up.

He hadn't actually seen her do it, but when he had gone back to the office and searched the chaos of his desk it had gone. It had to have been her. Who else would have done it?

'Have you asked her?'

Hugh shook his head.

'Why?'

'I didn't want to confront her, I suppose.' Hugh shrugged. Scowling, he levered himself out of his chair and paced restlessly up and down the floor a couple of times.

Thoughtfully Meryn watched him. Hugh was growing more agitated by the second.

'She doesn't realise what she has started!' Hugh burst out suddenly. He flung himself down on the chair again and drummed his fingers on his knee, staring into the fire.

'And what has she started?' Meryn's question was very soft as he studied the other man's expression.

'A war.' Hugh said the words almost absent-mindedly. 'She started a war. Stupid bitch!' His voice had changed. Deepened. Become raw with anger. 'She will pay for what she has done!'

Meryn raised an eyebrow. 'Strong words.' He was carefully scanning Hugh's face.

'Not strong enough!'

'Are we still talking about Dr Lloyd Rees?'

'No! I'm talking about Cartimandua!' Hugh's eyes were closed now, his mouth set in a grim line.

Meryn frowned, his senses alert. It wasn't Cartimandua who had started a war, it was the man whose essence was prowling through the room, the man whose anger and impatience was resonating in the shadows, whose voice had used Hugh's larynx, the man whom Hugh did not appear, as yet, to have seen.

'What do you think Dr Lloyd Rees took from you, Hugh?' he asked quietly.

'A brooch. Technically a gold fibula.' After a moment's hesitation Hugh's voice was his own again. The shadowy figure had gone.

Meryn nodded gravely. He relaxed. 'And why did she take it, do you know? Presumably she is not by nature a thief.'

'She wants it to show on a TV programme. Part of the publicity for her book.'

'So she hasn't stolen it ? She intends to give it back?'

Hugh shrugged. 'As far as I know.'

'And did she not ask if she could borrow it?'

Hugh nodded. 'I said no.'

'Why?'

'Because –' Hugh shook his head from side to side vehemently. 'Because I didn't want her to have it, Meryn!' He hesitated again. 'Don't ask me why. I was feeling uncooperative, perhaps. Or grouchy, as you so charmingly put it. Or just angry with her. But she shouldn't have taken it.'

'If indeed she has.'

'If indeed she has.' Hugh sighed. 'I lent it to Hamish Macleod.' He paused. 'He couldn't bring himself to touch it. He told me he left it in the box. He wouldn't let anyone else touch it either.' He looked up and met Meryn's steady gaze. 'There is something about the brooch which is odd.'

'What about you? Have you touched it, Hugh?'

Hugh nodded.

'What happened?' Meryn was looking thoughtful.

'Nothing happened. At least –' Hugh shrugged. 'It felt strange. Powerful. I assumed that was because I knew how old and rare it was. But . . .'

'But?' Meryn prompted after a minute or two.

Hugh shook his head. 'Artefacts like that have a powerful effect on the imagination.' He couldn't quite bring himself to say the word evil. His father had felt it. Perhaps so had Wheeler. He had always wondered why the latter had given up the brooch so easily. Maybe this irrational fear was experienced by anyone who came near it. That would explain everything.

71

Meryn was nodding sagely. 'So, what did you imagine, my friend?' There was a slight twinkle in his eye.

'That the brooch would give me an unpleasant insight into the head of the man to whom it had belonged.'

'Who was?'

'Venutios, King of the Brigantes.'

'And you don't want Dr Lloyd Rees to share your insight?'

Hugh opened his mouth to answer, said nothing, and shrugged. 'I didn't want her to be harmed.'

'Harmed in what way?'

Hugh sighed. 'Something happened when she left the room. The sudden cold. The atmosphere. It didn't make sense at the time. I thought it was me. The quarrel I'd had with her. But now,' he looked up with a frown, 'I'm frightened, Meryn. I think the brooch could be dangerous. That's why I came to see you.'

III

Meryn sat for a long time after Hugh left, staring deep into the smouldering embers of the fire, reaching with tentative fingers into the past. Hugh had left him a postcard of the brooch, its exquisite craftsmanship obvious in the intricate swirls of gold and the jewelled colours of the enamels as it sat on its black velvet plinth in the museum showcase. The card rested on his knee as his mind quested the darkness behind the glowing logs at his feet. The craftsman who had made it had been proud of this his most beautiful achievement. It was an artefact fit for a god. But it had not been given to a god. Meryn frowned. The shadowy figure who was stalking Hugh was not alone. There were others there, drifting in the room, conjured from the otherworld by the very thought of this piece of jewellery. Who else had been affected by it, he wondered. He shivered as his thoughts strayed to the museum where it had lain, the malign chill of its presence cut off from the world by its glass case. Conservators and curators had admitted to him more than once in private that they could feel the vibes coming off some of the treasures in their care. Alone, when the public had gone, in the empty galleries or the work rooms behind the scenes they saw and felt echoes of the past which were far from dormant. This brooch had probably done the same.

He lifted the picture off his knee and studied it in the flickering glow of the firelight. At some point in its existence it had been imbued with power which, whatever the original intention, was now malign. Why? By whom? How? Why had these sticky threads of danger remained to contaminate all who touched it? He looked back into the fire. Tendrils of grey smoke were seeping out into the room and he screwed up his eyes with a frown, sensing a swirl of conflict, of love and hate, of fear and tragedy as the last of the logs collapsed into the bed of ash and for the time being the window into the shadows closed.

IV

'So, Dr Lloyd Rees, are you coming to hand in your notice? As a popular author, you clearly no longer need the pittance you earn with us.' Hugh had just managed to ease his car into a much coveted parking space near George Square. He was pocketing his car keys as he turned and found himself face to face with Viv.

She could feel her face flaming in response to the comment. Somehow she clamped down on the retort which fizzed in her head. She would not give him the satisfaction of seeing her lose her temper again. She forced herself to smile. 'I'm afraid you'll have to put up with me a while, yet, Hugh. Someone has to try and bring our attitudes out of the ark and into the world of modern research, after all.'

Damn! Why had she said that? Why antagonise him further?

He had started it, though.

She gripped the strap of the tote bag on her shoulder until her knuckles turned white. Don't say another word, Viv. Wait for him to mention the brooch. Did he even know it was missing? If he didn't he soon would if he was heading into the office. She chewed her lips nervously, watching as he bent to retrieve from the pavement the heavy briefcase which he had just pulled out of the car.

For a moment they both stood unmoving there on the footpath. It was the professor who turned away first. Swinging on his heel without another word he strode off, carrying his heavy case with him. He had said nothing about the pin. At the corner he veered away from the office, walking briskly into the square. In spite of herself she smiled with relief. At least they were not going to the same place, but he wouldn't want to carry that briefcase far.

Following him at a safe distance she headed away from him, seeking the sanctuary of the small book-lined room she had called her own for five years now on the first floor of the small Georgian terraced building on the west side of the square.

Turning up the steps she ducked in through the door to look in at the office where the departmental secretary, Heather James, was sitting at her computer, her eyes fixed on the screen. The coffee machine was gurgling quietly. 'Can I grab one on my way upstairs?' Viv dropped her bag on the only empty chair and reached towards the tray of mugs. 'I suppose you saw that through the window?'

'Saw what?' Heather's large blue eyes seemed to grow larger behind her glasses as she glanced up, then went back to her letter.

'The Prof heading off towards the library rather than come in here with me.' Viv grinned. She poured herself a coffee, then realised that her legs were shaking. She sat down abruptly beside her bag, cupping her hands around the mug.

Heather raised an eyebrow. Her light-hearted daily flirtations with her devastatingly attractive boss were part of office life, as was her ability to soothe his notoriously short fuse. 'Don't let him get to you, Viv.' Her fingers flashed across the keyboard; her eyes didn't leave the screen.

'It's hard not to.'

'But not impossible. He's done it before, you know.'

'What?'

'Bullied people. I think it means he likes you.' There was an unexpected chortle from behind the piles of files on her desk. 'Keep cool. He's won if you lose it.'

Viv exhaled audibly. 'Lose what? Temper or job?' Heather clearly hadn't heard about her attempt at grand larceny.

'Either or both. Take some time out this summer and chill. Get right away from the department.'

It was a tempting idea. Upstairs Viv stared round her office. Book-lined walls, desk, chairs for students. Piles of papers and the view out across the square. How many days and months had she spent in this room in all? She didn't like to think. It was beginning to feel like a trap. It smelled dusty. Depressing. She could cross the floor in three paces. Throwing up the sash window with its old frayed cords juddering on the brink of stasis, she stood looking out. Hugh hadn't headed across towards the library as she had assumed after all. He was sitting in the square. She could see him easily from here. His briefcase on the bench beside him, he was leaning forward, his hands clenched between his knees, his face set in deep lines as he stared down at his feet, the dappled shadow of the trees playing over his features. He looked up briefly as someone walked past him, then he looked down again. His whole body language spelled out dejection. She frowned. She wasn't about to feel sorry for him.

Twice she looked out of the window again. He hadn't moved. Then as she was about to sit down at her desk at last she saw him climb to his feet and slowly turn back towards the department.

V

Standing in his office doorway, jingling his keys in his hand, Hugh was surveying the room as though he had never seen it before. The building was quiet. Further up the corridor Viv's door was closed. Taking a step inside he shut the door behind him, dropped his heavy bag on the floor, and stood, taking in the over-laden book-shelves, the piles of books and papers on the floor, the worn rugs, the untidy desk, the ancient chairs some of which also bore piles of books.

Slowly he walked across to the desk.

'Just make absolutely sure the brooch has actually gone, Hugh,' Meryn had said. 'Go for the obvious first. Check and double-check you haven't hidden it, lost it, dropped it. Then decide what you want to do.'

Methodically he began to tidy the desk, collecting files and letters into neat stacks, returning books to the shelves, capping pens and biros and putting them into the mug which sat beside his computer for that purpose. Twice he paused, looking round, listening. The room was empty. He had no sense that there was anything, or anyone, there. The strange overwhelming feeling that someone had been watching Viv as she left his room with the brooch, the feeling about which he had told Meryn, had gone. Emptying the two filing trays and refilling them methodically with the letters and reports and memos which they were supposed to contain but somehow didn't any more, he slowly began to bring order to the chaos. Before he was halfway through his task he knew for certain that the brooch wasn't there.

Finished at last, he sat down and considered the empty blotter, the tidy filing trays, the piles of files, the whole neat area in front of him, then he put his head in his hands. His mind was a blank.

'Do you want to sack her? Do you want to call the police?' Meryn had said before Hugh left. The blue eyes had held his for a second. 'If she has stolen the brooch, she's given you cause.'

Hugh sighed with frustration. What had possessed her to take the wretched thing? He pictured her standing there in front of him, a vision in magenta, her eyes betraying her every thought as she looked at him. Angry. Challenging. Frightened. Indignant and then guilty. Even before she had taken the darn thing. Guilty.

Guilty because she was the cause of the war.

Guilty because she had betrayed her people.

Hugh frowned and took a deep breath, clenching his fists on the blotter in front of him. He had done it again. For one frightening moment he had confused her in his mind with the woman who had owned the brooch nearly two millennia before.

'Be careful, Hugh,' Meryn had said quietly as they had sat together before the gently smouldering fire in the cottage in the Pentland hills. 'Don't let yourself identify too closely with Venutios. I don't know why yet, but his link with that brooch was only too real.'

Hugh had laughed.

VI

The sun had risen out of a bank of opal mist. Above it scraps of pink cloud floated like spun gauze in the clear blue bowl of the sky. The sea slumbered still, the colour of knapped flint, save where a path of light, carbuncle red, led towards the shore.

Her horse's rein over her arm, Carta stood on the clifftop watching. In a moment the gauze would be too flimsy, the sun's brilliance too strong and she would have to avert her eyes. The sweet symbol of the goddess of fire who hung her cloak upon its golden rays and whose warmth would sustain and comfort them through the summer would in a moment remind her of its implacable strength.

Dropping the rein she waited, ignoring the animal, who wandered a few paces away before beginning to graze, then as the crimson sliver broke through the mist she raised her arms in greeting.

She could feel the goddess's kiss of warmth on her skin. Feel her power touching the land. As her gentle fingers touched the horse's flank it raised its head and in turn it whickered greeting and acknowledgement before dropping its head once more to the grass.

The time of her marriage was coming close. Carta was a woman now. Several moons ago her bleeding time had started. There was a celebration for her in the women's hall and a blessing. The king's Druids and the king and his sons had met and messages had been sent to her father, recently elected high king of Brigantia. Her marriage portion had to be agreed and brought to Alba and her father and mother would come to celebrate the Beltane feast with gifts and feasting. Her husband was chosen and she was happy – so happy.

Were it not for one deep cloud like that which hovered across the sea and now covered the great rock out there amidst the gathering sun paths through the mist. Someone who did not want her to marry. Someone who had cursed her.

She shivered. The night before it had been the turn of Carta's bard, Conaire, to sing. He had risen to his feet and with a bow to the king reached for his small harp. The song he had sung was one of Carta's favourites. It told how she had raced across the moors against her three brothers and won. It told how well she rode, how she was one with her pony as it galloped through the Setantian mists. It told how she had won her name.

The men and women in the crowded hall listened as they lounged round the fire glancing from time to time at Carta who sat next to Riach, with Mellia beside her, the girl's eyes fixed on the young man's face with adoration. The servants and slaves had cleared away the dishes and the food. Fresh logs had been thrown on the hot ashes and mead and wine were being passed round the assembled company as, outside, the heavy spring rain watered the growing crops of the farms which spread out across the plain below the high terraces of the fort and drenched the roofs of the round houses, splattering on the mud beneath the eaves.

Carta stared down at her own small goblet, half embarrassed, pleased by the looks of admiration being cast in her direction. She was glowing with pride.

The music was slowing. Conaire drew his fingers across the strings in a vivid, dramatic chord.

> *Carta came to the court of a king,*
> *And all who looked upon her smiled.*

His voice rang to the roof timbers.

> *But deep in the heart of the friendly crowd*
> *Lurked a worm who her name reviled.*

There was a dramatic pause, then a gasp spread around the great chamber. The words of the bard implied that the sacred vow of hospitality and friendship had been violated. Such an accusation was unheard of, but the accusation of a trained bard had the blessing of the gods as his words came direct from them through their inspiration. It had to be heard.

The king rose to his feet and silence fell on the company. Carta could feel her cheeks flaming. She did not dare to look around at the faces of the king's family, her foster family. Beside her Mellia was holding her breath.

'You make a grave accusation, my friend.' Lugaid's voice was calm. 'And you make it in a public place.'

Conaire bowed. He set his harp down at his feet. 'I speak the truth.' His voice was quiet, but it carried to every man and woman there.

Carta found the courage to look up at last. Her eyes met Medb's.

The king's youngest wife was white to the lips, her eyes radiating anger and hatred. Carta looked away. Somehow she forced herself to stand up and face the crowds in the room. The silence was intense. 'I don't know what I have done to earn such dislike,' she said, her voice ringing out clearly, 'but I am sorry for it. I would have hoped to be a sister to every woman here.'

There was a second gasp and a rapid murmur of voices ran round the fire. She had added her support to the accusation; and she had confirmed that her enemy was a woman.

Truthac, the king's Druid leaned forward and murmured in his ear. Lugaid nodded and sat down as Truthac rose in his place and stood, leaning on his staff. 'This must be spoken about further. But for now I would invite our own bard to sing us another song; perhaps a song about Carta's family and her heritage of courage and dedication.' He smiled gravely at the silent crowd, his eyes resting for only a fraction longer on one face than on the others. His gaze was met by stony defiance.

By the fire Carta resumed her seat on the cushioned bench, so close to the woman who was her enemy. The nervous thudding of her heart had subsided a little. She glanced at Conaire as Mellia slipped away from her side and made her way towards him, shyly touching the young man's shoulder in a gesture of support. Carta hadn't realised he knew what was going on, but the gods had chosen to speak through him and all she could do now was to wait patiently and see what Truthac and Lugaid advised, and in the mean time she would pray to her goddesses to help her.

'Strong Lady of the sun; Sweet Lady of the moon; guardians of this place; spirits of this land; keep me safe. Shield me from her curses. Turn them back as arrows to her heart. Tell me what to do –'

'Viv? Are you asleep?'

The voice beside her made Viv jump violently. Heather was standing in the doorway with the coffee jug in her hand. 'I thought you might like a top up. You've been up here for ages.'

Outside her office the sun had moved on round. The bench where Hugh had been sitting was in deep shadow. And empty.

Viv stared at it for a moment, numb with shock, her heart thumping under her ribs. Carta had gone. Vanished in an instant in the middle of her prayer as though a door had slammed, separating them so abruptly that the shock she felt was like a pain. Taking a deep breath, she looked up at Heather and somehow she managed to pull herself together, forcing herself to concentrate on the present and put the dream behind her. Her first coherent thought was of the professor. 'Is Hugh here?'

'Yup. In his office. He's got a meeting with Hamish later.'

'I think I'll go home, then.' Viv reached for her mug and held it out. Her hand was shaking. 'Thanks, Heather. Just half. Then I'll go and work at the flat for the rest of the week. Keep out of his way. If you need me give me a call.'

The vision had come without invitation. Suddenly. Completely. For over an hour she had been sitting there in another world, unaware of anything around her. Not even hearing the door open. Aware of nothing until Heather spoke to her. Slowly she began to pile books and folders into her bag, realising as she did so that her hands were still trembling.

'There shouldn't be any problems. All the exam papers are marked. I don't think there will be any queries. There aren't any resits this year, thank goodness.'

After Heather disappeared she stopped her frenetic activity for a moment and took a deep breath. She mustn't forget the dream. She had to fix the details in her mind. The sounds and smells of the feasting hall, the haunting beauty of the song, the background noise and then the total silence, the bolt of fear that had shocked Carta as she sat and listened to the prophecy. Somehow she had to find her way back to the scene as soon as possible. As soon as she reached the privacy of her own flat.

Her desk cleared, she let herself out of her office and stood for a moment on the landing, listening. Hugh's door was closed. The building was silent. Holding her breath, she tiptoed along the corridor, pausing as the floor creaked beneath her feet. The last thing she needed now was another encounter with Hugh and the discussion which would surely follow about the Cartimandua Pin.

Heather was right. She needed to chill.

She had made her escape, pulling the heavy outside door behind her when, only a few paces from the building, a voice accosted her. 'Hi, Viv.'

She nearly jumped out of her skin.

It was Steve Steadman. The bag on his back hung open to reveal several books and files. 'I've just been to the library.'

'So I see.' She did not stop walking so he fell in step beside her, his long strides adapting at once to hers. He was smiling, his pleasant face relaxed and friendly.

'When are you planning to go home to Yorkshire?' She glanced across at him, pleased suddenly to have his cheerful, straightforward company.

'Next weekend.'

'You must be looking forward to it.' She was making conversation to compensate for not stopping; for walking so fast. She wanted to put as much distance between herself and the office and Hugh as possible.

'I am.' He nodded. 'I'll probably stay there for a bit over the summer and give them a hand on the farm. I can come back up to the library if I need to as I work on my thesis. So, might I see you down there?' He gave her his usual relaxed grin. 'It would be great if you could visit us.'

She hesitated. 'You know, I might. It's very tempting.' Tempting and frightening. To see Carta's home. The scenes of her early childhood. What would happen if she went there? They paused to wait for the traffic lights before turning into Forrest Road. She glanced at him in time to see his eyes fixed on her face. He looked away at once, as though embarrassed to be caught staring. Could he see something odd about her, she wondered. Sense the aura of the past which she could still feel hanging around her? She hoped not. She shivered. The street was busy, and for a moment the noise of a lorry changing gear beside them almost drowned out the quiet voice which spoke unexpectedly in her ear.

'So, Dr Lloyd Rees, has Mr Steadman been giving you his opinion of your book?'

Viv gasped audibly. Hugh Graham had walked up behind them, unnoticed. She faced him, her heart thudding. 'Indeed he has. He liked it.'

'Did you?' Hugh turned to her companion and peered at him over the top of his spectacles. 'Well, you're inexperienced as yet.' He smiled. 'I had hoped to see you in the department, Dr Lloyd Rees.' He paused, scanning her face . 'I would have appreciated the chance to speak to you alone.' He glanced at Steve, then he went on, 'But as you are here now, I may as well tell you. Amongst other things, I have been looking over the timetables for next year. Assuming you are still with us.' He paused for a fraction of a second, his eyes fixed on hers. For a moment she thought she saw a flicker of hesitation there, but if there was it was gone so fast she might have imagined it. He went on implacably, 'I'm sure you'll be pleased to see you've been given more time to lecture the new intake of undergraduates. I think your approach to history will intrigue them. The second years, where the standards of teaching are so much more important, will be supervised by Dr Grant. As you know Dr Macleod has resigned as from the end of this academic year to start his well-earned retirement, and I have decided that I will give the Readership to Dr Grant as a reward for his hard work and loyalty to the department.' He paused, waiting for a reaction as the lights changed once more and the traffic surged forward. 'He hasn't published as much as you, but his work is sound.'

Viv stared at him, dimly aware that Steve had moved closer to her and reached out to touch her elbow in a quiet gesture of support. For a moment she was too stunned to speak. When at last she managed to open her mouth it was to stutter, 'You're right. This is hardly the place to discuss this, Hugh!'

He shrugged. 'Why not? Surely you don't mind Mr Steadman knowing. Everyone will soon enough. As I warned you I have reviewed the situation and I have now made the right decision. We are a small department. I am afraid there is very little room for promotion and when a position does come up, it must go to the strongest candidate. The most reliable and honest candidate.'

'Honest?' Viv was intensely aware of Steve's eyes on her face again. He was looking very uncomfortable.

'Honest, Dr Lloyd Rees.' Hugh pursed his lips. 'There is, as I believe you know, something missing from my study.' Near them the lights turned red once more. People surged past them across the road. They did not move.

'I don't know what you mean.' Viv's mouth had gone dry.

'Don't you?'

They faced each other in silence for a moment, Steve at Viv's elbow. Holding her breath, she waited for Hugh's next blow; for him to laugh as he told her he had the perfect excuse now to sack her, an excuse which would be upheld by any court and any university council in the world. He didn't. He didn't know for sure, she realised suddenly. He couldn't prove it.

He gave her another long cold look then with a smile he bowed slightly and turned away, walking briskly up the road towards Greyfriars.

Steve shook his head. 'What the hell is he talking about? What is he thinking of, telling you like that, in the street, for God's sake?' He was furiously indignant for her. 'I'm so sorry, Viv.'

'You too?' Viv said somewhat grimly. 'Don't worry about it. I'm not. If he was out to humiliate me, it hasn't worked.' She managed to bring her attention back to his face. 'Look, I wish you hadn't had to witness that. I'm not the Prof's favourite person at the moment as you can see and he doesn't seem to be himself, does he.' She realised that she was shaking. 'This is nothing that can't be fixed, I'm sure. We differ in our approach to things, that's all. A nice long summer holiday and it will all blow over.' It wouldn't, of course. How could it? But there was no need for Steve to know that.

'Come to Ingleborough, Viv.' Steve reached out and touched her arm. 'Away from Hugh. Follow the footsteps of Cartimandua. Why don't you?'

She shivered. 'I'll let you know, Steve.' She punched his arm affectionately. 'See you soon.' And she ducked across the road just as the lights turned green again, leaving him standing looking after her.

6

I

Viv spotted the manuscript of her play on Cathy's desk at once, with the copy of her book resting on top of it, as she threw herself into one of the armchairs in front of the bookcase. Cathy and Pete were in the kitchen getting supper and Tasha was slumped in front of the TV in the living room. Pat had followed her into the study with a bottle of chilled white wine and two glasses. The other armchair was occupied with a certain air of defiance by Pablo, so after a moment's hesitation Pat pulled up a smaller chair next to the desk.

'This is fantastic!' She thumped the jacket of the book. 'Brilliant. I enjoyed it enormously. What a woman!'

Viv gave a wry grin. 'Indeed.' She waited to see what Pat was going to say next.

'And your stab at the play is not at all bad.' Pat put on a pair of green-rimmed spectacles and laid her hand on the manuscript. 'Much better than I expected, in fact.' She reached for the bottle and poured, pushing one of the glasses across the desk towards Viv. 'I like the approach you've taken. The drama. The narrative interludes. That works well.'

'Not according to Maddie.' Viv took a gulp from her glass.

'And I'll tell you why.' Pat glanced up. 'You don't mind? It's what I'm here for.'

'I don't mind.' Viv shrugged. She minded like hell, but she had no choice.

'You've become self-conscious. In the book you were relaxed and confident. On your own ground. You knew what you were doing. Your voice, and Cartimandua's voice are authentic. In the play you've lost that authenticity. It comes through from time to time almost by accident and those bits come alive. Like the first scene. It's brilliant. Then you rein yourself in again and I think that's the phrase you used yourself, and the style becomes –' Pat hesitated. 'Pedagogic. Even pedantic.' She groped in her pocket for her cigarettes. 'Do you think Cathy would notice if I smoke?'

'Yes.' Viv grinned. 'Yes, she would.'

'You're right. It's a bummer trying to give up.' Pushing the packet back into her jacket Pat reached for her glass again instead. 'Does what I'm saying make sense?' She raised an eyebrow.

Viv shrugged again. 'I suppose it does, yes.'

Cartimandua's voice – not authentic! She smiled grimly to herself.

'Do you mind if we do some deconstructing?' Pat went on. 'Shorter scenes. Punchier. More real. Your good ones are so good they make the hairs stand up on the back of my neck. That's why the others are such an anti-climax.' She shook her head. 'And the narrator's voice needs to be less tentative. This is you, right? Whether we use you in person, or an actor. You are the world authority on this woman. We need to be convinced of it.'

Viv let out a gasp of laughter. 'The world authority?'

'Too right!' Pat took off her glasses and looked at her earnestly. 'I've got such a good feeling about this. It will make a fabulous piece of radio. I've got a friend down in Cornwall who could compose us some music. Lots of ambient sound. Celtic stuff, you know. Pentatonic scale – all the black notes! Full of mystery and atmosphere. Maybe record it on site with the wind in the mike. I can hear it in my head already. Viv, this is going to be wonderful.' She took a sip of wine, then reached for her spectacles again. Opening the manuscript she glanced at it, running her finger down the text as though she were going to read a bit from it. Then she changed her mind. 'What we need is a new outline.' She studied Viv's face and hesitated. 'Can I ask you something?'

'What?'

Who is Maeve?'

'Maeve?' Viv echoed the name in shock. 'Why?'

Maeve. Medb.

Medb of the White Hands.

She was not in the play. Not in the book. She had no part to play in recorded history.

85

Pat was frowning. 'The name keeps coming to me. I dreamed about her last night, as though she was a character in your book. But she isn't. Is she? I checked the index and I couldn't find her.'

Viv shook her head. 'No, she's not in the book.' Her mouth had gone dry.

'But the name means something to you?' Pat cocked an eyebrow. She picked up her glass and standing up, wandered over to the other chair near Viv's where, careful not to disturb the cat, she perched on the arm. 'Who is she?'

Viv shook her head. 'I believe she was someone Cartimandua came across in her early life. A period not covered by the book because we know nothing about it officially.' She paused. Then she found herself unable to resist asking, 'What did she look like. In your dream?'

Pat was silent for a moment, remembering. 'She was young. Very beautiful. Tall. Slim. With amazingly striking eyes. Intense light steely-blue. A hard face.' She shook her head. 'I don't think she was very nice.'

The silence in the study drew out into a long pause as Pat swung one leg slowly back and forth, the shoe dangling from her foot. She was studying Viv's face.

'No.' Viv sounded worried. 'She wasn't very nice. But I don't know how we know that. We know nothing about Cartimandua's life apart from what the Roman historians tell us. They were not interested in anything much but politics.'

'A point you make very clearly in the book.'

Viv nodded.

'And yet you've put in a lot more than Roman politics.'

'Extrapolated from other sources,' Viv said, almost to herself. 'From archaeology for instance.'

'And Maeve's name is not mentioned anywhere.'

'No.'

'But she features in the story, doesn't she? Why haven't you mentioned her?'

It was Viv's turn to reach for the bottle. Lunging forward out of her chair she grabbed it and slopped a little wine into her glass with a shaking hand, spilling some onto the carpet. 'Nothing more than guesswork. Forget her. She's not part of this story.'

'Are you sure?' Pat was frowning. 'Why would I dream about her?'

'I can't imagine.'

For a moment the two women looked at each other, then at last Pat shrugged. She changed the subject. 'How do you want to work with this? Shall we get together each morning? I could come over to your place and we can concentrate on getting it done before you have to go away. I gather you have a publicity tour coming up?'

Viv nodded. 'A week or so talking about my book.'

'Right. Well, we'll try and get as much done as possible before that.' Pat paused. Then went on, 'Another idea has just occurred to me. Rather than do all this in a studio, I think it would be really effective to record some if not all of it on location. With sound effects. Like the music. It would be tremendously atmospheric. It works on radio. Something TV has taught us. Any editing we need I'll do myself initially on my laptop.'

'That sounds a wonderful idea.' Viv nodded vehemently, then she glanced round as the door opened and Pete put his head in. 'Supper's ready, girls.'

As they stood up and made their way after him towards the kitchen Pablo sat up and stretched, then he jumped down from the chair to follow them. In the doorway he stopped and glanced back over his shoulder into the empty room. For a moment he hesitated, eyes wide, his tail fluffing with fear, then he followed them.

There were five of them around the table this time including Tasha, and tonight's menu was once-more child friendly. Fishcakes made from a mixture of organic wild salmon and sustainably-sourced white fish, the name of which Cathy could not recall.

'You can help Viv and me choose a name for ourselves, Tash,' Pat said with a grin as she sat down. She was becoming quite fond of this precocious mixed-up child. 'Maddie has suggested we form a production company. And this could be the start of a very exciting new angle to Viv's career. You realise, Viv,' she added enthusiastically, 'if this is the success I think it is going to be, we needn't stop with Cartimandua. We could go on to make other historical drama documentaries for radio. The success of this will carry us forward and your name will be linked with the product rather than with the period. That would get your professor off your back.'

'But I'm a Celticist.'

'You're a talented woman with several strings to your bow,' Pat contradicted. She sat back in the chair, her arms outstretched on either side of her plate, eyeing her fishcake. She was dying for a cigarette. Opposite her Pablo the cat was sitting on the draining board watching the proceedings with inscrutable green eyes. 'So, what are we going to call ourselves?'

Half an hour later they were still arguing. Wearily Cathy stood up and went to rummage in the fridge for another bottle of wine. 'Do you think you'll find it easy to agree the script if you find it this difficult to decide on a name?' She picked up the corkscrew with a rueful smile.

'Sisters. That's good. Something sisters. Or sisters of something,' Pat went on, ignoring her. She too was growing impatient. They were going round in circles.

'Sounds too much like feminist stuff.' Pete shook his head. He helped himself to the last of the peas.

'Daughters, then.' Cathy topped up their glasses.

'That's less aggressive, certainly.' Pete nodded. He was keeping out of the argument.

'Daughters of Fire,' Viv said suddenly. 'That's it. Brigantia is a fire goddess, the Brigantes the people of fire and Cartimandua is a fiery woman.' She was conscious of Pablo watching her, his eyes unblinking.

'As are we! Perfect!' Pat punched the air. 'Yes! Then if we write other things we can specialise in feisty women. Mary, Queen of Scots. Elizabeth. Mary Tudor. Eleanor of Aquitaine –'

'They needn't be queens of course,' Cathy put in. 'Jane Austen. The Brontë Sisters, George Eliot.' The excitement was catching. 'Amelia Earhart, Mata Hari. Florence Nightingale.' She paused. 'So, as I said, no need to panic at being typecast as a Celticist who kicked over the traces, Viv!' She laughed. 'Right, now, one thing at a time. Don't forget you need a working title for the play.'

'The Forgotten Queen,' Viv put in quietly. 'That's what I've called it. After all, you'll find hardly anyone has heard of her.'

'Perfect.' Pat nodded. 'It's intriguing. Descriptive. Tantalising.' She didn't tell them it would probably be changed several times before the editors decided what was right. 'So, let's drink a toast. To the Daughters of Fire: Viv, Pat and Cartimandua, the Forgotten Queen.'

Tash was very silent. She had finished her fishcake, pushed aside the impeccably vegetarian peas and rice and the especially bought bottle of tomato sauce which was her exclusive property and which now stood untouched beside her plate. 'Do you want to drink to us, Tash?' Viv asked, uncomfortably aware that the child's eyes had been fixed on her face. There was a glass of orange beside her plate.

Tasha shook her head. 'She's there again,' she said, her small face screwed into a puzzled frown. 'That woman behind you.'

Viv froze, paralysed with terror. The room had grown very still.

The others fell silent. One by one they turned to look at Viv.

'Tasha!' Pete was very stern. 'We told you before.'

'It's true!' Tasha stood up. 'It's true!' she wailed again. 'Look!' She pointed. 'Can't you see her? Pablo can. Look at him.' The cat had risen to his feet, back arched, and was staring towards Viv, his fur on end.

There was a further second of utter silence. At last Cathy spoke. 'We can't see anyone, Tash,' she said gently. 'Pablo is just stretching.'

'I'm not making it up!' Tash screamed.

Pablo let out a screech of terror and jumped off the draining board, fleeing out of the door. Tasha paused for only a second before breaking into floods of tears and running from the kitchen after him.

'Wow!' Pat took a deep breath. 'Does she often do that?' She glanced at Viv, who had gone white as a sheet. Cartimandua was here in the room with them. She could feel her.

'She said the same thing last time I was here,' Viv replied shakily.

'And as before, we all know it's rubbish,' Cathy said firmly. 'Collect up the plates, Pete, would you? She got a wonderful reaction last time and she thought she'd try it again. Let her be. Ignore it.'

'I saw something,' Pete said quietly. He hadn't moved.

The three women looked at him. Viv blanched. Please, no.

'A shadow. Just for a second. There, immediately behind Viv.'

'Oh, for God's sake!' Cathy began to gather up the plates herself. 'Come on, Pete. Let's have a bit of stark reality here, please!'

He shook his head. 'Of course. It must have been a trick of the light.' He didn't sound convinced.

'Too right!' Cathy was cross.

Pete shrugged. He was watching Viv's face. 'You OK? Sorry, I didn't mean to frighten you.'

'Well, you did!' Viv stood up. Suddenly she found she couldn't breathe. 'I need some fresh air. I'm going home. I'm sorry. I'm all right . . .'

Ignoring the anxious voices behind her, Viv ran down the elegant curved stone staircase with its wrought-iron balustrade which climbed up through the house towards an oval skylight above her head. As she reached the entrance hall, she glanced over her shoulder with a shiver of terror. The street door was closed. The vestibule was silent, shadowy and cold, and smelled of pine disinfectant and, faintly, of cigarettes. Scrabbling frantically at the latch, she let herself out into the street. Behind her the light clicked off on its timer and left her in darkness.

II

Pat couldn't sleep. The so-called box room in which she had been installed boasted a narrow pine bed and a duvet decorated with fairy tale princesses, aimed she suspected at Tasha or her friends in earlier, more innocent incarnations. On the small chest of drawers she had laid out her notebooks and laptop. Her capacious red canvas bag acted as wardrobe and her cosmetics such as they were sat on the window sill where earlier she had rested on her elbows puffing the smoke from a guiltily smoked cigarette into the darkness. She left the window open as she turned out the light and climbed into the bed to lie staring up at the ceiling.

Sleep wouldn't come. Tense and uneasy, she kept playing back the extraordinary scene at the kitchen table. Tasha and Pete had both seen something. There was no doubt about that. And Pete had not just said it to show solidarity with his daughter. She pictured Viv's white face. She had often heard people described as looking like rabbits caught in a car's headlights. That was how she had looked. Disbelieving. Trapped. Terrified.

They hadn't wanted her to go home alone. Cathy was worried and cross. Cross with Tasha and with Pete. Protective. Pete and she had had a row after Viv had gone and Pat had left them to it, wandering into the sitting room where she had joined Tasha who was sitting on the sofa in front of the television. The news was just finishing and a map of the next day's weather was flashed on the screen. Tasha was hugging a large cushion. There were tears in her eyes. 'I did see something.'

'I know.' Pat was dying for a cigarette.

'You don't believe me.'

'I didn't say that. I didn't see anything myself, Tasha,' Pat said cautiously. 'But your dad said he did.' They were both staring at the screen.

'It was a woman.' Tasha's arms tightened on the cushion.

'Can you describe her?'

'She was looking at Viv. Trying to get her attention. She had reddish hair.'

Not Medb, then. Pat had felt a surge of relief. And not a shadow either.

She turned over and punched the pillow. Pete was going to drop her off at Viv's in the morning on his way to a meeting so that she and Viv could start on the play. Suddenly she was dreading it.

Somewhere outside a dog barked and she found herself tensing. The sound was eerie in the silence of the city streets.

She awoke suddenly some time later, aware that she was shouting out loud, her heart thumping in her chest. Staring round the dark room she held her breath, wondering if she had woken the others. There was no sound from the rest of the flat. Perhaps the shout had been in her dream. Groping for her watch, she squinted at it. One a.m. She had been asleep for less than half an hour.

Lying back on the pillow again with a groan she screwed her eyes up against the darkness, willing herself back to sleep.

Medb.

Her eyes flew open.

Medb must be in the play. She was a key character. Medb who wasn't in the index. Who wasn't in the book. Who did not exist at all, according to Viv who had shrugged and then admitted that she had heard of her. Somewhere. Pat saw again the pale clear eyes in her mind's eye and she shivered. The woman's implacable hatred was a physical presence in the room with her.

7

I

Vivienne! Help me!

With a sob Viv shook her head.

The wind amongst the chimney pots sometimes wailed strangely and it was a windy day. The early morning sun was throwing shadows from corbels and chimneys across the deep window-lined chasms where the wynd sliced back through the tall slab of buildings. Far above she could see the white cloud, shredded and spinning against the vivid blue of the sky. As she watched a gull, messenger of the sea gods, soared past the window, angling its wings as it headed back towards the Forth. What she had heard had been its ringing cry.

Vivienne
I need you
Help me
Lady, I bring you gifts!

Turning sharply back into the room she went and stood by her desk, looking down at the notebook where she had scribbled her descriptions of the world of Cartimandua, descriptions from some part of her brain hell-bent on writing fiction and destroying her street cred as a serious historian forever.

She had walked home fast the night before, her head down, her hands rammed into the pockets of her jacket, determined not to think about Tasha's revelation, concentrating instead on the city around her. It was beautiful at night. She loved it all. The secrecy that the luminous darkness threw across the elegant streets and gardens of the New Town. The contrast, as she crossed Princes

92

Street, between the brightly lit shop windows and the convoys of buses making their way towards the West End, with the darkness of the gardens beyond, the cavern of blackness over the railway line, set deep in its gorge below the castle. And she loved the steep ridge beyond the gardens on which crouched the Old Town where she lived, crowded, atmospheric, the shadows of the night hiding the twenty-first century, allowing memories of the past to filter up through the narrow streets and dark alleyways like a subtle, all-pervasive miasma.

Vivienne, Lady, hear my pleas!

Carta was crying, her voice echoing amongst the trees and bushes which clustered around the hilltop lochan.

I need your help, Lady. Where are you?

Viv had walked faster.

Daughters of Fire. It had a good ring to it. It made her cooperation with Pat official. It gave them a base from which to work. If they got on. There hadn't been an instant rapport between them, that much was certain, but she thought that they could respect each other for the experience each could bring to the project.

She had reached the bend in the Mound when she heard footsteps behind her. Light. Hurrying. She stopped dead and turned. There was no one there. The street was empty. Below her the city spread out like a colourful carpet of light and dark.

Cartimandua.

Or Maeve.

Medb.

Medb of the White Hands.

Where had Pat got that name? Viv felt a shiver playing again across her shoulders, and wished she had allowed Pete to bring her home.

Medb and Cartimandua. Who or what had Tasha and Pablo and then Pete, dear old unflappable, unimaginative Pete, seen as they stared at her across the kitchen table? They had certainly seen something, and whatever they may all have said afterwards about the child's vivid imagination, and the scatty cat, and the trick of the light, deep down inside, they all knew it.

'Mellia?' Carta had walked out of her bedroom and stared round the living chamber. It was empty. The fire burned quietly, unwatched, a full cauldron of water steaming gently as it hung from the chains above it. The women were outside in the sunshine about their various tasks. 'Mellia?' she called again. 'I want you to come with me to see Conaire about tonight's songs.' Mellia would enjoy that; Carta, not above a little matchmaking, smiled gleefully. She planned to bring Mellia into the discussion and then, remembering an urgent meeting with her groom, to leave the two of them together. She made her way outside and stood in the warm sunshine looking around. Mellia would not be far. She always stayed within earshot in case Carta should need her. 'Mellia?' She walked across the cobbled street, between two other houses and onto the broad grass terrace above the clifftop ramparts. From there a panorama of woods and hills stretched out towards the western horizon. Below her a blackbird broke cover, screeching its alarm note and she stepped forward, glancing down.

At the bottom of the flight of steep steps cut into the rockface a body lay in the shadows on a pile of fallen scree below the cliff. Carta stared down, her heart in her mouth. The green plaid mantle had been pulled half off in the fall and it lay fluttering and tangled in a bush of whin. It was a mantle that she herself had given to Mellia as a gift only a few days earlier. Mellia, who was like a sister to her.

'Mellia?' Her strangled whisper hardly made a sound. For a moment she stood still, paralysed with terror, then she ran frantically down the long flight of steps. 'Mellia? Mellia? Are you all right?'

Mellia's eyes were still open, her hand clutched around a lump of raw wool. Her spindle lay crushed beneath her.

'Mellia?' Carta touched the girl's face with incredulous fingers. 'Mellia? Speak to me!' She could feel the panic welling up in her throat. 'Mellia! Wake up!'

But the girl's skin was cold, her head twisted to one side at an impossible angle, her neck broken.

For a long time she knelt there, Mellia's cold hand clutched in her own, willing warmth back into the stiffening fingers, tears pouring down her cheeks. No one came. The busy township went about its business on the hill above her as usual, unaware of the tragedy.

It was a long time before someone appeared at the top of the steps. It was Éabha. She stood there for a moment, calling, 'Mellia? Where are you? Are you out here?' Then she looked down and saw.

'She tripped, child.' Truthac was summoned at once. Gently he raised Carta to her feet. 'See, the thongs of her shoe are unlaced. She was concentrating on her spinning as she walked.'

'It's not true.' Carta could not control her tears as Mairghread, summoned by Éabha's screams, put her arms around her. 'She was killed. Someone pushed her.' It was a certainty deep inside her. Something she had known the very moment she realised that Mellia was dead.

Truthac looked hard at her face. He did not attempt to contradict her, or to question. She could feel his mind reaching out to hers, questing, seeking the truth.

After a moment he nodded. He believed her, as he had believed her all along. 'I will consult with the gods. And so, child, must you. They watch over you, Carta. If you ask, they will answer.' He gave the order and Mellia's body was lifted and carried away.

Sadly Carta stepped away from Mairghread. She stooped and picked up the broken spindle. 'I will ask my goddess,' she muttered to herself. 'She sees everything. She will know what to do.' Anger was coming now and the tears were drying on her face. She knew who had done it, whether with her own hands or through someone else's action at her command, or by magic, by weaving a spell to unlace the thong around Mellia's ankle. By whatever method Mellia's death had been accomplished, Carta vowed she was going to find out the truth. Above all else, that was what mattered here. That was what the Druids taught. Truth and justice and finally retribution. Mourning could come later.

She stared round. Truthac had gone. Trying desperately to compose herself she sent the women away. For a moment they hesitated, then they moved back towards the house, shooing away the crowd of sightseers who had gathered to watch the young woman's body being carried back up the cliff. She was alone again now, save for the one pair of eyes that watched her constantly from the dark corners of the settlement, jealous, vicious eyes which could see her from wherever their owner was hidden. Eyes which held power and hatred. Carta shivered, then she turned and headed towards the shrine.

'What shall I do, Lady? The king will never believe me. How can I prove what she has done?'

She had brought offerings of milk and a pot of wild bee honey to the goddess.

As she looked up, her eyes were looking straight at Viv's. She was in the room, yet not in the room. Together, they were in some dark place that smelled of cold stone. Viv could hear the lap of water and somewhere in the distance the thin delicate sound of a flute. She held her breath, trying to concentrate, afraid to blink in case the young woman disappeared.

But nothing she could do would hold her. Carta was fading, dissolving. In seconds she had gone.

Viv shivered violently. The wind in Dun Pelder had been cold, in spite of the spring sunshine; the trickling water bringing memories of winter ice from deep beneath the ground. Going back to the window, she focussed on her neighbour's geraniums as she felt warmth seep back slowly into her body. She could feel the tears wet on her own cheeks, the misery tight inside her. Carta's misery. Her absolute desolation. Leaning with her elbows on the sill, Viv breathed in the comforting warm smell of stone. Far below she could hear the early morning traffic rattling down the Lawnmarket. In the distance someone gave a sharp indignant hoot. From one of the open windows across the wynd she heard the wail of a child. Far above, a gull gave a long drawn out raucous peel of laughter. The sound was drowned out as someone turned on the radio and pop music echoed round the close.

With a sigh she turned back into the room.

III

Seating herself on the rocking chair, Pat leaned back and crossed her legs. She scanned Viv's face. 'Are you OK after last night?'

Viv nodded. 'Did Tash or Pete say anything else about what happened?'

Pat shook her head. 'They didn't say anything about it to me. I don't think Tasha was making it up.'

'No.'

There was a moment's silence. It was Pat who spoke first. 'I dreamed about Medb again last night,' she said at last.

Viv paled. 'But how could you? You don't know anything about Medb,' she whispered.

'Apparently, I do.' Pat leaned over towards her bag, groped for her cigarettes, then changed her mind. 'So, where does she fit in?'

'She doesn't.' Viv stood up. 'I told you. She has no part in the play at all.'

'Are you sure?' Pat frowned. 'Who the hell is she, then?'

'She's –' Viv broke off with a deep sigh. 'I don't know. That's the point. Maybe I've dreamed about her as well, but whoever, what-ever she is, Pat, she is not in the play. She has no part in history. This is a drama documentary with the emphasis on documentary. We can guess some bits –' she paused with a wry inner smile, ' – but most of it is fact. Not fiction. There is no room for extraneous characters and sub-plots. Maddie made that clear. You said so yourself.'

'Fair enough.' Pat didn't sound convinced but she let it ride. 'So, let's make a start.' She reached into her bag for her notepad.

Medb.

The name seemed to hang in the air between them.

'Your first scene is good, as I said.' Pat said thoughtfully. 'But I think we need more narrative to introduce the subject before we launch into too much action. To anchor the scene.'

Vivienne

Viv tensed. The voice was in the room.

Vivienne. Tell me what to do.

Pat was flipping through the first few pages of the manuscript.

She gave no sign that she had heard anything out of the ordinary. 'Here. From this point we want the voice of the narrator.' She marked the page and held it out. Viv didn't move.

'Viv?' Pat stared at her.

'Did you hear it?'

'What?' Pat put the pile of manuscript down on her knee.

'The voice.' Viv closed her eyes, shaking her head slowly from side to side. 'No, of course you didn't. It was in my head. I'm sorry.'

Pat studied her face. 'What sort of voice?'

'I don't know. I can't describe it. A woman. No. No, it was nothing. Probably a gull. You hear them a lot up here.'

'Then it wasn't in your head.'

Viv returned her gaze steadily. 'No.' It wasn't Medb. She wanted to shout the words out loud.

It wasn't. It was Carta. She needs me.

She gave a watery grin. 'Sorry. Last night. Whatever it was, it spooked me a bit. I didn't sleep very well.'

'Do you want to put this off –' Pat gestured at the sheets of paper on her knee.

'No. No, I want to get it finished as soon as possible.' Viv sighed.

Think about the play.

Bring Cartimandua's voice alive. Allow her to speak for herself.

Fact.

Not fiction.

Concentrate. Think about what Pat was saying. Walking over to her desk she picked up a pad and pencil and returning to her chair she sat down and began to doodle on the paper.

By the time Pat left at about five Viv had a pounding headache.

'Same time tomorrow?' Pat slung her bag on her shoulder.

Viv nodded. All she wanted was to be alone.

Shutting the door behind her she took a deep breath, closing her eyes, pressing her fingers against her throbbing temples. The phone rang and she sat listening as the answering machine clicked on. 'Viv? It's Steve. I just wanted to make sure you were OK. Ring me if you want to.' He paused, giving her a chance to respond, then hung up.

She didn't move.

The room was very still.

Vivienne

Carta was there, waiting.

Vivienne

I have brought offerings. Help me, Vivienne. Tell me what to do.

All Viv needed to do was to ask what had happened and the story would unfold; a story unknown to history. The story about which she already knew more than any other person alive.

Or guessed.

Or imagined.

Fiction.

Not fact.

Can't be fact.

Wrapping her arms around herself she shivered violently. Push her away, Viv. That is what you should do. You are sick. Hearing voices. Mad.

Vivienne, receive my gifts.

I have brought you milk and honey. Help me!

'Go away!' Viv cried out loud. 'Please, go away. Leave me alone!'

She paced round the room a couple of times.

But she wanted to know what was happening. She wanted to know so badly. Would it really do any harm? As long as she kept a firm grip on reality. As long as she knew this was a day dream.

Fiction.

Not fact.

IV

Carta was standing looking down into the grave, tears pouring down her face. How was she going to live without her friend? How could she live with the guilt of knowing that Mellia had been killed because of her? She had never felt more alone.

As Carta's friend Mellia had been given a formal ceremony and interred with her broken spindle, her comb and mirror, her favourite strings of beads and bangles and a flagon of mead. With her went prayers and exhortations to the gods to guide her to the land of the ever young.

Now it was over, as they stood around the grave in one final moment of silence after the eulogies ended, Carta raised her eyes to those of the woman who was watching her across the freshly piled soil. Medb of the White Hands was smiling.

In her private bedchamber, one of many portioned off with wattle screens inside the wall of the women's house Carta set up a new little shrine. Her belongings were comparatively few. Beside the bed box filled with softly scented, tightly packed heather, topped with linen sheets and soft beautifully cured fur covers, there were two chests containing her personal possessions. Her jewellery, her clothes, folded away clean with dried wormwood and sweet gale and wild mountain thyme to keep away moth and mildew. Her mantles and cloaks hung on pegs on the wall. Her comb and mirror lay on a small table with the lamp by whose light she went to bed. Now on one of the coffers she placed a figure of the goddess, carved in holly wood, a silver bowl in which she piled her offerings and the bundle of little carved ogham staves which she used for divination when there was no fire and there were no clouds and no birds to speak to her of the omens.

Her Druid instructors had been thorough. She was a good reader. She could write and speak Latin and write in Greek reasonably fluently now as well as writing the Celtic language of her own people using both alphabets. She could recite poetry and sing and she knew something of the magic of the Druids, studying healing, divination and law.

'You are one of us, Cartimandua,' Truthac had said. 'By birth and by blood, you are of the royal house, a descendant of warriors, a daughter of kings and queens, and of the line of Druids. You have been more than thrice blessed. Your destiny is written in the stars which later you will study, and in the rocks and in the waters which circle this land. You are a daughter of Brigantia. A daughter of fire. The portents at your birth were favourable and the auguries now speak of great futures and fame for all time.' He laid a cool hand on her head. 'You will outshine me, child. When my name is forgotten yours will echo in the words of the bards. It is not for me to tell you how to avenge the death of your friend. Consult the staves; through them consult your gods; listen to what you are told. But be sure that you divine the truth. Remember, what is done cannot be undone.'

Rising from the stool on which he had been sitting he paused for a moment, looking down at her as he leaned on his staff and he nodded sagely as he saw the loss and misery in her eyes. 'You are no longer a child, Carta, you are now a woman. The rising sun is behind you, the setting sun many moons in front. It will take courage to tread the path you feel is right. But you have that courage.' Gravely he nodded once more. 'You have more courage than anyone I have taught, Cartimandua. All you need to do is summon it.'

She watched him walk away, dumbfounded. He had taught the king and the king's sons. He was senior tutor to the Druid school. He examined bards and seers and Druids on their long journey to wisdom. And yet he thought her brave. She remembered her tears and her face burned. He didn't know how frightened and angry and lonely she had felt; still felt in the secret dark of the night.

And he must never know. No one must know.

Except perhaps the goddess who knew everything and would give her courage.

Carta stood for a moment longer before the shrine she had created. She was frowning. Sometimes she was so sure the Lady had heard her and would help. Other times it felt as though there was no one there. No one at all.

It was late. Viv sat at her desk, writing without a break as the sun moved across into the west and sank out of sight. Outside it grew dark, and the street became more and more noisy, then quiet again as one by one people began to make for home. In her room Viv put down the pencil and stretched cramped fingers. Somewhere far below her windows a man shouted a drunken obscenity in the deep crevasse of the narrow wynd as he relieved himself against the wall. Behind him a group of young people, cheerfully rowdy from the pub, jeered and someone threw a bottle. Viv heard nothing. She was watching Carta. Who was watching Medb of the White Hands.

Medb was nervous. It had seemed so easy to torment the king's latest fosterling. Her naturally acerbic temperament and resentful nature had sought someone to pick on since the day she had arrived at Dun Pelder, the daughter of one of the king's best warriors. At first it had been assumed that she would marry his son, Riach. Then the king himself had chosen her. It was a great honour.

It was not what she wanted.

No one would force her into marriage. That was against the law, but who would want to refuse to mate with a king? The contracts were drawn up, her marriage portion stacked in the house the king gave her for her own and, save for the fact that there had been no children so far of the match, in her own way she was content. Until she realised that Riach was to marry someone else.

The king's senior wife was under no illusions about Medb. At first a little resentful herself that he was looking for younger flesh she had resigned herself to the situation with pragmatic grace. She had her sons and her two daughters to comfort her, she had her husband's respect and generosity. She could put up with his frequent absences from her bed, but she would not tolerate the young woman's vicious temper and her spiteful treatment of slaves and servants and the other women in the household. She did not know about Medb's latest vendetta. Medb was too clever for that.

It was easy to kill the dog. She had hidden wolfsbane in a lump of fresh venison and put some leftover gravy from the kitchens in the bowl for luck. The animal had swallowed it without hesitation. She was almost sad to see how it suffered, but Carta's pain more than made up for it. Medb was astonished how satisfied it made her feel.

Killing Mellia had been a spur of the moment action, not planned in any way. She had walked around the house on the cobbled path which led towards the kitchens and seen the woman standing there on the terrace at the top of the flight of steps, staring out across the fields, singing quietly to herself as she twisted the woollen threads between her fingers. Mellia had half turned and smiled at her. The smile had died on her lips as she saw Medb's face and read her fate in the other woman's eyes.

Medb would have to be careful how she dealt with Carta. People were suspicious now, the bard had seen to that, and Carta herself was wary. Medb saw the way the young woman looked at her. She read suspicion and angry resolution where once there had been nothing but open friendliness and she began to be afraid. But her hatred and jealousy did not abate. If anything they grew as she saw how the family of her husband, King Lugaid, who should be supporting and loving her, closed instead around this young woman, consoling her for the death of a mere servant and a dog. Month after month, year after year when she had failed to conceive, the king had frowned, and shrugged and patted her stomach and assured her that one day soon his seed would take root. That was all the comfort he gave her. He had sons and daughters already. It did not matter to him whether or not he had more. He did not recognise her gnawing pain or her loneliness. Nor did he see her jealousy of Carta growing.

Nurturing her bitterness, she went to see Aoife, the spell maker, and demanded a lead token on which a spell had been inscribed. 'I will write the name of the recipient myself.'

Aoife was affronted. 'The spell will not work unless I cast it fully, lady.'

'The spell will work.' Medb fixed her with a cold eye. 'Or it will rebound on you. And as it is the spell of barrenness you would do well to see that its power is correctly directed.' She stared at Aoife's belly, visibly swelling beneath her gown.

The seer turned white with fear as she stood transfixed by the other woman's hard gaze. 'It seems to me, lady,' she stuttered, 'that you have no need of my skills.'

'Maybe not. But I choose to do it this way.' Medb stretched out her hand for the amulet. The implication was clear. If the charm failed Aoife would be blamed. If it succeeded and there were repercussions the seer would be blamed equally.

Aoife went straight to Truthac. He listened to her story thoughtfully. 'You did right to tell me. It is every man and every woman's right to curse an enemy. If there is an enemy and if it is fully justified, but to do so out of mere spite or jealousy, that is a different matter. Was the amulet empowered?'

Aoife nodded miserably. 'She made me do it.'

'But was it properly done without the name of the person to be cursed written on it, that is the question.' The old man sighed. 'Even now sometimes I question the logic of the gods. Are they so easily won over, so easily bribed?' He smiled ruefully at Aoife, noting the hand resting protectively over her belly. 'Let us bless this child and ask for its safety. That will be a good place to start. Then we will ask the gods about the other matter.' He knew who the recipient of Medb's spite would be, and so, he guessed, did Aoife.

*

103

Viv stirred uncomfortably. Outside a seagull was calling in the luminous night sky. The sound echoed in her head.

Gulls don't cry at night.

Do they?

Carta, be careful. The omens are not good.

A hunting party had arrived, bringing in more food for the Beltane feast and cattle were being rounded up from the grazing grounds ready for slaughter. A king's wealth is judged on the numbers of his cattle, augmented regularly by raids on neighbouring tribes and King Lugaid's wealth was enormous.

Excitement was beginning to build at Dun Pelder. Wagons loaded with food and goods creaked and groaned as they made their way along the tracks towards the township. A party of Gaulish traders laden with wine and another with bales of richly-coloured silks from the eastern frontiers of the Roman Empire joined the crowds thronging the fields around the base of the hill.

Carta was sick with excitement. Her parents, the year before confirmed as High King and Queen of all Brigantia, would be arriving any day now and with them would come two of her brothers, Triganos, the eldest, and Bran, the youngest who several years before had accompanied her to Dun Pelder. With them would come Brigantian priests and Druids who would help officiate at the marriage.

It was while she tried to distract herself from the excitement by watching the grooms attending to her ponies in the stable lines that Riach sought her out at last. Darting out of the shadows he caught her hand.

'I hardly ever see you nowadays.'

She shrugged, suddenly shy. 'Then you have not tried hard enough. I sit at your father's feet often enough. I ride with your mother and your sisters.'

'And I have been into the hills with the hunting party.' He grinned. 'So I wasn't there to see. But I am now. Your parents are nearby. Word has come. Their baggage train has been seen on the road.'

Carta shivered with excitement. 'And the feast starts tomorrow at sundown.'

'And our wedding is the day after.' He reached into the leather bag that hung at his waist. 'I have a present for you. It is special.

We so seldom get the chance to be alone. Shall I give it to you now? No, not here.' He pushed whatever it was back into the bag. 'Come with me.' He caught her wrist and drew her away from the horses across the busy muddy yard and onto the track. Together they ran between the houses, across the warriors' training ground and scrambled down the ramparts, through the open gates, and giggling like the children they still were, dodged at last out between the gatehouses and into the fields. Riach led her over a bank and into an orchard. Around them sweet early blossom on the crab apple trees and thick creamy hawthorn flowers with their musky provocative scent cast a dappled shade on the grass. 'Here.' As they faced each other under the trees he produced a small bundle, wrapped in blue linen.

She glanced up at his face. He was excited, his eyes dancing as he pressed it into her hands.

Slowly, trying to prolong the anticipation, she began to unfold the material, conscious of the heavy flexible weight of the present in her fingers.

It was a golden chain and hanging from it a tiny enamelled golden horse. She gasped with delight. 'It's beautiful.'

'My wedding gift. Here, let me put it on.' He slipped the chain over her head and rearranged her hair carefully on her shoulders. 'A glossy pony. After your name. I had it made specially by my father's best goldsmith.'

She could guess which one, the old man who lived near the ironsmith. She had wandered into all the craft houses on the hill. Each one housed a family business. There were more scattered down amongst the farmhouses. Potters, harness makers, wood-turners, stone carvers, jewellery makers, weavers, three weapon makers and swordsmiths, but the best, the absolute best, were up there on the top of Dun Pelder near the king.

She glanced up. 'You are so generous.' The shyness vanished. She flung her arms around his neck and touched her lips against his.

The impetuous childish gesture hovered for a moment between them, then his arms closed around her. A man's arms, claiming his woman. The kiss deepened. Her eyes closed as their bodies pressed closer and she felt him pulling aside her tunic as his lips left hers to move down her neck into the nest of her shoulder and then on towards her breasts.

Pausing only a moment to tear off his cloak and throw it onto the ground beneath the trees, he pulled her down with him, and they lay there in one another's arms, exploring each other's bodies, touching and kissing throats, breasts, shoulders, until at last he pushed her legs apart with his knee, and then gasped with surprise and delight as with a shout of glee she gripped him with her thighs and pulled him inside her.

For a long time they were oblivious of the world about them. If anyone glanced over the bank into the orchard they smiled tolerantly and moved on. It was the spring. The blood was high. What else would a man and a maid do given half a chance beneath the newly warm sun?

Only one creature saw them and stayed to watch. A hoodie crow in the spiny apple boughs above them swayed in time with the gentle breeze, fixed them with a baleful eye and kept unaccountably silent.

'Watch out for the bird!' Viv was struggling to make herself heard. 'Can't you see it's a spy? Oh please, be careful.'

Her own voice in the silent room precipitated her out of her dream and she found herself sitting at her desk, trembling with cold and exhaustion. Carta and Riach were gone. It was 3.30 a.m.

8

I

Arriving early at the department next morning, Hugh glanced in at the office. There was no sign of Heather. The room was silent, the computer off, the coffee machine cold. He frowned in disappointment. His easy banter with her always cheered him up, but of course it was Saturday. He probably had the building to himself. Thoughtfully he climbed the stairs and walked along the narrow, dark corridor with its squeaky floorboards, past the three closed doors with their labels announcing Dr Hamish Macleod, Miss Mhairi Mackenzie and Dr Viv Lloyd Rees. He paused outside Viv's room and listened. There was no sound from within. Cautiously he reached out and turned the knob. The door was locked. He stood for a moment, lost in thought, then he turned and retraced his steps swiftly down the stairs and into the office. There behind Heather's impressive cheese plant, which was threatening to take over the entire room, was a small cupboard in which hung duplicates of all the department's keys. Scooping Viv's key off its hook, he turned and made his way once more towards the stairs.

Her room was unnaturally tidy, the desk cleared of its usual piles of books and papers, her bookcase neatly ordered, the chairs pushed back against the walls. She had taken most of her files, her boxes of old floppy disks, her CDs, her notepads, her correspondence. There was nothing of her there. The room felt abandoned. Walking over to her desk he sat down in her chair. For a moment he didn't move, sitting, staring into space, then slowly he leaned forward and began methodically to open the drawers of her desk. He wasn't sure what he was looking for. He knew the pin would not be there but somehow he couldn't stop himself searching. As he scanned the contents, the notepaper and envelopes, the old pens and biros, the notepads, the files of old papers and letters, a couple of unused birthday cards, still in their Cellophane slips, he found himself trying to gain a sense of her presence. A scent. A sound. There was nothing. Giving up abruptly he slammed the drawers shut and walking out of the door, locked it once more behind him. Going straight into his own room he flung himself down at his desk and thumped the surface with his fist.

'Stupid, silly woman! Why in God's name did you do it?'

There was no reply.

Pulling the phone towards him he lifted the receiver and punched in a number. 'Meryn? I've looked everywhere. The brooch has gone. I've more or less accused her but she pretended she didn't know what I was talking about! I couldn't bring myself to press the point. Not to her face. If she has taken it the implications are appalling.'

'Why not wait and give her the chance to return it after her programme?' The voice the other end sounded faintly amused. 'Don't dwell on it, Hugh.'

'But the insurance –'

'I'm sure it won't come to that. Trust her.'

'What if she's touched it? What if it's cursed?' He couldn't believe he had said the words, but that sense of chill, the feeling of evil, seemed to cling still to his fingertips. He shivered.

Meryn didn't balk at the word. 'If she's touched it, Hugh, it's already too late.'

Hugh was silent for a moment. 'You said the link with Venutios was real, Meryn.' He clenched his fist in front of him, asking the question in spite of himself. 'How do you know?'

There was a pause at the other end of the phone. 'You wouldn't believe me if I told you, Hugh, now would you.'

'Try me.' Hugh's voice was dry.

'OK.' There was a further silence. 'I sensed it strongly when you came here. There was a vibration in your auric field when you talked about it. I sensed him as a watching spirit.'

'I shouldn't have asked!' In his office Hugh glanced heavenwards and shook his head.

'No.' A quiet chuckle. 'But you need to be careful, Hugh. Believe that at least. Don't talk about the brooch. Don't think about it. Avoid thinking about Venutios at all if you can.'

'I'm writing a book about him, Meryn!'

'Don't. At least, not for now.' All the humour had disappeared from Meryn's voice. 'Concentrate on other aspects in the book. You told me it's about the Romans. Think about them for a bit. I'm serious, Hugh. Don't spare him any thoughts at the moment.'

'That is ridiculous! You know I can't do that. He's central to the whole thing –' Hugh broke off as a quiet tap sounded at the door. It opened and Steve poked his head around it. 'I'm sorry, Professor –'

'Meryn, I have to go. I'll call you back a bit later.' Hugh put down the phone and frowned. 'Yes? What are you doing here?'

'Could I have a word if you're not too busy?' Steve approached the desk. 'You kindly said you would lend me some of your notes about the northern tribes. I'm planning to go home for a few weeks fairly soon, and it would be great if I could take them with me.' He eyed the Professor thoughtfully. 'I gather you've started a new book on the subject. I shall look forward to reading it.'

Venutios.

It seemed to Hugh that the name hung in the air between them.

Staring up at the tall young man, casual and relaxed in a striped, open-necked shirt and faded jeans, Hugh gave a tight smile. He felt old just looking at him. No wonder Viv enjoyed his company so much. 'I wonder where you heard about that. Well, no matter. It will be some time before it's finished, Steve. I have a great deal of work to do yet but you are welcome to the lecture notes.' He stood up and walked over to the bookcase, riffling through a box file and extricating a pile of A4 sheets. 'Return them to me, if you would, when you've finished with them. I can let you have some books too if you like, but they are at home. You'll have to arrange to come and collect them.'

As Steve closed the door Hugh stood where he was, frowning, listening to the sound of the young man's footsteps as he walked back down the corridor and ran down the stairs.

In the silence that followed Hugh found himself staring round the room. The hair on the back of his neck was prickling suddenly and he was uncomfortably aware of a strange feeling that there was a presence there with him. He scanned the corners carefully. There was no one there. Nothing. Of course there was nothing. Just the echo of Meryn's voice with his usual brand of silly superstitious mumbo jumbo. For a moment he considered ringing Meryn back.

109

He should have asked him what he meant, why he should avoid thinking about Venutios. He stared down at his hand, the hand that had touched the brooch, and flexed his fingers cautiously, then shrugging his shoulders he walked back to his desk. The whole thing was a blatant nonsense. The only problem was what to do about Viv Lloyd Rees and perhaps for now he would take Meryn's advice on that one and do absolutely nothing.

II

'I can't work on the play today!' Viv stared at Pat in dismay. The sound of the doorbell at 9.30 a.m. had dragged her out of a deep exhausted sleep. She ran her hands through her hair leaving it standing on end, uncomfortably aware that Pat, in a pale blue blouse and cream trousers looked rested and alert while she herself was wearing nothing but a crumpled shirt, her customary sleeping attire, her legs and feet bare.

'I could make us some coffee while you jump in the shower,' Pat said, eyebrow raised. 'Please, don't make me go down all those damn stairs again. What on earth made you choose to live in a place like this without a lift?' She dropped her bag on the floor and pushing past Viv, walked into the living room.

'I live here because I like it,' Viv retorted.

'And it's fabulous. You're right,' Pat said quickly. 'It's just the stairs getting to me. I'm too unfit. Put it down to the smoking.' She changed the subject. 'I did some more work on the play last night. I can't wait to show it to you.'

In the shower Viv stood for a long time allowing tepid water to pour over her head and face and down her aching body. The story from the night before was coming back to her. The two young lovers in the orchard under the apple blossom. Carta's ecstatic passion. The sound of their laughter, the heat of their young bodies. Her eyes closed, she found she was smiling as languidly she sponged her own body beneath the water. Then she remembered the bird sitting high above them. Medb's messenger; Medb's spy. Abruptly she opened her eyes and reached out to turn off the tap. How did she know the bird was a spy? Somehow she had to get rid of Pat; go back to Carta's life. Find out about Medb.

Pat was waiting with a mug of black coffee. Sipping from it, Viv listened to her as she read from the pages on her knee. It was good. Fluent. Well written.

'This bit,' Pat said, glancing up, 'is straight narrative. And I think it should be your voice. You would be good at this –'

'Pat,' Viv interrupted. 'I'm really sorry, but I'm not in the mood.'

'You have to be, Viv. We have a deadline,' Pat said firmly. 'I'm sorry too, but we've got to keep at this if we can, to get it done.'

'No.' Viv stood up. 'No, Pat. I can't. Look, give me some space. We'll do this tomorrow. I promise.' She put down the mug. 'There is something I have to do now. Something important.'

Pat peered at her over her spectacles. 'You do look like shit.'

Viv scowled. 'No doubt.' She took a deep breath. 'I'm sorry. Really sorry.' She relented. 'I should have rung, but I overslept. I didn't get to bed till the early hours and I've got a foul headache. I won't make any sense today.' She just wanted Pat to go.

She needed to know what happened next.

She had to warn Carta about the bird.

'OK.' Pat did not look happy as she stood up. 'But for God's sake ring me next time. I didn't get a lift, you know. I had to make my own way here.' She gathered together her papers and slotted them into her bag. 'I'm up in Edinburgh to do you a favour,' she said sharply as she opened the door. 'You might give that fact some thought.'

'A favour that will be very well paid!' Viv retorted. 'Shit!' she muttered as the door banged and she heard Pat's heels clattering down the stairs outside. For a moment she entertained the idea of opening the door and shouting down after her to come back. But only for a moment.

In seconds Pat was forgotten.

III

'She has cursed me! Look!' Carta held out the amulet with a shaking hand. She had found it on her pillow. 'She has made me barren!'

Truthac took it from her soberly. 'This is bad work, daughter. Grave. But a curse can be unmade. The woman who put this on your bed is not a powerful seer and nor is the person who made this charm.'

'You know?' Carta stared at him through her tears. 'You know who did this?'

'I know.' He sighed. 'The spell maker came to me for advice after it was bought from her. It was undedicated and without power. You have nothing to fear.'

'And you know who it was who bought it?'

'And so do you, child. You have the strength and the knowledge to fight her viciousness.'

'I might have.' She didn't sound certain. 'But what about Mellia? She died.'

'Of an accident.'

'No. She was murdered. The gods have told me.' Carta's eyes flashed with anger. 'As was my Catia. Are they to go unavenged? Is Conaire to go unavenged?' Her voice rose passionately. 'He spoke out against this vicious woman at the feast. He loved Mellia too. You are a great judge. You must deliver justice!'

'And so I shall.' He paused. A scandal at Beltane when the fort was full and the surrounding settlements overflowing with visitors in celebratory mood would be unpropitious. 'It will be done at the right time, Carta. At Elembivios, you will bring me your charge and your evidence when I hold my court of justice, and at Edrinios, in the time of arbitration, I will give judgement.' He paused, seeing her shoulders slump. 'It's but three moons away, daughter of Brigantia, and then justice will be done.'

Medb was hiding in the shadows, watching the dancing.

Riach and Cartimandua were holding hands, their vows made before the whole world. Gifts had been exchanged, her marriage portion safely lodged in the Votadini warehouses and the three days of feasting had begun. On their marriage bed lay silken sheets, brought by trade routes from the east through Galatia to Gaul, and rich soft brown bearskins from the northern forests of the Caledones. On her arms were gold and silver bracelets. Round her neck she wore her enamelled pony on its golden chain.

Lugaid had given them their own house as a wedding present. Small, neat, newly thatched, it afforded them privacy as long as the members of their household – their servants and slaves and companions – were outside around the communal fire.

All night they made love, sometimes in their own deep heather bed in the new house, sometimes wrapped in Riach's cloak out in the hay meadows and orchards, staring up at Sarn Gwyddion, the great swathe of stars, which came to be known to the poets as the Milky Way. And then they danced, late into the night with their friends around them to the tune of pipe and lyre and harp. Or they sat with others listening to the songs of the bards and to the sennachies with their stories of long ago. Only Carta was aware of the sadness in Conaire's eyes and the wistful lilt to his music and deep in her heart she vowed she would make it up to him. He too would be avenged.

But all the time Medb was coming closer, her eyes narrowed, her heart locked in jealous rage.

In the second week of the festival, as slowly the farmers began to drift back to their fields and the hunters sharpened their spears and arrows and the warrior parties drew apart to plan new raids, Carta bade a sad farewell to her parents and her brothers and the friends who had accompanied them to see her married and watched them ride away. Then at last she decided to act. Her husband knew nothing of his stepmother's lustful rage. He had eyes for none but his wife. Truthac had still said nothing; whatever was to be done, it had to be done by her. It was her friend and her dog who had to be avenged. Her bard whose heart was broken. It was her life and the lives of her children to come that had to be saved. Even as she lay in Riach's arms she could feel the threat approaching. Somehow she had to be free of it.

Outside, at the street door someone rang the bell again and again. Viv did not react. In her dream there was no door. No sound other

113

than the crackle of the fire in the fire pit and the bubble of boiling water in the cauldron suspended over it, as Carta sat alone in her new house, deep in thought.

The first party of merchants of the year had arrived from Gaul. The members of the tribe were used to such visitors now. Traders from the Empire were commonplace in the coastal towns, but this far north it was unusual to see them in person. King Lugaid fêted them and talked with them long into the night, promising rich goods, wolfhounds and slaves from Erin, silver and gold and lead, skins and weapons, in exchange for their wine and olive oil, beautiful pottery, luxury fabrics, exotic herbs and spices.

Listening to them talk, Carta had begun to form the beginnings of a plan.

It would take three men of the Brigantes to carry it out. Men who would be richly rewarded and then sent home to her father's service; one of those men she suspected had been as much in love with Mellia as was Conaire, and would look to his young mistress to avenge any wrong that had been done to her. The others would follow without question. No one would ever know what became of Medb of the White Hands.

Two days after the Gaulish party had set off back towards the coast where they would embark into the Germanican Ocean and thence, down the coast and across to Gaul, Medb rode south with two of her maidens in response to an invitation to visit the dun of her friend, Étain. The small party travelled in an ornate wagon, escorted by three horsemen. What danger was there, after all, in the land of the king's allies and compatriots?

The raiders came upon them swiftly, weapons drawn. The warriors died hard, protecting their king's wife. The three women were captured. Horses and chariot were part of the booty. The bodies were buried so no trace would be found, given to the gods in the hungry depths of a local marsh.

The price for female slaves was high. The traders paid handsomely. No one believed women chained with neck rings and manacles when they cried that the king of the Votadini would pay handsomely for their release. Why should they? Slaves made claims like that all the time.

At Dun Pelder, Carta danced in a circle of women round the

114

fire and wondered with the rest of the township what could have happened to Medb of the White Hands.

It was a long time before she dared to hope that Mellia and Catia could rest in peace. That they were avenged and that she was safe.

Viv frowned, staring at the monitor. Page 143. She could see the numbers flashing at the bottom of the screen. 143 pages! Her arms were cramped, her fingers stiff and painful. In disbelief she clicked on the save icon and pushed back her chair. It was dark outside once more.

IV

'How many people sit down in this chair and announce that they think they're going mad?' Viv threw herself uneasily into the chair in Cathy's office.

'About sixty per cent.'

'Is that all?' Viv was silent for a moment.

'Viv, whatever it is, if it worries you, tell me about it. It won't go any further, I promise.'

'What if I told you I sat in front of the computer last night and typed 143 pages without being aware of it. It took me several hours.'

Cathy took off her glasses. 'Have you read what you wrote?'

'Not all of it, but it makes sense, if that's what you are wondering.'

'Can I ask what it is about?'

'Cartimandua.'

'Viv, we've been here before! You've just finished a book about her. She is very much on your mind for all sorts of reasons. This is normal.'

'This is about her life before the book starts. The part of her life no one knows about.'

Fiction.

The word hovered on Viv's lips but she didn't say it. It wasn't true. 'I'm not making it up, Cathy. I can't stop. She's talking to me.'

115

Cathy nodded. 'I'm sure it feels like that. Your brain has gone into overdrive. The exhaustion from writing the book and then the hassle with Professor Graham has probably triggered the same reflexes which give us nightmares and make us sleep walk. That, combined with your very real frustration at finding there are so many aspects of her life you can't ever know about.'

Viv slumped back in the chair. 'I suppose so. But it's so vivid!'

'As are a lot of dreams.'

Viv hesitated. 'So you don't think she is actually communicating with me?'

'No.' Cathy shook her head.

'Or that Tasha and Pete really saw her the other night?'

'No.'

'But you don't rule out the possibility of some sort of communication between the living and the dead?'

Cathy frowned. 'Like spiritualism, you mean? I think, on the whole, most of that is a con.' She paused. 'I'm not saying I don't believe in some paranormal stuff, in fact, yes, I do believe in some things, but not that you're being stalked by some Celtic female with tattoos, no.'

'So, Tasha told you what she looked like.'

Cathy nodded.

'It was Cartimandua.'

'I don't think so. Look,' Cathy leaned forward in her chair, 'you have a story to tell. You are putting on a radio play. So your brain is providing you with the story. It's as simple as that. It doesn't matter where this stuff is coming from. Who ever knows where creative stuff comes from? It is a wonderful story. You now have an extra scene or two to go at the beginning of your drama: her childhood; her marriage. Who cares if it's fact or fiction?'

'I care.' Viv shrugged. 'I care very much. I'm a serious academic.'

Behind them there was a slight click as the door opened a fraction and Pablo pushed his way into the room. He sat down, carefully surveying them both before beginning to wash his ears.

'You can't tackle this academically and I think that fact is at the root of your problem,' Cathy went on. 'Your brain is creating a let-out for you. Just use it. Tell Pat what's happening. Let her help you write it into the play.'

'And give Hugh Graham even more ammunition to use against me?'

116

There was a pause. 'Why do you really care so much what he thinks?'

'Because he is my professor. The head of department.'

'And?'

'What do you mean, and?'

'What is wrong with an academic writing a semi-fictional piece? I am not saying any of your book was sourced like this –' Cathy stopped abruptly. 'Or was it?'

Viv shook her head. 'No! No, of course not! At least . . .' She looked at Cathy in despair. 'I'm not sure. It's all got so muddled up.'

Cathy raised an eyebrow. 'Then you've got nothing to lose, if you ask me. Exploit your dreams and your creative visions. Turn them into, what do they call it, faction?' She grimaced. 'Use all this as a kind of catharsis to clear Cartimandua out of your system.'

'Catharsis, maybe.' Viv shook her head wearily. 'But for me professional suicide.'

'Why?' Cathy looked genuinely bewildered. 'I don't understand what you've got against it. You are an academic writing fiction. It's been done before.'

'No, Cathy, I'm not a fiction writer. I can't make these leaps of deduction. It's not allowed.'

'Who says?'

'It's just part of the rules.'

Behind them Pablo finished his ablutions and sat watching Viv intently. Neither woman noticed him.

'Yet in your book, if you don't mind my saying so,' Cathy said slowly, 'everything is supposition because it is pre-historic in the literal sense of the word, and all your sources are suspect in that they are Roman spin! Didn't you tell me that? So, how come that is allowed?'

'It just is.'

'Well, now you have Pat on board to keep the academic in check. Use her, Viv. You really upset her by chasing her away yesterday, you know. And then this morning. She is threatening to go back to London.'

'Perhaps it would be better if she does.' Viv was getting more and more stressed.

Behind them Pablo stood up. He was staring at her in a panic, eyes wide, ears flattened against his head, and leaping off the chair, he fled through the door. Once more neither of them noticed.

'You don't mean that,' said Cathy.

'I do. She's going to interfere.'

'That's what she's here for.' Cathy frowned. 'Be reasonable. Don't upset her. Listen to her.'

'And if she upsets me?' With her mentions of Medb, for instance. Where had they come from? She shuddered.

'She hasn't. Or if she did, she didn't mean to. You need her –'

Somewhere in the flat a door banged. Cathy sat back in her chair, breathing a quiet sigh of relief. 'Look, that must be Pete and Tash,' she said gently. 'Hang on a minute while I let them know we're here –'

Before she had a chance to move the door was flung open and Tasha stood there, an evil grin on her face. 'I thought so. You're hiding! Mummy's here. Don't you want to talk to her, Cathy?'

Cathy laughed uncomfortably. 'Tasha, we are having a meeting. I've asked you before not to burst into my office. I might have had a patient here.'

'But you haven't,' Tasha retorted.

Cathy groaned. 'Nevertheless, we are having a meeting. When it's finished Viv and I will come and say hello, OK?'

Tasha looked both quizzical and smug. It was an extraordinary feat of facial gymnastics which brought Viv to the conclusion that the child would go far on the stage.

'Should I surrender now?' Cathy smiled wryly as the door closed behind the girl. 'May as well.'

Greta greeted Viv and Cathy with a patently insincere smile. 'I'm so sorry not to be able to stay. I have an appointment.'

'That's all right.' Tasha smiled. 'We want to talk to Viv about her ghost, don't we, Cathy.' Turning, she reached for her mother's handbag. 'Mummy, please. You promised me some extra pocket money.'

'Ghost?' Greta frowned. 'What ghost?'

'It's nothing, Greta.' Cathy glared at Tasha repressively. 'A joke, that's all.'

'I'm glad to hear it.' Greta turned towards her daughter. 'Put my bag down!' She was peremptory.

Viv clenched her fists. Cartimandua was a ghost; not a dream, not imaginary, not a disembodied memory. She was a ghost and she had shown herself in this room.

'I'm frightened of ghosts!' Tasha continued firmly and glanced at her father as Cathy sighed.

He pursed his lips.

Greta stared at her. Then turned to Pete. 'What is this nonsense?'

'As Cathy said, Greta. A joke. Take no notice.' Pete glared at his daughter.

'Well, I have no time for jokes. I have to go,' Greta retorted. 'Tasha!' The name hurled across the kitchen made the child jump guiltily. Her hand was inside her mother's purse.

'Is this what you teach her?' Greta grabbed the bag. The accusation was aimed at Cathy.

'Certainly not.' Cathy was flustered.

Tasha scowled. 'Cathy was hiding from you, Mummy. In her study. She knew you were here and hid! She didn't want you to know about the ghost. It was in there with them. It follows Viv everywhere.'

There was a moment of silence. The kitchen seemed to have gone cold as Viv looked around at their faces, Tasha's smug, Greta's lip curling with disdain, Pete frowning, Cathy astonished.

'I think it's time for me to go.' Viv tried to smile and failed.

'No, wait. Our consultation . . .' Cathy reached out towards her.

'Was brilliant. You've given me lots to think about.' Viv gave an uncomfortable gesture of surrender. 'Tell Pat I'm sorry. I'll call her.'

Outside the door at the top of the stairs she paused, her heart thudding in terror.

Carta had been standing there next to her. Tasha was right. This time she had seen the hazy figure herself.

V

Slamming the door of her flat behind her, Viv tried to force herself to be calm. She sat down on the rocking chair and closed her eyes, rocking back and forth. Cathy was right! Her brain was dreaming up a story which her intellect had rejected. There was nothing sinister here. Tasha was only trying to stir things. Taking a deep breath, she opened her eyes. The flat was unusually quiet and cold. She looked round nervously. It was several seconds before it dawned on her that the computer was switched on. She frowned.

Surely it had been off when she left home? Standing up reluctantly she moved across to her desk and sat down again in front of the screen. Beside the keyboard her answer machine was flashing. She ignored it.

Carta was pregnant. Ecstatic and excited, she stood for long periods, her hands gently cupped over her belly where as yet there was barely any sign of the life not yet quickened inside her. For now Medb was forgotten.

Riach was as excited as she was. He presented her with an exquisitely carved and decorated chariot and two matched ponies to pull it. 'So you don't need to ride when the child is larger.' He rested his hand on the place where only moments before she had been stroking her own belly. 'A soft and gentle ride for my son!'

The young charioteer was called Fergal. He was the son of a warrior, one of Riach's older warrior comrades, elevated to a position of honour as her driver and her bodyguard.

She still rode daily, but the novelty of her own war cart was an exciting one and she planned excursions to visit the duns and homesteads of the women she had met at the Beltane and Lughnasadh gatherings in the fort. Fergal drove her all over the territories of the Votadini. He was a serious young man, tall and well-built, with fair wavy hair and blue eyes. By inclination he would have preferred to study as a bard, and later maybe as a Druid, but his father was adamant that he should carry weapons in the king's service and Fergal, good-natured and always willing to oblige, gave up his hopes. Driving the prince's young wife was a perfect compromise. As he escorted her around the district he listened to bards and learned their songs. He carried his lyre in the war cart with his sword and spears.

Carta's baby quickened at the time of the autumnal equinox as violent gales roared across the land from the west, tearing the leaves from the trees. The cailleach, goddess of the winter storm, had arrived early. It was time for hunting and reiving, the cattle raids which would augment the herds brought in for slaughter from the shielings. One man's feasting is another man's starvation. That was the way it was. No amount of grain would fill the belly in the same way as beef or mutton or venison salted down and stored away in safety for the long winter months.

'Do you want to go with them, Fergal?' Carta had been watching the young man's face as Riach called his men together. They had been sharpening and polishing their weapons for days, drawing up plans, waiting for the runners to return with news of when the herds were being brought down from the pastures of neighbouring tribes. Rich pickings, with the added excitement of the chance to capture slaves and take prisoners for ransom.

'I'd rather stay with you, lady.' Fergal gave a rueful grin. 'I have my orders. The king and Riach have spoken.'

'Poor Fergal.' Carta shook her head. 'Watching women is not much fun. Being a woman is not much fun either.' Her wry pout echoed his own. She had been feeling sick and uncomfortable and hated having to stay at home. 'But once this child is born then you and I will join the next raids with the men.' The glint in her eye showed the tomboy was still alive and well. 'My women can take care of the baby.'

They laughed easily together and he went to groom the ponies who had caught the excitement in the horse lines and were expecting to go out with the others.

Carta walked back out of the wind and rain into the small round house which was now her home and stood staring down at the central fire. The flames flickered in the draught. Riach had said his farewells the night before, holding her in his arms so that she was completely enfolded in his cloak. 'Take care of our son, my Carta,' he whispered. 'And of yourself. You are my two treasures. I don't know why I need more.'

She laughed, snuggling against his chest. 'To feed your men and your father's followers. That's why. A thousand hungry mouths.' She reached up and kissed him on the lips. 'And to make me proud. My husband must be the greatest warrior who ever lived.'

He gave a shout of laughter. 'I'll remember that. My bard goes with me to record my every move and when we return he will tell the whole court of my courage and feats of arms!'

'And I will listen to every detail as we sit together by the winter fires.' She wound her fingers into the fine linen of his tunic under his cloak. 'And sing them myself to your son as he waits to be born.'

She watched them ride away, her companion Mairghread by her side, a comforting presence as the horses, the chariots, the great wolfhounds from Erin baying at their heels drew away into the distance. It was then she found herself shivering with apprehension.

She felt it again now as she stared down into the fire. Mairghread, sensitive as always to her every mood had rounded up the other women and ushered them out of hearing so that she could be alone with her thoughts. Sitting there, she lost herself in her dreams, gazing at the tongues of flame licking around the glowing logs, hissing their message as they threaded patterns through the fragrant smoke.

Danger.

Her hand went automatically to her belly where her child, Riach's child, nestled in the darkness below her heart. It was safe there. The flames crackled and a log split with a bang. Suddenly her head was spinning. She was falling towards the fire.

There was an arm around her. Then another. 'Come on, lady. Let me take you to your bed.' It was Mairghread. 'I saw you grow dizzy. Lie down and rest.' Two other women reappeared from the far side of the room where they had been sitting talking, out of the cold wind. They guided her through to the bedchamber and drew the wicker screens around her.

'My baby . . .'

'Your baby is fine. Women often feel as you do now. It is quite usual. Your baby is greedy. He is sucking at your strength from within. It shows he is already big and strong.' Mairghread smiled reassuringly. She placed a cool hand on Carta's forehead. 'I'll bring you some chamomile infusion and you must sleep for a while. Then you will be yourself again, your own strength recovered. You'll see.'

In her sleeping chamber Mairghread went to her herb cupboard. There, neatly arranged on the shelves behind the door were bundles of dried herbs, gathered in the spring and summer, each neatly labelled with a small wooden tag engraved with a symbol. Twice married and twice widowed already, although she was less than ten years older than Carta, and childless herself, Mairghread had elected to remain unmarried and instead to study with the Druid healers and to look after her young mistress and companion, understanding the gap Mellia had left in Carta's life, and wishing she could fill it. She took some chamomile and went to ladle boiling water from the cauldron. Frowning, she waited while the herbs were steeping in their flagon, her eyes fixed on the dancing flames. What had Carta seen?

The whole fort had turned out to look for Medb of the White Hands when she disappeared. Search parties were sent far and wide, messengers despatched the length and breadth of the land, to Brigantia and beyond to the lands of the Selgovae and the Novantae, the Venicones and even further north, to the lands of the Picti. The seers consulted their auguries to see if she had been killed by wolves or bears, and the bards constructed magical lays to bring her home had she been stolen by the gods. There was no sign of her. It was as if she and her two slaves had never been. Only two people asked themselves if they could guess. Truthac, Archdruid of the Votadini, and Brigit, senior wife to the king. Both looked at Carta's wide-eyed innocence and concern and both wondered. Both kept their thoughts to themselves.

The Archdruid came to Carta's bedside, when her message reached him. She was lying wrapped in warm furs, the brazier near her throwing out heat which did not seem to be able to dispel the chill from her bones.

'The curse is working.' She was white-lipped. The small chamber was empty – they could hear the subdued chatter of the other women around the main fire pit beyond the wattle walls. Some were spinning in the firelight, others just sat listening to the soft voice of one of the women bards as she told a story, accompanying the narrative from time to time with a few chords on the small harp on the table at her side. At Carta's request Mairghread had gone to join the others so she could talk to Truthac alone.

'The curse that condemned me to barrenness. I can feel it worming its way into my womb.'

The Archdruid leaned his staff against the wall and, sitting down beside the bed, took her hand. It was ice-cold and clammy. He was frowning. 'Mairghread told me she thought you saw something in the flames.'

'I did. I saw blood.' Carta took a deep shaky breath, trying to still her own panic.

'But there is no issue of blood from your womb. The child lies securely?' His eyes were fixed steadily on her face. She was reminded of that other Druid years before who had saved her dog's life. He had had the same calm certainty, the same ability to reassure. She nodded.

'Then allow your ladies to take care of you. Rest. Do not ride horse or chariot for a while and do not consult the oracles yourself.' He gave a grave smile. 'It is commonplace, so I've noticed, for women in your condition to see troubles where there are none.'

'And the curse?'

'The curse tablet had not been awakened. It would not have worked.'

Carta bit her lip. 'Supposing –' She hesitated.

'Suppose nothing, princess.' He put a stern hand on hers. 'Think no more about it, or about the person who wanted it.' He raised his eyes to hers and held her gaze. 'The gods know the truth, Carta. They know who is honest and who deserves punishment here.' There was a pause. He saw the pupils of her eyes contract with fear. She looked away into the corner of the room. 'My goddess knows what happens in my heart,' she said quietly. 'And what happened to Medb. She is not dead. She did not come to harm.'

The old man frowned but he made no comment. He stood up slowly, drawing his robe around him and reached for his staff. 'Rest now, child, and forget Medb. And pray that your baby stays safe.'

Carta watched him disappear between the screens, then she huddled down into the bed, pulling the covers over her head.

The vision returned in her dreams that night. Three ravens were sitting in a storm-swept tree staring down at a blood-soaked body as the wind and rain tore through a narrow glen. 'Who is it? Who is dead?' Her screams woke the other women and they ran to her bedside, holding up lamps in the darkness. The central fire had been smoored for the night, carefully covered by a layer of peats so that in the morning it would be ready to stir back into life. Someone grabbed the poker and in a short while it was blazing, bringing warmth back to her chilled body.

'Someone is dead!' Carta was crying. She clutched at Mairghread's hand.

'No one is dead, Carta!' The young woman was trying to comfort her. 'Everyone is safe. See, your little one kicks. You have woken him.' They all saw the slight movement beneath her nightgown.

But someone was dead. Two days later the remnants of the hunting party returned. Riach's body was carried in the chariot in which he had so proudly ridden away from Dun Pelder. Four of the young men who had accompanied him had died with him, the others came home badly wounded.

Concentrating so completely on Carta's baby, no one had given a thought to the raiding party which had ridden with such optimism towards the western hills, the lands of the neighbouring Selgovae, favourite targets for autumn raids, so news of the hunters was not expected for a long time. Their arrival back was a devastating shock.

Mairghread tried to hold Carta back. 'Don't look. Stay in here by the fire. You don't want to see him.'

Carta swept her aside. Walking very straight, wrapped in a cloak against the icy wind she stood beside the chariot and stared down. For a few moments her composure held. He looked the same. So serene, so eager, so strong. The arms which had held her, the lips which had kissed every inch of her body, were undamaged. The terrible wounds which had drained his life were hidden beneath the fur rug.

'He fought with honour. It is we who survive who are dis-honoured.' His own arm nearly severed through, a gaping wound in his shoulder, Riach's charioteer gently wiped the mud from the prince's face. 'We could do nothing against them, my lady. There were two dozen of them. They came out of the clouds and mist. There was no warning. We read no omens.' He stood, staring down, his own eyes brimming with tears of shame. At least they had left him his head. Two of his companions had not been so fortunate.

Carta was biting her lips. 'I saw omens and I did nothing to help him.' She knelt beside her husband and kissed his cold, bloody forehead. It was then that her tears burst through the dam. Shaking with sobs she clung to his body and wept as though her heart would break.

When she rose at last to her feet she found the king and Brigit at her side. Lugaid was staring down at his son, weeping openly. Behind him men and women were flocking out of their houses as the news spread. They parted to let Carta through as she turned away, her face white and strained. She headed not towards the round house behind her but towards the shrine where she had made her offerings to her goddess.

'I gave you rich gifts. I begged you to take care of him!' Her voice rose to an anguished shriek of misery as she stood before the wooden statue in a darkness lit only by dim lamps fed by sweet oil. 'You promised. You promised you would watch over me and mine. You came to me and you assured me. Why did you let him die? Why?'

Her hand went to her stomach suddenly and she gave a sharp cry of pain. 'My baby!' She fell to her knees on the stones. 'Sweet Lady, forgive me. Help me!'

No one had followed her. They had held back in respect. As blood began to soak into her skirt, Carta screamed in her rage and fear and desolation, alone but for the woman who watched, helpless, two thousand years away.

VI

She didn't realise that she had picked up the phone. As she put it to her ear her eyes were fixed on the scene in the smoky shrine, her ears full of Carta's screams.

'Viv? It's Steve. Viv, are you there? Viv, is something wrong?' The voice in the receiver echoed into the past unheard.

Wrong? Of course something was wrong. Everything was wrong. Suddenly she was crying. Heart-rending sobs she couldn't hold back.

'Viv, it's Steve. Wait there. I'm coming over!'

Then the doorbell was ringing. The scene in the temple drew back into the shadows.

'Viv, let me in!' She could hear a voice calling; hear frantic banging on the door.

Wearily she dragged herself to her feet.

'Steve.' She saw him staring at her as she pulled the door open and realised after a second how she must look. She was pale and exhausted. Her eye make-up had run, leaving streaks of coppery green on her cheeks. Her hair was on end and her clothes crumpled.

'Are you all right? Viv, what's wrong!' He seized her hands and pulled her to him protectively. He was scanning the living room apprehensively. 'Is there someone here?'

'No. Yes.' Oh God! She shouldn't have opened the door. Gently she pushed him away, embarrassed. 'I'm sorry, Steve. There wasn't any need for you to come.'

'Of course I had to come. You're upset. You sounded so frightened.' He stepped past her, still looking round. 'What's happened? Is it Hugh?'

'Hugh?' She stared at him. 'No, it's not Hugh.' The tears were coming back. She was disorientated and confused. Shaking her head she pointed helplessly to the flickering computer monitor on the desk.

He followed the gesture, puzzled. 'What is it? Is there something wrong with the computer?'

'Look at it.'

He frowned. 'All I can see is text.'

'Read it.' She took a deep breath, trying to steady herself as Steve sat down at the desk but before he could start reading she had begun to talk, unable to stop herself, words falling over one another in her hurry to get the story out.

'She grabbed me by the throat!' Her hands were shaking. 'As soon as I came in she was in my head. It's automatic writing, Steve. Oh God, what am I going to do!' She sat down abruptly, rubbing her palms up and down her face.

Steve was silent; after glancing anxiously at her he turned back to the screen and was at once engrossed in the text unrolling before his eyes. 'You were certainly writing this very fast,' he commented cautiously. He glanced across at her again, puzzled. 'It's breathless.' The text was littered with little red squiggly lines denoting spelling errors.

He lapsed into silence again, reading intently while Viv, too restless to sit still, got to her feet and paced up and down the floor behind him. When he finished at last he turned away from the computer.

'That's incredible prose. So vivid.' He hesitated. 'You're writing a novel, yes?' He studied her face.

'No!' She came to a standstill behind him. 'It's not a novel, Steve. It's real!'

'What do you mean, real?'

'It's true!' Suddenly she was sobbing.

He frowned. 'It's weird and frightening.'

'And convincing.'

'It certainly reads convincingly.' He sounded dubious. 'But it is a novel you're writing. It must be.'

'No! No! I told you, it's true! You've got to believe it. I didn't make it up.'

He said nothing for a moment. 'I don't understand. I don't know what to think. How can it be real?' He scanned her face. 'Look, Viv. You must calm down. Tell me exactly what happened.' He was anxious.

'She is there. In my head. I can't stop her! I don't want to stop her!'

'You can't stop who?' Steve stood up and put his arms around her. She seemed so vulnerable. So unlike herself.

'Cartimandua. I told you.'

For a moment he was speechless. 'You don't mean you think she is dictating all this?'

'I just said so, didn't I!' She was trying to control her trembling. 'It's overwhelming. I can't fight it. She's there. All the time. Just out of sight. Not out of sight. Tasha saw her. And Pete.' She choked back a sob.

'Who are Tasha and Pete?' Steve was incredulous.

'Friends. They saw her. Oh God, what am I going to do?'

'You must calm down.'

'You mustn't tell anyone about this, Steve. Promise. I shouldn't have told you. Nobody must know. Especially not Hugh –'

'I won't tell a soul.' He stared at the screen again. 'It can't be real, Viv.'

'It is.' Her mouth was dry, her lips sore where she had chewed them. She moved away from him and sat down on the sofa. 'She's haunting me, Steve.'

He went and sat down beside her on the sofa. Taking the tissue out of her hand, he leaned forward and dabbed at her cheeks then hesitantly he put an arm around her shoulder again. They sat for a while, unmoving.

'Why don't I go and make some coffee,' he said at last. 'I know where everything is.'

When he came back she was still sitting where he had left her but she seemed calmer. 'Steve, I'm sorry.' She looked up at him wanly. 'I shouldn't have got you involved in all this. You rang at just the wrong moment.'

'I'm glad I did.' He put a mug into her hands. 'Look, you know this is not real, Viv. I don't have to tell you that. It can't be. You're not being haunted. It must be some kind of stream of consciousness creative thing, coming from deep inside you.'

She shook her head. God, he sounded just like Cathy. Rationalising. Always rationalising. Making it sound normal.

'Viv, it's –' He started, then stopped, unable to find the words. 'It's amazing, but it's not true.'

'It is!' She was anguished.

128

He sighed. 'Whatever it is, you have to stop.'

'I can't stop!' It was a whisper.

There was a long silence as they both contemplated the screen in the corner of the room. With a sigh, Viv climbed to her feet and went over to turn it off, then she threw herself back down on the sofa. 'I'm going mad.'

'No.' He turned to face her. 'Gifted. Honoured. Blessed. Maybe obsessive, and highly creative and fighting the tight restrictions of the rules of your – our – chosen profession. Mad, no.'

'Not yet, anyway.' She gave a wry smile.

'You are exhausted, Viv.' He reached for his own coffee thoughtfully. 'Before anything else, I think you should get some rest.' He paused. 'Unless – do you dream about her too?'

She shrugged. Those flashes of firelight. The thunder of hooves. The shouts and clashes of sword-blades. Were those part of her waking dream or part of a nightmare?

'Would you like me to stay?' He was watching her anxiously. 'I can sleep on the sofa. I don't think you should be alone.'

'No, Steve.' She shook her head. 'That's sweet of you, but I'll be fine.'

'Are you sure?' He was uncertain. 'I don't think you should do this any more. Not if it upsets you so much.'

'I don't have a choice. She forces herself into my consciousness. I'm not imagining this.' She was pleading with him. 'Besides,' she hesitated, 'I want to go on.'

He leaned over and took her hand. 'I think it could be dangerous.' He was looking very serious. 'Honestly. Whether it is coming from inside you, or from some sort of ghostly spirit it's not good if it's taken control of you like this. I wish my mother was here. She knows more about this sort of thing than I do. She would believe you.'

Viv gave a wan smile. 'Then I shall look forward to meeting your mother one day.'

'You must.' He paused. 'Are you sure I can't stay?'

'No. I'll be all right. Don't worry about me. It was really nice of you to come, Steve.' She hesitated. 'This is all secret. You realise that, don't you? I don't want anyone to know about it.'

'They won't. Not from me.' A thought struck him. 'Is this where those extra facts came from in the book?'

'I didn't mean to use them. I tried not to listen. I pushed her

129

away. I never wrote it down before!' She swallowed, looking down at her hands. 'I think I want you to go now, Steve.'

He stood up unhappily. 'You're sure you'll be all right?'

She nodded. 'Promise you won't say anything?'

'I promise.' He headed for the door. 'Call me if you need me. Any time.' He turned anxiously. 'I don't like to leave you alone –'

'I'm fine. Thanks for coming, Steve.'

Closing the door behind him, she shut her eyes with a sigh. Shit! She wouldn't blame him if he went straight to Hugh.

9

I

Steve rang at 8.30 the next morning. Standing beside the phone, Viv listened to his voice, her fists clenched, her forehead twisted into an agonised frown. She didn't pick it up.

She had to get out of the flat. She had to distract herself from the cacophony of voices whirling around her. She hadn't slept. She hadn't moved from the computer all night. She was exhausted.

Traprain. Carta wanted her to go to there.

By nine she was in her car, heading south on the A1, heading for the car park at the foot of Traprain Law. It was here that Carta had come to live with the Votadini. Here she had met and married her first love. Here she had fallen ill during her pregnancy. Sitting in the car, Viv stared up at the steep grass-sided hill climbing sheer out of the flat countryside around it. Then slowly she opened the car door.

Climbing over the stile from the car park she started to walk up the steep track, up the huge shoulder of the hill. In this life the place was deserted, but the view was still amazing. She could see for miles. To the east the sea was a brilliant, almost violet blue, with the viridian-topped Bass Rock rising vertically out of it in the distance. She shivered. Warm though it was, the wind was cold, whistling though the grass, drumming in her ears as she walked slowly across the empty terraces where once a thriving Iron Age community had lived.

Small yellow flowers of tormentil danced at her feet, and lush dandelions on the banks. Nearby she could hear a skylark as it soared overhead. She stopped, listening intently. The atmosphere had become jagged. She shivered again, plunging her hands into the pockets of her jacket as the wind whipped briskly across the grass, trying to marshal facts in her head. This place, desecrated now at one end by a quarry, had once been a busy township. Dozens, perhaps hundreds of houses had clustered on the flat top of this high, almost surreal volcanic mound. It had been called Dun Pelder then. Its present name, Traprain, also came, it was thought, from the Celtic or Welsh Tra Pren, which would mean something like the 'wooden town', from the palisades which had topped some of the great ramparts defending it and which would have been visible for miles. Over the span of the centuries, thousands of people had lived and loved and died here and in the township which had sprung up around the hill; kings and queens, the ancient Druids, the bards, the seers, the educated, aristocratic layer of people who with the warriors, the farmers and the servants and slaves made up the society of Britain two thousand years ago. The contemporaries of Boudica. The contemporaries of the Romans, who she had fought. The contemporaries of Cartimandua, Queen of the North.

Vivienne!

The ringing in her ears grew louder and she found herself turning round and round, unexpectedly finding herself at last looking down the sheer cliff face where Mellia had fallen to her death. Her eyes filled with tears. The memories here were too confused, too violent, too intense and she was quite alone. Why in God's name had she come? Turning quickly, she began to retrace her steps across the plateau towards the track, and once there she began to scramble down from the summit. Pausing to catch her breath, she smelled the wild thyme and sweet grasses and the subtle undertone of sheep dung. Once out of the wind the silence was an enormous relief. She could hear again the lark and in the distance the mewing of a buzzard as it circled over the wide farmland below her. Here the air was full of the scent of woodsmoke from a farmhouse down in the lea of the hill and the rich coconut scent of the gorse from the flanks of the terraces.

She sat down on a sheltered ridge of the ancient terracing, just visible still beneath the grass, and closed her eyes to the view.

They had carried Carta to her bed and sent for Gruoch, the Druid priestess who specialised at the college as a healer in women's problems. She arrived carrying her emergency bag of herb bundles and went straight to the bedside, dismissing the women who flocked anxiously around the room.

Her hands on Carta's belly were gentle and experienced, her voice soothing. She frowned as she felt the muscles under her fingers contract. 'Your babe is not happy, my dear.' She pulled aside the bloody skirts and frowned again. 'And you are still bleeding. We must pray to the blessed goddess to bring you succour. Lie still. I will give you something to help.' She pulled the blankets back and reached for her bag. Calling for warm wine in which to steep the herbs, she smiled across at the frightened young woman. 'Have no fear. If this child is destined to be born he will be. If there is no soul ready to come to rebirth then so be it. There will be others.' She opened a pouch of dried mosses and reached for some linen to make a pad to ease beneath the girl's hips as Mairghread brought in a goblet of wine and set it down carefully near the lamp beside the bed.

'But it's Riach's child.' Tears slid down Carta's cheeks.

'And Riach may require him in Tir n'an Og,' Gruoch said reassuringly. 'If that is so, then you must allow him to claim his son.' She sighed. She saw no future for this baby. Even if the birth pains stopped she doubted if it would go to term. She knew, as well as everyone else within the Druids' college, that Cartimandua's womb was blighted by a curse. Truthac had called a meeting of his senior colleagues after Riach's funeral, a ceremony Carta had been too sick to attend, and warned them. And he had told them then the future he saw for this young woman. He had foreseen her widowhood and he had foreseen what would happen next.

'No!' Viv was unaware that she had spoken out loud. Startled, two ramblers climbing the track nearby stopped and glanced at her. She appeared to be staring into the distance, lost in thought. With a quick look at each other they hurried on.

The pains and the bleeding stopped. Carta climbed wearily from her bed at last to make offerings to the goddess. From the wood-carver's stock of amulets and charms she bought a tiny carving of a baby and, with her favourite gold clip knelt before the sacred

133

lochan and dropped them in, allowing them to carry her prayers and pleas deep into the fern-draped depths of clear brown water.

'I am praying for you. I am,' Viv murmured. She, like Gruoch, knew it was to no avail. If Cartimandua had borne a child to the son of the king of the Votadini, surely history would know about it. On the hillside, only a hundred yards, did she but know it, from the spot where Carta's marriage bed had stood in the round house near the middle of the settlement, and within sight of the location of Riach's funeral pyre far below in what were now fields, Viv drew up her knees and hugged them thoughtfully, her eyes fixed unseeing on the North Sea.

The pains returned at midnight two days later as the moon moved from Samionos, the time of seedfall, to Dumannios, the darkest depth of winter and as the cold winter sun slid above the horizon Riach's tiny son was born. He never drew breath. His body, wrapped in soft fur, comforted with precious beads, a small carved toy bear and his mother's jewelled pony pendant, was consigned to the pit of offerings which would take him into the next world where his father's arms would gather him up and carry him towards the western shore.

Carta remained dry-eyed throughout the ceremony, then as her breasts began to leak precious unneeded milk beneath her linen tunic, she walked alone to the shrine.

'Why? I gave you offerings. I gave you my prayers. I gave you my husband! Why did you take my son as well?' Her anguished cry echoed round the settlement and men and women crept away, respecting her need to be alone. 'I see you watching me. Listening to me. Why? Why, if you do nothing to help me?'

And gradually Viv became aware of the pale tear-stained face, framed by wild uncombed hair, staring straight into her own with wide furious eyes.

She woke with a violent start and scrambled to her knees.

She was alone. The hillside was bare now, where in her trance it had been terraced, crowded with houses, busy with people. Only one part in her vision was empty. Sacred. Where the pit of sacrifice had been and the holy lochan and the temple that guarded it. She stared round, still trembling with the shock of seeing those grey-green eyes fixed so firmly on her own.

Slowly she stood up and at once she felt the wind catching her hair. All around her the Law was silent save for the distant song of the skylark and from somewhere in the fields far below the warning cry of a curlew. Retracing her steps, she found the lochan, on the very top. Small, insignificant. Its importance long forgotten. Overwhelmed by the need to make an offering of her own in memory of that little boy, she hunted through her pockets and brought out a coin. She looked at the water and back at the pound in her hand and shook her head. Carta had always left gold. This coin seemed tawdry, to say nothing of a gross intrusion on the memories and ecology of the place. Instead she stooped and picked a small perfect head of white saxifrage and dropped it into the water. It floated out into the centre of the pool and lay there in the sunshine.

'I'm sorry.' The words were ringing in her head. 'I'm so sorry. I couldn't save him for you.'

Gruoch would have done so if she could. She had been so calm. So confident. A Druidess, trained in the healing arts.

Viv stood there for a long time, her head bowed, then at last she turned and made her way back to the track. She was shivering. She had to pull herself together. Remember the detail, not the emotions. She was a historian. She had watched a healer at work. She must try and remember the details of what Gruoch had done. Perhaps this was something that could be checked and verified. What had the woman used? Red wine. Imported from Gaul presumably at this date, although the Romans cultivated vines when they came to southern Britain. A nice Burgundy or a Bordeaux, perhaps. She smiled sadly. It was used to steep the herbs which Gruoch had pulled from what appeared to be, in Native American terms, a medicine bundle and used to make a soothing mulled wine. What herbs were they? She repeated the names to herself like a mantra, trying to remember the unfamiliar terms which the woman had murmured as she added them to her concoction. At the end, as the baby was about to be born, Gruoch had given her rasps, presumably wild raspberries, and willow. And other things. Haws. Rosehips. She groped in her pocket for a notebook. Had those herbs been of any use? Did Gruoch, stately, reassuring Gruoch, know what she was doing? Did Carta survive?

But of course she survived. History was clear on that score.

Out to sea it was growing hazy. Once more a breeze stroked her skin, this time cold, smelling of salt.

She stood staring round. The other climbers and walkers if there had been any while she was in her trance had disappeared. There was no one in sight. Nothing on the top of the great hill of Traprain but fleeting memories, lost as soon as they surfaced, swept away by new gods and time.

II

'I told you so!' Pat looked across the desk at Maddie Corston with a grimace 'Still no answer. Just the machine.'

Maddie leaned back in her chair with a sigh. A slim, natural blonde with startlingly blue eyes she was dressed in voluminous trousers and a bright blue T-shirt which moulded tightly over the large, presumably fairly imminent bump of her belly.

'You say you got on well?' Maddie picked up the folder on her desk and stared at it.

'I thought so.' Pat shrugged. 'I still think so.'

'This is certainly good. A huge improvement.' Maddie tapped the folder with a bright red fingernail.

'It's a good book. I'm enjoying working on it.' Pat was watching Maddie's face closely. 'I could do it on my own, if necessary, you know,' she said cautiously. The idea had been growing slowly at the back of her mind, egged on by the subliminal presence of Medb, the stranger in her dreams who could prove the stronger, more dramatic character the play needed.

Maddie frowned. 'I don't think Viv is going to agree to that.'

'It would take the strain off her. She's very stressed.' Pat leaned forward. 'Let me suggest it to her if there is any more delay.' She looked away from Maddie and glanced towards the window for a moment, forcing herself to relax, willing herself not to care either way. Staring out at the columns of the monument on Calton Hill in the distance she took a deep breath. Don't seem too anxious. Keep this low key. She didn't understand herself why it was suddenly so important that she took charge, but it was.

'You say here you've some ideas on how to push the rest of the story through more dramatically,' Maddie went on as if on cue. She was flicking through the script. 'That's good, and now that we've rescheduled this for later in the year you've got much more time. That should give Viv the chance to de-stress, I hope. I really want her on board, Pat. This is her story,' she added firmly as she glanced at the woman sitting opposite her, half sensing that Pat was up to something.

Pat nodded. It was as if Medb was there in the room with them. 'Leave it with me. I'll do some work on it and speak to Viv, then I'll come back to you with the new ideas.'

Out in the street, she slung her bag over her shoulder and began to walk quickly up towards Princes Street. Reaching into her pocket for her mobile she called Viv yet again. She had left other messages, all of them prompted by Medb but so far there had been no response. 'Do you want to meet up? I've just been to see Maddie. Good news. She liked what we've done so far. She's made some good suggestions. Slight changes of emphasis, that sort of thing.' Best to let Viv think the alterations in plotline were Maddie's idea. Pat gave a quiet satisfied smile. That would please Medb. 'We must get together soon. Phone me. ASAP.'

Clicking off the phone and slipping it back into her bag she spotted a taxi. If she went back to Abercromby Place now, with luck Cathy would still be out and she could spend the rest of the day working on her new ideas.

Viv rang back that evening. 'I'm sorry, Pat. I've been out of town. When do you want to meet?' She sounded cheerful. Normal.

They settled on the following morning.

'Is she OK?' Cathy overheard the end of the call as she walked in.

'Fine.'

'You've been busy.'

Pat had been working on her laptop in the living room, *Cartimandua, Queen of the North* open on the table beside her, the floor covered in sheets of paper. 'I've still got a huge amount of rewriting to do.' Stretching her arms above her head, she yawned. 'Maddie's not happy with Viv's contribution. I'm not sure how we're going to handle this.' She hesitated, suddenly aware of what she had said. It wasn't true. She took a deep breath. 'We're changing the angle slightly. More about other, more interesting characters. Including the Romans.' That was true at least. Or it would be by the time she had talked Viv round. Leaning down to her capacious bag she dug for a pen and her battered, overstuffed Filofax. 'There are too many obscure Celtic names for a start. We need people with short easy names.'

Medb.

Maeve.

'I've convinced Maddie that Romans are more sexy, too. All that leather.'

Cathy shook her head in mock exasperation. 'This is radio, Pat, not TV.'

'Leather squeaks. And Romans march. Sound effects are doubly important on radio.' Pat laughed.

'Viv hasn't mentioned the Romans at all to me,' Cathy said. She was carrying a flat box and a bottle of wine. They had spoken briefly at tea time. On realising that neither Pete nor Tasha would be home that evening they had planned a girls' evening in. 'Are you sure they're relevant?'

'Of course. You still haven't read her book, have you? The Roman invasion of Britain in AD 43 took place in Cartimandua's time.' Pat glanced down at her notes. 'And I intend there to be some sexy Roman generals in the play. People can visualise Romans. Think *Ben Hur*. Think *Gladiator*.'

Cathy grimaced. 'So, you're going to have lots of romance and violence?'

Pat nodded. 'Buckets of it. The story does rather lend itself to all that.'

'Poor Viv. I'm not sure she sees it that way.'

'She will. You leave her to me.' Pushing her papers together and closing the Filofax, Pat shut the laptop. Time to change the subject. 'Is that our pizza?'

Nodding, Cathy slid the box down onto the table and produced a couple of glasses. 'I'm saving her book for the summer holidays,' she said, sitting beside Pat. 'Surely Maddie's not suggesting Viv hands the project over to you completely?' Opening the box, she returned to the subject as she passed Pat a plate and a paper napkin.

Shrugging, Pat helped herself to a slice of pizza. 'I suspect that's what's at the back of her mind.' At the back of Medb's mind. Pat frowned. She was beginning to believe this herself. 'It would be tricky to get Viv to pull out but I'm certain she'd rather do that than lose the chance to see her work on radio. She would still get a credit.' She was skilfully manoeuvring sticky strings of melted cheese.

Cathy grimaced, helping herself to a portion. 'I can't believe she would want that.'

Pat shrugged. 'I'll sound her out tomorrow.'

'Tactfully.'

'Of course tactfully!'

In her bedroom later Pat stood at the open window, the hand which held her cigarette resting outside on the window sill. Frowning, she watched the wisp of smoke drift out into the night as she leaned there on her elbows, thinking about the play.

All her notes this afternoon had been about Medb. Medb was the key character, a strong determined free spirit. An interesting foil for Cartimandua. A tough, resilient focus for dramatic tension. An alternative heroine. A fictional heroine according to Viv, but nevertheless a vital part of the story. She chewed her lip. She was imposing a storyline which was not in Viv's book, but this was after all why she had been brought in to help Viv out; she knew what was needed to make drama work.

With a sigh she took a final puff on the cigarette, ground it out on the sill and tossed it outside. Turning out the lamp she stood for a moment in the darkness, conscious of the pale silhouette of the open window. It was then she became gradually aware of the face near hers in the dark, the strange staring eyes, the transparent figure standing between her and the table. Gasping with fear, she groped for the switch and flooded the room with light again, blinking. There was no one there.

She sat down on the bed, her heart thumping unsteadily. How much had they had to drink? Taking a deep breath, she climbed into bed, leaving the light on, and lay back on the pillows, her eyes fixed on the spot by the table where for a fraction of a second the figure had shown itself.

Medb.

The new heroine of the play.

'Do you know what happened to Medb after Cartimandua had her kidnapped?' Ashen, with red-rimmed eyes Pat pushed past Viv and threw herself onto the sofa.

Viv stared at her, cold all over. 'How do you know Cartimandua had her kidnapped?' Her eyes strayed to her desk where an ever-increasing pile of notes lay beside the computer.

'I know all about it! Carta thought she was so clever, didn't she! Out of sight, out of mind! Sell her into slavery, what a wonderful vicious revenge. Did she ever give her another thought? I doubt it!'

Viv was speechless for a moment. This was the stuff of her own nightmares. They hadn't talked about it. She swallowed. 'Pat, how do you know all this?'

'Guess?' Pat said coldly. 'She told me last night.'

'Medb?' Viv could hardly bring herself to say the name out loud.

'Yes, Medb. Medb who was dragged away in chains. Sold to a merchant who threw her and her two companions into the hold of his ship and set sail for Gaul.' Pat paused with a shiver.

Viv was staring at her in horror. This couldn't be happening. Pat knew nothing about this. Nothing. She sat down on the edge of the rocker, her eyes fixed on Pat's face. 'So what happened?'

'What happened?' Pat almost spat out the words. 'I'll tell you what happened. They raped her!'

Viv was silent. 'She told you that?' she whispered at last.

'Yes, she told me. That is what they did to female slaves. To young beautiful female slaves.' Pat started crying.

Viv stared at her appalled. 'And you dreamed about her?'

Pat nodded.

'Oh God, Pat, what's happening to us?' Viv's voice was bleak. With a shiver she wrapped her arms around herself. 'They are taking us over.'

Pat took a deep breath. 'Don't you want to know what happened?' Her hands shaking, she groped in her bag for cigarettes. 'Or are you too wrapped up in Carta to care?'

'She tried to destroy Carta,' Viv said bitterly. 'She killed her friend. Her beloved dog. For all we know it was her fault Riach died and remember, Medb cursed her baby.'

'And she had good cause!' Pat flipped her lighter. It refused to ignite and she tried again.

'What cause? What had Carta ever done to her?' Viv asked indignantly. 'For goodness' sake, she had done nothing. And she didn't know what would happen. She just wanted Medb out of sight. Somewhere safe. Where she wouldn't hurt anyone any more. She didn't consider the repercussions.' She realised what Pat was doing. 'I'd rather you didn't smoke,' she said wearily. She rubbed her face with her hands.

'Tough.' The flame caught at last and Pat slammed the lighter down on the table. 'I think you should bloody well listen. See what you – what she – did!'

'Don't touch me!' Medb's voice was shrill. 'I'm the wife of a king!'

'Yes, darling, so you said!' The two men had been drinking heavily when they appeared in the doorway of the hold and dragged her out onto the deck. The huge sail creaked over head, bellying before the wind, and showers of icy spray cascaded over the decks, soaking them as they pulled her away from the gangway. Her two companions had been dragged out earlier that morning. She had not seen them since. Terrified, she struggled frantically as they laid hold of her, bleary-eyed, unsteady as the ship rose and fell to the ocean swell. 'Your friends weren't so fussy!' The younger man laughed.

'They are slaves!' Medb countered hotly.

'So are you now, darling, or hadn't you noticed!' The stout man bent and flipped the chain fastened round her wrists with a stubby, dirt-engrained finger.

There was a shuddering slam as the ship broached between two waves and the man toppled forward onto her, bearing her beneath him onto the deck and landing squarely on top of her. With a shout of laughter he dragged at her clothes, ripping open the neck of her gown and pulling up her skirt.

Medb screamed. Kicking desperately, she writhed beneath him as the younger man roared approval. 'Go for it, wild cat! When you've castrated him with your kneecaps there'll be all the more for me!'

141

He lurched again as the ship slammed another wave, mast creaking, the great brown sail beginning to flap.

The stout man groped for Medb's wrists, holding her arms above her head. 'One more kick like that darling and I'll smash your pretty face in.'

His friend turned and with a groan vomited into the scuppers. Wiping his mouth with his arm he turned back. 'Don't touch her face. We want a good price for her, remember.'

'We'll get a good price!' His companion thrust into Medb with brutal force. 'The more she practises the better she'll be, won't you sweetheart. Purchasers don't like their goods to be too fussy!'

By the time the two men had finished with her Medb lay half-conscious on the slimy boards. She did not cry. Dry-eyed, she lay in the brackish water as it sloshed backwards and forward to the pitching of the ship. The weather was worsening. Rain battered into the sail and streamed down onto her face, washing away the reek of sweat and alcohol and vomit from the men's slobbering lips, cooling the raw wounds under the iron manacles. Turning on her side with a groan she curled up, shielding her bruised body as best she could. The men had gone. She could hear nothing but the rush of the waves and the strumming of the wind in the rigging. Closing her eyes, she sought deep inside herself for a source of strength. She knew how she had come to this pass. She had recognised one of her original captors. He was a Brigantian warrior who served Cartimandua. As he had laid hold of her and thrust her into the arms of the waiting slave traders he had looked long and hard into her face to make sure she knew by whose orders this was happening to her.

If anything could bring her through this ordeal it was the full force of her hatred for Cartimandua and her desire to survive long enough to have her revenge.

'My lady?'

A voice dragged her back to consciousness at last. 'My lady, are you all right?'

Sibael, Medb's servant and companion, staggered across the deck towards her from the shelter of the cabin doorway. Clinging to anything within reach to keep her balance, she fell on her knees at Medb's side, her hair dripping with sea water, her clothes soaked, her face wet with tears. Her gown too was torn, her face bruised, a vicious bite mark visible on her breast at the gaping neck of her tunic. 'What's going to happen to us?' Around them the crew of the ship went about their business in the storm as if the women were not there, hauling on the ropes, swinging the great tiller to and fro as the wind caught the ship and it threatened to founder.

Medb dragged herself onto her knees groggily. 'Where is Anu? Is she all right?'

Sibael nodded. 'She is in the hold. They've sent me to fetch you. The storm is getting worse.' Her words turned to sobs. 'We are going to die!'

'Not if they can get money for us alive!' Medb's voice was harsh. She raised her chained hands to her face, pushing her wet hair out of her eyes.

Clinging together, the two women dragged themselves across the deck and half climbed, half fell down the steps which led to the hold where Anu huddled alone in the darkness.

Medb collapsed beside her, shivering violently, relieved to be out of the worst of the wind. 'Where are those men?'

'Through there.' Anu nodded towards the set of doors behind her. 'In the main cabin, where it is warm and dry.' She too was crying. 'They say we will make landfall before dark.'

'Make landfall where?' Medb, her teeth chattering, pulled a piece of sacking towards her, trying to cover herself. The cabin was stacked with sacks and barrels and boxes. It smelled sour and wet.

'Gaul.' Anu sobbed. 'They are going to sell us there like so many trade goods!' She let out a wail of misery. 'The man who,' her voice broke again, 'the man who raped me said we would be bought by a rich man. They will clean us up and give us dry clothes so they get a better price for us.'

'Will they indeed.' Medb clenched her fists. 'We will accommodate them as best we can until that happens, then –' she took a deep breath, 'then believe me, I shall see to it that the person who brought us to this pays dearly!'

There was a long silence after Pat stopped talking.

Viv was staring at her numbly. 'That's awful,' she said at last, her voice husky.

Pat ground out her cigarette in a saucer lying on the coffee table in front of her and reached for the packet again. Her hands were shaking. 'This has to go into the play.'

Viv shrugged. 'It can't.'

'You are joking! Of course it can. It is vital to the story. Dramatically it's dynamite.'

'It's not history. It's not relevant.' Wearily Viv stood up and walking over to the window, pushed it open. 'Pat, we are writing a drama documentary about Cartimandua. We have to stick to the known facts at least as a basis!' Turning back into the room she shook her head. 'I know we need more drama, but this is just not important in the context, wherever it comes from.'

'Not important!' Pat echoed. 'Cartimandua sent her to this fate deliberately!'

'She deserved it, Pat. Look what she had done. Murder. Vicious, deliberate murder.'

'You don't know that!' Pat shook her head. 'Why should she have murdered anyone?'

'God knows! She was a vindictive, jealous woman.'

'Viv, you are insane! Look at the facts!' Pat broke off as the phone rang.

Viv picked it up with an angry glance at her.

'We need to talk.' It was Hugh. 'There are things we have to discuss,' he said without preamble. 'Are you coming into the office today?'

Viv closed her eyes with an inward groan. 'That's not going to be possible. I'm in a meeting at the moment.' Her mind was still full of images of Medb.

'A meeting that's more important than discussing the Cartimandua fibula?' The voice in her ear was hard.

She went cold. She couldn't deal with this as well. Not now. Probably not ever. 'Hugh, we do need to discuss it,' she said at last. 'But not today. I will call you, I promise.'

'I don't know if that is good enough.'

'It has to be. Look, Hugh. There is someone here. I can't talk about it now.' Putting the receiver down she turned back to Pat. 'That was the Prof. The last person I wanted to hear from.' She paused. 'Pat? Are you all right?'

Pat was sitting, the cigarette between her fingers, staring into space. The anger had gone from her face which was blank. She did not appear to have heard anything Viv said.

'Pat?'

Going across to her, Viv touched her shoulder. 'Are you OK? You were miles away.'

144

For a moment Pat said nothing, then she shook her head. 'I don't know what's happening to me.' She sighed. 'I suppose I'm tired.' She reached into her bag and pulled out the script and her copy of *Queen of the North*. 'Where were we?'

Viv frowned. 'We hadn't really started,' she said cautiously. 'We were just tossing a few ideas around, remember?'

Pat shrugged. 'I've got a lot of stuff to show you. Maddie has seen it. She likes it.' She stubbed out the second cigarette and uncapped her pen. 'Let's see if we've got the introductory scenes right, shall we?'

It was as though Medb had never been mentioned at all.

10

I

Hugh. Please!

Alison turned and looked at him, her eyes intense with compassion. Her hair was a fluffy halo around her head, drifting in the wind as she stood on the top of Traprain Law staring out across the fields towards the sea.

Please. Be careful!

She held out her hands to him and taking a step forward, he reached out to clasp them but she was fading. Drawing away.

Desperately he moved towards her but she was going. Nothing would keep her there with him. In a second she was gone and he was alone.

It was then he heard it. The sound of the war trumpet echoing across the hillside. He found himself turning round, straining his ears, the hair on the back of his neck prickling even in the dream. 'Alison? Where are you?' His voice was thready, weak, echoing out across the distances and in response he heard it again, the carnyx, the war trumpet of the Celts. It was closer now and the shock of the sound woke him.

He lay staring up at the ceiling as the early sunlight pushed tentative fingers through the curtains. Twice he had heard that noise the day before. Once as he walked down the road, a newspaper under his arm, the sound echoing over the sound of traffic. It was beautiful. Wild. Imperious. Then again in the garden as he strolled out to look at the roses after speaking to Viv on the phone. He had been scared that time too. He wasn't sure how he knew what it was; he had never heard one before though he had seen one in the museum. It comprised an elegant, long bronze tube leading up to a bronze boar's head with a raised crest, a movable clapper-like jaw and fiery red enamelled eyes. The trumpeter carried it vertically so its great head was high above the heads of the warriors whence its eerie notes echoed over the din of battle. It was, he remembered reading somewhere, one of the loudest, most sophisticated and terrifying instruments ever made. The sound now was threatening and unearthly. And each time it was getting closer.

Rolling out of bed, he went and drew back the curtains, staring down at the back lawn. A pair of blackbirds were hopping about on the grass. The place was quiet, save for the birds and there was nothing threatening there now. Turning away he headed for the shower.

He rang Viv again as he waited for the kettle to boil. This morning she had turned on the answer machine and he didn't bother to leave a message. Annoyed, he slammed down the receiver. On his desk lay the letter from the museum. It was full of phrases like, 'If you could see your way to . . .' and, 'The fibula would of course be a central feature of the new exhibit . . .' and, 'We have been enormously grateful in the past for your generous decision to leave it in our care . . .'

So, they were forcing his arm. Now he would have to demand it back. He sighed. When was it she said she wanted to show it on the TV? *History Discussion Night* was on Wednesdays and her publication was coming up soon, so it would most likely be next week. With a frown he reached for the phone again. This time he called Steve Steadman.

Steve was there by 10.30. 'It's awfully good of you to lend me this stuff, Professor.' The young man gazed at the pile of notes and books on Hugh's desk. If he was puzzled by Hugh's imperious demand that he come and collect them from Aberlady at once he gave no sign of it. 'I'm probably going home at the weekend, so I can take it all with me.'

Hugh was watching him thoughtfully.

'Have you seen Dr Lloyd Rees in the last day or two?'

Steve tensed. 'I have seen her, yes,' he said guardedly.

'And how did she seem?'

Steve hesitated. 'A bit stressed.'

Hugh saw the wariness in the other man's eyes. 'She's upset

about not getting the Readership, no doubt. There are good reasons why I changed my mind.' He began methodically to roll up his shirtsleeves. 'Would you like a mug of coffee? One of my talents, coffee, though you must promise not to tell Heather. She thinks I can't even switch on her machine whereas I can open a jar with the best of them!' He strode through to the kitchen and reaching for the kettle, glanced out of the window. Steve's old blue Peugeot 205 GTi was parked outside the front of the house.

Hugh rummaged in a cupboard for mugs, then turned back to him. 'Would you like to do a bit of lecturing for me next year?'

Steve stared at him.

'I expect you could do with a bit of cash,' Hugh went on. 'And it would help Viv. She'll be stretched with all the teaching I've given her.' He reached for a jar and unscrewed the top, sniffing at it cautiously. 'Give it some thought, and perhaps a tutorial or two a week?'

'That's very good of you, Professor.' Steve frowned. 'But I would have to talk it over with Viv. I wouldn't want to tread on her toes.' He was firm.

'Of course.' Hugh managed an affable smile. 'You see quite a lot of her, don't you.' He paused, eyebrow raised. 'I should imagine she's a good friend.' He paused again. Steve made no comment so he went on, 'Well, when you do see her, would you remind her that I need the pin. The museum wants it back.'

'The pin?' Steve looked genuinely mystified.

'She borrowed a valuable artefact from my study.' Hugh said slowly. 'I've been trying to contact her about it without success. Her answer phone is permanently switched on, it seems.' His eyes met Steve's steadily. 'She needs to return it soon or I shall be forced to inform the police.'

Steve stared at him, stunned. 'Are you saying she stole it?'

'I am saying she borrowed it without permission. It is only stolen if it fails to return.'

'She wouldn't steal anything, Professor, you must know that,' Steve said hotly. 'You must have misunderstood. She wouldn't do a thing like that.'

'You know her that well, do you?' Hugh narrowed his eyes.

'Pretty well, yes,' Steve retorted.

Hugh nodded. 'I hope you're right. I'm sure a reminder from you is all she needs.' He added water to the granules in the mugs, topped them up with milk and pushed one across to Steve. 'I'm really very fond of Viv, you know,' he added. 'I'd hate anything to come between us permanently.'

Steve gave a wry grin. 'She speaks well of you, too.'

Hugh raised an eyebrow. 'Does she indeed.' He laughed. 'I'm sure this will all blow over. I miss her friendship, you know.' He put his mug down decisively. 'Right. Let me give you a hand with this stuff to your car.'

As they piled it all into the back, Hugh glanced up abruptly. He had heard it again. The wild call of the bronze war trumpet echoing in the gentle warmth of the breeze. He felt himself grow cold. 'Did you hear that?'

Steve pulled the hatchback down. 'What?' He paused, listening. 'I didn't hear anything except for the birds. This is a lovely garden, Professor.' He walked round to the side of the car with a smile and held out his hand. 'Thanks again for the notes and books. I really appreciate your lending them to me.'

Hugh shook his hand. 'It's a pleasure. Let me know if there is anything else I can do to help.' He stiffened, listening again. 'Are you sure you can't hear anything?'

Puzzled, Steve hesitated as he was opening the driver's door. 'What sort of thing?'

'A horn.' Hugh turned away from him, staring down the drive. 'A war trumpet.' He turned back, and seeing the expression on Steve's face burst out laughing. 'Probably the kids next door. Or tinnitus! Take no notice, my boy. I'm obviously heading for early onset senility!' He laughed again. 'Drive safely now.'

He watched as the Peugeot disappeared out of the gate and he stood for several minutes alone on the gravel listening to the birds. Then at last he turned back towards the house.

II

'I knew it!' Viv turned on Steve furiously. 'I asked you not to tell him!'

He had turned up early the next morning and the moment he

149

mentioned Hugh she exploded. 'You just had to run to him, didn't you!'

'Hey, wait a minute!' Steve followed her inside. 'For your information I told him nothing about what you showed me. Nothing at all. Just listen to me, please, before you blow a gasket!' Patiently he relayed all that Hugh had said. When he got to the fibula she erupted again. 'So that's it! He gets you to do his dirty work. And I suppose you believe him, that I stole it!' She was pacing up and down the floor, her lips pursed.

Steve perched on the corner of the sofa. 'I've no idea what you did', he said mildly. 'Perhaps if you didn't take it you ought to tell him because presumably someone else did!'

'But I did take it!' Viv swung round. 'I asked him if I could borrow it. Did he tell you that? For a TV show. On Channel 4 next week.'

She sat down abruptly and put her head in her hands. 'God knows what possessed me, Steve! I asked and he said no, and I was so cross! I wasn't thinking. He turned away almost daring me to take it –'

'Why not give it back?'

'Because –' She paused again. 'Because I would have to admit I'd done it. Because I would have to apologise. Because I need it!' She shook her head furiously. 'I've completely screwed up over this, Steve. I don't know what the hell to do.'

'Can I see it?' He was looking very serious. It made her feel worse, as though her confession had reversed their roles and now he was the elder, the teacher, the keeper of moral rectitude and she was the one who had fallen by the wayside.

She went over to the desk and opened the bottom drawer. The small box was hidden at the back under a whole lot of old papers. She held it out to him.

Taking it, he studied the brooch for a long time through the Perspex, without opening the lid. 'It's beautiful,' he said at last.

'And priceless.'

'Does it feature in your research?' He gestured towards her desk.

She shook her head. 'Not so far. I've no idea if it genuinely did belong to Cartimandua, but that's what it's called. The Cartimandua Pin.' She glanced up at him. 'You think I should give it back.'

'I think if you don't there could be real trouble.' He opened the lid and held it up, studying it more closely.

'It's not long till the TV programme. I only want to keep it until then.'

'When you will admit to millions of people that you have it? That you took it?'

'Do you think he'd want me to go to prison?' She stared at him. 'That would solve his problem, wouldn't it. How long do you reckon they'd give me? Five years?'

'Viv!'

She shook her head. 'I'm not giving it back, Steve!' She held out her hand for the box.

He hesitated, lifting a finger as though to stroke the cold enamels.

She froze. 'Don't touch it,' she said sharply.

'Sorry.' He withdrew his finger and refitted the lid carefully, then he handed it back to her. 'I'm going home at the weekend,' he said, glancing up. 'Do you want to come with me?' She was standing by the desk, the box in her hand. 'It would be a break for you. Get you away from Hugh. Give you a chance to think this over.'

She looked down at the pin. 'Do you think he'd really call the police?'

Behind them the front door was pushed wide and Pat appeared, out of breath from the stairs. 'What's this about the police?' She paused. 'Sorry. You left the door open – am I interrupting?' She dropped her bag on the floor. 'What's that?' She had spotted the gleam of gold in the sunlight which poured through the open window.

'The brooch.' Viv turned and slotted the box into the back of the drawer decisively. 'I was just showing it to Steve.'

Pat frowned as he stood up. 'I hope you didn't touch it.'

He grinned. 'Don't worry, I didn't.'

'Good.' She shrugged. 'It has dangerous powers!'

'Really!' He grinned even more broadly. 'Glad I wasn't tempted, then.' He glanced across at Viv before heading for the door. 'Let me know?'

She nodded. 'I'll ring you tonight, OK?'

'Who was that?' Pat began to unpack her bag as the door closed behind him.

'One of my graduate students.'

'Wow! I thought your students were all pimply faced adolescents. He's grown up. And gorgeous.'

Viv smiled. 'I'll tell him you think so.' She hesitated. 'Why did you tell him the brooch was dangerous?'

Pat shrugged. 'A momentary fancy,' She replied thoughtfully. 'Or an intuition, perhaps. Or common sense.'

151

Viv studied her face for a moment. She said nothing. Then she turned her attention to Pat's script. 'So, have you had any more dreams?' She glanced up warily.

To her relief Pat shook her head. 'I've written the next scene, though. Just skim through it and then we can move on.' She held out a few pages.

Viv took them. 'I'm beginning to get the impression you're writing this without me,' she said as she turned to the first page.

'Not at all. We discussed all this. Some of it is based on what you did in the first draft. I'm just tidying it up.' Pat sat down, not meeting her eye. 'So,' she went on as Viv turned over the first page, 'is this young man special, as it were?'

Viv didn't look up. 'Don't be daft.' She frowned. 'Pat, this is nothing like the outline we agreed.'

'Better, don't you agree?'

'No. I don't. You've put Medb in here.'

'We discussed that, Viv. She's too good a character to ignore.' Pat sighed. 'I talked this over with Maddie. I told you.'

Viv was shaking her head. 'No, this is all wrong. We are writing a drama documentary, Pat. There is no room for all this. It may be exciting. I'm sure it would be wonderful for a thriller. But this isn't a thriller. We have to keep within a framework of the known facts.' She gave a wry smile. 'I'm sorry. This won't do. Let's put our heads together and rewrite this bit without Medb. We agreed. There is only room for about five minutes about Carta's early life. If that. The story really starts just before her marriage.'

Her second marriage.

Pat stood up. 'I don't see any point in this.' Medb had to be in the play. Medb was the play.

Viv had picked up a pencil and was drawing a line through whole sections of the typescript. She looked up, startled. 'What do you mean?'

'I came here to help you because I know what makes a good play. If you are going to ignore my advice I may as well go back to London.'

'That's silly. I value your advice.' Viv sighed. 'You've done some fantastic writing in the first scene.'

'And so I have in this scene. What is it with you and Medb? You cannot bear the thought that people might hear what happened. That's it, isn't it.'

152

'Pat! Hang on a minute!'

'I told you Maddie is fine about this. And she wants the play finished soon. Before she goes on maternity leave. If you keep making problems the whole thing will be scrapped. I suggest you let me do the writing, Viv. That's what I'm here for. Just be pleased that the project is in good hands.' Pat stood up and swept her pages together. 'Look, I'll leave you to think about it. There's no point in even discussing it with you in this mood.' Heading for the door, she stopped. 'Ring me when you're ready to look at some more, OK? I do understand how hard this must be for you, but I know when you've considered it you'll agree it's for the best. If you want the play to be broadcast, that is.'

Viv sat staring at the door for fully two minutes after Pat had gone, stunned at the outburst, then she lowered her eyes to the script and read the scene through again. It was all about Medb.

III

They sold Anu on the quay. The women were still bedraggled and dripping with salt water, chained together in a miserable group while the cargo was being unloaded, when two men walked up to them and stood discussing them as though they were brood mares. Medb met the eyes of the taller of the two defiantly, daring him to approach. He did, circling them with a critical eye, exchanging quiet comments with his companion. Then they moved away to talk to the ship owner. 'I'll take the little blonde,' he said, loudly enough for them to hear. 'The other two look like trouble. You can send them to the slave market next week.'

And that was that. Anu was unchained and dragged away screaming. They never saw her again.

Medb and Sibael, in their dry clothes, with their hair combed, were bought by a Roman official to work in his household some two days' march inland. He kept twenty slaves, fifteen working on the farmstead around his villa and five working indoors. Sibael and Medb were to wait upon his wife, Lucilla, an austere woman with cold steel-grey eyes and rugged cheekbones who spoke the

153

language of Less Britain and therefore was able to converse with them more or less. Medb did not for one moment betray the fact that she understood Latin. 'Behave and work hard and you will find me a fair mistress,' Lucilla said to them on the first day. 'You will have clean clothing and good beds and decent food. When I know I can trust you your chains will be removed. You cannot work with chains. My other servants will tell you they have a good life here. Don't abuse my trust.'

Sure enough, several days later the chains were struck from their wrists by the blacksmith and their duties were allotted to them. Sibael was to work in the laundry and Medb was required to wait at their meals. 'You have a certain refinement,' her new mistress said to her. 'I suspect you have worked in a wealthy household. That is good. You can teach the others.'

Medb smiled and nodded and kept her counsel. She would tell her mistress who she was in good time.

The woman was indeed fair. She rewarded hard work with praise and small gifts which made their lives easier. She was popular with all the servants, free and unfree and, as they saw in time, with her friends and family as well. But the slaves were locked in at night and the house and grounds were patrolled by armed guards. Escaping would not be quite as easy as Medb had imagined. And even if she escaped from the villa she still had to work out a way to cross the ocean to go back home. Gritting her teeth she smiled and worked and earned Lucilla's trust. At night she lay awake and schemed. She never considered for a minute that she might have brought her misfortunes upon herself. Always in her dreams she saw the face of Cartimandua, the woman whom she blamed for all her misery. The woman who, once she was free, she intended to kill with her own hands.

Throwing down the pages, Viv looked up with a sigh. Where had Pat got this idea from? It had nothing to do with the story. It was a complete red herring. Medb had disappeared out of Carta's life the day she had been captured and spirited away. Her only relevance from then on had been the malign trail of devastation which had led to the death of Riach and then of Carta's baby. And that was over, surely. Walking over to the computer she hesitated for a moment, then she sat down and switched it on. There was only one way to find out what had happened next.

154

IV

'But this is my home!' Carta was staring at King Lugaid incredulously. 'You can't send me away!'

'Nor do I want to, child.' Lugaid was fond of this girl, his son's widow.

His first instinct had been to marry her to one of his other sons. Then he wondered if he could marry her himself. With Medb of the White Hands gone his bed was often cold. His senior wife would always be a friend and companion; he even loved her in his own way and she still knew how to give him pleasure, but for how much longer? She was past childbearing age. Her beauty and charm were no doubt prolonged by magical potions and spells and prayers to the goddesses. One day he might wake up and find a crone in his bed.

But the Archdruid had warned him off. 'Carta's destiny is with her own people, Lugaid. I have been reading it in the signs for some time. She has been studying with me and at the classes that Gruoch and Vivios run at the college. She learns fast. She has a natural aptitude.'

'So, you would claim her as a Druid?'

'She is already of the Druid caste, my friend, and I have no doubt if she pursues her studies for the set length of time she will one day become a fully fledged Druidess but no, that is not the primary future I see for her. The loss of the child has strengthened her. She has iron in her soul now. I would send her back to her father and send Gruoch with her. Then she can study with Artgenos at his Druidic school. She has much to learn, but the time will come soon when her people will seek a ruler of strength and wisdom.'

'And they will choose Carta?' Lugaid was disbelieving. 'But she has brothers. Her mother has brothers. There are several warriors to my knowledge of her royal house who would come before her. Almost anyone would come before her. She's a woman. And still a child!'

Truthac smiled. 'So?' He folded his arms more comfortably under his thick cloak. Outside the snow was falling out of a leaden sky. 'If she is chosen by the gods, she will be chosen by the people. Yes, by the men and women of her tribe.' He shrugged. 'I have done all I can to prepare her. She must go now to her own country.'

'But her marriage portion –'

'Will return with her and with it half of Riach's wealth as is her entitlement according to the law.' Truthac smiled at the king's expression. 'And with her will go also a firm alliance between the Votadini and the Brigantes, my friend. The omens suggest such close ties will need to be protected and reinforced in the future.'

V

Viv jumped as the phone rang. 'Hell and damnation!' She ran her hands through her hair. Why interrupt now, just as Carta was about to go back to Brigantia?

She had picked up the phone before she had time to come back down to earth.

'Hi there, Viv. It's Steve.' There was a pause. 'You were going to ring me? I'm sorry. Is this a bad time?'

She took a deep breath. 'Sorry Steve. I was a bit preoccupied.' She glanced at her watch. Once again the whole day had gone.

'You were going to tell me if you would like to come to Yorkshire for the weekend.'

To Brigantia.

Carta's home.

'Yes please.' Her reply was greeted by a long silence. 'Did you hear me, Steve? I said yes, I'd love to.' Away from Pat and away from Hugh. The perfect solution.

'Great!' It was spoken with such an exhalation of relief she almost laughed.

'On one condition,' she went on. 'We take my car. I need to be independent. And I can only come for a couple of days – there is so much I need to do here. Is that a problem?'

'No.' At the other end of the phone he grinned. Whether his old Peugeot would reach home was always a bit of an uncertain equation. And one of his friends would undoubtedly enjoy the chance to drive it down for him. They agreed to leave next morning and

Viv hung up the phone with a smile. She would reach Ingleborough at just about the same time as Carta.

'How long did you say your family have lived here?'

Steve had directed her along a series of increasingly small lanes until they headed at last through a gate and up a steeply rutted drive towards a grey limestone farmhouse, surrounded by dry stone walls and sheltered by old fruit trees, nestling in a beautiful fold of moorland on the flanks of the great humped hillside which was Ingleborough.

He shrugged. 'Around the Lancashire, Yorkshire border, for generations.' He had grown increasingly quiet as they drove south and west from Edinburgh into the farthest corners of North Yorkshire.

'As in hundreds of years?' Switching off the engine she sat back with a sigh. It had been a long drive. Around them the silence was broken only by the song of a lark high up in the brilliant azure sky.

He nodded. 'You'll have to ask Dad. Several, as far as I remember. Maybe thousands.' He laughed, then sobered abruptly. 'Mum takes the old gods very seriously. Sometimes I think too seriously. Tread carefully, won't you.'

She stared at him, studying his profile. 'What do you mean, seriously?'

He shrugged, concentrating on the view ahead of them. 'She still believes in them, Viv. Dad doesn't. It creates a bit of tension.'

'I can imagine.' She reached for the door handle. 'Don't worry. I'm hardly likely to contradict her! It's wonderful. Part of belonging here.' She pushed the door open. 'Imagine knowing that your family has lived in an area for thousands of years!'

'But sadly not for much longer, I suspect.'

'Why? Don't you want to stay?'

He shrugged. 'I'm not a farmer. Neither are my brother or my sister. We've seen too much of it.'

'That's sad.'

His answer, if any, was lost as he followed her round the back of the car to unstrap his bag which was perched on the luggage rack.

He led the way to the house, and down the entry hall over scrubbed flagstones towards a long low-ceilinged sitting room. It

157

was neat and well furnished with up-to-date magazines and a small modern TV with video and DVD and was aimed exclusively, Viv decided, at the B&B guests. Nice though the gently smouldering log fire was, it was not a family room. No room could be that tidy naturally. As she stood looking round Steve's mother appeared with outstretched arms to embrace her son. Having hugged him she turned to shake Viv's hand with a smile of welcome.

Peggy Steadman was the archetypal farmer's wife with pink cheeks, faded blue eyes and wispy grey-blonde hair. Slightly over-weight, she was dressed in blue cotton trousers and a V-necked grey sweater. 'Steve has told us so much about you!' she said as she led them back into the passage.

Steve frowned, embarrassed. 'Mum!'

'And why not?' Peggy was indignant. 'Come with me, love.' She turned to Viv. 'I'll show you your room, then you can make yourself at home.'

They climbed a broad, easy-rising stone staircase and then a second narrower flight. 'You'll have this whole floor to yourself this weekend. I have three double rooms for guests but there is no one else here just now, so you can choose which one you would like,' Peggy said over her shoulder as Viv followed her upstairs. She was panting slightly from the climb. Steve, having brought in the rest of their luggage, some from the boot, some strapped onto the luggage rack, some stuffed down the back of the seats of the two-seater car, had vanished somewhere into the back of the house.

The first door Peggy threw open showed a bright south-facing room which looked across the gardens. There were twin beds and all the usual comforts including another TV. 'This one – ' Viv would have been happy to stay there, but Peggy had already moved on down the passage, 'is north-facing, but you do have a view of the hill.' The room was darker than the first, but ancient stone-mullioned windows looked out across a narrow strip of garden up the valley towards Ingleborough itself. Viv shivered. 'It's beautiful.'

Peggy was watching her surreptitiously. She nodded. 'Well, take your time to choose and make yourself at home, then come down-stairs. If you don't mind being part of the family, follow the noise to the kitchen and join us for a cup of tea before you go out to explore.'

Slowly Viv moved across to the window. Kneeling down and resting her elbows on the stone sill, she stared out.

High clouds racing before a westerly wind were streaming huge shadows over the soft green of the steep-sided, rugged, flat-topped hill. No round houses on top, no high walls, no well-used track as far as she could see winding up its flank, but it was like coming home.

With a start Viv shook her head. Now was not the time. Ducking outside into the passage she hauled her holdall into the room together with the bag that contained her laptop and notebooks. Then she went to find the kitchen.

The long scrubbed refectory table held teapot, cups, a plate of scones and a huge chocolate cake. Steve was already seated there and Viv slid into a chair beside him. 'This place is heaven. I'm going to enjoy staying here.'

He smiled as his mother reached for the teapot and poured Viv a cup. 'You're certainly going to find it interesting. Climbing the hill. Visiting the site of the fort. Ghost hunting!'

'Steve.' His mother's voice was sharp. 'Don't talk about such things. You'll scare Viv away.'

'No, on the contrary. I'm very interested.' Viv accepted a scone. 'Steve told me you had heard things and I wanted to know all about it.'

Peggy gave her a quick shrewd glance from eyes very like her son's, then she sat down opposite Viv. 'This is an old house, at least six hundred years, probably older. I expect Steve has told you. There are bound to be noises. Creaking wood. Ceiling beams groaning in the night. You get used to it. And the wind. Wuthering as the guests always say. Always the wind. But then sometimes,' she hesitated, 'yes, people do hear other things as well.'

'In the house?'

Peggy nodded.

'And on the hill?'

'Oh yes, there especially. It's a long way up to the fort. Climbers go there. And ramblers. But when one is alone the memories start.'

'Memories?' Viv frowned. 'That's a strange word to use.'

Peggy nodded. 'Why don't you go and see for yourself? You must be longing to be outside after your long drive. It's a fair walk, but you could do it before supper if you've a mind. Steve can show you the way. Maybe you'll hear nothing. Maybe something will happen. You're not afraid?' She held Viv's gaze for a moment and Viv thought there was a challenge there.

'I'm not sure. I don't think so,' Viv replied thoughtfully. 'I hope not. How does one know until it happens?'

Steve walked beside her in silence as they followed a farm track across a small field, through a gate in the dry stone wall across another rough field and up onto the open hillside. The westering sun was throwing long shadows at their feet as they began to climb.

'I'm sorry if Mum was a bit brusque,' he said after a moment. 'It's only her way.'

Viv glanced at him. 'I liked her.'

'Good.' His face softened. 'She's defensive about some of the stories and myths. Visitors sometimes make fun of them.'

'Not me, Steve.' Viv raised an eyebrow. 'You know me better than that.' She changed the subject. 'Have you any idea what this place was called before it was Ingleborough? Is there a local folk memory of an old name?'

He shrugged. 'Not as far as I know.'

'I spent a long time researching names for my book,' she said thoughtfully. 'Before my alternative source kicked in' She glanced at him. 'The word Ingleborough isn't Celtic, of course. It's Old English. The fortification of the Englishman, something like that. Carta – Cartimandua,' she corrected herself quickly, 'called it Dun Righ.'

Steve grinned. 'The castle of the king. That makes sense. Pen y Ghent is over there,' he gestured with his thumb, 'the neighbouring hill. Obviously that's Celtic.'

Viv nodded at last, seeing that Steve was waiting for her to say something. 'The names of most of the old hill forts are forgotten or changed out of all recognition though we can guess at a few from the derivations and from analysing the compounds – British or Brythonic prefixes with later English endings. I had a lot of help with the philology from Mhairi. It is a help that the Romans so often just stuck a Latin ending on the native name. York for instance was Eboracum to the Romans. That probably came from something like Eborios.'

'So this could have been Rigodunum, the dun of the king,' Steve put in.

Viv nodded. 'Some people do think that's Ingleborough.' She was breathless. The track was very steep and rough in places and

160

occasionally as they climbed higher someone had cut steps to make the climb easier.

'What did you decide to do about the brooch?' Steve said suddenly. He stopped and waited for her.

'Nothing.'

'Was that wise?'

'Who knows.' She shrugged. 'Hugh can't do anything if he can't reach me. You haven't told him where we were going, have you?'

'No fear.' He glanced at her. 'You didn't bring it with you?'

She shook her head. 'It's not long till the programme. Then he can have it back and welcome.'

'Supposing there are police waiting for you at the TV studio?'

She gazed at him. 'You don't really believe he'd do that?'

'I don't think so, but our Prof is a law unto himself. I'm not sure I'd bet on it too heavily.'

She grimaced. She didn't want to think about it. 'This is so beautiful, Steve. Do you realise how lucky you are to live here?'

The view of farmland and moors and woods spread out beneath them with, beyond, a panorama of fells and cloud-painted skies. For a few minutes they stood without talking, drinking it in.

'Would you like to do the last bit to the top on your own? Steve asked. 'I know how special this is for you.'

Viv glanced at him. 'Are you sure you wouldn't mind?'

He shook his head. 'I'm just as happy to wait here. You go on up. Take it all in. Come down when you're ready. I'll be here.'

She smiled and leaning forward touched his hand. 'Thanks.' For a minute their eyes met. Then he turned away.

She watched as he retraced his steps, sometimes walking, sometimes loping over the soft stony grass until he reached a flat patch of grass near a clump of bobbing bog cotton, where with a wave of his hand he sat down, then lay back, his arm across his eyes.

Resolutely she turned back towards the summit alone.

11

I

In Edinburgh Cathy put down the phone. It was the third time she had called Viv. She had left messages each time on her home number and on the mobile which was switched off. Cathy frowned. A thread of worry was beginning to worm its way into the back of her mind.

She had shared her thoughts about Viv, without naming names, of course, with a couple of colleagues and they had discussed the implications of her experiences. 'No, she's not on drugs. Absolutely not.' That had been their first suggestion. She was fully aware of the voices. She wasn't being taken over by them or told to do things by them. It wasn't schizophrenia and it wasn't demonic possession, imagined or real, requiring the help of the church. On the contrary, the whole experience seemed to be wholly narrative as though she were tapping into a story.

A previous life, maybe? They had discussed that seriously. Even in orthodox psychology nowadays there were people prepared to believe the possibility of such things, or at least acknowledge that the vivid role-playing involved had a therapeutic purpose. But this did not seem to fit either. Viv did not become Cartimandua or any of the personalities around her. She was purely a spectator. Or an amanuensis. Putting the story on paper. Finally getting it right.

She was a goddess.

Wasn't that what Viv had said the last time they had spoken on the phone?

Cartimandua had spoken to her directly. 'She sees me, Cathy. I'm sure she can see me as clearly as I can see her. Not all the time.

162

Most of the time she's busy. She's in her own world, but then she pauses. She goes to the shrine. She opens herself to other worlds. Through prayer – meditation – I don't know how, but it's a direct channel into my head!'

'And do you speak back to her?' Cathy had asked that very quietly, frowning with concentration.

Viv shrugged. 'Sometimes. I can't stop myself. I should be able to advise her, help her. After all I know so much about what happens.'

'And does she hear you?'

Viv had shrugged again. 'I don't know. I can't hold it. As soon as I become involved I lose contact.'

That had been the last conversation they had had. The moment Cathy had suggested that she discuss this with Pat, Viv had become distant, almost suspicious. And now there was no answer from either of her phones.

At the far end of the flat a door banged and she heard voices. Pete's lower growl. Then a mellow mezzo. Damn it, Greta was still here. Still part of the family group. With a sigh, Cathy headed for the door of her study. Time to assert herself.

Pat was in the living room alone with her laptop. Sitting down opposite her, Cathy grimaced. 'Was that Pete and Greta?'

Pat shrugged. 'To be honest I wasn't taking much notice.'

Cathy nodded. Who could blame her. 'I've been trying to reach Viv again,' she said. 'I've even tried e-mailing her. There's no reply.'

Pat saved her document. 'I shouldn't worry. She'll turn up.'

'But haven't you got meetings with her every day?'

'Not for now. I've plenty to be getting on with.' Pat was evasive. She glanced up. 'Maddie is quite happy for me to do most of this, as I told you. I'm showing it to Viv but she seems to have lost interest.'

Cathy raised an eyebrow. 'That's odd, I can't imagine her doing that.' She paused, thinking of possible reasons for her friend's abrupt absence. 'She didn't tell you she was going away or anything?'

'No.'

'And she hasn't been in touch with Maddie?'

'Whatever for?' Pat was indignant. 'Maddie has left this all in my hands.' She stood up and tucked the laptop under her arm. 'I'll put this upstairs out of harm's way while you sort out your family.'

They could hear voices again now, Pete and Greta were arguing in the kitchen.

Pat stopped in her tracks. 'She couldn't be ill, could she?' She glanced back. 'Or had an accident or something? Is there anyone who would know? How about the university?'

'She's not flavour of the month there, at the moment,' said Cathy thoughtfully. 'But I suppose the departmental secretary might know if she's gone away. But why on earth should she disappear so unexpectedly when you are working together?'

'She was pretty strung up last time I saw her.' Pat shook her head. 'And, as I said, I suppose she realises I can get on pretty much without her.'

'Without who?' The door opened and Tasha bounced into the room in time to hear the last comment.

'Viv, if it's any of your business, brat!' Pat said tolerantly. She reached, absent-mindedly, for her cigarettes.

'I expect Professor Graham has murdered her,' Tash put in helpfully. 'Didn't she say that's what he wanted to do?'

'Something like that.' Cathy hid a smile.

'Like Mum wants to murder Dad,' Tash continued. 'Can you hear them? Dad forgot to arrange something he was supposed to and she's spitting nails.'

'Oh God!' Cathy stood up. It was too late. Greta was already in the doorway. Whatever she was about to say froze on her lips as she spotted the cigarette in Pat's hand. 'I hope you do not intend to inflict that disgusting thing on my child. I do not permit anyone to smoke in her presence. Anyone at all.'

Pat stared at the cigarette. Her mouth had fallen open and for a moment she seemed incapable of speech.

'I gave Pat permission to smoke here, Greta,' Cathy lied, as Tasha threw herself on the sofa and pulled a cushion over her head. 'This is my flat. And I was not expecting you or Tasha to be here this morning.' She pursed her lips. 'Perhaps you would both like to go back and join Pete in the kitchen?'

Greta gave Pat a look of utter disdain and disappeared back into the hall.

Pat stared after her. 'Wow!' she murmured. 'Poor Pete. Why on earth did he ever marry her?'

'For her legs,' Cathy replied tartly. 'Or so he says. Excuse me a moment.' Climbing to her feet she headed for the door.

Pat stubbed out her cigarette in the ashtray. 'Suddenly it doesn't seem worth it.'

'Not even as an act of healthy rebellion?' Cathy grinned over her shoulder.

'As you constantly point out, healthy is probably not the right word.' Pat gave a throaty laugh.

She waited as Cathy headed for the door and then followed her into the hall with a smile.

Upstairs in her bedroom Medb was waiting.

II

Viv was standing alone on the top of the hill staring out towards the eastern horizon. Shoulder after shoulder of misty hills and dales stretched away into the distance, whilst behind her the sun was disappearing into the haze. All she could hear was the hiss of the wind. High above a circling buzzard let out an eerie cry, mewing into the advancing mist.

She shivered, wishing that Steve was still beside her.

The actual area of the hill fort, inside its mile-long collapsed stone ramparts was about half the size of that at Traprain. She knew that from her notes, but the setting was so different. Traprain was surrounded by flat farmland, with the sea in the distance. Here there was nothing to see but lonely fells. The sea was probably there, somewhere far away on the western horizon, but she couldn't see it for the haze. There had been stone-built round houses here, a flourishing community just as there had been at Traprain. Craftsmen and lead miners as well as warriors and Druids. Someone had built some of the stones of those houses into a cross-shaped shelter where people could sit out of the wind. So much for preserving any archaeological clues there might have been. Other stones had been heaped into cairns. Apart from that only the trig point stood up here on top now. She felt suddenly terribly lonely.

A breath of icy wind touched her cheek. She shivered again, glancing at her watch. It was getting late and they were expecting them back at the farmhouse. Was she really hoping to make contact with Carta here? Just like that. Flick a switch. Pick up the phone.

She hesitated. Then as another icy breath of wind began to tease the tendrils of her hair she turned to retrace her steps down the steep track to the spot where she had left Steve.

Gordon Steadman had joined his wife by the time they had returned to the farmhouse. A stooped, wiry man in his late sixties, he had thinning grey hair and a weathered face, an older, more battered version of his son who, Viv had now realised, was very much the ewe lamb of his parents' later years, his brother and sister being respectively ten and twelve years older than he was. Gordon was washing his hands in the sink when she appeared, his two collies lying on the floor by the dresser. They wagged their tails in greeting but otherwise lay still as he welcomed her warmly and directed her to her place at the table. Talking to him as they ate Peggy's cottage pie and spring greens dressed in butter and nutmeg, Viv realised that this house, this valley, was his whole life.

He shrugged when Viv asked him how long his family had lived in the house. 'Since records began. And long before that.' He gave a slow, thoughtful smile. 'Since time began, I reckon.'

Viv felt a quick shiver of goose pimples across her arms. 'That must be the most amazing feeling. My parents have never lived longer than about ten years anywhere. I'm not sure my grand-parents did.'

'You've got a Welsh name?'

Viv nodded. 'We come from North Wales and are very proud of it. But my parents live in Australia now. The tradition is broken as it seems to be with most people these days.'

'These days a lot of things are less than ideal.' Gordon Steadman pursed his lips. 'I watched them slaughter my stock, which had been bred to this land for hundreds of years. Gone. Just like that. To the knacker's bullet by the order of some fool behind a desk far away in London. I'm not allowed to know if my own beasts are healthy or not. We are told we must get used to the idea that we no longer know best about anything.'

There was a moment's silence. Viv stared down at her plate, intensely embarrassed. She could not begin to imagine what life had been like during the foot and mouth epidemic and how people like the Steadmans had managed to come through it. Out of the corner of her eye she saw Peggy reach across and touch her husband's hand. He pulled away sharply and she saw a flash of anger cross Peggy's face.

Steve stood up hastily to collect the plates. 'Tell Viv about the ghosts, Mum. She is seriously interested.'

As a method of changing the subject it worked. Peggy turned to Viv. 'In the house or up at the fort?'

Viv shrugged. 'I suppose both. Iron Age ghosts for preference as that is the period of my research project.'

Peggy gave a small humourless laugh as she stood up and went to the fridge for a bowl of fresh fruit salad. 'People aren't usually that fussy. Mostly we just hear noises. People shouting in the distance. The clash of swords. All carried on the wind.'

'It's all imagination!' Gordon put in sharply.

Viv glanced at him. 'I should imagine it's spooky out here in the winter.' Outside the distant fells were lit by the slanting light of the setting sun.

'Not just in winter,' Steve put in cheerfully. He passed round the bowls as his mother filled them. 'You'd be surprised how eerie it gets when the mist comes up over the fells at night sometimes. When we hear Awd Goggie in the orchard.' He grinned at Peggy. 'Or the barguest out on the fell.'

'I'm sure Viv hasn't come up here to see ghosts and evil spirits, Steve,' his father said sternly. 'She's a serious historian.'

'Indeed I am.' Viv tried to resist the jug of fresh rich cream and failed. 'But I'm interested in ghosts. All sorts of phenomena. Who knows how much such things might be able to help us with our research if we only knew how to interpret or verify what we see.' She glanced at Steve, uncomfortable at the tension between his parents. He was concentrating on the fruit salad.

Peggy nodded solemnly. 'Aye, well, that's true enough. That is what I keep telling Steve. The world is not unforgivingly black and white. There are a million shades of grey – so hard to see, so beautiful under the starlight.'

Viv smiled. Steve was right. His mother would understand. But not Gordon. He did not look up from his plate, nor did he join any further in the conversation.

It was after they had finished supper that Viv noticed a book on herbs pushed in on the shelf amongst the well-thumbed cookbooks.

'It's something else to do with my research,' she explained. 'I

167

wanted to find out what sort of potions would have been used to prevent someone miscarrying a baby.'

'Oh, Mum can help you with that,' Steve said with a tolerant grin. He put an arm round his mother's shoulders and gave her a hug. 'She's more or less the local midwife.'

'Really?' Viv was astonished.

'No, not really.' Peggy was firm. 'I sometimes lend a hand when no one else can get here, that's all. The hill farms get cut off in the winter sometimes.' She glanced at her husband. Some of those times had been by order of the government. He had left the table and was shrugging on his jacket, the two dogs milling round him, tails wagging, and did not seem to have heard. 'Come with me.' She touched Viv's arm. 'We'll look it up. You go with your father, Steve.'

Peggy watched the two men leave the kitchen then she led the way down the long flagged passage and into a dark shelf-lined back room. Some of the shelves were laden with books, others with jars and bottles. In one corner was an old kneehole writing desk, in another a couch covered by a brightly coloured throw. 'My still room.' Peggy waved her in and closed the door behind them. 'This was my mother-in-law's room when I first came here. She taught me everything she knew about herbs. Sit you down, love.' She smiled. 'This is a woman's room. I don't allow Steve or Gordon in here.'

Viv hitched herself up onto the couch and sat, legs swinging like a child. 'It smells wonderful.'

Peggy smiled. 'That's the herbs. I used to use the kitchen for making remedies and things, but since the B&B I have to be a bit careful. I prefer to be private.'

'Regulations?' Viv raised a sympathetic eyebrow.

Peggy nodded after a moment. 'Regulations. Poor Gordon. Forgive his little rant out there at supper.'

'It must have been awful beyond belief. He's so lucky to have you there.'

'It's what wives do.' Peggy tightened her lips for a moment. 'Now, let's see about your miscarriages.'

'Perhaps it's easier if I tell you what I think was used. This was in the Iron Age. The woman was threatening to miscarry at I think about five or six months. I made some notes of the names and had our Celtic language expert check them for me and she came up

168

with what she thought they were in the Gaelic. *Copan an druichd* which I believe is dew cup or lady's mantle; *muca faileag* which are briar rose hips; *sgiteach* – haws, *preas subh chraobh* which were rasps or raspberries and *seilleach* which is willow.'

Peggy nodded. 'Couldn't have prescribed better myself. Three textbook herbs, raspberry leaves, rather than raspberries, with willow bark, that's the origin of aspirin, as a pain killer.'

'And would they have worked?'

Peggy shrugged. 'It depends why the woman was threatening to miscarry. If there are contractions and too much bleeding it is probably impossible to stop it, even today. Rest. Sedation. Something to soothe the cramps and relax the uterus. That's all you can do. Haws are a tonic; wonderful relaxants. Lady's mantle wouldn't be so good to try and stop the miscarriage, but once it was underway it would make things less painful, and the same with raspberry leaves which are one of the herbal remedies people still remember today. Roses are good for the female system as well. It sounds as though your Iron Age herbalist knew what she was doing.'

'It does, doesn't it.' Viv sat for a moment lost in thought.

'Did they find archaeological evidence of those remedies?' Peggy leaned against the desk, arms folded. 'They've been finding some amazing things at the hospital they are excavating up at Soutra, I believe. Steve told me about it.'

'That's more a medieval site.' Viv frowned. 'This is earlier. Much earlier.'

'They've found Roman remedies too,' Peggy prompted. 'Jars which still have traces of cream. That sort of thing. Haven't they?'

Viv nodded. 'But this is actually conjectural,' she said slowly. 'To be honest, with you, I –' She hesitated. 'I sort of dreamed it.'

'Sort of?'

'I'll tell you about it some time.' Viv stood up.

'Fair enough.' Peggy scrutinised her face for a minute. Her eyes were no longer soft. They were uncomfortably piercing. 'I hope you enjoy your stay with us, love. Ask me if you need anything at all and make yourself at home.' As they walked back in towards the kitchen Peggy paused at the foot of the stairs. 'Don't go up to the fort on your own, will you. It's very wild up there. Easy to fall and even easier to get lost.' She hesitated a moment as though about to say something else, changed her mind and walked back into the kitchen.

169

III

The city was basking in the glorious sunshine. It was the kind of day which made one glad to be alive and Hugh was sick with worry, thanks to Viv. Someone greeted him as they walked past. He hadn't recognised them; hadn't even seen them to be honest. Stopping, he turned and looked back. Amongst the crowds he recognised no one.

There had been no reply from Viv's flat, either on the phone or when he had climbed all those millions of steps and knocked on the door. Hugh frowned as he walked back down the High Street, past the High Kirk of St Giles, with its wonderful crown spire, past Parliament House and the Heart of Midlothian, dodging the dawdling tourists without really seeing them.

Making up his mind abruptly, he changed course and headed towards the department. To his surprise Heather was there even though it was Saturday. Greeting her with a smile he made his way up to his office. There he closed the door and stared round the room suspiciously. Someone had been in there. He could feel it. Walking across to the desk he scanned it carefully. Since his tidy up he could tell at once if anything had been touched. It was all exactly as he had left it. Meticulous. Organised. He pulled open the top drawers. Nothing had been moved, as far as he could see. He straightened and stared round the room again, then shaking his head he walked to the door and pulling it open strode down the landing.

'Heather?' he bellowed from the top of the stairs.

Her face appeared at her office door, and she looked up apprehensively.

'Has anyone been in my room?'

'No, Professor. No one.' She stepped out into the hall. 'Is anything wrong?'

He shook his head. 'No. Don't worry.' Turning abruptly he found that Mhairi Mackenzie had opened her door and was peering out at him. A pretty mousey-haired woman, she found Hugh terrifying at the best of times. Her face was white as she stared out at him. 'Is everything all right, Professor?'

He nodded. 'Sorry, I didn't realise anyone else was here. Mhairi, did you see anyone going into my room?'

She shook her head adamantly. 'No one. I'd have heard them if they went past my door. It's been quiet as the grave.'

'How apt!' The Professor's tart comment made her shrink back as he strode past her towards his office. With a quick look after him she retreated and closed her door.

Back in his study Hugh stared round again with a wave of apprehension. He could sense someone there and yet he could see no one. Not daring to move, he scanned the room. There was nowhere to hide. Next to the filing cabinets? Behind the door? Under the desk? Every space was crammed with things. Books. Boxes. Files. Chairs. The old fashioned curly-armed coatrack held only an old scarf, dropped by one of his students and never reclaimed.

Taking a firm grip on himself he walked over to the desk and sat down, gripping the edge with whitened fingers. It was then he heard it again. The distant call of the trumpet, and he was sure, the sound of horses hooves. Dear God, he was going mad!

Pushing back the chair he shot to his feet and going to the window threw it open. Leaning out he took a few deep breaths of fresh air, feeling the sweat cooling on his face, then he turned back into the room, slamming the window down behind him and was brought up short by a wave of anger.

He reeled back. What the hell was going on? Throwing himself into his chair he felt a film of sweat break out on his forehead again. This was because of the stolen pin. It was Viv's fault. Well, he had given her every chance. If he called the police now she only had herself to blame. Without giving himself time to think he picked up the phone.

12

I

High above a skylark was singing as early sunlight slanted across the soft tussocky grass. Wrapped in her jacket and scarf, Viv had woken early and now sat cross-legged in the lea of a stone wall, her notebook open on her lap. She was writing fast. In her head it was the end of June as well. The soft warm wind from the west contained the scents of summer two thousand years ago as surely as they did in her waking life.

Carta stood staring up at the great cliffs which guarded this side of her hilltop home and beyond them to the stone ramparts with their entry gatehouses, one here, to the north, the other two out of sight behind the flat plateau on the high hill where she had been born. She was listening as the echoing cry of the horn announced her arrival. Behind her the wagons and chariots of the men and women who accompanied her and all her belongings were strung out some mile or so along the trackways which traversed the territories of her father the king. Her fists were clenched on the guardrail at her side and she braced herself easily as the chariot, driven by Fergal, lurched over the rutted ground, following now the steep stony roadway which wound up the sloping side of the hill towards the walls.

Physically she had recovered quickly from the loss of her baby, and as far as those around her could see she had put the event behind her. That she still mourned Riach with a bitter intense sorrow and anger perhaps only four people guessed, Mairghread and Gruoch, who had both elected to return with her to her father's kingdom, Conaire, her bard, and Fergal at whose side in her chariot she spent so much time as she grew stronger. She had been away for some six years and the young woman who rode now into the hilltop fortress of the Setantii was an educated, self-possessed, more thoughtful version of the wild untameable child who had ridden out at the age of twelve.

As she stepped down from the vehicle in front of her father's great round house he was waiting to greet her with arms outstretched, Fidelma beside him. But his welcoming hug though warm, was feeble and she could see at once that something was wrong. The strong vital man who had attended her wedding was gone. His face was thin, his hair greying, his arms beneath their gold bracelets feeble.

Kissing her mother, Carta was surprised to see her turn away and walk back towards the women's house. Two tall, handsome warriors had taken her place at the king's side, their very vitality, their virility seeming to emphasise his weakness. One, Carta's eldest brother, Triganos, surreptitiously took their father's arm as soon as they turned towards the great house and once there, helped him to his seat, the other following closely behind. Carta frowned, resenting the presence of the stranger who had almost elbowed her mother away on such a special family occasion. She subjected him to a searching stare, meeting his eyes coldly and realising with a sudden shock of recognition that it was Venutios who stood there. The boy who had plagued her as a child was now, it appeared, chieftain and king in his own right of their neighbours, the Carvetii. He was a man in his prime, his face adorned with blue swirls and flourishes, his eyes still the deep rich agate which had seemed so hard and resentful when they were children and which, she saw wryly, were hard and resentful still. Whilst her brother and her father were smiling, he looked at her with nothing but hostility and challenge.

Tearing her eyes away from his with a shiver of distaste, she stared round as the dark round house filled with men and women. He was not alone in his resentment, it seemed. Instead of the unrestrained welcome she had been expecting, the atmosphere throughout the township was tense. It was Triganos who now stood to welcome her officially, Triganos's bard with his branch of silver bells, the symbol of his office, who spoke the words of praise and joy and welcome that she should have returned to her father's roof. Her father said nothing. Neither did Venutios.

At the feast which followed, amidst the noise and bustle and music she watched her father closely. He ate almost nothing. Her

173

mother did not reappear. Only the next day did she find a chance to speak to Triganos alone. 'What has happened to him? Why was Mama not at the feast? Why is no one pleased to see me?'

Her brother looked down at her sadly. 'We are pleased to see you, Carta. Do not doubt it. It is just that father's health is failing. He was ill some four months ago with a bad fever and he has not properly recovered. On top of that, when we were out hunting only a fortnight ago he was gored by a boar. Not badly, not enough to hurt him seriously, but it has left him scarred. We all hoped he would get better, continue to be our king, but it is not going to happen as we would wish it. The elders of the Setantii and of the Brigantes as a whole, feel a new king should be chosen. It is time. Mama does not agree. She is angry. That is why she didn't come to the feast. The worry of all that has distracted us from the welcome we should have given you. I'm sorry.'

Carta slumped down on the bench nearby. 'Poor Father.'

'He can no longer claim the respect of his men, Carta. He can't lead them any more. It is time to stand back and enjoy the pleasures of old age.' He shrugged. 'Talk to him. He'll tell you, he doesn't want to fight the decision. He is prepared to stand down at Samhain. And in the meantime his chosen successor will lead the men should the need arise.'

'And his chosen successor will be?' Carta raised an eyebrow.

'Almost certainly me. There is no one else in contention.' Her brother grinned at her. He was a tall, well-built man, handsome, unscarred, exactly the choice the gods would make. And the people.

'So, your dream comes true.' She gave a wistful smile. 'What about Fintan, or Bran or Oisín? Do they agree?' Their brothers or the son of their father's sister were all of the royal blood, all eligible for choice. The Setantii would want the best man of the tribe to lead them, but to lead the whole confederation? That was different. 'What about the leaders of some of the other tribes?' she asked quietly. 'They will have a view. After all, it does not follow that the leader of the Brigantes should come from the Setantii.' She looked up at him quizzically.

'No, but it helps.' He grinned.

'What about Venutios? Why is he not back amongst his own people?' She studied Triganos's face, trying to keep the suspicion out of her voice.

The young man raised an eyebrow. 'You remember him then?'

174

'Of course I remember him!' she replied hotly. 'How could I forget! Why is he here?'

Triganos shrugged. 'He visits from time to time. Perhaps he's come to greet you.'

Carta snorted. 'I don't think that is likely. Perhaps he has another reason. Perhaps he wants to become high king.'

Triganos shook his head. 'He knows the position is mine.'

Carta nodded doubtfully. Perhaps he was right. Her own childhood dream to be a queen had died with Riach. Had he been chosen to succeed his father as leader of the Votadini she would have been his consort, his senior wife, his only wife – he had sworn it – and his queen. But that was not to be either. Not now. Folding her arms across her chest she half turned away from her brother. 'And what will become of me?' She hated saying it. It was weak. To her own ears her voice sounded pathetic, almost pleading.

Triganos stared at her in surprise as though the answer was too obvious to need voicing. 'It will be for me to find you a new husband, sister.' He followed her and gave her a quick hug. 'I'll find you someone special, sweetheart. A lusty chieftain. Perhaps even a king. We'll draw up a shortlist and you can choose. You know I wouldn't force you to take someone you didn't like.'

'Indeed you won't!' She spoke more sharply than she intended. 'For that would be against the law.' Extricating herself from his arms, she went to stand in the doorway. The chieftain's house was shadowy and empty at this time of the day. The sun had moved on and the low south-facing doorway no longer caught the long warm rays. Only the fire, smouldering gently in the centre of the floor, glowed with gentle light. Outside, the township was quiet. From the forge came the sound of hammering and from the stonemason's house on the far side of the township the regular sharp chink of chisel on rock. A group of women were sitting with their querns in the sunshine outside or spinning and sewing as they chatted and sang. Most of the male population were out, far away from the hill, working in the fields or with the slaves in the lead mines, or with the cattle and sheep on the surrounding moors. The warriors were practising their skills with sword and bow and sling. The men and women of her own train had dispersed, some to the horse lines, some to the men's lodgings, some to the servants' quarters.

Carta was not staying in her father's house. She had been given one of the largest guest houses as her own. There with Mairghread and Gruoch and her closest attendants she would settle for the time being. Around the circular stone walls of the house were the small private rooms much as there had been at Dun Pelder. Her father's township was shabby though, in comparison. In places the walls of the houses were crumbling; the thatch pulled by the birds; the great rampart walls falling down. She stared out across the compound with a sinking heart. A flock of small chickens were scratching in the dust. Nearby a dog slept in the sun, ignoring them. She frowned at the sight. The animal reminded her of Catia. It was probably related to Catia. Her heart ached for a moment for the faithful dog which had been such a friend to her. There had been no animal since to fill that special place. She loved all her dogs and horses equally but there was no hound now constantly at her heels or sleeping across her threshold. She had been content with Riach's dogs and they had stayed behind.

'What's happened, Triganos?' She turned back inside. 'Father may be ill, but he is High King of the Brigantian peoples. He is rich in cattle and gold. He has a dozen high forts to choose from, so why stay here?' This was a place she had loved, the home of her own special goddess, but there was no disguising the shabbiness and lack of care.

'We are here only for the summer.' Triganos shrugged. 'Father has ordered the building of a great new township at Dinas Dwr at the other side of the mountains. The roofs are being replaced and the walls refurbished and the place extended as a trading centre. We will go there before next winter.' He seemed a little uncertain; he had not looked at his home before with such a dispassionate eye. As long as it provided food and shelter and sport it served him well enough.

Carta stared at him. 'And in the meantime this, the great township of the king of The Setantii, Dun Righ on Pen y Righ, the king's hill, looks like a cluster of peasants' hovels!' She frowned. 'Are you saying that father has allowed everything to fall into this state?'

Triganos shrugged sulkily. 'It's not his fault. The cattle did not breed well this year. The gods did not watch over us and father has lost their favour.'

'Then it is his fault.' She pursed her lips. 'And it is for you,' she added tartly, 'to win their favour back.' She could feel her old impatience with her brother returning. The streak of indolence, of lazy arrogance, was still there.

'I'm doing so.' He looked angry. 'I am waiting for the advice of the Druids. I have asked what sacrifices the gods need and while I await their deliberations I am making plans of my own.' He pulled her away from the doorway and lowered his voice. 'I am planning a raid on the territory of the Parisii. They are rich in cattle. They wouldn't miss a few head.'

'They are our allies, Triganos!' Carta was shocked. 'They are part of the Brigantian federation. Or they were under father's rule. You will not succeed if you alienate our closest friends. That is foolish. And these cattle raids are senseless. Better far to trade new stock if it is needed.'

'Nonsense!' he contradicted her scornfully. 'They will enjoy a good scrap as much as we would. There's nothing like a battle or two to get the blood moving!' He did not see the tactlessness of his remark, or the pain in his sister's face as almost on cue a group of young men passed the doorway on their way to the training ground, their cheerful shouts finding their way into the silent room.

'And what about trade. How is that?' Carta was tight-lipped. 'The Brigantes control the routes bringing gold and slaves and dogs from Erin into our Setantian harbours and rivers. We produce lead in the fells and dales and corn from our fields. We should be rich!'

'We are rich.' He was very much on the defensive now. 'Father has ordered all this work to be done at Dinas Dwr – and some building here, too. That is expensive. And the chieftains resent paying too much in taxes. It is hard to collect from them if they don't cooperate.' He turned and headed towards the door. 'Leave it, Carta. It is enough that you are home. Don't stir things up. Everything is in hand. Come. You haven't yet met my wife, Essylt. It is time you greeted her.'

She followed him, her heart sinking. Of course he was married. How could he not be? Yet no one had told her. Another wave of loneliness swept over her as they entered the room where Essylt was sitting beside the fire, a baby at her breast. Younger than Carta by some five years, with pale, almost white hair hanging in heavy plaits and eyes of soft cornflower blue she smiled a welcome. 'Greeting, sister. I have so looked forward to meeting you.' Her voice was gentle and shy. 'Come. Kiss your new nephew.' Detaching the child she held him out.

Carta hesitated. A wave of anguish shot through her as she stared at the baby. For a moment she couldn't move, overwhelmed by her sense of loss and longing.

'Carta?' Triganos didn't understand why she was hanging back. 'Take him.' He was full of pride. 'Isn't he splendid? This is Finn. My eldest son!'

Stooping, he kissed his wife on the top of her head and she looked up at him in adoration.

Carta forced herself to smile. Somehow she managed to hold out her arms and take the baby, hugging it to her as she looked down at the small face with its fuzz of blond hair, its wildly waving little hands, the milky bubbles at the rosebud mouth. It fixed her with a serious stare and then suddenly smiled.

She kissed his head gently, biting back her anguished tears. 'He's lovely. May the blessings of the goddess be upon him.' Her voice was husky.

'Triganos!' Fidelma walked into the room. 'Were you not going to tell me that Cartimandua was here?' She took in the situation at a glance. At once the baby was returned to its mother, Triganos was despatched elsewhere and Fidelma had led her daughter to an alcove where they could sit in private as Essylt returned to her milky worship of her child.

By the time she was facing her mother's astute gaze Carta had brushed away her tears and won the fight to regain her composure.

'It will get better with time, child.' The older woman was not fooled for a second. 'You will have other babies of your own. I lost children. It happens. But I have you and your brothers as comfort.' The quizzical glance she sent after Triganos underlined the wry smile which hovered for a moment round her mouth. 'Don't be in too much of a hurry to marry again Carta,' she added softly. 'Wait to choose the right man.'

Carta took her hand. 'The right man died, Mama. No one will be able to replace him.'

'But you will remarry.' It was not a question.

'Of course. In time.' Carta grimaced. 'When I see someone suitable.'

Fidelma chuckled. Carta had grown up indeed She doubted if anyone married to her daughter would have an easy life, or a boring one. But she would be a rich prize in more ways than one.

'Why were you not at the feast yesterday, Mama?' Carta scanned her mother's face. Even in the dim rushlight she could see the lines of strain.

'I felt I should stay with Essylt.' Fidelma's mouth set in a stubborn line. 'There were enough people there without me.'

'You don't approve of Triganos's desire to take father's place?'

Fidelma shrugged. 'It's not up to me. If his Druid advisers think it best then it must happen.' She paused. 'Your father is tired, Carta,' she conceded. 'Perhaps it is time to step back. But is Triganos the right man to follow him?'

Carta frowned. 'Triganos is your son!'

'And I look on him with a mother's pride. But I can be dispassionate.' Fidelma sighed. 'I see his faults as well as his strengths.'

'He only needs experience, Mama.' Carta defended him

Fidelma nodded.

Her daughter frowned. 'You wouldn't want Venutios to succeed father as high king?'

'Indeed not.'

'Then support Triganos, Mama. Give him the benefit of your strength and your experience.' Carta smiled. 'He'll take it from you!'

Fidelma gave a low chuckle. 'I shall try, my dear. Indeed. I shall try.'

Walking later onto the hillside outside the walls Carta stood, her back to the fort, staring out towards the Western Sea. On a clear day it was possible to see right out across the gilded waters towards the Manannan's Isle, halfway to Erin. Today it was hazy. Fold upon fold of cloud shrouded the distant hills. She missed, she realised, the clear bright view of the cold Northern Ocean with its great rocks, shrouded in gannets. Its ever-changing freshness. She had become a stranger in her own soft, rain-swept lands.

Below her, in a fold of the moor on the edge of the forest nestled the Druid college, one of the most respected in the whole of the Pretannic Isles. Gruoch had promised to stay at Carta's side as long as she was needed, but above all, she wanted to make her way down to the guest house at the college. 'It is important I meet my colleagues here and continue my studies.' She had laid a gentle hand on Carta's arm. 'As you must if you are to fulfil your destiny.' The two young women had held one another's gaze for a moment.

'And what is my destiny?' Carta whispered. 'When will I marry again? Who will it be? Will I have another baby one day? I have begged the gods to tell me and they say nothing. Will Medb's curse last forever?' Tears filled her eyes.

Gruoch shrugged. 'That is not for me to know, Carta. That is for you to learn from the gods. Consult the omens. Your teachers say you are a talented seer. Now is the time to put your gifts to good use. Consult the signs. See what is required of you.'

Praying to her gods was as natural to Carta as breathing. She consulted them, railed against them, pleaded with them, made them offerings. Their voices were everywhere. In the wind in the trees, in the song of the birds, in the rippling of the water over the broad sweeping rivers, the roar of the waterfalls and in the echoes of the hollow hills. Making her way now across the steep hillside, avoiding the sink holes which led down into those echoing hollows where only the gods dared go, she paused again to listen. The west wind was whispering across the soft fell grasses as she stood deep in thought, the hood of her cloak pulled up over her hair. She was alone. No one would accost her here and there was no danger from strangers on these her homeland hills and yet the whispers spoke of danger.

Vivienne?

She whispered the name out loud.

Vivienne! Tell me of the future. Tell me where my destiny lies!

There was no answer.

Then as she stood there a flock of small birds flew out of the gorse bushes ahead of her. She watched them automatically, listening to their gossip, noting the direction of their flight, tuning her mind to the messages they had for her. In the space of a heartbeat she saw the birds wheel as one and turn and dive back into the bushes as a shadow passed across the grass at her feet. Squinting up from beneath her hood she saw, high up, the drifting watchful silhouette of a sea eagle and she heard it scream.

She felt the hairs on the back of her neck stir. The whispers of the grass were true. There was danger lurking in the future, distant danger, not imminent, not close but somewhere in the shadows it was there, waiting.

Viv woke to find herself sitting staring out across the fells and fields towards the west. The sun was high in the sky now and it was growing warm. She tensed, listening. From far away she could hear the sound of galloping hooves. For a moment she didn't move, then slowly she stood up and turned, shading her eyes as she stared up towards the folded ramparts and beyond into the distant haze. The sound was coming closer. Several horses, moving fast. She could hear the chink of harness now, the click of hoof on stone but she could see nothing. High above, a buzzard wheeled, riding the thermals and she heard its plaintive wild mewing echoing off the distant scar. The sound grew louder. It was on her. Then it passed and almost at once had drawn away with a rattle of hooves on the scree until it had died away into silence. She had seen nothing. Shaken, she turned round, staring in every direction. There was nothing and no one to be seen. If any horsemen had passed close by on the faint track they were invisible.

Peggy was alone in the kitchen when she finally reached the farm, exhausted by her second long walk in two days. The men, it appeared, had gone out early to the lower fields, haymaking. 'You must have left soon after them.' Peggy put down a pot of coffee and some toast in front of her. 'Are you sure you wouldn't like a cooked breakfast, love?'

Viv shook her head. Her fear had evaporated considerably on the long walk back down from the summit, but she was still shaken. After a moment's hesitation she told Peggy what had happened. 'It was as though they rode right past me. I could feel the ground shake.'

Peggy nodded. She sat down across the table from Viv. 'So many people have mentioned it over the years I've got used to hearing about it.'

'Is it some kind of trick of geology? An echo through the ground, through the caves and potholes, of people riding miles away?' Relieved at Peggy's matter-of-fact reaction, Viv found she was ravenous. She reached for the homemade marmalade.

Peggy was shaking her head. 'Nothing like that. Several people have been up and investigated it. Even the local TV news came up once. It is horses galloping. Everyone agrees on that. You can hear the squeak of leather, the snorting, and breathing of the horses sometimes. They tried to record it, but nothing came out.'

Viv stopped eating for a moment to study her hostess's face. 'You don't really think it's ghosts?'

Peggy shrugged comfortably. 'I don't have a view. It happens. All sorts of strange things happen round here. It's part of what makes it so special. The land is alive. It's full of memories of the past and, who knows, echoes of the future as well.' She leaned across to top up Viv's coffee cup. 'You've written about the fort in your book, Steve tells me.'

Viv nodded. 'Can I tell you something about that? Something that's been happening to me?' She hesitated, her eyes fixed anxiously on Peggy's. Steve had said she would understand. 'I'm nervous talking about this because I think maybe I'm going mad.' She paused. Then she plunged on. 'My best friend is a psychologist. I've told her about this, and she's calm and reassuring and has lots of professional suggestions to make about me being obsessed with the subject of my book, but –' She hesitated again. 'Well, I think you'll know what I'm talking about.'

Peggy listened without comment as Viv told her the whole story, interrupting once to answer the phone and once to replenish the coffee pot. Otherwise the kitchen was silent save for the sound of Viv's voice and the ticking of the old clock on the shelf above the Aga. When she had finished Viv sat nursing her empty mug, staring down into the dregs.

Peggy looked up at last. 'I think your friend is wrong,' she said slowly. 'As a psychologist she is looking for orthodox answers to your problem. That is not necessarily helpful. Tell me, does all this frighten you or does it interest you?'

Viv shrugged. 'A bit of both.'

Peggy nodded. 'I think you need to decide which feeling is the stronger, love. If it's the former you must stop doing it now. Forget it. Fight it. Never let yourself do it again.' She glanced up and held Viv's gaze. 'If you're not going to stop, then you need to lay down some ground rules. Whatever – whoever – she is, she's in your head and you only want her there on your terms.'

'So you believe she's real. Do you think I'm being possessed?'

'No. No, I don't think that. But I think maybe you are being used and I think that at least to start with that was by your invitation.

You've opened up a line of communication, but that needs to stay open only as long as you want it to.'

Peggy stood up and went over to lean against the Aga rail. 'I'm not a clever psychologist like your friend and I'm no church-goer.' Again she paused and scanned Viv's face for a reaction. 'So I speak as I find. These things happen. There are people out there,' she gestured towards the ceiling, 'from other times, maybe from other dimensions, who knows where they come from, but they have stories to tell. We can welcome them and listen or we can push them away. That's up to us. It's our business and theirs. But it is natural. You needn't be afraid of it. But you must be strong.'

'You're saying it's normal.'

'It would be if people would open themselves up.'

Viv, elbows on table, rested her chin on her hands.

Peggy pushed the kettle onto the hotplate again. 'You said there is stuff this Carta is telling you that you didn't know before. That nobody knows?'

Viv nodded. 'It could all be rubbish.'

'It could. Or it could be true. Stop worrying about that. Listen to her.' She smiled. 'That is what you want, isn't it.'

Viv nodded.

'Well, go on writing down what she tells you. You are a writer first and foremost, my Steve says, so write. Only when you've got it all down and the story is finished one way or another do you have to make a decision about what to do about it. My guess is, she'll go once she's told you everything.'

Viv grinned. 'I knew I was right to talk to you. Thank you. You've made it all sound so simple.'

'It is simple.' Waiting for the kettle to boil, Peggy moved across to the fridge and lifted out a huge lump of crumbly cheese. 'Now, I'm going to make some sandwiches for my haymakers and if you like you can come down to the fields with me and on the way back I'll show you the Druid's Well.'

It was down three steep limestone steps at the bottom of a steeply folded valley near the hayfields. As Peggy led her towards it, Viv felt her throat constricting. There was something about the place, the line of the tumbling beck, the outline of the hills, she recognised as they picked their way between lichen-draped trees and through

183

waist-high grasses feathery with seed, deeper into the tumbled limestone cliffs which closed the end of the valley.

Peggy stood back on the path and waved Viv past her. 'There's only room for one at a time in there. Be careful. The steps can be slippery.'

The well head was cold and dank and smelled of musty rock and water. The sound of the beck behind them echoed in her ears. Carefully stepping down out of the sunlight she was immediately in a different world, the liminal halfway house so beloved of the Celts, neither one thing nor the other, neither light nor dark, neither wet not dry, neither outdoors nor in, gateway to the underworld. Someone had put a small candleholder on a natural shelf in the rock and near it lay a spray of wilted flowers.

It was just possible to squat down under the low rock roof and sit on the edge of the stone basin where the water lay unreflecting in a pool of darkness. Cautiously she reached down and dipped her fingers in the pool. The smooth surface broke and moved and for a second she saw the reflection of her own face then it was gone.

It was coincidence, of course, that this should look so like Carta's sacred spring. Probably they all looked much the same. She had seen them in Cornwall – secret, special hidden places, their presence often advertised by a nearby tree festooned with ribbons and rags. Clooties, they called them in Scotland, left by people as a plea or a promise, an offering or a thank you to whoever or whatever spirit looked after the well, be it one of the ancient Celtic gods, or a Christian saint, or the Virgin Mary herself.

She gave a wry smile, aware of an unlooked for atavistic urge within herself to leave her own gift here by the dark water.

Vivienne

The voice was little more than a whisper of the water outside. Viv shivered and climbed to her feet. It was her imagination.

Turning towards the daylight she looked up and saw Peggy seated on a rock near the entrance, her back to the well, staring down towards the gurgling water of the beck. Hesitating, she glanced back, then groped in her pocket to see if there was a coin there she would offer to the gods. What she found was a sweet smelling head of lavender she had broken from the clump near Peggy's kitchen door. It seemed a fitting offering and she laid it near the flowers and candle and imagined for a second that its sweetness was powerful enough to fill the whole valley.

Peggy glanced up as she re-emerged and came to sit beside her. 'Wonderful, isn't it.' She scanned Viv's face with steady blue eyes which seemed to be able to read her soul.

Viv nodded. 'Very special.'

'I come up here sometimes on my own and light a candle.' Peggy looked away again. 'It's a place of immense power and healing.'

'Do many people know it's here?' Viv kicked off her sandals and let her feet rest on the soft moss on the edge of the waterfall.

'The locals. Of course it's not in any guidebooks as far as I know. Once these places become too popular they lose part of their specialness.' She glanced back at Viv and once more the intensity of her gaze was almost uncomfortable. 'Can you keep it to yourself?'

'Of course.'

'It's just that not everyone has the right respect these days and even those that do don't always behave appropriately. It's a sad fact of life.'

'I won't tell anyone.' Viv was silent for a moment. 'Why do you call it the Druid's Well?'

Peggy shrugged. 'It's always been called that. The Celts honoured water just as they honoured the sun and the moon, the stars, the rocks, the trees, the soil beneath their feet; they knew it all as sacred. They must have known this place as a spring, so near the hill fort but the ordinary people would have been afraid to come here, so it must have been a Druid sanctuary.' She laughed cheerfully. Then, sobering, she glanced sideways at Viv. 'Did you feel anything in there? A sense of the sacred, perhaps?'

Viv nodded. She was staring down at the glittering gurgling stream pouring over the rocks at her feet. There was a strange red tinge to the water. 'It's odd. I feel as though –' She shook her head. 'I feel as though I've seen it before, but I suppose holy wells often look and feel the same?' She looked up almost pleadingly.

'I suppose they do. Or you've seen it through someone else's eyes. If that's the case, don't let it worry you. Accept it for what it is. A gift.' She put her hand on Viv's shoulder for a minute. 'The people who lived in the ancient world had a respectful attitude to life. They would have thanked a tree before cutting it down. They would have acknowledged that an animal had to die so they could eat it but thank it for that sacrifice. They had a generosity of spirit as opposed to our selfishness. It's something I like to think still happens here.' She fell silent. For a while they sat quietly, listening

185

to the sounds of the water, then at last Peggy stirred. 'Do you want to wait here for a bit and come back to the farm later, or come back with me now? I've another guest coming this evening and I have to get ready for her. She's booked a week's painting holiday.' She hesitated, then she stood up. 'You wait a bit. See what happens. Who knows, perhaps the goddess will bless you.'

Viv sat there for a long time, listening to the water. The sound filled the whole valley, swirling into the silences, drowning every other sound as she gazed down into the glittering ripples. She wasn't sure when Steve arrived, but after a while he was there, watching her, sitting on a rock a couple of yards from her. He smiled when he saw she had noticed him at last. 'Any interesting dreams?' He had to raise his voice to make himself heard above the water.

She shook her head. 'This is a fabulous place.'

He nodded. 'Very special.'

'Your mum is a wonderful woman.'

'I'm glad you think so.' He climbed to his feet and held out his hand. 'Come on, we need to go back or you'll miss your lunch. I've left Dad to it for a while.'

They walked back up the fields side by side, in companionable silence. As the farmhouse came in sight, nestling in the fold of the hillside above them Viv reached over and took his hand again. 'I'm enjoying this so much. I wish I could stay longer.'

He grinned, squeezing her fingers back. 'So do I. When do you have to go?'

'After lunch tomorrow. So, I need to make the most of every second here. What do you suggest I see next?'

'The waterfalls. We'll go this afternoon.'

He was, she realised, still holding her hand. She pulled away gently. 'I'll look forward to that.'

The walk was spectacular. They climbed through woodland and cliffs, alongside the river as it hurtled down from the moors above through gorges and glens towards the river valley beneath. From time to time they would come to a viewpoint where the water was particularly dramatic. She paused on one of these, staring down into the foaming pool beneath, feeling the ground tremble under her feet. Ahead of her Steve strode easily up the path beneath tangled ash and hazel and great bushes of yew. He reached a corner where the path turned around an overhanging outcrop of rock and stopping for a moment, he looked back. Then he walked on out of sight.

The water thundered in her ears, sunlight catching the torrent, reflecting into her eyes, mesmerising, sliding in great sheets, stained reddish-brown by the minerals on the high moors, thundering past her in spate. She stood for several minutes, overwhelmed by its beauty and power before she gradually became aware of the image of a face looking at her from the mist of spray that hung in front of the fall. Not Carta. These eyes were pale, the hair the colour of moonlight, the gaze implacably hostile. Viv could feel the power of the questing mind reaching out, searching.

Medb.

Viv took a step back, feeling the spray cold on her face. The intrusion was brutal. The threat unmistakable. There was evil here. Hatred. Jealousy.

Slipping on the wet rock, she turned back towards the path, pushing past curtains of ferns and hanging mosses, her feet sliding in the puddles of spray as she hurried to catch up with Steve. Once she paused and looked back. There was nothing there but a glittering sheet of falling water. Where she had been standing two figures in red cagoules were poised photographing the water. The face had gone.

Steve was waiting for her at the next viewpoint. 'Isn't it awesome? We've had a lot of rain this year, so they're especially good. I've loved this place since I was a child.'

She nodded, trying to catch her breath.

'You can feel the power of the water making the ground shake.' He laughed. 'This is a sacred place! You can feel it, can't you. Druids would have worshipped here. It's a place to talk to the gods. I sometimes think it draws you in. You feel you could fly out into the water and soar towards the heavens all at the same moment!' He raised his arms.

'Be careful, Steve!' With a cry of alarm, Viv grabbed his arm. 'Don't go too near the edge!'

He laughed. 'Don't worry. I'm not. Do you see the rainbows in the sunlight? Castles and ramparts and figures dancing in the water. Naiads. Undines. Water sprites. Goddesses!'

But no face. Viv gazed into the spray. The pale vicious face of Medb of the White Hands had gone.

'Please, Steve! Come away!'

He stepped back and turned towards her, still laughing and for a moment they found themselves staring at each other. She realised she still had her hand on the sleeve of his shirt. She could feel the warmth of his skin under the cotton which was damp from the spray. 'I hate you going too near the edge. It gives me vertigo.' Letting him go, she gave an awkward little laugh.

'Sorry. I didn't mean to frighten you.' His fingertips brushed against hers as he turned back to the path. It was just the lightest of touches. Almost accidental. 'Come on, I'll race you to the top!'

13

Viv arrived home the following evening after driving straight into the tail of the rush hour. Most of it was going the other way but even so she found herself crawling impatiently through the suburbs and it was after seven when at last she climbed, exhausted, up the worn stone steps towards her door, lugging her holdall after her.

She had been reluctant to leave Winter Gill Farm. It was a place of magic and warmth. A home from home. But the arrival of a stranger the night before, and the knowledge that she had so much to do in Edinburgh had helped her stick to her decision to return. Besides, it was difficult to get her head around the feelings which were flooding through her. Being there in the place where Carta had lived, in the place which featured in her dreams, was over-whelming. More so even than Traprain this was a place of Druid magic, of Celtic mysticism. A place where the past still clung to the mist-shrouded cliffs and rivers. It was all too much; too immediate; too close to Carta.

And, there were facts she wanted to check.

'Come back and see us, as soon as your book tour is finished,' Peggy had said as she gave her a farewell hug. 'You're a friend of the family now, love. I'd be very cross if you didn't come!' She held Viv's gaze for a moment, then she smiled. 'Steve will miss you too. It's nice for him to have a bit of company. So, come back soon.'

Viv didn't bother to unpack. Throwing her bag down just inside the door she went straight to the computer.

Steve and Peggy were forgotten. Ingleborough, Dun Righ, Dinas Dwr. This was what she wanted to look up. The possible sites of the royal family's bases. Did they live in one place and visit the others or was the court peripatetic? Did they select one place and live there because it was convenient or they liked it, or like medieval kings move around from place to place to feed the entourage of fighting men and the household which accompanied them. In her book she had mentioned possible sites for the Brigantian capital: Stanwick St John. Barwick in Elmet. Aldbrough. Which was right? Or were they all right? How much was actually known about Ingleborough? Now that she had been there, really been there, she needed to know at once.

As the programme loaded she glanced down at her box files. There was nothing there to help her. She was pretty sure of that. For this kind of information she needed the latest archaeological data. The results of excavations, if any, that had been conducted since her original research. Standing up she stared at the screen for a second or two then she turned and went into the kitchen, returning a moment later, a glass of apple juice in her hand to sense the impatient tension in the room. Her throat tightened with fear.

Peggy had told her to be firm. To learn to take control. Determinedly she sat down at the keyboard. At the moment she wanted archaeological facts. A hoard. The remains of a house amongst the others large enough to be the equivalent of a palace. Jewellery. A grave like those over on the eastern side of Yorkshire at Wetwang. Was Wetwang the burial ground of the Brigantian kings or just of the Parisii? Those graves, with their chariots and grave goods and horses and dogs, were of very special high-ranking people. One of them was a woman's. Could the grave be that of Cartimandua herself? No, wrong date. She clicked the mouse impatiently. Refuse pits. Always of interest, but weren't always refuse pits at all. Some were for storage – a safe cool place to keep things just outside the houses, often created out of the places where they dug the clay to make mud and wattle walls, though perhaps not in these mountain settlements. Others were obviously for sacrifice. But not sacrifice in the sense of killing things by chucking them down a hole. A sacred, special place to lower beloved animals and special offerings, and even the body of a baby, so that it would be nearer to the gods, a place to begin the journey to Tir n'an Og, the land of the ever young.

The computer wasn't responding. Suddenly the screen went blank. She stared at it. Hell and damnation! What was the matter with the thing? But no amount of coaxing or swearing could bring it back to life. Glancing round the room she felt a jolt of fear. She was there. Somewhere. Waiting in the shadows. Standing up, Viv grabbed her department keys off the shelf and headed for the door.

The streets were busy. It was a beautiful warm evening, encouraging people out to wander round the city. Walking down the High Street she could smell the various delights of the restaurants and bars. Garlic and pasta. That was obviously Italian. Stale beer – one of a dozen dark doors leading into heavy masses of humanity. Wine. Bright, trendy and no less crowded. Meat and noodles, cooking in woks. Chinese. Curry. Indian. In the distance she could hear the steady thump of music coming from an upstairs window and drifting up from Princes Street the inevitable haunting drone of the bagpipes.

The DPCHC was deserted. Inserting her key she pushed open the door and then locked it behind her. Her office smelled of stale old books. The window was closed and there was dust on the computer monitor as she sat down and switched on. In minutes she had the latest archaeological finds record and was scrolling down towards the Iron Age. There was a lot of information there. Each year it seemed to increase exponentially and it was hard to keep up with the latest discoveries. Leaning forward she scanned the screen, completely engrossed until somewhere in the depths of the building the sound of a door closing interrupted her concentration. She looked up with a frown, conscious now of how quiet it had been as she sat reading the closely spaced lines in front of her. With a sigh she rubbed her eyes wearily and glanced at her watch. It was nearly ten. Then she heard it again. A sound from outside her door, this time the creak of a floorboard. She listened intently, suddenly nervous. She was about to stand up to go to investigate when her door opened. Hugh was standing there. Dressed in an open-necked, checked shirt, and with a cluster of cardboard files under his arm he stood surveying her from beneath frowning eyebrows.

For a moment she stared at him blankly, aware only of what a strong presence he had. It filled the room, distracting her from her task. Seeing him dispassionately like that, as though he was a stranger, she realised inconsequentially what a good-looking man he was and how overwhelmingly attractive. His words brought her back to herself with a jolt. 'What exactly are you doing here at this time of night?'

'Working.' She could hear the defiance in her own voice.

'Indeed?' He stepped into the room. 'Am I supposed to be impressed by your keenness, Dr Lloyd Rees?'

'On the contrary. I was trying very hard to avoid you knowing about it at all.' Viv resisted the urge to stand up so that she could face him. Somehow she managed to relax into her chair. It was important that he didn't see how much his unexpected appearance had rattled her. 'And, by the way, may I ask again, why this formality, *Professor*?' She emphasised the word. 'I seem to remember that in the days before I wrote a book, I was Viv.'

'Were you?'

She wasn't sure how to interpret his tone. Was he being vague or sarcastic? Either way it was, as she supposed he intended, hurtful.

'Looking up the Iron Age, I see.' She realised too late that he was looking past her at the screen. 'Checking your facts? A bit late for that, I would have thought. Surely your book is finished?'

'I am doing further research, certainly.' She managed the retort in as casual a way as possible. 'Unlike some, I like to be on the ball with the latest discoveries and theories.'

'And, let's face it, you're not sure of your facts now they are being queried by an expert in the field.' He gave a half-smile which broadened as he noticed the flicker of uncertainty which crossed her face.

She sighed. She didn't need this. She was tired and now that he had interrupted her train of thought, all she wanted was to go home. On the other hand her pride dictated that she couldn't allow him to think he had managed to chase her out. 'It seems very late for you to be working, Hugh.' She caught him off balance, she noticed, by the sudden use of his Christian name, the gentle tone. 'You look very tired. You should take more care of yourself.'

'I am very grateful for your concern.' His voice hardened. 'But I can assure you, I don't need it.' He hesitated for a fraction of a second. 'The Cartimandua Pin is reputed to have a curse on it. Did you know?' He held her gaze for a second.

Viv frowned. 'I am surprised you of all people believe in curses, Hugh,' she said. She looked up and forced a smile. 'Not your sort of thing at all, surely.'

He seemed rooted to the spot, staring at her with uncomfortable intensity.

'I'll be here some time yet,' she went on at last. 'Perhaps I should get on.' She turned her back on him, deftly flicking the screen away from the website before he could scrutinise it any more closely. 'By the way,' she added before she could stop herself, 'did you call the police in the end. About the brooch?' She managed to sound casual.

She turned and looked at him over her shoulder, holding her breath as she waited for a reply. For several seconds he said nothing then he gave a quiet chuckle. 'That, my dear Viv, remains to be seen, doesn't it.'

For a moment he stood motionless behind her, then she heard him move away. He walked out of the room, leaving her door open and she heard the creak of the floorboards as he strode down the corridor towards his own room. She waited for a moment until she heard his door bang then she stood up and went over to close her own. She leaned against it with her eyes closed, breathing deeply. Damn. Damn. Damn! That was all she needed.

She turned back to her desk. He hadn't spoken to the police. She was sure of it. Otherwise they would have been waiting on her doorstep. Or would they. She sat still, staring at the screen. And now she would have to outstay him as a matter of principle when all she wanted was to print up her findings to study later and go home and have a long hot bath.

He seemed to have conceded defeat however. After only ten minutes she heard his door opening again and the sound of his footsteps on the stairs. She listened for the bang of the outer door and then cautiously went over to the window and peered round the blind. She saw him stride down the road, groping in his pocket for his car keys. Then he rounded the corner and was out of sight.

When, after switching off the computer and collecting some more books, she opened her study door she found he had switched off all the lights in the building. How pathetic could you get?

Outside, she realised it had started to rain. The crowds had melted away and the streets smelled wonderfully fresh, the dust laid, the traffic less heavy, the scent of grass and leaves and flowers drifting across the streets from the gardens and squares and the dark brooding outline of Arthur's Seat.

Swinging the heavy bag of books onto her shoulder she walked fast, pausing automatically at the traffic lights even though no cars were coming, then walking on.

Vivienne

The voice in her head was clear and slightly fretful.

193

Vivienne?

Viv stopped, her heart thudding. What had she been thinking about? Not Carta. Not Ingleborough.

Vivienne!

She put a hand to her forehead. This wasn't the same as sitting at her desk and inviting the voice in. This wasn't like sitting within the fallen ramparts of a hill fort, meditating on the past. She was walking down the street thinking about something else.

Vivienne

'Stop it! Go away!' She realised, shocked, that she had spoken out loud. She paused, easing the bag higher onto her shoulder, staring round, wondering if there was someone there, hiding in the shadows, playing a joke on her. No one called her Vivienne. Ever. No one except an Iron Age queen!

She took a deep breath and walked on fast, her head down against the soft mizzle of rain. Preoccupied, she barely noticed that the streets were busier here or that a crowd of youths was hanging around outside the pub. She registered that they were shouting. Someone kicked an empty beer can along the gutter. The air was heavy with the fumes of stale beer and the acrid tang of vomit. Normally she would have crossed the road and taken another turning to avoid them. She strode on and as she approached they fell silent.

'Fucking hell!' The comment was almost awed as they stared at her. They fell back out of her way and she passed without even appearing to notice them. 'Did you fucking see that?'

Viv shivered. She kept on walking, aware suddenly of what had happened and wondering with a second's blinding terror what – or who – they thought they had seen.

II

Sitting quietly in the darkness of the cave near the sacred spring Peggy reached at last for her matches and lit a fresh candle before her statue of the goddess. The sound of water was everywhere. Outside, the rain was slapping onto the leaves, smacking the path, pitting the gurgling torrent of the river, reinforcing the constant splashing of the falls at the top of the rocks and here, inside, the steady gentle drip of the trickling water in which she found so much reassurance and strength. The cave was cold after the warmth of the woods outside and slick with damp, but the dripping ferns and mosses gave a velvety green glow to the candlelight.

'Sweet Lady, hear me.' She breathed her prayer out loud. 'Tell me that she is one of us. I sensed it in everything she said and did, but she is naïve as yet, not understanding; untutored in our ways. I can teach her, Sweet Lady, if that is your wish. My son can bring her to you. She will be good for him and he for her.' She paused in the prayer with a frown. Viv was his teacher. Would that make things difficult? On the other hand she had seen how attracted he was to her and she to him. 'She's not that much older than he is,' she went on in a whisper, 'but her age gives her wisdom and understanding which is rare. I sense her potential, Sweet Lady. Queen Cartimandua was one of us. She has marked her already as chosen. I will not gainsay her.'

The cave was very still. The sound of the water retreated, leaving a heavy breathing silence. The candle burned steadily, without a flicker, and in the depths of the dark waters of the well she saw at last a pinpoint of light. It was the sign she was looking for.

III

Hugh drove straight home to Aberlady. Parking in the drive he sat for a moment staring at the house until the raindrops on the windscreen blurred and then finally obscured his view. With a sigh he climbed out, lugging his briefcase behind him and locking the car, walked towards the front door.

Turning on the lights as he made his way through the dark house he found himself wishing he hadn't turned the lights out like that in George Square. That was petty. Reaching into the cupboard for a glass, he helped himself to a hefty tot of Talisker. He pictured Viv sitting at her computer, turning round so guiltily as he walked in. He would have known she was there as soon as he had let himself into the department even if he hadn't seen the light on in her study. It was that scent she wore – never too strong, often hardly noticeable at all, but nevertheless a part of her. Not flowery. Slightly spicy. Mysterious. He swallowed a mouthful of the whisky, unlocked the back door and stood looking out into the garden, letting the warm damp air seep past him into the house. The rain sounded heavier out here, smacking the broad leathery leaves of the magnolia, trickling down from a broken gutter and splashing onto the terrace. Stupid woman. She would realise what he thought of her and her lightweight populist travesty of a history when she saw he had not bothered to review it. He sighed. She had so much ability and she was wasting it. But then, there was no place for lightweights in his department and she would soon get the message that it would be better for everyone if she packed her bags and moved on.

Turning back into the house he wandered into the hall, sipping his drink, and picked up the mail that had been lying on the floor, pushed back against the wall by the opening front door. Amongst it was a jiffy bag. He ripped it open. He drew out the book eagerly and then gave an exclamation of disgust. It was another copy of *Cartimandua, Queen of the North.* Why the hell had they sent him another copy? He shook the book indignantly and a letter fell out.

Dear Hugh,
I wondered whether you would be interested in saying some-
thing about the enclosed for us in order to add your personal
accolade to Viv's wonderful book . . .'

He threw the letter down with a sigh. What was the matter with these people? Did they never give up? He had already made it clear he had no interest in reviewing the book – not after reading that trashy article she had written in the *Sunday Times* supplement. God damn it, the *Sunday Times* themselves would ask him to review it next, and he would find himself the recipient of yet another copy!

Flipping open the cover as he walked through into his den and turned on the light, he glanced down at the blurb.

In her vivid and well-researched account of the life and times of Cartimandua, Queen of the North, Dr Lloyd Rees brings to life the glamorous and mysterious age of the Iron Age Celts. She charts the progress of the invading

196

Romans and describes the beginning of the end of Britain's native culture at the hands of the all powerful conquerors . . .

Hugh snorted as he flung himself down in his chair. He glanced at the back flap. There was a colour photograph of Viv there, smiling, her green eyes slightly narrowed against the sunlight, the dappled leaves of a flowery bush behind her left shoulder. She looked hesitant, slightly uncertain. As well she might. He studied it for a moment, then he sighed. It was in fact rather a good picture. It conveyed her charm and energy while at the same time doing nothing to detract from her so-called academic background. He flicked through the book slowly, something he had not actually bothered to do before he had passed the last copy on to Steve. It was well illustrated with good quality coloured plates. He glanced at them critically. The usual stuff: the chariot burials, the gold torcs, the beautiful pieces of horse harness, scabbards, the Battersea Shield. He snorted. What had that to do with Cartimandua? Viv was obviously scraping the barrel here. She had not used the Cartimandua Pin. That above all else should have been illustrated in the book. He gave a further snort of derision. Opening a page at random he glanced down it and for several minutes found himself locked into the narrative. She was a good writer – fluent. Lucid. But of course as her teacher he had recognised that years ago, so why, oh why had she chosen to take this idiotic route? His eye was caught by a sentence:

Almost certainly Cartimandua spent her formative years at the court of a neighbouring tribe, fostered into the leading household. The Parisii, maybe, or the Votadini.

Rubbish! Guesswork! Exactly the sort of inventive 'intuitive' idiocies he knew he would find in it. The worst kind of ill-informed fact stuffing! Her reputation as a scholar was not going to survive this and by association, neither would his.

Artefacts found in excavations at Traprain Law, for instance, may lead us to guess . . .

Guess!

He frowned. What, he wondered suddenly, did she have to say about Venutios. Flipping over the pages he began to read again.

197

Twenty minutes later he slammed the book shut and stood up. Venutios was the villain of her story, of course. It was an unbalanced, uninformed, pro-Roman confection of half-truths and misrepresentations. Behind him a gust of wind blew in through the open French doors and the curtains billowed into the room.

The sound of the horn was very close this time. Paralysed, he stood staring out into the darkness.

Venutios.

The name came to him out of the garden. Venutios demanding recognition. Venutios insisting on the truth. Venutios, who had been traduced in the book which lay on the table beside his chair.

IV

Viv dragged herself up to her front door, let herself in and switched on the lights. Dumping the bag of books on the floor near her desk she went straight over to stare at the mirror. Her mouth was dry with fear, her hands shaking, but the face that looked back at her was her own, her hair tousled, her eyes strained and exhausted.

With a sigh of relief she turned away, then she paused and glanced back. Was that a shadow at her shoulder? Another woman looking at her? The woman Tasha saw? And Pete? And the crowd of youths outside the pub?

There was nothing – no one – there.

Taking a deep breath, she headed for the kitchen to get a glass of wine. The message light was flashing on her phone. Twelve missed calls.

'Viv, where are you?' 'Viv, we need to talk urgently. Where are you?' 'Viv, are you OK?' 'Viv, listen, call me. Your mobile is switched off.' There were several from Pat, one from Maddie, two from her editor, one from Sandy, the publicist who was planning her book tour, and all the rest were from Cathy. No doubt there were e-mails as well – she hadn't logged in to her account for days. Viv sighed. There had been no network coverage at Winter Gill Farm and she had turned off her mobile while she was there. Strangely it hadn't occurred to her to turn it on again when she got back to civilisation. Well, it was too late to call any of them now. They would have to wait till morning.

The glass in her hand, she went to the window and looked out at the darkened roofs, then with a rush of claustrophobia she pushed it open. She stood listening to the quiet hiss of the rain on the roof slates, wishing suddenly, illogically, that Alison's had been one of the voices on the machine, remembering how in the old days she had been able to confide in her friend, count on her support, be certain of her reassurance.

Vivienne

Viv jumped. The call was like a punch inside the head, somewhere between her eyes.

Vivienne

She gulped some more wine, moving her head uncomfortably as though she had a stiff neck. Go away!

Vivienne

His name was Diarmaid. A warrior of noble birth, he often marched and trained at Triganos's side and once or twice, sitting idly watching the men on the parade ground, Carta's eyes strayed to follow him. He had a lithe feral grace as he wielded the sword, the sunlight catching the planes of his face, the painted whirl of muscle and sinew as the blade flashed in the air, the arrogant set of his mouth and the secret smile as he threw the sword in the air and deftly caught it before thrusting it home its sheath. As he ran from the ground with the others, joining their shouts of laughter, she looked away. But somewhere, deep inside, she could feel a deep yearning. She was lonely. Two years had passed since the death of Riach and their baby. It was little enough time in her mind to mourn, but her body was eager again for the comfort of a man's arms around her; for the excitement of his touch. For several days she watched Diarmaid cautiously, content to let her imagination take the lead, never speaking to him, never showing any outward signs of interest, but he knew. Now and then their eyes met and a spark seemed to fly between them.

She was in the stables, running her hand down the foreleg of her mother's favourite mare, sensing the heat and tension in the fetlock, gentling the animal and crooning words of healing spells when she became aware suddenly of someone standing behind her.

Straightening abruptly, she turned to find herself staring into his eyes. 'You never speak to me, lady.' His voice was deep and musical. 'But I know you want to.'

She felt a deep blush mantling her cheeks.

'Do you know anything of horses, Diarmaid?' The mare nudged her, resentful of the interruption.

He smiled, his face suddenly boyish and open. 'Only how to ride them. You are the expert.'

For several seconds neither moved, then he leaned forward and gently kissed her on the lips. 'If I can be of service in any other way,' he murmured, 'you have only to call.'

She had raised her hand and rested it for a moment on his chest, overwhelmed with the violence of her sudden longing for him to take her in his arms when the horse behind her let out a shrill whinny and at the other end of the building they heard the clank of a bucket. He stood back as a stable lad ducked into one of the stalls.

'I'll think about it.' She raised a finger and touched his lips gently, then she dodged away beneath the horse's head. When she turned back he had gone.

As a free woman she was entitled to take whomsoever she pleased as a lover. Walking up and down her darkening bed-chamber as the light faded she chewed her lip in an agony of indecision. What would Triganos say if she took his henchman to her bed? And did she care? She had no desire for a new husband and her brother had shown no signs of coming up with the list he had so fulsomely promised. So why not? No one's honour would be harmed. Caught between her passionate longing for the man, the touch of whose lips she could still feel on her own, and her pragmatic common sense, common sense lost out.

She waited until Mairghread had smoored the fire in her chamber and bade her goodnight then snatching up her cloak she tiptoed from the house. The young men were lounging around the fire on the edge of the training ground drinking, exchanging jokes, one by one rolling themselves in their cloaks and turning their backs on the fire to sleep as exhaustion overcame them. From the shadows she watched, her face shrouded by her hood, scanning the shadowy figures until she saw him. Her body was alive with anticipation; she could feel a fluttering on her skin, an excitement which caught at her throat and sent tremors through her belly. Quietly she stepped closer. The men had their backs to her. No one could see her. Her eyes lighted on some stones. With a silent chuckle she picked up a small pebble and lobbed it at Diarmaid. It was one of the childhood skills which had not deserted her and she hit him squarely in the small of the back. He turned, staring into the darkness, frowning. She could see his face clearly in the firelight. Not seeing her, he shrugged and turned away again. With a grin she scooped up another pebble, slightly larger this time. This one caught him on the back of the head. Clapping his hand to his hair he leaped to his feet. The men around him glanced up idly, then went back to their ale. She waved and this time he saw her as, pulling her cloak around her, she ran towards the stables.

He caught her in the harness room, enfolding her in his arms, pressing his mouth to hers, his hands fumbling for the brooch that held her cloak fastened. Gasping with pleasure and excitement she pulled him close, her hair slipping from her hood, reaching for his hands, guiding them to her breasts as the door creaked open behind them and a lantern was thrust into the darkness.

'I thought so.' For a moment she didn't recognise the harsh voice. Frozen to the spot they both stood staring at the flickering light, unable to see the face of the man holding it.

'Get out, Diarmaid. Do you dare to meddle with the king's sister! Men have died for less.'

Suddenly she recognised him. It was Venutios.

Pulling her cloak tightly around her and pushing her hair out of her eyes she stepped forward into the circle of light. 'How dare you! What business is this of yours?'

He smiled. She could see his face clearly now as he lowered the lantern and the light shone upward over the line of his jaw. 'It is very much my business. If your brother seeks a husband for you he'll find it hard if you are known to have spread your favours around the clachan.'

Beside her, Diarmaid stepped forward, his dagger in his hand.

'Don't!' Carta grabbed his wrist. 'Get out of here, Venutios! Leave me to be the keeper of my own reputation!' she flashed at him, her eyes blazing. 'If and when I marry it will be on my terms, not my brother's.'

'It will be on my terms, if I'm to be your husband!' Venutios threw the words back in her face.

She laughed. 'Don't worry on that score. I would rather die than come to your bed!' She whirled round towards the door. 'Come, Diarmaid. I have had enough of this conversation!' She ran a few steps past the long line of bridles hanging from their pegs, then she stopped and turning, flung a final word: 'Why would you ever think that I would even consider you as a husband, Venutios?'

He laughed harshly. 'Because your brother wants you to marry a king, Carta. And there aren't very many of them around!'

The next morning Diarmaid had left Dun Righ. When she asked Triganos where he was her brother gazed down at her thoughtfully for several seconds before telling her that he had been sent on a mission south to the lands of the Cantiaci and would be gone for several months.

Venutios himself rode north that afternoon, but not before wishing her a polite farewell, bowing as he took her hand and raised it to her lips. When he straightened his eyes were full of triumphant laughter.

Her brother was weak. It took her a while to notice it, but once she had she saw the signs everywhere. When he had been elected with general acclaim to succeed their father at last he had everything it took to be a successful leader. But he found it hard to take the advice of his council of Druids and warriors. His judgement was poor. He lavished riches on some men to secure them as his allies when they were already handfasted to his cause, while others whom he should have wooed he ignored or worse, insulted. He would go with enthusiasm to the feasting and the mock battles but he ignored the council of elders. As the months passed it was Carta who attended these meetings under the great oak tree in the forest or in the chieftains' hall, slowly taking her place as a right which no one questioned, between Artgenos, the Archdruid of Brigantia, and Brochan, King of the Parisii. At least in the matter of attacking their closest allies Triganos had deferred to her advice, claiming it had never been his serious intention to do such a thing at any time. Firmly putting thoughts of husbands and babies and lovers behind her, she listened quietly to the men's discussions, unconscious of the fact that at some meetings she was the only woman present and that at others she was by far the youngest; the women who gave advice to kings and warriors were normally old in their wisdom and experienced in the ways of politics and war.

Her father was there too, as advisor and counsellor. He had set down his leadership with relief, no longer trying to hide the stiffening of his joints, and his words were listened to with respect for his experience and his knowledge of the law, almost as great now in his fortieth summer as that of the Druid sitting next to him.

In front of them on these occasions, whether indoors or out, the fire smouldered, fed by branches of juniper and rowan, blessed by the seers to spread wisdom with the fragrant smoke. Behind them the best harpists in the land took turns to play tunes designed to bring the wisdom of the gods to their deliberations.

Carta did not speak much. Once or twice her opinion was sought by Artgenos and listened to with respectful attention by all who were present. Once she was questioned about her opinions of the King of the Votadini by Venutios, who had returned to Dun Righ and sat in the seat where her brother should have been. She had stiffened at the question, searching his face with narrowed eyes, seeking for some mocking ulterior motive which would discredit her, but it had been well founded and he had listened with every appearance of respect to her answer. Venutios, like the other men, experienced warriors all, gave her the respect which was her due when her responses showed wisdom. For now.

These meetings were very different from the more usual informal gatherings, held in the feasting hall where men already drunk on mead or Gaulish wine or ale deliberated, argued and, their voices rising as their faces reddened, from time to time rose unsteadily to their feet, their hands reaching for their weapons as the debate escalated swiftly into a brawl. Carta loved them. The discussions fascinated her. In her studies as a seer she was becoming more and more learned in the interpretation of the auguries, in consulting the omens, considering the prophesies and she had learned to prophesy herself. But this was an extra layer of learning. This was the planning, and the making of leaders. The combination of experience, something of which she had little herself as yet, with intuition, common sense, the knowledge of one's potential adversaries, be they the men of neighbouring tribes or the gods of the wind and storm, the movements of the sun and the moon and the stars, famine or plenty. Trade was one of their most important topics. The trade routes which crossed the Brigantian country had made them rich; and they were crucial for the import of the tin which could not be found in their own country. The current confederacy had taken a long time to establish. It consisted of a loosely linked collection of large and small tribes under one high king, whose aim was to preserve as much peace as possible between its members. Hard, within a society whose love of fighting was legendary, but something which the Druid advisers to the chieftains and kings worked hard to promote.

Artgenos sometimes called Carta to his house within the walls of the college at the foot of the hill, where he would explain things further to her, encourage her to have confidence in her opinions and to have the courage to voice them clearly. She never wondered why she was singled out for such attention, never suspected that her intelligence and learning were greater than those of the men around her. They wondered, though, and muttered into their moustaches about the tall, slim young woman who had become a part of their deliberations, occasionally at her brother's side, but more often without him.

'Why don't you come to the meeting?' She confronted him on the second day of Beltane as he stood, his hand on his pony's bridle, his small group of chosen companions already mounted, jeering at him to hurry and stop lingering to discuss spinning with his sister. None of the other leaders was there.

He gentled the excited horse. 'Because it bores me. I'm a man of action, not words, Carta.' He swung himself easily into the saddle of the small sturdy garron, his favourite mount. His feet nearly touched the ground but the creature was strong and as agile as a goat on the moors. 'You go. Speak for me, sister. I trust you to decide what's best.'

And he was gone, with his men around him, their shouts and whoops of excitement echoing across the hillside, horses bucking, dogs barking at their heels as they disappeared through the eastern gate in the rampart wall plunging down the hillside towards the forest, leaving her standing alone as the noise died away into the distance.

Carta stared after him in dismay. For days men and women had been arriving from every corner of Brigantia. Laden wagons, war chariots, ox-carts full of gifts and wares to be traded, horses, dogs, servants, slaves, had wound their way through the glorious last bright days of Giamonios, in the time of the waxing moon, to arrive in time for the Beltane feast. The township was filling up with market stalls, and tents and awnings to shelter the overflow of new arrivals, impromptu playing fields were being cleared of stones with picket lines for the hundreds of extra horses. Young men were practising their skills at the sword and spear, the sling and bow, in boisterous competitions. The place was full of noise and bustle and the eyes of the entire northern confederation were upon them. They were all here. As well as the whole tribe of the Setantii, representatives from the Corionototae, the Parisii, the Lopocares, the Textoverdi, the Carvetii, and even the Cornovii from their south-western borders were there and more besides. There was a bigger than usual gathering because the Druids had sent word that on this occasion there was an extra item on the agenda. The escalation of the threat from Rome. And Triganos, High King of the Brigantes, could not be bothered to attend.

With a sigh she turned and made her way towards the great round house where as the weather was too bad for the traditional meeting ground beneath the three oaks at the foot of the hill, the meetings were to be held. Taking her place amongst the leaders of the tribes, Carta felt many eyes upon her. Most of them knew her. Some had not seen her before except at the feast the previous night. Word that the sister of the leader of the Brigantes was a power to reckon with was filtering through the community. Men were eyeing her with curiosity. She was as tall as her brother, broad-shouldered yet slim with hair naturally the colour of sun-baked barley, eyes that were brilliant green in some lights, in others the colour of the dawn grey sea. A handsome woman, still young, already a widow but as yet without a new husband. There were quite a few men present who were considering her with the professional eye of a marriage-maker seeking a wife for one of their sons or indeed for themselves.

For the meeting she had dressed with some care, aware at last that it mattered to others what you wore even if it did not matter to you. She had put on a new cream woollen gown covered with a tunic of the softest doeskin and her best plaid fastened at the shoulders with gold. There were gold bracelets on her arms and a heavy plaited gold necklet about her throat. She did not speak at first. Taking her brother's seat, the seat of the high king, under the nose of Venutios who was about to seat himself there, she deferred to her father instead, who sat on her right, and it was he who stood to greet their guests. Venutios scowled as he found himself another place, further from the centre of the circle. Carta ignored him. She was scanning the other faces amongst the people seated around the fire. She was not the only woman there, though as usual now, her mother was absent. Several men had brought their wives, not just to the feasting and the games, but also to this meeting, respecting their views or, the thought struck Carta with sudden humour, too afraid of them to leave them behind. As her gaze moved on round she came back at last to Venutios and found he was studying her with equal interest. He had seen the smile flicker across her eyes and the expression had caught his attention. For a moment they considered each other, almost thoughtfully, before Carta looked away. She was careful to school her features into stillness. He was a handsome man, this king from the north-western corner of their territories who as a boy had been her sworn enemy, and he was powerful. Artgenos had already mentioned to her quietly that he was ambitious, as she had seen by his readiness to take Triganos's place in the high seat and his readiness to interfere in her affairs. She narrowed her eyes. If a list of possible suitors was ever to appear she would personally see that his name was not on it.

She sat back thoughtfully and returned her attention to the discussions which were already under way around her, listening intently as Brochan of the Parisii rose to his feet and held up his hand for silence.

'I have received messages from my sister who is married to the king of the Cantiaci that Roman armies are massing on the coast of Gaul. They are planning another invasion of our Isles.'

There was a moment of stunned silence. Then everyone was talking at once.

'Wait.' The voice was loud and demanded silence. Carta frowned, trying to locate its owner. 'Julius Caesar tried to conquer these islands some eighty summers ago, my friends. He went home with his tail between his legs. If they come, we can send them packing again.'

'Rome might have abandoned these shores, but it has kept a close eye on us.' Artgenos rose stiffly to his feet as he spoke. Immediately the others fell into a respectful silence. 'What Brochan says is confirmed by Druid intelligence. An army is gathering to invade us. Two legions, so I have heard, plus a great number of auxiliaries.' He paused, looking round. The faces staring back at his were shocked, intent on his every word. 'It is the Roman way,' he went on, 'to expand their empire. Their gods, so we are told, have assured them that their conquests will stretch as far as the ends of the earth.

They have been given what in their language they call *imperium sine fine* and they believe that all the world should be ruled by Rome. And they wish to challenge our Ocean gods. Since the death of Cunobelinus of the Catuvellauni the balance of power amongst the southern tribes of these islands has changed. If you remember three years ago the Emperor Gaius threatened to invade. He, too, brought his troops to the shores of Gaul. Then he changed his mind. There was no invasion. Things are different now under Claudius. He needs success to pacify his opponents in Rome.'

There was a long silence.

'Will the Cantiaci fight?' A voice came from the shadows.

'Undoubtedly. As will the sons of Cunobelinus. And as will our gods of wind and storm and sea which have before terrified the Roman invader and sent him packing.'

A whisper went round the circle and Artgenos held up his hand. 'Each kingdom in this land must hold itself ready to send war bands and levies to their aid if necessary. We will watch developments carefully. There are Druid spies throughout the Empire, and I have my best seers studying the portents and the signs so that we can react at once, before they know themselves what they will do. My friends, our confederation forms the largest kingdom on this island. Our decisions will be vital to the outcome of any invasion. This time, if the Romans come, in my opinion they will be determined to stay. They have failed twice before. There will not be a third failure. We cannot allow them to gain a foothold here.'

As the meeting disbanded Artgenos gestured at Carta to remain. Together they watched the senior members of the gathering as they walked away in groups of twos and threes, still in earnest discussion.

'They are worried.' Carta shook her head slowly as they stood just outside the door of the meeting house, sheltering from the rain under the broad eaves of the heather thatch. Heavy drifts of cloud were settling into the creases of the hills and she took a deep breath of the soft air, refreshing after the smoky heat of the meeting.

'Come with me down to the college.' Artgenos strode ahead of her for a few paces, drawing his hood over his head against the rain. He paused well out of hearing of any stragglers from the meeting and waited for her as she pulled her fur cloak around her and walked after him. 'Where was your brother, Carta?' He stopped and faced her, folding his arms across his chest.

She met his gaze firmly, aware of the blend of wisdom and strength in the old man's deep blue eyes. 'He went hunting with some of his friends.'

He gave an exasperated sigh. 'Even though I told him how important this discussion was! We needed to decide policy. If Rome invades these islands every tribe will need to make decisions. These people are organised. They take war seriously. To our men it is a sport no more.' He shook his head. 'The Druids will coordinate opposition from our base on the sacred Isle of Môn, but if important men like your brother ignore the omens and treat the threat as trivial we are doomed to defeat.'

'He will listen to you, Artgenos.'

'Will he?' He frowned. 'I hope so. I tell you in confidence, the longterm omens are worrying. A stand has to be made. In the south, to be sure, but we have to send our support. We have to make decisions.'

'Triganos doesn't like decisions.' Carta shrugged. 'He enjoys planning tactics for a hunt because he understands the ways of the stag or the roebuck; he can follow a wolf or a bear. To him the Roman is a rare creature, not worth thinking about. They trade, they visit. Their army came three, four, lifetimes ago and it went without trace. He does not believe the Emperor will bother with the Pretannic Isles again. He thinks we are nothing to him.'

'He is wrong, Carta. We are rich. Our nations trade wheat, silver, slaves, gold, dogs, lead, tin, pearls to the Empire. The Emperor covets our wealth.' Artgenos frowned. 'And when he turns his attention to us, nothing will deflect him this time. He claims his gods have given him every land and every sea he can conquer. He sees opposition as an inconvenience at best, a challenge at worst. We are flies to be swatted out of his way.' He paused. 'He particularly does not like Druids,' he added almost as an afterthought. 'I have spoken to senior Druids from Gaul who know the Roman officials well. The Emperor sees us as the greatest danger. Without our advice and influence kings and chieftains would not have the knowledge or the organisation to oppose them.'

Carta walked a few paces from him on the track, and stood staring down across the murky moorland, her cloak blowing around her.

Medb was out there somewhere in Gaul, if she was still alive. She frowned. She was alive. Carta had felt the woman's mind, searching, probing the secret pathways of the gods, planning her revenge, her anger unabated. With a shudder she put the thought behind her. This was not the time to think about Medb.

'My brother is not interested in politics, Artgenos. You must have realised that when you put him forward for election. But he will fight with the best if the time comes and lead his men with supreme courage. But for now he lives for the hunt and for the training of his warriors and the raids to win more cattle and slaves. Such is the usual business of kings.' Her shiver spoke as much of her memories of Riach's death, never far from her mind, as of the weather.

Artgenos snorted. 'He is a child in some ways. I have always known that. When he attended the school with the other children of the chieftains he lagged far behind all of them.' He paused, eyeing her as she stood half-turned away from him, her hair blowing back from her face around the fur trim of her hood. She had outstripped the other children in the classes and under the careful tutoring of Truthac at Dun Pelder her education had continued. The two men had kept in close touch over the years, aware that in this world where men normally led the way they were nurturing an exceptional talent.

Once a year the most senior Druids of all the nations gathered together on Môn. The subjects of debate, political and spiritual, were a closely guarded secret, the outcome never written or revealed, but twice now the subject of Cartimandua of the Brigantes had come high on the list of matters to be discussed.

'Triganos will be a good war leader.' She turned back, surveying his face. Her eyes were, he always thought, disconcertingly far-seeing, as though already she could read his thoughts even when they were scarcely formed in his own mind. 'Convince him the legions are worthy foes; a quarry to be hunted, their heads trophies worth collecting and he will fight with the best. With a purpose like that he will lead his men to victory. He will prove himself, Artgenos.'

'I don't doubt it.' Artgenos's voice was dry. 'But will he then be able to negotiate with the Emperor? Will he be able to turn his back on the spoils and sit down to discussions while the smell of the meat juices of the victory feast drift in from the camp?'

She turned away again without comment and he nodded grimly. 'He will have to change, Carta. He will have to change a great deal in order to grow into a general. At the moment he is merely a man.'

14

I

'Viv!'

The banging was from the spring flap on the letter box. As the post was always left on the bottom step of the stairs by whoever took it out of the box on the outer door it was never used.

'Viv! Come on! I know you're in there.'

With a groan Viv sat up. The dream vanished in an instant, the past rolled up and gone as completely as a drawing in the sand as the tide sweeps over it.

'Wait.' She managed to croak a response. 'I'm coming.'

'Bloody hell, Viv! Where have you been? What's happened?'

Cathy strode past her into the room, staring at the bags still on the floor where Viv had left them the night before. 'I was ready to call the police!'

'Why?' Viv sat down on the sofa and ran her fingers through her hair. Her eyes didn't appear to be focussing properly as, haltingly, she told Cathy about the farm and the late-night encounter with Hugh. 'Then last night . . .' She paused at last. 'I dreamed about Carta again. I must have done. Even though I didn't want to. Even though I said no.' Suddenly she was crying. 'I'm sorry. I'm just so tired. It was a long drive back and I ran into Hugh –'

'And then Carta came into your dreams even though you said no,' Cathy repeated her words thoughtfully.

'Peggy at the farm said I must make some ground rules. Say when I wanted to talk to her. But she just came.'

'You've got to stop this, Viv.' Cathy frowned. 'It's getting out of hand.'

'I know.'

'Peggy-at-the-farm, whoever she may be, is right. It is up to you. But if you're not strong enough to control your imagination and this – entity – whatever it – she – is, that you have created in your own mind, then you must stop altogether. It could destroy you.'

'Not just in my mind, Cathy, remember. Tasha saw her. And so did Pete. And I thought you said it wasn't dangerous. You said I was just having trouble adjusting after finishing the book,' Viv retorted. 'Anyway, that's irrelevant. I want to go on.' She groped in her pocket for tissues. 'I have to go on, Cathy. I want to know what happens. This is so important. I am finding out things that no one knows about. No one at all. So much happened last night. I thought it had all gone, you know, the way a dream goes if you wake up and think about something else too quickly, but it's coming back It always comes back. And it's crucial.'

Cathy sighed. 'Then will you at least let Pat help you? It's important that you stay grounded. Talking to her will let you keep this all in perspective.'

Viv shook her head. 'No. Pat doesn't understand.'

'She does, Viv.' Cathy looked anxious.

Viv frowned. 'No, she doesn't. She's got completely the wrong end of the stick. The last stuff she showed me had nothing to do with my book at all. It was a great scene, but irrelevant. Rubbish. You know, the more I think about this, Cathy, the more I feel I don't want to go ahead with this play idea at all. Not at the moment. I want to write another book.'

Cathy took a deep breath. 'Pat and Maddie would be very upset to hear you say that, Viv.' She paused. 'And Pat would be very hard to put off now that she's got her teeth into this.'

'Tough.' Viv shook her head. 'It's my book. My story. If I say no, that's the end of it. No play. No subsidiary rights of any sort. Nothing.'

Cathy studied her face thoughtfully. 'Have you spoken to Maddie about this?'

Viv shook her head. 'I know there's this tight deadline and everything. And they will want their advance back, but I can't help that. I don't think this play is what Carta wants.'

'Viv.' Cathy stood up anxiously.

'No. Listen. This story is the biggest thing that has ever happened

211

to me. I'm being allowed to witness something incredible.' Viv spread her hands out on the table. 'Nothing must get in its way.'

Fiction?

Fact.

'I'll speak to Maddie about it. I'm sure she'll understand.'

'And Pat?'

'Pat will have to understand too. She's way off track anyway. She wants to write about Medb.'

'Who's Medb?' Cathy looked puzzled.

'Medb?' Viv shook her head. 'Medb is no one. She doesn't exist!'

II

The hillside was totally silent, the fields empty, tractor and baler back in the yard behind the farmhouse. The gentle babble of the water and the soughing of the wind in Steve's ears was soothing, lulling him almost to sleep. Sheltered by the dry stone walls and the deep fold in the hillside he couldn't see the top of the hill from here. He was in a small private world, a world where anything could happen.

His mother had brought Viv here and that puzzled him. She never brought anyone here. It was their special place. His father obviously knew about it, but he never mentioned it or appeared interested in any of the more inaccessible corners of the land, except where in the old days they might prove dangerous to the sheep. Now the gates lay open. Some of the wire had gone. The fields were being mown for their hay rather than cut for silage. That was one good thing. More ecologically sound. He turned his face up towards the sun with a deep sigh of contentment, aware that his candle still burned down there in the dark and that his offering to the goddess would lie there undisturbed until he or his mother replaced it. Flowers. Seeds. Grains. Raisins. The latter would in fact probably swiftly disappear, carried off by the smaller hungrier inhabitants of the place, but that was fine. That was the intention. To give freely to the shrine and its occupants.

But Viv. Why had his mother brought Viv here? This place was for people who believed. Did it mean that she too was a follower of the old religion?

He gave a wry smile. Who would have thought it. No wonder Hugh Graham was antagonistic. He was one of the old school. Almost defensive in his study. Keeping it scientific. Not wanting to 'feel' too much about his subject in case he got too close. This was much too close.

Slowly he stood up. Well, her secret was safe with him, but he was sorry she had gone so soon. He had been hoping she might stay to do some writing in the farmhouse, using it as a site base for her research. He glanced back towards the shadows where the beck came tumbling out into the sunshine. She had promised she would come back as soon as her book promotion was finished. Perhaps he could hold her to that.

III

Hugh was sitting on the veranda at the back of his house, a glass of white wine on the wrought iron table at his elbow, a notebook on the arm of his chair, Viv's book on his knee.

He was torn between a deep enjoyment of the moment – book and wine – and extreme irritation at the fluent, almost glib style with which she wrote. She was too confident, too knowing. Had she stuck to the old theories about the Celts he could have been tolerantly condescending. So many people still believed in the wholesale immigration theory and in the fact that the native Brit was a pretty primitive chap waiting to be saved by his Roman superiors. She didn't just contradict this, however, which would have been all right in its way. She seemed to imply that the Celts – and she didn't seem sure such a race even existed – were probably vastly superior to the Romans! Somewhere she even suggested that they were Pythagoreans long before Pythagoras; that Pythagoras was instructed in his theorem by his Celtic, presumably Druidic, slave rather than the other way round and that Pythagoras might have himself travelled west to learn from the Druids in Gaul or who knows where! What a travesty! New Age bunk.

He liked her theories about a Druid network of spies, though. Europe wide. Caesar had of course hinted as much in *De Bello Gallico*. She should just learn to be more tentative about putting her ideas forward as just that, theories, not implying they were historical fact and that old farts like him knew nothing. Not that she mentioned him by name. Anywhere. He put the book down and took a sip from his glass, sighing. The garden, in spite of his lack of care, was exquisite, full of flowers and birdsong and the deeply satisfying hum of bees. He closed his eyes for a moment, savouring the crisp cold sauvignon flavour on his tongue. When he opened them again there was a woman standing on the terrace only six feet from him. He let out a shout of surprise, the glass flying in the air to shatter on the stone flags, the book sliding between his knees to disappear beneath the chair. When he looked again, she had gone.

'Jesus Christ!' He stood up, staring around. 'Where are you? Hello?' She had been watching him. Closely. A hippy. Matted hair, tatty weird clothes and eyes of a vivid blue-green. 'Come on out. I know you're there!' But he didn't know. Where could she have gone? There was nowhere to hide closer than the laurel bushes at the edge of the lawn and she couldn't have moved that fast. Could she? He strode down off the terrace onto the grass and proceeded to search the lawn and garden beyond. There was no one there.

In the distance he heard the note of the bronze war trumpet. The sound made his blood run cold.

IV

'Do not question my decisions!' Triganos's face was contorted with fury. 'I am King of the Brigantes. What I decide is law!'

'What your Druids decide is law, brother!' Carta stood her ground, hands on hips, eyes mirroring his in their anger. 'Above anything you may decide. They advise you and their advice is good. If you go against it you will be the loser. As will our people. They rely on you to lead them well!' She emphasised the last word.

Time had passed; Dun Righ had been enlarged; improved;

214

strengthened. Where there were no natural cliffs, the ramparts were now huge, the wall and stockade above them substantial. Inside it was a bustling village comprising round houses, workshops, the larger houses of the king and the meeting house, the feasting hall, the warriors' hall, where the young men lived. Carta and her brother were standing immediately outside the latter; behind them a group of warriors, carrying bows and spears and shields, waited in grim silence as nearby their horses were being harnessed into light fighting chariots, lined up on the practice ground.

This was only the latest of a series of increasingly violent and public quarrels between brother and sister. This time it was about his determination to lead a war party south to aid the stand against Rome and this time Venutios was once more at his side.

The subject was contentious. Discussion at the council meetings under the great oak tree in the forest had raged back and forth between the petty kings of the tribes, their advisers and their most experienced warriors. The Roman legions had invaded the south coast and the question was simple. Did they go south and fight, or did they wait? If the legions defeated the Cantiaci and the Catuvellauni would they then turn their attention further north or would they settle down content with the richer land and the wealth of the more compliant southern kingdoms?

'They will not be satisfied until they have conquered all the Pretannic Isles!' Her brother was beside himself with impatience. 'How can you imagine otherwise? They have crossed the ocean! The last defence that divides us from Gaul. The gods did not stop them and now there is nothing to keep them from our doors unless we fight.'

'There is a lot to keep them from our doors.' It was his sister who retorted before the others had time to open their mouths. 'The tribes of the south and the middle lands and then our own mountains. We are Brigantians; the warriors of the high places. They will not defeat us, unless –' she raised her hand in his face as he took a deep breath to shout her down, 'unless we come down out of the hills and expose ourselves to them. Their armies fight best in the flat lands.'

'Who told you that?' His eyes were hard and angry.

'I have seen them.' She held his gaze defiantly. 'I have seen them in the waters of the sacred well, with their armour and their shields

215

and their great eagles. Thousands of them, drawn up in squares across the land.'

He swallowed his retort. He too often forgot that his sister was a seer, training as a Druidess as well as a princess of his own blood. Visions such as hers could not be gainsaid. 'Even so,' he continued to glare at her sulkily, 'they are not unstoppable. They can be sent back where they came from. We have done it before.'

'He speaks the truth, Cartimandua.' Venutios had been standing nearby, watching her face with a quizzical sneer. 'I would have thought it was obvious. If the tribes ally we can defeat them. Send them back to Gaul.'

'And have them return with even more legions and greater determination still?' Carta snapped at him, his patronising tone instantly goading her further. 'You do not understand these people.'

'And you do, little sister?' her brother put in, smirking beneath his moustaches. 'You turn your face against war because you lost your husband in a skirmish and it's turned you lily-livered. You know nothing of the subject!'

There was a moment's intense silence. Carta tensed, aware of Venutios's eyes on her face, waiting with a half-smile to see how she handled Triganos's deliberate cruelty. Taking a deep breath she ignored the jibe. 'I understand war, brother, because I listen to the Druids who have colleagues all over the Empire, because I listened to Lugaid of the Votadini and because I listen to the gods. They send us warnings, and if we disregard those warnings it is at our own peril.'

'There are Druids who advise resistance,' Venutios contradicted at once. 'Our advisers are not all of the same mind over this.' He raised an eyebrow in Triganos's direction. 'I don't understand my friend, why you put up with these arguments from your sister. You would do better to send her packing to the women's fireside! She is better fitted to gossip about her lust for meaty thighs than political realities.'

Carta clenched her fists. 'He puts up with me, Venutios, because he knows that my advice is sound,' she said through gritted teeth.

'I don't think so.' Venutios retorted. 'The man is in danger of being pussy whipped by his own baby sister. Tell her, Triganos.'

Triganos shrugged. He glanced warily from his sister to his friend and back. 'She does know about these things, Venutios,' he conceded carefully. 'There are two sides to the argument.'

216

'So, while the Druids dither, we wait for defeat?' Venutios was suddenly beside himself with impatience, striding a few paces away from them and then back again.

'And the gods? They dither too, I suppose?' Carta was furious.

'The gods never seem to agree on anything, to my mind.' Venutios scowled at her. 'The Romans, after all, now say that their gods have given them the world. Do their gods fight with our gods? Do they fight with the gods of Greece and Egypt and Libya? The gods of Scandia? Of Ind and far Cathay? Of the lands across the seas far beyond Erin? Or this new god the Druids tell us about who challenges those of the Romans in Palestine? I don't think so! Do they parcel the world up between themselves but allow us mortals to work out the borders? Of course they don't. They leave it to us!'

Carta hesitated. Venutios was clearly better informed than she had given him credit for; better informed by far than her brother. She gave him a calculating glance from beneath her eyelashes. 'Our gods, the gods of Brigantia would expect us to protect the lands they have given us,' she said thoughtfully. 'But they would not expect us to fight without thought or reason.'

'Well spoken.' Artgenos had joined them unnoticed. He stood leaning on his staff. 'To behave like hot heads is to risk losing your best men for no reason. Be canny. Don't rush in like fools . . .'

Viv started violently and the scene vanished as her brain had kicked in with sudden infuriating logic. It was that list of places that had done it. The known world. Scandinavia. Ultima Thule. Egypt. Libya. Palestine. Cathay. West beyond Erin – surely that wasn't, couldn't be, America? Who knows, perhaps the Celts had found Australia too and the deep snows of Antarctica. After all they had sophisticated knowledge of astronomy which the whole world respected. They could navigate. They knew the world was round. Get the notion of primitive small islanders out of your head, Rees! That was the kind of history that Hugh still embraced. Primitive Celts against sophisticated Romans. No. No. No. That was believing the propaganda. She gave a grim smile.

In the corner of the room, Carta was waiting. A shadow. A thought form. A ghost. She was growing stronger and she was growing impatient.

V

'You've got to do some hefty fence-building. Viv's on the point of giving up on the play completely.' Cathy stood staring down at Pat as she sat before her laptop in the living room. The book on the coffee table beside her had sprouted red Post-its on dozens of pages, and the sheaf of papers scattered about her on the carpet was liberally marked with yellow and pink marker pen.

Pat looked up over spectacles which had slid down her nose. 'I half expected that. It makes it easier for me.'

'No. You don't understand. She doesn't want it to go ahead at all.'

Pat shook her head. She was typing again, her fingers flying over the keyboard. 'She can't do that.'

'It's her book.'

'Not by the time I've finished with it. We can alter the wording on the contract. Or take her name off the play all together.' Pat paused, squinting at the screen then backspaced a few places. She glanced up. 'I'll ring her.'

'I think you'd better.' Cathy sat down heavily. 'You can't just take over her project, Pat.'

'Why not?' Pat took off the specs and stretched, flexing her fingers wearily. 'She was going nowhere without me. I am going to conduct some auditions and we are going to get this show on the road. All Viv's trances and dreaming and rows and contradictions have been getting in the way of what we're about here. Daughters of Fire needs to establish a reputation for fantastic drama documentary, slick production, and efficient scheduling.' She glanced up. 'I'll need to borrow your printer again, Cathy, then I can show her these new scenes. I think you'll find she'll change her mind about it when she's read them.'

Privately Cathy doubted it. She raised an eyebrow. 'There seems to be an awful lot there.'

'There is.' Pat glanced at the pile of typescript already sitting on the corner of the table. 'It'll have to be cut. And probably changed as we work on it. Don't worry. I'll sort Viv out. There is stuff she can do. Ideally I would like her to read the narrator's role if she's up for it. I'm waiting to see how she performs on TV tomorrow.'

She glanced round cautiously. 'Talking of performances, where's the psychic child prodigy?'

Cathy grimaced. 'Hopefully getting ready to go to Sweden for the holidays.'

'Go on, you'll miss her.'

'Probably.'

'Pete will, certainly.'

Cathy nodded.

'Do you think she really did see Viv's alter ego?' Pat closed the laptop at last and leaned back against the cushions.

Cathy shrugged. 'Of course not. She's pretty acute. She's capable of picking up on what's going on and using it to stir things up.'

'But her description –'

'Could have come from anywhere.'

Pat stared thoughtfully into space in front of her. It had not taken very much fishing to find out from Cathy the full extent of Viv's involvement with this strange world she was inventing for herself. She glanced up at Cathy. 'You know I've been dreaming about this stuff as well.'

Cathy stared at her. 'Oh, Pat. Come on.'

Pat ignored the reproach in the tone. 'The thing is,' she folded her arms, 'should I worry about it?'

Cathy scratched her head. 'I think you both need a bit more exercise!'

'So you don't rate the possession theory?'

Cathy studied her face. 'No, I don't. And I don't believe it's reincarnation, either.'

'And you reckon Viv is just being obsessive.'

'She's finding it hard to separate herself –'

'Yes, you said that before. And what's my excuse?'

'You think you've found a storyline that will upstage Viv's.' Cathy grimaced.

'So why am I dreaming it and not just writing it down?'

'Maybe because you have a guilty conscience. You are trying to sideline her and steal her play.' Cathy stood up. 'Think about that.'

Pat gave a humourless grin. Maybe Cathy was right.

Two days after her chains were removed and she was given the free run of the villa during the daytime, Medb stole a bodkin from the dressmaking room. The guard on the door of the slaves' quarters died before he was properly awake, his life bubbling from his throat in a small pool of frothy blood. For several seconds Medb stood looking down at him debating whether to seek out Lucilla for the same treatment. The villa lay in darkness, passages lit here and there by oil lamps. The guards were lazy. It would probably be easy. But it was an unnecessary risk. If she was caught wandering around she would be flogged and shackled; once they found the guard she would be put to death. Better to get out now while she had the chance. On tiptoe she made her way over the mosaic floors and out into the villa kitchens. There she helped herself to bread and biscuits, cheese and cold meat, wrapped them in a linen cloth and stowed them in a bag she found hanging on the back of a door. Then she let herself out silently into the summer night. Creeping through the gardens she unbolted the door in the wall. She was away from the fields and into the forest before daybreak. She had not brought Sibael with her, a calculated decision. Sibael would slow her up, would have had qualms about murdering the guard. She could fend for herself.

Medb travelled by night under the stars and the thin slivered moon, making steady but slow progress, hiding during the day, keeping away from roads and habitation. She eked out her store of food with birds' eggs and stolen milk and fish she charmed with gentle fingers from the streams where she stopped to drink, constantly heading north-west towards the coast.

Once or twice in the first days she thought she heard hounds baying in the distance. Grimly she slipped into the river to wade downstream, losing her trail in the water. After that she didn't hear them again.

Scrying in a dark pool of stream water she watched Carta leave Dun Pelder. There was no sign of a baby. Thoughtfully she scanned the brackish depths trying to hold the vision as it wavered in the shadows. There were horses and wagons, many people with her. Where would the nurses travel? If there were nurses.

Then she smiled. Her curse had worked. The baby was lost. She leaned closer to the water, watching grimly, a lock of her hair trailing like pale weed across its surface. So, where was Cartimandua going with such a large entourage? She tried to see if there were any landmarks but the woman rode in a watery world of shadows and reflections. No matter. She had an ocean to cross before she need worry about finding Cartimandua.

Thoughtfully she let the vision go and moved away from the water's edge. The sun was rising as she slipped back into the forest out of sight and a white mist rose to cover the stream.

15

I

The sacred well was dark after the sunlight and silent save for the dripping of the water. Leaning towards the surface of the spring, Carta made offerings to the goddess.

Vivienne?

She whispered the name into the green depths.

Vivienne. Where are you?

There was no response. Outside a breeze touched the trees in the fold of the hillside above the beck and rustled the leaves. She heard the sound above the drip of the water and frowned. The hillside was speaking to her.

Vivienne?

Far away, in another time, Viv struggled to reply, but no sound came.

Triganos, Bran and Venutios had ridden onto the moors that morning with their companions and a troop of warriors, leaving the township all but unguarded. They had not invited her to join them.

Watching them leave, she had been overwhelmed without warning by a wave of misery and loneliness. She fitted nowhere here. At the discussions beneath the sacred oak, only Artgenos and his fellow Druids respected her opinions. The men, following the lead of Triganos and Venutios, resented the fact that she was there at all and argued with her or teased her constantly. Only elderwomen had wisdom and experience. By virtue of her youth she had neither. And if she went to the women's hearths she was treated with suspicion and reserve, fitting in neither with the younger maidens, nor with the married women who had husbands and children about whom to gossip. More and more she found herself riding alone or walking with Conaire through the forests or in the chariot with Fergal at the reins.

Riach was there in her dreams. Aching with love and loss she would hold out her arms to him, begging him to come to her and smiling, he would move towards her; then as she ran into his embrace he would be gone, withdrawing into the mists, leaving her to weep into her pillow alone.

'Riach!' She cried his name into the wind. 'Riach! Wait!'

She never saw her baby in these dreams at all.

Vivienne! Help me. Is my baby reborn? Is he with his father? Tell me where he is!

But the goddess was silent. Leaning again towards the spring, Carta saw the splash of her tears like raindrops on the water, then they were gone.

It was then in the depths of the pool beneath the rocks near the bank that she saw the face, the pale hard eyes, the long fair hair trailing amongst the ferns.

Medb of the White Hands had found her.

II

'Shit!' The scene had gone. The drip of the water in the well chamber had receded.

Medb.

Medb was there. She was spying on Carta. And Carta was afraid!

Viv's head was spinning, her body stiff and exhausted. However much she wanted to return to the scene she couldn't; however much Carta invaded her head she was too tired to go on. Staggering stiffly into the kitchen, she began opening the cupboards and the fridge. She couldn't even remember when had she last been shopping. Going back into the living room she grabbed her purse and keys.

Sitting on the floor in front of the coffee table with her takeaway half an hour later, she scanned her notes whilst she ate. Whatever she had said to Cathy, she was still thinking about the play. And Medb. Perhaps Pat was right and there was a small place for Medb in the story as a focus point of tension. It would make it more exciting. Heaping rice and chicken Madras onto her fork she leaned forward, shuffling through her notebook. The food was making her feel better. More focussed. There was so much to do. She needed to reread her draft of the play and at the same time choose passages to talk about on TV tomorrow; decide at what point she was going to produce the pin. Finishing the curry and rice she reached for a poppadum as her notepad filled page by page.

It was very late when at last she put down her pen and stretched her arms, yawning. Climbing to her feet she picked up her plate and headed for the kitchen. Gathering up the empty foil containers she dumped them in the bin, switched off the lights and went into the bathroom. She was exhausted, physically and emotionally, and all she wanted now was to sleep. Turning on the taps she hunted on the shelf over the bath and found some exotic bubbly stuff to swirl into the steam. Undressing slowly she turned off the taps at last and was about to step into the water when she decided to bring some music into the bathroom.

The living room was dark, the window still open on the warm night air. Outside the sounds of the street had died away. An occasional car, its tyres rattling over the stone sets in the High Street, broke the silence, then it was quiet again. Reaching for her CD player she was about to turn back towards the bathroom when she caught sight of a movement in the doorway to the hall out of the corner of her eye and she became suddenly acutely aware that she was naked.

'Who is it? Who's there?' She was clutching the disc player against her breasts. At this time of year the sky had a luminosity which reflected down even into the wynds and closes of the old town. It gave the room a faint glow as her eyes attuned. She held her breath. The room was completely silent now. But it was a strange silence. Thick. Impenetrable. Self-conscious. All she could hear was her own heartbeat in her ears. She wanted it to stop so she could listen; she wanted it to stop so she couldn't be heard.

'Who is it?' she whispered. More tentatively this time.

The wedge of black where the half-open doorway led into the hall was dense and unmoving. Cautiously she stepped towards the rocking chair. Setting down the player she grabbed the sweater which lay thrown over the chair and pulled it quickly on, then with a swift movement she reached for the light switch. The room in the harsh light of three lamps was empty as she had known, in some deep core of herself below the irrational panic, that it would be. She moved towards the door, then she paused. A fresh damp waft of air came to her from the hall. She reached to turn on that light as well, afraid suddenly that the front door was open onto the cold stone of the winding stair, but it was closed and locked and almost as soon as she had registered the smell it had gone.

She shivered. It had been the smell of the dales and the Yorkshire moors.

'Carta?' Her whisper was hesitant. She did not want an answer. 'Carta? Is that you?' Carta was angry; impatient. She wanted Viv to go on.

But whatever gateway might have temporarily opened between Carta's world and Viv's had closed. The fresh air of the Brigantian hills was once more locked away into the past and she was left with an empty flat and the faint smell of the curry she had eaten only a few short hours before.

III

With a scowl Hugh turned his back on the dripping garden and walked back to his desk. He glanced at the transcript of his review lying beside the keyboard and read it through again while he drank a mug of black coffee. At best Viv's book was a jolly romp through a historical theme. A slow and careful reading of the full text hadn't changed his mind. Sitting down, he stared at the computer monitor. Either way the book was a disaster and not something he wanted either his own name or that of his department associated with.

The offending book itself was sitting on the far corner of his desk. Like Pat's copy it was bristling with Post-its but in this case every one represented an inaccuracy or a guess. Every one flagged an insult to historical truth. Just as well they had sent him this second copy after he had handed his first to Steve or he would never have read it; never have had the chance to accept the *Daily Post*'s

225

invitation to review the book and to do it properly with a full range of damaging quotes, emphasising particularly the travesty she had made out of the role of Venutios in her story. Venutios, who was one of the greatest leaders of the period, outshining even Caratacus.

Well, she couldn't claim he hadn't given her the chance to retract. Or withdraw it. Or pulp it. Whatever one did with unwanted books. He had warned her; he had begged her and she had remained adamant. Whatever happened now, it was her own fault. He picked up the mouse and called up his e-mail. One click and the review was on its way.

He frowned. The day it appeared, he realised abruptly, Viv Lloyd Rees would be a public laughing stock. Did he really want that?

He sat for a moment staring at the screen. **Message sent**. Not too late to change his mind. He could withdraw it. Poor Viv. Alison would have hated him for this. But if Alison was still there he probably wouldn't have done it. He was more mellow in those days. More tolerant. Probably, he had to admit, a nicer person. But then he wasn't doing this to prove his niceness or otherwise. He was doing it to maintain the integrity of his department and everything he believed in, in the field of research. In the long run this was in Viv's own interest. Some day she would even thank him for it. Flipping open the book's cover, he sat staring at her photo inside the jacket. For a moment he wondered if he should ring her; warn her what he had done. He put his hand out to the phone then he withdrew it again. Tonight she would be appearing on TV to talk about the wretched book and presumably produce the stolen pin in full view of the whole world. It would be even more important after that for him to distance himself from her.

Standing up, he went back to his survey of the wet garden. He hadn't told the police. Of course he hadn't told the police. Not yet. He couldn't do that to her.

Cartimandua's pin.

No. Venutios's pin.

He frowned uncomfortably. Where had that thought come from?

With a sudden bolt of irrational fear he knew that he was about to hear the brazen note of the carnyx even before it was there, echoing across the garden, drowning out the sound of the rain.

'I'm not stopping long!' Pat waved a paper bag enticingly as Viv opened the door. 'Peace offering. Doughnuts! Can I come in?' She shook the rain out of her hair.

Viv stepped back and led the way into the living room. She had slept heavily, still swathed in the jumper and had woken with a headache which a shower had done little to dissipate. She had also changed her mind about Medb.

'I've been crass,' Pat said as she followed her in. 'I admit it. I got so excited by the story I went into rough-shod mode. A fault of mine and I know it. Mea Culpa!' She put her briefcase down on the sofa and flung herself down beside it. 'Can we start again?'

Viv studied her face for a moment in silence before seating herself on the rocker. 'No Medb?'

Pat opened her mouth then closed it. She put her head on one side. 'Less Medb?'

'No Medb. There's no space for Medb. No actual place for Medb!' Cartimandua had vetoed the woman's part in the play.

Pat exhaled sharply. 'Maybe you're right.' She didn't sound convinced. 'So, where do we go from here?' She left her briefcase unopened.

Viv shrugged. 'I've got the TV programme this evening. I can't really think straight until that is over.'

'Live?'

Viv grimaced. 'Live.'

'But you're good at this sort of thing, right? I've heard you're a natural.'

'I don't know. I'm nervous.'

Pat shook her head. 'That's a good sign. You'll be terrific.' She stood up. 'Tomorrow, OK? We'll slot some scenes together with the narrative and see how it reads.'

She left Viv both doughnuts.

In the TV studios late that night Viv found herself seated opposite the presenter, Selwyn Briggs. She had placed the Perspex box between her glass of water and the small bowl of flowers which stood on the low table between them.

A grey-haired man, with a craggy face and eccentric taste in luminous shirts, Selwyn eyed it. 'When do you want to produce it?'

'About halfway through my segment?' She shrugged. Behind the spotlights the cameras were lining up. Cables snaked across the floor into the distance. Someone was checking the small mike pinned to her blouse. 'I'll lead into it naturally if that's OK with you, when I talk about Cartimandua's life style.'

'That's fine.' He grinned at her. 'Don't forget you've only got about ten minutes in all. Don't go into too much detail. Keep it general.'

On the studio wall the clock ticked round towards the hour. Listening to the signature tune Viv found her mouth had gone dry. Selwyn was smiling at her now, engaged, his professional persona in place, his introduction as always word perfect.

'This evening our programme comes to you from Edinburgh and in it we have three practical historians who are here to talk about their work. First up we have Dr Vivienne Lloyd Rees who is a Celticist at Edinburgh University. Good evening, Viv.' His smile broadened. 'Your new book, *Cartimandua, Queen of the North* will be on our shelves any day now. Can you tell us briefly what it's about?'

The camera crept nearer, focussed on her face. Viv smiled back at him and her nerves disappeared. She made a couple of passable jokes. She flirted with the lens. She was a natural; relaxed; charismatic. The camera adored her. The first few minutes seemed to fly. At last she reached for the box. 'I have something here, Selwyn, which I think will interest the viewers.' She removed the lid and picked up the pin, holding it on her palm. 'This brooch – technically it's called a fibula – a safety pin, if you like, came from a place called Stanwick in Yorkshire, the site of one of the largest Brigantian settlements, the place which many people think was their capital. In Celtic times I believe it was called Dinas Dwr, which means the castle on the water. The river there is tiny now, no more than a brook, a tributary of the Tees but in earlier times it was larger. As you can see, this is a beautiful object, made of gold and the most exquisite enamelling.' She moved her hand in front of the camera so the brooch caught the light. Even here, in the heat of the studios it was cold. 'By rights, it should be in the museum, of course,' she paused, eyebrow raised, 'and it will go back there straight after the programme, but its owner, Professor Hugh Graham, allowed me to borrow it especially for tonight.' She glanced up at the camera nearest to her and grinned. 'There's no way of knowing if it really belonged to Cartimandua, but that's what it has come to be called. The Cartimandua Pin.'

Selwyn leaned forward. 'A very talented craftsman made this.' He held out his hand and reluctantly she placed the brooch on his palm.

'Indeed. These were sophisticated, artistic people.'

Selwyn nodded sagely, staring down at it for a few seconds before hastily handing it back. She saw him surreptitiously rub his palm on his knee as he smiled at her again. So, he felt it too. 'You obviously have amazing pull, Viv. People aren't usually allowed to "borrow" things from museums. Professor Graham must look on you with great favour. Not to say trust.' He gave her a wolfish grin.

Viv met his eye, startled. 'He's certainly taken a great interest in my book,' she said cautiously. He knew.

'And has been very supportive, no doubt?' He left the question hanging.

'He has backed me in his own inimitable way,' Viv commented dryly. 'Professor Graham and I have different ways of pursuing our research. Ways which I think complement each other very well.' She gave a wry smile. Did he know about the row, or were his comments merely shrewd? She put the pin down on the table. 'In fact he's probably sent an armoured car to collect this and make sure it gets back safely,' she commented. She managed a humorous shrug.

Selwyn laughed. 'I'm sure he trusts you, Viv,' he said. 'So, where next?' He changed the subject adroitly. 'Another book, perhaps?'

'Indeed.' She looked straight into the camera. 'I've been doing further, tremendously exciting research and I have already started on a sequel. I am also working on a radio drama documentary about Cartimandua.'

'So, we should watch this space?'

Viv smiled. 'I hope you will.'

There was a pause. The floor manager made a thumbs up sign and taking off his headphones, slung them round his neck. It was time for the break. Selwyn sat back with a grin. 'Great. Thanks, Viv.' There was an infinitesimal pause. 'You believe in living dangerously!' He raised an eyebrow. 'Hugh was on the phone to me about that pin.'

She waited while the mike was unfastened from her blouse and then stood up. 'Thanks for not relaying the full force of his fury to the nation.'

'I wouldn't call it fury.' Selwyn reached across to shake her hand. 'A touch of professional jealousy maybe? Go carefully, sweetie!'

The next guest – a TV presenter from Glasgow whose new series on rescue archaeology would start in a couple of weeks – was waiting for her chair. Viv picked up the brooch, put it back into the box and made her way off the sound stage, past the cameras towards the green room where she had left her jacket as the show restarted behind her. What had he meant by 'go carefully'? With a shiver she zipped the brooch into the inner pocket of her bag and put the strap over her shoulder.

It was almost midnight. The studios were for the most part in darkness. The reception desk was unmanned, the corridors deserted. Only the one studio was in use tonight. At the outer door she paused to let herself out, half expecting her prediction to be right, but there was no one around. No armoured car. No police. No heavies – she gave wry grin at the thought. No one at all.

The car park was nearly empty, the tarmac between the rows of small neatly planted cherry trees reflecting the rain under the tall security lights. Pulling her car key out of her pocket she headed for the Mazda which she had left on the far side of the car park, which when she had arrived a couple of hours before, had been nearly full. She stopped abruptly, listening to the rain hissing down on a bank of laurels nearby as she narrowed her eyes in the glare of the lights. There was a figure standing near her car. She glanced round nervously. It was Carta. She was sure of it. She could feel the terror tightening her throat as she looked back towards the studio. The door had clicked shut behind her. She was completely alone.

Vivienne!

She could hear the voice above the sound of the rain.

Vivienne. Come back!

It was the voice of her narrator. The voice of the ghost. The hair was standing up on the back of her neck. With a moan of fear she broke into a run and headed back to the building behind her, splashing through puddles, water soaking her shoes. Banging on the locked door frantically she glanced behind her. The car park was deserted once more. She could see no sign of the figure. 'Please. Let me in!' She searched desperately for a bell or a buzzer. There seemed to be nothing. Once again she banged on the glass panels with her fist. There was no response. With a cry of anguish she turned, her back to the door. There was no one in sight. Her car stood alone in the rain beneath the bank of lights.

Her mouth dry with fear, she took a deep breath. There was nothing for it. She had to go. Running as fast as she could she headed for the far side of the car park and the safety of the little car.

For a moment she couldn't slot the key into the lock. She could feel the panic mounting. Her hands shaking, her fingers wet with rain she stabbed at the lock, and then at last felt it slide in and turn. Pulling open the door she dived in and slammed the locks shut. Only then did she take a deep breath and look round, wiping the rain from her eyes. The car park was still deserted. The shadows were empty.

V

She had been very watchable. He had to give her that. Standing up, Hugh went over to the sideboard to replenish his whisky. She was relaxed. Attractive. Charismatic, that was probably the word. Enthusiastic about the wretched book and, God help us, already writing another. He raised the glass and took a swig. That old sod Selwyn had been a damn sight too tactful about the brooch. He had had the chance to pillory her and all he had done was make a joke of it. Hugh walked over to the window. He hadn't drawn the curtains and outside the world was black and wet. He could hear the rain on the glass above the sound of the adverts. The wind had whipped some brown and dying rose petals into the air and plastered them against the panes. The larches at the bottom of the garden were thrashing up and down, their branches sounding like waves on the beach. With a shiver he pulled the curtains across and turned back to the TV where Selwyn was already smiling benignly at his next guest.

It was after midnight when Hugh finally turned off the set. He returned his glass to the sideboard, contemplated another top-up

231

and realised that he was already slightly unsteady on his feet. Too much whisky would negate the desired effect of a quick and deep sleep. If one wasn't careful there was that uncomfortable transition state before unconsciousness when one lay awake, the room beginning to spin unpleasantly when the regret set in. He never used to drink so heavily. He didn't like being drunk. Firmly putting down the glass he walked out of the room and turned the lights off in time to see the sweep of car headlights through the hall window as someone drew up on the gravel outside the front door. He heard a car door slam. Seconds later his doorbell rang.

Viv was standing on the doorstep, her hair plastered flat by the rain, the shoulders of her jacket soaked. Under it she wore the cream trousers and rust-coloured blouse she had worn on TV and the sexy pointed shoes.

He stood back and let her in without a word. It was the first time she had been in the house since Alison had died.

'Here you are.' She groped in her bag as they stood there, facing each other in the hall. 'I've brought it back as promised. Perfect. Undamaged. The loan much appreciated!' She managed a small smile. 'Did you watch?'

'I did.' He found himself grudgingly returning the smile. Her presence in the dark lonely house was like a breath of sunshine. An unsuitable simile perhaps in view of her rain-soaked state, but apt, nevertheless. 'You were good. I have to admit it.'

'But hopelessly inaccurate and shaming to the department?' She was still smiling. Just. Behind the smile her face was white and strained.

He shrugged. 'I didn't spot anything too controversial.'

She had produced the box and was holding it out towards him. Ignoring it, he turned towards the kitchen. 'Come in and have a drink. It's a foul night. You needn't have come straight here, you know.' Turning on the switch he flooded the room with cold light. The window beyond the sink looked out at the black rain-soaked gardens and the drive. He made no attempt to close the blind before he filled the kettle.

Viv followed him in and put the box carefully in the centre of the bare table. She was still feeling scared and shaky after her ordeal in the car park. 'You're not going to the police, then.'

He gave a grim laugh. 'As long as it's not a replica.' Plugging in the kettle he pushed the switch.

232

She grimaced 'I never thought of that.'

'Then we'll leave it at that.' He glanced up. 'Did you take it out of its box? But of course you did. I saw you. And anyway, how could you resist?' He sighed as he answered his own question. 'I'll take it back to the museum as soon as possible. They want it for a special display.'

She shrugged. 'It seems a shame to lock it away behind glass forever. It's such a personal thing. Someone must have loved and admired it very much.' She glanced at it doubtfully, then at his face. 'Holding it in your hand,' she paused, cautiously, 'you can almost feel the last person to wear it is watching you.'

He shivered.

Venutios.

The name hung in the air between them. Venutios. Not Cartimandua.

'You don't really believe it's cursed, do you?' she asked softly.

He shrugged. 'As you say, when you hold it –' He broke off and she saw his eyes shift abruptly from her face towards the window. He was frowning and there was something like fear in his eyes. 'Did you hear that?'

'It's windy out there.' All she could hear was the kettle.

'The carnyx.' He half-whispered the word.

Viv stared at him, shocked. There was no doubt about it. He too was scared.

'Can't you hear it?' He clapped his hands over his ears.

Viv followed his gaze. All she could see in the window were the reflections of the stark room. Tidy. Neat. No dishes. No food. Clean empty worktops, table, cooker, sink. Just the kettle, belching out steam and the two people facing each other across the table, both looking towards the window. She felt a moment of her old affection and of intense pity for his loneliness, then it was gone, replaced by a feeling of unease. His fear was infectious.

'It was his brooch, not hers,' he said at last. 'Strange, as the crane is a bird more usually associated with women.'

'Hugh –'

'He is so angry. Can you hear him? He wants it back. It's the key to everything. To love and hate and revenge! Beyond the roar of the wind and the lash of the rain he is shouting out his frustration and fury!'

She stepped back from the table. 'Hugh, have you been drinking?'

She knew he had. She'd smelled it on his breath when she arrived. But not a huge amount. Nothing serious, surely.

He ignored the question. Instead he went across to the table and picking up the box he opened it and took out the brooch, holding it on the palm of his hand. 'It's beautiful. Exquisite. A bird of the underworld.' He smiled grimly.

'And a bird that brings luck in time of war, a servant of the war gods, and nearly two thousand years old,' she reminded him, afraid of what he might be going to do with it.

'He's out there. In the garden,' Hugh said, very quietly. 'Waiting for me.'

'Who?' Her mouth had gone dry.

'Venutios. I told you.'

'Don't be silly.' She was really frightened now. This was her territory. Even Pat's. But not Hugh Graham's. Never Hugh. He must be a lot drunker than she had suspected. 'Shall I make us a coffee?' With a quick glance at him she went over to the cupboards and started to pull them open, searching for cups, coffee and milk. There was almost nothing in the fridge, she discovered, just half a loaf of bread and some marmalade and about a quarter of a bottle of milk. She sniffed it cautiously, with a wave of sadness, thinking how bleak it all was now, without Alison and her passion for cooking which had always left the kitchen warm, chaotic and overflowing with food. It was a relief to switch off the frantically boiling kettle and watch the steam disperse as she made the coffee, but the sudden silence brought the sound of the wind and rain closer.

'Can you hear it?' Hugh had walked over to the window. He still had the brooch in his hand. His face was white.

'I can hear the storm.' She grimaced. 'Here you are.' She held out the mug. 'Have it while it's hot.'

He was staring out through the rain-streaked glass, his hands cupped round the brooch in front of him as though he was cupping the body of a real bird which at any moment might escape and fly out into the night.

'There it is again. Listen!' She could hear the fear in his voice. 'He wants it. He wants the brooch!'

'Hugh, don't be silly.' Cautiously she went and stood beside him. 'Have your coffee, then why don't you lock it up somewhere safe.'

His face was grey now, and she realised that he was shaking.

'Hugh? What is it?' She put her hand on his arm. Then she heard

234

it too. Far away, beyond the sound of the rain, a deep ethereal note echoing in the distance. 'What is it?' she whispered. But she had heard it before at Ingleborough and in her own small flat amongst the rooftops of Edinburgh. The haughty baying call of the carnyx.

'He's out there.' Hugh was still staring at the window.

Viv put down the mug and put her arm around his shoulders. 'Come away. It's the wind. It has to be.'

He turned towards her and she saw the despair and fear in his face.

'There's no one there.' She tried to draw him away from the window and for a moment he resisted, then suddenly he gave in and turning, he put his arms around her and buried his face in her hair, inhaling the smell of rain and shampoo and the sweet musky scent of her skin. 'Oh God, Viv. What's happening to me?'

She didn't move. His arms were strong. Secure. Briefly she felt herself relax against him, her own lonely longing intense, remembering just how much she had loved him; longed for him – her friend's husband. How agonising it had been to pretend she just liked him as a friend and colleague. How much his antagonism since Alison had died had hurt her. Gently she pushed him away. 'Hugh? Come on. Come away from the window. There are too many eyes out there. Let me draw the blind.'

He stood quite still, staring unseeing into the distance, as she went over to it. He was listening intently. 'There it is again. Can you hear it?' It was a whisper.

She nodded grimly.

'He wants the brooch.' He grabbed it off the table. 'Take it. Don't let him have it.' He pushed it into her hand. 'Take it now. Take it away. And go. Quickly. It's me he's after! He won't hurt you!' Without warning he was pushing her towards the door.

'Why does he want it?' she protested.

He shrugged. 'It's part of his story. Who knows. Just go away and take it with you!'

'Hugh!' His panic was infectious. She ran into the front hall ahead of him. She grabbed her bag and shoving the brooch, just as it was, into her jacket pocket, dug for her car keys.

'Hugh, I don't want to go out there! I can't leave you!' She was frantic. 'Come with me. Come back to Edinburgh. You can't stay here alone.'

'I have to. Don't you understand? He's made me angry so that he can feed off my anger. I'm frightened of what he'll do. Of what he might make me do! Go, quickly!'

Somehow the door was open and she found herself outside, running across the gravel. Throwing herself into the car in a complete panic for the second time that night she stabbed frantically at the ignition, turning the key at last, revving the engine. Behind her Hugh had slammed the front door. As she turned the car, gravel spitting beneath the wheels, the house was once more in total darkness.

She drove out of the gate and onto the road, and she had gone at least a mile before she pulled onto the verge. Her heart slamming under her ribs, her breath coming in quick small jerks she banged the door locks shut, then she rummaged in her bag for her mobile. Punching out Hugh's number she let it ring for a while before cutting the call and dropping the phone down on the seat beside her. She glanced in the mirror. The road was deserted, the rain drumming on the soft top of the car, lashing the windscreen, streaming down the windows. She couldn't leave him like that. He was drunk and he was frightened. She should have insisted he come with her. God, what should she do? She stared ahead along the road in the bright beam of the headlights. She would have to find somewhere to turn the car. Shakily she engaged gear and set off, more slowly this time, scanning the hedges for a gateway where she could turn. It was several minutes before she found somewhere and reversed into someone's driveway. Pausing, she tried the phone again. Again there was no answer.

Turning the car into Hugh's gate she drew up, the headlights trained on the front door. The house was still in darkness. She crept closer easing up the clutch in first gear until she was as close to the door as possible. Tucking the brooch into the glove pocket of the car she leaned on the hooter. There was no response. Staring round for a minute as she tried to pluck up the courage to get out, she studied the rain-swept flower beds, the shadowy trees, the darkness of the lawns. They were all deserted. Taking a deep breath she opened the door, she flung herself out and ran to the front door. 'Hugh!' she rang the bell and hammered on the oak panelling. 'Hugh! It's me, Viv. Come with me. You can't stay here on your own.' She crouched down and opened the letter box, peering inside. The hall was in total darkness. 'Hugh! Can you hear me?'

There was no reply.

With a sob she turned back to the car and locked herself inside again. She was drenched and cold and very frightened. She tried the mobile again. Still no reply.

Of course he wasn't answering. He had probably gone up to bed to sleep off the whisky. He had heard neither the phone nor her knocking. She sat back in the seat forcing herself to breathe slowly and deeply, trying to master her panic. Should she ring the police? But what would she say? A drunken man thought an Iron Age war lord was after him? Probably not. All she could do was go home and ring him again in the morning. Slowly she reversed the car and turned back towards the gate.

16

I

'I have seen your death, brother!' Carta was holding Triganos's forearms in a furious grip. 'Can you not listen and be warned?'

She had dragged him away from the township on foot, through the gates in the ramparts down the track out onto the moss where they would not be overheard. Nearby the red-stained waters of a mountain beck poured over the falls at the cliff edge with a roar which almost drowned her voice. 'I have seen you, with blood on your back. I have seen you fall, a sword between your shoulders!'

He was staring at her, his face white with shock beneath the tan and the carefully symmetrical tattoos. 'I don't believe you.' He was furiously angry.

'Why not? When have I ever lied?' Her eyes blazed back at his. 'Listen.' She gestured frantically at the waterfall. 'Can you not hear, even the waters are keening. Do not go, Triganos. You have a choice. The gods will not demand such a sacrifice. This land can be protected in other ways.' They were so close to the water now that droplets clung to her eyelashes and her hair.

'But it can't!' He was shouting against the roar of the falls. 'The Romans need nothing but the power of the sword to win. They have cut their way through the south of these islands like iron through butter. Tribe after tribe has fallen into slavery. No one has the power, alone, to gainsay them. They need experienced warriors to hold them back, men such as mine who can hurl them back into the sea!'

It was bravado. He had been frightened of his sister's visionary powers since he had first realised her talent when they were children. She had done it so naturally. It was a part of her, a misty smokiness behind those intense eyes, a part of her power and her fascination, and a lethal weapon when she wanted her own way. Now she was a trained seer and she was, he was beginning to think, formidable. He was determined not to let her see how wary he was of her. Stepping away from her, he was relieved to see the passion subsiding as she shook her head sadly. She followed him, scrambling down the muddy track which followed the river, steep as a ladder here and there as they made their way down into the gorge.

'You are a fool, brother. A stupid fool. You cannot defeat the Romans with a few hundred men. Nor even a few thousand. They have four legions now on British soil,' she shouted after him. 'Listen to me! Artgenos's spies report that there are twenty thousand men at their command, with as many again auxiliaries.'

Triganos frowned. He stopped, waiting for her on the slippery rocks. 'So many?'

'Have you not been listening during the council meetings?' She was exasperated. 'But of course not. You have not even been there half the time. But your friend, Venutios. He's been listening. He understands the gravity of the situation. Why in the name of all the gods does he not stop this insanity of yours?'

'The whole of the Catuvellauni and the Trinovantes have risen –'

'Rome defeated the Cantiaci and the Catuvellauni, brother. They have walked through thousands, perhaps hundreds of thousands, of men and women as though the land was undefended.' Carta shook her head. He was not going to listen to her. Already she could see the shadow of death growing closer about his shoulders. 'Does Venutios advocate this foolish charge down the country?' she asked sharply. She frowned. Venutios, she was loathe to admit, was the leader her eldest brother was not and as king of the Carvetii he had, so she had heard, more than proved himself to his own tribes-men. He was devious but he was rugged and implacable, more experienced in battle and he had been listening. All the time. And taking note. She frowned. Did he think she hadn't noticed how recently he had encouraged Triganos to go off with his companions while he himself stayed behind? Without doubt he had the makings of a first-rate commander, she would grant him that much. He listened to the Druids who brought news and advice daily from the south and he heeded the words of their own wise men. He was

239

astute and ambitious and she didn't trust him further than she could have thrown the mountain.

'Oh yes, he wants to go with us.' Triganos looked defiant. 'Indeed he does. He'll go with me, you'll see. Get back to your women's work, Carta, and leave us men to protect you.' He slapped himself on the chest with a grin, full of bravado. 'By the first snows these invaders will be back in Gaul and running for their fancy villas!'

She let him go, watching sadly as he strode back up the hillside and out of sight. Then she turned to the water. She had no offerings for the goddess save the gold bangle around her wrist. She stood for a moment on a wet outcrop of limestone, watching the roaring waters, like boiling milk with the tell-tale streaks and patches of red. Signs of blood to come.

'Sweet goddess, save him. Save us from these savages,' she cried. Pulling the bangle off she held it high for a moment over the edge of the rock. The whole area trembled beneath the thunder of the water. 'If it is your wish, protect this land and its people and guide me so that, if it has to be, I may rule them in my brother's stead.'

And not Venutios. She didn't say the words out loud. The goddess would know her thoughts.

The gold arced up as she threw it, for a second catching a stray ray of sunshine, then it fell into the greedy water and vanished. She stood for a moment looking down into the churning cauldron below the rock, staring into the foaming waters, mesmerised by the swirl and roar of the whirlpool, then at last she turned away and began the slow steep climb back to the summit of the hill. The bangle did not reappear. The goddess had accepted it.

Two days later Triganos rode out at the head of a band of warriors. 300 horsemen and women, 122 war chariots, each carrying a driver and a warrior with a full compliment of weapons and several hundred levied men. With him, as he had predicted, went Venutios of the Carvetii and Brochan of the Parisii each with nearly 1000 men and women of their own. It was an impressive sight. On their way south they would collect more from the forts and settlements along the trackways and high drove roads until by the time they crossed the Trisantona, which later men would call the River Trent, they would have more than 10,000 followers. That was the plan.

The whole settlement had gathered to see them leave. With tears and cheers the remaining women and the children, the old men and the lame had waved until they were out of sight, then slowly they turned away. Carta sighed, standing in the doorway of the feasting hall which was silent and empty. She knew she would not see her brother again. Behind her, quiet footsteps rustled through the dried heather on the floor. Their father came to stand beside her. He put his arm round her shoulders. 'A brave man, your brother,' he said softly.

She nodded.

'I have decided –' He spoke huskily. He cleared his throat and tried again. 'With Artgenos's advice and agreement, to call upon your cousin Oisín to lead the tribe while Triganos and Fintan and Bran are away. We need a strong decision-maker to take Triganos's place for the time being.'

'What!' Carta turned in disbelief. 'You can't do that! I will lead our people –'

'No, Carta. Not yet.' He sighed. 'You are not ready, sweetheart, ambitious though you are. Maybe you will never be ready. Who knows. You will need to marry again before you can think of leading us, and Oisín is a sound steady man.'

'He is wounded!'

'Which is why he cannot fight at your brothers' side. But his injuries do not incapacitate him. They are healed.'

'They disqualify him from being king!' She clenched her fists. 'The king must be unblemished or the gods will not bless him –' She broke off in mid-sentence but it was too late. Her father's rueful smile was serene however. 'As I know to my cost, daughter. I lost the throne because I was wounded, remember?' He shrugged. 'Without a council to elect him Oisín will not be our king. He is our leader for the time being.'

'And will tell me, as my brother did, to go and sit with Essylt and attend to women's work?' She spoke through clenched teeth. 'Our men despise Rome and talk of chasing away the Roman legions but they are quick enough to copy the Roman way with women, relegating them to their beds and their kitchens as though they are slaves!' Her face was flushed with anger. 'Well, I for one will not stay to be ruled by him!'

'I'm sure he will try and do no such thing!' Her father laughed out loud. 'I don't think he would have the courage.'

But already she had swept out of the house towards her own. The heather thatch was slick beneath the rain, the smoke flattened and heavy as she ducked inside. There were no lamps lit and her

241

women had not yet returned to her fireside. It did not matter. She did not intend to stay there. Her belongings bundled into a leather bag, her thickest beaver fur cloak snatched from its peg and wrapped around her shoulders, she was outside again before her father had made his way back to his own fireside. He watched sadly from the doorway as she splashed her way through the township towards the great gates which still stood open and disappeared between the ramparts. She was heading towards the Druid college in the valley. There was no need for him to have her followed to make sure she was safe. Artgenos had told him what she would do. Bellacos chuckled. Headstrong but determined, his daughter was nothing if not predictable. So be it. It would make life easier for Oisín as he looked after the remaining men, women and children and helped them prepare for winter without their menfolk there to protect and support them.

Carta did not go straight to the Druid college below the falls. First she went to the hidden cavern of the goddess.

Every part of this mountain was sacred. Every tree, every stone had its living spirit. Every part of the whole land was blessed and alive, watched over and guarded by the gods and goddesses of place, of the elements, of the seasons themselves, but some places came closer, far closer, to those other secret realms than others. Places of power, marked by the great stones of the ancients, by the sacred Cursus, and by the caves and hollows of the earth. And this place was one of them, guarded by an angry spirit that roared and howled its rage into the night when the storms sped over the high peaks and the waters rose in the rivers and streams. But she had braved it alone, initially in the dark, later with a torch lit by iron and tinder and she had gasped at the beauty and awesome grandeur of the goddess's home. A low tunnel led a long way into the hillside hidden behind gorse and thorn, both trees sacred to the goddess, then abruptly the passage opened into a vast cave, snug within the huge belly of the high peak itself. The flaming torch, held high above her head revealed stalactites and stalagmites of giant proportions, patterns of rock, dark, still waters and everywhere the reverberation of greater hidden rivers somewhere beneath her feet.

On one wall she found drawings of creatures the goddess especi-

242

ally called her own. Bears. Great deer. Aurochs, and in a corner she found their bones.

She brought offerings of gold and silver, food and wine and left them there at the entrance to the goddess's own house. Then she put out her torch and sat down alone in the dark to meditate and to pray.

'Goddess. Great spirit of the mountains and of our land, Brigantia, our queen, come to me here. Advise me. Give me the knowledge and strength I need to rule my people.' She waited in the dark, aware of a strange glow amongst the rocks and coming from the water itself. This ordeal would make her strong. And after that she would summon the handmaid of the goddess, the woman who listened and spoke to her amongst the rocks and from the sacred well and from the heart of the land itself. *Vivienne*

'Oh God!' Had she wanted this? Had she deliberately summoned Carta in the small hours of the morning or had Carta forced her way into the flat? Stiffly Viv climbed to her feet, glancing at the clock on the bookcase and with a violent shock realised it was midday.

Hugh! She had to speak to Hugh! Punching out the number, she sat listening to the phone ringing and ringing the other end. No answer. No answer machine. Just the ring tone, on and on. At last she rang off and dialled the department. 'Heather? Is Hugh there?'

He wasn't.

The Cartimandua Pin was sitting on her desk. Its box had been left behind. Staring at it almost distastefully for several seconds she picked it up at last and carefully wrapping it in tissues, she tucked it back into the drawer where it had lain for so many days, then she went to find her car.

Hugh's house was deserted. Cautiously she made her way through the rain and peered in through the kitchen window. Their mugs still stood on the central table where they had put them down the night before, and the empty Perspex box was still there as well. Walking round the back she found the curtains in the living room open and she stared in. There was no one there. The French doors when she tried them were locked. It was only then that it occurred to her to look in the garage. His car was gone. Relieved, she walked back round the front. All the upstairs curtains were open as well. If he had driven off in the night after she had left he would have

243

left them closed, surely, so wherever he had gone he had gone there this morning, and hopefully, a great deal more sober than he had been the night before.

She stood for several seconds, listening. Had they really heard the sound of a trumpet in the night? Unlikely. Had he really put his arms around her and for that short split second held her close? She gave a small wistful smile. That was probably her imagination as well. Rooting through the glove box in the car, she found a notebook and tore out a page. Her message was brief: 'Called to make sure you were OK. Ring me about the pin. V.' Pushing it through the letter box she gave another quick glance round, then she climbed back into her car.

II

Standing on the summit of Traprain Law, Hugh stared out towards the sea. The clouds were low on the ground, the rain still pouring down his neck, splashing the grass, turning the trackways to mud. The car park had been empty. There was no one on the hill at all. His head was throbbing, his eyes sore, and his mouth felt like sandpaper. He stood for several minutes feeling the cold rain running down his face and into the collar of his shirt without registering any discomfort, then at last he began to move, walking slowly across the spongy grass towards the lochan.

It was here, according to Viv on TV last night, that Cartimandua had met and married her Votadini prince. He smiled grimly. Here she had learned her arts and her skills. Here in this small muddy pool she had gazed down into the eyes of her goddess.

He laughed, an awkward harsh sound above the pattering of the rain on the surface of the water. A sound quite unlike his own voice. The voice of Venutios. Foolish woman. Did she really think she could hold her head high as a queen and a warrior among men like him?

He groped in his pocket and finding a coin flipped it carelessly into the water. A gift for the gods. Her gods. To his gods he would give something far more valuable, the gift of life blood.

It was several minutes before he moved, retracing his steps

towards the eastern slope of the hill. This time when he heard the call of the carnyx, he smiled. His men had found him. He was ready to join them.

III

Pat knew there was something wrong as soon as she pushed open the door. She dropped her bag on the carpet and listened intently. The flat had a strange congested feeling, as though dozens of people were there. Or had just left.

'Viv? Are you here?' She headed for the living room.

Viv was standing by the desk.

'Are you OK?' Pat stood in the doorway, suddenly apprehensive.

Viv didn't answer.

'Viv? Did you hear me?'

Again there was no reply.

Cautiously Pat stepped into the room and tapped Viv on the shoulder. 'Are you all right?'

'Can you see her?' Viv's voice was tight with fear.

'See who?' Pat glanced round the room. She could feel the hairs on the back of her neck beginning to stir.

'There.' Viv seemed paralysed. She gave a half-nod towards the window.

'I can't see anyone.' Pat stared round. She could feel something, though. The tense, swirling anger, rage, frustration. And then it was gone. The room was empty.

Viv gave a small cry and put her hands to her face. 'Oh shit!'

'It's all right.' Pat exhaled rapidly. 'She's gone. It's gone. Oh, Viv. What was it?'

But she knew. That was Cartimandua. Queen of the North.

The two women sat down side by side. Viv was shaking.

'After you rang to say you were coming over I thought I would cook us some supper. I came through to put some music on and all at once she was there in my head.' Viv was almost in tears, speaking through gritted teeth. 'I didn't want to do it. I'm so tired. I couldn't face any more, but she wanted to talk – and she was angry. I don't

245

know why. It's as though she blames me for something.' She raced on incoherently. 'Perhaps I'm not listening hard enough, but I'm getting so tired with all this writing and trying to sleep, and when I do she comes into my dreams as well.'

Pat glanced round the room with another shiver. 'I thought this was something you were doing deliberately,' she said hesitantly. 'Something you initiated.'

'I was.' Viv ran her fingers thorough her hair in agitation. 'But she's taking over.' It had happened when she came back from Aberlady. Carta was angry. Unstoppable. All consuming.

'And you couldn't walk away from it?'

'No.'

Pat shook her head. 'What do you want to do? Shall I ring Cathy?'

'What can Cathy do? She's already told me there's nothing wrong with me! She thinks it's my imagination. She thinks I can switch it off if I try.'

Pat grimaced. 'I tell you what. Let's have a drink. That'll make you feel better. I've brought some wine.' She hesitated. 'Are you sure you can't stop?'

'I can't. And I don't want to.' Viv stood up wearily. 'That's the point. I want to know. I have to know what happened. I just don't want to do it non-stop, all the time. I want to pick my moment.'

Pat found some glasses in the kitchen and a corkscrew and brought them through. She glanced at Viv cautiously as she opened the bottle. 'I saw you on TV last night. You were great.'

'Thanks.'

'And it's confirmed in my mind that you should do the narrative in the play yourself. You'd be a natural at it.' She passed Viv a glass. 'I've written some more of the dramatic scenes for you to read through when you feel up to it, but I think we should try recording a bit of the narrator's introduction soon to see how it sounds.'

'Record it? Ourselves?'

'Why not?'

'How will we find the people to play the other parts?' Viv sat down shakily on the sofa and took a gulp from her glass.

'Audition.' Pat smiled. It would take some juggling to get Viv to relinquish her hold on the script, but this would appease her; let her play the part of the academic which she craved. Distract her from the terrifying visions. Make way for Medb.

*

246

Viv woke suddenly, staring round in fright.

She had lain for a while in a hot bath after Pat had finally left, trying to soak away her increasing fears but it hadn't worked. The insistence of the voice in her head, her worry about Hugh, the ever-growing suspicion that Pat was up to something, her own exhaustion and her restlessness had all contributed to an uneasy sleep.

She lay still for a while trying to recall her dream. It had not been about Cartimandua and the people of Dun Righ but about Andrew Brennan, the man she had left behind in Dublin. In her dream he had held her in his arms, and tipping her face up towards his with an imperious hand, he had kissed her long and firmly on the mouth. She was, she realised, aching with longing. Which was idiotic. Andrew had been firmly consigned to the past. She could guess what had given rise to the dream. The feel of Hugh's arms around her. Her body's recognition of its utter loneliness. The knowledge that when she had left Ireland and returned to Edinburgh she had fallen hopelessly in love with another married man. She gave a wry grimace in the darkness. Hugh. Widowed, technically free, she supposed, since poor Alison had died but now her arch enemy. Her undeniably attractive arch enemy, driven into her arms not by love but by a phantom Iron Age king.

It was a long time before she eventually dozed off again but her sleep was still uneasy and suddenly she found herself fully awake once more, her senses alert. It had not been a dream which awoke her this time. She listened. Nothing. The flat was silent. Cautiously she sat up and pushing her feet out from under the bedclothes she stood up. Without turning on the light she made her way towards the door and quietly reached for the handle. The hall was in darkness, as was the sitting room beyond. She could see the outline of the open doorway clearly. On tiptoe she made her way towards it.

There was a figure standing by her desk in the shadowy darkness.

'Pat? Is that you? Why've you come back?' She groped for the light switch. As she clicked it on she caught a fleeting half-glance of a woman standing by the desk, bending over the drawer which held the brooch. It was not Pat. This woman had long red-blonde hair, thick bundled clothes, startled aggressive grey-green eyes. For two seconds she met Viv's gaze, then she was gone.

'Oh my God!' Viv clung to the doorknob. Her knees buckled. For several seconds she couldn't move, once again overwhelmed by a fear she couldn't control. At last she managed to straighten and step into the room. There was nothing there. No sign. No smell. No feeling to substantiate what she had seen.

'It's my imagination.' She whispered the words to herself firmly. 'Or a dream.'

Or a reality.

It was Cartimandua.

IV

Some messages come on horseback. Some are carried on the wind like thistledown. Carta had known the moment her brother died. She knew before he did. She knew he hadn't even been killed honourably in battle. There was a skirmish with a Roman outpost. His pony had stumbled and as it fell one of the men had hurled his sword like a spear with such force it pierced his flesh to lodge in his spine. He took only minutes to die. Fourteen of his men died that day. It was all that was needed to persuade the others to turn back.

The tribesmen had divided at Isurios, travelling in two war bands. Triganos and Fintan had taken the main roadway down through the flat eastern side of the country, following the well-used trade route through the lands of the Corieltauvi. Venutios had led the others further to the west, venturing more cautiously towards the Roman-held south-east through the lands of the Cornovii and the Dobunni.

Taking Essylt by the hand, Carta led her away from the fireside, leaving the latest baby asleep in his cradle as the women crooned their weaving songs around him. 'I must prepare you for bad news, sister,' she said gently. 'Triganos is dead.'

Essylt stared at her, her face white, her eyes enormous. 'No.' It was a protest, not disbelief.

'I'm so sorry.' Carta's eyes filled with tears. 'When the messengers come, I wanted you to be prepared.'

Essylt did not question her knowledge or hold out any hope. She sat for several minutes staring before her, her shoulders slumped, tears pouring down her face while Carta held her hand. Gradually the other women became aware of their distress and one by one they crept closer. The signs had been there for all to see. The raven of death had sat upon the roof of the royal house only two days before, two of them had seen it. Another had dropped her brooch on the floor and pricked her finger picking it up. She had thought the omen was for her. As the sound of keening began to spread through the town Carta made her way towards her father's house. The hardest task of all would be to tell him and Fidelma what, she suspected, they too would already know. When the messengers reached Dun Righ at last, the township was already in mourning.

Carta made offerings to the gods for the safe passage of Triganos's soul to the land of the ever young, and vowed to give him a piece of her mind when they met in their next lives. When she wept, she wept alone in the silence of her bedchamber late at night. She wept for the handsome carefree boy who had taught her to ride, to climb trees, to fight with a sword. She wept for the adoring brother who had given her the name 'Sleek Pony' and laughed with her when to their delight the family and then the tribe adopted it as her proper name. She could cry for him, and rage against the gods who had taken him so young, just as they had taken Riach. But for the stubborn, thoughtless young warrior who had become a king and given no more thought to the honour than he had to the bestowal of his first tattoo, and for his wasted chances, she felt nothing but anger.

Over the next few weeks the remnants of the Setantian war party trickled back to the north. Brochan with his Parisians, it appeared, had continued south towards their destiny with the invaders; of Venutios and his army there was no word.

With the high king dead, Oisín had no choice but to declare that another must succeed to the leadership and word went out that any contestants for the title should declare themselves before the next full moon. Bran had returned, but he had been wounded by his brother's attackers and was weak and unsteady on his feet. He had no desire to put himself forward. Fintan had not yet returned, though word had come that he was alive. Brochan sent messengers that he would not put himself forward. From Venutios there was no word.

Carta went to see Artgenos. 'I want to stand for election. I can rule the Brigantians. I am ready.' She fixed him with a steady gaze. 'You can't deny that I could do it far better than Triganos.'

Artgenos nodded sagely. 'It would be hard to deny that, my child.'

'And better than any of the others who are suggesting themselves for the position.'

'That too may be true.'

'Then I shall do it!' Her eyes blazed with triumph.

'I think the time has come when you can put your name forward, Cartimandua.' The old man nodded slowly. 'But it is up to the people. They will have to choose you.'

'They will choose me!'

'Then pray to the goddess to support you.' He rubbed his chin thoughtfully. 'Has there been word yet from Venutios?'

She frowned. 'None that I have heard. Why?'

'Because I would have expected him to put in a claim. He covets the high kingship as you must realise. Perhaps we should wait until he returns.'

'No!' Carta slammed her fist down on the table between them. 'If he doesn't come, then he loses his chance. He is not going to win anyway. The people will choose the heir to the Setantian claim.'

'Not necessarily.' Artgenos shook his head. 'Venutios has the advantage of experience, and age and strength, child. Could you win him over, do you think?' The old eyes twinkled.

That night Carta went to the sacred spring. Overhead the moon swam through a sea of cloud, four days from the full. With her she took offerings and her divination sticks. If the waters would not tell her what she wanted to know, perhaps the slivers of yew wood would do so.

'Where is Venutios? Do I need to fear him?' She whispered the words into the cool dark waters, conscious of the flickering candle flame behind her. Her breath seemed to clutch at her throat; her heart thudded unsteadily as she peered down. The water glowed with refracted light but the goddess was silent. She bit her lip. Feeling in the bag at her waist she brought out the bundle of sticks, with their secret markings, and held them to her breast. 'Tell me the truth,' she murmured. 'Do I need to fear Venutios?'

As the sticks fell onto the rock beside her she held her breath for a moment, eyes closed. Then at last she opened them and read the prediction of the trees: 'Yes.' She hissed the word between her teeth. Yes, she should fear him.

'And will he contest the kingship?' She gathered them up and tossed them again onto the ground.

'Yes.'

She sat for a long time there beside the water, then at last she gathered her sticks into their bag and with a bow to the goddess within her watery bower she walked slowly back up the track towards the township gates.

That night he came to her in her dreams. With his strong, handsome face, tall muscular body, hard agate eyes, he appeared in her bedroom, arms folded, golden torc around his neck, a cloak of bearskin over his shoulders. For a moment he watched her in silence, then at last he raised a hand and pointed at her. 'Do not dare to steal my throne!' His voice echoed with the thunder over the fells.

She woke with a start and lay staring up at the darkness of the roof. Far away the thunder rumbled again and she heard the hiss of rain beyond the doorway. Venutios had called upon the thunder god Taranis to support him.

On the day of the full moon before the council of the Druids and the warriors and princes of the confederation only three men stood up to claim their right by descent to the high kingship of Brigantia, two of them sons of the Setantii, one, the young king of the Textoverdi, a cousin of Fidelma, and one woman. Cartimandua. From Venutios there was still no word.

Carta's grieving for her brother had been done. His soul had moved on. Now it was her turn. Her ambition, so long damped down, burned up brightly, fired by certainty that she was the best candidate and that the gods would smile on her success. She wore a scarlet gown, with a gold headband and armlets at the gathering, and fixed the senior men and women of the tribes with a gaze so determined that they quailed. Her Setantian cousins almost at once resigned their claim without argument; Fidelma's nephew surrendered with a smile and a bow and vowed to support her to the death. Even so, it was a near thing. Without the support of Artgenos and her father and mother she would not have been chosen. It was the former who stood and argued that she was ready and Artgenos who called upon the gods to send a sign if she was not fit to be queen. In the silence that followed his challenge she waited with a thousand others, holding her breath, for a sign from the thunder god, but there was none. It was Artgenos, also, who when the

251

choosing was finished under the branches of the great oak, and her name had been shouted to the skies by the assembled tribes of the people of the high hills, saw the great rainbow arc across the forest and touch the bare peaks with a kiss of approval.

Alone in her bedchamber that night as Carta prepared for the ceremony that would bring her before the gods and confirm her marriage to the land of her fathers and mothers, she smiled at herself in the polished bronze mirror, seeing her reflection faintly in the candlelight. There were no shadows there. No black penumbra. No sign of Venutios. The gods and goddesses were at last looking on her with favour.

She had just allowed Mairghread to clasp her cloak around her shoulders against the sharp cold of the night when Artgenos was announced. Now in his early seventies, he was as upright and sure of foot as he had been when she was a child. He dismissed her women with a snap of his fingers. 'So, you have achieved your dream, Carta.'

'Indeed.' She pushed her bangles up her arm and began to select rings from the box on her candle stand. There was a fluttering of nerves in her stomach and firmly she suppressed it.

'I trust you appreciate the burden you take on your shoulders tonight. When you stand in the footprints of the gods, up on the sacred rocks, and sit upon the stone of enthronement, you take responsibility for thousands of people.' He was very stern.

'Do you think Triganos ever really realised what he was doing when he stood there?' She glanced at him, watching his face in the flickering candlelight. Her mouth was dry with fear now that the time had come.

'No. I don't. I would not have had him chosen as king. But the goddess did not feel that you were ready, Carta. So Triganos was put on the throne to keep it in trust for you. And he has died to make room for you, so give him thanks in your prayers, Carta, for his sacrifice. This is a heavy burden you are taking on, my lady, and you are young. You have not finished your full training as a Druidess, and now you won't do so. But you must never forget what you have learned. You are a Druid by blood and our learning and strength will always be yours.' He paused. 'You have picked up another weight of duties, Carta,' he went on thoughtfully, 'and they are duties you cannot be expected to perform unaided. You must marry again. And soon.'

252

'I don't need a husband to be queen.' She raised her chin.

'Maybe not, in theory. But the warriors will not all be happy to follow a woman at such a time as this. The skies to the south are red with bloodshed. The auguries are full of warnings. The Brigantian federation is large. It could split asunder very easily. Be warned. Think about this and pray to the goddess Brigantia. It is my belief she has already chosen your mate.'

Carta smiled warily. 'You think so?' She was fond of this old man, who had steered her so carefully through her childhood and through these last years. 'And the goddess has no doubt confided in you who this man is?'

Artgenos chose to look enigmatic. 'I believe so, but it is important that you consult her yourself.'

'Only after I am enthroned and blessed by all the gods of the tribe tomorrow.' She set her chin stubbornly. 'Then I will take a husband, if I choose to, as queen, and he will have to recognise me as such. Otherwise there will be no marriage.'

His eyes narrowed as he studied her face but he said nothing. The gods would decide how she should rule and only the gods.

Suddenly he was full of misgivings.

17

I

Hugh sat for a long time in the car, outside his own front door, staring at the house without seeing it, his hands clamped to the wheel, his face damp with sweat, his body ice-cold and shaking. He wasn't sure how he had managed to drive home.

He remembered walking, running, sliding, down the hillside. He remembered seeing faces, hearing the sounds of men, of shouting, the notes of horns and above them all that floating deep bay of the carnyx. Somehow he had dragged himself into the car and locked the doors. Had he really seen faces at the windscreen, shouting at him, banging on the glass? He wasn't sure. There had been so much pressure inside his head. The anger. The arrogance. The certainties.

He must have sat there for ages, fighting for his sanity, his face running with sweat, his body gripped by a succession of rigors which racked him with violent shivers. He might have sat there all day had it not been for the arrival of another car. It had pulled in beside his, all four doors had opened and people and dogs had leaped out. They were talking and laughing and one of them stooped beside Hugh's door to adjust a bootlace. As the man straightened to follow his companions towards the stile he glanced at Hugh and shouted a cheery greeting. In a flash Hugh's tormentors had gone. The scene changed. The world was normal again.

Suppressing the growing waves of nausea as best he could, Hugh had backed the car out onto the road and headed for home, but it was a long time before he managed to climb out and stagger across to the front door. Fumbling for his keys he found them at last and let himself in, slammed the door behind him and stood, his heart thundering in his chest, waiting for it to steady before he groped his way along the wall towards his study. Flinging himself down in the chair at his desk he reached for the phone. He had not noticed Viv's note lying on the floor in the hall. With a shaking hand he punched out a number. 'Meryn? I need you. Can you come?'

He was drinking black coffee when the phone on his desk rang. 'Meryn? Where are you?' His voice was steadier now and his hands had stopped shaking.

'Sorry, old boy. I think you've got the wrong chap.' The editor of the *Daily Post*'s book page, Roland McCafferty, sounded puzzled. 'I thought I'd give you a buzz and see how you are.' He was at his most affable and urbane.

'I'm fine.' Hugh took a deep breath, groping for normality. Pulling himself together as best he could, he frowned, thinking back to yesterday's review writing. It seemed a lifetime away. Normally his reviews were acknowledged by e-mail. He and Roland met infrequently for lunch. Otherwise their relationship was elegantly minimal. 'Is there a problem with the review?' He was in no mood to discuss it. His hand on the receiver was trembling again.

'No problem, old boy. Very much to the point as always.' There was an infinitesimal hesitation. 'You meant this to be a public execution, did you?'

Hugh hesitated. 'I think that's a bit of an exaggeration, Roland.'

'So, you don't want any changes? No second thoughts?'

'No. The book was a mistake. That needs to be pointed out. For the author's own sake.'

There was a moment's silence. 'Right then. OK. I thought you'd like to know we'll run it next week to coincide with publication. Catch the publicity.' He chuckled. 'Good work, old boy.'

As he hung up at the other end of the line, Roland grinned to himself wryly and shook his head. What in God's name could the poor cow have done to Hugh!

Hugh sat there, looking down at his desk, lost in thought. Had he been too harsh? If so, it was no more than Viv deserved. She could have been such a fine historian if she had been able to discipline herself more. She still could be; perhaps this was what she needed to spur her into a more accurate mindset.

He sighed, running his fingers through his thick hair. The sound of Roland's voice had re-established a sense of reality. The echoes had gone. Suddenly he was thinking properly again. Taking a deep breath he straightened his shoulders. Somehow he had to face Viv; he had to talk to her again, to explain what he was trying to do.

What was he trying to do?

He shook his head. He wanted to help her. He wanted to encourage her. Damn it, he wanted to hold her in his arms.

For a few seconds his mind drifted, conjuring up the feel and the sound of her, the scent of the rain in her hair when he had taken her in his arms before, then suddenly he tensed, swinging round to face the window, every sense alert, Viv forgotten, adrenaline pumping. Venutios was back!

He was still staring paralysed at the window when, only seconds later the doorbell rang into the silence of the house.

'Meryn!' He gawped at his visitor. 'How on earth did you get here so quickly?' He grabbed Meryn's arm and, Roland and the review forgotten as completely as Viv, pulled him inside, closing the door behind him and leading Meryn into his study as the clouds drew back and sunlight began to flood through the windows at last. 'Venutios!' He could hardly bring himself to say the word as he scanned Meryn's face. 'He's here. He followed me!'

Striding over to the leather armchair by the bookshelf Meryn sat down, stretching his long legs out in front of him. Dressed in a dark threadbare shirt of the black watch tartan, his sleeves rolled up to the elbow, and a pair of faded jeans he leaned back and fixed Hugh with a thoughtful gaze. A silver charm hung on a leather thong around his neck almost out of sight. As he moved it caught the light. 'Tell me what's been happening.'

By the end of his increasingly agitated account, Hugh was pacing up and down the room, his fists clenched, his face drawn and exhausted.

'So, where is the brooch now?' Meryn asked calmly after a moment's thoughtful silence. He did not allow Hugh to see how shocked he was.

Hugh shrugged. 'I told her to take it away.' He felt himself colouring slightly as he remembered the hug; the feel of her warm body in his arms.

'Thereby possibly putting her at risk instead of yourself,' Meryn pointed out.

Hugh sat down abruptly. 'That didn't occur to me. Dear God, I didn't mean that to happen –' He paused. 'I know you said anyone who touched it could be affected by its, what did you call it, psychometry? But she's had it for weeks and nothing's happened to her –'

'As far as you know.'

'As far as I know. It can't have done. She would have said.'

'Would she?' Meryn smiled wryly. 'It doesn't sound to me as though you two have much of a dialogue going at the moment.'

Hugh didn't answer.

'Have you spoken to her since?' Meryn went on.

Hugh shook his head.

'Then you must contact her and make sure she is all right,' Meryn said firmly. 'But first, we need to sort you out.' He stood up. 'I need my bag of tricks from the car.' He grinned easily, determined not to let Hugh see the depth of his anxiety. 'I take it you are going to leave this to me, Hugh? No protestations of cynical mirth? You do understand that this is serious, my friend?'

'I wouldn't have rung you otherwise,' Hugh said slowly. 'I admit defeat. There are more things in heaven and earth and all that. I am scared.'

He followed Meryn back into the hall and watched warily as Meryn pulled open the front door. Sunlight streamed in and Meryn stooped to pick up the piece of paper lying on the mat. He glanced down at it. 'Well, here is the answer to at least one of our questions,' he commented quietly. ' "Called to make sure you were OK. Ring me about the pin. V",' he read out loud.

'She must have come while I was up at Traprain,' Hugh said shamefacedly. 'I didn't see it.' He held out his hand and Meryn put the scrap of paper into it, then watched as Meryn went over to the old green MG and pulled out a battered leather holdall.

Shoving Viv's note into his pocket, Hugh managed a watery smile. 'Mumbo jumbo?'

Meryn nodded tolerantly. 'Lots.'

'Shall I tell you what Venutios would probably have done if he were in your position and being threatened in his own home,' Meryn said affably as he put the bags down in the study and opened the holdall. 'He would have planted a circle of skulls around the garden, facing outwards, to ward off the enemy.'

Hugh blanched. 'A ghost fence,' he said weakly. 'The archaeologists found traces of them at Stanwick. His last stand against the Romans. I'd hoped we might have become rather more sophisticated in our techniques. Please tell me you haven't got a bunch of skulls in there.'

257

Meryn smiled. 'Don't talk about sophistication in that superior way, Hugh. We are the ones who are unsophisticated. In our wild rush over the last few hundred years for what we now consider to be rational and scientific we have lost so much which has been known and valued for thousands of years and which is vital to our survival as human beings. Venutios would consider us naïve babes in arms if he could see what we believe now. He probably can see it,' he added, with a mischievous smile.

'When you say, we,' Hugh added quietly, 'you obviously exclude yourself from the generalisation. You mean me.'

Meryn shrugged. 'It's not your fault, old son. It's our culture. Remember the world he lived in was an animistic, rainbow world of links and connections which included vast echelons of spirits and gods and ancestors, people dead and people yet to be born, all of whom could be summoned to his aid.' He unpacked various bags and boxes. 'To fight him we have to use techniques which he will understand and which will work.'

'Is he a ghost, then?' Hugh sat down. He rubbed his face with his hands wearily.

Meryn was piling his containers on Hugh's desk. 'The Celts believed in the immortality of the soul. They believed in reincarnation and transmigration of the soul, what the Irish Celts called *tuirigin*, which means that they believed one could come back as more or less anything until the experience of one's soul was complete. People, yes. But also animals. Birds. There is a wonderful poem in the Irish tradition called the "Song of Amergin". In it the narrator recalls being a salmon, a bull, the wind, a wave. Or Taliesin, from the Welsh – he remembered being a spade, and fire tongs! As well as a stag, a stallion, and a cockerel. "I was dead. I was alive."'

'I know the literature.' Hugh scowled.

'Of course you do. Then you know that Venutios could have come back a thousand times in any form. His soul is still alive. Will always be alive. At present I am assuming it is between existences, ducking back and forth between this world and the otherworld, and very interested in you and your views on what went on in the life he lived in the first century Anno Domini.'

'We call it the Common Era now,' Hugh objected weakly.

'Why? Politically correct tosh.' Meryn grinned. 'The counting of our history in our current Western calendar starts from the birth of Christ. Why try and pretend it doesn't?' He straightened and looked at Hugh. 'No, don't tell me. It's all arbitrary anyway. Now. Let me show you what I have here.'

He waited for Hugh to drag himself out of the chair and come over to the desk. 'This is a Druid's protection kit,' he said with a smile. 'Luckily you don't have to believe in it. All that matters is that Venutios does.'

Hugh watched while Meryn produced a bag of white pebbles, a jar of crushed herbs, a censor and charcoal, a small bronze bowl, various packages, a bottle of spring water and other things he couldn't identify. He managed a feeble grin. 'Forget mumbo jumbo. This is hocus pocus!'

Meryn laughed out loud. 'Indeed. Even more powerful. What I am going to do is to protect your house. Like the ring of skulls but maybe more hygienic; less liable for European Community interference. I am going to protect you, and then I am going to send you to bed for a rest because you look, to put no finer point upon it, knackered. I will see to it that you do not dream and that you are not attacked in any way so you can get a decent rest and while you are doing that I will work out our plan of strategy.'

'Do I actually have to be here for any of it?' Hugh managed a self-deprecating grimace. This was very hard. In the past their relationship had always degenerated into unconfrontational banter when they touched on topics which were to Hugh completely incomprehensible. That was thanks to Alison. She had been so good at easing him past no-go areas like this. Now he had invited Meryn here to do the very things he ridiculed and he was feeling increasingly uncomfortable.

Meryn glanced up at him. He relented. Too much scepticism would be counter-productive. 'Probably not. Go on up and have a shower and a few hours' kip. Leave me in charge down here.'

Hugh did not argue. Mounting the stairs he realised just how stiff and tired he was. Not letting himself think about what might be happening in his study, he walked into his bedroom and threw himself down on the bed. It did not occur to him that Meryn had not yet had time to do more than unpack his bag; that Venutios might already be waiting for him.

It had been so easy to cut round behind Triganos and his brothers. Venutios, with a hand-picked band of followers, had broken away from his own army and cut across the country, keeping to the deep forest, following the broad river valley where there were no settlements, until they had found Triganos's encampment. Luring him away from the main band of men was child's play. A secret challenge to single combat, delivered by hand, attended only by his brothers and the fool accepted. Venutios himself had thrust the blade into his friend's back. He would make it up to him in another life. This was no dishonour. This was to save the great Brigantian alliance from annihilation; the sons of Bellacos and Fidelma were not the right men to take on the mantle of the high kingship at such a crucial time. Triganos's reign at the head of the tribes had been a disaster. With him and his two brothers dead there could be no one to contest the high king's throne.

The murders completed, he and his companions slipped away. The abandoned stolen Roman broadswords would be enough to throw suspicion elsewhere. No one would suspect him anyway. Leaving Triganos's followers to find the body of their king he melted away into the night, leaving six bodies on the ground – The three brothers and their three charioteers. The challenge, accepted with so much excitement and bravado, was over. As always Triganos had misjudged the situation. That two of the sons of Bellacos were not actually dead did not occur to Venutios. If it had it didn't matter. They would not have recognised the faces of their attackers, masked as they were by wolves' heads, and, dishonoured by their brother's death, wounded and scarred, neither would be fit anyway now to contend for the title of high king.

Returning to his own army, Venutios waited for word of the murder. It was four days in coming, four days during which he champed with impatience and fury. As soon as the news came, appropriately shocked and angry, he ordered his two most senior warriors to lead his troops south to rendezvous with Brochan and his army, heading for the Roman front. He himself planned to set off with two companions on the long ride north, back towards Dun Righ. There he would have himself declared high king.

Riding through the territory of the Corieltauvi, they were following the ridgeways and forest roads, avoiding hamlets and farms where curious strangers might delay them, heading north as fast as their horses would carry them. There was a three-quarter moon to light their way and before dawn they had made camp, eating, resting the horses, taking turns at sleeping, then they rode on.

They were once more approaching the Trisantona, riding in single file beneath the trees of the great forest when they were attacked. Exhausted, unprepared and greatly outnumbered, they were overpowered by their attackers before they knew what had happened. When it was over they had been left for dead without weapons, stripped and without their horses, lying unconscious under the trees.

When Venutios awoke it was dark. He was lying on a bed in a small room, a rushlight on a table there. Putting his hand to his head he groaned. Immediately there was someone beside him. A cool hand rested for a moment on his forehead. Dragging his eyelids open, he tried to see. A young man in the white robe of a Druid was standing beside his bed.

'Rest, good sir. You have been very ill.' The voice was gentle.

'Where am I?' His mouth was dry. It felt as though it had been scoured with ash.

'You are in our temple of healing, my friend. We found you unconscious on the track. You had been robbed of everything, even your clothes.' The young man glanced at Venutios cautiously. 'I'm afraid your two companions were dead, friend,' he went on, gently. 'Their souls had already begun their onward journey when we found you.'

Venutios lay looking up at the ceiling. He frowned, trying to think. To remember. For a long time his mind remained a blank. He submitted to the healing ministrations of the Druids, accepting food and remedies, simple woollen clothing and a healing amulet around his neck and it was only on the third day that his memory began to return. Aching from his bruises, he made his way to the chamber of the senior Druid who ran the temple complex and informed his hosts that they had been caring for the king of the Carvetii. The old Druid bowed and smiled. 'Sir, as is our sacred duty we entertain all who come here without asking their name or fortune. I am only sorry you received such poor treatment from whoever waylaid you on the forest road. Sadly there are all too many outlaws living out there these days.' He shrugged.

Venutios grimaced. 'I am going to have to beg a further lien on your hospitality, my friend. The loan of a horse and a sword so I can make my way northward again. I have to reach Dun Righ in the land of the Setantii before they receive news of the high king's death. He was murdered a few days ago by Roman war bands.'

The Druid raised an eyebrow. 'I had heard that sad news, sir. I fear you are too late to bear the tidings to the Brigantian people. They heard it many weeks ago. They have already chosen a new leader.'

Venutios stared at him, white to the lips. 'That is not possible. There hasn't been time!'

'It is two moons since Triganos died, sir king.'

'Two moons?' Venutios echoed the words soundlessly. 'I have been ill for two moons?'

The Druid nodded.

'And who –' Venutios could hardly bring himself to ask the question. 'Who has been chosen in his place?'

'His sister, Queen Cartimandua. I believe the ceremonies are to be held at the next full moon in two days' time.'

Venutios sat down on the old man's stool and put his head in his hands. The room was suddenly spinning, the blood pounding in his veins. Blindly he grabbed the flagon of mead that was pushed into his hands. He tipped it back and felt the sweetness flood his throat. 'Too late!' he whispered.

'You can be there for her coronation, if you ride fast,' the old man said solicitously. 'I'm not sure you are well enough, though.'

'I'm well enough.' Venutios spoke through gritted teeth. 'Give me a horse and a guide, my friend. I will repay you, you have my word.'

He left the temple within the hour. If he could reach Dun Righ before she was put upon the throne, by the gods he could stop the coronation!

'Stop the coronation!' Flinging his head from side to side on the pillow Hugh moaned out loud, his fingers shredding the bedspread. 'It cannot be allowed! It has to be stopped!'

262

'Hugh?' Meryn opened the door and looked in. 'Hugh, are you all right?'

One look told him he wasn't. It was too late. Venutios was already in the house. No amount of boundary protection would work now.

It was a long time since he had gone into shamanic trance to encounter spirits in their own world and it was dangerous, but what was the alternative? With one more look at the man thrashing back and forth on the bed, Meryn turned and ran down the stairs to his car. With his Druid cloak, his deerskin bodhran, and his own personal amulet of protection, Meryn sat himself cross-legged on the floor in the corner of Hugh's bedroom and quietly began to pick out a rhythm on the drum. Not only did he have to try and save his friend, but, he suspected, he had to save the woman who had charge of Cartimandua's brooch as well. As the low rhythmic beat of the drum set the shadows vibrating he heard it answered by the deep resonating note of the carnyx from the misty distances closing in around the house.

III

Cathy was already in bed. The curtains were undrawn, the windows open onto the warm night air. By the light of the single lamp on the side table the room looked calm and inviting. It was peaceful in there. Reaching into her briefcase Pat pulled out the typescript which she had taken to Viv's but not shown her. The typescript about Medb. It would have to be edited of course, she recognised that. There wouldn't be room for the full account of Medb's journey across France – Gaul, she corrected herself – nor her agonising wait at the port before she found a ship which would carry her across to Albion, her soulful promises to the ship's master, her trip with him to the market to buy new shoes and a warm cloak, the voyage during which she had been too sick to fulfil her side of any bargain with her rescuer and then her journey north, giving him the slip, avoiding the Roman invaders and the native townships with the cunning of the night-eyed owl. She was in the territories of the Corieltauvi, dressed in the white woollen robe and veil of a

Druidess, when she heard about the death of Triganos. Still there when news came of who had been chosen as his successor.

Pat threw the file down on the table with a satisfied sigh. It was good; exciting. Suspenseful. Climbing to her feet, she wandered into the kitchen. Opening the fridge and scanning the contents she found a half-drunk bottle of white wine. Helping herself to a glass, she went back into the living room.

Medb was standing by the table. With a gasp of fear Pat dropped the glass, pinned to the spot by those clear pale eyes as the glass rolled harmlessly across the rug and lay there in a pool of crystal-clear sauvignon.

'What do you want?' Pat's voice was a husky croak.

The figure did not respond.

'I'm telling your story.' Pat was starting to shake. 'Please, go away.'

The figure didn't move. It seemed solid. Pat could see every detail of the woman's face. Her blonde hair was braided into tresses beneath the woven veil which had embroidery along its edge. She wore no make-up or tattoos; her face was hard, with an unhappy line etched from the mouth downwards; the eyes were almost colourless, like the water of a mountain stream and they bored deep into Pat's soul.

'Please, go,' Pat repeated faintly. 'I've done everything you wanted. I've written your story down.'

Behind her a light came on in the hall. 'Pat? Is that you?' Cathy's voice rang out from the stairs.

The figure vanished.

Pat closed her eyes. She took a deep gasping breath as Cathy came into the room.

'Pat, what's happening –' Cathy looked round and spotted the glass on the carpet. Are you drunk?'

Pat pointed towards the table. 'There! Medb! She was there.'

Cathy wrinkled her nose. 'Oh, Pat! For God's sake!' Stooping, she picked up the glass and set it down on the coffee table with a bang. 'I'll get a cloth for the wine. Why don't you go to bed! Sleep it off!'

Pat scowled. Picking up the manuscript, she headed for the stairs. 'Sorry. But I did see her. And I hadn't had a drop. I never got that far!'

Lying in bed later she stared up at the ceiling, too scared to close her eyes. Medb was prowling round the room. She could feel her. Her mouth dry, her eyes gritty with lack of sleep, Pat clenched her fists under the sheet, hardly daring to breathe. When at last, unable to keep them open a moment longer, she felt her lids begin to close it was in the knowledge that Medb was already inside her head.

Cartimandua must die.

Was it an order? A statement? She didn't know. The voice that filled her head was angry; bitter; vicious in its insistence. As it filled Pat's whole being she knew she couldn't fight it any longer. Drifting further and further into sleep, she surrendered to the darkness.

IV

Hugh gradually was aware of a strange low thudding sound somewhere in the room near him. He frowned. It was not unpleasant. In fact it was strangely soothing, leading him out of the grey silences of sleep back towards the daylight. The sound was growing louder. More insistent. It was telling him to open his eyes.

With a groan he stretched and sat up. The drumming stopped.

'How are you?' Meryn was sitting on the floor in the corner of the room.

Hugh stared at him in astonishment. 'What?'

'We've been on a journey.' Meryn set the drum down beside him. 'A very interesting journey. To the Brigantia of your nightmares.'

Hugh swallowed. Swinging his feet to the floor he groaned again. 'What happened?'

Meryn rose and stood looking down at him thoughtfully. 'I followed you into your dreams in order to confront Venutios if he would let me.' For the first time Meryn frowned.

Hugh grimaced. 'Did he?' He couldn't quite hide the scepticism in his voice.

Meryn shook his head. His approach had been met with anger and derision.

'So, he's going to go on haunting me?' Hugh could not keep the fear hidden. 'Why?'

Meryn was silent for a moment. His glimpse of the whirling distances which surrounded Hugh had been terrifying and confusing. The past had been reawakened, and like a sleeping giant who has been prodded and goaded into life it was gaining strength and momentum with every second that passed.

Venutios was not amenable to reason or persuasion. Nor were the two women whose shadows swirled around him.

'Hugh, I want you to listen to me.' Meryn spoke slowly and thoughtfully, his eyes on Hugh's face. 'Venutios has gone for now but he is dangerous and I believe he poses a real threat to you and to anyone involved with this brooch of yours. You must retrieve it. As long as Viv has it in her possession she is in danger.'

'Danger?' Hugh stared at him. 'What sort of danger?'

Meryn remained silent for a moment or two, thinking. 'Danger of possession; of physical harm.'

Hugh blanched. 'Then what. What do I do with it?'

'I suggest you give it back to the museum. It has lain there for a long time without interference. It may be that it is safe there.'

Or maybe not. Was the brooch the catalyst that had awoken this angry man from the sleep of ages, and if so, why did he want it back so badly? Meryn sighed. 'Ring her, Hugh. Ask for it back and bring it to me.'

His cottage was a safe environment. Venutios would not be welcome there. On his own ground, maybe Meryn could fight him.

V

'Pat!' Viv caught her arm and pulled her in through the door. It was just after nine a.m. and Pat was panting from the stairs. Her face was white and strained and drawn with exhaustion. 'The brooch has gone. It's been stolen!'

Pat put down her bag and, hand to chest, tried to regain her breath. 'What do you mean, stolen?'

'It has gone. Look!' Viv gestured towards her desk. The drawer in which she had put the brooch was lying on the floor, the contents scattered on the rug. 'After the TV programme I took it back to

Hugh. He told me to keep it until it could be returned to the museum so I put it back in that drawer.'

Pat sat down on the rocking chair. 'Christ! Did someone break in? Have you called the police?'

Viv shook her head. 'It was Carta.'

'What?' Pat froze.

'Carta was here again last night. Standing there –' She pointed towards the desk.

They both stared at the spot, then at each other. 'Something happened to me last night, too,' Pat said quietly. 'When I got back. Medb was there.' She shivered, eyeing Viv's face 'What's happening to us?'

Viv sat down on the sofa. 'I don't know what to do. I brought the brooch back because Hugh thinks he is being haunted as well – by Venutios.'

'Have you told Hugh it's gone?' Pat's eyes were fixed on the drawer still lying on the floor.

Viv shook her head.

'Do you think, if Carta took it, it will all stop?'

Viv shrugged. 'It's worth a fortune. It can't disappear. Who would believe us?'

'Hugh would.' Pat looked at her hopefully. 'Wouldn't he?'

'I don't know. I've tried ringing him. There's no reply.'

They sat for a moment in silence, then Viv stood up. Wearily she stooped and began to collect the bits and pieces lying on the floor around the drawer. Throwing them inside it she slotted it back into place.

'What about fingerprints?' Pat said suddenly. 'Does it matter that you've touched it?'

'Fingerprints!' Viv retorted. 'Do you think a ghost has fingerprints? No one else was here last night. The door was locked –' She stopped abruptly. Once before the door had opened in the night when she had thought it closed. She shook her head. 'Besides, I saw her standing there.'

Pat stood up. 'I can't stand this any more. Let's get out of here.' She turned towards the door. 'Are you coming? Let's get some breakfast as Georgio's, then go for a walk or something. Let's just get out of this flat.'

As they headed down the winding stone stairs towards the street neither woman heard the crash and splinter of breaking glass or sensed the wave of anguish and frustrated anger which exploded behind them.

VI

They went to Traprain.

'Bloody hell!' Pat was bright red in the face. 'Remind me to give up smoking, somebody. You mean these people lived on the top of this thing?'

Viv laughed. Think of the view when you reach the top. It'll be worth it, I promise. The Celts followed on in the tradition of making a point of living in high places where possible. Some people think that is what Brigantia means. People of the high places.'

'Shit!' Pat was not seeing the romance of the setting. She paused, catching her breath. 'But hang on, this isn't Brigantia, is it.'

'This is the land of the Votadini. Their northern neighbours and at least in my book, allies.'

'And your professor doesn't agree with this, right?'

'No, he thinks we should avoid all supposition.'

'And from your point of view it's not supposition.'

'No way. I'm certain.'

'Good enough for us.' Pat laughed. 'OK. Race you to the top!'

The excursion cheered them both and windblown and tired, they returned just before four.

'What next?' Pat waited while Viv fumbled with her keys. 'A trip to Brigantia proper?'

'Why not.' Viv pushed open the lower door and they stepped into the chilly vestibule at the foot of the stairs.

Pat frowned. She could feel it already. The strange oppressiveness which had permeated the flat that morning. They climbed the stairs, then she waited as Viv slotted her key into the lock. As she pushed open the door Pat heard her give an exclamation of irritation. 'It smells awfully odd in here –' Her next words were cut off by a small cry of fear. 'The mirror! Oh God, the mirror!'

'Viv, what is it? What's wrong?' Pat moved forward but was brought up short as the door slammed in her face.

'Viv, let me in!' She banged on it with her fist. 'What's wrong? Oh God! Viv! Let me in!' She knelt down and forced open the flap of the letter box, trying to see through it. There was a strong smell of damp and an icy coldness coming from the flat. And total silence. There was no sign or sound from Viv. Desperately Pat banged on the door with her fists, then at last with a sob of frustration she sat down on the top step of the stairs and dragging her bag off her shoulder began to rummage in it for her mobile.

VII

The ceremony began before dawn. Dressed in plain undyed linen, her feet bare, Cartimandua was led in a procession of her Druids, bards and seers to the place on the hillside ordained by the gods for her union to the goddess of the earth. In days gone by, as told by the bards, such ceremonies were prolonged and secret, but now in a celebration before the tribes she was elevated onto the place where her foot would fit the footprints of the goddess and onto the stone upon which she sat, and which held all the knowledge of the earth and the sun and moon and stars.

Artgenos, Archdruid of the Brigantes, stood before her in his finest robes and turned to face the people. 'Cartimandua has been brought here before you to take up the mantle of high kingship which was worn by her brother and before that by her father. She has been chosen by the Druids after consultation with our gods, and by the warriors who will follow her leadership. Before I place upon her head the diadem of the gods, is there any here who will challenge her right?'

He paused. Silence fell over the hundreds of men and women who were crowded around the high rock. Every pair of eyes was focused on her. Cartimandua held her breath. No sound was heard. No voice. If anyone was going to contend for the title they could do so now. They could claim precedence. A man could claim he could better lead men into battle. Then from the distance a circling eagle let out a yelping cry. There was a sharp intake of breath from those around her. Was this a message from the gods? Did the eagle support their queen or was it crying out in its despair? Every eye switched to Artgenos who stared up, his hand shading his eyes to follow the great bird with its golden feathers catching the light of the hidden sun as the horizon in the east grew ever brighter.

Carta swallowed. She could feel the chill of the dawn creeping over her. Her bare feet on the rock were like ice. It seemed an age before Artgenos turned back to the people. 'The gods have spoken,' he shouted. 'They confirm their choice. Cartimandua is high queen of all Brigantia.'

As the cheers rang out around them he reached for the golden diadem and as the sun broke the horizon in a blaze of glory he set it upon her brow, then as the sun rose clear of the hill he anointed her with blessed water and sacred oil. Into her hands he placed a wand of sacred wood, and an orb of rock crystal. Then he bade her stand and repeat the sacred words of the tribes after him.

Her vows made, the tribe's genealogy recited by the sennachie, her praises sung by three bards and three harpers, the people's songs of praise and rejoicing sung, echoing across the fells, she led the procession back down to the forest where, beneath the great council oak she was placed on her high seat, and there safely within the circle of her tribe she ordered the first of the three days of feasting and celebrations to begin.

Conaire, having sung her praises until he was hoarse, had disappeared into the crowds to replenish his cup of mead. When he returned he fought his way through the crowds to her side, his face white. 'I have just seen an outrider from the fells. Brochan is approaching at the head of a huge army, great queen.'

Carta met his gaze. 'You think he comes to oppose my election?' She glanced across at Artgenos who was seated some way from her. The old man caught the look and wearily he rose to his feet and approached her. He frowned at the news. 'He is too late to oppose your election in law, but that is not to say that he might oppose it by force.' He shook his head. 'I saw no signs of opposition in the stars. Nor in the auguries I performed last night.'

'Then there are none.' Carta rose to her feet. Stepping forward she lifted her arms for silence, feeling the weight of the great gold bracelets slide up her arm, and slowly the shouts and laughter and singing died away. 'My people,' she cried as she stood before them, an imposing figure in her white gown and tunic and her golden diadem and torcs. 'It seems that our neighbours the king of the

270

Parisii and the king of the Carvetii are on their way with the armies they led to fight against Rome. We must bid them welcome and have our feast prepared in readiness for their arrival.'

Sitting down again as a great cheer rang out around them she grinned at Artgenos. 'At least they are prepared for visitors,' she said. 'I would not believe that Brochan would oppose me. Never in a dozen lifetimes would he put himself forward as high king.'

Artgenos shrugged. The decision was made. Her fate was sealed. All he could do now was leave it in the hands of the gods.

Her estimation of Brochan's reaction proved right. When the vast army drew up to camp on the fells outside the walls he came at once and knelt before her, offering his homage and support. He brought news of her missing brother. Fintan was still sick from his wounds and being cared for in a healing temple far to the south but sent her his blessing; Bran was far more sorely wounded. He had not yet awoken though he still breathed.

'And Venutios?' Carta had scanned the crowds around Brochan and seen no sign of him. 'Is he not with you?'

Brochan frowned. 'I had thought Venutios would be here already, my queen. He left a fortnight before we turned back north, anxious to be at your side.' He looked away suddenly and she read his embarrassment correctly.

'He set off to stand in opposition to my claim?'

Brochan shrugged. 'Who knows what he decided. Perhaps he changed his mind. Perhaps he rode back to Caer Lugus.' He glanced over his shoulder. 'I have many of his men in my army, lady. He left them under my command.'

Carta smiled at him. 'Then let it be your command that all your men, and his, join our celebrations.'

That night she lay awake for a long time in her lonely bed going over the events of the day in her mind. Amongst all the glory and excitement and beauty of the ceremonies and celebrations, one thing stood out as a dark shadow cast over the sun. The absence of Venutios. His presence there would have conveyed his approbation; his approval; his blessing. The fact that he was not there denied her all three. She thought back over the ceremony and again heard the cry of the eagle above her as the sun rose. Was Artgenos wrong? Had Venutios returned home to the centre of the land of the Carvetii to invoke the great god, Lugh, the protector of his tribe, the god of victory and light against her?

271

Unable to sleep she rose and, wrapping her cloak around her shoulders, walked out into the central chamber of the house. It was deserted. Her guards remained outside, her ladies were asleep at last in their own quarters. Walking over to the fire she stirred the peats, kindling a flame from the smoky embers and sat down in the flickering light, reaching into her bag for the bundle of yew slips she used for prophesy. Praying over them, she let them fall upon the floor and leant forward to read their message.

There was a blackness which she could not read in the pattern of the staves though they showed clearly that Venutios was not at Caer Lugus. Puzzled, she shuffled them and tossed them down again. He had gone to Dinas Dwr. Why? And who was the woman there with him? A shiver of apprehension settled across her shoulders as a figure appeared from the shadows behind her. 'My queen?' It was Mairghread. 'You need your sleep. There is so much to do tomorrow.' The woman stood looking down at the pattern of the sticks on the floor at Carta's feet. 'Do you see blessings in the future?'

Carta shuffled them together and put them back in their linen bag. 'I see many things, Mairghread.' She rose to her feet with a smile. 'Will you bank the fire again, my dear, while I go back to my bed. I need to wake at dawn.'

She was woken by the clear fluting of the blackbird and she lay still for a moment listening to its message. The gates to the other worlds were open. In the cold dawn light the township slept in silence as she made her way to the shrine among the rocks and knelt before the stone head of the goddess. She made her offerings, then she bent to look into the dark depths of the ice-cold water. There the picture was clear; Venutios lay on a bed of furs. In the crook of his arm she could see the woman's blonde hair spread across the pillows. Even though those chilling eyes were closed she recognised the face. The woman in his arms was Medb of the White Hands.

18

I

It was half an hour before Pete and Cathy arrived, one of the longest half-hours of Pat's life. Every few minutes she stood up and called and rattled the door but there was no reply, no sign that Viv was in there at all. By the time they had joined her on the landing, Pat was trembling with shock and fear. 'I didn't know what to do. Perhaps I should have called the police.'

'Have you any keys?' Pete banged on the door.

Pat shook her head. 'It's Cartimandua,' she said softly.

'Oh come on, Pat!' Cathy eyed her sternly.

Pete snorted. 'Let's get a grip on reality here.'

'No, Pete. She's angry. She wants the brooch. Viv thought she'd taken it, but –' Pat shrugged.

Cathy and Pete stared at her in silence for several seconds, then they glanced at each other.

'Whatever is happening, we have to get in here,' Cathy said at last.

'Can't you break the door down?' Pat looked from one to the other desperately.

Pete gave a wry grin. 'That's an old oak door. None of your modern plywood stuff.' He ran his fingers down the wood. 'Is there another way in? Windows, for instance. If there's even a remote chance there are burglars in there, how would they get in?'

Pat shook her head. 'There are lots of little windows, facing in all directions, some onto the roofs, but they are all too high.'

'Then it has to be the police.' Pete looked from one to the other. I don't see what else we can do.' He turned one last time towards the door and putting his shoulder to it, threw his full weight against it. It flew open, precipitating him into the hall.

'Viv!' Cathy pushed past him as he tried to regain his balance. 'Viv, are you all right?'

There was no reply.

'Wait! Let me go first.' Pete caught her arm.

Viv was sitting in the rocking chair, her eyes on the opposite wall, a half-smile on her lips. She was alone, but the mirror that had hung above her desk was lying on the floor, smashed into a thousand pieces.

'Viv? Are you OK?' Cathy went to her and crouched in front of her. 'Didn't you hear us knocking?'

Viv did not react. She was rocking gently back and forth.

'Viv, can you hear me?' Cathy spoke a little more loudly. Behind her Pete had quickly looked round the flat. Satisfied there were no intruders, he was examining the door.

'Viv!' Cathy's voice was louder now, more commanding. 'Wake up! Do you hear me. Now!' She snapped her fingers in front of Viv's nose. For a moment nothing happened, then with a start Viv sat up, her eyes focussing with difficulty on Cathy's face.

'Cathy? What are you doing here?' She looked confused.

'Pat called us, when she couldn't get in.'

'What's happened to the mirror?' Viv cried out suddenly. 'It's broken!' She was staring down at it in horror.

Pete stooped over the broken glass. 'Don't worry. We'll clear it up.'

'It was Carta, wasn't it.' Viv clutched at the arms of the chair. 'She was angry we went out.'

'I'm sure there's a rational reason, Viv,' Pete said calmly. 'The wire must have broken.'

'The mirror was bolted to the wall, Pete.' Viv tried to smile. 'No, It was Carta. I know it was.'

'Come on, Viv.' Cathy pulled the desk chair over towards her, hearing it crunch over the broken glass and sat down. 'What really happened?'

'Happened?' Viv still appeared to be confused.

'The door was locked. None of us could get in.'

'Couldn't you?' Viv's confusion was genuine. 'Did I fall asleep?'

'You were in some kind of trance state.'

Viv shook her head. 'No. I'd remember if I was. I always remember, so I can write everything down.'

274

'And you don't remember anything?'

'No.'

'How you slammed the door in Pat's face?'

'I didn't. I wouldn't.'

'Well, someone did.'

'It was the draught.'

'I doubt it. If it was the draught why didn't you open it for her?'

There was a moment's silence. Viv shook her head slowly. 'She was here, wasn't she. Like before. Cartimandua.'

'No, Viv. It was you.' Cathy was looking very stern. 'I think you resent Pat being here because she comes between you and this obsession of yours. I think you deliberately locked her out.'

'No.'

'Yes. You may not realise it. You may genuinely not remember doing it, but I think that's what happened. Then when you realised we were talking about calling the police you came and unlocked it.'

'Cathy, that is insane. I did no such thing.'

'Are you sure?' Cathy held her gaze.

'Of course I'm sure.' Viv looked down at her hands. 'I'd remember if I'd done something like that.'

'Would you?' Cathy smiled reassuringly. 'Not necessarily. And no, I'm not saying you're insane. Far from it. You're stressed and very tired. Perhaps we should leave you to rest.'

'But I don't want you to go!' Viv cried. 'Please. I need you here. I'm scared on my own.' She paused, looking round the room at the three of them in real anguish. 'I'm so scared.'

There was a long silence. No one moved. Viv was shredding a tissue between nervously twitching fingers.

Pete retreated to the sofa. 'Would you like to come and stay with us, Viv?' He said gently. 'There's plenty of room. You're right, you shouldn't be here on your own.'

Viv shook her head. She glanced up. 'There is nothing wrong with this flat. Christ! There's nothing wrong with me!'

'No one said there was,' Cathy put in. 'You just need some sleep, love, that's all.'

Viv shook her head. 'I've slept. I'm not tired.'

'I think Viv is right. It was Carta,' Pat said at last. She sat down next to Pete. 'There was half an hour at least while I was out on the stairs. She was here with you, wasn't she. You were so

275

engrossed you didn't hear me knocking. I don't think you locked me out. I think she did. And I think she opened the door only when you had stopped listening to her because you were too tired to listen any more. Are you sure you haven't written something down?'

Viv shook her head. She glanced round helplessly. 'I haven't got a notebook here –' They were all still neatly stacked on her desk next to the computer which was turned off.

'But you want to write it down before you forget.'

'I have forgotten.' Viv looked down dully at her hands, folded between her knees. She was near tears.

'So you are saying that Carta – whoever, whatever she is – is capable of locking and opening doors?' Pete asked wryly.

All three women looked at him. Pat gave an involuntary shiver. 'She is also capable of doing that.' She pointed down at the broken glass. 'Scary thought.' She frowned and leaned forward suddenly. There, amongst the glass lay the brooch. She picked it up and held it out to Viv on the palm of her hand. 'She brought it back. Why? What is she trying to tell us?'

Viv stared at it in silence. The atmosphere of the room had changed. It was tense, dark, as though a storm cloud had drifted between them as they sat looking at the jewel on Viv's palm. For a moment the four of them were transfixed.

'She's getting more real and stronger every time,' Viv said quietly. Her mouth had gone dry. 'And the awful thing is, I don't want it to stop. Whatever she's doing, I don't want the story to stop.'

'It has to,' Cathy put in sternly. 'This has gone far enough.'

Viv shook her head wearily. 'On the contrary. It hasn't gone nearly far enough.'

'Cathy's right, Viv. This is getting dangerous,' Pat put in. 'You must see it is. Look what she can do!'

'If it is her,' Pete said quizzically. 'We haven't established that, have we? Not beyond all doubt.'

'I don't think we need to. We will just assume that whatever is happening it is not good for Viv's wellbeing,' Cathy said firmly. She paused abruptly. 'You can't stay here on your own. You must come back with us.'

Viv shook her head. 'Hasn't it dawned on you, Cathy? It doesn't matter where I am. If I come to your flat she'll come with me. Time and place mean nothing to her. She's dead, for God's sake!'

Medb had seen Venutios in the clouds and in the waters of the river and in the flight of the birds: a man who would be her ally. A man who hated Cartimandua as much as she did. It was easy finding him. She followed the direction of the wind and the stories of the foresters she met on her journey towards Brigantia. At first she thought they were directing her to Dun Righ where Cartimandua had been chosen as high queen, but the gods were more subtle than that. The hero of her dreams was wounded. He was weak and he travelled slowly. At first he had followed the tracks north-west, towards the crowning, then he had veered away from the direct route and followed the secret paths towards the home of the north wind. When he reached Dinas Dwr he had resumed his own identity at last and as king of the Carvetii he had been fêted and made welcome by those who remained in the township, and there he stayed for a few days while he regained his strength. Many of the warriors and their wives had gone to Dun Righ for the great celebrations. Those who remained were pleased to entertain him.

Medb arrived on foot, late at night as the gates were about to close. A tall, beautiful woman, in the white robe and veil of a priestess of the woods, she was shown at her request into the guest house where Venutios was awaiting his supper. Looking up he took in the beautiful face, the fair silken hair, the clear eyes and he rose to his feet to greet her.

Within minutes he was ensnared. They ate together and later they lay together on the heaps of furs which had been lavished on the bed in the guest chamber. Her body was as beautiful as her face, this lithe, exquisite woman who had wandered in from the darkness of the forest. Venutios did not enquire where she came from. Enough that she was a priestess; a Druidess who served the goddess of the forest.

'And why, great king, did you not challenge Cartimandua for the high kingship of Brigantia?' she whispered as she lay in his arms. 'Surely you are the one they would have chosen?'

He lay back, staring up at the ceiling. 'So I thought. But the gods must have decided otherwise. Why else would they have waylaid me on my way to Dun Righ? Why else would they have scarred me?' The wound the robbers had inflicted across his chest had still not knitted properly. That was the reason he had not gone straight to the crowning. No one would elect a wounded man who could barely sit in the saddle.

She smiled, running her fingers across the raw, jagged skin. 'I think we can do something about that, my lord,' she said softly. 'Cartimandua will go nowhere for a while. She will wait for you.' She bent and ran her tongue lightly across the wound, leaving him shuddering with desire. 'Then you will go and challenge her.' She looked up and narrowed her eyes. 'I have seen the future, King Venutios. I have seen you as high king of all Brigantia. It will be you and no one else who brings Cartimandua to her knees.'

III

'I convinced them to go on without me,' Pat said, shutting the door. 'I've been thinking about what's happened. They don't understand.'

Viv raised an eyebrow. 'I thought Cathy of all people would believe me.' The others had stayed to help clear up the glass and finally left about an hour before.

'She's a scientist, Viv. There's no chance she's going to admit any of this is real.' Pat came over and stood staring down at the brooch which lay on the table by the window. 'What are you going to do with this?'

'I want to give it back to Hugh, but he's not answering the phone.'

'Don't give it to Hugh!'

'Why?'

'You mustn't.' Pat frowned. 'Perhaps he doesn't realise the power of Venutios, Viv.' She narrowed her eyes, studying the brooch. 'You can feel it.' She held her hand about six inches above the brooch, palm down, as though assessing its warmth.

Viv frowned, watching her. She swallowed nervously. 'Don't touch it, Pat.'

'I'm not going to.' Pat hadn't shifted her gaze. 'I'll tell you what we're going to do. We'll take it back to Stanwick.'

'What?' Viv stared at her incredulously.

'You heard. That's where it came from, didn't it? We'll hide it there.'

'That's insane. It's valuable –'

'And it was perfectly safe for two thousand or so years, give or take. Wasn't it?' Pat faced her with determination. 'It's the perfect solution.'

'What if someone else finds it?'

'They won't. We'll put it somewhere no one will find it. Then Cartimandua will stop pestering you. And so will Hugh.' She smiled.

Viv sat down abruptly. 'It's certainly an idea.'

'It makes sense, doesn't it.' Pat was persuasive. 'Then at the same time you can introduce me to the wonders of Brigantia. Let's go for the weekend.'

19

I

'It's not a high place! I thought hill forts were all dramatic like Traprain.' Feeling obscurely cheated, Pat stared round as Viv pulled the car into the side of the road. They were in a lush area of farmland on the edge of a small Yorkshire village. Nearby, half-obscured by the hedge was a gate and a bank, and above it the grass mound which was, according to the Heritage sign nearby, the way up to the Stanwick Fortifications.

They stood for a moment, staring at the sign, taking in the extent of the area. The walk around the walls it informed them would be about six miles; the original area was developed into a huge town-ship covering some 650 acres.

'But I suspect at the time we're dealing with, the start of Carta's reign, this was a relatively small place,' Viv said thoughtfully. 'She developed it later. Or someone did. But even so we shouldn't underestimate the size of the population in her time. We're not talking just a few souls hiding in the woods.'

'Yet the Romans defeated them.' Pat frowned. 'Why? How?'

They opened the gate and climbed the steps to the top of the earth rampart.

'That is what our play is about,' Viv replied. 'Why the Romans won when they were far outnumbered.'

The banks of the rampart were wooded and thick with brambles and nettle. Viv shivered. She could feel Carta here. Almost see the shadows of those long ago Brigantians flitting through the trees. After a night of silence, Carta was back.

'Are you OK?' Pat had noticed her hesitation.

Viv nodded. The brooch was in her pocket, wrapped in several layers of protective foam and polythene inside a small airtight plastic box. 'I'm still not sure this is the right thing to do.'

'It is.' Pat was very positive. She smiled. 'Come on. Let's decide where to put it. Stooping beneath the tree branches they pushed their way along the top of the dyke until they came to an area which had been cleared below it. 'Wow.' Pat lowered herself down the bank, sliding through nettles and dock until she reached the bottom. 'Look at this. Is this original?' The ditch had been carefully excavated at some time; there were signs of building and a stretch of the ancient wall stood out clearly above them on the top of the rampart.

Viv followed her down. 'I think Wheeler rebuilt this bit,' she said, staring round. 'But there are places here we could hide it.'

'Under rocks. Or in the wall itself. I wonder if any of the stones are loose?' Pat tried to climb the rampart to the base of the wall, slipped and fell forward on her hands and knees. 'Here! Look, Viv. These stones seem to be unsteady.' She pulled at one or two and they fell around her feet.

'I don't know. Isn't this a bit obvious? Supposing someone came here and found it? Supposing people came with metal detectors?'

'They're not going to detect a wall,' Pat said, scanning the area in front of her. 'Especially if they knew it's already been excavated. There would be nothing to find.' She was feeling her way along the stones. 'Do you know where they found it in the first place?'

Viv shook her head. She was walking along the flat bottom of the excavated ditch. Carta was there, at her side. She could feel her. She could feel anxiety. Anger.

'I don't think she wants me to leave it here,' she called. 'I can feel her.'

Pat paused. She closed her eyes and took a deep breath. Medb wanted it. Medb wanted the brooch to be put exactly where it had been found. Medb had brought them here because . . .

'I have a present for my king.' Medb was in his arms as they stood on the ramparts, looking north towards the forest. All around them the wall had crumbled. They could see where Bellacos's workmen had made a start on the new defences, but they had stopped, leaving steps cut into the rampart and the stone wall no more than a few courses high.

Venutios smiled down at her. 'Indeed?' He dropped a kiss on her head. 'It seems to me you have already given me enough presents, little Medb. My health and strength and by your magic arts a vanishing scar. What more could I want?'

'This.' She reached into the pocket of her robe and produced a small package. It was something she had brought from the gold-smith who lived near the western wall of the township. A man of unparalleled skill, he had settled in Dinas Dwr only the year before and had been reluctant to part with one of his most beautiful pieces. He was still uncertain how she had persuaded him.

Unwrapping it, he raised an eyebrow as the beautiful jewelled bird flashed in the sunlight. 'This is indeed lovely.'

'Wear it on your tunic.' She reached for it and pinned it onto his cloak. 'It is a magic pin. It will bring you luck and health and strength whenever you need them.' The enchantments she had performed herself this time. She no longer had need of anyone else to install blessings or curses on her behalf.

He laughed. 'I am truly blessed. Thank you.'

'And you will keep it forever.'

'I will keep it forever.' Taking her into his arms he drew her close and kissed her again. Unknown to her, he had already despatched a coronation gift to Cartimandua. It was only polite, and it would keep the lady guessing.

'Pat? Are you all right?'

Viv was looking up at her, as Pat stood, unmoving, balanced at the foot of the wall.

'I'm OK. Fine.' Pat turned round. Her face was white and she was sweating profusely. 'Look. Here. There's a rabbit hole or some-thing at the foot of the wall. It goes in miles. We could shove it in there and then block it with smaller stones. What do you think?'

'Perfect.'

It took them only a few minutes, then they scrambled back to the top of the rampart and stood looking down. There was no sign from any angle of where they had been.

'We will be able to find it again?' Pat laughed. She knew she would find it. Medb would see to that.

Viv nodded. 'I have made a note. Don't worry.'

'Good. Then let's go on a bit, shall we? How long is this path?'

'Six miles. It said so on the notice.'

'Oh.' Pat deflated visibly. 'OK. We can do this. Think of the weight falling off.'

She led the way for a few paces further. When she turned back to face Viv she was herself again. 'OK. I give up. Do you know what I want to do? I've brought my digital voice recorder with me. I think we should try a bit of dialogue here. On site.'

Viv frowned. 'Won't it sound odd?'

'No! That's the whole point. It will sound outdoors. It will give atmosphere. And it is the real place. It may not work, but I think we should try it.' She led the way to a fallen tree and sitting down on the trunk, rummaged in her bag for the recorder. Her hands were shaking. She could feel Medb there watching them. 'It will give us an idea of how it would sound. The wind in the trees, the outdoor ambience. That sort of thing.'

'Who's going to speak?' Viv sat down beside her.

'Both of us.'

'Did you bring the script?'

Pat nodded. 'Here you are. You start. A bit of Cartimandua, or that lovely piece you wrote for the intro by the narrator, perhaps.'

They both had muddy hands after the burial of the brooch. Clicking the little machine on, Pat held it out.

II

For three days Artgenos did not mention the subject of husbands, but Carta knew he would not let the matter rest, so now, as she enjoyed her exalted position on the raised seat at the centre of her warriors she allowed herself to scrutinise the kings of the visiting tribes.

There were only two contenders when it came down to a serious choice. Brochan of the Parisii. His would be a useful and much-needed alliance, though he was older than she would have liked. He was a good-looking man, twice widowed, strong-willed, much respected by his warriors, a wise man who would rule at her side with strength and diplomacy. And there was Artios, of the Gabrantovices, seated beside her now, attentive, handsome, adorned with the latest tattoos, bejewelled. A man with a dozen trophy heads at his door. A tough extrovert with a wonderful singing voice and a string of concubines but as yet no senior wife.

There would have been one more: Venutios of the Carvetii, but even had he been there she would not have considered him; he would not be a man to lie quietly beside a wife who was a queen in her own right even had she been able to countenance the thought of him as husband. At first she had wondered if he would appear at the crowning after all. Amongst the hundreds of on-lookers it was easy to miss a face, but he, as a king in his own right and an ally should have been there, with his hand beneath her elbow as Brochan's and Artios's hands had been as she was raised towards the sun. He had not appeared. It was a studied insult.

At the great feast it was Artios, beside her, who had taken the warrior's portion of the meat. A horrified silence spread from guest to guest. Surely this should be the queen's.

Artios stood up, the succulent joint in his hands. He raised it as though offering it to the gods of the fire, then turning he presented it to her. His jewelled dagger in his hand, he cut off a tender portion and held it out. 'Queen of sunlight and of the moon. Daughter of fire, Lady of the stars, your portion by right and by inheritance.'

She took it, smiling, and found to her delight, skewered to the meat, by a small silver pin, a beautifully worked golden ring, the interlaced design depicting a horse's head, the flowing mane drawn round to form the circle for her finger. For a moment she hesitated, thinking of another jewelled horse, another man, but she put the thought resolutely behind her. Riach and her little son inhabited another world.

'A sleek pony, for a sleeker, golden queen.' He bowed and she laughed and the men nearest to them roared their approval.

Already Conaire was moving closer, drawing his fingers across the strings of his harp, working a verse into his song to capture the occasion.

Not to be outdone by his rival, Brochan came forward. Raising his hand he beckoned a servant from the back of the room and the man approached bringing with him two young wolfhounds. Each had a jewelled collar with a plaited soft leather leash. 'A gift fit for our great queen,' he said with a bow. He took the leads and handed them to her. 'Trained by my best hound master they will serve you with their lives, great lady. As will I.' He held her gaze and she was aware for the first time of the strange topaz colour of his eyes.

So, they would court her openly, before the world, these kings, and as publicly she would have to choose one of them.

Artgenos was sitting in the shadows watching, his arms folded beneath his cloak. Feeling her gaze on him he looked up but he gave no sign.

Conaire was spinning his tale again, bringing in the dogs, and they were waiting now for her to name them, so he could carry on with his song. She frowned. His fingers hovered over the strings. The great feasting hall was falling silent. She had to think quickly and her decision had to be astute and witty and strong. She stood up, the supple leather in her hands and leaned down to her plate, picking up two pieces of meat, one for each of the great dogs, conscious of the strings of saliva dripping from their jaws as they spotted the coming rewards.

'These great creatures will guard me well. I thank you, Brochan. And as they will be there for my rising in the morning and for my sleeping at night, I shall call them Sun –' she turned to the larger, darker dog, 'and Moon.' She indicated the smaller, cream bitch.

There was a delighted roar from the hall, the dogs took their titbits and licked their lips and Conaire, drawing his fingers across the strings in a series of wild arpeggios, continued his song.

There was no sign of Venutios. As man after man came forward and pledged allegiance and presented their gifts and the afternoon drew on she realised he was not there. She frowned. Was he not prepared to pledge allegiance to her as high queen of all Brigantia? Did he not think her worthy of a present? Or of a wooing?

She sat back in her high seat and waved away the food. Another bard had come forward now. This man came from the land of the Silures. He was small, with a twisted leg but he wore, she noted, a jewelled brooch on his shoulder and a golden necklet. His silver branch was exquisitely carved, the chime of the tiny bells very sweet. A man of means, this bard. And as he started to sing she realised why. The man had the voice of a god. By the time he had finished the first verse of his song the hall had fallen silent, and every eye was upon his face. He sang on, spinning a wild tale of daring and might and loss and sorrow, carrying his audience with him up into the heights of excitement and then down into the depths of despair. Not until he had finished and put down his harp was there a sound in the hall. Then there was an explosion of applause.

Carta beckoned him forward and gestured to one of the slaves to bring the customary reward for the best entertainer. 'A bag of gold, sir. Without dispute, you win the accolade today.'

He knelt before her and took the small bag in his hand.

'May I ask where you come from?' She liked his face, weather-beaten and of dark complexion which set off his eyes which were the brightest blue.

'From Caer Isca, oh great queen.'

'And whose court do you serve?' She was curious that such a fine singer should be a travelling bard.

'I am yours, lady.' He smiled at her, a touch of mischief in the twitch of his mouth. 'I believe I am a gift.'

She was speechless for a moment. 'Are you not a freeman, then? I didn't take you for a slave.'

'I am a freeman, lady. I go of my own free will to a great queen at the behest of a great king.'

'Venutios.' She had whispered the name without realising it and only afterwards as he nodded did she smile. So, he had not forgotten.

Later that night, as she lay back on her heather bed and pulled sheets and furs over her, she thought again about Venutios. One by one the faces of the men at the feast rose before her and she considered them, wondering how it would feel to welcome them to her bed, how their bodies would curve against hers, how their manhood would tease her to desire and one by one, her body told her that no one would please her and tease her and love her as Riach had. But Riach had been a boy as she had been a girl. He had been a friend, a companion, and a co-conspirator against the world. These were men parading themselves before a woman.

Venutios's was the last face she allowed herself to view, the last physique she allowed herself to imagine. The fantasy did not please her. With a shiver she put the thought aside and turned over, hugging her pillows, waiting for sleep to wash away her exhaustion and her loneliness as outside the rain began to fall.

III

'Viv!' Pat's hand on her shoulder brought Viv back to reality with a cry of fright. 'Sorry, but it's raining.'

Viv closed her eyes, her heart thundering unsteadily under her ribs, trying to claw back the dream, but it had gone. 'Don't ever do that again!' She was furious, 'You nearly gave me a heart attack!'

'Sorry.' Pat stood up. 'It was weird. There was a clear blue sky. Sunshine. Glorious. Warm. Then the storm comes out of nowhere and it's so bloody cold!' She shivered. 'You weren't saying anything, Viv. Not to the mike.'

They were both aware suddenly that the rain on the leaves above their heads had stopped.

Viv looked round, disoriented. The storm had been a part of her dream. The storm had been in Carta's time, and it had been nightfall at Dun Righ. Here it was a clear day with no clouds in the sky at all. She gazed round her at the nettles and brambles and the trees clinging to the rampart, the glimpses through the undergrowth of green fields in an area where the walls had been. Acres of emptiness where once there had been houses, people, animals, workshops, store rooms and the smoke from a hundred smoke holes and ovens and kilns. She was trying to regain her grip on reality.

'For any scenes set here we'll need domestic noises,' Pat went on. 'Children. Dogs. Hens. That sort of stuff? Not something we can record here these days!'

Viv nodded. 'Wagon wheels on cobbles. Probably sheep and cows from time to time as they are brought in from the fields. Men shouting. Women laughing. Distant chatter. No recognisable words, of course. Can we fade out for indoor scenes and dialogue with maybe indoor noises of a fire, snapping, crackling twigs, that sort of thing?' She sounded dreamy.

Pat nodded again. ''Exactly! I was hoping it would work with this small recorder just to get the effect. I'll get hold of a better quality mike if necessary. Then I'll download it all onto my laptop and I can edit it after that.' She fumbled in her bag for the tiny digital recorder which she had put away as it started to rain. 'Do you want to try again? Tell me what was happening just now in

287

your head.' She plugged the microphone back into the small device and held it out. 'OK. I've switched on. And . . .' She paused as a blackbird started to sing nearby. 'That's perfect.'

Viv hesitated. 'It's jumbled. I woke up so quickly most of it vanished. Like a dream.' The blackbird stopped singing and exploded out of the thicket, its alarm call ringing in their ears.

'Go back.' Pat was business-like. 'And this time speak out loud as it happens.'

'It doesn't work like that.'

'Try.' Pat reached into her pocket for her cigarettes. 'Sorry. I'll sit down wind. And when you're ready we'll record a bit of downtown Stanwick. OK. I want you to talk to me. And I don't want you to wake up. Just talk quietly out loud. Can you hear me?'

Viv's eyes were closed.

'Good. Now begin.'

IV

As spring turned into summer Carta's father died suddenly. His parting left her bereft, though he had taken no part in public affairs for a long time. Lonely and lost without his support her grief became an excuse not to consider the subject of a husband, though potential suitors were arriving from all over the country.

Artgenos was becoming impatient. 'You cannot expect all the warriors to follow you, lady, without a strong man at your side to lead them into battle. I know you can do it alone,' he forestalled her furious retort with a raised hand,' but you should not have to. The gods need you to stay safe. You saw what happens when the king dies. Your brother could not be spared so soon. And decisions must be made. The Romans are advancing daily across the south. No one is fighting save my cousin Caradoc, now his brother Togodumnos is dead, and he won't last long. The situation becomes more serious by the day.'

Carta frowned. They were sitting facing one another in one of the small side rooms built onto the outer wall of the circular great house at Dinas Dwr. They had travelled here, as Carta's father had before her, for the Lughnasadh fair in this rich, lowland side of her kingdom – the side more vulnerable perhaps to attack should the Romans come. They were alone, screened from interested eyes and ears so that they could talk in private. 'The gods are growing impatient, Carta. Listen to them grumble.'

Although it was high summer it had been raining for three days and the surrounding moors were slick with moisture, the peat like a sponge. The fields and pastures had turned to mud. A steady stream of raindrops was finding its way through the smoke hole and hissing in the hot ashes of the fire. Beside the hearth, Carta's two new dogs lay bored, idly scratching as they stared into the flames. She put out her hand and at once they came to her and nuzzled her fingers as another growl of thunder echoed across the township. In the distance she could hear the strum of the harp. Her new bard, Dafydd, sat beside the central fire quietly playing to the women who were spinning near him. As soon as Dafydd had arrived she had lost Conaire and she missed him sorely. 'I crave your leave to go to the Druid college, lady,' he had said, the day after the new bard had arrived. 'You don't need me now. I will always be your friend and I will always sing for you, but in my heart I have wanted to train as a seer and maybe a Druid if I am blessed by the gods.' And she had nodded and given him her blessing and had let him go.

She sighed. 'The gods do not have to make this decision! They will not have to make the man their husband!' She replied to Artgenos at last.

'But they will help you to choose wisely.' He glared at her. 'Throw the divination sticks and ask. Visit the sacred waters and consult the goddess herself. Consult the omens, woman!' His patience was all but at an end.

'And if I do these things, what will they tell me?' She was tired of hedging. 'Why not tell me now, Artgenos, and save me from this uncertainty.' Her eyes were flashing with anger.

'They will tell you to pick Venutios.'

'I knew it!' She stood up furiously and both dogs sat up, ears pricked. He had been there waiting when they rode into the township, full of apologies for his absence from the coronation. Carta had scanned the faces at his side. There was no sign of Medb.

'So. What is wrong with him? He is a strong man. A king. He will father healthy sons and lead your men well.'

'Yes, I am sure he would do all those things.' Her eyes were hard.

'But would he bow the knee to me as his queen? Would he obey my command in battle? Would he stand back if I desired it and allow me to take my war bands where I choose?'

'He is a king in his own right, Cartimandua.' Artgenos put his head on one side. 'An experienced, popular king.'

'In other words, no. He would do none of those things.'

'He would make a strong consort.'

'He will not suit me, Artgenos.' She folded her arms. 'And now, I am sick of sitting here listening to the gods argue above my roof tree. I am going out.'

She swept her cloak around her shoulders and stepped out into the larger room outside. 'Send a groom to fetch my pony,' she called into the shadows. 'I intend to go riding and I take no one with me, save the dogs!'

She felt the horse slide as she put it to the path into the forest but she steadied it, pulling her plaid around her hair, conscious of Sun and Moon close at the animal's heels. It was foolish to come out like this. She could see nothing as the cloud nestled in the trees and before long the rain had worked its way through her mantle. She would have to be cautious as the pony hurried on, keeping to the track as she ducked beneath overhanging branches, feeling the brush of wet leaves on her face, smelling the keen scents of the forest and the earth.

When she heard the hoofbeats thundering after her she let out an exclamation of anger. In her frustration, all she wanted was to be alone. She reined in the pony and turned to face her pursuer. It was Brochan. 'It is not safe for you to be out alone in this weather, Great Queen. Please, let me escort you.' His hair was plastered to his head, his brown eyes anxious. 'You should not go out into the forest at all. It is not safe. You could get lost.'

'You dare to tell me where I can or cannot go!' She was furious. 'I have the gods to protect me, and the dogs you yourself gave me. Are they not enough?'

'No, not in this weather.' He held her gaze steadily and she liked him for it. He was handsome and charming and he would make a useful ally. She studied him for a moment, as the rain poured down. And she would enjoy him in her bed. Maybe he read something of her thoughts in her eyes because suddenly he grinned. 'We could take shelter under the trees somewhere quiet, lady. This rain must stop soon.' He glanced past her into the mist.

'I know where we are, Brochan.' She was smiling. 'I know this place better than you, my friend, remember? This is the centre of my kingdom.' It was a gentle rebuke.

He bowed his head. 'Of course.' For a moment she was tempted, oh so tempted, then reluctantly she shook her head. 'Probably it would be better to return within the walls. I wouldn't like them to send out a search party. The reason for my ride is gone. I have stretched my legs and shaken loose the gremlins in my soul.'

He laughed out loud. 'A trail of gremlins would be a fearful sight. I trust they do not litter the track.' His hand went to the wooden charm around his neck to ward off the insult to the little people. 'Ride on, my lady, and I will follow at a respectful distance as befits your obedient kinsman.'

She was laughing too, now. 'Very well. I will lead the way.' She was drawing on the pony's reins, kicking him round when the dogs at her side began to growl.

Brochan edged his own pony closer to hers. 'What is it?' He strained his eyes into the mist where the track disappeared into the trees.

They could hear nothing above the wind and rain on the leaves above their heads.

'Wolves maybe, in the forest?' Carta could see nothing. She gentled the pony, sensing its fear.

Brochan drew his sword. 'Come on, back to the fort. Curse this rain, we can see nothing!'

'Do not curse the rain.' Carta urged her mount into a canter. 'It could be our saving. It wraps us in its arms and provides us with a disguise.'

They were still a half-mile ride away from the gates when out of the mist behind them a band of horsemen appeared, moving fast towards them. Glancing over their shoulders Carta and Brochan saw the glint of metal through the rain. The men were riding with drawn swords.

The hoofbeats grew closer. There was no possibility of running. In seconds their own horses were surrounded.

'So. Our queen rides without an escort? And where any man could take her captive! Not sensible, I think.' It was Venutios, circling her on his sweating brown pony. He wore his war helmet and a waterproofed cloak against the storm. Ramming his sword back into the ornate scabbard at his belt he leaned forward and caught her rein, dragging her pony next to his.

291

As his men surrounded her Carta felt a wave of fury engulf her. 'Let go! How dare you!' She drew the dagger from the sheath she wore at her own girdle beneath her cloak and slashed at his hand. 'Don't you dare touch me! Brochan! Where is Brochan?' It gave her enormous satisfaction to see the bloody welt bloom across the back of Venutios's wrist as with a curse he dropped her rein. 'Withdraw your men, sir. I cannot believe you would threaten me within sight of my own walls!'

'I do not threaten you, my Queen.' He reined back and to her fury she saw he was laughing. 'I'm sorry if my wooing was too rough! Please, forgive my ardour!'

'Your ardour!' She sheathed her own dagger after wiping it across her knees. 'I call it an insulting assault –'

'Not meant, I assure you.'

'And was it "not meant" to charge me with drawn swords?' She was not going to be cajoled. 'And where is Brochan?'

'Here. I am here, Carta. Lady.' He was on foot, one eye blackened, a trickle of blood dripping from his nose. 'Venutios shall pay with his life for this insult!'

With a horrified glance at the man with whom she had been riding, she turned on Venutios. 'How dare you! I cannot believe you would do this! This man is king of the Parisii as you well know. How *dare* you!'

'It was an accident, my Queen.' One of Venutios's men stepped forward. 'Forgive me. I unseated him by mistake.'

'Then I suggest you find his horse and help him mount, then beg his forgiveness on your knees!' She narrowed her eyes. 'You call this a wooing, Venutios? I call it an attack. You will leave Dinas Dwr with your men today. At once. Go back to Caer Lugus and don't dare to return to my presence until I tell you that you may.'

'But my lady . . .' He was still laughing.

'But nothing!' She was beside herself with anger. 'Go, and think yourself lucky that the Parisii do not declare war on you for your insult to their king!'

Behind her Brochan's horse had been found. He was unceremoniously boosted into the saddle and someone smacked the animal on the rump, sending it bolting down the track.

'So much for his royal pretensions!' Venutios chuckled. 'You need a real man, madam, not a poet who cannot hold his horse!'

'He was my companion and he is my friend.' Her voice dropped dangerously. 'And he was my escort. Now, thanks to you, I have to persuade him not to declare war on you, a declaration to which he would be absolutely entitled. And at this moment, I have to return to my fort alone and unescorted.'

'No. That would be unthinkable. I shall escort you myself and my men shall form a guard.'

'I do not need a guard, Venutios,' she spat back. 'And I do not choose to have you at my side. Leave me.'

'Out of the question.'

'Are you defying me?'

'I am ensuring your safety, which is my duty before the gods.' He had turned his pony alongside hers. His hand she noticed was bleeding profusely as he held his reins. He did not deign to notice.

Pat stubbed out her cigarette with a sigh of impatience as the silence lengthened. It was obviously all happening for Viv, but not out loud and she was missing it. She narrowed her eyes thoughtfully. You could tell people who were sleepwalking to go back to bed and they would hear you and obey your instructions. She moved closer.

'Viv, can you hear me? I want you to tell me what you're seeing.' Her voice was quiet but firm. 'Tell me what you're hearing.' She paused expectantly. Viv didn't react. 'Viv. Can you hear me? I don't want you to wake up. I just want you to speak to me.'

She moved closer still, the mike in her hand. 'Tell me what is happening, Viv. What can you see?'

Viv's eyes were almost closed. Beneath her lids her eyes were moving rapidly from side to side. She did not appear to hear Pat, but after a moment she moved slightly and a frown appeared on her face, as hesitantly she began to speak.

'Yes!' Exultantly, Pat pushed the mike closer.

Carta rode ahead, her eyes fixed on the fort entrance, ignoring Venutios who pushed his pony into a trot to keep up with hers. Behind them the other riders bunched together, keeping a healthy distance between their king and the high queen and themselves. Secretly many of them were smiling at their lord's discomfiture. It would take a lot for him to redeem his dignity after today.

At the entrance he reined back a little to allow her to enter the gates first. She rode straight to her own house where she slid from her mount, threw the reins to one of the loitering boys and disappeared inside followed by the dogs.

Venutios hesitated. He was well aware of what the men behind him must think. 'Dismount. Go and find a bivouac and food,' he yelled at them, then he too slid off his pony and disappeared into the royal house.

The main room was deserted, the fire banked low, the benches pushed back against the walls, stacked with cushions and neatly folded rugs. She must have made her way directly to one of the other rooms. He waited, dripping where he stood in his soaking cloak and breeks, his boots covered in mud, and glanced at the curtained doorways, listening intently. The muffled sounds of everyday life came to him through the main door, but in here it was completely silent. He strode across the floor, aware of the rattle of his sword in its hanger and the slight squeak of leather from his belt as he approached the largest curtained door and pulled back the hanging with a rattle of wooden rings. He had guessed rightly. Carta was standing in the room, her face and wet hair illuminated by the lamps on the dressing chest and on the tables. Two women were with her, one unfastening the brooch which held her sodden mantle, the other searching through a coffer for soft woollen towels. The women looked up with exclamations of fright and anger as he strode in.

'Leave us!' His command was peremptory and they stepped away from the queen in shock.

'Don't move!' Carta's voice was like iron. 'Stay here, Mairghread, please. Sibáel, I want you to call for help. This man is to be removed.'

'I don't think so.' He seized her arm, sending Sibáel reeling towards the bed with one quick push of his hand. 'You and I have to talk.'

'There is no question of talking.' She was blazing with fury. 'I want you out of this fort. I want you out of Brigantia!' Behind them Sibáel slipped out of the doorway as Mairghread reached silently for Carta's dagger, discarded with her girdle on the bed.

He had pulled her close to him and she could feel the heat of his body against hers; the strength of his hand was hurting her wrist.

'You need me, Cartimandua. The gods have spelled it out!' he whispered in her ear.

'Then the gods are mistaken! They contradict themselves!' She held his gaze without a trace of fear. 'The omens were clear to me.

294

I forbid you to touch me!' Their faces were only inches apart. She could feel the bones of her wrist being crushed in his fist.

'Venutios!' Artgenos's voice was like a whiplash.

Venutios dropped Carta's wrist and stepped back reluctantly. His expression was dark with fury as the old man walked into the room, followed by Sibael and Fergal, Carta's charioteer, who held a drawn sword.

Carta turned away, rubbing her wrist. 'Take him away, Artgenos. He is to leave this fort today.' She spoke through gritted teeth.

'You heard her,' Artgenos said sternly. 'Take your men and leave.'

'But Artgenos, the gods have decreed –'

'The gods have never decreed that you should use violence against your queen! You will go now.' Artgenos turned his back on Venutios and went to Carta. Gently he took her hand, running his fingers across her wrist. 'Let your ladies tend you. I will go and find some salve for this bruising,' he said quietly. 'Fergal, please escort the king of the Carvetii to his men and see they have all the supplies they need to start their ride back to Caer Lugus today.'

Venutios strode out of the room across the outer chamber and out into the rain with Fergal behind him.

'He won't bother you again. I'll see to it he leaves the fort at once.' Artgenos sighed. 'He is a man of mettle. It will be hard for him to take a wife who outranks him.'

'Then it's a good thing he won't have to.' Her wet mantle had fallen to the floor at her feet leaving her dressed in a blue tunic and a soft green gown, both as wet as her hair. She was shivering. 'He was on your list of possible suitors, Artgenos, but no longer. I would rather marry my shoemaker!' She turned to the two women who were standing waiting. Sibael picked up a towel. 'I want him gone before dark.'

'I think you will find he has already gone, Carta.' Artgenos stood for a moment, listening to the sound of horses outside the door of the house. He shook his head ruefully, then he too turned towards the door. 'Get warm and dry, and I will return with the salve.'

'Wow! Real fireworks!' Pat breathed as Viv fell silent. She turned off the mike and stared down at the recorder, flicking off the switch with her fingernail.

She was stunned. She could hardly believe what she had heard. Viv's voice, certainly, but overlaid with a dozen others. Her descriptions; her anguish – the anger that had erupted from her as she described Carta's fury. She stared at Viv's face. It was relaxed now and her eyes were closed, almost as though now this instalment of the story had been told the spirit that animated her had left.

She frowned and touched Viv on the shoulder. 'Are you OK?'

There was no response.

'Viv? Can you hear me?'

She had started packing her equipment away in her bag when Viv began to speak again.

Her voice was a low monotone; her eyes were open, but she was not looking at Pat or anywhere other than into the distant past, this time as an observer, not a participant.

'It is the next morning. The sun is rising. Carta is standing in the centre of the circle, her arms raised as she faces east. I can see the red-gold light spilling across the heather towards her, illuminating her face, her hair. She is alone as she smiles in welcome to the morning, but behind her in the west the clouds are building. They race across the land and within minutes the long sun shadows of the trees are gone, the sky is grey and the sun has withdrawn. She lets her arms fall to her sides, aware that overhead two buzzards are circling. Their mewing cries echo on the wind as they spiral ever higher. She watches them, listening. They can hear the war eagles, the tramp of marching feet. They are warning her of death and slavery. Only she can save her people now. But to save them she must be sly like a fox. The gods of war bid her fight, but the goddess is more subtle. She has drawn a veil across the face of the Roman Apollo. She must learn to dissemble.'

Viv fell silent again. She was as white as a sheet and for several seconds Pat watched, holding her breath. 'Viv? Are you OK? Wake up. I think you'd better stop this now.' She pushed the recorder into her bag. 'Viv? Come on. That's enough.' She shook her shoulder. Viv's head rolled back, her eyes still closed. 'Shit!' Pat recoiled. 'Oh God! Viv!' She hesitated, then she pressed her fingers onto Viv's wrist. The pulse was strong and steady.

Pat glanced up at the canopy of leaves above their heads. 'I hate to tell you, but I think the rain is starting again. We need to get back to the car.'

There was no response.

'Viv, come on. I want you to wake up now. Do you hear? I want you to wake up and talk to me!'

V

'You did what?'

In the car they were sitting staring out at the pouring rain as they wiped condensation from the windows. Pat turned and leaned back against the passenger door. 'I recorded it all. You talking, describing the whole thing. Hang on. Let me find the recorder.' She had dumped the bag behind the seat as they dived into the car while the first clap of thunder echoed across the fields.

'But I tried to do that before. There was nothing. I wasn't speaking out loud.'

'You did this time.' Pat took the digital voice recorder out of the bag.

'But I don't understand. Why, suddenly?'

'Because I asked you to once you were in a trance.'

'You asked me to?'

'You access Cartimandua in some sort of hypnotic state – a bit like talking in your sleep, so I figured if I talked to you, you would respond as people do when they are sleepwalking, and you did! Listen.' Pat was triumphant. She switched on the machine and Viv's voice spoke out. Behind it they could hear birds, and the sound of rustling leaves. At one point there was the patter of rain, but it was what she was saying that riveted them.

Sometimes she was telling the story, describing what was happening. Sometimes she was hesitant, trying to set the scene. 'There's a dog barking, can you hear it? Not a hound. A small dog of some kind, someone's pet. Goats and sheep and a cow, lowing in the distance. Children shouting. A hammer on metal in the forge. I can smell woodsmoke and cooking. Meat roasting. Carta's putting on her mantle; it's damp and cold from last time she wore it. It smells

297

of wet wool and horses. Not unpleasant. It's an earthy, outdoor sort of smell. It's only a small site at this period. Perhaps fifteen acres? I don't know how to judge.

'There are quite a lot of houses of different sizes. Carta's is dark inside, well insulated. A bit stuffy with the fire and woodsmoke. The smoke is seeping out of the roof. I don't think there is any sort of smoke hole or chimney. The inside of the roof is blackened, it's smooth with a sort of wattle and daub. The whole effect is exotic. More like an Arab nomad's tent than a peasant hut. Wall hangings, beautifully worked, bright colours. Woven rugs. Decorated pots. The supporting pillars for the roof are intricately carved. One has a dragon or a serpent winding round it. There is a vase of flowers standing on a coffer chest next to a silver jug. These people are civilised. Rich. They like their comfort. And their food. If I go into the kitchen – it's another building – the ovens are outside. Clay, I suppose. Covered and steaming, but a rich lovely smell coming from them.' There was a pause, almost as though Viv was walking through this scene she was describing. 'There is a large table in here. It's raining now outside and the cooks are indoors – though there is a table outside too, under the eaves. There are jugs and bowls and spoons. Some wooden, some metal. Sharp knives. Bunches of herbs. Vegetables. Not sure what they are. Green. Small leaves. There are strings of dried apple rings like my mother used to do,' she sounded delighted. 'And dried mushrooms. And a huge cheese covered by a net. Butter. A pretty pottery jar of honey. Conserves of some sort. You know, I don't think these people just gnawed bloody bones! This food looks and smells good.

'I'm going to find Carta. She's outside now. With her pony. It shoves at her affectionately with its nose and she pets it a bit just as we would. The young man holding its reins smiles at her and they talk briefly and laugh. Then she pulls herself onto its back. She has a saddle but no stirrups. And the bridle looks just like ours would. A jointed snaffle bit. Reins. But that's where the likeness ends. This is really fancy. The leather is gilded and red and quite beautiful.

'Brochan is beside her. He is short; shorter than Carta. With fair hair all clogged with clay of some sort, but he's good-looking. He laughs a lot. He has blue dots tattooed on his temples and across his cheekbones and a necklace and a brooch on his shoulder. He is wearing loose tartan trousers held up with a gorgeous leather belt. A soft shirt. Leather boots – baggy, not fitted, and a warm cloak.

'Side by side they ride towards the gate. There is a wooden palisade on top of the rampart and big gates in it, but they're open and unguarded and judging by the grass growing in front of them they haven't been shut for a long time.' There was a long pause. Viv sounded out of breath. 'Let me get closer. I want to hear what they are saying.' Then her voice changed. It was the voice of Cartimandua. Speaking English. When it was Brochan's turn to speak, the voice they heard was deeper. More masculine. It was definitely the voice of a man.

They listened to the end of the recording, then Pat switched off.

For a long time neither of them said anything, then at last Pat spoke. 'What do you think?'

Viv seemed incapable of speech. After a moment she shook her head. 'I remember that last bit. Like a dream. In patches. But all that description.' She bit her lip. 'It's just –' She paused again. 'It's fantastic!'

'Isn't it!' Pat was triumphant. 'You know,' she went on, 'you have time travelled. You weren't making that up.'

Viv sat back in the seat and closed her eyes, exhausted. 'No one is going to believe all that wasn't scripted.'

'Nor will we ask them to.' Pat was suddenly very focussed. 'Listen. We are sitting on dynamite, here. There are two programmes, not one. First we do the play, as we planned. Using your info only where we need to as just that. Background and sequencing. Then, later, we produce these recordings! Another book, as you said to Selwyn. Transcripts and another programme where we actually play them the tapes. This could rock the world. Imagine the publicity!'

'Yes, imagine.' Viv scowled. Her eyes were still shut. 'Dr Vivien Lloyd Rees, former historian, carted off to the funny farm after losing her marbles in faked hypnosis stunt!'

Pat's mouth dropped open. 'Rubbish. No one is going to say that! Well, that old scrooge of a professor might, but the rest of the world would love it. There are some very lucrative deals to be made here, Viv. You were fantastic in that recording! It completely bowled me over. I'm covered in goosepimples even now. Look.' She pushed her arm in front of Viv. 'Wait till we tell Maddie about this.'

'No.' Viv shook her head. 'Pat, you mustn't tell anyone about it. I want you to promise. Not at this stage.'

'You're kidding!' Pat frowned, then shrugging she forced a smile.

'OK. Whatever you say.' She turned and tucked the bag with the recorder back behind the seat. 'Come on. Let's go. This rain is getting worse. Where are we going to spend the night?'

In her head Medb smiled. The brooch was safe. The story hers.

20

I

'It would mean rewriting *Cartimandua, Queen of the North.*' Viv was giving in. 'Any new book will make a nonsense of everything I've said so far.' She rubbed her face with her hands. 'It has been superseded before it even appears in the shops.'

They spent the night at a small hotel near Aldborough, which Carta had called Isurios, and which to the Romans became Isurium Brigantum. To her surprise Viv slept deeply and without dreams. After looking round the museum they had headed west towards Nidderdale and the moors.

'Not for the general reader,' Pat commented lazily. 'Don't underestimate *Queen of the North*. It's fantastic. Every page is alive. You may not have been aware of Carta while you were writing it, or at least not consciously, but she was there, hovering over your shoulder. That is what makes it so vivid.'

Viv clenched and unclenched her fists uncomfortably. 'I wish I thought Hugh would agree with you.' She sighed. Where was Hugh? Why hadn't he contacted her?

They were sitting on a grassy plateau between two of the huge Brimham Rocks. A strange wonderful landscape surrounded them, of grotesque rock formations balanced and stacked and carved by ice and wind over thousands of years out of millstone grit into a collection of wild and wonderful shapes standing high above the surrounding moor. There was no proof that Cartimandua or any of her contemporaries had been here, but nearby there was a tantalisingly named 'Druid's cave' and how could anyone doubt that any Druid worth his salt would have paused here to talk with his gods.

Pat sat up, crossed her legs, and reached for an apple, resisting the urge to close her eyes in the warm sunshine. This picnic had been a spontaneous idea as they passed the signpost to the rocks and they had allowed themselves to be tempted.

'You're wrong. With *Queen of the North*, you have given an authoritative and scholarly overview. The second book would have to be written with the proviso that it is intuitive and even clairvoyant in its origins, and in a different category, albeit one that never contradicts or misleads the possibilities of the earlier work.'

'Clairvoyant,' Viv echoed with a hollow laugh. 'Great! That's all Hugh needs.'

'Stuff Hugh!' Lying back, Pat spoke from beneath the folded newspaper which she had spread over her face to protect her from the sun. 'I'm beginning to think you're obsessed with that man.'

'He's my boss.'

'Are you sure that's all he is?' There was an earthy chuckle from under the paper.

'Yes, I'm sure.' Viv stood up. 'I'm going to climb that rock. See you in ten minutes.'

Pat didn't move.

Sitting on the top of the rock staring out towards the distant moors, Viv closed her eyes and tried to still her mind. It was very hot. The rock burned her hands and she found a patch of alpine flowers and grasses to sit on, aware of the sounds around her – a buzzard in the sky out of sight in the glare, a party of noisy children, all dressed in identical blue boiler suits and hard hats, practising their mountaineering skills in spite of the heat, a stonechat pinking monotonously in the background. Slowly they faded from her consciousness. But nothing replaced it. Just a pleasant emptiness. It was as though the shock and excitement at hearing her own voice at last the day before had switched off whatever facility she had acquired. And she needed it. She wanted badly to see if she could ask direct questions. Did you come here? Did your Druids use this place to commune with their gods? Was Dinas Dwr your capital? She closed her eyes again. 'Carta?' She tried to picture the township as she had seen it. Recall the sounds; the smells. They had gone.

'Carta? Where are you?'

Suddenly she felt panicky. Supposing Carta had been scared off or neutralised in some way by Pat's recording? Supposing it had all gone, this strange, wonderful, frightening contact with another world? Supposing Carta was furious that they had left the brooch at Stanwick buried once more in the depths of the stones. Supposing when they went back, if they went back, it had gone? What would she do?

She drew up her knees, hugging them thoughtfully and without warning she knew she was going to cry.

'We've got to go back.' When she returned to Pat she was dry-eyed again. 'We can't leave the brooch there. I don't know what we were thinking about!'

Pat sat up and stared at her. 'What do you mean. Of course we can leave it there. It'll be perfectly safe.'

'Not if someone else finds it.'

'They won't.' Pat narrowed her eyes and her voice was suddenly hard. 'Forget it, Viv. Just put it out of your mind. It is back where it belongs.'

Viv stared at her. Pat's voice had changed. It was as though she had slipped into someone else's skin. She was acting a part and it was not a part that Viv liked at all. It was Medb.

She stared at Pat, shocked and frightened. 'If I say we should fetch it, we will,' she said quietly.

The change in her tone pulled Pat up. She frowned uneasily. 'Sorry. I just think it would be stupid. It is perfectly safe.' Her voice was her own again. 'So, which place is to be her capital in the play?' she went on. 'Stanwick makes sense. It's accessible. It's on a trade route between the south and Scotland. It is in gentle flat lands. Fertile. Civilised. Farmed.'

They were still discussing it when they climbed back into the car. Viv shrugged as she pulled onto the road. 'Somehow I want it to be somewhere like Ingleborough. Wait till you see it.' There were other contenders. Barwick in Elmet for instance, which was smaller, near the later Roman town, Isurium Brigantium. That too was beautiful and accessible and civilised.

'Ask her.' Pat sat back in her seat and fished in her pocket for a packet of gum. 'It's a straightforward question. Look her in the eye and ask. People claim to be able to direct the action in lucid dreams. Why not you?' She sighed impatiently. 'You're being too reactive,

Viv. You're acting like a victim instead of a bus driver.' She shifted the gum from one cheek to the other. 'You spoke for Cartimandua on the recording. "This is my people. I am their queen".' She mimicked Viv as Cartimandua in ringing tones. '"Vivienne, my goddess, ask and I will reply. My city is at Stanwick St John, or as I call it, Dinas Dwr".' She paused, coming out of character. 'We don't know the Celtic names for many of these places, do we? But we don't need them for the play. They are too confusing. "This is my seat. My palace. My capital.".' She was back in character. 'We could hold a séance!' she added thoughtfully. 'Under controlled conditions. Invite Cartimandua to talk to us and record it just like yesterday afternoon.'

'Carta has been talking to me for months,' Viv put in. 'I haven't needed a séance.'

'But this way I can be part of it.' Pat gave up on the gum and reached for her cigarettes. 'And the best part is we can invite other people in as well. Imagine Medb on line! What a performer she would be!'

'No!' Viv shook her head. 'Absolutely not! Leave it alone, Pat. Let Carta come if and when she wants and to whom she wants.' She frowned. 'But not Medb. For God's sake!'

'OK.' Pat sighed. 'Back to the site of the action: "It is here I sit in state and show the Romans what a great queen I am. I rule on my terms, not theirs, because I am the greatest queen there has ever been in Britain.".' She paused. 'Well?'

Viv smiled. 'Pretty good. Very good, actually.'

'Good. Perhaps I should play Cartimandua. I'd be fantastic in the part.' Pat raised an eyebrow and waited for the response.

'I don't know. You are good, but Carta is younger –'

'So, I talk younger.' Pat raised her voice a tone. Immediately it was lighter. Less mature. 'As long as they can't see me they can't count the wrinkles.' She laughed. 'I'd be wonderful, Viv. With you as the narrator.'

'That would give the right balance, I suppose,' Viv said thoughtfully. 'Me the author and narrator. You the lead actress and co-script writer. We need some men, of course. Strong male actors.'

Pat nodded. 'No problem. I've already got ideas about who can play the parts.'

Medb. She wanted to play Medb, not Cartimandua.

Dangerous, fascinating Medb.

'Still no word from Viv?'

Hugh was standing in Meryn's garden staring down at the rows of herbs and vegetables with a worried frown. 'She's got the brooch because I gave it back to her; because I'm a coward. She's in danger. I don't know where she is. She doesn't answer the phone or return any messages and I'm sitting here doing nothing about it.'

He felt safe in here. There had been no massive confrontation with Venutios. No shadowy visitors from another world, no brazen sounds echoing on the wind.

Meryn stooped to pull some spinach. 'Do you sense danger?'

Hugh frowned. 'Isn't that your department? Can't you look into your crystal ball and see what she's done with it? See if she's all right.' He glanced over the hedge and shivered. 'He's still lurking out there somewhere, isn't he.'

'Maybe.'

'Is he frightened of you? Because you're a Druid?' Hugh cocked an eyebrow in Meryn's direction.

'Possibly.' Meryn gave an enigmatic smile.

'What happens if I go out there?' He nodded towards the fence.

Meryn straightened his back and stood, the bowl of fresh green spinach leaves in his hand. 'Probably nothing.'

'Meaning there is a possibility that something could?'

Meryn smiled again. Turning towards the door he shrugged. 'We won't know until you try, Hugh. When you feel ready you will have to leave.'

Hugh stared at his retreating back. 'You're telling me to go?' he called after him. He stood for a moment considering the glorious crop of dandelions which flourished around the edge of the spinach patch, then he hurried after Meryn into the kitchen. 'Is that what you're saying?'

'Unless you want to live here forever.' Meryn put the bowl in the sink. 'There are things I can show you. Techniques to use to protect yourself.'

Hugh sat down at the kitchen table. 'Hocus pocus?'

'Undoubtedly.'

Hugh groaned.

Meryn picked a slug off the spinach. 'It's your call, Hugh. I can't do anything unless you want me to. You believe in the hocus pocus enough to stay here, so why not stick a small amulet round your neck on a piece of thread and forget it's there.'

'And that would save me?'

Meryn went over to the door and threw the slug out into the flower bed. 'You believe in Venutios?' He had not answered the question.

'I couldn't very well not believe that something is happening, but it could just be in my own head.'

'True. It's up to you. You need to leave soon anyway. Didn't you say you had an interview with someone on the radio?' Meryn put his hands on the table and leaned forward, studying Hugh's face. 'One of the things I do is to make amulets for people who need them. I can make one which will strengthen you should you encounter Venutios again out there in the big wide world or inside your head in a nightmare, whichever it may be. Pretend you are trendy enough to wear some jewellery.' He chuckled.

Hugh shook his head. 'It just doesn't do it for me. I'm sorry. It's not rational. How could a charm possibly work? It's just superstition.'

Meryn sighed. He dried his hands on a towel. 'Fair enough.'

'You don't really believe all this, in your heart of hearts, do you.' Hugh went on after a moment. 'It's all very romantic and beautiful and touchy feely, but you must have reservations. You're an intelligent man.'

Meryn held up his hands. 'Enough, Hugh. We've agreed to differ on this one so many times it's not worth pursuing it again. I believe completely and wholly in what I do. It's because of that you called me in such a panic, remember? And I'll be there for you should you need me again.'

'But that's it.'

'That's it.'

Hugh shrugged. He stood up. 'OK. I'll go home this afternoon. You're right. I'm a coward. I had a nightmare or two and then I let my imagination run away with me. A helping or two of spinach quiche,' he paused, gazing at the sink with a wry grin, 'will bolster my will power enough to get me out of here.'

Meryn laughed. 'It did it for Popeye, my friend.' As he watched Hugh wander back into the garden the worried frown returned.

For an equally intelligent and educated man, Hugh could be a complete fool at times. He sighed. How often had he encountered rational 'scientifically' literate men and women who had shared Hugh's blinkered opinions and lived to regret it? If only they could be made to see what was all around them. If only they could be brought to believe in the evidence of their own eyes and ears. But no. The hocus pocus factor kicked in and sometimes a man would rather die than admit that something paranormal was at work near him. He frowned again. That was an unfortunate choice of words; he hoped it wouldn't prove prophetic.

III

'I've just spoken to Maddie.' It was Pat who, barely an hour earlier Viv had dropped off at Abercromby Place. 'I wanted her to know what's going on. She is fantastically keen on the idea of the second programme!'

'Pat!' Viv was livid. 'I asked you not to say anything yet! I'm not at all sure I want anyone to know about this.'

'Don't worry, she'll keep it quiet. We don't want anything to spoil it.' Pat was breezy and enthusiastic. 'I'll be over tomorrow to go on with the script, OK?'

Slamming down the phone, Viv sighed. She went to pick up a pile of mail off the mat and threw it down on the desk. There was a letter with Australian stamps on top. Turning it over in her hands she felt an overwhelming pang of loneliness at the sight of her mother's writing. Her mother still prefered letters to e-mail. Turning to the answer machine she punched the button as she stared cautiously round the room. The atmosphere was peaceful. In spite of the missing mirror, the room felt ordinary. It smelled as it usually did when she had been away, of musty books and coffee and the jasmine plant which scrambled around the wall towards the window.

There were three messages from Hugh asking her to call urgently, but when she tried there was no reply from his phone or from the department. There were two messages from Maddie asking how she was and for news of progress on the play, one from Sandy

307

about a talk she had been asked to give to the WI in Taunton and one from Cathy. When she called them back she heard answer-phone messages from them all.

With a sigh she glanced round the room again. The emptiness was back. Suddenly she began to panic. Carta wasn't there. Supposing it had all been spoiled by Pat's recording; by leaving the brooch?

Sitting down she closed her eyes. 'Carta?'

The room was very quiet.

'Carta? I'm sorry.' She was overwhelmed with misery.

Nothing happened. Outside, the sky was grey and the wynd below was for once silent. There were no gulls to call out the messages of the gods.

IV

Medb was furious. Venutios had sent her away from Dinas Dwr as soon as he heard that Carta was approaching, giving her a pony and a servant and an escort for the four-day ride to Caer Lugus. With her he sent a letter to his brother, Brucetos. He was under no illusions about Medb's talents. He knew she would read it. *Take care of this lady who is very dear to me. Give her anything she needs and see that she is content until I come.* He had also given her a necklace of carved jet and amber beads and a tunic of the softest doeskin which he had bought for her from the best tanner at Dinas Dwr.

Medb was not happy but she was prepared to bide her time. The road was mountainous and rough but on this occasion she was travelling in some style with a good pony and servants to guard her. She saw to it that they were terrified of her. All she needed to do was to let it be known that she spoke nightly with her gods, and that the gods were prepared to act on her every whim.

In the water of the burns and becks of the north, in the lakes and in the bowls which had been brought for her to wash in, she watched Venutios's every move. He was still wearing the brooch; she saw the gold glitter on his shoulder and she smiled. She saw him talking with the warriors and Druids; she saw his encounter with Cartimandua and she saw the new queen throw his advances back into his face. In her fury she whipped her pony until the blood ran while she watched him walk away from Carta's house and she saw the anger in his eyes. It was then that he set off after her, so she knew to the very hour when he would arrive at Caer Lugus and claim her in his bed.

Running her hands across his body she kissed his throat, his shoulders, his belly. Then she snatched up the brooch which had been holding his cloak in place and ran the pin across his chest, leaving a line of blood welling into the dark chest hair. When he protested, wrenching it out of her hand, she laughed and stopped his mouth with her lips.

'That was to show you what would happen if you betray me,' she whispered. 'No one plays double with Medb of the White Hands. No one. Remember, you will keep that brooch forever, to remind you that you and I are joined as one in our desires and our plans to bring down Cartimandua.'

'Jesus!' Pat woke with a jolt of fear. Her room was dark and she could smell burning. Leaping out of bed, she scrabbled for the light switch and stared round. She couldn't have left a cigarette burning somewhere. Searching, she found nothing. The smell of burning had come from the fire in the bedchamber in Caer Lugus.

Cathy heard her as she fumbled with the tap in the kitchen, her hands shaking. 'Pat, this is stupid. You can't go on like this!' She yawned, drawing the belt of her dressing gown more tightly round her. 'Every time you go and see Viv you come back and have a nightmare. It's ludicrous.'

Pat shook her head. Her heart was still hammering with fear 'No. You don't understand. It all makes sense. It's about the brooch. It was real. What they are doing. Carta and Medb were practising something called remote viewing. The CIA trains people how to do that, for goodness' sake.' She was gabbling. 'It wasn't magic or imagination! It is a real skill. I produced a programme once about the subject for Channel 4. That's how she watched what Carta was doing. That's how she knew what had happened to the brooch.'

'I don't want to hear about the brooch!' Cathy was exhausted. 'I have never heard such a load of nonsense in my life. You are winding each other up, Pat. Stop it! As for leaving that thing buried in the middle of nowhere, I have never heard such idiocy. The museum or the professor or someone will probably sue you both if it's lost!'

'It's not lost. Medb will find it.'

'Medb?' Cathy stared at her. 'Stop it, Pat. You're scaring me.'

'I'm scaring myself!' Pat drained her water. 'If I could stop this, I would. But it has to be settled.' She slammed the glass down on the draining board. 'I can't sleep.'

'I'm not surprised.'

'I'm scared shitless, if you want to know.'

'Then stop doing this!'

'I'm not doing it on purpose!' Pat stood for a moment, then she shrugged. 'I'm going back to bed.' As she headed for the door she stopped abruptly. Medb was standing in the corner of the kitchen. 'Cathy?' Pat whispered. Chilled to the marrow, paralysed with fear, she pointed her finger. 'Look.'

'What?' Cathy gave an irritated sigh. 'Look at what, Pat?'

'There,' Pat gasped. 'There.' Why couldn't Cathy see her?

'What's going on?' Tasha appeared in the doorway, yawning. The child stared for several seconds where Pat was pointing, her eyes growing enormous in her pale face, then she let out a blood-curdling scream.

Medb vanished.

Cathy ran to the child and scooped her into her arms. 'Tasha, Tasha, be quiet, love. It's all right.' Hugging her, Cathy stared up helplessly at Pete as he ran into the room. 'It's OK. She had a bit of a fright. It's all over.'

'What? What happened?' As his daughter extricated herself from Cathy's arms and ran to him, Pete looked from Pat to Cathy and back. 'What happened, for God's sake?'

'Medb,' Pat said. Her mouth was dry; she was shivering violently. 'She's gone. She was standing there.' She pointed.

Pete scowled. 'No. That's enough! You are scaring everybody with your stupid stories. Just leave it. Please. Go to bed.'

Pat left them. Miserably she climbed the stairs back to her room. She stood still for a few moments, just inside the door, taking slow deep breaths with her eyes closed then warily she moved towards the bed. There, lying on the pillow, she saw the brooch. She froze, staring at it.

Please God, no.

Slowly she reached out her hand and drew back the covers. The sheets were soaked in blood.

21

I

Viv woke to a furious knocking on the front door of the flat. Still knotting the belt of her dressing gown, she stood back and let Pete in. He was tight-lipped. 'I'm sorry to call round so early,' he followed her through into the living room, 'but I had to talk to you. All this stuff about Cartimandua and ghosts and brooches has got to stop. You are upsetting everyone. Pat and Cathy were up all night. They were in a complete panic. You have to stop this play! Stop writing completely. Forget it. You are going to make yourselves mad. You're both getting hysterical. Give it a rest, OK?'

Viv stared at him. 'Pete –'

'I mean it, Viv. This has all gone long past a joke. I'm going to suggest that Pat goes back to London.'

'You can't.' Suddenly Viv was defensive and angry.

'Cathy thinks it's best. I think you'll find that Pat will agree.'

'No, Pete. I'm sorry. Why don't you just mind your own business. You and Cathy. This is nonsense. Pat was as keen as I was on the play. She still is. I only dropped her off last night, for God's sake! She hadn't changed her mind then. Far from it –'

'Something happened last night which frightened her.'

Viv was silent. 'What?' she asked at last.

'She announced that she could see some woman called Maeve there in the kitchen in the middle of the night. She freaked out and Cathy got upset. The cat went ballistic. Tasha was screaming the place down. The woman from downstairs came up to see if someone was being murdered . . .' He ran his fingers through his hair. 'Then on top of all that, when Pat went back to bed she found blood all

311

over the place where some brooch had scratched her and they had to change the sheets. No, I'm sorry, Viv. I really am. But you see the position I'm in.'

Viv was speechless for several seconds. 'Pat can come and stay here,' she said at last.

'I think you'll find she doesn't want to.' Pete stood up. 'Just give us all a break, will you? I'm going to persuade Cathy to come with me when I take Tasha to Stockholm on Friday and we'll spend a few days over there. I don't like leaving you alone, but this has to stop. Just pull yourself together, Viv, please!'

She stood listening to the sound of his footsteps as he ran down the stairs, then she pushed the door shut. She was white with shock.

Sitting down on the rocking chair she began to rock backwards and forwards gently, the only sound in the room the quiet squeak of the floorboard under the rockers. If the brooch had been in Pat's bed, Pat must have brought it back with her.

Or Medb.

II

'You summoned me, my Queen.' Venutios gave a small bow as he greeted Carta. He was dressed in his finest cloak and tunic, the gold and enamelled bird brooch on his shoulder. He did not smile as he straightened and met her eye. 'You find you cannot do without me after all?' He couldn't keep the irony out of his voice.

Carta's lips tightened angrily as she held his gaze. 'I summoned you because the kings of the Brigantian tribes must stand shoulder to shoulder before the Romans. I have also summoned Brochan. We have to maintain a united front. An envoy is on his way here from the Emperor as we speak.'

Venutios raised an eyebrow. 'And you think Brochan will impress him?' He gave a wintry laugh. 'Do you know what this Roman is going to say? Or does he merely wish to see how sharp our weapons are?'

Carta smiled. 'I know why he is coming. Artgenos's spies have already told me. I need my kings at my side and my Druids behind me when I greet him.' She stepped forward. 'You look better than when I saw you last, Venutios. I trust you have recovered from your wound and that your new clothes have put you in a better temper.' She reached forward, almost touching the bird on his shoulder, her gaze challenging his, then she gave a half-smile and stepped back as though aware of the eyes that watched her from far away.

Cartimandua had been impressed when word had arrived of the impending invitation from Aulus Plautius, commander of the invading Roman forces and now newly appointed governor of Britannia, to a meeting with him and the leaders of all the tribes of Britain, before the Emperor of Rome. She planned to receive the envoy in her feasting hall at Dun Righ. The Roman advance had halted. Their enemies were waiting to see what they would do next. The leaders of the tribes of Albion had not expected diplomacy after the appalling violence of the invasion. Impressed by the state and importance of her visitor and curious to see what these Roman invaders were like face to face, Carta ordered a feast in his honour which was designed to impress him and fill him with awe.

On one side she was flanked by Artgenos, and his colleague in the Druid college, Culann, a younger, more ascetic version of himself; on the other there was Brochan and Venutios, as the most senior kings of the northern tribes, a feat of diplomacy in itself to bring them together under the same roof without either drawing a sword. Venutios had been summoned by his high queen to the meeting with the envoy at three days' notice. She had not expected him to come.

The envoy was dressed in the uniform of a military tribune of the XX Legion Valeria Victrix, and accompanied by twenty-five legionaries. His name was Gaius Flavius Cerialis. He was tall, dark-haired, with high cheekbones and even, handsome features.

Going down on one knee before her, he handed her the scroll which contained the invitation. If he was surprised to find himself confronting the woman leader of these wild northern tribes he hid it well. If he was even more surprised that she was young and beautiful and that these seasoned warriors all treated her with respect he made no comment until he penned his report back to Plautius later.

An even greater surprise was in store. 'If you will permit, lady, I will read you the message from the governor.' He held out his hand to take back the scroll, but Cartimandua had already unrolled it and was scanning the close-written lines with every appearance of being able to read and understand Latin. He glanced at her warily. He had heard rumours about the powerful warrior queen of the Brigantes, none of which he had believed. The whole concept of a queen was fascinating to the young Roman. Women did not rule in their own name in the Empire. Even the fearsome wives of the emperors were not rulers in their own right.

There was silence in the room, broken only by the crackling of the fire as she read, then he realised that she was looking at him. He straightened his shoulders imperceptibly. She was good-looking; strong-featured, with haunting eyes. Red-gold hair, not stiff with lye as some of her countrymen and women, but luxurious and shining, plaited into heavy ropes and pinned in place with golden combs. For a moment as she lowered the document and looked at him their eyes met and he was tempted to smile.

'So, I am commanded to meet your Emperor.' If she was impressed she gave no sign of it. She handed the document to Artgenos. The envoy watched the old Druid read it, who in turn passed it on to one of the other men. Gaius had been told that unlike the southern tribes, who were closer to Gaul and in more contact already with Rome, these northern peoples were backwoodsmen and illiterate. That was clearly not the case. His information was wrong.

He glanced round surreptitiously, noting the richly woven hangings, the carved wooden furniture, the intricately decorated pottery – some of it undoubtedly imported from Gaul and expensive – on the tray which a slave was carrying towards him loaded with refreshments. Above all, he noted this young queen with her gold neckring and armlets, her soft, brightly coloured mantle trimmed with fur over a pale linen gown, the two great wolfhounds which lay at her feet watching him, and beside her the two formidable stern-faced warrior kings, with behind them the tall old Druid with his staff and his deep-set, all-seeing eyes. Gaius glanced at Queen Cartimandua's face again and was embarrassed to find her eyes once more on his. Her expression was shrewdly focussed.

Though he didn't know it, Carta was equally fascinated by her visitor. The handsome Roman was clean-shaven, and wore a long-sleeved tunic with a leather corselet trimmed with metal. He carried

314

his plumed helmet under his arm and had been allowed to keep his sword. His shield bearer and two of his officers stood immediately behind him.

When the presentation of the invitation was over and he had been shown to the guest house to refresh himself and prepare for the feast, she turned to her advisers.

'I have no intention of going. At the head of a war band, yes. As a supplicant to Rome, no.'

'I agree.' Venutios leaned towards the fire thoughtfully. His quarrel with Brochan, or for that matter with Cartimandua, was not at the forefront of his mind for the moment. Time enough for that later. Besides, he might be able to turn her position as high queen to his own advantage later. 'Compliance will be seen as weakness.'

Carta glanced at him. 'On the other hand, it would be interesting to see these people for myself and judge their position. They have treated me with respect. They have brought gifts.' Not many, but nevertheless the quality of the gold-engraved cup which had been passed over was exquisite and Gaius's explanation that the gift was small only because of the speed with which he had been required to travel had been accepted.

'I wouldn't go.' Venutios scowled. 'These men are two-faced. They invite with one hand and stab you in the back with the other.'

'That is not their intention here,' Artgenos put in at last. 'They are thinly spread on this island and they are seeking allies. Why else would the Emperor of Rome himself have come here? It is unthinkable that we would agree to an alliance but it would do no harm to talk to them. To judge their strength and the pattern of their intentions. Cartimandua is right. I think she should go. And I think you two should accompany her.' He frowned sternly. 'You must put your enmity behind you. Unless the tribes are allies, we have no chance against their people. Watch these men. See how disciplined they are and learn.'

He was right. Carta studied the Roman at the feast that night with great care. She sat him next to her and saw that he was plied with dishes, and watched his every move. He had changed from his armour in honour of the feast and the men of the tribe stared at him in astonishment as he strode in, swathed in a toga with the narrow stripe of a career officer.

Carta found him easy to talk to. He was intelligent, charming, a little formal, but she put that down to the fact that he was undoubtedly awed by the circumstances in which he found himself. And he was, she had to admit it, attractive. He was a hand-span taller even than Venutios. Plied with wine, he talked freely of the invasion, the war, his experience on the battlefield and the building which was starting at Camulodunum, the capital of the Catuvellaunian-Trinovantian alliance and now the new capital of the province of Britannia.

While the men and women around him drank freely and the noise in the feasting hall grew louder, Gaius kept his head. He waved away the constant refills from the wine jug, and ate sparingly. Aware that his hostess too was keeping her drinking carefully in control he talked expansively and with a certain bravado as he had been instructed. He was not sure if she was fooled by his wide-eyed bonhomie, but he did, he had to admit, rather enjoy her company. After the Spartan order and discipline of the unmarried officers' quarters this riot of noise and colour and music and indulgence was decidedly pleasing.

The next morning he had expected to find the whole place still locked in drunken sleep when he and his men mounted to begin their journey south. He had also expected her to play for time and delay the decision as to whether or not she accepted the governor's invitation. To his astonishment she was there to bid him farewell, and in her hand she carried a fresh scroll, the reply to the invitation, penned with all the flurries and courtesies that could be wished for, agreeing to come to Camulodunum.

She inclined her head gravely in response to his salute. 'I trust you have a safe journey, Gaius Flavius Cerialis.' She held his gaze for a moment and then she smiled. 'And I trust that we will meet again.' Just for a second he thought he had seen a certain calculation in her eyes, but whether she was judging him as an enemy or as a potential ally he could not decide. The thought worried him on his way back south.

III

The sound of the rocking chair slowly brought Viv back to wakeful-
ness. She smiled. She had seen the feast. Watched Carta taking
her first steps in diplomatic dealings with the Romans. Watched
Venutios wearing the brooch.

She frowned abruptly. So Hugh was right. The brooch was his.
But where had he got it from? Since Carta had noticed it so obviously, she hadn't given it to him.

Viv sat for a minute in silence. Outside somewhere on the rooftops a blackbird was singing, the liquid trill soaring above the muted
roar of traffic. She frowned. Was it a warning? She must learn to
listen to the birds like Carta. Listen to the wind, the rain; heed the
messages the gods sent her. Alert now, she concentrated on the
sound, attuned to the slightest nuance, her mind still half in
the past.

How had the brooch come back to Edinburgh? Had Pat tricked
her? Had she somehow retrieved it? Had Medb brought it?

'Carta?' She whispered the name tentatively. 'Carta, are you
there?'

The only answer was the distant wheezing and rumble of an
early morning milk float stopping and starting on its way up the
street and the cheerful chink of bottles in the rain.

She must ring Cathy. Find out what had happened. The bird
wasn't going to tell her. His message spoke of otherworldly things.
Standing up unsteadily she went to the phone. Cathy's number
rang on and on without an answer. Pete had virtually forbidden
her to see Pat or Cathy again. What was he thinking of? With a
shaking hand she dialled Pat's mobile. It was switched off. Frowning, she slammed down the receiver. They couldn't just cut her out
like this. It was nonsense. She would go over there and see them.
Now.

She didn't. Instead she rang Hugh. There was no reply.

Finally she called Winter Gill Farm. Peggy answered. 'Steve is
out on the fell with his father,' she said when Viv enquired. 'How
are you, my dear? When are you coming back?'

Viv smiled with relief. The genuine warmth in Peggy's voice was

317

just what she needed. 'I have the book launch tomorrow, Peggy, and then I'm away for a few days doing book signings and things, but I would love to come down again when that is over.' She hesitated. 'Is Steve coming up to Edinburgh at all?'

'I'm sure he'll come if you'd like him to,' Peggy said quickly. 'Shall I get him to ring you?'

'I was going to ask him to the launch party tomorrow if he'd like to come,' Viv said. 'Don't worry him. Just pass on the invitation. I'll understand if it's too lovely down there for him to drag himself away.'

Walking through into her bedroom she flung herself down on the bed wearily. No Pat. No Cathy. No Hugh and now no Steve. Tomorrow her book would be published and Carta's life would be public property and she was scared and lonely and utterly miserable.

'Carta? Are you there? I need you. Tell me about your visit to the Emperor.' She put her arm across her eyes. 'Tell me about the brooch. I'm sorry I didn't keep it for you. I didn't understand.'

IV

The journey to Camulodunum took ten days. She travelled in style as befitted a queen, with several chariots, her most beautiful horses and an escort of fifty of her most experienced warriors. With her went Venutios as king of the Carvetii, and Brochan of the Parisii, both invited in the end not just by her but by Plautius in their own right as petty kings of the Brigantian alliance.

The road they followed led down the flat lands, through forests and across ancient causeways. Once over the Wash and through the fens they made their way downwards on newer, straighter roads, already widened and reinforced by the Romans, and realised that now they were in the area which had been designated as the new province of Britannia.

The Brigantian party made camp on the banks of the River Colne and found themselves a part of a gathering of a dozen or so tribal kings all summoned before the Emperor Claudius. The ancient town of Cunobelinos was already in the process of being rebuilt by the Roman army, who had erected a fort in the middle of the British fortifications. It was clear immediately that the visiting rulers were in a conquered land where already the camp of the XX legion with its thousands of regimented tents and stores was in total command.

The Emperor himself was lodged with his entourage within the newly built area of fortifications and it was on the first morning after their arrival that Cartimandua was informed that an audience had been arranged. Followed by her own attendants, and arrayed in her finest gown and mantle and her richest jewellery, she made her way slowly from the chariot in which Fergal had driven her from the riverside camp. Venutios and Brochan were not invited.

Her heart was thudding uncomfortably as she looked around at the stern-faced sentries, the fluttering banners, the massed troops standing to attention in the meadows outside the fort and the spectacle, no doubt carefully arranged, but none the less awesome for that, of Claudius's famous elephants, each with its attendant keeper, striding slowly around the outer ditch.

Taking a deep breath she strode towards the entrance, only hesitating slightly as the sentries crossed their spears immediately behind her, denying entry to her followers.

The Emperor was seated on a throne upon a dais at the far end of an imposing if quickly erected barrack house. Flanked by men on both sides, he stood as she approached him.

'Queen Cartimandua, sir, High Queen of the Brigantian peoples.' A voice announced her from the shadows behind the Emperor's shoulder.

She stopped several yards from the dais so that she would not have to look up at him, her nervousness counterbalanced by a growing determination not to bow the knee to the invader. Claudius might rule a large part of the known world, but to her at least, he was not a god; indeed, on close inspection he was to all intents and purposes just a middle-aged man, thin and grey-haired beneath his splendid purple toga.

Behind him Aulus Plautius was flanked in his turn by other men in togas and many wearing military uniform. Along the side walls, shoulder to shoulder, stood more armed men, all smartly to attention, all looking curiously at this strange phenomenon, a barbarian queen. As far as she could see, in the quick glance she threw in their direction, Gaius was not there.

319

Her head high, her shoulders back, she met Claudius's gaze squarely. She was not a defeated supplicant here. She was queen in her own right of an independent unconquered and unconquerable people.

Unsure what to do or how to address him, she waited in silence and was pleased at last to see him look away. He glanced back at Plautius and reached up for the scroll that was passed to him.

'The Emperor is pleased to greet the Queen of the Brigantes,' he said slowly. There was a slight hesitation in his voice as he spoke, the final trace of a stammer that had plagued him as a boy. 'It is our wish that an alliance be made between the Roman Province of Britannia and the lands of the Brigantes. Such an alliance would be an honour and a great benefit to your peoples and you would be richly rewarded.' His words were instantaneously translated into her own tongue by a man at his elbow. He looked at her again and unexpectedly he smiled. The fearsome cold face was transformed into that of a rather ordinary but essentially friendly man.

Carta felt her own mouth soften in response, an almost unavoidable urge to smile back, but she managed to keep her face grave. 'The Queen of the Brigantes thanks the Emperor for his gracious offer.' Her Latin, thanks to Truthac of the Votadini, was fluent and she saw his eyebrow rise a fraction. 'She will consider his offer with the aid of her tribal leaders and Druids.'

She saw his face harden for a second and she felt a flash of fear. She had been intended, she realised, to accept immediately with delighted relief and thus ensure the northern part of Britain was his ally and no danger to the new province.

'The Queen of the Brigantes is no doubt aware that the penalty for opposing the wishes of Rome is death. For herself and for her people.' His voice was cold now. He waved away the interpreter. 'But I will be gracious. I understand that a queen without a husband must turn for advice to others.' He gave her a grim smile. 'My gifts will perhaps help you to make up your mind.' He waved his arm and several slaves hurried forward carrying chests. These they laid before her and at a nod from the Emperor they flung back the lids. Carta bit back an exclamation of surprise and wonder at the glint of gold. Two were full of coins, two of jewellery.

As grave as he, schooling her face to absolute impassivity she bowed, not too low, but enough to acknowledge the richness of the gift. 'The Emperor is too generous,' she added.

320

'The Emperor is always generous to his allies.' Claudius narrowed his eyes. 'And to seal what I hope will be a lasting alliance I invite you to a feast this evening, together with the other British kings and queens who have accepted our offer of friendship.'

They were all there, the kings and queens who had made peace with Rome and thereby, at least for now, kept their kingdoms: Prasutagus and Boudica of the Iceni, Cogidubnus of the Regni, the new king of the Votadini, Lugaid's nephew, and the king of the Orcades amongst them, as well as Venutios and Brochan as two of the most senior tribal kings of the Brigantian peoples.

Lounging in the Roman fashion on couches before the laden boards, Cartimandua had been placed at the Emperor's right hand, Venutios at her own. The latter glanced at her several times during the course of the evening and once or twice he caught her eye. His thoughts were easy to read. Do not be seduced by this demonstration; don't be fooled. This man is dangerous.

He was, but he was also fascinating; the most powerful man in the world and charming now he put his mind to it, intent on winning her friendship and alliance. She enjoyed the evening, the more so because in the distance she had spotted the envoy, Gaius Flavius Cerialis, seated lower down the table, his eyes fixed on her face. She acknowledged his gaze with a raised eyebrow and was pleased to see him blush.

Later, in their own encampment, Venutios came to her fireside as she sat, sipping from a goblet of thin beer, trying to clear her head of the heavy wine from Appulio.

'The sooner we're away from here, the better I'll be pleased.' He sat down beside her, uninvited.

She did not reply. Thoughtfully she took another sip from the cup. 'How many troops does he have?'

'Five thousand men to a legion. I believe there are now four legions in *Britannia*.' He emphasised the word sarcastically. 'Plus auxiliaries, plus the traitors who gobbled like pigs at a trough at his table tonight. The Dobunni, the Dumnonii, the Catuvellauni.'

'Still not enough to win the whole land.' She was staring thoughtfully into the fire. 'We are safe for the time being. These southern tribes lie open to attack. No one is fighting save my cousin, Caradoc, and he won't last long by all accounts.' A gust of wind blew through the camp, scattering sparks from the fires, blowing rags of smoke amongst their tents. She shivered, pulling her soft bearskin cloak more closely around her shoulders. 'We have to accept that the Roman eagle casts a long shadow over this island. It has power and strength, and probably infinite resources. Our gods bid us be very wary.'

He frowned, making the sign against the evil eye. 'Our gods are mighty. They will help sustain us if we are strong.' He was studying her face in the light of the leaping flames. 'They will not respect weakness.' He glanced up beyond the smoke towards the sky where Mars, Roman god of war, shone red on the western horizon and he too gave an involuntary shiver.

The room had grown dark. The fireside and the companionship of the Brigantians had disappeared into the night and Viv was shivering uncontrollably now that the heat of the camp fire had gone. She looked around for a notebook.

Eleven. There were eleven kings at Camulodunum on that occasion. She frowned, trying to recall the facts. It was recorded on the inscription on the triumphal arch in Rome, which was erected after Claudius's return after his six-month absence. His state visit to Britannia had lasted sixteen days and during that time he had received the submission of eleven kings. Or ten kings and a queen, presumably. Slowly she began to scribble down what she remembered.

Through the open door of her bedroom Viv could hear the faint noises of the street from the open window. Otherwise the flat was silent. It was almost tomorrow, when *Cartimandua, Queen of the North* would be published and her new life as an author would begin.

22

'I've rewritten your schedule, Viv.' Sandy Collingham, the publicity manager in charge of Viv's book launch, dropped her shoulderbag and laptop carrier on the floor and put a fat file down on the table. 'You're feeling strong, I hope?' She grinned. 'The book has gone straight into the bestseller list at number twenty! That's fantastic! We've several new events scheduled,' she went on. 'Bookshops are queuing up for you, lady.' She glanced up. 'People want to meet you.'

'Why?' Viv was overwhelmed.

'Because they are fascinated by the sound of the book. They saw you on the telly and that review has done you nothing but good.'

Viv stared at her. 'What review?'

Sandy paused. 'Oh shit. You haven't seen it? The one by Professor Graham?'

'We were driving back from Yorkshire. We didn't see any papers. And I didn't go out yesterday.' Viv clenched her fists. Why had no one told her? 'Have you got a copy?'

Sandy nodded. 'Hold on to your hat, Viv. Don't let it upset you.'

The review was crucifying. Viv put down the paper with tears in her eyes. Her face was white.

'Why?'

'It's a bit unkind, that's for sure.' Sandy shrugged. 'Ride it. Take no notice. In fact it's so over the top it will be counter-productive from his point of view. And good from yours. People will read the book to see why he's so vitriolic. It'll help sell copies and that's what matters. Now,' she dismissed the topic briskly, 'to the schedule. We're starting this morning with a radio interview. Then the launch party tonight. Tomorrow afternoon we take a train to York. And then as you know it's all points south, coming back up the west coast route.'

Viv barely heard. She was thinking, numbly, about Hugh's review. Why? Why was he still doing this to her?

The interviewer, Mike Malone, stood up, shook hands, waved Viv towards the microphone and returned to his bank of controls. 'This is going out tonight, OK? Part of the Books about Britain fortnight.' He glanced at her quizzically. 'Nervous?'

She nodded.

'You'll be fine. Just be natural.'

As always she enjoyed it once she had started talking. He was friendly, well informed. He appeared to have read the book. He didn't mention the review. They stopped after ten minutes or so and he grinned at her. 'We'll be pausing here for some music. Then for the second half I'll be a bit more aggressive.'

'Aggressive?' Viv frowned apprehensively.

'You'll be fine.' It was obviously his stock phrase.

He waited for a fraction of a second, watching the clock, then he clicked a switch. 'Listen to this and then we'll talk afterwards, OK?'

Viv reached for the earphones.

The voice in her ear was Mike's. 'Now, Professor Graham. You have read Dr Lloyd Rees's book. What did you think of it?'

'There's a base of good stuff.' Hugh's voice was warm. 'Not bad at all. But there are too many inaccuracies to make this a book I could recommend. Viv is a talented writer but she's allowed her imagination to run away with her here.' It went on and on. Or that's what it felt like. In reality it was probably no more than a couple of minutes. It stopped and Mike turned back to her.

'So, Viv. How would you reply to your professor's criticisms?' Mike glanced at her, his face impersonal.

Viv could feel herself sweating. The red light was on. Her reply was being recorded. 'Unfair. Small-minded. Mean.' She forced herself to laugh. 'We have to have progress, Mike. Without leaps of deduction made through the latest research into archaeology, philology, forensic techniques, we would stay with the Victorian take on history. Or in this case the Roman. We have to learn to expand our views.'

'You have anticipated Professor Graham's own book on the subject. Do you expect to be asked to review it in your turn when it comes out?'

Viv stared across the table. Mike raised his eyebrows gesturing at her to speak.

'I did know he was writing a book, of course,' she said at last. 'And perhaps that explains his angst. And if and when he completes it, oh yes, I would be delighted to review it and I hope in my case I can give a fair and considered opinion.'

Mike grinned. He raised finger and thumb circled in triumph. Seconds later he had rounded off the interview and switched off.

'That was a rotten trick!' She glared at him. 'Why didn't you tell me you had spoken to him?'

His shrug was mischievous.' Your reaction was perfect. Natural. If I'd told you, you would have been nervous and angry.'

'And you think I'm not angry now?'

'Oh yes. You are. Great radio!'

'Where is he?' Viv had rung the DPCHC at once.

'At home. He didn't come in today.' Heather didn't have to ask who she meant.

Viv was on his doorstep in under an hour.

'Why? Why are you doing this to me?'

Hugh was standing in the doorway, in an old cotton sweatshirt, sleeves rolled above the elbows and threadbare jeans, a pair of spectacles swinging from his left hand. As he stared at her she found herself incongruously noticing how the tight jeans suited him, but this was a different Hugh to the Hugh she had visited in the night the week before. He stared at her for several seconds, almost as if he didn't recognise her. 'Come in, Viv.' When he spoke at last he sounded bored; even patronising. 'Don't make a scene on the doorstep.' He turned into the hall.

'Why not? It's not as though anyone can see.' She didn't move.

He swung round to face her. 'Did you bring the brooch?'

'Ah. At last you've remembered I've got it; and have you remembered you were so frightened you begged me to take it away again?'

'A stupid thing to do. I'm sorry.' He straightened his shoulders. 'A very stupid thing to do. I need it back.'

325

She frowned. 'Are you all right, Hugh?' Her voice softened.

He laughed. 'Why shouldn't I be?'

'You sound odd.'

'Odd?'

'Different.' She eyed him suspiciously.

'Perhaps because I dared to criticise your book.'

'You call that criticism? It was vicious and hurtful!'

'OK.' He shrugged. 'There's nothing more to say. I'm sorry you can't take criticism. With study and discipline I'm sure one of these days you could find your way back into the academic world, but if you persist with this rubbish –'

'Rubbish?' To her embarrassment she found she was near tears. 'You are trying to destroy me!'

'No, no.' He leaned against the doorpost. 'You're destroying yourself. This book is a disaster and it needs to be pointed out to people who might otherwise read it as serious history.'

'It is serious history.' She was beside herself with anger. 'If you read it dispassionately, Hugh, you'd see that.'

He folded his arms. 'Come on, Viv. You've entered novelistic territory. You are making stuff up.'

'I see. OK.' She laughed dryly. 'Now we have it. You are terrified I have sources you don't know about. I have done original research which you have not seen and you are afraid. Suddenly you are no longer the authority. I am. Poor Hugh.' She began to move away from him. 'Poor Professor Graham, fighting for mastery.'

'The brooch, Viv,' he called after her.

She paused and glanced at him with a frown. 'It's somewhere safe.'

'I want it back. For the museum.'

'For the museum, or for Venutios?'

For a while he didn't reply. 'Venutios was a dream. A hallucination,' he said at last. 'I was not myself when that happened.'

'No, Hugh. You were almost a human being.' Turning, she walked back to her car and climbed in. 'Don't worry about the brooch. It's safe.' As she reversed and turned the car towards the gate, to her amazement she was smiling.

Behind her he stood watching as the car disappeared between the banks of rhododendrons. Without realising it he was listening for the sound of the carnyx. All he heard was the crunch of her car tyres on the gravel.

326

II

Steve caught the train to Edinburgh. It was a fantastic idea, holding the party in the Museum of Scotland. Brilliant. Upmarket, a visible sign of faith from Viv's publishers, and it was in full swing when he arrived. For a few minutes he could not see Viv at all, but he recognised Pat almost at once. Threading his way through the crowd he tapped her lightly on the shoulder and she turned.

'Steve!'

'Hi! Small world!' he smiled. 'How are you?'

'I'm fine.' Pat frowned. She looked pale and ill at ease; anything but fine.

He scanned her face 'What is it?'

'I don't know.' She shivered. A little champagne slopped from her glass over her hand. 'A draught. It's cold in here suddenly.'

They both looked round the huge room. Whatever else it was, it was not cold. She took a deep gulp from her glass. Someone pushed between them and for a moment he lost sight of her. He didn't notice the slight frisson in the air around him. Plunging after her, he saw her talking to a group of media people. She raised a hand, he waved and moved on.

Someone tapped him on the shoulder and he spun round. 'Hello, Steve.' It was Viv. She was dressed in black trousers and a vivid scarlet top. Off the shoulder. Sexy.

'Congratulations, Viv.' He leaned across and kissed her on the cheek.

'I'm so pleased you came, Steve.' She reached up and touched his face.

'Of course I came. You knew I would.' Steve reached for her hand, but Viv had gone, swept away by someone from her publishers to confront a man with a camera. With a grimace he held his glass out for a refill.

Hugh stood in the doorway, staring around him. It was a good turn-out. A media-fest. Why, for an unknown? He grabbed a glass of champagne from a passing tray and stepped into the room. Alison would have loved this. She would have been proud of Viv. Support-ive. She would have told him to stop being such a horrible selfish grouch. She would have called him a dog-in-the-manger. She would have said – what she had said only a week before she had died: 'You must marry again, Hugh. Don't mope about, thinking of me. Marry someone like Viv. I've always suspected you fancied her a little bit. You do, don't you!' And she had lifted her poor thin arm and attempted to punch him and she had laughed.

As though Viv could replace her. As though anyone could.

'Hello, Hugh.' Steve Steadman was standing in front of him. He gave a puzzled smile, a bit wary, as though unsure what to say next. 'Were you looking for Viv? She's over there.'

Hugh frowned. Steve. Always Steve, constantly hanging around her. He shook his head. Were they having an affair? That was grounds to sack her if anything was. Inappropriate behaviour with a student. Steve shouldn't be here. But then he wasn't a student as such, was he, and he was obviously her friend. Hugh sighed. He was the one who shouldn't be here. He should allow her this one piece of celebration at least. But it was too late. Viv was there in front of him. She hadn't seen him. She looked stunning, beautiful, as she talked animatedly to a man in a green shirt. She was laugh-ing, vivacious, happy and so very alive.

He stepped forward. Without thinking, he touched her arm.

She stopped in mid-sentence and swung round to face him, staring at him, frozen, a rabbit in the headlights.

'Why have you come?' In the noise of the room he had to lip-read the words. Perhaps she hadn't actually spoken them out loud. Per-haps she could hear the distant sound of the carnyx in the back-ground. Strange thing to have at a party, but perhaps not in the museum where there were the remains of real carnyxes on display.

'I was invited.' He smiled. 'Presumably by you? She is too gener-ous, but I am the head of her department.' He was speaking to the man in the green shirt now. Explaining. 'She can't believe I think the book is crap. Can't believe it at all.' The man was smiling. Someone else was coming. A photographer. He felt drunk. But he hadn't drunk anything at all. Had he? There was an empty glass in his hand. And she was shouting at him.

'Why did you come? I didn't ask you! Why did you have to do this?' Camera bulbs were flashing. The man in the green shirt had produced a notebook. Hugh smiled sadly. Alison would not have been pleased with him. Not at all pleased. He was quite relieved when Heather appeared out of the crowds and gently took him by the arm. Perhaps she would drive him home. He couldn't quite remember where he had left his car.

'You OK, Viv?' Sandy was standing on the doorstep beside her as Viv groped for her keys. Behind them a taxi was drawn up at the kerb, engine running. Viv nodded. She was exhausted.

'Get a good night's sleep. Tomorrow we hit the world.' Sandy chuckled. 'I'll be here with a taxi at nine, OK?'

'Was that all as much of a disaster as I think it was?' Viv had the door open and was standing in the hall at the foot of the stairs.

'No, not at all. Viv, love, one would pay money for that kind of publicity. I'd be very surprised if you haven't made the front page of every paper in the land! Publicity departments kill for that kind of scene. Don't worry about it. Your sales will rocket. Hundreds, even thousands of people will buy your book just to see what all the fuss is about! Believe me, your drunken professor has done you a huge favour!' She paused. 'He's a handsome devil, isn't he!' She laughed and leaning forward gave Viv a quick hug. 'Go on. Get your beauty sleep. I'll see you tomorrow, bright and early.'

III

Cartimandua was thoughtful as they rode at last out of the Roman encampment at Camulodunum heading north. Venutios reined his pony back beside hers as behind them the long train of chariots and riders and packhorses wound out onto the newly built road.

'He impressed you, the Emperor?' He glanced across at her.

She nodded. 'It would be foolish to deny it. He is the most powerful man in the world. And with reason. He is clever, a statesman. He has the power to make or break us.'

'Which is why you grovelled before him like a slave?' Venutios was scathing. 'Why do it? Why agree to his plans and accept his

329

bribes without consulting me or Brochan? Above all, without consulting Artgenos? Do you realise what you have done?'

She looked across at him and nodded, her face grave. 'I have used statesmanship, Venutios. I have bought us time and I have bought us wealth. Those mules,' she gestured behind them, 'are laden with gold. Do not berate me! I have done what is best for the Brigantians. I have kept my head. I have negotiated with an emperor and I have made him respect me. What would you have done? Shouted? Sworn? Drawn your sword?'

'I am not that stupid, woman!' His face flushed with anger. 'But I would not have kissed his hand!'

Carta laughed. 'No? Perhaps not. But do not forget, that he also kissed mine!' She kicked her pony into a trot, the finely tooled leather of the reins held loosely in one hand, Sun and Moon running effortlessly at the animal's heels. 'And now I am returning to my kingdom free of fear, without any threat of invasion hanging over me and we have all the time in the world to plan our strategy for the future, and no one has been waylaid on the journey. No one has died.' She glanced at him again, as his horse paced alongside hers. 'And in the meantime you might be interested to know that the Emperor asked if I had any plans to marry.'

'He's not the only one who wants to know that!' Venutios retorted. He glanced at her from beneath his eyebrows. 'And did the Emperor also suggest who should be your consort?'

She smiled. 'He did as a matter of fact. Or at least, I told him who I had in mind, and he gave the union his approval.' Her pony sidestepped and shook its bridle. Their escort was several paces behind them now. They were not being overheard.

'So?' He leaned across and grabbed her reins. 'Don't play coy with me! Who are you going to choose?'

'I'm not sure I should tell you until we return home.' She pushed his arm away.

For a moment she thought his anger would overwhelm him, but he pulled his horse back. 'Have it your own way.' He was biting down visibly on his impatience.

She shook her head. 'First I need to consult the gods and then Artgenos and Culann. Then I will reveal my choice to the man I have selected. It will be a hard choice. Not only do I want an ally and a friend and a companion, I want a man who will please me in bed and father strong children.' She was concentrating on her horse's ears. 'A man who will support my decisions and my alliance with Rome. A man who will bow to my leadership as high queen of the Brigantes.' She looked at him at last. 'He will be a hard man to find.' Their eyes locked for an instant.

Her pony bared its teeth and took a nip at the neck of his as they rode on side by side. He swore under his breath.

'Don't look to me, madam, for a man to bring you posies of flowers and pretty trinkets!' he growled at last. 'A king of the Carvetii bends the knee to no one, never mind a woman.'

'Then the king of the Carvetii will never marry a high queen,' she retorted. She was soothing her pony's neck. 'He will kick his heels at her fireside as one of her advisers, but never as one of her trusted confidants.' With a kick she sent her pony into a canter, leaving him reining in his own mount as it jibbed and bucked, trying to follow.

That night they camped at the edge of a broad, slow-moving river, the wagons and horses pulled up into a circle, the queen's tent of skins and poles in the centre near the fire where the cooks began at once to prepare a meal of cold meats and biscuits and cheeses with hot broth and bread slops to wash it down.

A mist was rising from the water as Carta, leaving her ladies and attendants behind in the encampment, made her way along the bank. The water was dark, softly moving in amongst the reeds at the river's edge. Somewhere a bird called out in warning and she heard a splash from a leaping fish.

'Sweet goddess? Are you there? Come to me. Advise me. Have I done right to ally myself with these men of Rome?' She groped at her girdle for a small pouch that hung there and drew out offerings for the spirit of the river. Some coins. Some grain. Some seed heads. Symbols of fertility and hope.

'Vivienne?'

Her voice echoed for a moment across the water. The mist swirled, lapping at her cloak, dappling it with droplets of moisture.

There was no answer from the waters as she stood staring out into the darkness, shivering, unable to concentrate, aware suddenly of a movement in the mists nearby. Turning, she scanned the river bank, wishing she had brought Fergal or a guard, or her hounds with her. The voice that spoke without warning so close to her was not that of a goddess or a spirit of the river waters or of the woods and gentle mossy banks. It was the voice of a man.

'So, my queen. Have you finished your prayers?'

Venutios materialised out of the darkness. 'Then I think you and I need to talk some more about your choice of a husband, don't you?'

He was very close. For all her height and strength he was the taller and now they were no longer on horseback, physically at a huge advantage. 'My politics and my abilities as an adviser and a leader of men you have already tried but you have not taken me to your bed, madam. Should you not put my potential as a mate to the test?'

He was very close. She could smell the sweat on his skin, the leather of his jerkin, the wet wool of his cloak, pinned at the shoulder with the golden bird. His eyes were fixed on hers, his hands now on her shoulders as he pulled her towards him.

'Would you rape me, Venutios?' Her voice, as cold as ice, stopped him in his tracks.

His arms dropped to his sides. 'Venutios does not need to rape a woman. Most would beg for his attention.'

'Did you hear me beg?'

For a moment she thought he would hit her. Then he grinned. 'I had assumed that a queen merely had to snap her fingers and raise an eyebrow. Perhaps I misinterpreted the signs. Would you like me to beg instead?' He went down on one knee, lightly, on the wet grass. Then as she looked down at him in astonishment he seized her wrist. He pulled her off balance and she found herself on the ground beneath him. In the dark the whites of his eyes were very clear. 'If you scream, my queen, I will throw myself into the river and give myself to the gods.' His mouth was on hers, his hands dragging at her cloak, ripping the material away from her body, before tearing off his own and throwing his clothes aside into the reeds.

She did not scream. Breathlessly she felt her body respond to his, his strength and violence triggering a response in her, movement for movement, kiss for kiss. Only when at last their bodies had exploded into mutual orgasm did he slump exhausted across her, his head on her breasts, his shoulders heaving as he tried to catch his breath.

She gave a quiet laugh. 'So. He is tired already. If this is your test performance, Venutios, I have to ask myself if a younger man might not have more stamina.'

This time she did scream, but it was not a scream of fear.

Exhausted they rolled apart and lay in the cold wet grass. He recovered first, staggering to his feet, making his way to the river bank where he knelt. 'Blessed gods, I salute you! May my seed prove fruitful and my strength all that is desired by my queen!' He splashed his face with the icy water and turned away to gather up his clothes.

She was lying staring up at the stars. 'See. Caer Gwyddion, Llys Don, the Harp of Idris . . .'

He picked up her cloak. Throwing it over her he knelt and scooped her into his arms. 'The stars and their gods are witness to my triumph tonight, Cartimandua and now the men and women of our party will witness it as well.' As he staggered to his feet she struggled to free herself but somehow he had managed to pinion her arms with the cloak.

'Put me down!' Her fury was overwhelming. He was carrying, her, naked inside the cloak, like a trophy, heading towards the light of the fire and the noise of the camp, singing, shouting, laughter in the night.

'I advise you to lie still in my arms.' He chuckled. 'Should I drop you, you would roll naked onto the grass at the feet of your servants and that would not be dignified.'

Her language, learned from a lifetime in the horse lines and amongst the tribe's most seasoned warriors made him laugh out loud. Carrying her past the guards in between the wagons and across the fire-lit grass he strode directly into the middle of the camp. She was aware of the sudden silence. Closing her eyes she groaned.

Venutios laughed again. 'Your queen and I have plans for this evening, my friends. Continue with preparing the food. We will join you later.'

Ducking into her tent he rolled her onto the pile of furs which had been put there as her bed and threw himself on top of her. 'So, do you still think me too old, my queen?' As he entered her again with a shout of triumph she was capable only of a small moan. Neither of them were conscious of the silence outside the tent or the immense roar of laughter and approval as the sound of his triumph was clearly audible in the night.

*

333

In her bath Viv dozed, the launch party long forgotten. The water had grown cold, the foam settled into a soapy scum. The only sound in the silent flat was the drip from one of the taps.

IV

Watching from the distance, Medb scowled He had taken off his clothes, tossed his cloak and the brooch aside and ravaged Cartimandua there on the ground, rutting with her like a boar in the woods. And he was going to take her as wife.

Sitting up, Medb overturned the bowl of water into which she had been gazing with a shout of anger and watched it splash across the floor. All but a prisoner at Caer Lugus, she could do nothing but wait and watch and scheme, alone, while Venutios danced attendance on his high queen.

In her sleep Pat groaned and turned over in bed.

'So, Viv will be away for a week or so.' She faced Cathy across the café table next morning. Both were drinking their coffee black. 'Just as well, after that row with the Prof last night.'

Cathy raised an eyebrow. 'What is the matter with the man? How small-minded and mean can you get!'

'I keep telling you what the matter is. He fancies her.' Pat reached for her cigarettes. 'You should have gone, Cathy. She was really hurt that you weren't there.' She and Viv had finally confronted one another amidst the crowds, with Pat shouting above the noise. 'I didn't take it! I swear it! The brooch wasn't there! Cathy and I searched for it and it had disappeared again! I imagined it! Imagined the blood! When we looked at the sheets in the laundry basket, there was no trace of blood anywhere! It was all a dream. We were all dreaming!'

She had moved out of the flat and, temporarily, into Maddie's spare room by the time Pete got back from his showdown with Viv.

'This will all blow over, Pat. Once we come back from Sweden I'll get in touch with Viv and explain. It's just,' Cathy paused, 'she's going to make herself ill. If she goes on like this she really will need a psychiatrist. And so will you.' She glanced up at Pat. 'I mean it, Pat. You've got to stop all this stuff. No more Medb. No more dreams and nightmares and ghosts and –' she shuddered, 'blood!'

Pat shrugged. 'I didn't imagine it, Cathy. And neither did you.' There was a long pause. 'I think we all had too much excitement and booze at the party last night,' she went on with a grimace. 'Don't worry. You go to Sweden and enjoy yourself and I'll see you when you come back.'

Cathy gave a wry grin. 'Too much booze and now too much publicity.' She nodded towards the paper lying folded between them. There was a picture of Viv and Hugh on page three under the headline: '**Academic Rancour explodes at Museum.**'

'All publicity is good publicity,' Pat repeated the mantra solemnly. 'Don't worry about her. I think some time in the hard-headed company of a publicist and a non-stop schedule of talks and book signings will distract her sufficiently from her dreams and take her mind off the whole business.'

Hugh had not seen the paper Pat and Cathy were perusing. He was studying the *Scotsman*. It wasn't a headline. In fact he had only spotted it by chance. 'Amongst other projects under production is one by a new company, Daughters of Fire, who plan to turn Viv Lloyd Rees's controversial book, *Cartimandua Queen of the North* into a drama documentary to hit the radio schedules this winter. As part of the BBC's policy of producing good quality programmes to meet the public's current passion for history, this kind of enterprise can only be encouraged.'

Hugh stared at the paper in front of him. That morning he had woken with a violent hangover and a feeling of overwhelming remorse. What was the matter with him? Why had he hurt Viv so badly yet again and probably trashed her academic career forever? He was contemplating ringing her to apologise for his crass behaviour, perhaps ask her out to dinner to see if he could mend some fences when the newspapers hit the mat. Scanning the article, his remorse had vanished. Career indeed. Obviously her career in his department was irrelevant. She had already sold out. She wouldn't want her job any more. Well, he could easily fix that. He knew people at the BBC. It would only take one phone call to make them pull it from the schedules. Then where would this bright, clever innovative writer be? She'd be begging for her job back, that's where. He was working himself up into a fury again. This was going to lead to yet more publicity for Cartimandua and once again she would take the opportunity to traduce Venutios.

Venutios!

Hugh gripped the edge of his desk, aware of the tension in the room around him. No. Please God, no! Not again. He shouldn't even have thought the word!

'Leave me alone, you bastard!' he shouted out loud. He looked round nervously. It was all right. The room was normal again. Whatever had threatened to appear had changed its mind and drawn back. He listened fearfully but there was no call of the carnyx in the distance. Only the sound of the clock on the bookcase broke the silence.

23

I

Viv and Sandy walked slowly back through the streets of York to their hotel and sat in the bar for half an hour, unwinding after a tiring day which had culminated in a book signing which had seemed to go on for hours. Tomorrow they were going to Nottingham, the day after that to London. It was midnight when they wished each other goodnight and Viv wearily unlocked her bedroom door.

Cartimandua, High Queen of the Brigantes and Venutios, King of the Carvetii, were married at the feast of Beltane. There were a thousand guests in attendance, including Carta's mother, her younger brothers Bran and Fintan, both recovered at last from their wounds, and the rest of the family, Venutios's brother Brucetos, his wife and baby, his uncle and his cousins, Prasutagus and Boudica of the Iceni and their baby daughter, the kings of the Atrebates and of the Dobunni, all of whom where now allies of Rome. Medb was not there. When Venutios had returned to Caer Lugus to prepare for the wedding he had been furious to find she had evaded those set to watch over her. He had no idea where she had gone. His anger had lasted only a few hours. He was glad to be rid of her.

Two days before the ceremony Aulus Plautius, governor of Britannia, arrived in person with ten wagons of wine in amphorae and furs, spices and gold, wedding gifts to impress and hold firm the loyalty of these new allies, so crucial to the north-western frontier of the Empire.

The ceremony was held at Dinas Dwr, the site selected by Cartimandua and her consort to be the new capital of their great confederacy, following her father's original decision to enlarge it and embellish the buildings there, creating what the Romans called an oppidum. They would after all need a centre from which to trade and negotiate with their new allies, who were nothing if not reluctant to make their way into the high hills and moors of the Brigantian kingdom, so this sheltered rich valley would be perfect.

The line of the new walls would be chosen and marked and blessed and men brought in from all over the north to start constructing the great new ramparts and build dozens of extra houses.

The gods smiled upon the wedding day. The sun shone, the winds were soft and smelled of the sweet grasses of the hills and Carta, wearing a gown of green and pink as befit a queen, linked hands with her husband-to-be and walked out of the gates, down the path garlanded with flowers and strewn with herbs, into the forest to the great oak tree under which Artgenos and Culann stood ready to bless them in the presence of their followers and friends and guests. At the right hand of Aulus Plautius stood his military tribune, Gaius Flavius Cerialis, his eyes fixed on the figure of the barbarian queen.

At the feast and dancing that followed the ceremony Cartimandua of the Brigantes danced late into the night. Once she was partnered by the governor himself, once by his tribune, who passed her in the circle dance, broke away, touched her hands with his own, bowed and danced on. She had met his eye and bowed and laughed, reaching out to touch his cheek and then she was gone in the thick of the dance again, whirled away on the sound of pipes and harps and drums as the sparks flew up from the dozens of fires and the luminous night closed in across the countryside.

Two days later the Romans were gone.

As soon as the building of the new walls had commenced, Carta and Venutios set off on a tour of their northern kingdoms, anxious to reinforce their own authority and the alliance with Rome, heading first up towards the lands of the Textoverdi and then onwards to visit the Votadini, still secure under the strong rule of Lugaid and part of the northern alliance as clients of Rome.

In the main guest house on Dun Pelder, Venutios sat down and bent to unlace the thongs of his sandals with a groan. 'Too long on horseback. It will be good to stop here a while with friends. These are good people. We will enjoy our visit here. Come, wife, can you not undo this knot for your husband?' He extended a foot in her direction. Carta turned from the mirror where she had been contemplating her dusty, dishevelled hair, remembering another arrival here, another day, when her hair had looked like a birds' nest, remembering the young man who had laughed her out of her bad humour.

'A queen does not unlace anyone's shoes, not even her own. Call a servant, if you cannot do it yourself.' She softened the words with a smile. 'Why don't you go and have a bath and spend some time in the sweat house? Lugaid plans a great feast for us at dusk.'

'Are you sending me away?' He had undone the knot. Kicking the sandal towards the wall, he stood up. 'Because I don't intend to be banished so easily.' In two strides he was beside her, grabbing her wrists, wrestling her down onto the deep heather bed. 'My wife, queen or not, does not dismiss her husband like a servant. She does his bidding first!'

He knew just how much he could anger her, and what it took to arouse her, diverting her passionate fury into lust. He had done it many times now, mostly in the privacy of their bedchamber, but from time to time outside, careless of who saw them. To hold the high queen helpless and obedient by the touch of his hand and his thighs gave him the same satisfaction he felt as he mastered an unbroken horse. He rode her exultantly and at last fell beside her on the bed, exhausted.

When Carta extricated herself from the sheets he was already asleep. Wrapping herself in a cloak, she went to the door and stood in its lee, staring round the camp. Once more she was remembering Riach and her eyes filled with tears.

'Lady?' A gentle voice at her elbow made her start. It was Vellocatus, her husband's shield bearer. 'Are you all right?' The young man was clearly torn between embarrassment and concern. 'I'm sorry, lady. The king told me to wait for him out here.'

She straightened her shoulders, vividly aware of how weak and dishevelled she must appear. 'The king is asleep. Leave him for now. Find Mairghread for me, then go to your companions in the warriors' house. I doubt if the king will need you again tonight.'

As she lay back in the large wooden bath in the women's house, luxuriating in water warmed by stones straight from the firebed, wearily soaping her arms as a slave poured jugs of warm water over

339

her back, Carta had a vision suddenly of Aulus Plautius, governor of all Britannia and his envoy, Gaius Flavius Cerialis in the bath. The picture of Gaius, with his muscled, well-built body was not altogether unpleasing. The Romans, so she had been told, never used soap to make them clean. The Romans did not know what soap was. They oiled themselves, apparently, like haunches of meat and scraped off the dirt with their knives. The thought made her laugh out loud.

II

Viv dropped her bags on the floor of the flat and stared round. The taxi had dropped Sandy at Waverley to catch her train back to London after two last book signings, one in Glasgow and then this morning in Dundee. The book promotion was over. It was time to go back to being a writer. Viv went to open the window. The whirlwind tour, the plaudits of her audiences, a handful of complimentary reviews and some really good radio and TV interviews had restored her faith in herself and in her book. It was good to be home.

Sighing, she threw the pile of post onto her desk and pressed the play button on the answer machine. The first message was from Steve. 'Viv? I didn't see you again after the party. I came round but you had already gone. Sorry to miss you. Ring me when you get back.' Bugger! She had forgotten all about him. The slight reproach in his tone was unmistakable. Poor Steve, she had brought him all the way back to Edinburgh for the party and then only spoken to him for a few seconds. She would ring him back today. Shuffling through the letters, she listened to the second message. It was from her editor. 'Congratulations, Viv! The book has rocketed to number nine in the bestsellers. All that publicity worked, my dear. Well done! Talk soon!' Viv grimaced. Most of that publicity had not been intentional, far from it, but still it was fantastic to be in the top ten. She could hardly believe it. The next message was from Pat. 'Ring me as soon as you get back. We need to do some work. Hope the trip was good. I'm back at Abercromby Place – catsitting while the others are away!'

One of the letters had an Irish postmark. She stared at it puzzled as she listened to the third message. It was from Hugh. 'I believe I owe you an apology. And I need to collect the brooch. Ring me.'

Tearing the letter open she gaped in astonishment as her eyes skimmed the contents. '. . . impressed by your scholarship . . . you would be a senior part of a friendly department here in south-west Ireland . . . we invite you to come and look round to discuss our proposition . . .' They were offering her an academic post, in spite of, perhaps because of, everything that had happened! A prestigious job. Stunned, she sat down. She was still staring at the letter five minutes later when there was a sharp double ring on the doorbell.

Hugh was standing on the landing. 'I have come to apologise.' He stepped in uninvited and walked straight past her into the living room, skirting her suitcase and holdall as if they were not there. 'Whatever I thought of your research methods I should have been more supportive.'

Viv stared at him, the letter forgotten as her hurt and anger came flooding back. 'After trashing me in public! In the most public way possible, you are apologising in private? Now that it's too late? Now my book tour is over!' She threw the letter down on the desk.

'Book tour?' He looked puzzled for a moment, and then seeming to see her bags for the first time, nodded. 'I see. Of course. The celebrity tour. Something us academics seldom get to indulge in.'

'Probably because you are sour and embittered old fogies!' she retorted. 'I've only been back a few minutes. How on earth did you know I was here? Did you set up a watch on my doorstep?'

The idea had clearly never occurred to him. 'No, I was passing. I was afraid I might have been too harsh and it was unfair of me to speak to Maddie Corston. After all, what harm can a play do? But you still have a job at the department, Viv. I am sure we can resolve our differences –'

Viv stared at him. She didn't even hear the last conciliatory sentence. 'You've spoken to Maddie?'

He nodded almost sadly. 'I told her to bin the play. Hasn't she told you?'

For a moment Viv was too stunned to speak. 'And she listened to you?' At last she managed a husky response.

'Oh yes. I've known Maddie for years She was a student of mine. Before your time of course.' He smiled apologetically.

341

'So you can speak to her again. Tell her to unbin it. We have a contract, Hugh! You can't do this!'

'I think you'll find I can.' He folded his arms. She was looking exhausted. Untidy. Her hair on end, her face pale, her shirt unbuttoned just low enough to show her cleavage. She was wearing some sort of pendant on a chain, he noticed. It had slid down between her breasts so he could not identify it. An amulet, maybe. Not for the first time it crossed his mind that he had been stupid in refusing Meryn's suggestion that he wear one. But, for goodness' sake, this was the twenty-first century! And there had been no further appearances from Venutios, beyond that one scary moment in his study when he was reading the paper, nor ghostly fanfares of the carnyx, which confirmed his suspicion that it had all been in his imagination, for all he knew triggered by something Viv had said in the first place!

He was staring at her, he realised, but he couldn't help himself. He wasn't sure why he kept on harassing her like this. Because that's what it was. Harassment. Perhaps it was because she refused to be impressed by him. Maybe she even despised him a little. The thought hurt.

'You could make her change her mind. Hugh, this is important to me. You can't wreck everything like this!'

She was devastated, off guard. Transparent with shock. She was, he realised, about to beg. It did not make him feel better. Turning towards the door he shrugged. 'Clearly you were about to unpack so we won't discuss it now.'

'Please, Hugh. Don't do this.' She hadn't moved from the centre of the floor, pinned to the spot.

He shrugged. 'It's done, I'm afraid.'

'Hugh.' She followed him and put her hand on his arm. 'You don't need to be like this!'

She saw his face soften as he stood looking down at her. He reached up and touched her cheek lightly with his finger. 'Viv.' He shook his head, almost sadly as he whispered her name and Viv knew with absolute certainty that more than anything in the world she wanted him to kiss her. She could feel herself being drawn towards him irresistibly. They were very close when she looked up into his eyes.

And saw the eyes of someone else.

She jerked away with a cry of fright.

'Where is the brooch?' His voice was deeper suddenly and threat-ening. It was the voice of a stranger. 'By all the gods why do you think I came here?' He seized her arm and she screamed as his fingers tightened on her wrist. 'Give it to me and I'll go.'

'Hugh! Fight him!' Viv screamed in terror. She was struggling frantically, trying to free herself. His fingers were ice cold, like an iron clamp on her skin. 'For God's sake, fight him!'

'Viv! What's going on?' Pat's voice in the doorway interrupted them and suddenly it was over. Hugh, white as a sheet, slumped back, releasing her. He reeled towards the door. 'Dear God! I'm sorry. I'm so sorry!' Pushing past Pat, he headed blindly for the stairs and disappeared, the sound of his footsteps pounding into the distance.

Pat looked at Viv, astonished. 'What in heaven's name was going on?'

'He was possessed! Literally.' Viv was trying to stop herself shak-ing. Sitting down on the rocking chair she put her head in her hands. 'I thought he was going to kill me. He wanted the brooch.'

'Did you tell him where it is?' Pat walked over and closed the door. Turning the key in the lock, she came back and sat down opposite Viv. Her eyes narrowed.

Viv shook her head. 'It all happened so quickly. We were talking about the play and suddenly he changed. His eyes changed. He was somebody else.'

'Who?'

'Venutios.' It was a whisper.

'Shit!' Pat dived into her bag and brought out her cigarettes.

'Where is the brooch, Pat?' Viv frowned. 'Pete said you had it at the flat.'

Pat shook her head. 'No. That was all a bad dream. It wasn't real. It's still at Stanwick. It must be.' She blew out a cloud of smoke.

Viv bit her lip, looking down again at her hands. 'What's happen-ing to us?'

Pat shrugged. 'They want it, don't they. They all want it. Carta. Venutios.' She paused. 'And Medb.' She took another drag on the cigarette. 'Why? What is so special about it? Christ, this is scary.' She glanced at Viv. 'So what did Hugh say about the play before he was dragged away by our friend ?'

'That he's had a word with Maddie, who he knows, apparently, and he told her to bin it.' Viv's hands were still shaking.

'What?' Pat stared at her, her mouth hanging open.

'I know. I don't believe it either.' Viv gave a stilted laugh. 'Don't worry. I'm sure we can sort it.'

'Too bloody right we can sort it!' Pat stared at her. 'I've never heard such nonsense. We've got a contract! I'll ring her now. That man's impossible!' Her mobile was already in her hand and in a matter of seconds she was through to Maddie's office.

The short conversation with Maddie's assistant was inconclusive. Pat switched the phone off impatiently. 'She's out. I think I'll go round there. I'll camp on her doorstep if necessary. I'm not letting that bastard spoil everything now.' She paused. 'You know, in spite of himself I'll bet Hugh has done you a bit of good. The book is selling like mad – mostly to people who want to know what the row is all about!'

Viv gave a watery grin. 'Thank you, Hugh!' The irony made her feel better.

With a sigh she stood up and walked over to the desk as soon as Pat had gone. What had happened to Hugh just now? She had seen Venutios. Felt Venutios. Dear God, Venutios had taken him over so completely he might have done anything in his rage. She shuddered. Picking up the letter, she read it through again. It hadn't been a dream. It was true. She had been offered a job. A prestigious job, far away from Edinburgh and away from Hugh. A job which presumably was not dependent on a reference from him as it implied that the author of the letter knew all about their quarrel. The question was, did she want it?

It was three hours before Pat rang her back. 'Viv? I've spoken to Maddie. It's OK. She had no intention of listening to the mad professor. None at all. She said she let him rant away and assume he'd persuaded her. It was easier that way. What is it with the guy? Anyway, she's going off on maternity leave at the end of the week but she thinks they'll be scheduling the play probably for the late autumn or early winter. So, my darling co-writer, we have a deadline. Does that make you feel better? Nothing but writing for the next week or so, OK?'

Carta, watching from the shadows, frowned. Venutios and Medb. Their story was nothing. They were leaves blowing in the wind. She smiled grimly. Venutios she had dealt with at once. He knew where he stood.

'They are your own people!' Venutios was furious.

'They disobeyed me.'

More than a hundred men had died, the rebellion suppressed as fast as it had flared into being, and now she was confronted by the surviving ringleaders. In chains they awaited summary justice here at Dun Righ, in the place of judgement under the great oak near the falls.

She had given orders that no Brigantian would fight Rome. In exchange Plautius confirmed the guarantee that Rome would not attack Brigantia. That was the way the client status worked. They were allies. She would hold the northern frontier and her people would keep their weapons. They were a free people. So, if Brigantians broke the agreement and sent men to support her cousin Caradoc in his war against the legions, she had to act swiftly and she had to act hard to stop them.

Artgenos and Culann, like Venutios, counselled restraint.

'They have been punished enough. They have lost face; they have lost their best warriors. Leave well alone,' Artgenos advised, sitting by her fireside, wrapped in his undyed woollen mantle, his face grey with fatigue. He sensed Carta rapidly moving out of his control. The woman was wilful. And she had strength. He sighed again.

Cartimandua's popularity amongst her people was enormous. She was bringing them peace and prosperity. Through her intervention the gods had smiled on Brigantia. Their granaries were full, their beasts fat and fertile and unlike their conquered southern neighbours in the province they did not have to watch endless wagons of food and provisions that should have been their own, plodding down the trackways to feed the ever-hungry legions of their conquerors. If her warriors needed to fight there were distant northern tribes to be raided for cattle and women. The cream of the fighting men were part of her own army. Her personal prae-torian guard! Any doubts she harboured deep in her heart were buried and hidden. She was determined no one would ever see her weakened by uncertainty or by misplaced compassion.

She sat, the heavy gold torcs, symbols of her power and status at neck and wrists, within the sacred grove with Artgenos and his fellow Druids seated on either side of her. Behind them the tribe was gath-ered in awed silence. The prisoners had, to a man, chosen their death. Better by far to elect to die in the sacred grove as messengers carrying offerings to the gods than to be executed as cowards and criminals. These men were brave warriors. They would die full of honour and explain their rebellion to their gods, confident of life and contentment in the land of the ever young until such time as their souls chose to be reborn. One was barely more than a boy, by far the youngest; the son of the tribal chieftain and a mere stripling, he stood close to his father, his face set, trying with every last ounce of courage he possessed not to cry. Every now and then his eyes strayed from Carta's face, up into the great branches of the tree, and she could see him watching the leaves, the sunlight, feeling for the last few minutes the warmth on his face. He could see a squirrel, carefree, leaping about in the topmost branches and she guessed how desperately he longed to join the squirrel in its freedom.

Carta did not allow herself to flinch as she watched the men die. If they could be strong, so could she. Only once, when the boy knelt in the bloody place of death, next to his father's body to receive the triple death blows did she close her eyes and sigh. She saw him glance up. Saw him look one last time on the green leaves of the oak and the sunshine and the life that would never now be his, then he closed his eyes and waited for the blow. His would be one of the heads she would take as a trophy, making herself the keeper of his soul and the inheritor of his valour and his strength and finally, in private, she would tell him how sad his death had made her.

As the men, women and children of the tribe watched, the boy's body slumped to the earth. Above the trees the kites and buzzards were already circling. The squirrel fled.

For a moment she saw the boy's shadow hover over the body, then it had gone. He had made the crossing into the land of the gods. She looked across at Artgenos, who nodded. He too had seen the boy's soul leave. It was well done.

It was strange how the Romans, brave men undeniably, did not

346

understand this transition of the soul. They professed shock and horror at stories of the priests being present at executions and supervising this the most important moment in a man's life. Their own prisoners they butchered without honour, condemning the frightened souls to roam eternally. Such crude viciousness was beyond comprehension.

Slowly she stood up, signalling the end of the ceremony and the end of the rebellion. However bravely a man met his death he did not court it. Better to serve the queen than defy her. The message had gone home.

She paused, allowing Venutios to walk beside her and realised that he was watching her with something like awe. Behind him Vellocatus was following them slowly, carrying his king's sword. His handsome young face was ravaged with grief and shock at what he had witnessed.

Venutios glanced at his wife again. 'You were strong today.' He sounded almost impressed.

She met his gaze gravely. 'I had to be. There must be no more defiance of my authority.'

His face was grim. 'I doubt there will be.'

'Then the deaths have served their purpose. I gave Artgenos the order that their heads be preserved. They were all brave men, if misguided. We will honour that bravery.' She reached out to touch his arm. Behind her the two dogs which followed her everywhere were, like her husband, uneasy. They had smelled the blood and sensed her resolution and perhaps, unlike him, her inner sorrow, and their hackles were up.

Venutios looked across at her, his jaw set, his eyes veiled. She had made her first big mistake.

Viv shuddered violently. She awakened without warning to find herself sitting on the edge of the rocking chair. She was sweating and shaking with horror and she was, she realised, about to be violently sick. Running to the bathroom she vomited again and again, the sight and stench of the killing grounds still inside her head. So, those were the bloodsoaked groves described with such horror by historians, the human sacrifice so abhorred by the hypocritical Romans who preferred to throw their prisoners to the lions and watch them die as a spectacle in the arena.

347

How could she? How could she order it? Stand and watch. Not flinch. But then she was a queen and all her reputation and power depended on the fact that she could be strong. Besides, she was warning Venutios that she would not be defied. Venutios, whose eyes Viv had seen looking out at her from Hugh's.

Splashing water on her face, Viv groped for a towel and pressed it hard against her eyes. She was still shaking uncontrollably.

24

I

Hugh slammed down the phone and walked over to the French windows. The heat from the terrace was rising like a tangible wave as he stood staring out. He grimaced. He had been ringing Viv all morning. He ought to go back to Edinburgh now. Camp on her doorstep. Search her flat by force if necessary. He clenched his fists. He could feel it again, the strange overpowering anger which seemed to lurk out here in the garden. Cautiously he looked round. The place was silent; nothing stirred. The heat from the stones and the walls radiated out into a stillness which was uncanny and suddenly he knew why. Venutios was there. He listened. There wasn't a breath of wind; not a bird sang. He could hear nothing. He looked down at his hands and cautiously he flexed his fingers. Had Venutios really invaded his soul for a few terrifying seconds or had it been his imagination? He had felt the man's anger and his strength. For a paralysing moment he had known what it would feel like to want to kill and to know himself capable of violence such as he had never contemplated. In those same seconds, while he had been on the phone, he had also realised that, however much he tried to deny it to himself, he loved Viv Lloyd Rees, but that one day he might be forced to hurt her.

When he saw the tall figure, over by the laurels, it was with a sense of inevitability and overwhelming defeat. Venutios was standing on the grass, his hands on his hips. His handsome face was hard and set, the blue painted swirls around the temples terrifying, the long hair tangled by a wind Hugh couldn't feel. Frozen with fear, he watched as Venutios strode towards him, knowing he should turn back inside and slam the doors; knowing he should ring Meryn; knowing he should throw himself into the car and drive. Drive anywhere, as fast as he could. He didn't move.

When at last the tall figure was standing only a few feet from him he merely shook his head. 'I couldn't find the brooch,' he said quietly. 'I did my best. It's not Viv's fault. Leave her alone. If you want to blame anyone, blame me.'

II

'Viv, we've got to talk!' Hugh's voice echoed through the flat. 'I have to have the brooch. It's the only way to get him off my back. I'm sorry. I didn't mean to frighten you. Help me, Viv!'

Miserably she stared at the phone. It was the third time he had called her that morning. Fifteen minutes later she was still seated at the keyboard when the phone rang again. This time she switched it off. A mug of coffee, cold and skimmed with a milk slick, lay untouched beside the monitor as her fingers rattled over the keys and the documentation of Cartimandua's life grew longer and longer, the story loud and insistent in her head.

CARTA: I will lead these men into battle myself.
VENUTIOS: No, I will lead them. That is what men do.
CARTA: But I am queen.
VENUTIOS: You may be queen, but you are only a woman!

That was all wrong. Venutios would never say that. Elected as high queen, she must have been able to lead her men herself. Boudica did. And Carta had proved herself. She was strong. And she was ruthless.

CARTA: I have ridden into battle, sir, at the head of my troops and I shall do so again. And I have ordered the death of traitors. Remember that.

How would she address him? How did she address him in the dreams? Viv bit her lip, staring back at her notes.

350

VENUTIOS: My queen, this is a job for a man!

Oh God, how corny!

CARTA: I think not! I shall lead my men, and the women of the tribe shall as always accompany us. That way we shall be sure of success.

Viv began to write again. By the time Pat arrived she had several pages to show her. They sat reading, passing notes and pages of dialogue to each other and then at last they put the sheets down and looked at one other.

'Well?' Viv was eyeing Pat nervously.

Pat exhaled slowly. 'It's good as far as it goes. But it's still too self-conscious. You need to lift bits out of your notes in toto. Real language as you've noted it down. As we recorded it before. You've edited it back into history speak. We need to bring in earlier more of a feel of what Carta's beliefs – Medb's beliefs – meant to them. Lift it out of the ordinary. Convey something of the amazing Celtic world view'. She paused thoughtfully. 'I've had a glimpse of what it means to live and breathe a native spirituality from a programme I've worked on about the Native Americans. Living as part of the world around them, not top species laying down the law, but being one with it. That's what we need here. To think as Carta thought.'

There was a moment's silence. Viv put down her pen. 'You're right.'

'Sound effects are going to be important to help with this,' Pat went on. 'Nothing too spooky, but we're going to need some atmospherics to back up the spiritual link to nature. Waterfalls. Wind on the high moors, that sort of thing.' She shrugged. 'I haven't really got to grips with what Carta's world looked like, you know. Your descriptions in the book are great as far as they go, but obviously it's a history book. I want to go and see it all myself.'

'I suppose we could go to Winter Gill Farm.' Viv put in. 'It would be a great place to record sound effects. You could climb Ingleborough. You're in training now you've been up Traprain.' She smiled.

'That would be great –' Pat stopped. 'You know, I'm learning to notice things I never used to. How one can look into a stream or a pool of water and see the future and the past, for instance. We can do it, just as they did.' Medb was teaching her.

Viv gave a wry laugh. 'I should be putting stuff like that into the

351

dialogue.' She sounded subdued. 'I've seen it through Carta's eyes, but when I write I still see it as a historian. I'm as bad as Hugh. I see her beliefs as quaint. Primitive. Pagan. And I am unconsciously editing it accordingly.'

'Well, she was a pagan in that hers was a pre-Christian world.' Pat nodded.

'But I'm using pagan as a pejorative term. You are right. I wouldn't dare call in question Native American spirituality these days, would I? And Celtic religion is similar. It dramatically effects their attitude to death. That's important. That's what we have to get in very early in the dialogue. It effects how she feels about Riach and about Triganos and her baby. She obviously felt sad on a day to day basis, sad because they weren't there any more, but not as sad as someone feels who thinks "that's it, gone for good". If they communicated with their ancestors and their gods, surely they communicated with their dead.' She broke off with a curse as the phone rang again. Hugh had called half a dozen times since Pat had arrived. 'He's not going to give up, is he? And he's going to keep on threatening to come round.'

This time, though, the message was longer. 'Listen, Viv. This is important. Don't let anyone else touch the brooch, or touch it yourself again. It was cursed.' He paused, and they could almost hear his embarrassment down the phone. 'I've been told by someone who knows about these things, that that is how Venutios got to me. And it might affect other people. You. Anyone who touches it!' There was a pause, then the line went dead.

Pat's face had drained of colour. 'I touched it, Viv! I touched that brooch. I held it in my hand.'

Viv stared at her. She was biting her lip. 'That's where Medb came from, Pat,' she said at last. 'She gave Venutios the brooch. It's imbued with her power.'

For a moment neither of them said anything. When Pat spoke at last it was one word. 'Shit!'

In the long silence that followed the phone rang again. They ignored it.

'You need to move out for a bit,' Pat whispered. 'Get right away. Come and stay at Abercromby Place. He won't know where you are.'

'No. 'Viv shook her head. 'Don't you see, Pat. I have to get it back to him.'

352

'You can't! It's dangerous! He just said so.'

'If it is, it's too late for us.' Viv shrugged. 'We've both touched it.' She glanced at Pat with a shudder. 'You have to fight Medb. She's evil.' She was scanning Pat's face carefully.

'Thanks!' Pat scowled. 'How exactly am I supposed to fight her?'

'Don't listen to her.' Viv looked down at the manuscript in front of them. 'Don't keep writing about her.' She stood up and walked towards the window uneasily, then she turned and faced Pat again. 'Medb hated Cartimandua.'

'Yes.' Pat gave a small tight laugh.

'She wanted to see her brought down. She wanted to drive a wedge between her and Venutios.'

'I shouldn't think that was hard,' Pat retorted.

'You suggested taking the brooch to Stanwick,' Viv went on thoughtfully. 'You were the one who didn't want to give it back to Hugh once the programme was over.'

'So? You agreed with me.'

'Did Medb put that idea in your head, Pat? Was it Medb who wants to keep it away from Venutios?'

'If it's cursed you'd think she would want him to have it!' Pat scrabbled for her cigarettes again and shook the packet. It was empty.

'There is something we are not seeing.' Viv shivered. 'I don't know what to do.'

'Then don't do anything. Concentrate on the play.' Pat stood up. 'I need to buy some more cigarettes.'

'Let's leave it there for tonight.' Viv was suddenly exhausted. 'Talk about it some more tomorrow.'

'When you've consulted Carta?' Pat raised an eyebrow sarcastically. 'She knows nothing about Medb. And she doesn't care! She never gave Medb another thought after she had her kidnapped.'

'Maybe not.' Viv frowned.

'The truth will come out in the play.'

'Will it?' Viv watched as Pat pushed her papers into her bag and slung it onto her shoulder. 'We'll see.'

III

Vivienne.

The voice woke Viv from an uneasy sleep.

Vivienne. Sweet goddess, protect me and protect my people!

It was just growing light. In the distance she could hear the blackbird. She frowned. Blackbirds sing at dawn because every dawn has a message. A sheaf of messages. She glanced towards the phone, then she shook her head. Every dawn is also a potential gateway, a magical time. Not a time for modern technology. A time to listen to the voices from the past. And to act.

She had to retrieve the brooch. And she had to do it without Pat knowing.

It was still early when she drove out of Edinburgh and the streets were comparatively empty. By nine she was almost there.

Drawing up in the place they had parked before, she headed up onto the rampart wall.

The day was airless and the trees which hung over the track were still. In the short time since they had been there last the undergrowth had grown up even more thickly. Nettles and brambles crossed the track and in places it was hard to see where she was going. Cautiously she made her way down the steep bank to the bottom of the reconstructed piece of wall and began to feel along the stones. It was here somewhere. She paused uncomfortably. She could feel someone watching her. She turned round slowly. The clearing was very hot. No breath of wind stirred down here in the lee of the wall. 'Carta?' The word faded into silence. 'Medb?'

Turning back, she scrabbled amongst the stones, pulling at them, patting the moss, trying to find which one was loose. She had counted the courses of stone. She knew where it was. Batting a fly away from her face she pulled at some grass and then let out an exclamation of triumph. Dropping the large stone on the ground, she pushed her hand into the space behind it. In seconds she had brought out the plastic box.

She tore off the lid and stared down at the package inside. It seemed untouched. Pushing the stone back into place in the wall, she turned round to scramble up the bank once more. The trees remained still. There was no sound from the path ahead where it vanished into the tangled bushes. In the distance she could hear the low mournful mooing of a cow.

She stopped and stared back over her shoulder into the undergrowth. There was someone there all right. Someone who did not want to be seen.

Carta.

Or Medb?

IV

'I'm sorry to come unannounced! It was on the spur of the moment!' Viv looked at Peggy, pleadingly.

Sitting in the car with the brooch in its box locked in the glove compartment, she had realised that she didn't want to go back to Edinburgh. Not yet. She couldn't face Pat, and she wasn't ready to make contact with Hugh or listen to any more of his messages. Not yet. Making up her mind at last she had driven on south. The weather had changed and successive showers of rain greeted her head on as she drove west down Nidderdale. Then as she drew up at the farm gate, brilliant sunshine reflected off the house windows and raindrops spangled the flowers. Behind the blue sky another black cloud was powering up the dale.

Steve greeted her with a hug. Then he took her into the kitchen. The atmosphere at the farm had changed. 'Dad went away without telling anyone.' Steve shrugged. 'It's upset Mum a bit.' It was obviously an understatement. As he glanced at his mother Viv felt a wave of sympathy for him. His anguish was palpable. There was a moment's uncomfortable silence. 'He left the dogs with one of our old farm workers up the dale,' he went on, 'which is odd, to say the least, and it's kind of quiet without them, isn't it, Ma.'

Peggy, her face shiny with heat, lifted a cake out of the oven and slammed it down on the table. She ignored his comment. 'You're not planning to go up the hill tonight, I hope?' she said to Viv, with a glance towards the kitchen window where the next rainstorm was streaking the glass and lashing the apple trees. The great shoulder of the hill was out of sight, girdled by black cloud.

'No. Not tonight.' Viv shook her head. She paused awkwardly, watching Peggy turn the cake out onto a rack, before she looked back at Steve. 'I am so sorry I didn't see you again at the party. The row with Hugh completely threw me and then I was whisked away with Sandy. I hoped you'd understand.'

He nodded. 'Of course. I knew you'd come back here in the end.' Lifting three mugs down from the dresser, he lined them up on the table.

Peggy had seated herself in the armchair at the head of the table and was watching Viv and Steve through narrowed eyes. Wearily she reached for the teapot. 'Well, those folk we've just seen off this afternoon – they heard your ghosts up on the top.'

Viv accepted a mug of tea from her gratefully. 'Really?'

'Really.' Peggy clasped her own mug between her hands with a sigh. 'They spent all day up there yesterday, didn't they, Steve?' It was almost a plea. There had clearly been a row between Peggy and Steve as well. 'And what a to-do! Heard hooves, even though the hill was empty. Heard voices. Thought they saw a load of horsemen with swords.'

'Swords?' Viv's attention snapped away from Steve and she felt the colour drain from her face.

'So they said. It's the second time they've been here. Remember, Steve, love?' Peggy glanced at him again. 'They were here last back end. And they heard something then. They were going to tell the local ghost club or something.'

Steve was concentrating on Viv. 'I told them they were hearing noises from the boggart holes.'

'Men on horses,' Viv repeated thoughtfully. 'With swords.'

'Imagination, Viv.' Steve reached for a knife. 'Shall I cut this up?' He turned to Peggy at last. 'It'll cool quicker.'

Peggy gave her a pretty, low-ceilinged room in the attic looking out over the front garden. She didn't comment on Viv's lack of luggage. She had brought her walking gear and a small overnight bag, thrown into the car at the last minute in case she decided to spend the weekend near Stanwick. No computer. No notes. 'You've the whole floor to yourself up here and you won't be disturbed by

356

my other guests.' Two other couples were arriving to occupy the rooms on the first floor where Viv had stayed before and that first evening she found herself sitting around the large dining table with Steve and several strangers. After a flicker of resentment, she relaxed. It was good to ground herself. To forget, however briefly, Pat and Hugh and Cartimandua and the brooch tucked into the bottom of her small holdall. Glancing at the others as they tucked into Peggy's smoked chicken terrine she listened as they talked about their visit to Mother Shipton's Cave.

Later she went to sit outside on a bench in the garden, staring out towards the hill. Her dinner companions had dispersed, one couple for an early night and one for an evening stroll. Moths were hovering above the grass and bats were swooping after them. Viv was watching them thoughtfully when Steve wandered out. He sat down beside her. 'Enjoying the view?' It was nearly dark.

Viv nodded. She shivered, huddling into her sweater. They sat side by side in companionable silence.

'Do you reckon Mother Shipton's spring was a Druid place too?' she said at last.

'Bound to have been.' Steve nodded. 'On the edge of a great river, water emerging from the womb of the earth and strange water, capable of turning things to stone. A kind of alchemy. Magic in everything. But not magic as we know it. The perfect place.'

'The Celts lived in such a wonderfully vivid world, didn't they.' She smiled dreamily. 'Even the silence of the hills and moors was special. They had no radio or TV. There was no newspaper popping through the letter box at breakfast time, no phone to warn them when visitors, welcome or unwelcome, were on the way. Their senses weren't dulled by noise and bright lights. They couldn't afford to let that happen. Instead they listened to everything. If a robin sang unexpectedly on a bush nearby they heard not just the beauty but what he was saying. Was he warning you off his territory or telling his friends – and you – that a fox or a cat or a human was lying in wait? When a blackbird sang at the liminal time of dawn and dusk they walked gently and with respect, for blackbirds were special. They were believed to guard the secret sacred places.'

He glanced at her. 'You make it sound romantic, but it must have been a bit scary, don't you think?'

'What world isn't?' Viv shrugged.

There was another long silence. In the distance they heard the call of an owl. 'Are you escaping Hugh?' Steve asked at last. He wasn't looking at her now, concentrating instead on the misty view in front of them.

She nodded. 'He won't find me here.'

'He's been giving you a bloody hard time, hasn't he? And it's more than professional antagonism, that's obvious. It's very personal, isn't it?'

Viv did not reply. She sat staring at the mist closing in across the fields. It was growing cold. 'We used to be such friends,' she said after a long pause. 'When Alison, his wife, was alive, I often went over to their house. He changed after she died. I mean, you'd expect him to of course, but he changed towards me. Even before he read the book something was different.'

'I suppose the whole dynamic of his relationships with people would alter after losing someone close like that.' He sighed. 'It would be bound to. You were a friend of his wife's. And you're an attractive younger woman, remember.'

Viv gave a wry laugh. 'Thanks for the compliment.' She smiled at him, conscious suddenly of the warmth of his body as he sat so close beside her. 'I don't think that's it, though.' She turned back towards the hill.

'That's always it.' Steve nodded. 'At some level, acknowledged or not.' He paused, giving her a sideways glance. She didn't see it. 'The book is a fantastic bestseller, I gather,' he went on. 'It'll be the launch pad for your new career as a whiz kid trendy historian. Simon Schama, Michael Wood, eat your hearts out. Viv Lloyd Rees has hit the headlines!'

She laughed again. 'You make it sound very glamorous.'

'And so it is. You deserve the success.' He rested his arm along the back of the bench behind her. 'And the play will only consolidate your reputation.'

'It would be fun to record some of it here.' She was not going to think about Pat tonight. Enough time for that when she had decided what to do with the brooch.

'I'm looking forward to seeing what happens.' Gently he touched her hair. She didn't notice.

There was another pause. 'Steve,' Viv said slowly. 'Your mother didn't mind me arriving like this, did she?'

'On the contrary. She's terribly pleased. Why?'

'Without your father being around it makes extra work for her.'

She turned and scanned his face. 'There's nothing seriously wrong, is there? She seems a bit strained.'

He shrugged. 'Dad and she had a row. A bad row,' he said, after a long pause. 'Then she and I had a bit of a barney as well. They've been under a lot of pressure over the last few years. We all have. He needed to get away for a bit, that's all. But don't you worry about staying. It's good to have someone else here, and he never helps with the guests anyway; there's a lady from the village who does that, and Ma was really pleased to see you. She's a bit tired today, that's all.' He stood up and stared thoughtfully up at the hill, then he shivered. 'It's getting a bit parky. Come in soon or you'll get chilled.'

25

Viv woke early and lay listening to the silence. Sliding out of bed she went to the window and, pushing it open she took a deep breath of the cold air. Outside the dawn lay like a pure veil across the hills and dales. She stared up at the table top of the hill with its drifting mist and knew with a stab of excitement that she wouldn't be able to go back to sleep.

A few minutes later, fully dressed except for her shoes, she tiptoed down the passage, pausing with a wince at every creak of the floorboards. Padding downstairs and along the hall where the only sound came from the slow tick of the grandfather clock, she stopped in the kitchen to put on her boots and quietly let herself out of the back door.

It was very cold and the dew lay across the grass as a shimmering layer laced with spiders' webs. She hurried towards the gate, past the lichen-draped apple trees and out into the lane. With a quick glance over her shoulder towards the sleeping farmhouse, she headed for the steps over the stone wall which would take her onto the track which led across the fields and up the hillside towards the summit. Her hands firmly wedged in her pockets against the cold, she set off up the steep track towards Carta's birthplace; the place where the high queen of Brigantia had had her first encounter with a Roman and where she had begun to try her wings as a politician and a leader of men.

Pausing to catch her breath, Viv turned to look back the way she had come. Down there in the valley, the trees along the rivers and the valley bottom probably showed where the ancient oak forests had long ago grown up to the edge of the escarpment. Somewhere down there, in a shadowy sacred grove, Carta had witnessed that bloody sacrifice and established herself as a strong and ruthless leader. What had happened after that? Finding herself a flat rock to sit on, Viv put her hands in her pockets, huddled into her jacket and closed her eyes. She did not have to wait more than a second.

Carta was standing with her back against the great oak. Sun and Moon were seated at her feet, watching the three men who stood in front of her. A light breeze stirred the thick foliage over their heads as they spoke and Carta was aware of the gods nearby, listening to their every word. She shivered. The lives of men and women for generations to come depended on her decisions. In the south and west the fight against the Roman invasion continued. Messengers had kept them informed of Caradoc's progress as he led the native opposition to Rome. His two brothers dead, he was the only surviving son of Cunobelinos, and the only man left who could defeat the invaders and chase them back to the coast.

Venutios was determined to send him support. 'The more successful he is the more tribes will join him and the moment will come when the scale begins to tip in his favour and we should be there when that moment comes. Chase the bastards back into the sea!'

Carta had folded her arms, her chin set, taking strength from the tree. She was aware that Artgenos and Culann were nodding at her husband's words. It was happening again. She was being made to feel the one in the wrong.

'I have sworn to uphold the Roman governor.' Aulus Plautius had returned to Rome. The new governor was Publius Ostorius Scapula, as yet an unknown quantity. 'The Brigantians will not support Caradoc against him. Not yet.' She was adamant.

Venutios gave an exclamation of disgust. 'You do not have to stick to your oath! You are high queen. You do not bend the knee to the imperial lap dog. You have sworn no oath at all to Scapula.'

'No, but I entered into an agreement to do what is best for the people of our hills.' She narrowed her eyes. 'Do not contradict me, husband.'

'But you in your turn, great queen, should not contradict the urgings of the gods,' Culann put in quietly. 'Have you thought,

361

lady, why the Romans are so anxious to move west and capture the lands of the Silures and the Ordovices? Their mountains protect the most sacred place in the Pretannic Isles. The Island of Môn.'

Carta hesitated. 'They would not attack Môn. Surely the gods would not tolerate that.' She closed her eyes, trying to think, aware of the rustle amongst the branches overhead as the messengers of the gods leaned closer in the west wind.

'Ah, there you underestimate them,' Culann continued. 'They would indeed. They see us Druids at the heart of opposition to them. They see us behind every insurrection in Gaul and now in Britannia, as they choose to call the lands of the southern tribes who have been defeated by them or become their clients. They see the Druids supporting Caradoc, as indeed we do as he is now our only protector.' He paused with a reproachful grimace in her direction. 'The gods warn that the Romans mean to destroy us. They are not fools, Cartimandua. Far from it. Do not underestimate these people.'

She turned away sharply and walked a few paces away from them. Her dogs stood up at once and followed her. 'I don't underestimate them. Not for a moment!' His rebuke had stung. 'The gods are with us, Culann, not with the Romans.' She threw a glance at Artgenos, who had remained silent. The old man did not respond. He knew as well as she did that the portents were not favourable. The eagles were circling over the fells.

As dusk fell she was once more at the shrine in the forest. She had to be certain what she did was right. Silently she knelt beside the dark water and gazed into its depths.

Vivienne?

It was a long time since she had called upon her own personal goddess.

Vivienne!

Whatever the goddess demanded, she would obey. To ensure success and victory only the greatest and most valuable offering would suffice.

Viv stirred uneasily.

What? What was the greatest and most valuable offering? Not a human life. She, as goddess, would never demand a human life. But as she looked deep into the eyes of the queen she felt her implacable resolve with a shudder of primitive fear. One day Carta would feel the need to offer human sacrifice to her goddess. She knew it in the depths of her soul. And when she did, nothing Viv could do would prevent it from happening.

II

What a brilliant start to a Monday morning! Hugh put down the phone and whistled. The bollocking Maddie Corston had just given him had taken him completely by surprise. All he had done was to warn her that she would be putting her credibility on the line if she persisted in scheduling any kind of programme based on Viv's book.

'What's the matter with you, Hugh? You're behaving like a spoilt, jealous, mean-minded vicious old goat!' Maddie's voice had filled the study, so loud he had had to hold the receiver away from his ear and check the door was shut.

'Now, back off! Academic squabbles are all very well, but this is a nonsense. Go away and write your own book and leave Viv alone. I'm not having you interfere with my scheduling and I'm not having you trying to destroy my script writers. These two women have all the makings of a fantastic team and you will not poke your nose in. Is that clear?'

Suddenly, he laughed. He had really stirred up a wasps' nest; maenads, all of them. Maddie was right. He should leave them to it and get on with his own research. And he owed Viv an apology. Another apology. He shouldn't have done it. He was already regretting his interference, regretting everything, even before Maddie rang. But he had only wanted to stop Viv making a complete idiot of herself.

He shook his head. If truth were told, he was missing her around the department, and if she had gone for good, it was going to be his own damn fault.

Pushing back his chair, he got to his feet and went in search of Heather. Perhaps she could arrange some flowers or something by way of an apology.

In Heather's office downstairs the room was full of sunshine and busyness; her computer was frantically updating itself; her telephone was ringing on and off every few minutes; the coffee machine was making strange cranky noises and Heather was full of the joys of spring.

For a few happy moments he felt almost himself again. Viv, she told him sternly, had probably gone away to get some peace after the book tour and he should just leave the poor woman alone and give her some space. It seemed a good suggestion.

III

'You took the brooch!' Pat was waiting for her on the bench outside the front door when Viv returned later that morning. 'What have you done with it?'

Viv stared at her, stunned. 'How did you get here?'

'I borrowed Maddic's car. She won't need it for a bit. Not very friendly of you to rush off like that.'

'I'm sorry. I needed to be alone.' Viv was flustered and angry. 'What makes you think I took the brooch?'

'Because I went back to Stanwick to look for it. I take it you've got it here? You haven't sent it back to Hugh, I hope.'

'You had no business to check up on me!'

'Why not? We're partners. Remember?'

Viv sat down beside her. 'How did you know I'd come here?'

Pat laughed. 'Medb told me.'

Viv blanched. 'Oh God, Pat –'

'No, no! You told me the name of the farm. It wasn't hard to find it.'

Behind them Steve appeared in the doorway. 'Breakfast is ready, ladies. Isn't it great Pat came too, Viv.' Steve glanced at her. 'We've put her in the room next to yours.'

Pat had brought her script and all her recording equipment. She had, it seemed, abandoned Pablo and her catsitting duties to Cathy's downstairs neighbour – Cathy and Pete would anyway be back on Friday – so Daughters of Fire made their first official ascent of Ingleborough Hill later that morning, laden with Peggy's picnic lunch, notebooks and recording equipment. The air was clear and gloriously sharp and they found they had the place to themselves.

Surrendering as gracefully as she could to the fact of Pat's arrival, once she had recovered from the shock Viv allowed her to select a couple of scenes and a section of narrative and if the ambient sound proved right up here they were going to try recording. If the idea worked out they planned to record trial sections in other places as well. Ingleton Falls, perhaps, with the thunder of water in the background, and somewhere where the muffled resonances of damp mossy limestone and caves with their echoing mysterious acoustics would fit in with the script. There were all sorts of possibilities.

For their first attempt to create some of the background atmosphere, they bivouacked in the lee of the shelter on the very top of the hill where the faint signs of the round houses of two thousand years ago were still visible within the ramparts. Around them the views stretched out over the full 360°: to the west the Irish Sea, a brilliant sparkling blue line, and in the distance the Isle of Man, hazy on the horizon. Northwards they would see the great Lakeland hills, nearer at hand the two sister peaks of Peny Ghent and Whernside.

The soundtrack to Viv's introductory section was the gentle whisper of wind over the long dry grasses and the distant mew of a buzzard.

NARRATOR: Just over two thousand years ago on a hilltop seven hundred and twenty-one metres above sea level in what is now the Yorkshire Dales National Park a queen was born. No one knew she would be a queen. Her father was a tribal leader. Her mother the granddaughter of the king of the Trinovantes in a region that would one day be called Essex. But for now, in this Iron Age fortress behind ramparts already hundreds of years old, the bright courageous little girl grew up, a tomboy amongst her brothers and her cousins.

'Cut!' Pat brought her hand down, beaming. Engrossed in their work, they had both put their earlier animosity behind them. 'Perfect! At this point I think we should add in the sound of some young children playing and laughing. Maybe a dog barking. We'll ask Peggy to find us some kids.'

Almost on cue they heard shouts in the distance. It was male laughter. Adult laughter. Pat swore. She had hoped to have the area to themselves a little longer. They stared round, trying to spot the intruders. There was no sign of anyone.

'Ghosts?' Viv whispered to Pat. She shivered, remembering Peggy's account of the visitors' experiences on the hill.

Pat shook her head. 'If they're ghosts, they're very loud ghosts,' she retorted. 'I'll check out where they are. We can't risk them interrupting.' Walking swiftly, she headed down towards a stone wall built at an angle across the hillside. From behind it she could just make out a wisp of smoke rising into the clear sky. As she approached a man rose to his feet from behind the wall. He was dressed in a tunic and leggings, a tartan mantle round his shoulders pinned with a large circular silver pin. He sported a large drooping moustache.

Staring at him, Pat let out a scream.

'It's OK. I'm not a ghost!' The accent was modern Yorkshire.

For a moment she was too shocked to move.

He came towards her. 'We're up here for the weekend. Re-enactors? You know, Ancient Celts!' He paused, gauging her reaction. 'Not dangerous, I promise.'

Pat breathed again. She was laughing. There were behind him some dozen or so people, all in costume, clustered round a fire pit full of carefully smouldering peats. Their tents had been painted to look like skins. In fact, she realised, they had draped furs and blankets over the nylon. Nearby lay a stack of weapons. Swords. Spears. Bows. Shields.

Suddenly she had an idea.

It worked like a dream. Jake, Art, Dave, Lugh and their colleagues slogged it out with a will for the microphone. The clash of iron blades, the thwack of shields and twang of bow strings, the shouts and shrieks and groans were all Pat could have wished for. She and Viv pooled their twenty-first century farmhouse picnic with slightly underdone barbecued rabbit, doughy homemade bread, local cheeses and vast quantities of mead and then went on to record the sounds of girlish laughter, women's gossip without words, difficult, but made easier by the mead and the ever-strengthening wind. No children, though; children would still have to be found down in the village, but now they had a wonderful repertoire of noises off to be used as and when required.

By the time the sun was beginning to sink towards the west they had gained an audience of climbers, plus a few intrepid Sunday afternoon walkers and had discovered that Jake and Art were drama students from Manchester. They were beginning to find their cast. At least six of them were planning to spend the whole week on the hill and would be available for further sound effects and auditions when needed. It seemed too good to be true.

As the distant sea disappeared into a turquoise haze they began the long walk home, tired but, Viv had to admit, triumphant.

Pat was astounded to find that she was enjoying herself. 'Can you imagine living here for real!' The fury which had driven her from Edinburgh in the hired Fiesta had dissipated; her certainty that even one day away from the emotional support of the city landscape would terrify her had not happened and here she was in the middle of nowhere, exhausted, her feet covered in blisters in borrowed boots, her skin sticky with sun cream and insect repellent, wearing a hat belonging to the farm which made her feel like a refugee from the outback and she was unutterably content. Sinking down on an outcrop of limestone she slipped off her rucksack and stretched out her arms.

Viv was staring out into the distance. 'This is the place of my ancestors! The cradle of my blood and my bones!' She raised her arms towards the west. 'Sweet goddess, keep this place between your breasts; guard it in your hands; nestle it within your womb. Let no enemy come within its walls, no weapon strike in anger, no voice cry out in pain. This is a sacred place. May it be heavy with your blessings, fertile with the blood of your creation, kissed with sweet heaven's tears and hidden from the world by the veils of sacredness.'

Pat narrowed her eyes. This was Cartimandua speaking. Her contentment vanished and she felt a wave of anger. Medb's anger. She hesitated, then, remembering the play again, she dived into the rucksack for the recorder. 'Go on,' she whispered.

Viv shook her head. Her arms dropped to her sides and she slumped down on the rock beside Pat. She gave a short uncomfortable laugh. 'That re-enactment was all very real as far as it went, but we have to listen too.' She shivered as though she could see the shadow of Pat's alter ego standing between them. 'Come on, Pat. Let's be honest about this. Medb brought you here, didn't she. So, why don't you try. See what happens.'

'Ask Medb to speak?' Pat was nervous suddenly.

Viv hesitated. Then she nodded. 'Why not. You made me do it.'

Pat shrugged. Why not indeed. She closed her eyes and waited, frowning.

There was a long silence.

'Pat?' Viv whispered. 'Are you OK?'

Pat laughed. 'He thinks I can't see what's going on. He thinks I have gone away to leave him with you. He's betrayed me.' The voice was quite different from her own. Lighter. Harsher. Medb.

'I can see him, standing with you under the trees. You think the oaks have blessed your union. You think he will follow like the puppy dogs which fawn at your heels.' Pat got up and walked a few steps away towards the edge of the track where she stood staring out towards the north. There was a strange silvery light in her eyes. 'You are so wrong.' She turned and looked at Viv – looked straight through Viv. There was real hatred in her expression. 'I will take Venutios away from you and make you crawl before me and I'll see him eat the dust under my shoes.'

Viv stepped back, shocked. 'Pat?' Her voice was husky with fear. 'Pat! That's enough.' She took a couple of steps forward, grabbed Pat's arm and shook her. 'Pat!'

'Let go of me!' Pat pushed her away violently. She took a deep breath. 'Bloody hell, Viv!' She paused. 'What happened?' She was speaking with her own voice again.

Viv was staring at her, her face white. 'You were Medb! You were speaking for her; threatening Venutios. You sounded vicious.'

Pat bit her lip. 'It was that easy?' she said softly.

Viv nodded.

Pat sat down on the outcrop of rock and put her head in her hands. 'I didn't think it would work. I thought it was only in my dreams.'

Viv sat down beside her. 'You scared me.'

'Shit!'

'As you say.' They were both silent for a long time.

'What are we going to do?' Pat said at last.

Viv made a face. 'Go on. We have to. We owe it to history. We have to find out the truth.' She sighed, staring at the ground. When she looked up at last her eyes were blazing with excitement. 'This is too interesting to stop, Pat, don't you see! We've seen the most amazing things; heard history being made. Both of us! This is incredible. We can't give up.'

'But we're being taken over.'

'Are we? Or are we just mouthpieces for –' Viv hesitated, spreading her hands helplessly, 'spirits. Shadows. Echoes from the past. We're not possessed.'

Pat grimaced. 'Are you sure?'

'Did you feel possessed?'

'I didn't feel anything. I didn't know it was happening that time.'

'Exactly! That's not possession.'

'Isn't it? Are you sure we're not being set up against each other?'

Viv stared at her suspiciously. 'No. No, Pat.' She was dismissive. 'Come on, don't you see how exciting this is? We are mediums. Look at all the thousands of people all over the country who act as mediums. They don't think it's dangerous. They just relay what they are hearing. That's all we're doing. I wasn't expecting it when it started, so it scared me, but now, up here, I understand what's going on. It's fantastic. And exciting. And after all, we know what happens. We know the history. No one gets hurt; no one gets killed. 'She paused. 'If we're frightened by anything we can stop before it happens. Can't we?'

IV

It was very dark in the narrow river ravine. Stumbling and slipping on the loose stone scree, Viv made her way down the path towards the sacred well, every now and then flashing the beam of torchlight in front of her feet as she drew nearer the small waterfall. Behind her the house was in darkness. Everyone else was asleep.

In the chamber it was cold and damp and very still. Carefully she dug in her pocket for matches and a nightlight, setting the little candle on the rocks beside the water basin. Someone else had been there recently. Fresh flowers in a small cut-glass vase were standing on the shelf in the rock and something else had changed too. She frowned, trying to see what it was and realised after a minute that the small figure of the goddess had been moved to the back of the shelf. In its place there stood a crude stone head. She felt herself grow cold. In the light of the candle the head stared at her balefully; carved from gritstone, its two round eyes and circular mouth were

369

dark holes in the flat expressionless face. It was old. There was no doubt about that. As old as time itself. Repelled, she stepped back, staring back at it. If this was the true ancient god of this place it was to this head that Carta had prayed; this cold stone she had touched with her own hands. Dragging her eyes away from the impassive stare, Viv forced herself to sit down at the edge of the pool and study the reflections in the red-brown water.

'Carta? Are you there?' Her whisper was lost in the dripping and splashes of the spring and of the beck outside as it plunged over the limestone boulders, out of sight into the valley.

'Carta?' She raised her voice. 'Speak to me. Where are you?'

There was no answer.

V

Hugh's good mood had lasted all the way home from the department, but now as he hauled his briefcase out of the car and slammed the door, he hesitated. Something was different. Wrong. Cautiously he surveyed the house front. The grey stone building stood four-square to the gravel parking space where he had pulled up. There were two windows evenly placed on either side of the square front door with its small cracked Corinthian pillars. Upstairs there were five windows, the central one arched, giving a slightly supercilious expression to the otherwise dour face of the house which was only softened by its shroud of honeysuckle and clematis. One of the things he loved about coming home to the house in the summer was the smell of those flowers.

He could smell nothing. Putting down the briefcase at his feet, he took a deep lungful of air. Nothing. No flowers. No grass. Nothing. All around him the garden was totally silent. Yet he could see the trees moving in the breeze. Cautiously he put out his hand in front of him, half expecting to touch something, a sheet of glass perhaps. His fingers shimmered slightly and then he heard it. The bronze note of the carnyx.

He froze. 'Venutios.' His lips framed the word, but no sound came. For several more seconds he remained immobile, trapped by his own fear, then he turned and bolted for the car. Throwing himself inside and slamming the door, he could feel his heart thudding inside his chest as he pushed down the locks and grasped the wheel white-knuckled, trying to steady himself. As he groped for his mobile and stabbed in Meryn's number, he could see his briefcase standing where he had left it on the gravel. The garden looked completely deserted.

26

I

They were once more at Dun Righ.

Venutios had come to her bed late. The room was lit by smoking lamps as the rain lashed the roofs of the houses and the wind howled down the dales from the west.

Carta was sitting before her mirror thoughtfully combing her hair, all her women dismissed for the night save Mairghread who was sitting near her singing softly as she stitched up the hem of one of Carta's tunics. Staring into the depths of the bronze, Carta realised suddenly that another face was there behind her own. She frowned for a moment, seeing the outline, then she realised who it was and turned to look up at him.

He bent, his hand behind her head to hold her still as he kissed her fiercely. She could smell the wine on his breath and for a moment was tempted to send him away but as ever he knew how to excite her. He pulled her to her feet, took the comb from her hand and threw it on the floor. 'Go away, woman!' he shouted at Mairghread and Mairghread stood up hastily. She glanced at Carta seeking permission but Carta was not looking at her. Her eyes were fixed on those of her husband. As Venutios lifted Carta in his arms and carried her to the bed, Mairghread slipped out of the room and pulled the heavy curtain across the doorway.

Carta and Venutios had disagreed in council again that afternoon and again she had overruled him, well aware of the simmering anger of some of the men there. Venutios had summoned his brother, Brucetos, from Caer Lugus the week before and the two men, shoulder to shoulder, had tried yet again to persuade her to give up her support for Rome. She could sense the discomfort of the others, leaders of the various tribes of Brigantia, who had come here to the west to talk, far away from any possible listening ears. In spite of all her efforts they were polarising into two factions. On the one side, Venutios, Brucetos and the men of the wild central moors and hills who treasured their freedom and despised the wealth the Romans brought as bribes. They had no wish to be part of the Empire, not as a client kingdom, certainly not as part of the province under the Roman yoke. On the other side were the men who supported her without question, the men from the eastern territories, the rich grazing lands, the cleared arable lowlands, where they had grown used to the traders from Gaul and the olive-skinned merchants from the south around the Mediterranean with their luxurious goods packed into ox-drawn wagons and onto mules. These were men who paid for gold and silver and all the other highly prized goods from Erin and the western lands of Pritannia that came into the western Brigantian ports and round over the estuary from Deceanglia and then on over the high pack trails. It took all her powers of diplomacy to hold them together, these diverse, strong men of her council and hardest of all to rein in was her own husband.

As he threw her down onto the deep heather bed she felt the accustomed bolt of excitement and fear explode through her belly. In the council chamber she could control him. In bed it was a different matter.

This time she tired long before him, but still he held her down, thrusting savagely deep inside her. Her body had a life of its own. Still it responded, time after time, shuddering with pleasure and pain as he held her wrists pinioned to the pillows.

At last he stopped. He didn't slump beside her as usual. He was still above her, his eyes narrowed, staring down at her in the smoky lamplight. 'So, why no child, wife? Why do I have no son?'

She tensed and turned her face away. 'Because it has not pleased the gods to send one yet.' She gasped as his fists tightened round her wrists, determined not to let him see how much he hurt her. She could feel the flaccid penis lying possessively across her thigh, the weight of the man crushing her and suddenly he disgusted her. 'When it is time for the high queen to bear a child, the goddess will send her one. Until then we can but wait.' She tried to push him off, but he was a dead weight on top of her and his hands still held hers prisoner.

Gruoch had taught her long ago how to study the rhythms of her body as it ripened and waned with the moon and how, to be sure, to use the herbs and waxes which would keep her belly empty, her body fit and young. As queen she had no time for pregnancy. Besides, her child was dead. Hers and Riach's. However much she might long for another baby deep in her heart, he could never be replaced. When the time was right, if he chose to be reborn, or if another soul chose to visit the earth again as the child of a queen, the goddess would tell her. Until then, she would keep the hard body of a warrior-woman and no amount of rutting by her great bull husband would plant a seed that would take.

She realised that he was studying her face again, his eyes so close to hers that she could see through the darkness of his pupils into his very soul and again she felt that sudden shaft of fear. By the ancient laws of the tribes it was her right to deny him a child until such time as she and the goddess decided it was auspicious; her right to send him away from her bed. Yet those deep-set brooding eyes held a power and a menace and an excitement which made it very hard for her refuse him anything.

'My queen? My lord Venutios?'

The voice from the doorway was discrete, but sufficiently loud to make Venutios roll aside with a groan and sit up. Beside him Carta pulled the sheets over her with a shiver, conscious of the bliss of cool soft linen after the hard sweating body.

'Vellocatus?' Venutios barked at his shield bearer. 'You had better have a good reason for disturbing us!'

'I am sorry, my lord. The queen has to come.' The young man stepped forward out of the darkness into the lamp-shadowed room. 'My queen.' He looked at her at last, aware of her dishevelled hair, the voluptuous bare shoulders and heavy breasts as she sat up. He looked away again quickly. 'Prince Caradoc is here.'

'What?' Venutios hauled himself out of the bed.

Carta felt her heart sink. Caradoc was the last person she wanted to see in Brigantia. His presence could only bode ill for her and for everything she believed and put her in an impossible position.

It took them only short minutes to fling on their clothes. By the time they had walked over to the meeting house and taken their seats the fire was roaring and a servant was ready to serve mead and wine to their unexpected guest.

Caradoc was a tall, well-built man of some thirty-five summers.

Normally strong and commanding in appearance, he stood before them exhausted now, with an ugly oozing sword wound to the upper arm and his shoulder wrapped in blood-stained bandages.

Carta surveyed him coolly. 'Greetings, cousin. I am sorry to see you so wounded.' This man was the implacable enemy of Rome. Even by being here he was compromising her position. 'Have you brought men with you?' She was frantically working out the implications of his arrival.

'A dozen only, cousin.' He emphasised the last word as though reminding her of her duty to him as his kinswoman as well as his host. 'My army has withdrawn into the mountains of Eryri for the time being. We confronted the Romans first in the upper valleys of the Sabrina.' He shook his head. 'Scapula was at the head of two legions. Perhaps more. But my men outnumbered them. The tribes had flocked to my standard.' There was an infinitesimal pause. Where were the Brigantians this time, when he had needed their support? Where were the Brigantians who had fought under his banner before?

'They fought like heroes. I could have defeated them with more men.' Again a pause. He shrugged and shook his head. 'The trouble is, the legions fight like gods. All fall before them. They march like knives through cheese. Nothing could stop them, not this time. But we'll drive them out yet. With your help, cousin, and yours Venutios, my friend.'

Carta beckoned a servant. 'Fetch Artgenos, and tell him to bring a healer with him. Our guest is wounded.'

As the man disappeared she waved Caradoc, who had been standing awkwardly, leaning on a staff, to a seat. 'Rest now. We will tend your wounds before we decide what is to be done.' She had not smiled at him or given him the kiss of welcome. 'Are you being pursued?'

He shook his head with a bitter laugh. 'Maybe they think they have killed me. They no doubt claim victory. But I had few losses. My men have vanished into the mist leaving Scapula scratching his head in confusion. We'll fight again. And soon.' He made an effort to straighten his shoulders and winced at the pain.

Carta studied his face thoughtfully. 'Those sound brave and defiant words, but I sense you have not told me all there is to know.' Beside her, Venutios stood up and himself brought a cup of wine to their guest.

Caradoc tipped it down his throat. It brought a flush of colour to his grey cheeks. 'I speak the truth about my men. We will live to fight again.' He took a deep shaky breath. 'But Scapula captured a fort on the flank of the action. My wife and children were there.'

There was a long pause.

'You have my sympathy, my friend.' Venutios spoke at last.

'If he puts them to the sword –'

'He won't.' Carta shook her head. She was torn with indecision. Caradoc's family were her family. The bonds of kinship were sacred, yet she was bound also by treaty. 'I have not met Scapula, but I hear he is shrewd and experienced. He will use them as bargaining counters. They have too much value as hostages for him to kill them. Be assured on that score. He will take them back to Camulodunum.'

'To lure me from the hills? He wouldn't think it that easy?' Caradoc managed a note of defiance.

'Who knows what he thinks!' Venutios put in. 'Perhaps Carta can tell you more. She's the client of the Romans here. She studies their every move.' His voice was heavy with scorn.

'And as such, I am pledged to uphold their cause in the interests of peace. Peace for my people.' She was looking very serious as Artgenos came in. With him was Gruoch, followed by a young Druidess carrying a bag of herbs and potions.

Artgenos raised his hand in blessing and joined the circle. Gruoch, after a careful examination of Caradoc's wound, bade her companion clean it and put on a fresh dressing. She took two phials from the bag and tipping their contents into Caradoc's cup beckoned another servant forward to fill it once more with wine before joining the circle herself, drawing up a stool closer to the fire.

'We will support you, Caradoc,' Artgenos stated flatly. 'The Romans are heading for nys Môn. There is no question that that is their ultimate goal. They have never trusted the Druids. They see us as the source of strength and unity behind all opposition to their attempt to conquer these isles, just as we opposed their inroads into Gaul. They will not be content until we are destroyed totally. The portents and the omens all say the same.'

There was another long silence. Carta was watching the young Druidess's nimble fingers as she packed Caradoc's wound with healing ointment and bound it with a pad of moss and the linen bandages. They had all seen the vicious jaggedly raw edges of the wound.

'That is not true, Artgenos.' She cleared her throat at last. 'Plautius assured me, as did the Emperor himself – '

'Plautius is not governor now,' Venutios broke in. 'And Claudius is long gone from these shores. They bought you off temporarily with their flattery and their gifts. Now events have moved on. Can't you see it, woman? We are not bound by your agreement. Particularly if they now threaten our very gods!'

'Our gods are not threatened!' Carta was angry. 'How could they be? I do what is right for our people. The tribes of the south are taxed to starvation levels. They are enslaved. They are murdered and tortured if they are found with so much as a knife to cut up their meagre bread. Is that what we want for the Brigantians? We are wealthy and at peace. We do not have to watch our dead sons and husbands brought home on litters.' She stood up and strode out of the circle seated round the fire, her mantle brushing the wounded man's shoulder as she passed. He flinched. 'It is our duty to support Rome up here on the northern borders of the province.' She spoke firmly from near the doorway. Beside the fire, Gruoch frowned. None of the men moved. 'I put to death the men of Brigantia who defied me and went to support you, Caradoc. And I would do it again.'

Caradoc stood up. Nearby, two of Carta's men put their hands on the hilts of their swords. Slowly the room had been filling up as one by one they filed in, stooping at the low doorway, warriors, council members, Vellocatus – all there now.

'I have to honour my oath to the Emperor, Caradoc,' she went on. 'You are my cousin but you have led an insurrection and rebellion and it is my duty to give you up to the Romans, according to our agreement, to prove my loyalty and keep my people free and safe – '

'No!' Caradoc's face was white to the lips. 'We are tied by blood!'

'It is the teaching of our gods and of our judges that we must keep our promises and our oaths above all else, otherwise we are dishonoured.' Carta's mouth was dry. She felt the resentment round her in the room like a black cloud. Somehow she kept her voice strong.

'You are wrong, Cartimandua.' Artgenos hauled himself to his feet with a groan. 'In this case you are wrong. Do not do this, I beg you.'

'I have to.' Could they not understand that she had given her oath? That she had done all this to save her people?

377

'No!' Venutios, too, was on his feet now. 'I forbid it! Caradoc came here to claim sanctuary and aid. You would break every code of honour if you did not render him hospitality.'

'You do not forbid your high queen anything!' Her voice was icy as she confronted her husband. She stepped forward into the firelight. 'How dare you question my decisions? Caradoc shall have our hospitality and food and warmth and attention for his wounds and he will remain here until he is well. But he will do so as my prisoner. Then I shall send him to the governor. I will not break my oath and endanger the lives of every man, woman and child in Brigantia for one man!' She was facing Venutios now, glaring at him, daring him to defy her.

'You cannot do this, Cartimandua. It would bring disgrace on your name and on that of the Brigantian peoples.' Artgenos laid his hand on her arm as he spoke. 'You are queen only by choice of the gods. The gods could remove you from power if you defy their wishes.'

She span round to face him. 'I have the ear of the gods! My gods! And the people are behind me.'

'Not all of them.' Venutios spoke through gritted teeth. 'You will divide the tribes.'

'The tribes will remain united,' she retorted. 'Those who defy their queen will die.' She beckoned the two armed warriors over. 'Place the Lord Caradoc in chains. Give him the best of everything as befits a prince and king of his own people and see his wounds are tended regularly. But see he is closely guarded. I shall send messengers tonight to Ostorius Scapula to tell him that I hold his enemy. I shall demand assurances for the safety of his wife and children in exchange for surrendering him to Rome. And you, my husband,' she turned on Venutios, 'will add your name to my message. You will support your queen in her decisions.'

Gathering her mantle around her, she swept out of the council room, the dogs at her heels. Outside she stood for a moment, staring up at the sky. She was trembling. The heavy clouds were rolling away towards the east. The rain had stopped and she could see the stars appearing, one by one. She took a deep breath. The starlight was a sign. The gods supported her. They were drawing away the clouds.

'Lady? May I escort you back to your house?' She jumped at the soft voice behind her. It was Vellocatus. She gave him a quick hard look, glancing behind him to see if he was alone then she nodded, her expression softening as it always did when she saw the young man who followed Venutios everywhere as was his duty. 'You should be attending my husband.' It was a gentle reproof.

'I shall do so, later.' He put his hand under her arm. She could feel the warmth of his fingers through the wool of her mantle. He was strong and yet gentle; a gentleness which almost shocked her after the customary violence in her husband's touch.

'That was a brave deed, my queen. To stand up for your beliefs against so many shows you to be very strong.'

She gave a grim smile. 'Very strong or very foolish.'

'They respect you for strength, not foolishness. You have done the right thing.'

She paused, looking at him. Then abruptly she laughed. 'Thank you for your support, Vellocatus. I shall remember where your loyalties lie, my friend. But for now, return to your king.'

He bowed and stood back. She was aware of his eyes following her as she walked towards her house. At the doorway she paused. Two human heads hung there, moving slightly in the breeze. They smelled of the precious imported cedar oil in which they had been embalmed. 'I do this for you,' she murmured. She touched them lightly as she walked past. 'For my principles you died and for my principles I must live or die also.'

In her sleep Viv cried out. The farmhouse lay swathed in mist and silence. There was no one to hear.

Mairghread was waiting for her in the central chamber. The fire had been rebuilt and soothing herbs thrown on the smouldering peats.

'Is it true that you are going to hand the Lord Caradoc over to the Romans?' she asked.

Carta closed her eyes briefly. 'Are you questioning my decisions?' Taking a deep breath she faced the other woman sternly.

'No!' Mairghread stepped back hastily. 'No, my queen. Never.' Her eyes narrowed.

'I'm glad to hear it.'

'Nevertheless you need to beware,' Mairghread persisted. She paused. 'There is much talk amongst the people. They believe the king is right.'

'Then they are disloyal!' Carta walked past her into her bed-chamber. Suddenly she was furiously angry. She was being made to feel the traitor. Caradoc knew where her loyalty lay; he should not have tried to sway her. It was his choice to come here. His choice to put his life at risk. She stood staring down at the bed. The servants had smoothed the sheets and there was no trace now of their earlier love-making. She gave a bitter smile. Venutios would not forgive her easily for this. He would not dare show his fury openly but he would punish her subtly by avoiding her. By sleeping elsewhere. Well, that would be no loss. There were other fish in the sea if she felt the need of a man. Young Vellocatus, for example. She considered him for a moment, glad of the distraction from her sombre thoughts. He wasn't of noble birth; he was all but a servant, but he was good-looking and gentle and had had the courage to give her his support when higher-born men had stood silent. And it would be very satisfying to suborn her husband's closest attendant.

'So, are you revelling in your powers, lady?'

She froze. She was wrong. Venutios was going to face her. She turned. 'Do not dare to contradict me! Brigantia will honour her agreements with the Emperor.'

He was standing in the doorway. 'Then the world will despise Brigantia until the end of time!'

Turning on his heel he walked out. The curtain fell across the doorway behind him. She was alone.

Half-awake now, Viv stirred. How right Venutios was. Except that the world had not despised Brigantia. It had despised Cartimandua.

Through the window she heard in the distance a sheep calling, the sound echoing strangely in the rising mist. It was a lonely noise. Two thousand years ago she would have heard after it the eerie cry of a wolf.

II

The rain started next morning as they sat round the breakfast table. Huge bronze thunderheads were piling up in the west and in the distance a low rumble announced the coming storm.

'Perfect!' Viv glanced at Pat. 'Are you game to go up the hill and record during the storm? The effects would be stunning.'

'And suicidal.' Pat reached for the coffee pot. She was exhausted after the previous day's climb and her head had begun to ache. 'People get struck by lightning in storms!'

'Not if we use the shelters up there. Or get down behind some rocks. We needn't go very far up. Come on. We can't miss a chance like this.'

'Why not go into town with Steve? You'd be mad to go out on the fells in this weather.' Peggy came in with a tray of empty plates in time to hear the tail end of the conversation.

'Mad but inspired!' Pat grinned. 'Viv's right.'

'Can't you record it in the house?' Peggy commented over her shoulder as she carried fresh toast to the dining room for the other guests.

'It wouldn't be the same,' Pat called after her.

Viv grinned. The story in her head was too insistent to give up the chance of seeing the sullen beauty of the hill when Taranis the thunder god was angry.

There was no sign of the re-enactors. They had packed their tents and gone.

'They've got more sense than us.' Viv swung the bag off her back and crouched down behind a low stone wall where it strode across the side of the hill. 'Shall we stop here? I don't want to go too far. We've got to have some shelter before it hits us for real.'

As if to underline her words a fork of lightning cut through the sky and they flinched at the almost instant crash of thunder reverberating across the moorland. Pat subsided beside her.

'Go on, Pat. You play Cartimandua; this is the first speech she makes as she returns from Colchester. She addresses the tribal leaders in a storm. 'Don't improvise here. This bit is important. It

381

shows her motivation for the whole of the rest of the play.' Viv handed her the page in its plastic sleeve.

Pat nodded, turning on the recorder inside its weatherproof bag.

The sound of the rain on their waterproofs, on the stone, on the grass was deafening. As another thunderclap echoed round them Pat began to speak. Water ran across the lines of typescript. She couldn't read it. Her words were snatched from her lips by the wind. Another thunderclap broke almost overhead. With a shrug she rose to her knees. 'I can't do this, Viv. Sorry. Perhaps this wasn't such a good idea after all.'

'Then I will,' Viv said impatiently. 'Here. Give me the mike.' And suddenly she was shouting, belting the speech out into the storm. It was not what was written on the script in her hand.

'Can you not understand? It is my honour that is at stake here! I gave my oath to the Emperor only to protect my people. To bring them prosperity and peace. If I break that oath the Romans will attack us as they have attacked the Silures and the Ordovices. As they have attacked the south. They are all disarmed. Destroyed. Slaughtered. Is that what you want for the Brigantes? Annihilation? I see disaster on the horizon. This storm carries portents from the gods! If I give in and release this man, the mountains will fall, our civilisation will disappear, our gods will be defeated. The only hope for us is to honour my agreement as the Romans will honour it. It can be no other way!'

The sizzle and crack of the lightning bolt seemed to hit the ground beside them and the crash of thunder drowned Viv's next words. She ducked down behind the wall, shaking the rain out of her eyes.

'Viv, that wasn't in the script!' Pat muttered.

Viv ignored the interruption. She was staring out cross the broad valley into the rain.

'The Druids do not understand this changing world! How, with all their wisdom and their knowledge can they not see what will happen? It is the Druids that the Romans distrust the most. They see them as spies nurturing the opposition. Artgenos only proves their point. He demands that I release Caradoc. If I do so, it will seal their fate as surely as my own and that of my people!'

'Viv!' The recorder had stopped. The light had gone out. Pat reached over and took the script out of Viv's wet hands.

'I cannot do it. I will not let him go. The Romans are on their way to collect him. My messengers will have reached the legion already!'

'Viv!' Pat grabbed her arm. 'We've stopped recording!'

'Do not touch me!' Viv rounded on her. 'I will call my guards!'

Pat shrank back. The fury in Viv's eyes was overwhelming, the sense of power coming off her in tangible waves.

'Viv!' Pat leaned across and touched Viv's shoulder. 'Stop it! Stop it now!' She was afraid. Whoever it was crouching next to her against the old stone wall it was not Viv Lloyd Rees. She took a deep breath, leaned over and shook Viv's shoulder again. 'For God's sake, wake up! Come back!'

Another rumble of thunder deafened them, but it was further away now, moving eastwards.

'Viv!' The rain was pouring down their waterproofs, forming huge puddles at the base of the wall.

'Viv, wake up now.' Pat spoke through clenched teeth.

Viv exhaled violently. She slumped back against the wall and closed her eyes. For a moment she didn't move. She didn't breathe. Then slowly she gave a deep, agonised sigh as she struggled to rise to her feet.

'Viv, stay put. There is still lightning about.' Pat pushed her back against the wall. 'It's over. We've recorded the sequence.' She studied Viv's face. The anger and the power had gone. She was herself again.

III

Pat lay soaking thoughtfully in the scented water of her bath, listening to the rain lashing the window. Downstairs, Peggy was orchestrating the delectable smells which were issuing from the kitchen and drifting up the stairs. Viv had disappeared into her own room. Viv's turn was over. Now it was Medb's.

Medb laughed. Watching him from the homestead in the hills where she had taken shelter, she saw it all. Venutios wanted her.

He wore the brooch which held him to her and he scanned the signs for clues to the whereabouts of the woman who pleased him so much better than did his wife.

He had sent men to track her down when she disappeared from Caer Lugus but she had taken care that they did not find her. Now, as she watched him and listened to the news which spread like wildfire across the fells of the arrival of Caradoc and of the quarrel of Cartimandua and her husband, she changed her mind. It was time to let herself be found.

Beautiful. Seductive. Entrancing. Medb of the White Hands arrived at Dun Righ, veiled and in secret, and was installed in a small guest house on the edge of the township. There she gathered all the things around her that she needed to be comfortable and powerful. The hand of Venutios was sufficient to ensure that she was given anything she asked for and guaranteed her privacy when she walked in the forest at dusk, selecting herbs and stones, leaves and branches, all items of power and magic. It was no time at all before word began to spread amongst the men and women of the township that their king had been ensnared by an enchantress. No one dared to tell the queen.

IV

'What happened up there?' Peggy had been listening to their conversation as she hung up their waterproofs to drip in the boot room, and when Viv appeared on her own before supper she led her into her small healing room and closed the door behind them. Her face was pale and strained and she sounded abrupt.

Viv eyed her warily. 'Cartimandua spoke through me in the storm. It was the most amazing experience. And Pat –' She paused with a shiver. Pat had scared her.

'And Pat?' Peggy prompted.

Viv frowned uncomfortably. She glanced up, aware of Peggy's scrutiny. 'I'm sorry Pat arrived without warning like that, Peggy. I hope you didn't mind.'

Peggy shrugged. 'I don't want you to take her to the well.'

Viv gazed at her for a moment. 'Of course not, if you don't want me to.'

'You haven't mentioned it to her?'

'No.' Viv thought for a second. 'No, I'm pretty sure I haven't.'

Peggy nodded again. 'It's not for everybody, Viv. Best keep it that way.' She shivered.

'You have reservations about Pat?' Viv asked cautiously.

Peggy's eyes narrowed. 'Of course I do. And you know as well as I do why.'

'Supposing you tell me.'

'She is being overshadowed. By a woman.'

'And you've seen this woman?' Viv felt a chill run up her spine. Peggy nodded.

Viv hesitated. 'She's called Medb of the White Hands. She was an enemy of Cartimandua. She isn't – shouldn't be – in my story. It's all to do with the Celtic brooch I showed on the TV, the Cartimandua Pin. Touching it seems to release the spirits of the people who once owned it. Cartimandua and Venutios.' She paused. 'And Medb.'

'You should not have brought Pat here,' Peggy said slowly. 'You have stirred up memories and resentments from the past between you which are not going to go away. This is a powerful place. A special place. It's vulnerable. Easily unbalanced. There are energies here which shouldn't be disturbed, don't you see? And Pat is making it worse. She's a loose cannon. She doesn't understand that she's playing with powers which are way beyond her. You must stop your research, give up the recording. Forget your play. Cartimandua was a great queen. I honour her, but Medb is evil. I can feel the danger in the air. Read it in the storm. Hear it from the gods. I've lived here all my life and I know. The more attention you give folk like Medb, the stronger they grow. Leave it alone now. Get Pat away from here and go. Please.'

'But Peggy –'

Peggy shook her head. 'You have to stop.'

'We can't do that. It's too late.'

The truth! They must know the truth!

The words echoed in Viv's head.

She took a deep breath. 'We need to know what happened! Cartimandua wants us to know the truth. Why she acted as she did. She wants the world to know she was not a traitor.'

There was a moment's intense silence.

'Even if you pay with your lives?' Peggy asked at last. She spoke very softly.

'Our lives?' Viv echoed.

'Around here, on the fells, on the moors, in the woods and dales, by the becks and waterfalls the old gods still exist. And they still demand their dues.' Peggy levered herself off the table where she had seated herself and walked to the door. 'If I were in your shoes, I would go back to Edinburgh and stay there. Forget your play. If you decide to remain here, well, that's up to you. You are my guests and I'll not order you out, but don't expect me to help you.'

'You don't mean that, Peggy.' Viv was frowning. 'Please. You showed me the well yourself.'

'I shouldn't have done that.' Peggy shook her head. She opened the door, then she turned and looked back at Viv with a frown. 'The gods of these hills demand heavy dues. Remember that. You'll get your programme if you persist. But will the price be too high?'

V

The rain had released a thousand scents into the air. Standing at the back door Pat was staring out into the garden. Fumbling in her pocket she brought out her cigarettes. Exhaling smoke out into the rain she closed her eyes and took a deep breath, drawing the nicotine down into her lungs. The bloody woman had been inside her head. Taken her over. Used her mouth. Her brain. She leaned against the doorpost, unsure if she was more angry or frightened. Or maybe she should just be excited, like Viv. Was she a medium? Some kind of spiritualist? She took another draw at the cigarette.

'Are you all right there?' Peggy had walked into the kitchen behind her.

Pat jumped guiltily. 'I'm sorry. I needed a cigarette.'

She flung it down on the wet flagstones and stepped on it, then she turned. Peggy was holding an armful of neatly folded towels. She put them down on the end of the table as Pat came back inside, closing the door on the rain.

'Did Viv tell you about our contact with the dear departed?' She gave a sharp little laugh. 'I'm not sure how to react. I'm indignant. Cross. Frightened. Excited. Viv is very excited. For her this is historical research of the most unbelievable kind.' She sat down at the table, running her fingers through her hair. 'Where is Viv?'

'She's gone upstairs.' Peggy sat down opposite her. She eyed Pat. 'We need to talk. I've told Viv that I think you should both go.'

Pat tensed. 'Because of what happened to me?'

'Because of what's happened to both of you.' Peggy nodded. She reached for a bottle and two glasses from the dresser. 'But you in particular. The lady in question – the lady who spoke through you – I'm not going to mention her name and give her any more strength than she has already. She's very powerful. Viv told me about the brooch and that she's contacted you before. Coming here has made it easier for her. You are thinking about her in a place where her spirit feels it still has work to do and it's made her stronger. I can feel her now, too, and I don't want to.' Peggy shook her head adamantly. 'The old folk are everywhere on these fells. I do what has to be done to appease their gods and their shades. I can't do any more than that; I don't want people here who are going to do the opposite.'

Pat picked up a glass. The drink was homemade and rich and sweet and very potent.

Peggy frowned. 'You have presented her with an empty vessel to fill as she sees fit.' Somehow it did not sound like a compliment.

'How do you know all this stuff?' Pat asked at last. 'Can you see her?'

Peggy nodded. 'I can see her. She's following you.'

'Christ!' Pat gulped. 'Can you get rid of her?' She found she was shivering suddenly.

'I doubt it.' Peggy stood up and, walking over to the Aga, reached for her oven gloves. 'Better if you go.'

'We can't go. We have to finish. Give us a bit more time. Just a couple of days. Please.' Pat sighed, elbows on the table, chin on interlinked fingers staring down into the glass. She could feel Medb stirring inside her head and she shifted uneasily in her seat. 'Could you do something about the brooch, Peggy? De-activate it, or remove its power?'

'The brooch?'

'You said Viv told you about it. She's brought it here.'

Peggy stared at her, appalled. 'Sweet Lady!' She closed her eyes. 'No, you don't understand, Medb won't hurt anyone.' Suddenly Pat was her apologist again. 'She just wants her story told, as Cartimandua does. There's nothing to be afraid of. I'm sure there isn't. It was a shock when it happened to me, I admit it, but that's all.' She shook her head earnestly. 'If I promise to control her, won't that make it all right? I can do that. I'm sure I can.' She paused, studying Peggy's face.

That wasn't quite true, she realised uncomfortably. What about what had happened just now. In the bath. Unable to bear Peggy's close scrutiny for a moment longer she stood up abruptly. 'I'll go and change for supper and we can discuss it with Viv when she comes down.'

Peggy watched her disappear into the hall. She sighed. Stupid woman. Was she really that naïve? Medb had returned for one reason only. Revenge.

27

I

'I want to know what happens next and I want you to monitor it, so that we don't miss anything,' Viv said. Steve had not appeared for supper and she and Pat had reconvened later in her bedroom. As Pat was here, she might as well make use of her. Viv glanced at her, firmly suppressing any doubts she might feel about trusting her. 'I want you to ask me questions. Guide what I'm saying.'

Pat eyed her doubtfully. 'I don't think we should. I'm scared. Peggy can see Medb, Viv. She's afraid of her and so am I! I don't want to risk her coming back.'

'We won't let her. This is about Cartimandua.' Viv pushed open the windows, The sharp scents of peat and grass and sheep and the sweet overlay of honeysuckle and roses drifted into the room. She stared out briefly at the mist shrouded height above them. The brooding silence of the hilltop was overwhelming. She stifled her momentary fear and turned to face Pat. 'Let's do it. Peggy won't know and I have to find out what happens.'

'What about Medb?'

Viv shook her head. 'Forget Medb. This isn't her story.'

'I think you'll find it is. Medb came here to Dun Righ.'

Viv frowned. 'She can't have!' She didn't want to hear this. She was biting down on her fear, concentrating on Carta.

'She did. I don't think she's a very nice person, Viv. I don't want to get involved.'

'Then don't. Refuse to listen.'

'Easier said than done. Peggy thinks she's dangerous.'

'She told you that?'

Pat nodded. 'And I told her about the brooch, Viv. You shouldn't have brought it here. Why did you? Is it somewhere safe?'

Viv nodded.

'Just don't tell me where, OK?' Pat sighed and reached into her bag for the voice recorder, setting it on the sill and pinning the mike to Viv's shirt as she sat on the window seat. Then she went and switched off the light. She had a bad feeling about this.

The room grew damp and cold as the night air seeped into the open window.

'Carta?' Pat's voice was husky suddenly. 'Are you there? Talk to me.'

Somewhere in the distance a dog barked.

Venutios was white with anger. He strode up and down the chamber several times before coming to a halt in front of his wife. 'There is still time to release him. You can still save the day.'

'No.' She looked up at him wearily. 'I have made my decision. I do not want to discuss this any further.'

'But I do!' He seized her wrists and pulled her to her feet. 'You cannot allow him to be taken! You cannot do this!' Beside her the two dogs were growling. Venutios ignored them.

'Let me go!' She did not flinch. 'If you touch me again I will call my guards.'

'Your guards!' His tone was scornful. He released her and moved away from her. 'Your guards, trained by me. Loyal to me, if truth were known!' He folded his arms and stood facing her. 'Are you going to put their loyalty to the test?'

She drew herself upright, then unexpectedly doubled over with a groan.

He frowned, taken aback. 'What is it? Are you ill?'

She nodded. 'Call Mairghread. I'm sick.' Her face had grown hot and clammy. The walls were spinning before her eyes.

Venutios strode from the room. When Mairghread appeared he did not follow her.

'You know what is wrong, of course.' Mairghread sponged her forehead gently.

'I've eaten something bad.' Carta lay back on her bed with a groan.

'You're breeding at last.' Mairghread smiled. 'About time, too.

390

That will distract you from politics, my lady, and remind you of your duties as queen.'

'My duties as queen,' Carta repeated slowly. 'You dare to tell me my duties as queen! Perhaps I had better instruct you. My duties are to my people.' She put her arm across her eyes. 'I am bound to do the best I can for them. And you're wrong. I am not with child. I can't be.'

She had made sure of that. Or had she? She frowned. The day Caradoc arrived Venutios had come to her room and forced himself on her. She had not been expecting him that night. She had not used the herbs which would prevent a man's seed implanting.

'The gods make their own decisions, lady.' Mairghread had been watching her closely, seeing the various expressions fleetingly written on the queen's face. 'Perhaps they do it to remind you of your place as their representative and the protector of their wishes.' She pursed her lips primly.

'Don't presume to criticise me!' Carta did not move her arm from her eyes. 'You understand nothing of my decisions.' With a groan she rolled over onto her side. 'I have eaten bad meat, that is all. Bring me some snakeweed steeped in hot water. It will settle my stomach.'

Venutios strode back into the room as she finished the drink. 'So, is it true? Are you with child?'

'No.' Mairghread hadn't taken long to allow that little piece of speculation loose on the township. Swinging her legs over the side of the bed she stood up wearily. 'Do not even hope for it.'

'Then perhaps I had better replant my seed.' He reached for her. 'A child would no doubt distract you.'

'Don't touch me!' She pushed him violently as he tried to grab her wrist. Off balance, he stepped back. His face darkened. Furious, he made a second grab for her and she countered with a stinging slap. Sun and Moon edged closer to her protectively, growling furiously at him and cursing loudly. Venutios aimed a kick at them.

Outside the room Mairghread stood, uncertain whether or not to go in. Her nerve failed her and she turned away from the door.

The next morning there was no sign of Venutios. He had ridden out before dawn. When the queen appeared a swollen bruise had shadowed her cheekbone below her left eye.

*

391

Her sickness passed as quickly as it had come, but as she donned her finery to greet the Roman escort sent to collect Caradoc, two weeks later, her face was grim. One by one she drew on the golden armlets, the torc, fastened the brooches to her finest gown and mantle, then she went to stand in the council chamber amongst her men. All the senior Druids were there and all the Brigantian kings save one. She looked around, her eyes narrowed, as from the watch tower a bronze horn announced the arrival of the Romans.

'Is any one here going to defy me and argue against handing over Caradoc?' One by one she scanned their faces. One by one the men looked away. Many were uneasy; none defied her.

At the head of the deputation was the military tribune of the XX legion, Gaius Flavius Cerialis. He saluted with outstretched hand, his face grave. 'The governor sends his greetings, great queen. He has told me to thank you personally for your loyalty. It will be well rewarded.'

She bowed. As they waited for Caradoc, Artgenos on one side, her brothers, Fintan and Bran on the other, her warriors and her advisers forming a sullen ring around them, Carta saw Gaius move uncomfortably from foot to foot. Drawing himself up stiffly he squared his shoulders, distracting himself by looking away from the men around him, scanning the building. She watched him surreptitiously, following his gaze, trying to see the huge room as he did, comparing its comfort and richness perhaps to the austerity of his barracks. The great chamber smelled of woodsmoke and scented herbs and the flowers which stood near them in silver jugs. Under their feet lay a woven rug, another lay across her seat. Everywhere the colours of the tartans and curled designs that he would have seen before perhaps in the houses of the Keltoi in Gaul brought life to the dimness of the interior of the house. She could see that he was, however reluctantly, impressed and she suspected that the feeling did not change when Caradoc was brought in. His wrists were chained, but she had given orders that as always he be treated with courtesy and honour by the guards who escorted him, orders which were, she knew, superfluous. Everyone at Dun Righ respected and admired this man.

He was brought to a halt in front of the Roman and he gave a small bow, acknowledging defeat but losing none of his dignity by the action. He was a man who would never beg for his life. Carta, watching intently, bit her lip as she saw Gaius bow back. These

392

were two soldiers, summing one another up, man to man. She saw their mutual respect and for a moment she felt excluded by it. Suddenly she was full of doubts.

'Prince Caradoc has been wounded. He is not yet fit to travel with you,' she said to Gaius abruptly. 'Your men may wait outside the walls, Gaius Flavius Cerialis.'

She toyed with his name as though it were an exotic trifle and she saw him raise an eyebrow. She had not realised that it might occur to him that she found him as strange and exciting as he probably found her and there was a challenge in her glance as she addressed him. 'You and your officers will remain as our guests until the Prince has recovered sufficiently to ride.'

She saw that Gaius noticed the sudden light of hope on Caradoc's face and saw his wry inward chuckle as he realised that, sadly for the prisoner, the game, if it was a game she was playing, was with him, not with her cousin. If she wanted to keep the Romans dangling so be it. He was in no hurry. If she wanted to trifle with him for a few days then he would be happy to oblige. More than happy. Poor Caradoc. It merely prolonged the man's suffering.

Carta met the Roman's eyes. This man was sensitive and intelligent; he was observant. Her thoughts had been carefully guarded as she exchanged glances with him but it occurred to her suddenly now that he understood her far better than she had realised. The thought was not reassuring.

II

Pat couldn't sleep when she returned to her room. She showered and put on her pyjamas, then she sat for a while in the lamplight, staring at her laptop, the recording equipment and a pile of books and papers on the table near her. They were making progress. Viv's recording had been fantastic. There would easily be enough material for at least two programmes.

About Medb . . .

She stiffened. No. Not about Medb. She did not want to think about Medb.

She stood up abruptly. 'Go away!'

The sound of her own voice in the silence was unnerving.

She held her breath, listening.

The house was quiet, the night very still outside the window. She glanced round the room suspiciously. Had something changed? She thought she could feel a presence there in the shadows, watching. 'Go away!' she said again, more loudly this time. 'I am not listening!'

Oh God, someone was laughing. A quiet chuckle. A cynical, evil, female chuckle. It was the most frightening thing she had ever heard. She took two steps backwards and stood, her back to the wall, staring round the room again. There was no one there. The room was small, low-ceilinged, pretty. Furnished with chintzy prints and dried flowers, with a small armchair, a dressing table, a writing table in the window, the table where all her notebooks were stacked, a cupboard and the stand on which she had put her large scarlet holdall. There was nowhere to hide. Taking a deep breath she tiptoed towards the cupboard and after a moment's hesitation she dragged the door open. It was empty except for her own clothes and a folded down ironing board. She slammed it shut again and spun round.

'OK, lady. Listen. I am not getting involved in this. This play is only a job!' Her fists clenched, she took another deep breath. 'Do you hear me? I don't want to know. I don't want to be involved in your nasty vicious little schemes. Count me out.'

She walked over to the door and flicked the switch, throwing the light of the central hanging lamp over the room. It was dazzling after the low light of the lamp in the corner. Blinking, she surveyed the scene again. She was still standing there when both lights suddenly went out.

'Shit!'

She licked her lips nervously. Don't be frightened. She had overloaded some ancient circuit by turning them both on together. This wasn't sinister. There was a scented candle in a pretty dish on the writing table. All she had to do was find her lighter. Her bag. Where had she left her bag?

She groped her way towards the window and drew back the curtains. The room filled with moonlight suddenly and with a sigh of relief she turned.

Medb was standing right behind her.

III

Viv too had found it impossible to sleep. Part of her was hyped with excitement, part of her desperate to go on with the story; part of her was afraid. It was all getting too easy. With Pat as line manager, director, Svengali, the story had become ever more dramatic and real. She had to stop. For her own sanity she had to stop. Come back to the real world. But she couldn't. Not now that Pat had Medb under control and was happy to continue with Carta's story. Wearily she sat up. An hour later she was still scribbling in her notebook by the light of her bedside lamp, putting down every detail before it slipped away. Seeing the Celts through Roman eyes she had become more acutely aware of the differences between the two races. This was interesting. This was history! The round house of Cartimandua had acquired the wild beauty and sophistication of the tent of a desert sheik. The Roman spin that these Northern tribes were primitive backwoodsmen was true maybe of the peasants as it was throughout the ages, but there was learning here and artistic exuberance. Because they built round houses in hilltop compounds and disliked the concept of town dwelling so beloved of the Romans, that did not make them uncivilised. Conflict between town and country; mutual suspicion and incomprehension. Nothing changes!

Rubbing her eyes she wrote faster. His clothes. Her clothes. The way their eyes met. Measuring each other up. Thoughtful. Calculating. Both intensely conscious of the greater stage upon which they played, but aware, too, of a personal interaction. To be experienced before the audience around them. Hidden. Subtle. Challenging. Suddenly the history had become personal again.

Viv stopped writing and stretched out her fingers with a quizzical smile. 'My God, they fancied each other!' Her whisper was full of admiration.

Throwing down her pen at last she lay back on the pillows with a sigh. There was so much to write. So much to describe. How could she get it all down on paper? This was going to be an electrifying book.

*

The Roman and his junior officers fed that evening with the queen and her tribal leaders. In the face of the constant music and laughter, poetry and loud exuberant conversation he sat almost silent at her side. He did not eat much, Carta noticed, and she scanned the board, trying to see the food as he saw it. Flavoured with wild garlic and mustard and mint, chives and horseradish and watercress and juniper berries. There were meats, obviously. Fish. Game. Bread. There was butter and cheeses and fruit. Was nothing to his taste? He drank moderately too, though there was wine and mead and ale. There was even milk for the children. When the Brigantian chieftains were deep in their cups, squabbling and shouting and one by one falling asleep where they sat, he remained alert. So did she.

At length she stood up. Those who kept their wits about them rose too, bowed and waited. Once the queen had departed their drinking would continue until no one was left conscious.

Artgenos and Culann had long ago gone back to the Druid college in the forest, preferring not to share meat with the Romans. Caradoc too had withdrawn after eating only a small amount seated at Cartimandua's left hand, pleading weakness from his unhealed wounds.

She glanced at the Roman. 'Accompany me to my private rooms. We can talk there more easily.' As if to underline the reason for her words, two drunken men embarked upon a loud and tuneless song to the beat of a goatskin drum.

Gaius stood up and bowed. She was followed, he noted, by the tight-lipped female servant who had stood behind her all evening. Two of his officers rose with him. He gestured at them to remain. He was intrigued by what she would do. If she had messages for Scapula which she did not want to impart in front of the tribesmen or the Druid spies he would be happy to carry them. A messenger with welcome news was always rewarded.

The fire in her own rooms was bright and fragrant with neatly chopped lichen-covered apple logs. Warmed wine and honey cakes awaited them. To his delight, after seeing they had all they needed, the sour-faced woman withdrew, motioning the servants and attendants to follow her. He waited to see what would happen.

Cartimandua, Queen of the Brigantes, stood for a moment, staring down into the fire, then she seated herself on one of the cushioned stools drawn up to the circular hearth. He didn't move, nor did she bid him be seated. For a while she ignored him completely and he found himself wondering if she had forgotten he was there. Then at last she looked up and smiled. She had kept him waiting long enough to intrigue him. She beckoned him forward. 'Sit down.' She gestured at the floor.

He tensed. Was she telling him to sit at her feet? The two other stools were on the far side of the fire. He moved towards the nearest, picked it up and brought it to stand near hers. Not too near. Then he seated himself on the cushion, leaning forward towards her, elbow on knee, aware that in comparison to the trousered legs of the tribesmen his own knees beneath his armoured skirt were all too bare above the thongs of his sandals. He was aware also that he was assuming the position of an equal and possibly making a huge mistake.

She remained inscrutable, staring down at the fire, affecting not to notice what he had done. Perhaps she genuinely had not noticed. Her concentration on the fire was too intense. Too focussed to be casual. Suddenly he was aware of what she was doing. Like some temple priestess she was reading the omens in the flames. Perhaps at this very moment her gods were deciding his destiny. He felt the short hairs rise up on the back of his neck. A brave and experienced soldier, he did not shrink before a man's sword or a javelin. A woman – a queen – speaking to the gods was a different matter. He felt the sweat starting on the palms of his hands but he did not move. She would never be allowed to guess at the wave of terror which had swept over him as he became aware of the human heads – two of them – hanging by the doorway in the shadows. Were they real? He knew the Celtic tribesmen pickled the heads of their enemies and collected them as trophies. He sniffed cautiously. There was nothing putrid in the room. It smelled of the fire. Smoky. Spicy. Pleasant.

He realised suddenly that she was watching him. He saw the amusement in her eyes and wondered, just as she had, if she had read his mind.

'If you wish to drink you will have to serve yourself. The servants have gone,' she said at last. 'And you may bring me some wine as well.' She was speaking careful Latin.

He stood up and went to the side table where a jug of ornately beaten silver stood on a tray beside two goblets. Clever. She had made him stand up. Made him serve her. He obeyed, pouring the wine with a steady hand, aware that she was still watching him.

She took the wine from him, her fingers just brushing his and gestured him back to his seat. Clever again. Now she had invited him to sit, keeping the initiative. He took a deep gulp of the wine. It was good. Better than the wine at their meal. So, she had kept a stash for herself of the best vintage. The thought cheered him. He glanced at her and again saw the humour in her eyes.

'So, why did they choose you to come and collect my captive?' she asked at last.

He inclined his head. 'The governor knew that I had been to Brigantia before.'

'So, he knew you wouldn't get lost?' She raised an eyebrow. 'And this time as well, you have brought thanks and recompense from Scapula in exchange for me handing over Caradoc.' He caught a note of bitterness in her voice. And not to be wondered at judging by the hostility he had sensed amongst the men in the feasting chamber.

'It was the right decision, to hand him over, great lady,' he replied carefully. 'Rome appreciates your loyalty,' he paused, 'and your courage.'

'And will show her appreciation?' She looked at him sharply. She wondered if he realised just how unpopular her decision had been.

'And will show much appreciation.' There were indeed two wagons of silver and gold at the foot of the hill with his men at this moment. Or he hoped so. The wealth had been rounded up for delivery to the legionary fort of Viroconium for the slow journey north and east. He and his men had ridden *expediti*, fast and unladen, from the south-east. The hope was that they would arrive at about the same time in Brigantia. He took a deep breath. 'There will be more, great queen, once Caratacus reaches Camulodunum. Much more.'

'Caratacus?'

'Forgive me. You call him Caradoc, I notice. Our scribes have rendered his name into the Latin. I will see it is amended in the records.' He gave her an encouraging smile.

She studied him gravely. 'If the Brigantians are not sufficiently rewarded I cannot guarantee to persuade them next time to uphold our treaty with Rome.'

By the gods! He was not qualified to make these promises. Did she think him of higher rank than he was? But she probably did think him of high rank. After all she had seen him in the company of the Emperor; and he had been designated as a go-between for the governor, an undertaking he had not entirely welcomed. 'I will see that your message reaches the governor, great queen.' He managed to keep his voice steady.

She was, he reckoned, no older than he was. But her authority here was absolute. If she raised one finger her men would no doubt flock in and drag him away to be offered as some gory sacrifice to her bloodthirsty gods. He glanced in spite of himself towards the heads hanging at her doorway. Reaching for his goblet, he gulped the rest of his wine.

Again the look of amusement. 'Perhaps you should fetch the jug. We will keep it warm on the hearthstone.'

He did as he was bid, filling her goblet first. This time he was sure of it. Her fingers touched his deliberately. He met her eyes, startled. He did not know of her quarrel with Venutios, or her longing to feel a man take her in his arms without violence. Did not know that this good-looking Roman intrigued her. Or that she had wanted him from the first moment she had seen him, intrigued, tempted, hungry for a handsome man who would not cause mayhem in the township because she had taken one of her own tribesmen to her bed. A handsome man who had the added allure of being different and dangerous.

She played him like a fish on a line, pulling him in, letting him go, herself refilling his goblet, touching his hands and his face, his knees beneath the aproned tunic. When at last she stood up and moved towards her bedchamber he was in thrall.

'Finish your wine and follow me.'

'Is that a royal command?' He was not too drunk to know what he was doing.

'It is.'

He finished it slowly, savouring every sip, then he stood up. The fire had died down to ashes. The lamps had burned low and nobody had come to replenish them. He moved slowly towards the curtained doorway and ducked inside. She was lying on the bed naked but for her jewellery. He stared at her body. By Jove, but she was beautiful. He eyed the heavy breasts. The curve of her hip. The delicate swirling tattoos on one shoulder and across her back and thighs and he reached up to unpin his mantle.

She eyed his body critically. Well muscled. Nicely proportioned. But strangely pale in parts. She chuckled. Her own men frequently fought and hunted naked. They were tanned, tattooed and painted. Their bodies were works of art. This white-skinned Roman, only his arms and legs and face browned by sun and wind was, all said and done, strangely beautiful, like marble. And where it mattered most he was far from lacking in size and power.

It was good. Very good. But to her disappointment he tired before she did. Watching him sleep, still curious about this foreign stranger in her bed, she assumed it was the unaccustomed quantities of wine that had sapped his vigour. It did not matter. There would be other times. Tracing the lines of his cheekbones and his strangely smooth clean-shaven upper lip and chin with her finger, she wondered if it would be amusing to send him back to Camulodunum sporting a tattoo or two to identify him as a trophy of the Brigantian queen. Then at last she lay back and slept herself.

When he awoke next morning she was long gone from her bed and from the township. Her servants brought him hot water and shaving gear and served him breakfast and he found himself the recipient of a lavish gift from the queen – a young wolfhound of the best breeding.

He did not see her again before he left for the south with his prisoner. He was not sure whether to be flattered by the gift, relieved at her absence or insulted that she had left so abruptly. At least his head had not joined the other trophies in her collection. Perhaps she had not thought him worth it.

Half asleep, Viv grasped at the dream. What a triumph. Cartimandua had seduced a Roman. She smiled. And what a dish. She might have fancied him herself given half a chance. Did this explain Carta's strange loyalty to Rome, her fascination with all things Roman, or was it just curiosity? Or something altogether more pragmatic? Was she playing deeper politics or was she just pissed off with Venutios?

The creak of boards on the far side of the room sent the dream out of her head. She froze. Her eyes flew open. The only movement in the room came from the shadows of the leaves around the window, thrown by the rising sun as it appeared for a moment in a distant notch between the hills. In minutes it had swung southwards behind the lowering moors and the room was dull again as she clutched the sheet to her chin.

'Who is it? Who's there?' She held her breath, frightened. Was that a figure near the door? Someone was in the room with her. She edged herself up in bed. 'Pat? Is that you?'

There was no reply.

Then she heard a quiet click as the door closed. Leaping out of bed she ran to it and dragged it open. The landing was deserted. There was no one there. Closing it again thoughtfully she turned the key in the lock and went to climb shivering back into bed. Someone had been in her room. Pat? Or Carta? Or Medb?

The next time she woke it was full daylight and there was only one thought in her head. The brooch. Whoever had been in her room had been trying to find it. Leaping out of bed she went straight to her bag and rummaged in its depths. To her relief she found it at once, still zipped into the inner pocket where she had left it. Taking it into the little bathroom she looked round. There was a small cupboard above the towel rail where she had found a supply of miniature soaps and shampoos and after a moment's hesitation she tucked it in behind them. The plastic box blended perfectly. It would have to do as a temporary hiding place until she thought of somewhere better.

Pulling on her clothes after her shower, she sat down at the dressing table and began working her comb through her wet tangled curls, wondering if Pat was awake. It was Pat who had warned her not to divulge the hiding place of the brooch to anyone, Pat who was her colleague; her partner; a Daughter of Fire. But Pat was Medb.

And Medb was Pat.

28

I

Viv was already seated at the kitchen table when Pat finally appeared. Viv eyed her suspiciously. 'You look as knackered as I feel. Didn't you sleep?'

'No.'

Pat slid behind the table. She was pale and her hand was shaking slightly as she reached for the coffee pot. On the far side of the kitchen Peggy pulled a pan of bacon and eggs out of the oven and stood them on the hot plate.

'Guess what,' Viv went on. She was not about to talk about the brooch in front of Peggy. 'Carta slept with her Roman soldier.'

'What?' Pat took a sip of black coffee.

'She slept with him! Everyone in the township must have known. She pulled the tribune!'

Pat scanned her face. 'You went on with the story after I'd gone to bed?'

Viv shrugged. 'I dreamed about her. It was fantastic!'

'I bet.' Pat took another sip. 'And what did Venutios think about that?'

'I doubt if she told him!' She had seen Cartimandua as young and vulnerable, uncertain, afraid; now as she grew older, as strong, tough and loud and powerful. She knew Celtic women had a huge degree of licence to choose their own men but this sexy, devious lady was a revelation. 'If he's a military tribune there might be a record of his name somewhere,' she went on. 'We're getting into real history now, Pat. Something that can be checked.' She reached for the milk jug.

'Lucky old Carta.' Pat helped herself to a slice of toast then almost at once pushed it aside. What she really wanted for breakfast was a cigarette.

Viv shook her head. 'I don't think Tacitus mentions him, but I'll check as soon as I get back to Edinburgh.'

'I wonder if Medb knows about him.' Pat was slowly stirring her coffee.

Viv frowned, and looked at Pat cautiously. 'He seems to have been especially trusted, first by Plautius and then by Scapula,' she persisted thoughtfully. 'Perhaps he didn't go with the legion when they were posted to Gloucester and he stayed in Camulodunum as some kind of special negotiator? And one-night-stand. Good in bed. Very.' She chuckled.

As Peggy set the hot plates in front of them the door opened and Steve came in, a couple of newspapers under his arm. 'I've been down to the village. I thought I'd pick these up for the visitors if anyone is interested. You're still in the top ten, Viv!' He dropped them on the end of the table and slid into the chair next to her. 'So, how is it going? Are you going to do some more recording today? I wish I could come with you but I have to go into Lancaster.'

'I've told you, you don't have to go, Steve!' his mother said abruptly. 'Why not leave it.'

'I can't.' He frowned. 'You know I can't. In fact I'd better go now. See you, ladies! Sorry to run out on you again.' He smiled, his glance lingering for a moment on Viv's face and he was gone.

Peggy seemed unusually put out as she turned abruptly from the Aga and glared at Viv and Pat. 'Have you thought about my warnings?'

'Peggy, please.' Viv glanced at Pat. 'We would like to stay a bit longer. I promise we won't do anything silly.'

Peggy shrugged. 'I can't force you to go. Just be careful. Especially you.' She looked at Pat.

When she was out of the room taking a fresh pot of coffee into the dining room Viv turned to her. 'What did she mean by that?' She paused. 'Did you come into my room early this morning? Before dawn?'

'No, of course I didn't. Why?'

'Someone did.'

'It was probably Carta!' 'She's everywhere, isn't she. Wonderful, beautiful, sexy, Cartimandua.' Pat's voice was heavy with sarcasm.

'I can see why Medb wants to kill her!' She gave a strange little laugh. 'You did realise that is what she plans, didn't you?' She stood up. 'I'm going outside to have a smoke. See you soon.'

Viv didn't move.

When Peggy returned, she found Viv alone. Her face was white. Peggy frowned. 'What's wrong?'

'I gather you can actually see Medb.'

Peggy nodded. 'She is getting stronger every hour. Can't you sense it?'

'Stronger in what way?' Viv's mouth went dry. She found her hands were shaking.

'In every way.' Peggy paused. 'Where has Pat gone?'

'Out for a smoke.'

Peggy glanced at the back door and shook her head 'You stay here.'

Untying her apron, she followed Pat outside, leaving Viv sitting in front of her coffee.

II

'I warned you!' Peggy said.

'What do you mean?' Pat took a deep drag on her cigarette. She was staring out across the garden.

'She's all over you.'

Pat turned. 'You can see her now? This minute?'

Peggy nodded.

'Shit!' Pat took another pull on the cigarette. She shuddered. 'How can I get rid of her?'

'Fight her. Go away from here. Leave us alone.'

Pat screwed up her face. 'Why is she doing this to me? What does she want?'

'Power. You have opened yourself to her. She's going to use you.'

'What for?' Pat stared at her, appalled. She thought back to the moments she had seen Medb; the dreams, the visions, her own powerlessness and she shivered again. She had a feeling she already knew the answer.

Peggy's eyes narrowed, suddenly thoughtful. 'She hates Cartimandua, doesn't she.'

The colour drained from Pat's face.

'She's there now,' Peggy whispered. 'If you won't send her away, listen to her. What is she saying?'

'You're a good woman, Peggy. You serve the goddess.' It was Medb's voice. Then Pat's again. 'Why didn't you tell me about the spring?'

Peggy stared at her suspiciously. 'Viv showed it to you?'

'No. You asked her not to.' Pat drew on the cigarette again and flicked the ash into the bed of catmint.

'Then how –' Peggy was still scrutinising her face. 'I was right. But it's too late to fight her, isn't it? She's inside you.'

'I serve the same gods of the hills as you do, Peggy,' Pat went on, her voice growing stronger. This was Medb's voice again. 'I'm on your side. There's nothing for you to be afraid of. We're sisters, you and I.' She threw down the cigarette end and stamped on it. 'I want you to take me to the sacred spring. Just you and me.' She held Peggy's gaze for a moment. Her eyes were hard, boring into Peggy's skull. 'There are things we have to do there.' She paused. 'Has Steve gone?'

Peggy nodded.

'Good. We don't want a man here, do we.' She was still holding Peggy's gaze. 'That's why you got rid of your husband, isn't it.'

Peggy stared. Her already white face blanched. 'I didn't. He left –'

'He wanted to fill in the spring,' Pat interrupted.

Peggy was dismayed. 'How did you know?' It was a whisper.

'I watched. I watch everything.' There was a long pause. The cold dead eyes looking out of Pat's face were fixed unblinking on Peggy, pinning her to the spot. 'He was frightened of it, wasn't he?'

'He thought it brought us bad luck. He blamed the foot and mouth on it; the new subsidy rules. Everything. On the head of the goddess.'

Medb smiled. 'Who knows, perhaps he was right if he didn't pay his proper dues.' She paused. 'Forget him.' Her tone was icy. 'He's gone. You know what we have to do next, don't you? We have to find the brooch. That brooch contains my power. And then we have to punish Cartimandua.'

Peggy took a step backwards. 'Pat? Medb?' It was a whisper.

Pat was frowning. She reached for her cigarette packet, hesitated, then pushed it back into her pocket, throwing back her shoulders, her eyes still hard, the colour of Arctic ice. 'Let's go now,' she said, ignoring Peggy's plea. 'Before we do anything else we need to make an offering to the goddess. We don't want her to think we haven't paid our dues, do we.'

'We have paid our dues, Medb,' Peggy whispered. 'And you know it.'

Medb gave a wintry smile. 'I don't think so. Not in full. Not yet.'

III

Meryn was standing on the doorstep of Hugh's house, a worried frown on his face. He leaned on the doorbell once more, then turned and walked along the wall to peer in at the kitchen window. The house was empty. He could feel it.

It was several hours since Hugh's frantic phone call had been abruptly cut off. He had come as soon as he could, pushing his ancient car to its limit on the busy roads, but Hugh had gone. There was no sign of him or the car. Just the briefcase, abandoned on the gravel.

He sighed. Following the path he walked round to the back of the house and peered in through living room and study windows. There was still no sign of Hugh. Doors and windows were locked. Walking onto the lawn and turning, he stood scrutinising the rear of the building. He was listening. Hugh had said something about silence. No birds. No sound at all he had said.

A blackbird broke out of the bushes suddenly, shouting its alarm call and making Meryn jump. A warning? A message? Perhaps a suggestion. He groped in his pocket for his mobile and scanned it. Nothing. Tapping in Hugh's number he waited while it rang, slowly turning round to survey the garden as he did so. The call was picked up by the message service. 'Hugh? I'm at your house. Where are you?' With a sigh he cut the call and headed back towards his car. It was as he was walking past the bird bath, centred in the formal rose bed, that he paused. A few pink petals floated on the surface of the water. He looked down into the moss-lined depths. What he

406

saw, reflected behind the rose petals, was the golden enamelled head of a bird.

IV

'Pat? Peggy?' Viv stood at the kitchen door and stared out into the back garden. 'Where are you?'

There was no sign of them. Puzzled, she turned and walked back through the house to glance into the empty guest sitting room. Through the window she could see the other guests outside standing round their cars, packing in the last of their cases. From today they would have the place to themselves. She shivered. For a moment the thought scared her.

Taking the stairs two at a time she made her way upstairs and tapped on Pat's door. There was no reply. Opening her own door, she frowned. Someone had been in there. The bed had been made and the place tidied. Peggy's cleaning lady must have been in while they were all at breakfast. She remembered the woman walking through into the old washhouse with an armful of sheets for the washing machine. She glanced into the bathroom and saw clean towels on the radiator. And a new bar of soap. With sudden misgivings she went to the cupboard and opened it. It had been rearranged and restocked with a new selection of soaps and gels. There was no sign of the package with the brooch. Her heart in her mouth, she turned back into the bedroom, frantically scanning every surface.

The box was on the dressing table with her hairbrush and comb. Grabbing it, she tore off the lid and unwrapped the plastic. The brooch was safe. She sat down, her heart thudding with fright. What if the woman had taken it; or thrown it away? She glanced round the room once again, wondering where to hide it. Her case was too obvious. There was nowhere else. Then suddenly she knew what she had to do.

The sun was warm on her back as she climbed over the stone wall and set off. She already knew where she was going to put it. Not so far up that she couldn't retrieve it if necessary, but somewhere no one, not even Pat, or Medb, would think to hunt for it.

She skirted the rocky outcrops, heading towards a large area of limestone pavement, colonised by a few stunted thorn trees. When they had climbed to the summit they had avoided this area, but this time she moved carefully out across the uneven stone with its deep cracks, heading towards one of the trees. Ramming the plastic box inside one of the deep fissures at its foot, she covered it with loose scree. The perfect hiding place.

Retracing her steps to the track she sat down on a patch of short grass to get her breath back, feeling the sun beating down on her head, listening to the lonely call of a curlew in the distance. She could see the farmhouse far below, the grey stone roof, the apple trees, just visible below a ridge of folded hillside. The garden was deserted.

With a sigh she lay back and put her arm across her eyes.

V

Carta was once more vomiting into a basin.

'Do you still doubt you are with child?' Mairghread handed it to a servant and sponged Carta's face none too gently. 'Too much riding has made you ill. Rest, my queen. Unless you want to lose it.'

This time she had to admit that Mairghread was right. Her pregnancy was confirmed by Gruoch and then by Artgenos.

The old Druid had read the signs in the clouds. What he had seen was potential. Then hope and expectation. Then disaster. He looked for portents of Venutios's future and saw nothing but strife; he read Cartimandua's future and saw only confusion. In despair he sought out portents for the Roman, Gaius. There he saw turmoil and anger. Fear and something else. Rage. He paused in his readings with a frown. There was no threat there to the queen, yet threat there was. The man was dangerous in a way he could not yet fathom. Quietly he made his way out into the forest which filled the ravine on either side of the great waterfalls. As always he knew himself close to the gods here. There was a sacred grove hidden deep in the trees, far even from the Druid's college, and one that no one but

he frequented. Here there had been no sacrifice, no official ceremonies, no tradition of ten thousand years of worship. Here he
walked quietly to the centre of the trees which he greeted as friends
and colleagues and there he sat quietly to commune with the gods,
the ancestors and the children of the tribes as yet unborn.

As his mind stilled and opened to the infinite spaces, he watched
a succession of scenes unfold before him. He had schooled himself
not to react. Only by watching dispassionately would he see all the
gods chose to reveal. Later he would consider what he had seen
and begin the long struggle to interpret it all. To judge whether
they came from the past or from the future and decide whether the
events were cast in stone and rock; if not they might contain the
possibility for avoidance or for the manipulation of potential desti-
nies. Glancing up as night fell he noted the position of the great
wheel of stars, then slowly he subsided to his knees and closed his
eyes in prayer.

Later, much later, he returned stiffly to his chamber and sat for
a long time alone. Behind him on the table, by the small shrine he
kept there, lay the silver cauldron and the engraved sickle, symbols
of his station and the tools of sacrifice. Near them a golden flagon,
studded with smoky topaz, had been filled with flowering herbs.
At length, with a deep sigh, he stood up and went to consult the
calendar of beaten bronze on the wall. There were listed all the
months and days of the year; the positions of the stars; the days
which were propitious and the days which would prove disaster.
Only after that did he make his way slowly and painfully up to the
township to Carta's chamber to confirm with a sinking heart what
she already knew. That she was pregnant. When she asked the
child's destiny he sighed and turned away. 'I saw nothing,' he said
gently. 'Nothing for this child; nothing, save the spread of the
eagle's wing across this land.'

Carta froze on the spot. 'The eagle? The Roman eagle?'

He bowed slightly in acquiescence.

'But the eagle is our friend,' she went on. 'Our ally.'

'Indeed. At present.'

'And my actions have confirmed that alliance.'

Which action, he wondered. The alliance with the Emperor of
Rome or the bedding with the legionary from Camulodunum?

'Rest, my child. We will talk further when the gods have revealed
more to me. In the meantime, stay within these walls.' He reached

over and patted her hand. 'Let Mairghread and Gruoch take care of you.'

'Did you see when Venutios will return?' she asked suddenly, as he rose and rested his weight on his staff. She had not had the strength to seek for portents herself.

He sighed. Since their last quarrel Venutios had sought refuge with his brother Brucetos at Caer Lugus. 'He will come back soon, my daughter. And when he does you will need all your strength, so conserve it now.'

She watched him leave with a frown. There were things he was not telling her. Normally she would have pursued him, ordered him to return, demanded to know what was wrong, but something in his face stopped her. Maybe it was sometimes better not to know the future.

Wearily she walked over to the little statue of the goddess and stroked her fingers down the rounded belly of the figure. Tomorrow she would go out and give offerings at the spring for the safe delivery of her child.

'Viv! What are you doing!' The voice in her ear brought her back to herself with a jolt.

Pat was standing in front of her, panting from the climb.

'What possessed you to come up here on your own?'

For a moment Viv was silent, confused. She blinked, trying to gather her wits as Pat stood looking down at her. 'I couldn't find you Pat. So I came out for a walk. Where were you?'

'Peggy took me to see the sacred spring.' Pat sat down on the grass beside her.

Viv stared at her. 'But she made me promise – ' She broke off.

'Not to tell me. I know.' Pat smiled coldly. 'I changed her mind.'

'Why didn't you tell me? I would have gone with you.'

'I wanted to go with her alone,' Pat said. 'To get the atmosphere of the place.' There was a long pause. 'It would be a good place to record the play,' she went on at last. 'The acoustics are brilliant. The sound of dripping water; the falls in the background. That's where you should put the brooch.' She was staring out into the distance. 'As an offering to the goddess. It's the only possible destination for something which contains so much power.'

Viv sat very still for a moment, then she turned to stare at her.

410

'What kind of power exactly? Why don't you tell me, now that you seem to be such an expert on it.'

Pat glanced at her. 'Do you still not know? Medb imbued it with her magic. It can inspire and control. It can protect and it can kill. It's her link with immortality. It's the reason she and Cartimandua and Venutios still walk these hills, their destiny unresolved. It's worthy of becoming a gift for the gods for any one of those reasons, don't you think?'

'And because of all this Peggy suggested we throw it into the well?' Viv's mouth had gone dry.

'No, but it is the obvious place.' Pat lay back in the sun. 'Have you got it with you now? I looked in your room and I couldn't find it.'

'So you did search my room?' Viv was furious. 'You had no business to do that!' She looked down at her, full of misgivings. 'I don't carry it around, Pat, so don't bother to look. I've hidden it now and it's in a safe place.'

Pat sat up. 'Where?'

Viv shook her head. 'You told me not to tell you, remember? You were obviously right!' She gave a hard uncomfortable laugh. 'If you can't trust yourself, why should I?'

Pat smiled. Her head on one side she studied Viv coldly. She would find it. All she had to do was to consult the waters of the well as Medb had shown her. For the rest of her plan, she would wait for Venutios. It had been easy to contact Hugh. She had left a message with Heather, telling him where they all were. He wasn't going to get the brooch, she would see to that, but he could certainly deal with Cartimandua!

29

I

Climbing out of his car the next afternoon, Hugh stared for several seconds at the cottage. He had looked up an old bed and breakfast directory and found the phone number of the cottage only about three miles from Winter Gill Farm. At the end of the small picturesque village it nestled into its garden at the foot of a gentle hillside, the windows of the first floor open beneath the heavy thatch. It was very pretty. With a sigh he picked up his case and walked towards the door. It was opened by a grey-haired man in his late sixties. Dressed in an open-necked shirt, the sleeves rolled up over tanned, rope-veined arms, and with deeply weathered skin he beamed his welcome. 'James Oakley. You must be Hugh Graham? Welcome, sir. Come in. My wife is out at present but I can show you to your room and I'm capable of putting on a kettle.'

Having seen the small attractive bedroom and the neatly appointed shower and loo which would be, he was assured, his alone, Hugh dropped his bag on the bed and ran his fingers through his windblown hair, a gesture to tidiness, before following his host back downstairs. He had immediately liked the man, sensing a kindred spirit perhaps, and warming at once to his host's gentle enthusiasm. As they walked through the cottage to the kitchen he noted a pretty chintzy sitting room with a fire smouldering in the inglenook, a small dining room and a well-used study. All had low ceilings and were lined with books. Ignoring a plea to make himself comfortable in the sitting room, Hugh followed his host's example, ducked under the murderously low lintel of the kitchen door and stood just inside the room watching him fill the kettle. He did indeed seem competent.

'You appear to be something of a scholar, Mr Oakley,' he commented. There were books in here as well. Some cookery, but by no means all.

'Our passion and our failing – books.' James Oakley reached down a tea caddy. 'My wife and I collect them. And I plan to add to them with one of my own.'

'Indeed?' Hugh leaned against the doorpost. 'May I ask what about?'

'Christ.' Two spoons of leaves – not teabags – were carefully measured into the pot. 'I should explain, I'm a clergyman. A retired clergyman. I've always been intrigued – perhaps seduced would be a better word – by the idea that Our Lord may have come to England – to Britain, perhaps I should say. "And did those feet in ancient time, walk upon England's mountains green". You are aware of Blake's words, of course. Who isn't.' He picked up the kettle and began to fill the pot, unaware of his guest's quizzical expression. 'I like to think he came as a young man or a boy with his uncle Joseph of Arimathaea, to Glastonbury as legend has it, and that he then stayed during at least some of the hidden years to study with the Druids at one of their colleges.' He turned and put the pot on the tray. 'Ah.' At last he caught sight of Hugh's face as incredulity, horror and finally benevolent amusement chased one another across his guest's features. 'I see I have a sceptic here. Never mind. If you are interested, perhaps I can try and convince you. We have a holy well some four miles from here, you know. I think Jesus may have visited it on his tour round Britain. For many reasons, this is a very special part of the world.'

II

Fidelma was dead. Called suddenly to her mother's bedside after she had collapsed unconscious at her loom, Carta had watched as Gruoch and Artgenos frowned over her and shook their heads. There was nothing to be done. She sat throughout the night holding her mother's hand as her life ebbed away and as the first rays of sunlight warmed the rain-soaked fells she knew Fidelma's soul had departed. Leaning forward she kissed the papery skin of her forehead and saw her own tears falling onto her mother's hair. 'Bless me, Mama and watch over me,' she whispered. She reached for her mother's cold hand and pressed it against her own gently swelling belly. 'And bless your grandchild, too.' She bit her lip, aware of a terrible loneliness sweeping over her, a loneliness compounded only weeks later when her brother Bran fell victim to a vicious fever which left him dead after two short days of torment. In a township full of men and women, family and kinsmen, nothing would be the same again.

By the time Venutios returned, Carta had moved her court south over the high moors and down through the forests to Elmet. He followed her there with a large party of Carvetian warriors from Caer Lugus, leaving them encamped on the far side of the beck opposite the north gate of the township, and it wasn't until the day after his arrival that he finally strode to greet her, followed as always by Vellocatus.

She was waiting for him seated in the sun, with Culann on one side of her and Mairghread on the other, the dogs lying at her feet.

'So, have you come at last to offer your condolences over the death of my mother?' she asked wearily.

He raised an eyebrow and gave a small bow. 'It had not occurred to me, but of course you have them.'

She reined in her anger at the slight. 'So, you came to beg forgiveness for your disloyalty in not supporting me; in leaving my court without permission? And to acknowledge that I made the right decision. Rome has rewarded me well for giving up Caradoc.'

'So I hear.' He did not greet her with a kiss. 'It was clever of them to isolate us. Brigantia has no friends now amongst the free kingdoms. You may be rich, wife, decked in Roman gold, but you have no friends amongst the gods or amongst the peoples. Does that feel good and honourable to you? Does it feel good to you, Culann?' He turned to the tall Druid who stood beside her. 'No, I can see that it does not. It's written all over your face.'

Artgenos had declined to travel south with her, pleading old age and stiffness in his bones. So it had been Culann, thinner and more austere than ever, who accompanied her to Elmet as her senior Druid; Culann, who, she knew, strongly disapproved of her actions.

Carta's gaze had shifted from the face of her implacable husband to the young man behind him. Vellocatus, bearing her husband's sword and armed with a dagger, looked uncomfortable. He did not meet her eye.

'Tell me, husband,' she asked suddenly, 'why you feel it necessary to bring an army with you?'

'I frequently travel with my warriors,' he retorted. 'Not so long ago you were glad to have them around.'

'As I am now,' she said coolly. 'Provided I am certain of their loyalty to their queen.'

His face darkened. 'I hope you are not accusing me of disloyalty!'

'Indeed not.' She pursed her lips. 'But I expect support from my husband in my dealings with Rome. And I expect his warriors to be there at my command should I need them. We do not need them at the moment.' She clenched her teeth. 'Rome is our ally, Venutios.'

'And the Corieltauvi and the Cornovii and the Selgovae –'

'Are our neighbours. We respect their boundaries as long as they respect ours. If or when they become part of the Roman province, that is no longer our business.'

Venutios snorted. 'You will regret the day you believed Plautius's platitudes, you mark my words! You may trust Scapula and his gifts. I do not. And I do not intend to leave our boundaries open to visitors. If you will not defend them, I will.'

'Part of our agreement leaves our people fully armed, Venutios,' she warned. 'So that we can defend our borders.' Why was he incapable of understanding? 'Those of our neighbours who have been defeated have been stripped of everything with which they might have defended themselves. The penalty they pay if so much as a sword is found in one house is terrible. Don't open us to such a possibility. We are trusted.'

'More fool them! I doubt if the Romans trust me.' He was standing before her, hands on hips, his chin jutting aggressively as he looked down at her. Beside her she could hear Sun growling quietly deep in his throat. She put a warning hand on the dog's head as Venutios went on. 'Now that Caradoc has gone, the tribes are looking in my direction for a new leader. They are trying to persuade me to take up his mantle. I tell them we must wait until we know his fate. Whether he lives or dies.'

Culann raised his head. He looked from one to the other. 'My

415

spies tell me that the lord Caradoc and his family have been sent to Rome,' he said dryly.

Carta closed her eyes as she whispered a silent prayer. It was Venutios who spoke. 'Then may the gods help them,' he said with a shudder. 'And may he remember, when he steps into the arena to be torn apart by lions, who it was who sent him there.'

Carta went cold. In the pause which followed his words Culann stepped forward. 'My queen, King Venutios, may I suggest that if we talk further it is in private. Such discussions should not be held in the hearing of the entire township where who knows what wind will carry Venutios's doubts to the four corners of Albion and to our enemies, if such they be.' He gave a grim smile.

Venutios glared at him aggressively. 'Right. But my wife and I will talk in private and we will talk alone, Culann.' Venutios moved towards the queen's house.

'Vellocatus, my friend, send these folks back to their work and see my men are settled in their encampment and I will speak to you later.' He turned back to Culann. 'I will come to your lodging after I have spoken to my wife. I have word from nys Môn.'

He strode after Carta, ducking into the entrance behind her. Inside he dismissed her women.

Carta opened her mouth to contradict, but already they had fled. She rounded on him. 'Is what you have to tell me so private my ladies are to be sent away like slaves? That you dismiss a senior Druid like a horse boy?'

'Yes.' He grabbed her arm. 'Culann will understand. Now, listen to me once and for all. Why did Artgenos not attend the Archdruid on Môn when he was summoned to the meeting of the most senior Druids? They came from as far away as Armorica and eastern Gaul to consult our gods.'

'Artgenos is no longer strong, Venutios.' Carta felt suddenly guilty. He had asked her permission to leave her and travel to the Island of Môn and she had begged him not to go. She had not forbidden his journey. Not even the high queen of Brigantia could forbid a Druid from visiting one of the most sacred places on earth but he had sighed and agreed she needed him with her. She did not know that he had consulted the gods as well and they had warned him to stay close to her, that he would be needed in Brigantia and soon, or of his despair when his illness had made him so weak he could not come with her to Elmet.

416

Venutios was staring at Carta, his eyes narrowed. 'Something is different about you.' It was as if he had only just looked at her.

She gave a faint smile. 'I am with child.'

His face lit with delight, then it darkened again. 'Mine?'

'Of course yours, husband. There has been no one else – ' She paused.

No one save the Roman.

He saw the doubt in her eyes at once. Again he seized her wrist. 'So, the great queen has had lovers while I was away.'

'I take whomever I like to my bed, Venutios, as does every free-born woman. Do not question me!' she flared at him. She refused to let him cow her.

'I'll question you on this. I'll question every man, woman and child in this township. I'll question your bards and your servants and your slaves. Don't doubt it, woman! I'll not recognise a child that is not mine.' His voice was rising in fury.

'It is yours.' She wrenched her wrist away from him. 'Ask Mairghread. She saw I was breeding before you left.'

'But still you took a lover!' He leaned closer to her. 'I saw it in your eyes. Who?'

'I told you, Venutios. Whoever it was, if there was such a person, it was my business. It is not for you to question me.'

'And I told you, Cartimandua, that it is my business – ' He grabbed her shoulder and spun her to face him. 'Is he here, in Elmet?'

'No.' She couldn't free herself from his grip as she struggled, too proud to call for help. Closing her eyes she breathed deeply, trying to calm her panic.

He pulled her against him. 'My lovely, honourable queen – '

'No.' She turned her head away from him.

'Now, who I wonder, would lure you into his bed? Who, amongst the warriors and princes of Brigantia could tempt a queen?'

'Stop it, Venutios!'

'I need to know. I need to know who could have sired the child that will call me father.'

'It was you, Venutios.' He was holding her arm so tightly she thought the bones would crack. 'Ask Mairghread.'

'Perhaps I will.' He turned and shouted towards the doorway. Mairghread came in so fast it was obvious she had heard every word.

'So, Mairghread, tell me. Has my wife entertained a man alone while I was away?'

'No, my king.' Mairghread was pale. 'No one save Artgenos and Culann.' There was a pause. 'And the Roman.'

There was a long silence. Venutios felt the tension in her body like a charge. Slowly he dropped her arm.

'So. I do not suspect the Druids. Such would be a treason against their gods and against their own wives. But the Roman.' He paused, then suddenly he was shouting. 'So now we know why you are so keen on this Roman alliance, so eager to please, so anxious to flatter. They fascinate you, do they, wife? They intrigue you, these powerful men? And was he good? Was he as strong as a Brigantian warrior? Was he as virile? Did he satisfy you? Did you reward him for his dalliance, or did he reward you?'

Grabbing her by the shoulders he shook her hard, then spitefully he punched her in the stomach. 'That is what I think of the Roman. And that!' Another blow, harder this time, that left her doubled up on the floor, retching.

With a furious bark Sun launched himself at Venutios's throat. With a yell of fury he dragged a knife from his belt and thrusting it into the dog's side he pushed the animal away from him and stood panting as with a scream of pain Sun fell to the floor, twitching, then lay still.

Carta let out a cry of agony, reaching in despair for the dog as he drew back his foot and aimed another kick at the animal's body.

'My lord! Stop!' Mairghread was screaming. 'The queen was with child before you left. Before the Roman came. It is your child, King Venutios. I swear it. May I be cast beyond the ninth wave if I tell a lie! Stop, my lord, please . . . !'

It was too late. Already the first blood was seeping through onto the skirt of Carta's gown. Collapsing back onto the ground, she lost consciousness as Moon sniffed at her brother's body and raised her head in a howl of misery.

Mairghread and two of her slaves carried Carta to her bed and called Gruoch to attend her. Venutios had gone and by dusk the Carvetians had packed their tents and vanished into the rolling mists. Carta was unaware of anything around her, lost in a swirling sea of pain. As Gruoch bent over her sweating, contorted body she tossed and twisted and screamed in her agony.

Twice she awoke briefly, staring up at the roof above her bed. Putting her hand down to the bedside she felt Moon's cold muzzle touch her fingers. The dog had refused to leave her and no one had

418

the heart to force her out of the room. Hugging the animal in despair, Carta closed her eyes and wept. Then she opened them and screamed at Venutios in her anger and her pain, calling down the curses of the gods against him. Then she wept again. Hands tended her gently and changed her linen as she bled, and sponged her forehead. Through the haze she dimly recognised Gruoch's gentle face bending over her. Another woman was there with her, helping, holding the silver bowl of rose water. Tossing and turning in her pain, Carta caught sight of the woman's face in the dim light, as her veil slipped from her hair. She tensed, a shaft of terror cutting through the pain as the woman reached forward with the damp wash cloth and Carta cried out in fear. It was Medb.

'You?' She groaned as her body went into spasm again.

Medb smiled. 'I am here to help, great queen.' A touch of sarcasm tainted the words. 'The lady Gruoch is my teacher.' She lowered her eyes meekly, then rinsed the cloth once more in the silver basin of fragrant water and pressed it on Carta's brow. 'It is so sad, is it not, lady, that you can never bear a child,' she whispered. 'Never!' For an instant the gentle smile was replaced by a look of utter hatred. As Carta struggled to sit up, the woman pushed her back against the pillow. 'There is nothing you can do, Cartimandua,' Medb whispered again. 'Nothing you can do at all.'

When Carta awoke Gruoch was alone, with Mairghread to help her. By moonset she had been delivered of a tiny female foetus. By sun up Gruoch had given the child's body to the gods.

III

'Are you OK now?' Pat had been watching her closely as Viv went on with the story. She was clutching the microphone after rescuing it from the rocks where it had fallen as Viv leaped to her feet.

Viv nodded, rubbing the tears from her eyes. 'That was too real; too close! Childbirth is not something I know anything about!' She shuddered. 'And Medb. There, in the room.' She looked up. 'Did you know this was going to happen?' She rubbed the back of her

419

hand across her mouth. 'I don't think I can do this any more. It was –' She shook her head, unable to finish the sentence.

'It was awful.' Pat did it for her. She was as much in shock as Viv. 'No, I didn't know that was going to happen. Do you think Gaius was the father?' She perched on a flat piece of rock, her arms around her knees. Nearby a patch of bog cotton nodded in the breeze.

'She swore he wasn't.'

'Of course she swore it, but do you think he could have been?' Pat leaned forward and tucked the voice recorder into the small rucksack at her feet.

'She had morning sickness before he arrived.'

'She said it was food poisoning,' Pat sighed. 'Maybe she was lying. I suppose we'll never know.'

Viv stood up. 'Medb was there. You did know that was going to happen, didn't you! She was there, as Gruoch's helper.'

Pat shrugged. She smiled. 'I told you this was Medb's story as well.'

Viv rubbed her face with her hands. 'Did she make Carta lose the baby?'

'I think Venutios did that.'

Viv shuddered.

'Every time you do this –' Pat gave a wry smile, ' – describing it all, the experience gets more vivid and more violent doesn't it? Does it frighten you?' She glanced up.

'Yes, it does.' Viv nodded.

'But it's exciting?' Pat went on thoughtfully. 'And you're not going to stop, are you.'

Viv shook her head. Her misgivings were returning.

'Aren't you afraid of what might happen if Venutios gets too angry?' Pat went on after a pause. 'Supposing he hurts her. Supposing he kills her.' There was a long silence.

'He doesn't,' Viv said slowly. She wrapped her arms around herself miserably. 'He doesn't kill her and to my amazement she didn't kill him! We know what happens. It's all there, in the Roman histories.'

'Is it?' Pat raised an eyebrow. 'But did they know the truth?'

'Of course they did. Something important like this.' Viv's uncertainty was deepening.

'Then why don't we go on.' Pat looked at her watch. 'Peggy's not

420

expecting us back until supper. Why don't we go on and find out what happened next.'

Viv hesitated. 'I don't know.'

'I think you do. I think you want to know really badly. I think you want to know what happened to Medb.' Pat smiled. She reached in her bag again. 'And I think you're going to tell me.'

Cartimandua had walked into the forest with Gruoch at her side, Mairghread following a few paces a behind, carrying a basket. It was nearly dusk. Two months had passed since her miscarriage, two months without a word or sign from Venutios, and the royal household had moved back to Dun Righ. For the first time in her life Carta had allowed Fergal to drive her almost all of the way. Her ponies were led at the back of the long train of horses and wagons as, sore and exhausted and still weak from loss of blood, she huddled in the chariot, Moon at her side, and for some of the journey even lay on a bed of rugs and furs in one of the wagons as it jostled over the rough mountain tracks.

Of Medb there had been no sign. She had vanished into the mists as though she had never been, and Gruoch, questioned about her assistant, had shrugged and admitted only that the woman had been knowledgeable, studious and keen to please.

Now, still tired and in pain, Carta moved slowly, her head held high by sheer willpower. The place of offering and sacrifice was shadowy in the mist which rose over the river and the falls. In the bushes clinging to the sides of the ravine, a blackbird let out its ringing alarm call. The women stopped.

'*Druidh dubh*, the black watcher is guarding the entrance to other worlds. That is a good sign,' Gruoch whispered. 'He has announced you, and left the gateway open.'

Carta turned to Mairghread and held out her hands for the basket. Inside were two golden bangles, a bag of Roman coins and a carved wooden doll, the representation of a baby.

Taking them out, Carta gave the basket back and stepped forward to the edge of the falls alone, feeling the cold spray clinging to her skirts. She was at the sacred meeting place of the gods, between earth and water, between night and day, between forest and river, the place of nowhere and of no time. Behind her Mairghread and Gruoch withdrew along the bank of the river where the birch and ash, hazel and wych elm grew right down to the edge of the water, clustering thickly at the very edge of the torrent. Above them on the cliffs clung sacred yew trees, dark in the shadow of the rocks. Glancing at each other the two women stopped to wait.

Carta was alone.

'Vivienne?' Her voice was trembling. 'Why did you take my baby from me? What must I do to bear a child?' She stood staring out into the spray, the crude wooden baby cradled in her arms. 'Sweet Lady, take this offering. Do not ask of me another child of my body. Save me from Medb's curse, I implore you.' Tears were pouring down her cheeks. 'Bless me with fertility and strength.' She stood for a long time without moving, waiting in silence. In the distance a bird cried once up on the moor high above her head. It was growing darker.

'Vivienne? Why don't you answer?'

Pat was smiling.

Viv swallowed. 'Carta, I hear you,' she said softly in her own voice. 'This child was not meant to be. Say farewell, and leave her to the gods.' She paused. 'Go back. Become strong and well again. More babies will come in due time,' Viv went on. 'I can help you. I will see the curse is lifted.'

Pat frowned and shook her head. 'Don't make promises you can't keep. You're not really a goddess!' she mouthed.

Viv ignored her. 'Farewell, Cartimandua, Queen of Brigantia. Tend your kingdom. Leave the rest to the gods.'

There was a long silence, then at last Viv's voice resumed, speaking into the microphone. 'She has kissed the doll's head, pressed two fingers against its mouth in the sign of blessing and farewell and now she has thrown it into the waterfall where it disappears, sucked into the curtain of water. It bobs out for a moment on its torrential journey down the long fall then it is lost in the great whirlpool at the bottom. Now she has thrown in the bracelets and the bag of coins. They too are dragged out of sight. There is no chance the goddess is going to reject these. Her maw is ever greedy for gold. Carta watches the distant pool at the bottom for a long time, then she turns and walks slowly back along the bank towards the spot where her women are waiting amongst the trees.'

The Reverend James Oakley lay back in his chair and surveyed his visitor with a certain smug pleasure as the two men sipped his best brandy. At his own suggestion Hugh had eaten with him and his wife Margaret, and now that Margaret had retired to her own little sitting room to watch TV, the two men had settled down to a comfortable gossip. Now that he was here Hugh found himself in no hurry to contact Viv. Venutios seemed a million miles away, a figment of his imagination, and the whole sorry episode was best forgotten. The rector had taken a while to fathom the fact that this Hugh Graham was THE Hugh Graham, the Celtic scholar. He had, it appeared, all of Hugh's books in his library. He had also bought a copy of *Cartimandua, Queen of the North*.

'Have you read it?' Hugh raised a quizzical eyebrow. He was not going to allow anything to spoil the evening.

'Not yet, I must confess.' James Oakley took a sip from his glass. 'I read your review, of course.' He glanced up cautiously.

Hugh smiled. 'I feel now that I was a bit hard on her but then I'm a purist.' He crossed his legs, flicking an imaginary piece of lint off his knee. 'Tell me,' he changed the subject hastily, 'do you know the Steadmans? Their son is one of my graduate students.'

'Peg and Gordon?' James nodded. 'Salt of the earth. Gordon's family have farmed around here for hundreds of years.'

'They run a B&B, I gather?'

James laughed. 'Indeed. Much more elaborate than this, I fear. Margaret and I have only the one room. Well, one and a half, perhaps. I think they have about six. It's a rambling old place.'

Nodding, Hugh thought for a few seconds. 'I believe that Dr Lloyd Rees is staying there. To research a new enterprise. She believes Cartimandua lived up on Ingleborough.' He paused, waiting for a reaction, his eyes on the golden liquid in his glass.

James shrugged. 'Who knows. She must have come from somewhere. It is frustrating, you must admit, to know we may never be able to find out more about our more distant past. If only they had written something down!'

'Of course forensic archaeology improves all the time.' Was it Viv who had pointed out that very fact to him? Hugh took another small sip, unsure if he would be offered a top up, and so making the glorious experience last. 'I would like to stroll up there while I'm here. This is not an area I know at all, I'm sorry to say.'

'A bit more than a stroll, old boy.' James smiled. 'But you look fit and dapper. You could do it all right. The forecast is good for tomorrow. Perhaps you should take the opportunity while it's nice. And do please feel free to use the phone if you want to ring the Steadmans. I'm afraid most people's mobiles don't work around here.'

Hugh gave a small smile by way of acknowledgement. 'Perhaps I'll just surprise them,' he said.

30

I

Viv looked up at the quiet knock on the door. She had come upstairs after supper and was sitting on her bed, deep in thought.

'Come on, we're going out again.' Pat pushed the door open and stood there, silhouetted against the hall light.

'Tonight?' Viv glanced at the window. 'I don't think so.'

Pat nodded. 'We needn't go far. Just out onto the hillside to get the right ambiance to the sound; so it matches up.'

Viv shook her head. 'Not now, Pat,' she said uneasily.

'You're not losing interest?'

'Of course not! It's just it's late. I'm tired. I don't want to.'

'I think you do.' Pat's eyes were strange. Unfocussed. Viv felt a bolt of fear go through her. 'No, Pat. Not tonight. I'm sorry.'

Medb. Medb was there in the room with them. All over Pat. Viv could feel her skin crawling. 'Pat,' she whispered. 'Go away. Please.'

Pat merely smiled some more. 'Find your shoes, Viv. We want to know what happened next. You do, as much as me, don't you.'

For a moment Viv said nothing. She couldn't tear her eyes away from Pat's. Something strange was happening. Desperately she tried to fight it but she felt herself sigh. She was agreeing. Every part of her screamed in protest, but she was agreeing.

'OK. I suppose you're right.' It was as though someone else was speaking for her. She was powerless to resist. In two minutes they were making their way along the passage and down the stairs.

The evening was clear and cool, the sky luminous; a mass of purple clouds hung on the horizon but above them they could see the evening star as they let themselves out into the lane. They were heading for what Pat had dubbed Base Camp One – an outcrop of rocks a few hundred yards up the track once they were over the dry stone wall and up onto the open hillside.

In the distance a curlew cried mournfully at the cloud-striped moon. 'A bit spooky,' Pat said. She laughed. 'I hope we can get that on disc.' She sounded quite normal again now they were outside.

Viv glanced over her shoulder nervously. The cloud moved on and the moon shone more brightly casting deep shadows behind them.

Ten minutes later the cloud was back, more thickly this time. The moon vanished.

'Where are we going?' Viv was finding it difficult to keep up as Pat scrambled ahead of her. They had passed base camp and turned off the track.

'Not much further.' Pat was heading towards the limestone pavement.

Viv stopped, suddenly suspicious. 'I'm not sure we should go any further.' She shivered. 'We can't afford to lose our way. It could be really dangerous up here in the dark. It would be so easy to fall and break a leg.'

Pat was gazing into the distance. 'I agree. ' She turned to look up towards the summit, barely visible in the darkness. Wisps of mist were clinging to the northern cliffs. She was staring up at the hill. The half-moon had appeared again, through trails of cloud streaming towards the east. The wind was strengthening as they watched, dispersing the mist, rustling the grasses.

'Why don't we go back?' Viv said.

'No. No, that would be such a waste. Now we've come this far, let's do it. We can sit here, out of the wind behind this stone wall. We needn't stay long. All I need to know is where you've put the brooch.' Pat's voice was harsh suddenly. 'Medb wants it back.'

'Don't be silly!'

'It's not silly.' Pat sighed. 'Medb is quite anxious about it.'

'Right, that's it. I'm going!' Viv turned away.

'No.' Pat caught her arm. 'No! Sit down!' She gave her a sharp push and Viv found herself falling. Frantically she tried to regain her balance. When she recovered Pat was standing over her, the recorder in her hand.

They waited for five minutes. Nothing happened. Now that they were sitting still and Viv seemed to have acquiesced, Pat relaxed.

Around them the grasses rustled faintly. Down in the valley an owl hooted. Pat closed her eyes. 'Lady Brighid, goddess of the silver stars, comfort our queen, Cartimandua,' she whispered. 'Goddess of the land, keeper of the rocks, sacred spirit of the waters, grant her the blessing of another child.'

She lapsed once more into silence.

Viv glanced at her. 'You don't mean that.' Her skin was crawling.

'Oh but I do!' Pat smiled. 'Cartimandua, Queen of the North, We are here. Speak to us,' she said softly.

Viv bit her lip, fighting the urge to reply but it was overwhelming. When at last she spoke into the deepening silence, it was with the voice of the queen.

Vivienne. I gave you gold. I gave you blessings. I gave you the body of my child. What more can I give?

When Viv said nothing, Pat leaned towards her. 'Go on. Answer.'

Viv hesitated, her mouth dry with fear. 'Your prayers and blessings, lady, are all that I require.'

She glanced at Pat. She remained unmoving as the wind rose round them, lifting their hair. Then at last Carta began to speak again.

'Venutios has gone, lady.' Mairghread helped Carta on with her mantle. 'It's for the best.' She knew it was not her place to speak so, but she could not stand silently and watch them tear themselves and the whole of Brigantia apart in their fury and their mutual distrust. By the fire, in the fields, in the kitchens, on the training grounds since they had both returned at last to Dinas Dwr, people were beginning to align, some for her, some for him. If they stayed apart, matters could lie quietly and healing begin.

Carta frowned.

It had been a long time before she had brought herself to speak to Mairghread again. She blamed her, in some secret inner part of herself, for the loss of her baby. She blamed her for allowing Medb near her. She blamed her for Venutios's rage and now, she blamed her for supporting him.

She and Venutios had not spoken again since his return to Dinas Dwr with Brucetos from Caer Lugus. Although he was there, in the township, often near her, often at table with her, he somehow contrived to avoid her and the silence irked her. It challenged her authority as it was probably meant to do. She shivered. A gale howled down the dales outside and the fire smoked in a sullen refusal to burn clear. She sighed and pulled the heavy woollen folds around her against the cold, still not fully recovered from her miscarriage. That morning he had ridden down from the township into the forest. He had not returned.

'Berthe has made honey cakes, and there is fresh buttermilk to drink. It will make you feel better,' Mairghread coaxed, busying herself by tidying the room. 'Perhaps you might go for a short ride later? You like to ride in the storm. Or Fergal could take you in your chariot?'

Carta shook her head. 'I'll stay here for a while, then I'll come and join the others to listen to the music. Is Finley still here? I hear he has a fine repertoire of songs for all he is so young.' Dafydd, the bard given by Venutios as a gift on her accession, had gone. He had stood, and before the entire township he had spun a song of anger and betrayal, a song which pointed the finger at her and the Roman. A song designed to cut and wound; a song designed to destroy her.

Before she had a chance to respond, a young bard from the Druid college had stood up, incensed, to out-sing him, to stand for her as her bardic champion, but the damage was done, the poisoned dart had lodged home. She did not have to dismiss the older man. By next morning he had gone, back to the mountains of Eryri where he had come from. She gave the young bard, Finley, his position, a place he would hold as he continued his studies at the college under Artgenos, a position which would be hard to maintain as whispers flew around the firesides and men and women began to look at her askance.

'Go away, Mairghread. Leave me.' She put her hand down on Moon's head and fondled her ears. When the woman glanced in later, her queen was sitting by the fire, staring deep into the flames.

By noon, however, she had called for her pony and a warrior band to accompany her as she set off into the storm, Moon at her heels.

She caught up with Venutios in the end at a small fortress near Eburos. He was in bed with a pretty servant girl when Carta strode into the guest chamber soaked with rain, her hair matted, her colour high.

The girl tumbled from the bed with a squeak of fear and ran for the doorway. Carta ignored her. 'I did not give you leave to come

428

here. How dare you ride out of Dinas Dwr without seeking my permission.'

'I need no permission to travel the kingdoms.' He pulled on his tunic and breeks angrily. 'What am I? Some kind of servant? I am a king, madam, in my own right and I go where I wish, and like you, I bed when and with whom I wish!'

'And you foment rebellion where you wish too?' Ignoring his jibe she stared at him for a long moment with narrowed eyes. 'Do not push me too far, Venutios. You attacked me. You killed our child. I could have you executed for less.'

'Our child!' He retorted. 'A foreign bastard!' He spat on the floor.

'Our child.' She repeated coldly. 'A child of double royal blood and a child of the goddess.' She stared at him disdainfully. 'Did you please that girl?'

'I did. Greatly.'

She smiled. 'How strange. She knew no better, I suppose.'

There was a moment of total silence. Venutios's face suffused with scarlet. 'You whore!'

'I am a queen, Venutios, and a free woman. I take whomsoever I please to my bed, but I don't need to take slaves.'

She turned and walked out of the house.

Vellocatus was waiting just outside the doorway. 'Are you all right, lady?' He glanced over his shoulder. 'Venutios is not in the best of moods. His temper rules his head, and his sword arm.' He grimaced. 'He will calm soon.'

Carta paused. 'No doubt so will I. Escort me to a guest house, Vellocatus, if there is such a place and send for the headman so that I can meet him and explain why his high queen has arrived unannounced, and then send for Artgenos. I will speak to him as soon as he can ride here.' She hesitated. 'It may take him a few days. I will wait here.' She took a breath. 'The Roman, Gaius Flavius Cerialis told me between our romps in the bedchamber, that Eburos and Isurion would make fine trading posts.' She laughed bitterly. 'He did not like the moors and mountains and forests of our kingdom, they made him nervous, but these rich eastern lands, where the forests have been cleared and we have good fields rich in wheat and barley are different. No doubt they remind him of the south.'

'We encountered several traders when we arrived, lady.' Vellocatus was profoundly embarrassed at her remark. He refused to meet her eye. 'They brought fine wine and fabrics with them and

429

they were interested in the horse harnesses made by Oengus and his family here.'

'One of our best craftsmen.' Carta raised an eyebrow. 'Did they trade?'

Vellocatus sighed. 'Venutios chased them away, lady, before they had a chance.' He was hesitant, uncomfortable about telling her what had occurred. 'He kept the wares they had brought north to trade with.'

'Without payment?'

She scanned his face intently. The young man's handsome demeanour was incapable of guile. Every emotion swept over it as he met her gaze with large blue eyes. Anger, embarrassment again, shame and then reluctant acquiescence: they were all there in their turn. 'My king does not care for the Romans or those who trade on their behalf.'

'He doesn't, does he.' She pursed her lips. 'Come to my chamber as soon as I am settled and I will give you some coins. The Romans like to be paid in Celtic gold. See it is sent after the traders and see it is fair. I will not have them reporting to the governor, or to Gaius Flavius Cerialis, that they have been cheated by Cartimandua.' She paused. 'Or her husband.'

Vellocatus watched her walk away, his discomfort forgotten, and with something like hero worship in his eyes. She was strong and honest and let her head rule her heart. That gave her power. And she was the most beautiful woman he had ever seen.

He pulled himself together guiltily. Before all else he must see to the king, who was, after all, his master and his battle companion and his friend.

He turned back towards the house and was brought up short by the sight of Venutios standing in the entrance passage. 'So, you crawl to my wife!' he snarled.

Vellocatus blushed. 'I must obey the queen's orders, Venutios, as you do.' He squared his shoulders.

'Indeed? "Venutios chased them away, lady."' Venutios quoted him with high-pitched sarcasm. 'She did not command you to tell her what she did not know!'

'She guessed,' Vellocatus retorted hotly. 'It would not have been hard to do! The Roman wagons are standing out there on the trackway! Yet, there is no one to guard them. Not a merchant in the place. She could hardly have missed them.'

Venutios took a step towards him. 'Go, then. Run her errands. But be careful.' He narrowed his eyes threateningly, his voice an angry growl. 'Remember where your loyalty lies.'

Artgenos was not pleased to have been asked to ride the long miles to Eburos. His legs were aching and his back hurt. Wrapped in his woollen mantle, with a second one of furs over the top he laid his staff beside him on the ground with a sigh as he sat down and reached for the cup of spiced mead the servant passed him. Coel, the headman of the township, had joined Cartimandua and Venutios by the fire to greet him.

'So, is the debt paid?' Artgenos looked at Venutios with a raised eyebrow.

Venutios inclined his head. 'I was not to know they were peaceful traders,' he snarled. 'To me, every Roman sympathiser is an enemy, as she was –' he glanced at his wife, 'to Caradoc.'

'And rightly so, in present circumstances.' Artgenos took another sip from his cup. The mead was particularly good, flavoured with borage and anise. 'If we are to fight the Romans effectively and ensure our continuing independence we must use the cunning and diplomacy of the fox,' he glanced at Venutios, 'and the patience and discretion of the crane as she stands in the shallows of the pool, unmoving, waiting to strike at the unsuspecting fish.' He looked straight at Carta. 'My spies tell me we are right to be wary. Right to be cautious. 'It is not yet time –' he paused, once more looking at Venutios, 'to act. All over the Empire, Druids are watching and waiting. Brothers have come from Gaul. They warn of conspiracies against us.'

'From Gaul?' Carta frowned. 'I spoke to no Druids from Gaul.'

He took another sip of the mead and gave a small groan of pleasure as it began to reach his aching joints. 'They came to see me, lady. Silently, through the oak forest, wrapped in the cloak of invisibility.' He gave a cold smile. 'They did not expect to be intercepted by anyone who was not expecting them.'

Carta remained silent, stung by the rebuke.

'You see, Carta, they no longer trust you!' Venutios had no such qualms. 'You must take care or you will find yourself pushed aside and indeed, one of the enemy!'

Artgenos raised his hand before she could retort. 'Enough! Carta

431

is not our enemy. She is one of us. A Druidess, dedicated to the service of her goddess,' he reprimanded sternly. 'But she is not an Archdruid, nor was she at the gathering at Ynys Môn where these matters were discussed.'

'Nor were you!' she retorted. She knew she sounded childish as soon as she said the words.

Artgenos stood up painfully. He put his cup on the table. It teetered for a moment on the edge and then fell to the floor. He ignored it. 'At your command, if you remember,' he said reproachfully. 'Are you questioning my integrity?' He looked from one to the other of the three people seated at the fire. It was Coel, who had not yet spoken, who replied. 'No one would dare question you, Artgenos,' he growled.

As if echoing his words a low rumble of thunder resounded around the stone walls of the round house. Carta shivered. 'The gods are displeased.'

'As well they might be!' Artgenos agreed.

A flicker of lightning had found its way through the screened entrance. Moments later it was followed by a second, louder crash of thunder.

'Dear God, where did that come from!' Viv ducked as the lightning lanced across the hillside. A sheet of rain was heading towards them like a curtain.

Pat sat without moving. 'It's the voice of the gods,' she said slowly. 'They are angry.' She shook her head. Her mind was still in the round house by the fire with the three men and one woman as the rolling goblet came to rest against the stones of the hearth. There were no servants in the room to retrieve it. That meeting was private. Secret. Important.

Medb had been outside, listening from the shadowy doorway.

'This storm is going to get worse.' Viv glanced round apprehensively. The moon had gone and the hillside had been completely blotted out. They could see nothing in the dark as the slanting rain hid the distant lights in the valley.

'Perhaps it would be better not to move until the storm has passed over,' Pat said doubtfully. 'That lightning was very close!' As though in answer to her words another flash zigzagged almost at their feet. Both women ducked down behind the wall. Pat reached over and

432

snatched the small mike away from Viv, stowing it in her bag out of the rain, aware that ice-cold fingers of damp were finding their way down inside her collar. 'It looks as though we're stuck here! We can't risk losing our way in the dark.' She sounded almost triumphant. 'So, maybe you should go on. The sound effects are fantastic!'

'What about the recorder? Surely it mustn't get wet?'

'No.' Pat shrugged. 'So, we'll do without.'

Medb was there, waiting, and Medb did not care about the storm.

II

Medb turned and made her way back into the shadows. She knew enough. She had seen Venutios dragged from a whore's bed by his wife. Seen him wriggle like a fish on a hook. Seen Cartimandua lash him with her scorn, and then quail in her turn before the Druid. To push a wedge between the king and queen would be so easy. To boost Venutios in his arrogance to stand up against his wife would take no skill at all.

As he stormed out of the meeting she slid out of the shadows and caught his arm, drawing him silently back with her towards the guest house where she was lodged and behind the curtain which hid her bed. There she pulled off his tunic and his mantle and his breeches and ran her hands over his body, teasing him to eagerness. 'Your wife does not respect you, great king,' she whispered. She leaned closer, pressing her lips to his chest. 'Why do you let her walk all over you like that?'

He gasped as she knelt and her lips moved lower. 'How do you know what we were talking about?'

'I know everything, my lord.' She drew him down towards her. 'And I know how to help you.'

It was a long time before he could speak again.

Lying sweating, staring up at her as she knelt astride him he grinned, breathless with triumph. 'You know how to please a man, Medb, I'll grant you that.' He was exhausted.

'And how to instruct him in the ways of women.' She leaned

forward a little, allowing her hair to fall like heavy silk across his chest. 'How to manage your wife so she obeys you.'

He gave a snort. 'Not even you could do that, Medb.'

'Oh but I can.' Her eyes grew hard. 'Listen.'

Viv was staring at Pat as the storm rumbled away towards the east. 'Pat?' She whispered. 'Go on!'

Pat had fallen silent.

'What happened next?' Viv moved towards her, rummaged in the bag and gently put the mike between Pat's hands. This was incredible. Somehow they had changed roles. In the drumming rain and storm, Pat had started to speak, her voice filled with venom as she drew Venutios to her and poured out her plan.

Suddenly Pat laughed. 'Venutios will kill his wife. I won't have to do it. But I will make sure she knows who set the sword in his hand.'

Viv shuddered. She could barely see her face in the dark.

Medb had risen to her feet. She stood for a moment ethereal in her nakedness, her white skin and pale hair glowing in the darkness. As Venutios stood up beside her she reached for his mantle and pulled it round his shoulders, fastening the brooch and touching the bird's head with gentle fingers. Viv could see them clearly. Then Medb turned away and drifted into the darkness.

Shocked, Viv stared after her, then down at Pat who was smiling.

'You can't fight her,' Pat said quietly.

'You saw her?' Viv was paralysed with fear.

'I saw her.' Pat climbed stiffly to her feet.

Viv stepped back. The recorder fell to the ground between them.

'Venutios didn't kill Cartimandua,' Viv said after a minute. Her teeth were chattering.

'No?' Pat smiled. 'Can you be sure of that?'

Viv bent slowly to pick up the recorder. It was wet and she rubbed it against the sleeve of her jacket. 'I suppose not.'

'We'll see, won't we.' Pat put out her hand for it and tucked it into her bag. Her fingers were ice cold.

Viv nodded numbly. She glanced round. The hillside was empty. The moon reappeared through a gap in the clouds and for an instant the fells were illuminated with silvery light.

'Where have you been?' Peggy was waiting at the door, her hair untidy, her eyes wild. She dragged them inside and slammed it behind them.

Pat led the way down the hall, shivering. 'We wanted to record the storm. We're fine. We'll tell you about it later, Peggy. I don't know about you, Viv, but I want a soak in a hot bath for half an hour before I die of hypothermia.' And that was it. She had gone.

Viv stared after her. Peggy too watched her head off up the passage, her socks leaving wet footmarks on the flagstones, then she turned to Viv. 'What happened out there?' she snapped.

'Medb was there. She took her over.' Viv shook her head. 'I was so scared, Peggy.' Kicking off her own shoes she followed Peggy into the kitchen. She was shivering violently, her hair dripping down her neck as she went to stand near the comforting warmth of the Aga. 'It was just dreadful. Pat was –' She couldn't think of a word that would describe it. 'She was evil.'

Peggy handed her a towel, then automatically she slid the kettle onto the hob. 'I warned you.'

'This was different. It was threatening.' Viv could hardly speak. 'Pat was frightening.' She rubbed at her hair. 'She's changed. Medb seems to have made her stronger.' She shook her head. 'Why did you show her the well?' she asked suddenly.

Peggy went over to the fridge and brought out a jug of milk. 'She asked.'

'And you told her about the goddess?'

'I had to.' Pursing her lips, Peggy took three mugs down from the dresser.

'When I went to the well yesterday there was an ancient head there,' Viv went on.

'So.'

'It wasn't there when you took me there before.'

Peggy shrugged. 'It comes and goes,' she said evasively.

'By itself?'

'Maybe.'

'You hide it sometimes?' Peggy didn't answer. 'It felt very –' Viv

435

hesitated. She had been going to say evil. 'It felt very powerful.'

'Oh, it is. She is Brigantia.'

'Has she always been there?'

Peggy nodded. Behind them the kettle had begun to bubble. A wisp of steam escaped from the spout.

Viv could feel herself trembling again as she rubbed her hair. It wasn't entirely from the cold.

'When is Steve coming back?' she asked suddenly.

Peggy froze. She glanced at Viv, her eyes veiled. 'I don't know.' She smiled humourlessly. 'It doesn't matter. It's better he's not here. We don't want any men here at the moment.' Her knuckles had whitened as her fists clenched.

'Why?' Viv pulled the towel away from her head and stared at her.

'This is women's business.' Peggy's expression hardened. 'You have woken the sleepers. I'm sure it was not your intention, but it has happened. Cartimandua slept beneath this hill. You have brought her here to this house and you must face the consequences.'

Viv could feel the cold settling deep into her bones. 'Do you mean to say that Cartimandua died here?'

'No, I don't mean that.'

'What, then? You're frightening me.'

'Good. You should be frightened.' Peggy shook her head. 'Unless you do what I tell you.'

'Did Pat do what you told her?' Viv was suddenly suspicious. 'Is that why you've shown her the well?'

'I misjudged Pat.' Peggy handed her a mug of tea. It was a gesture of such normality Viv took it. She found herself sipping it gratefully.

'Medb, and through her, Pat, have embraced the goddess and all she stands for,' Peggy went on thoughtfully. 'I've changed my mind they are no danger to me.'

'And am I in danger?' Viv was holding her breath.

Peggy smiled. 'Cartimandua was a traitor; I realise that now. Steve has shown me your book. She betrayed Brigantia; and the other gods of these hills, but she paid the price. If she has woken, we have to lay her ghost and Medb is here to help us do that.'

Viv could feel her fingers tightening around the mug in her hands as Peggy sat down at the table opposite her.

Peggy stared thoughtfully down into the tea. 'The goddess will tell us what to do.' She looked up. 'Where is the brooch?'

436

Viv shook her head. 'That is safe.'

'I need it.'

'That's not possible, Peggy. It's not mine to give to you or to the gods. I have to keep it. But it's not in the house, I promise you. I have hidden it outside, far away, where no one will find it.'

'On the hill?' Peggy narrowed her eyes.

'On the hill.' She was studying Peggy's face nervously, and suddenly desperate to get away from her, she turned and hung the towel on the rail. 'Peggy, forgive me, but I'm very tired and cold. I think I'll go up and have a bath and go to bed. We can talk some more in the morning.'

Peggy shrugged. She made no move to stop her.

In her bedroom, Viv turned the key and stood for a moment, her back against the door, breathing deeply. This was insane. For a while she had been really scared. She glanced round the room. Had anything been moved? Had Pat been in, searching for the brooch while she was outside? Or Peggy? She couldn't see signs of anything being touched, but she couldn't be sure. Thoughtfully she walked over to the window and looked out. The moon was hanging low in the sky now. Soon it would have dropped below the apple trees on the lawn at the side of the house. When it had gone all would be dark.

Double-checking the lock on the door, she ran a bath and climbing in, lay back gratefully, feeling the warm water easing the cold out of her bones. In the morning everything would make sense again and she would wonder why she had been so frightened, and in the meantime, she would give in to Carta's incessant demand to tell her story by conjuring up another scene; a scene which Pat would not be overseeing with her digital recorder and her microphone and her computer; a part without Medb.

IV

It was autumn. The leaves were russet and rustled beneath the horses' hooves. Carta had ridden through the gateway at Dinas Dwr with as always, a quick critical glance at the ramparts and the wall on top of it, the great oak gates, the watch towers, to check that all was well and properly maintained. She liked it here. More woods had been felled around the township now, and a large area of fields and meadows surrounded the place, bisected by its gently meandering stream. In the centre of each field, as was proper, a single oak remained, the refuge for the gods of the woods that had gone. No one would ever cut down those trees, and when in the fullness of time, hundreds of years hence they fell of their own accord, each would be faithfully replaced by a successor.

Behind her the huntsmen and women straggled homewards in a long untidy file with two noble stags tied to the backs of sturdy moorland garrons. It had been a good chase, exhilarating and exciting. Horses, dogs, men and women were exhausted, but well pleased.

Carta reined in with a frown at the sight of two wagons pulled up outside the great house. She glanced across at Catuaros, the township elder. 'We have visitors, it seems.'

On the trackway which served as main street between the crowded houses and workshops and barns within the walls, a group of men appeared. Catuaros's eldest son and his Druid were escorting a group of Romans. Catuaros froze, his hand on his dagger, but his queen too had dismounted and she walked towards them with evident recognition.

'Gaius Flavius Cerialis! So, you honour us with another visit.' If she had any worries as to the reason for his appearance she did not show it.

He gave a slight bow, scanning her face warily, as if not knowing how to react to her greeting. The queen was suntanned, dishevelled, dusty and mud-splattered from the chase, unlike any highborn woman of the Roman empire that he had ever seen. He reminded himself hastily that she was a native Briton with all their barbaric habits, remembering the scornful incomprehension with which he had first noted the blue swirls painted on her temples. In spite of it all she still had that magnetic beauty he found so alluring.

He realised he was staring when she laughed at him. 'So, my friend, do I have birds' nests in my hair? Do Roman ladies not ride out on the hunt and come back blooded from the chase?'

So, she could still read his thoughts. He felt himself colouring slightly. 'You look wonderful, lady.' He bowed again, aware of the sniggers of her followers and the shocked silence of the men of his troop.

There was no sign of her husband, he noted, and he wondered if the rumours the spies had brought to Scapula about their increasing animosity were true.

'We have brought messages and gifts from the Governor of Britannia, great queen,' he said formally, aware of the intense interest immediately shown by the men around her and especially by the Druid standing beside her.

The man had greeted him with outward friendliness and dignity and with that strange sense of power all these Druids seemed to possess, when he had ridden into the township to find it all but empty and unguarded. It had shocked him that the place would be left to women and children and a few priests whilst most of the fit population had, it appeared, gone hunting. He glanced enviously at the two fine stags. He would have enjoyed such an excursion himself.

'Had you sent messengers ahead, tribune, the queen would have been here to greet you formally.' The Druid's reproachful tone was designed to irk him. To make him feel guilty and ill-mannered.

'I thought you people could see the future,' he retorted. 'Why did you not tell the queen yourself?'

The man had smiled gravely. 'An oversight. I shall see it does not happen again,' he said, mildly enough, but something in his tone made Gaius's skin crawl.

Bathed, dressed in one of her best mantles and laden with gold bangles, Carta joined Catuatos to receive Gaius formally that evening at a feast in his honour. Regaled with music, stories and dancing, he sat back on his cushioned stool and prepared to enjoy himself. The queen had received her gifts of wine amphorae, the furs and rich fabrics from the east with quizzical good humour. He wasn't entirely sure if she was pleased.

The food set before him as he sat at her right hand before the long trestle table was as before as good as any he would be served at home, he noted. There was venison and beef, there was rich mutton stew and there were wild mushrooms, bean cakes, breads and cheeses, wine and mead and barley beer. To follow there were huge polished wooden bowls of blackberries and vast ewers of milk and cream, honey cakes and nut dumplings.

More than once as he ate he found her looking at him. At first he looked away, embarrassed, then at last he straightened his shoulders and held her gaze. 'I trust the governor's gifts meet with your approval?' He spoke quietly as the music ceased for a moment. The bard who had been singing picked up his small harp, bowed, and retired to the back of the crowd for some refreshment. His place was taken almost at once by another performer. This one had brought his pipes.

As he started to play, she leaned towards Gaius. 'And why does the Governor send yet more gifts, my friend? Grateful though we are, there must be another reason for this visit.'

He saw the interest of the Druid next to her quicken and was intensely aware as she spoke of her eyes on his. 'Keep her on side. Make sure she is still compliant.' The Governor's words rang in his ear. He managed a smile. 'Does there have to be a reason, great queen? He wished to compliment you, no more.'

'I see.' She smiled. 'So, tell me, are you still a part of the gift?'

As she held his gaze, he was intensely aware of how much he wanted her. He hesitated. He was a Roman officer. Her tone implied that he was a plaything. And, he reminded himself of how she had discarded him before. A night of passion, the start of a friendship or so he had thought, and the gift of the valuable dog and then – nothing. Not even goodbye. He couldn't tear his gaze away from hers and at last he found himself replying, 'I'm sure that could be arranged if it is the queen's wish.'

She smiled. 'It is the queen's wish.' And suddenly she was standing up in front of the entire assembly, reaching out for his hand, pulling him to his feet. He saw faces watching him. He saw his own men look up for a moment, alert to possible trouble, then he saw them relax and laugh. One of them cheered, thumb up, from the far end of the table.

Some of the richly woven cloaks he had brought with him as gifts had been thrown across her bed. The room smelled of herbs and crushed grass and hay and the sweet beeswax of the best candles. There was no trace here of the sour echo of tallow or the stink of the latrine pits at the edge of the township. This was, he realised happily as he glanced round the room, as exotic as he remembered it, as exotic as some of the eastern palaces he had seen on his tour of duty in Macedonia and Galatia.

Only the sound of music in the distance broke the silence now. Three harpists were playing together, a glorious rich medley of sound. There were no servants or slaves in sight, although someone must have lit the candles, trimmed the lamp and filled it with sweet oil and thrown herbs on the fire.

'It shocks you, doesn't it, that a woman of our people may have any man she wishes,' she said with a chuckle. She put her hands on his forearms, drawing him to her. 'Roman women do not have that choice, I hear.'

'Not if they are honest women.' He reached out to touch her face, stroking the strangely beautiful decoration on her temples. She did not paint herself heavily as did some of her warriors or the other women, but the decorations were intricate and elegant. 'I would kill my wife if she went with another man.'

'So, you are married now.' She seemed to find the idea amusing.

'I am, lady. I have a wife in the south. She travels with the legion as do the other wives.'

'But she did not travel here.'

He shook his head. 'No. Not here.'

'And what is her name?' She ran her finger down the side of his face, echoing the gesture he himself had made. He had a scar down the edge of his jaw – a glancing blow from a spear which had it been an inch or so to the right would have killed him.

'She is called Portia, lady.'

'And is she faithful to you?' She looked deep into his eyes for a moment and he tried to read her expression, suspicious suddenly that she could read not only his thoughts but, with the strange power these Celts seemed to possess, the future as well. She remained inscrutable. 'More to the point, gift of the governor, are you going to be faithful to her?' She leaned forward and pressed her lips against his.

Slowly, almost against his will, he found he had put his arms around her. His eyes closed and he began to return her kisses more and more eagerly. Her forehead, her mouth, her throat. He stopped short, his hand on the gold necklet she wore, unsure how to unfasten it and with a throaty chuckle she removed it herself, aware that with her arms raised to her own throat she was vulnerable and provocative, her breasts thrust against the soft wool of her tunic.

She was naked before him and watched amused as he groped with the fastenings of his armoured tunic and the thongs of his sandals, then at last he turned to her and pushed her back onto the bed.

This time when he awoke she was still there beside him, asleep, her hair spread across the pillows. While they slept the candles had

441

been replaced and the lamp filled, the wick trimmed. Outside he could hear the rain smacking the limestone paving slabs on the pathway. He shivered. This accursed country. Did it ever do anything other than rain?

Someone was watching him, he realised suddenly. He made a grab for the sheet and pulled it over them both. Her attendant, the boot-faced one who disapproved of him with every fibre of her being, was watching him from the shadows.

'Good morning.' He yawned widely and scratched his head. The woman turned and left the room.

Cartimandua stirred. Her eyes were open suddenly and she smiled at him.

He stretched luxuriantly. 'So, did you enjoy your gift?'

She nodded. 'But today you must go. Back to your governor. Tell him how obedient we are; how we honour the treaty. How we enjoyed our gifts.'

'I don't have to go. Not yet.' He raised himself on his elbow and leaned across to kiss her breast.

'Maybe not.' She pushed him away. 'But I do. I have meetings to attend. So, off you go. Back to your Portia.' She had remembered the name.

She slid from the bed and stood for a moment, looking down at him. 'Will you tell her that you slept with a queen?' She raised an eyebrow.

Mairghread reappeared as if at some secret signal and stepped forward with her mantle. Within seconds the two women were gone, leaving him feeling as though he was a discarded toy with which she had grown bored. He scowled and climbed from the bed. Within an hour he and his men were on the road south. That his men knew what had happened, that he had been tossed from her bed and forgotten was obvious. Behind their hands they were laughing, he was sure of it. His humiliation and anger at himself for letting her use him yet again were total.

Viv lay awake for a long time, staring at the ceiling. In the distance the thunder had returned. It rumbled over the dales more and more softly until she could no longer hear it and the cloud began to clear. By dawn the thick mist which filled the river valleys was beginning to disperse and the brilliant blue sky heralded a beautiful day. She

442

climbed out of bed and went to kneel on the window seat, staring out at the glittering rain-washed garden.

Just before six she went back to bed, fell asleep at last and dreamed of Venutios. He stood at the end of her bed, staring at her from his strange tawny eyes.

She couldn't breathe. Shrinking back against the pillows she heard herself give a small whimper of fear. There was a sword in his hand. Short, stubby, sharp. Vicious.

'No. Please.' Her voice came out as a husky whisper.

He took a step towards her. 'You can't escape me! I will follow you wherever you go and I will kill you!'

With a cry of terror she raised her arm to ward off the blow as he lifted his arm, but his face changed. The man had gone. In his place stood a woman in a white gown – her hair veiled and her eyes as hard as granite.

Medb.

Viv woke up with a gasp and lay, her heart pumping adrenaline around her body, staring round the room. There was no one there.

31

I

'I'm sorry I can't walk with you.' The Reverend James Oakley dropped Hugh off in a lay-by at the foot of the hill. He had given him a map, a walking stick and copious instructions. 'My rheumatism plays up dreadfully in the damp. You'll enjoy the walk, though. It is the most wonderful view. Well worth it. As a Celtic scholar you'll be interested, whatever your views of the Setantii. And just for a moment if you can bring yourself to do it,' the rector gave an almost mischievous smile, 'imagine Our Lord striding with just such a staff in his hand, across hills much like this one – if not these very moors.'

Chuckling, Hugh had raised his hand in farewell and set off up the track.

His host was right. It was a wonderful, exhilarating walk. He stopped often, leaning on the stick, looking across to admire the view. There were other walkers around, straggling up the track, but he managed to avoid most of them, preferring to keep to himself. Near the top he sat down, panting, on a limestone knuckle protruding from the grass, staring into the distance.

Venutios was there at once. There was no carnyx this time. No warning at all.

In the interests of the Brigantian federation Carta had wooed him back to her bed. 'We have quarrelled enough, husband.' She lay on her elbow, staring into his eyes. 'It is time for us to form a new alliance. We have to be seen to be united by our tribesmen.'

She reached out and touched his face gently and she smiled. 'Why do we always fight?'

Hugh nodded grimly. Why indeed?

Venutios closed his eyes with a groan. His passion for this wife of his was as intense as ever. 'Because you try me sorely, woman.' He grabbed her hand and put her fingers between his teeth. 'You cannot see how your determination to ally with Rome damages you; damages all of us. It is insane.'

'It is the sensible route to follow. For our people's safety and prosperity.' She repeated the words yet again.

'Can you not think of anything else?' He sat up, infuriated. 'What about our freedom. Our pride!'

'Our future and our very existence.' She smiled and pushed him back on the pillows. 'That is what I think about.' Bending over him, she pressed her lips against his. The kiss was long and deep.

Their love-making was passionate but it held an edge of anger and it was short-lived. Rolling away from her, spent, Venutios rose to don his clothes. He did not turn back to the bed with any words of endearment.

Carta stood up and pulled a bed robe around her shoulders. 'Are you going hunting later?'

He nodded. He reached for his mantle and began to pin it at the shoulder. 'Wait. Let me help you.' She did not want them to part angrily again. It had become too much of a habit. She reached for the pin and took it from him. 'This is very beautiful.'

'It is indeed.' He put out his hand for it.

'It would go well with my best cloak.' She managed a wheedling note.

He frowned. 'You have many brooches, Carta. You do not need this one.'

'I shall swap one of my own for it.' She went to the coffer on the table near the door and opened it. 'Here. This is larger; more beautiful, more befitting a warrior.' She picked one out which was worked from solid gold. He hesitated. She was right. It was larger and contained a heavier weight of metal. Already the enamelled bird had been stowed away in her coffer. She turned with the gold brooch and pinned it on his shoulder. Then she reached up and gave him a quick kiss on the lips. 'There, Venutios. An exchange of gifts. An exchange of kisses. A pledge of our love.' For a moment she paused and looked at him closely, then she turned away. Her

445

kiss did not, he realised, contain any warmth. He shivered. His wife did not frighten him nearly as much as the thought of what Medb would say when she found her gift had been so easily spirited away.

II

Pat was waiting for her in the kitchen when Viv appeared at last. Looking remarkably cheerful in a scarlet cotton sweater and dark blue jeans she was boiling the kettle. 'Peggy's out and Steve's still not back, so we've got to make our own breakfast!' She reached for the coffee jar. ' Shall we go out again this morning?' She was enthusiastic. Her old, bubbly self. There was no sign of Medb. 'The re-enactors might be back. I would like to get some more of their sound effects. They were brilliant.'

Viv sat down heavily at the table. Her head was aching and she felt exhausted. It was a relief that Peggy wasn't there. 'Pat, when you went to the sacred well with Peggy, did she seem OK about it?'

'Fine. Why?' Pat sawed a couple of slices off the loaf of bread which was sitting on the table.

'I just wondered. We talked about it last night.' She hesitated. 'Did you see the grotesque head in there?'

'Grotesque?' Pat paused for a moment and considered the word. 'The old stone head?'

Viv nodded. 'That is the real thing. Thousands of years old.'

'Wow.' Pat carried the slices over, sandwiched them in the hinged wire Aga toaster and shoved it on the hob.

'Did it seem powerful to you?'

Pat nodded. 'Gordon hates it, apparently. You know he threatened to fill in the well?'

'What?'

'That's what the row was about before he walked out. That's where Steve has gone. To try and find him.'

'Why would Gordon want to fill it in?'

'Scared of it?' Pat shrugged. 'It's a bit too much of a woman thing.

446

Goddess stuff.' She seemed uninvolved. Distanced. She reached for some butter out of the fridge.

Viv grimaced. 'The Goddess as such wasn't really a Celtic thing you know; they had dozens of gods and goddesses. Carta worshipped Brigantia, the goddess of these hills. Britannia, if you like. Or Brighid. All versions of the same goddess probably, but not "The Goddess" of the feminists.'

'And Vivienne.' Pat raised an eyebrow.

Viv laughed uncomfortably.

'I don't see Peggy as a feminist,' Pat went on. 'But I do see her as a worshipper of the old gods and keeper of the shrine. I reckon she's been following on in an ancient tradition.'

Viv nodded. 'You're right about that. It scares me.'

Pat took the toaster off the hob and handed her a slice. 'Why?'

'It's too powerful. Too single-minded.'

'I wonder where she's gone,' Pat said thoughtfully. She reached for Peggy's homemade marmalade.

'So do I.' Viv glanced at her. They were both silent for a minute or two. It was as if Peggy's presence was suddenly in the room with them.

III

In her private chamber, Medb was staring down into the bronze bowl of vervain purified water, eyes narrowed with fury. She had seen it all. Venutios in the arms of his wife. Their sparring; their rising; their dressing. And she had seen Cartimandua standing holding the brooch in triumph as her husband walked out of the chamber, his mantle pinned with a great wheel of gold.

Cursing, she dashed the bowl to the ground and watched the water seep between the floorboards into the earth beneath. She had imbued that brooch with special powers; it held the owner in thrall to her every whim. It had been configured especially for Venutios, to keep him enslaved as long as she needed him but something had gone wrong. He had escaped its entanglement; worse, Cartimandua had tucked it away in her jewellery casket

447

with a smile of triumph which could only mean she knew what it could do and that she had somehow found a way to use it to her own advantage.

Medb let out a scream of fury and stamped her foot. Outside two women, spinning in the sunlight, glanced at each other and shivered. They made the sign against the evil eye and of one accord stood up and moved away.

Venutios had left his wife's presence and gone at once to the practice ground, where he found some of his warriors idly competing with their slings as to who could decapitate a straw figure set up on a wagon at the far end of the field. With a shout of greeting he took a sling from one of the men, picked up a stone and hurled it at the figure. The head spun off to a yell of triumph from the men. He grinned. He wasn't going to tell them the name he had given his target.

Medb knew. Her eyes narrowed like a cat watching a rat in the granary. He would pay for that. And so would his wife. She would see to it that the whole of Brigantia paid for what she had suffered and history for all time would know it.

IV

'Does Venutios not require you to drive his chariot today?' Carta looked at Vellocatus enquiringly. 'I don't want you to make him angry.'

The voice came to Hugh indistinctly from the other side of the rocks, then as he began to listen more carefully, more and more clearly. It was a woman's voice, at once familiar and at the same time alien. When at last he began to make out the words what he heard stunned him.

'He is hunting on foot, my queen, with his brother, Brucetos and his brother's son and a few chosen companions.' If Vellocatus was hurt not to have been selected as one of those companions he didn't show it. 'I know one of your team is lame. I wondered whether you would enjoy a drive in the king's chariot.'

Carta looked at him thoughtfully. She had a dozen charioteers and a hundred war chariots at her command. Why should this one be so special?

For an instant she looked inside, deep within her soul, to seek for an inner warning, an instruction that this might be a trap. There was none. She held his gaze and saw only an eagerness to please, to make amends for her husband's boorishness. 'Very well, that would indeed be a pleasure.' She called for a cloak and watched as he harnessed two of Venutios's best ponies, a matched team of black stallions, then allowed him to hand her up onto the driving platform beside him. She did not use Venutios's bird brooch.

They trotted down the long trackway away from the township, then gaining the more even valley bottom he whipped the horses into a canter and then into a gallop. Carta clutched the side rail of the chariot as it thundered over the ground, keeping her balance with difficulty as she was thrown back and forth against Vellocatus as he braced himself to hold the reins.

At last he slowed the horses, turning them off the moorland and onto a trail which led into the forest, beginning to circle round towards home. The horses were walking now, steam rising from their flanks, tossing their heads with a jangle of bits and harness.

'Fast enough for you?' He turned to her and grinned.

She nodded. Her hair had been whipped into tangles, her cloak almost torn from her shoulders. She was breathless. She laughed out loud. 'Fergal takes good care of me and of the horses' legs. He would not have dared to gallop so.'

'Then he doesn't understand you.' Vellocatus was exultant.

'No. Maybe he doesn't.' She eyed him. 'I don't require my charioteer to understand me,' she said quietly. 'I require him to obey me.'

'As I would.' He gave a small bow. 'As I will.'

There was a moment of silence.

She raised her hand and gently touched his cheek. 'You are sworn to my husband, Vellocatus. You are his shield bearer; his charioteer. You carry his weapons. You fight at his right hand.'

'And I read the message in the eyes of his wife,' he whispered. The horses had stopped and, taking the chance, were snatching mouthfuls of the long lush grass at the trackside under the trees. 'She feels betrayed by him. He abuses her trust and her standing as his queen. And he leaves her lonely.' He paused.

She said nothing.

'I am at your command, lady. Yours absolutely.'

449

The silence lengthened between them. One of the horses moved forward a pace to snatch another mouthful of grass and the chariot jerked slightly at the pull on the yoke, unbalancing her and nudging her towards him. He caught her and pulled her close. There was another split second's hesitation, then he reached down to kiss her lips.

V

'More research, Viv?' Hugh was standing immediately behind them, leaning on his staff, within easy earshot.

Viv turned incredulously. She stared at him wide-eyed. 'Hugh?' Dragged suddenly out of the past, she was confused and angry. 'What are you doing here?'

'Listening.' He stepped closer, still leaning on the stick.

With a sigh Pat switched off the recorder. 'Bad timing, to say the least!' She climbed wearily to her feet. 'But then your entrance stage left was imminent, wasn't it. Greetings, Venutios!'

Viv spun round. 'Pat?' She was furious and embarrassed. How much had he heard?

Pat nodded. 'I called him. Medb needs his services. I did warn you, Viv.'

'How could you!' Viv looked from one to the other in horror, finally focussing on Hugh's face. 'Venutios?' she whispered.

He shook his head violently. 'No! He's gone. You mustn't be frightened. I just need the brooch, then I'll leave.'

'He hasn't gone!' Pat's eyes narrowed in the sunlight. She pushed the recorder and microphone into her bag. 'But you are not going to get the brooch. Of that you can be certain. That's not why I brought you here. You gave it away to Cartimandua, Venutios, after Medb had given it to you!' She stepped towards him. 'Didn't you?' she accused.

'Pat! Stop it!' Viv snapped.

'Why? Does he scare you? He should!' Pat turned back to Hugh. 'You can't have the brooch back! It's mine.' Her voice had changed. It was lighter. Harsher. 'And I want it back. I will never let you have it. I will find it, whatever I have to do.' She eyed him scornfully.

'What's the matter with this woman? What's happening?' Hugh backed away from her.

'I'll tell you what's happening,' Viv cried. 'Don't you see? Us three. We're being forced to fight each other. We're being forced to re-enact their drama! And we've colluded in their plan! Pat and I are writing a play, for Christ's sake! And you, Hugh, are writing about Venutios! We're just puppets and they are pulling the strings!'

For a moment all three were silent.

Hugh swallowed hard. 'That's an insane suggestion,' he said at last.

'Is it?' Her eyes blazed. 'Why did you come then? And why, in God's name, Pat, did you tell him where I was?'

'So that he can kill Cartimandua.' Pat's eyes were silver slits.

'No!' Viv grabbed Pat's arm and shook her. 'Don't do this, Pat! You don't mean it. Don't listen to Medb!'

'I'll listen to whoever I please!' Pat pulled away. She laughed. 'I'm off. The recording is spoiled, anyway.' She turned and swinging her bag onto her shoulder she headed off down the track.

Hugh stared after her in silence, then he turned to Viv. 'That woman terrifies me!'

Viv bit her lip. She didn't disagree.

'Can we talk, Viv, please? This whole thing has to stop.'

'I agree.'

'I'm sorry,' he said. 'I really am.'

'For what? Coming here? Eavesdropping? Attacking me in the press? Destroying my life or planning to kill me?' Viv picked up her own bag. 'If we can't be on the same side, Hugh, there's no point in you and I even discussing this.'

'We are on the same side.'

She shook her head. 'No. It's too late, Hugh. I'm going.'

Hugh stood watching as she set off after Pat, then sitting down on an outcrop of rock he put his head in his hands.

The air was clear and hot. The stones in the wall near him were almost too hot to touch in the sun. It was hazy now in the distance and he could smell newly cut hay and sweet herbs. In the west the clouds seemed to be banking up on the horizon. He was stupid to have come. The best thing would be to go home. To leave them

451

alone. To hell with the brooch. And Viv's book. And their play. And that mad woman. He shuddered. Wearily he stood up again and turned back towards the track. Before he reached the first rampart, Venutios was back.

'Where is the brooch? I have to have the brooch!' He dragged Mairghread by the arm into Carta's sleeping chamber and threw her against the wall. 'She put it in one of her coffers. Find it. Quickly.'

'I don't know where it is, King Venutios. I swear by all the gods!' Mairghread was terrified. 'Look, lord. Look!' One by one she pulled open the lids.

He tipped the contents of the smaller boxes onto the bed. The jewelled crane was not there.

'Was she wearing it?' he growled. 'By the great god, Lugh, tell me!'

'I did not see it, lord.' Mairghread stepped away from him. Somehow she managed to recover some of her dignity. 'She was wearing silver pins on her gown this morning; she didn't have it with her.'

She did not tell him that Carta had shown her the brooch and that both women had shuddered. They could sense the evil coming from it.

'Is it cursed?' Mairghread had whispered as she had stretched out her hand and then withdrawn it again without touching it.

Carta had nodded. 'Oh yes, it is cursed. I have done him a service, taking it from him. And I will dispose of it for him.' She had smiled grimly. She could feel the impotent rage of the woman who had pinned the brooch on her husband.

VI

Hugh found the cottage empty when he got back at last. He walked back outside and climbed straight into his car.

'I want to apologise.' He shrugged. 'Please don't throw me out. We have to talk.' Viv had shown him into the visitors' sitting room at the farm, tight-lipped. To his intense relief there was no sign of Pat. 'I truly didn't know you were up there,' he went on. 'Not this afternoon.'

She raised an eyebrow. 'Why do I find that hard to believe?'

'Nevertheless, it is true. And I didn't realise you were recording your play. I really thought for a moment –' He paused. 'I don't quite know what I thought. It all seemed very realistic.' He shivered.

She said nothing.

'Listen.' He sat down, leaning forward earnestly as he looked up at her. 'This has all got out of hand. You're right. I've been unfair.'

'That's an understatement!' She spoke at last. 'You've tried to ruin me, Hugh.' She couldn't keep the hurt out of her voice.

He looked down at his feet. 'I hated to see you making claims you couldn't justify. You were – are – such a good scholar.'

'Thanks!' Her voice was heavy with sarcasm.

'You were improvising up there, weren't you,' he went on quietly. 'Making it up as you went along? You didn't have a script.'

Viv closed her eyes briefly. 'We were performing a play, Hugh. We make no claims for accuracy. We are making it up.'

'But there was no script.'

'No, there was no script at that stage. We have used scripts for most of it. It will be edited later.'

'I see.' He looked uncomfortable.

'Pat is a professional actress.'

'Right.' He nodded. He was still uncertain. 'And you made all that stuff up? Guessed it ? Dreamed it?' Watching her face, he saw something like panic in her eyes. 'That's it, isn't it. You dreamed your book.' He smiled sadly. 'Your source – your impeccable, unimpeachable source is a dream!' He stood up. 'Your dream? Or that actress woman's dream? That's why you're so protective. It seems real to you, doesn't it. It seems so bloody real you're prepared to put your reputation on the line. Jesus Christ! I just can't believe it. I can't!' He paused.

'A dream like yours, Hugh,' she said slowly. 'I dream of Cartimandua and you dream of Venutios. We are part of the same dream. Perhaps we are part of theirs.'

He blanched. 'What have we got ourselves into?'

'History.' She smiled sadly.

'What was Pat talking about up there on the hill?'

'She's convinced Venutios wanted to kill Cartimandua.'

453

'She had only to read the history books to know that.'

'She – Medb – thinks you might want to kill me.' She looked at him uncomfortably. 'You thought that yourself, didn't you?'

'No!'

'You did, Hugh.' Her voice softened. 'Please. You said we were on the same side but you have to mean it,' she said gently. 'Tell me what to do. The brooch is at the centre of all this. Venutios wants it. Carta wants it. Medb wants it. The museum wants it.' She laughed uncomfortably. 'You can't deny all this is happening.'

'I'm not denying it.' He shrugged angrily. 'I just find it hard to believe.'

'So do I. I didn't want all this to happen. I don't want us to be enemies.'

They looked at each other silently.

'Did you bring the brooch here?' he asked at last.

She nodded.

'I think I'd better have it back.'

'Yes, I think you'd better,' she said quietly. 'It's hidden. Up there, on the hillside. I'll retrieve it tomorrow.'

He nodded. 'I'll go now. I'm sorry to have inflicted myself on you,' he said. He hesitated, then unexpectedly he moved forward and kissed her on the cheek. For a moment they gazed at each other then he said softly, 'I'll ring you tomorrow?'

Viv watched him through the window as he walked out to the car, climbed in and drove away. When she turned round she found Peggy standing behind her.

'I thought I told you I don't want any men in my house!' Peggy's voice was harsh.

Startled, Viv stepped back. The cold anger was back in the other woman's eyes. 'He wanted the brooch, didn't he,' Peggy went on. She grabbed Viv's wrist. 'I think it would be best for everyone if you let me have it. Whatever happens you must not give it to him. Did you see Venutios?'

Viv gasped. 'You could see him?'

'Of course I could see him.' Peggy studied her face for a full ten seconds. 'Just as I can see Cartimandua and Medb. My dear, don't imagine these people care who they use. Or who they hurt. Don't you see,' she gave a cold humourless laugh, 'you and your friends have created a cast of monsters!'

VII

As the sun set and the mist began to gather in the folds of the hillside it grew colder, but Pat didn't feel it as she sat on the bench in the orchard. The voice in her head was too insistent, too loud, to allow any coherent thought.

'I gave you the brooch for a reason, Venutios! Get it back.' Medb was incandescent with anger.

He eyed her coldly, wondering not for the first time why he had ever felt attracted to this woman with her pale eyes and her vicious temper. 'Why is it so important?' He leaned forward and took hold of her arms.

She didn't flinch. 'Because I imbued it with power, you fool. To protect you. Do you want it to serve your wife?'

He held her gaze. 'I don't believe you.'

'Then leave it!' She tore herself out of his grasp. 'See what happens!'

He smiled. 'I think I will do just that. It is time you moved on, Medb. Your constant meddling annoys me.' He folded his arms. 'I'll give you a pension and a horse. Perhaps you should go home to Dun Pelder. Would they want you back there? Are you not a queen in your own country?'

Her eyes narrowed. 'You know I was never queen.'

He raised an eyebrow. 'Of course. I had forgotten. You were a murderess who cast spells upon anyone who you thought might be a rival. And when my astute wife saw through you and sought, I think with commendable restraint, to dispose of you without resorting to your own foul methods, you decided to hound her for the rest of her days.'

Medb scowled at him. 'No one treats me like that and gets away with it.'

'Yet you treat everyone else with vile disdain.' He shook his head. 'No. I don't think I should take back that brooch. For all I know it binds me to you forever –' He broke off and then gave a short hard laugh. 'I see I have hit the mark. You are nothing but a sorceress! Get out of my sight! I am an honourable man and I will pay as I said I would for such services as you have rendered, but no more. Get out of Dinas Dwr today and never come back.'

Medb stood white-faced, watching him as he turned on his heel and walked away from her. 'Oh yes, you will pay for this, my friend,' she murmured at his retreating back. 'Do not think a few fine brave words can release you from your debt to me.' She gave a grim smile. 'You accuse me of casting spells. Believe me, Venutios of the Carvetii, you have seen nothing yet, neither you, nor your scheming, Roman-loving wife.'

On her bench in the orchard Pat wiped a fleck of foam from the corner of her mouth. The brooch. She had to retrieve the brooch before Venutios found it. She stared up at the hill rising in the distance above the roofs of the house. Somewhere up there it was hidden where no one could find it. Only one person could retrieve it for her. After that she would let destiny takes its course and leave Viv to Venutios's rage.

32

I

Carta and Venutios were at Dinas Dwr. 'The ramparts are nearly finished.' Venutios strode along the inside of the wall approvingly. 'But they will still have to be strengthened in places. They would not withstand an attack.'

'There will be no attack.' Cartimandua turned her back on the wall and surveyed the township which had swelled in size to fill the huge area inside the new walls. Houses, workshops, granaries, store houses, craftsmen's dwellings, sweat houses, temple, barns, all prosperous and new, together with a new parade ground where the young men of the township were playing Hurley, had sprung up around the main central enclosure within which stood the great round house.

Some of the round houses were linked now by passages. Her private lodging, her bedroom, her meeting house led off the high council chambers to the west. The guest house was in the far side of the compound and between were a dozen new dwellings.

'There will undoubtedly be an attack.'

They had been quarrelling all day. Sometimes, it felt to Carta, all their lives. He was pushing at her constantly, undermining her, countermanding her orders. He leaned back against the warm stone and squinted into the sun. 'Don't delude yourself, woman. These Romans are not going to be content to stop at the Trisantona. Once they have caught their breath they will cross the river and start looking north!'

'When will you believe that the Romans are our allies.' Carta sighed wearily. 'They won't attack unless we provoke them.'

'But we will provoke them.' Venutios laughed grimly. 'As soon as we're ready, that is exactly what we'll do.'

She narrowed her eyes. So, it started again. Would he never learn? 'Luckily you are in no position to dictate the policy of Brigantia.'

'No?' He glared at her. 'I think you'll find I am. Culann will be chief Druid to the Brigantians after Artgenos's time. He is for a war. So is Artgenos, if truth were told. And my brother. Brucetos has a good head on his shoulders. He studies the way the Romans think. And the men. Ask every chieftain and king when they assemble here for Samhain. To a man they will follow me.'

'Then they will die as rebels.' She drew herself up to her full height. 'Don't defy me, Venutios. You cannot deny that I have brought peace and prosperity to my people. Look at this place if you do not believe me. And I do not intend to let it all slip through my fingers.'

'Pah!' He looked at her in exasperation. 'No one wants peace. And prosperity can be obtained by force. All we need to do is capture some Roman wagons and liberate some of the stores they extort from the peoples they have conquered. Have you any idea of the amount of grain they are demanding from the next harvest? Men and women and children will starve, while the legions grow fat!'

'Then it is our duty to try and persuade them to lessen the burden of taxation. But we will not do it by adding ourselves to the list of their victims.' Her voice had grown hard. 'Leave me, Venutios. Your endless hectoring bores me.'

'Does it indeed.' His eyes narrowed. 'Perhaps it would be better if you left me to deal with these matters and turn to something less complicated, wife. Politics obviously confuses you!'

She could feel the anger boiling up inside her. Their truces were so short-lived and every time they were ended by a quarrel; a quarrel which each time was more violent. More bitter. 'Don't insult me, Venutios! The gods will not tolerate such infamy and neither will I.' Nevertheless, it was she who turned and walked away from him, aware that many pairs of eyes were watching surreptitiously.

That night he came to her bedchamber after the meal. He was very drunk. Tripping in the doorway, he almost fell into the room.

'So, wife.' He slurred his words. 'I think it is time to put another child into your womb. A Brigantian child, who will fight against Rome alongside his father.' He staggered towards her.

Carta was sitting in the lamplight playing *gwyddbwyll* with Mairghread. As Venutios approached them he staggered, knocking the wooden board off the chest between them scattering the little silver and gold pieces in all directions.

Carta stood up, furious. 'Lay one finger on me and I will call my guards. I forbid you to touch me.'

As Mairghread retreated into the outer chamber, Carta dodged away but he lunged after her and caught her arm. 'My beautiful, vicious wife. It is time for bed –'

She wrenched herself away from him and he cursed, grabbing at her. She lurched away from him again, tearing her gown, and gasped as he slapped her hard across the face.

Her punch to the side of his head sent him reeling. He lost his grip on her and fell to his knees.

'That is the last time you attack me!' she hissed at him. Her lip was bleeding. 'The last time you hit me! Leave this house now.'

'Never, my love.' He gave a drunken laugh. 'Not till I have sired that little Roman-hater!' He threw himself after her, slipped and, cursing, landed once more on his knees. He was clawing at her when Culann walked into the room with Mairghread behind him.

'Venutios, do you dare to hit your wife?' The Druid's voice cut like acid though the sound of Venutios's heavy breathing.

'Oh yes, I dare.' Venutios let out a furious bellow. 'Indeed I dare. And I'll hit her again if I can just lay my hands on her!'

'That is enough!' Carta spoke very quietly, but the tone of her voice had the effect of stopping Venutios in his tracks as she pulled her mantle more tightly round her shoulders. She grabbed at a rough linen towel hanging near the bronze basin on a stand beside the bed and dabbed at her lip. 'This has happened too often. You conspire against me; you ally yourself to my enemies; you lay hands on me, your wife and your queen. And you come to me drunk and stinking! I divorce you, Venutios. You are no longer my husband. You have insulted me and betrayed me and threatened and assaulted me and I call on the laws of our peoples to end this marriage. I have more than enough just cause. I shall declare it tomorrow before the whole gathering.'

'You can't!' He staggered away from her, sobering rapidly. 'I am your husband before the gods.'

'And you have betrayed your promises and your position. You have forfeited your status as my husband.'

459

'She is right, Venutios.' Culann spoke with rigid authority. 'Leave this house now. We will consult with Artgenos in the morning and with the queen's leave you may plead your case, but I do not believe her to be in the wrong.'

Carta turned her back on her husband. She walked over to the lamp, holding the towel to her face. 'I shall not change my mind.'

'Then may the gods protect you, woman!' Venutios spat out the words. 'Because you and I shall be at war!'

II

'What an extraordinary story.' The Reverend James Oakley had cooked dinner and proved himself an excellent chef. His wife, he explained, had retired to bed with a migraine. He and Hugh had finished the zabaglione which he had whipped up for dessert and had adjourned once more to the book-lined snug with their coffee and brandy. Apple logs smouldered in the fireplace and Hugh felt himself to be extraordinarily content. Or he would have been, but for a niggling sense of guilt and fear.

'I have persecuted the woman. I confess it,' he said slowly, astonished at himself for finding how comforting confession to a man of the cloth could be. 'And now I've discovered why she's been making these claims. This actress person –' He said the words with the same distaste with which he would have described a peculiarly disgusting piece of litter sticking to his shoe, 'has been encouraging her to go into some sort of trance and declaim like a Greek oracle while they record the process for a radio play.'

'Really?' James stared at him over the rims of his glasses. 'How incredibly interesting. Some kind of spiritualist contact, you think? Or is she merely improvising?'

Hugh was contemplating the gently hissing logs. 'Surely a man of your calling doesn't believe in spiritualism?'

James sipped his brandy. 'Not as a religion, of course. Or as a do-it-yourself shortcut to proof of the afterlife, but as a philosophical concept and as an esoteric reality, yes, I do.'

Hugh sat back in his chair. 'You astound me.' He shivered.

'I'm surprised myself, that you as a historian don't have an open mind to the cycles of existence,' James went on mildly. 'And as a Celticist, how could you not have absorbed some of the more palatable of their beliefs?'

Hugh chuckled. 'More palatable? You mean not human sacrifice? I confess that that idea has occurred to me once or twice,' he said dryly. He glanced at the bookshelves near him. 'I see you have books on modern Druidry here as well as historical. I have to say that astonishes me. If you are a Christian, how can you study such a thing?'

'The Druids have much to teach us, and I study it, as do quite a few Christians, including the Archbishop, as you know.' James smiled in quiet reproof. 'I think of it as a philosophy, not a religion. And as I told you I happen to believe the Druids may well have taught Our Lord.'

There was a long silence. Hugh leaned forward in his chair again and pulled a book from the shelf near him. 'This one. By Meryn Jones. What do you think of him?'

'A great scholar. And a genuine Druid in every sense.' James smiled again.

'I know him,' Hugh said thoughtfully. 'Like you he believes in intuitive knowledge and the reality of the supernatural. But I have great respect for his scholarship. His books are deeply intelligent. We have often agreed to differ, but I wouldn't hesitate to turn to him for advice on occasions.' He paused. 'I have turned to him.'

'For instance in the matter of your enthusiastic playwrights and the shade of Cartimandua?' James probed gently.

Hugh nodded. 'This all worries me. I can't get the sound of Viv declaiming to the heavens out of my head. I should have been impressed. I was impressed, but it frightened me. A great deal about this frightens me.' He hesitated. 'Can I tell you a bit more about it?'

James listened in silence as Hugh, at first hesitantly and then with more and more candour related what had been happening to him. 'I am terrified that I shall find myself doing something I have no control over. Venutios wants Cartimandua dead. I'm not sure even now, if this man, this person, this spirit,' he hesitated, unable to describe Venutios with any certainty. 'My character, the hero of my book, the hero, no the villain of Viv's book – is he haunting me? Possessing me? I don't know. And I don't know what to do.'

'What about Meryn Jones, where does he fit in?' James was studying Hugh through half-closed eyes.

Hugh shrugged. 'I phoned him. But I didn't wait. There was no time.'

'Does he know where you are?'

Hugh shook his head.

'In my opinion it might be wise to call him. I am very willing to help, old chap, but I don't think my brand of spirituality will be of much use when it comes to banishing an Iron Age king.'

'No! We don't need Meryn.' It was a flat denial.

James frowned. 'I beg your pardon?' He put down his brandy glass.

'I said no.' Hugh shook his head violently. There was a buzzing in his ears which alarmed him. 'And I don't need you.' He stood up agitatedly. Something was happening. Venutios was there in the room with them. 'I need to see Viv. And I need to get that brooch back. She said she had hidden it. I have to find out where.'

'Maybe. But not tonight.' James spoke quietly but there was a firmness in his voice which pulled Hugh up. 'Go in the morning,' he went on. 'Have another brandy and relax now. I am sure nothing can be done in the dark.'

'You're probably right.' Hugh sat down restlessly. He noticed that James was studying him with some care. 'Can you see him?' he asked abruptly.

James looked thoughtfully down at his hands. 'I'm not sure. I am not in any way psychic, to my intense sorrow,' he smiled. 'But I do get a very strong impression –'

'God Almighty!' Hugh leaped to his feet. 'What?'

'A shadow. A presence in here with us.'

'And it doesn't scare you?' Hugh's eyes widened.

'No.'

'Well, it scares me.' Hugh shook his head. 'I'm sorry. I've got to get out of here!' Turning, he headed for the door and let himself out into the night.

III

Tiptoeing down the landing, Viv paused outside Pat's room. There was no sound from inside. 'Pat?' Cautiously she knocked. 'Pat, are you there?' There had been no sign of Pat all evening. She tried the handle. The door opened. The room inside was dark and she reached for the light switch. The window was open and the curtain flapped in the wind as she surveyed the litter of Pat's clothes and papers and books. Her headphones and a pile of CDs lay on the table beside her laptop. She had disappeared.

Turning out the light, she pulled the door closed and crept to the top of the stairs. The light was on in the hallway but there was no sound from any of the rooms. Her heart in her mouth, she made her way downstairs. Pat. Peggy. Hugh. Suddenly they were all enemies. She didn't know what to do. She wanted to leave, to run away and never come back. Only one thing stopped her. Carta. The voice was there, in her head, constant and insistent until she thought she too was going mad.

The farm office, beside the front door, was in darkness. Quietly she pushed open the door and slipped inside. Picking up the phone she stood for a moment listening to the silence in the house behind her, then she punched in the number of Steve's mobile. The sound of his voice, even as a recorded message was reassuring. 'Steve? It's Viv. Can you come back to the farm? I need you. Please. It's really urgent.' She slotted the receiver gently back onto its base, then she paused, staring round. She had heard something; a slight scraping sound on the flagstones in the hall. She froze. She wasn't alone after all. There was someone standing immediately outside the room. She could hear breathing. Soundlessly she flattened herself against the wall, waiting for the door to open. It didn't and after a minute she heard cautious footsteps heading down the passage. Seconds later the front door opened. It closed again and she was left with a cool waft of night air, then nothing. Whoever it was, had gone.

Silently she pulled open the office door and ran on tiptoe to the front window. Pat was hurrying up the path. She let herself out of the gate into the lane and turned up towards the hill.

Without a sound Viv eased open the door and with a cautious look back at the sleeping house, followed her.

Pat walked swiftly up the track to the steps over the wall, climbed over them and set off across the hillside, walking easily in the bright moonlight. Cautiously Viv followed her, hoping she wouldn't turn round. Once they were on the open hill there was nowhere to hide. Almost at once Pat veered off the track across the rough grass, skirting limestone outcrops and tell-tale patches of bog cotton with ease. Viv walked more slowly. This was dangerous country but Pat seemed to know exactly where she was going. She was heading for the limestone pavement. Her heart in her mouth, Viv closed the gap between them, out of breath now as she hurried on. Pat was walking at the most extraordinary speed, heading directly for the spot where Viv had hidden the brooch.

Medb.

Medb knew where she had put it and she mustn't be allowed to get her hands on it!

Stumbling on the rough ground, Viv swore to herself. How was it possible that this was happening? Hurrying again, she tripped and half fell, catching her knee on an outcrop of rock. A shaft of pain shot through her leg, but already Pat was drawing away again. Forcing herself to her feet, Viv stood up and hurried on, limping.

Reaching the pavement, Pat climbed onto it and at last she stopped, looking round. Viv was only about ten yards from her when Pat turned and looked back the way she had come. Viv froze but Pat didn't seem to see her. Viv could see her face clearly in the moonlight. It was closed and angry and in a strange way totally blank. Viv crept closer. 'Pat?' she whispered. 'What are you doing?'

Pat continued her scan of the horizon as if looking for landmarks. Slowly she turned away from Viv. There had been no hint of recognition in her face. Viv bit her lip, trying to steady her breathing. She crept closer. 'Pat? Can you hear me?'

Again there was no response.

Turning, Pat walked a few steps further on. The pavement was like moon rock beneath the moonlight, the stunted thorns contorted figures throwing black skeletal fingers of shadow across the fissures in the smooth limestone, leading deep into the underworld. Viv stared round. By this strange eerie light she couldn't tell herself where she had hidden the brooch. Every area of rock, every thorn, looked the same. She felt a bolt of panic shoot through her. What if she couldn't find it again herself?

Pat moved on, looking down now at her feet. 'Where is it?' Her voice was clear in the silence of the night.

Viv was only a couple of yards from her now. 'Leave it, Pat,' she whispered. 'You won't find it.'

Pat didn't react.

'Leave it, Medb,' Viv tried again. 'The brooch is not for you.'

Nothing. In the distance a flicker on the horizon showed where another storm was drifting across the hills. She could smell the rock and the grass and the pale, sweet meadowsweet growing in the deep cracks in the stone around her feet.

'It's gone, Medb. Back to the gods,' Viv whispered.

Pat moved on a few steps. She stared round again, pausing as she looked at Viv, so close beside her, then looking away without comment, continuing her sweep of the countryside. 'It must be here,' she said, suddenly. She sounded petulant. Was it Pat's voice, or Medb's? Viv wasn't sure. 'But there is nowhere to hide it.'

Viv smiled. On the contrary, there were a thousand places to hide it; the problem would be finding the right one.

'You won't find it, Pat,' she said softly. 'Let's go home. The storm is coming back.'

'I have to find it.' Pat's voice suddenly sounded nervous. Viv wasn't sure if she was responding to her or speaking to herself. 'I can't go without it.'

'You have to go without it. It's gone. The gods have taken it.' Viv grimaced. For all she knew that was true, and she couldn't look for it herself with Pat here. There was a rumble of thunder from far away. 'Did you hear that? Come on. You don't want to get wet again.'

Pat walked a few paces further on. She was standing very near one of the twisted thorn trees. Its shadow lay before it, a grotesque silhouette across the ground, but was it the right one? Viv bit her lip. She was looking down studying the area as behind them black shadows were racing across the limestone as clouds streamed across the sky. The wind was rising; she could hear it moaning in the distance. The fells were coming alive with the sounds of the night and suddenly they were enveloped in darkness as the clouds obscured the moon. Viv didn't dare move. 'Pat?' There was no response. 'Pat, be careful. One could so easily fall in the dark.' Why

465

hadn't she brought a torch, that was stupid. 'Pat, can you hear me?' She was no longer whispering.

A patch of moonlight showed up in the distance, illuminating part of the ramparts above them. It shifted and the spot of moonlight moved swiftly across the ground towards them. It reached Viv's feet and she gasped. Pat had gone.

She scanned the rocks desperately, and at last saw a movement in the distance. Pat was walking back the way they had come, once again moving with astonishing speed down the hillside. As she plunged into the darkness, she did not appear to slow down.

It took Viv a long time to find her own way back to the track and walk down to the farm. The house was once more bathed in moonlight as she opened the gate and headed up the path. There was no sign of Pat. Pushing open the front door, Viv stood for a moment in the hall, listening, before creeping upstairs and back to her own room. She had no idea if Pat had come back and she was not sure if she cared.

IV

'Steve? . . . I need you!'

When Steve picked up Viv's message he was sitting in the almost empty bar of a small pub in the Scottish borders. He frowned, glancing at his watch. If he got in the car now he could be back at the farm in the early hours. He glanced at the half-drunk pint on the table in front of him and pushing it away, got up and walked out into the rain.

He had had no luck in tracing his father. Every possible avenue he had followed had drawn a blank and he was seriously worried. More than worried. Frightened. He had even driven up to see his sister in Stirling. That was where he had been earlier in the day, wondering if Gordon had gone to his daughter's and asked her not to tell Peggy where he was. It turned out that she had been telling him the truth when she said on the phone that she hadn't seen their father for months. Now she was as worried as he was.

Pulling open the car door he threw himself inside with a sigh.

What could have happened to upset Viv? She had sounded really scared. Backing out of the car park he swung the car onto the deserted road and put his foot down, his anxiety deepening with every second.

Cartimandua. Pat. Medb. Peggy. The energies whirling round the farmhouse had been building for days. It had been a relief to get away, but he hadn't stopped thinking about Viv.

He would never stop thinking about Viv.

She was fond of him, he knew that. The fact that she could turn to him in a crisis proved she relied on him. If Hugh would just bugger off and leave her alone she would be able to relax and enjoy her success. And maybe see what was under her nose. That he, Steve, was there for her. Was always there for her when she needed him.

He swore as a signpost flashed towards him out of the rain and he hauled the car onto a side road. It was a shortcut home.

33

I

Viv hardly slept at all. Exhausted, she had locked her door and put the key under her pillow, then she lay awake, her eyes fixed on the window, her ears listening for any sound from the passage outside. The rain had stopped and the sky outside was the colour of forget-me-nots when at eight o'clock the next morning she tapped on Pat's door. Pat, her hair wet from the shower, was up and dressed. Her clothes from the night before were lying in a heap on the floor.

'You look tired.' Viv raised an eyebrow sarcastically.

Pat nodded. She didn't rise to the remark and Viv left it for the time being. 'I wanted to tell you, I'm going back to Edinburgh today.'

Pat had been combing her hair. She sat down on the end of her bed, her face wan. 'Not yet.'

'Why not? We've seen more than enough of Ingleborough. We've experienced the atmosphere. Haven't we just!' Viv gave a hollow laugh. 'We've got far more material for the play than we could ever use, and if I need any more when I come to write my book, then I can always come back.'

'But there are still things to do,' Pat said slowly. 'The re-enactors –'

'Have gone. The weather is too unsettled for them, I expect. We don't have to be here to record children playing. I've had enough, Pat.' She paused. 'I don't feel comfortable here any more. I want to go home. Peggy frightens me.' And so do you. The last words were unsaid.

Pat let her brush fall on the blanket and sat, looking down at her hands. 'Peggy's probably always been a bit odd, if you ask me,' she said wearily.

'Well, it's getting worse. Haven't you noticed? Her reaction to men. She's becoming, sort of,' Viv hesitated, 'obdurate. She's threatening. And obsessed. I don't like it.'

'That's strange, coming from you. Obsession and possession seem to be the name of the game round here.' Pat's laugh had a bitter edge.

Viv sat down next to her on the bed. She gave her a quick look. 'Pat, did you know you went out last night?'

'Out?'

'You walked up the hill in the moonlight.'

Pat laughed. 'I don't think so.'

'You did. You went up the track quite a way.'

'Why?' Pat frowned.

Viv shrugged. 'I followed you. I tried to persuade you to turn back, but you didn't register that I was there.'

'Shit!' Pat began chewing her lip. She glanced up. 'Medb?'

Viv shrugged again. 'Who else would it be?'

'Was I looking for the brooch?'

Viv nodded. 'I think so.'

'Are you going to give it to Hugh?'

'Of course. It's his.'

Pat shook her head. 'It's more complicated than that. He might want it, but Venutios must not get it. Don't you see? If you give it to Hugh, you are handing it to Venutios.'

'Well, the problem might have solved itself,' Viv said with a shake of her head. 'I'm not sure I'll be able to find it again, anyway. When I hid it, I thought it would be easy to find the place. Now I'm not so sure.'

'Do I gather Medb knows where it is?'

'I don't think she can know exactly or you would have found it.' Viv stood up. 'We ought to go down.'

'Don't say anything to Peggy about leaving. Not yet,' Pat said quickly.

Peggy was sitting at the kitchen table. Steve was standing by the Aga. They appeared to be in the middle of a heated argument.

Peggy swung round the moment Viv opened the door. 'You had no business to ring Steve and tell him to come back!' She looked furious.

469

'I was coming back anyway, Mum,' Steve put in. 'I told you, I can't find any sign of where Dad went. He hasn't been in touch with Uncle Bob or the Cowans. Nobody has heard from him for days. He's disappeared.'

'Rubbish.' Peggy clenched her fists on the table in front of her. 'He was in a pique because we had words. He's gone off to sulk somewhere.' She turned back to Viv. 'Why did you ring Steve? Our affairs are none of your business!'

'I'm sorry.' Viv sat down across the table from her. 'I felt things were getting a bit –' she shifted on her chair, 'out of balance.' She hesitated again as she looked at Steve. 'We were missing you.'

There was a pause. Peggy's face softened a little 'Of course. Of course you'd miss him.' She looked at Steve. 'Well, are you going to give us all a cup of that coffee, or are you just going to watch it sit there?'

Steve reached for the mugs and began to pour. His face was set grimly. He glanced at Viv and then at Pat. 'I think I'll go and speak to Dave later. See if the dogs are OK. See if he's heard from Dad.'

'I wouldn't bother.' Peggy sipped her coffee black. 'You'll just unsettle them. Leave be, Steve. He'll come back when he's good and ready. If he wants to.'

Steve exchanged a glance with Viv. 'Dave'll think it strange that none of us has been in touch.'

'No!' Peggy said sharply. 'Leave it! I told you!'

'I can't do that, Ma.' Steve looked at his mother with a frown, then he turned to Viv. 'I'll stroll over there this morning. Do you want to walk over with me?' It would be a chance to talk alone.

II

Peggy stood up as soon as they had gone. 'I need to go to the well. You come with me, Pat.' She walked into the garden and picked some flowers in stony silence, then Pat followed her across the paddocks towards the river. Peggy went into the cave first. She brought out the vase, threw away the dead flowers, filled it with water from the falls and then went back inside. It was a long time before she reappeared and came to sit beside Pat in the sunshine.

'Why didn't you want Steve here?' Pat asked cautiously. She glanced at Peggy, Viv's warning very much in her mind.

'I told you. This is women's business.'

'But Steve believes in the old gods, doesn't he?' It seemed like a good bet. 'Isn't that how he got interested in Celtic studies?'

Peggy nodded. 'He's a good boy. That was why I welcomed Viv into the house. He's so in love with her.'

Pat smiled. 'I thought perhaps he was.'

'She believes in the goddess too, of course.'

Pat said nothing. After a few hours of blessed peace Medb was suddenly there with them. She could feel those questing ice-cold fingers probing her soul; her body. She shivered.

'Let her come to you, Pat.' Peggy had seen her too. 'Don't fight her all the time. You could learn from her.'

'She wants the brooch.'

'We'll find it.'

'I went to look last night.' Pat paused, trying to remember. 'Viv followed me. She says I went up on the hillside and wandered round.'

'Did you find it?' Peggy looked at her sharply.

Pat shook her head. 'I didn't know where to search.'

'Then we have to make Viv tell us where it is.' Peggy's eyes narrowed.

'She won't. She wants Hugh to have it back for the museum.'

Peggy frowned. 'That's not going to be possible. No man should have that brooch. Ever. It contains female power.'

Pat sat up. 'What do you mean?'

'As I say.' Peggy fell silent for a few moments. 'Viv told me all about her quarrel with the professor. He has to be disposed of. He is dangerous.'

'Disposed of?' Pat echoed.

Peggy smiled. 'You're not squeamish, I hope.'

'Not usually.' Pat was cautious.

Peggy laughed. It was a light, carefree happy sound. 'Don't worry. If you find it hard, I am sure we can call on Medb to help you.'

'Find what hard, Peggy?' Pat could feel her skin crawling at the other woman's words. There was a cruel hardness in her eyes which hadn't been there before.

471

Peggy shook her head. 'You're still fighting her. Don't try. She is more powerful than you. Let her come.' She paused again. 'Maybe we should wait for Lughnasadh.' She saw Pat's look of incomprehension. 'August the first. Lammas. The festival of the god, Lugh.' She paused. 'But Venutios is particularly devoted to Lugh, isn't he,' she added thoughtfully, 'so perhaps that's not a good idea. Perhaps we shouldn't wait that long anyway. Leave it with me. I shall plan something appropriate.'

'With Steve's help?' Pat had begun to feel sick.

'No, bless him. This is nowt to do with him. He can distract Viv when the time comes.' Peggy paused. Again that happy gentle laugh, so at odds with everything she was saying. 'Once Cartimandua is gone they can come and live here when they're married. That will be nice.'

Pat frowned. 'Married?' She was finding it harder and harder to follow this conversation which veered from the bizarre to the ordinary and back.

'Why not? I know she's a little older than he is, but that doesn't matter.'

'Peggy, Viv doesn't love Steve,' Pat said incredulously. She laughed. 'She's fond of him, but she's not in love with him!'

Peggy stared at her, shocked. 'Of course she is.'

'No. She likes him. She finds him fun. That's all.'

'But I thought –'

Pat shook her head. 'If Viv is in love with anyone, I think it's with Hugh. That's the whole problem. That's why they keep sniping at each other. Neither of them realises it yet.' She stopped suddenly, seeing Peggy's face, wishing she could bite off her tongue.

Peggy had gone red. 'She doesn't love Steve?' she repeated.

'I don't think so.'

'But they've gone out together. They're out together now.'

'As friends. To look for Mr Steadman.' Pat hugged her knees nervously. 'I'm so sorry. I shouldn't have said anything.'

'No. You were right to tell me.' Peggy's face looked pinched and angry. 'That changes everything.'

'In what way?'

For a long time Peggy didn't answer. They sat in silence, the sound of the falls behind them, then she smiled again. This was a different smile. Cold and hard. 'It makes it easier to deal with the situation. I will consult with the goddess. Go home. I'll join you in

472

a little while. Go and wait. When they come back we'll be ready for them.'

Standing up, she ducked back into the cave, leaving Pat alone.

III

'So, what was wrong? Why did you ring?' Steve asked as soon as they were out of earshot of the house. 'It sounded urgent.'

'It was. I was scared. Pat and your mum were behaving so oddly.' Viv shrugged. 'I feel much safer with you here, Steve.' She smiled at him and reaching out touched his arm gently. 'I'm sorry, maybe I shouldn't have rung you. It all seems different in daylight, but the whole thing was getting on top of me. I felt really threatened.' They turned up the lane, their feet slipping on the loose stones. Within seconds the farmhouse was out of sight. 'Did you know your dad and mum had a row about the well?' Viv went on at last.

Steve nodded. 'Dad has been threatening to fill it in for years. It's such a special place. He doesn't understand and Ma gets apoplectic about it.'

'So he doesn't worship the old gods like your mother?'

'No.'

'Do you believe in them, Steve?' She asked it cautiously, watching his profile as he walked beside her.

He paused, staring out across the fells. 'Yes.' He didn't look at her.

'Does your father know?'

He gave a wry smile. 'Why court danger? No, he doesn't. He thinks I'm a bit of a nancy boy, as he puts it, anyway, for studying history!'

'That's tough.' She was silent for a few moments as they walked on up the track. 'The old gods have never gone away from these hills, have they?' She shivered.

He shook his head. 'Do they ever? They go underground. They wait for people to find them; they wait to be woken up.'

They stopped again, staring out across the hillside, and after a moment she levered herself up onto the wall to sit, swinging her legs. 'Living history.'

He nodded. They were silent for a while, then he pulled himself onto the wall close to her. The stones shifted slightly. She glanced at him. 'I'm going back to Edinburgh this afternoon, Steve.' She saw his face fall and she reached for his hand. 'It's been great here, but I need to get away. Hugh turned up yesterday. I'm not going to hang around and wait for him to cause more chaos. Besides, I have decisions to make. I've been offered a job in Ireland.'

Steve stared at her in dismay. 'So you really are leaving?'

'I don't suppose I have any choice. I want to go on teaching; I want to go on researching.'

'Hugh will be gutted.' He tried to hide his own devastation.

'You think so?'

'I do. Yes.' He looked down at his feet. 'Are you going back to your bloke?' He pursed his lips.

'Andrew?' She shook her head vehemently. 'No way. Anyway, he's in Dublin. The job is down in the south-west.'

Suddenly she found she was shivering again. She could feel the small hairs on the back of her neck stirring as the silence of the countryside flowed round them. She glanced at Steve. 'We'll still be friends, Steve. Won't we?'

He nodded sadly. 'Of course.' He grimaced. 'What about Cartimandua?' He could, he realised suddenly, see the shadowy figure of the woman standing there beside them. Feel her power. He shuddered violently. Viv was going nowhere until the Queen of Brigantia said so.

Tears were pouring down Carta's face as she stood looking down at the dog's body, unable to believe that she was dead. Her beloved Moon, old and grizzled, had licked her hand the night before, a last kiss and farewell, and gone to lie on her accustomed mat. In the night her soul had fled to join that of her brother, Sun, in the lands of the ever young.

Behind her Mairghread shook her head and sighed. Yet another blow; another friend gone. Gently she touched Carta's shoulder. 'I'll call two men to carry her away.'

Carta nodded bleakly. She couldn't speak. Numbly she watched as the men came in and carefully lifted the giant dog on her mat. As they passed, Carta touched Moon's head gently with her finger.

'There will be another,' Mairghread whispered. 'A puppy to love you as much.'

Carta shrugged. She shook her head. Later she would supervise the dog's burial and send her on her way with her blessing. Now she had to find the strength to attend a council meeting.

Miserably she let Mairghread help her dress. The room seemed so empty suddenly without Moon sitting watching the proceedings, ready to follow wherever she went, always there at her side, always loyal. Always loving.

One by one automatically she drew on her bangles, then she paused at the sound of raised voices in the outer chamber. A moment later the curtain was pushed aside and a figure appeared in the doorway.

Vellocatus was exhausted. Covered in mud and with a huge gash across his cheek, he staggered into the room and stood reeling as his eyes grew accustomed to the semi-darkness. Carta stared at him in horror. 'What happened?' She waved Mairghread away.

'I have left Venutios's service, lady. He is no longer my lord or my leader. He is not a warrior I choose to serve. I pledge my service and my life to you.' He went down on one knee before her and took her hand.

Dashing away her tears, she stared down at him. 'Did you tell him this?'

'Of course. I am a man of honour. I do not sneak away in the dark.'

'He was your friend, Vellocatus.' She stood looking down at him, her hand still in his. 'As well as your king.'

'He was once, lady.' He held her gaze.

Mairghread cleared her throat from the doorway. She gave Vellocatus a look of intense dislike. 'The council is ready, my queen. The Druids will not be pleased to be kept waiting.'

'Then go ahead of me and tell them I have been delayed,' Carta retorted sharply. 'Now,' she added as Mairghread hesitated.

The moment they were alone she gestured at Vellocatus to stand up and gently she touched his face. 'Is that a sword cut?'

He shrugged. 'Venutios and I had a slight exchange.'

'He fought his own sword bearer?' She was shocked.

'He called me a traitor for supporting you.' He shrugged. 'I was lucky to escape with my life.'

'And where is he now?'

'He has ridden back to Caer Lugus with Brucetos and the other Carvetian warriors. And he is vowing to be avenged against you,

475

my queen, for the thousand wrongs he claims you have done. He is planning to depose you. He claims you are not fit to be high queen of Brigantia.'

She stared at him in silence for a few seconds, trying to steady herself, aware of the young man's gaze upon her. He glanced round the room suddenly. 'Where's Moon?' He had never seen her without the dog before.

She shook her head blindly.

'Oh, my dear. I'm so sorry.' He took her hand again and kissed it.

She took a deep breath and managed to smile at him bleakly. 'Come with me. You will have to repeat what you have just told me to the council.'

The warriors and Druids listened gravely. Artgenos stood up at last, stiff and gaunt as he leaned on his staff. 'You were foolish to divorce him, Cartimandua. The man is now an open enemy. And he has a large following. This finally will divide Brigantia.'

'You would have had me stay married to a man who threatened me? A man who deliberately flouted my decision to form an alliance with Rome? A man who crossed me at every opportunity? A man who,' she laid her hand for a moment on her stomach, 'deliberately killed our child?' She still would not allow herself to feel the pain of those words. Her eyes were hard as she looked round. 'I can't believe you – any of you – would support him!' She paused, staring in turn into the face of every man and woman present. There was total silence around her.

Artgenos sighed. The omens were bad; the information he had received from his spies worse. He could see darkness ahead. He turned his thoughtful gaze towards Vellocatus. Standing in front of the firelight, the man's silhouette was ringed with blood.

Steve was staring at Viv in silence as she sat looking across the vale. He could hear the church bells calling people to Matins from the village in the distance. Dressed in a sweater and jeans and tough boots and with no make-up, she looked the perfect hill walker out for an morning stroll. Except for her face. He shivered miserably. This was Cartimandua's face. Strong, broad cheekbones, hard green-blue eyes, determined mouth and a voice ringing with power. This was the face of a barbarian queen. The face of a woman who ruled thousands of warriors and a dozen wild powerful tribes. The

476

face of a woman who deep inside could still cry over her lost child, her dog, her lonely longing for a man; a woman who was about to make the greatest mistake of her life.

'Viv?' he said. There was no response so he had no choice but to listen in ever increasing wonder to what she was saying. 'Go on,' he whispered. 'What happened next?'

Dismissing her women, Cartimandua led Vellocatus into her private chamber. 'We need to discuss Venutios's next moves,' she said soberly. She sat down near the fire and rubbed her hands together, trying to warm them.

'He will attack.' Vellocatus sat down at her feet. 'He is too full of hatred to desist now; and he truly believes he is right.' He glanced up at her.

She reached down to touch his shoulder. It was an absent-minded gesture; a gesture little different from the way she used to lean over to fondle the ears of her dog, but Vellocatus seized her hand and brought it to his lips.

For a moment she pulled away, shocked. Then she relaxed.

She knew how much he was in love with her and for a long time she had known herself to be strongly attracted to him. Why not? It would bring them both comfort in their loneliness.

With a smile she leaned down as he looked up at her and their lips touched. 'My queen!' He pulled her towards him and as she slid from her stool she found herself lying in his arms beside the fire. 'You'll be my downfall, Vellocatus!' She smiled as she ran her hands across his chest. 'You must not distract me. We have to plan battles, you and I.'

He laughed out loud. 'And so we shall, lady. Battles of love and ecstasy!'

He was still in her chamber at dawn.

Mairghread had listened with disgust to the sound of love-making behind the curtains of the queen's chamber for as long as she could stand it. The Roman she could just about tolerate. He was a mere plaything. The king's servant she could not. Drawing her cloak around her shoulders she walked out into the night in search of the Archdruid.

*

477

'Take him as your lover, if you must!' Thin and brittle as a twig, but still powerful with the eyes of a hawk, Artgenos drew himself up to his full height as he stood opposite Cartimandua. They were alone now, under the ancient oak which stood by the stream. 'But for pity's sake, do not show him too much favour. Vellocatus was your husband's shield bearer, his charioteer. Scarce more than a servant. Yet you treat him as a warrior and a counsellor. You ask his opinion at every turn. You act like a woman obsessed, and your people resent it deeply.'

Carta pulled her mantle tightly round her shoulders. There were snowflakes in the wind which was screaming down the dale. In the distance she heard the lonely cry of a wolf.

'Who better to advise me? He understands the way Venutios thinks. He knows what he will do.'

'And what does he say he will do?' Artgenos looked at her coldly.

'Nothing. He will mutter into his beard and swear and drink more than usual and he will take out his resentment on the Selgovae or the Novantae and in time he will forget.'

Artgenos let out a groan. 'Do you really believe that? No, of course you don't. You are not that naïve! He is at this moment mustering his warriors to attack you! He is calling the Selgovae and the Novantae to his banner against you and against Rome.'

'He wouldn't dare.'

'Of course he would dare! He knows he has only to lift a finger and half the people of Brigantia will flock to his side. You are losing them, Carta. Unless you are very careful and very strong he will win himself the high kingship.'

She looked at him in silence, stunned. 'He is nothing without me. Not even a king –'

'He is king of the Carvetii and he has proved himself strong. By divorcing him you have taken from him the status of husband of the high queen, but that is all. And now he is determined to earn his own place at the head of our peoples.' He sighed patiently, the sound losing itself in the whispering of the winter-day oak leaves over their heads. 'The gods are not happy.'

She smiled grimly. 'They will be. Vellocatus tells me that Brucetos and his sons are travelling south. They plan to recruit support of some sort for Venutios in the land of the Cornovii.'

Artgenos swung to face her again. 'So, he has warned you of a specific planned attack?'

'He warned me so I can intercept them.' She smiled. 'They have to come through my territories to reach the south. I will be waiting for them. With his brother as my hostage, Artgenos, Venutios will do nothing.'

Vellocatus drove her war chariot and she stood beside him, her hair stiff with pine-scented hair resins imported from Hispania, her face painted as a warrior, a sword in her hand, her spears in the chariot beside her. At the head of her warriors she made a stirring sight. Wild with anger and excitement she shouted the men onward behind her as they confronted Brucetos and his followers. Two men died at her hand. Vellocatus impaled another on his spear and stabbed another to the heart. Thirty more died at the hands of her followers. Ten of her own men fell to Brucetos before he was captured with his sons and she took him back at last to Dun Righ in chains.

'Don't be foolish, lady.' Brucetos was a brave man and had immense respect for her courage, more so, perhaps than his brother. 'Don't you see how your men will fall away if you fight Venutios?'

She studied his face through narrowed eyes. 'No one will have to fight Venutios if I hold his brother hostage.'

He shook his head sadly. 'How little you know him, Cartimandua. If anything this,' he lifted his chained wrists and shook them over his head, 'will provoke an attack all the sooner.'

She laughed. 'I doubt it. To make sure, I have sent south for help from the Governor of Britannia.'

There was a stunned silence. Brucetos stared at her. 'You have summoned Roman help?' He was shocked to the roots of his soul. 'And will you give me to them as you gave them Caradoc?'

She shrugged. 'Perhaps that threat will keep Venutios at a safe distance.'

'Oh, lady.' Brucetos shook his head. 'How wrong you are.'

Viv hadn't spoken for ten minutes. Her eyes were closed. Steve slid down off the wall and stretched. At first he had been terrified by her words, then completely captivated. Now her stillness and silence frightened him again. 'Viv?' He touched her shoulder lightly. 'Can you hear me?' She didn't move and he rested the back of his hand against her cheek for a moment. Her skin was ice cold.

'Viv? We must go on.' He shivered. The sky was cloudless but the air on the hillside had grown chill. 'Viv!' He had watched her describe Carta making love; seen the passion and the longing in her face. He reached out again, his fingers just touching her mouth. She didn't seem to register his presence. Leaning forward he kissed her gently on the lips. Still she didn't react.

'Come on, lady. We need to go.' It was a whisper.

She blinked. Then at last she moved. 'Steve?'

'You dozed off in the sunshine.' He smiled at her fondly. She would never know about the stolen kiss.

'I was dreaming. About Carta and Vellocatus.' She sounded blurry, as though she was not quite awake. For a moment she didn't move, then at last she slid off the wall beside him. 'It was amazing.'

'I heard you. You described them.'

She glanced at him and he saw a faint blush rise across her cheeks.

He laughed. 'Yes. It was quite graphic. I've always been rather a fan of Vellocatus. He was a lucky man.'

'Indeed.' She looked away. 'You're right. We need to go. Is it far?'

They were greeted at the gate of the cottage at the end of the dale by two ecstatic collies.

'Am I glad you're come to take the dogs back, young Steve!' Dave was a tall wizened man in his early seventies, his face the colour of polished hazelnuts, his eyes piercing blue. 'I've had the devil's own job keeping them up here. When your Ma brought them, I told her they wouldn't stay.'

'Ma brought them up here?' Steve looked at the old man, astonished.

He nodded. 'Said it would only be a couple of days she did.'

Steve and Viv exchanged puzzled glances. Steve shook his head. 'I don't understand any of this.'

'Your dad were ill, she said. Couldn't cope with them.' Dave went on. 'That didn't sound right to me.' The old man scanned their faces and they both saw the uncertainty and suspicion in his gaze.

'No.' Steve's voice was bleak. 'That doesn't sound right at all.'

'You'll take 'em back now?'

Steve nodded. 'We'll take them back.'

The dogs streaked ahead of them up the track. Viv glanced at Steve. 'They're keen to get home.'

Steve nodded, frowning anxiously. 'I don't get it. If Ma took them over to Dave, why did she tell me it was my dad? Where is he, Viv?'

The farmhouse was deserted when they arrived home. There was no sign of Peggy or of Pat.

'I suppose they followed your father everywhere?' Viv said. She was thinking of Sun and Moon.

'Everywhere.' Steve was fondling the dogs' heads as they sat at his feet looking up at him expectantly. 'They'd never leave him.'

They exchanged glances. 'You think something's happened to him, don't you,' Viv said softly.

Steve nodded.

'Your mother wouldn't –'

'No, of course she wouldn't. She and my dad adore each other. The only thing they can't agree on is the sacred well. Her beliefs. He's not a churchgoing man, but he doesn't hold with paganism.'

One of the dogs had wandered over to the back door. He barked to be let out. Steve opened it and both dogs ran outside and into the garden. With a glance at Viv, Steve followed.

She didn't move. Carta was coming back. She clenched her fingers around the edge of the table. She didn't want this. Not now.

It was no use. The shadow was there; the strange shimmer; the miasma which folded round her like a second skin.

V

Carta had brought two white bulls for sacrifice to Camulos, the god of war, and now she had brought doves. To send them to seek peace for Brigantia, the goddess of her peoples. The priests had slain the bulls. The doves she meant to kill with her own hands. She picked up the wicker basket and carried it into the centre of the grove.

'Sweet Lady? Are you there?'

She stared round, hearing the silence of the great trees. There was no breath of wind and the leaves hung motionless. She felt terribly alone.

'*Vivienne?*' Her cry was loud and long. 'Where are you? Why have you abandoned me?'

Unfastening the hasps which held the lid of the basket closed, she picked up her knife.

The two doves huddled side by side trembling, crouched in the bottom of the basket. She stared down at them for a moment, then with a sigh she shook her head. Dropping the knife, she tipped the basket on its side. The birds, after a moment's hesitation, flew out, circled the grove once, then headed towards the setting sun.

'Viv? Viv, can you hear me?'

She opened her eyes.

Steve was standing over her as she sat at the kitchen table, the two dogs panting at his side.

She lurched to her feet. 'I've got to go to the sacred spring.'

'Why?'

Viv wasn't listening. She barely saw him. He watched as she walked away, heading towards the paddock and the lower fields, then cautiously he followed her with the dogs.

The spring was running high after all the rain. The small stone chamber echoed with the sound of the falls outside. It smelled of wet moss and stone. There was a slight taste of iron on her tongue. Or blood. She shivered. Someone had removed the old flowers which lay before the old stone head and replaced them with roses and honeysuckle and feathery cosmos.

She sat for a long time in silence, listening to the water. Praying was not something she did as a rule. Oh yes, the odd quick throw-away prayer, the kind which must make God smile cynically and turn away. 'Please God, make it all right. If it's all right this time I'll go to church. I promise. Just this once, God . . .'

Vivienne

The voice echoed up out of the stone, filling the chamber with echoes.

Vivienne. Help me.

Viv clenched her fingers on the edge of the stone basin.

Vivienne. I need help. I have sent messengers. Send me the Roman!

Viv could feel the fine mist of spray from the water on her face. The dark corners of the chamber were very still. She could hardly breathe.

'Carta? The Romans will come. They will save you.'

She was sure. She knew the future. She was the time traveller, speaking backwards into the past.

Vivienne. Do you want more? More gifts? More sacrifices? Speak to me, goddess.

Viv licked her lips nervously. 'Carta? Be patient. Be strong.'

She leaned forward, staring down into the water in the basin, almost expecting to see a face; to meet the eyes of the woman from the past who also stared down into this small pool. There was nothing. Just the clear depthless water that separated as well as joined them.

34

I

When he woke, Hugh was pouring with sweat. He could smell blood, terror, and in the background the sweet scent of the trampled grass and heather; he could hear shouts and groans and the screams of horses and above it all the fearful baying note of the carnyx. With a groan he staggered out of bed and went to stand in the shower under the cool clean water, trying to clear his head.

Towelling himself dry at last, he wiped the steam from the mirror and peered at himself, afraid of what he might see. His own face looked back at him, haggard, exhausted, but his own.

Silently he let himself out of the cottage into the dawn and climbed back into the car. He couldn't feel Venutios any more. He couldn't see him. As far as he could tell he was safe in the car. Somehow it protected him, but he couldn't stay in there forever.

The hill was deserted as he climbed and for a while he was content and confident. It was exhilarating to be up so early. He could hear a skylark and in the distance the bubbling call of a curlew and for a few short minutes he allowed himself to feel happy. It didn't last. Between one second and the next the terror returned as, in the distance, he heard it again, echoing across the hills, the deep war cry of the carnyx. He clenched his fists, sweat breaking out on his forehead. This could not happen again!

He turned back, running, frantically scanning the lane at the foot of the hill for the gateway where he had left his car. Slipping and sliding on the grass and stones he reached it at last, and throwing himself inside slammed down the locks, then he sat back, eyes closed, feeling his heart thudding in his chest. His first thought was for Viv. He groped in his pocket for his mobile. He had to warn her. The bastard had followed him. He was still trying to find the brooch. Venutios mustn't get her; he mustn't find her. Somehow he had to keep her safe.

The mobile was dead.

He glanced up at the great flank of hillside and with a curse chucked the phone into the footwell beside him. He had to get back to the cottage and ring her on a landline.

James was standing in the doorway, sipping from a mug of tea as he quietly watched the road for his guest. The honeysuckle near him was alive with bees.

He greeted him cheerfully as Hugh pushed open the gate. 'I thought perhaps you'd gone for a walk. I hope you're ready for breakfast. Margaret has decided to spend a few days in Lancaster, so you and I are on our own. I don't suppose, as it's Sunday, that you'd care to come to church later?' He glanced at his guest and frowned. 'Perhaps not. Something has happened, hasn't it.'

'Venutios was out there on the hill. I heard that damn trumpet again; his signature tune. What am I going to do?'

James paused as he led the way towards the kitchen and gave Hugh a long hard look, then he gave a sheepish grin. 'I think I need to make a confession. When you rushed out last night I thought about what you told me and I consulted with the boss man.' He pointed at the ceiling. When Hugh looked blank he explained. 'I prayed for guidance. I thought in my unforgivably nosy way that you looked like a man who could do with some help. The boss suggested I talk to your friend, Meryn Jones.'

'What?' Hugh stared at him.

'I wasn't sure how to get in touch with him, but I rang a colleague in Edinburgh who I thought might know about the research you said Meryn was doing. To cut a long story short, he gave me his number and we talked.'

There was a long silence. Hugh subsided onto a kitchen chair. 'I suppose I should be grateful.'

James nodded. 'Meryn was worried. Apparently he's been looking for you.'

'He didn't know I had come here.'

'At Venutios's instigation?' James picked up the teapot and poured Hugh a cup of thick black tea.

'Probably.' Hugh shivered. 'I wanted to warn Viv. To make sure she was safe.'

'You care very much about Viv, don't you,' James said quietly. He smiled. 'Meryn is coming here today. We thought it best.'

There was a long silence. Hugh took a gulp of tea and winced at the tannin on his tongue. 'Thank you,' he said. 'I'd better ring her and warn her that Venutios is on the rampage again,' he said at last. 'I've seen inside his head. I know he will stop at nothing to get his revenge on Cartimandua; and he wants that brooch back so badly.' He paused and gave a quick harsh laugh as he headed for the phone in the hall. 'Listen to me! You'd think I believed all this stuff, wouldn't you!'

A couple of minutes later he was back in the kitchen. 'I spoke to Mrs Steadman. She was less than helpful.' He shrugged. 'She said Viv was out with Steve and wouldn't be back all day.'

James rubbed his nose thoughtfully. 'That would appear to remove her from any danger in the short-term.'

'I suppose so.' Hugh did not sound convinced.

'Don't you trust this young man?'

'I don't trust myself!' Hugh stood up. 'I'm going to go over there.'

'I don't think that's a good idea.' James shook his head.

Hugh stared down at him. 'Can you see him?' He meant Venutios.

James looked up through half-closed eyes. 'Not at the moment, no. But I wouldn't take my word for it.'

Hugh shuddered. 'It's like having some foul disease lurking inside me. I can't stand this! It's insane. It's not real. It can't be.' It was a desperate appeal.

James grimaced. 'I do sincerely believe such things can happen, my friend. The survival of the soul is, of course, a given of my belief, and what most Christians believe, or want to believe, is that the departed trots happily off to a place called, for want of a better term, "heaven", where it is engaged in happy hobbies for all eternity. We tend to skip over the concept of hell these days, preferring to believe that is a self-inflicted punishment in this life. What I think actually happens is that the soul is remarkably like the living person. It carries on with its obsessions and its loves and hates as long as these are unresolved. And being a sociable sort of a thing it is happy from time to time to hitch a lift with someone who is still here with mortal coil intact.'

Hugh sat down again. 'Scary.' He gave a heartfelt shudder. 'And

486

our Celtic friends believed quite passionately in the continuation of the soul's journey, of course.'

'Of course.' James was thoughtful. 'Whether what happens is dependent on one's beliefs – in other words one gets what one is expecting – or whether it is an objective end game for all, I don't know. My bishop would have great difficulty with what I am saying, I suspect. But one can't live up here and not get feelings about immortality which sink deep into the psyche.' He smiled. 'Your friend Mrs Steadman is one such. She believes passionately in the old gods, so I've heard.'

Hugh frowned. 'Would Viv have told her what is happening?'

'I've no idea. She is a moody lady.' James chuckled. 'I know those who are terrified of her; others who swear she is Florence Nightingale in person.'

II

At first Steve did not recognise the car bumping up the lane towards him. Only when it stopped did he realise it was Hugh. He walked towards the gate.

'Viv is not here, if you are looking for her.'

Hugh, in shirtsleeves, was alone. He paused, looking suspiciously at Steve over the stone wall. 'Your mother told me you were out together.'

'We were earlier.'

'When will Viv be back?'

Steve shrugged. 'To be honest, I don't think she wants to see you at the moment.'

'Well, I need to see her.' Hugh could feel Venutios's unrest, sense his jealousy. There was a resonance here between the young, good-looking charioteer who had subverted the king's affections and was trusted and loved by Cartimandua, and this handsome young man with his suntanned, freckled skin and untidy hair, standing so blatantly before him talking about Viv with such confidence. Hugh clenched his fists and glanced over his shoulder, looking up at the hill above them, listening intently. The heat haze had returned, shrouding its flat top, lapping down the soft mountain grasses, licking at the great limestone crags on the northern escarpment as the sun moved round the horizon and was lost at last in the banks of haze. This was Steve, not Vellocatus, he reminded himself firmly.

'I need to see Viv urgently,' he repeated, turning back. He caught his breath abruptly. 'There it is again. Did you hear it?'

'What?' Steve eyed him uncomfortably.

'Venutios. He's out there. He's looking for her.' Hugh couldn't hide the fear in his eyes.

Steve swallowed. 'I'm not going to let you in. We don't want you here, and we don't want him here either.'

'Don't you?' Hugh laughed bitterly. 'And you're going to stop him, are you?' He stepped forward aggressively.

'Yes.'

'How?'

'I'll think of a way.' Steve stood his ground, arms folded. 'Please go away, Hugh.'

'I need that brooch.' Hugh took another step forward. 'Can't you understand? If I get the brooch I will go back to Edinburgh and he will follow me. Until I do that, Viv is in danger. Venutios will kill to get it.' He paused and the two men looked at each other in silence. 'He is a soldier, Steve. He is completely unsentimental. He knows its power. Women's power. He will do anything to keep it out of a woman's grasp. He will kill,' he repeated softly. 'Please God, not with my hands.' For a moment he held Steve's gaze, then at last he turned and he climbed back into the car.

Steve stared after him as he drove off, cold with horror. For a moment he had been truly scared.

Something touched his hand and he glanced down fondly. One of the dogs was nuzzling him. It whined.

'This is all going crazy, boy.' Steve grimaced. At the sound of his voice both dogs sat in front of him expectantly. He turned and looked back at the house. There was still no sign of his mother or Pat.

When Viv came back from the well, tired and walking slowly across the garden to his side, he smiled and reached out his hand to hers. 'Hugh was here looking for you. He was ranting on about Venutios.'

She bit her lip. 'Even more reason to leave, Steve. I can't cope with all this any more. I'm sorry. If Pat wants to stay, that's up to her.' She glanced at him. 'I don't suppose you'd come too?' She

488

paused, as if waiting for him to say something. When he didn't she turned sadly, more pale and strained than ever after his news about Hugh's visit, to go back into the house.

He looked down at the dogs. 'I can't go, can I, boys. Not till we've found my dad.' He glanced at the old quad bike parked near the wall of the yard. He could cover a lot of ground on that. Slowly he walked towards it. 'Where's Gordon, dogs?' It was what his mother always said. It was the signal to run out into the yard, barking with excitement, tails wagging, to find him. Steve repeated the command and the dogs turned as one and headed round the side of the house towards the fields. Climbing onto the bike, Steve gunned the engine and set out to follow them.

III

Vellocatus had raised himself on one elbow. He was staring down at the beautiful woman beside him, watching her as she slept.

Dawn light filtered through the doorway and the township was still silent. He could hear the breathing of the half-grown pup, Moon's successor, lying near the foot of the bed. Head on paws, she was watching him. He could feel it. Just as every man, woman and child in the township was watching him.

To start with he had been popular. He had deserted his post and risked his honour by leaving Venutios, something no man would condone, but he had done it to serve his queen and to save her from a brutal husband and he had transferred his allegiance and his life to her service. That made him a hero with the women and more importantly with most of the bards who sang the story around the northern fires as the weather grew colder.

She had been without a man too long. Once he had come to her bed on that first long night, as cascades of shooting stars lit the skies, and she had made love to this strong, handsome, adoring man she could not stop. Once, twice, sometimes three times a day she would drag him away from the eyes of the men and women around them and pulling his tunic off his shoulders, and releasing his belt so his breeks fell about his ankles she would feast her eyes on his hard muscular body, groaning with ecstasy as he touched her, submitting with something like worship as he pushed her down and thrust again and again into her willing body.

Artgenos and Culann had tried to make her cool her ardour. 'Beware. Your people are restless. You neglect your duties to them and to the gods. Not everyone is happy to see this man who was your husband's servant, so high in your favour.'

Not since her bedding with Riach had she felt so completely overwhelmed by passion. Vellocatus had only to look at her for her breath to grow short. Her breasts would ache for his touch. She could feel herself dissolving with longing.

Then she had found she was pregnant. She had forgotten to count the phases of the moon. Forgotten everything in her need for this man. It did not matter. The goddess was giving her a son.

'The child will have to be fostered away. The people will not approve of their queen giving birth to the child of a servant.' Artgenos did not mince his words.

'Vellocatus is no servant!' Her eyes blazed with anger. 'He is a freeman. His family were farmers – '

'And not warriors.' Artgenos nodded. 'Do not hope to rear this child as a prince of the ruling family, Carta. You are pushing people's tolerance beyond all bearing. You will bring disaster upon yourself and your family.'

'Then I will make sure that this child, my son, is the son of a king!' She stared him down defiantly. 'Did you hear me, Artgenos? Vellocatus will be my husband and I shall make him king!'

'No!'

'Yes!' She was almost spitting with anger that he should deny her what she wanted above all else. 'And you and your priests shall marry us. That is my command.'

'And it is a command I will not obey. The portents already spell disaster. The skies are full of black birds reeling in from the west. The ravens scream of blood and death. Last night the wolves howled all night in the forest. Can you not see what you are doing, Carta? Send Vellocatus away. Keep him somewhere quietly for your pleasure. No one would grudge you that. But do not dare to try and rear this child as a prince. I repeat. You will bring death and destruction to this country.'

But she had not waited to hear the end of the sentence. She had turned in a swirl of skirts and cloaks and disappeared into the darkness outside, no doubt to find her lover yet again. Artgenos had frowned. He could smell the heat and musk on her. There would be no reasoning with her until this obsession had run its course.

In the township of Dun Righ they supported Cartimandua to a man, and it was here that Ban, the chief Druid of the township and senior Druid of the Setantii, under Artgenos and Culann, officiated at the rites of marriage and the legal processes that accompanied them, between Cartimandua of the Setantii and Vellocatus, formerly of the Carvetii. Her name meant Sleek Pony. His, Good Fighter. It had been given him by Venutios.

The ceremony heralded the outbreak of civil war and she sent another plea to Gaius for help.

Venutios attacked with a hand-picked army of warriors. The confederation of small tribes which had made up this the largest and strongest kingdom in the Pretannic Isles broke apart. Those who supported Cartimandua and believed in a peaceful relationship with Rome congregated around her in Elmet with the tacit support of the Votadini in the north. Those who supported Venutios, bent on removing Cartimandua as queen and pushing the Romans out of the island, rallied round Venutios at Dinas Dwr. His supporters far outnumbered hers.

Vellocatus reviewed the army of which he was now leader with a sinking heart. There would be no hope for them without the help she was so sure of from the south. No hope at all. The men had resented him from the start. A well-respected, brave and proven warrior at his king's side, he was no king himself. Their allegiance was grudging. For Carta's sake they would follow him, but for no other. The fact that she had declared him king at her side held no weight with their followers. Vellocatus, who was not of royal blood, could not be a king however much Cartimandua might wish it. And where were the Romans she promised? There had been no word.

She had written to Gaius, sent the letter by messenger, begging him to come. He had to pass the message on, of course. He couldn't help on his own. The XX legion was in Wales, close enough to go to her aid but the governor sent instead to Lindum and the commander there sent an auxiliary cavalry unit to help. They fought Venutios. He couldn't win against the experienced Roman army. Of course he couldn't. He ran away.

Carta reclaimed the allegiance of her people as she knew she would. There had been a battle and a victory. They liked that. They celebrated. The Romans gave her even more gifts and money to reward the men who supported her. They were always generous, the Romans, to their client queen. Everyone was happy for the time being.

She wrote to Gaius and thanked him.

IV

Gordon was lying on his back at the foot of a small ravine at the edge of the wood. Someone had made an attempt to cover him with earth and then piled branches over him.

Steve stood staring down, a dog on either side of him, his eyes full of tears. It looked as though his father had slipped. The edge of the bank had fallen away and the bushes had been crushed and torn as he had crashed down into the undergrowth. Whoever had found him had made no attempt to go for help. They had gone to great pains to cover his body.

Peggy.

In sudden revulsion and shock Steve turned away and vomited into the nettles, then, sitting down on a fallen log, he put his head in his hands. He was shaking violently, tears pouring down his face.

'Steve?' For a moment he thought the voice was in his head, but he saw the dogs leap up and go to greet her and he turned. Peggy was standing a few feet away.

'I knew they'd find him. That's why I wanted them to stay at Dave's.' She was matter-of-fact.

'What happened?' He could hardly speak.

'We were arguing. He slipped and fell.'

'And you didn't get help?'

She shrugged. 'There was no point. He was dead.'

'So you don't just leave him there, Ma. You go for help! You bring him home!' Steve stood up. He was staring at her with blind incredulity.

She sighed. 'It was his fault, Steve. He was going to destroy the well. You do see, he couldn't be allowed to do that.'

Steve froze. 'You did it on purpose? You killed him?'

'No. He fell.'

'But you didn't bring help.'

She shook her head. 'He would have desecrated it. I couldn't let him do that. I left it to the goddess.' She pursed her lips.

'He was still alive? You left him to die?'

She nodded. 'When I went back, he'd gone. He would have died anyway, Steve. He was too badly hurt. I couldn't have saved him. No one could.'

'An air ambulance might have. First aid might have!' Steve clenched his fists. 'So, were you going to leave him here forever?'

She shook her head. 'I don't know. It's what he would have wanted. To be on the farm.' She sounded completely detached.

'Picked clean by birds and foxes, I suppose!' Steve was beside himself. He scrambled to his feet. 'I'm going to ring the police!'

'No, Steve. You can't!'

'I can. I can't leave it like this.' He was sobbing out loud. 'Even if we say it was an accident – but how can we? No normal person would leave someone – their husband – to rot in the fields!' He turned and began to climb up the bank.

'Steve!' His mother reached out, clutching at him as he pushed past her. 'Steve! You can't tell anyone!'

'I can. And I will.' He was already walking blindly across the field. The two dogs turned and with a glance back at the ravine where their master lay, followed him.

V

'Steve? What on earth's the matter?' Pat threw down her cigarette as Steve ran towards her. She had been sitting in the garden, deep in thought.

'My dad's dead.' Steve stopped. His face was ravaged with grief. He closed his eyes and took a deep breath, trying to steady himself. 'Down there, in the ravine. He fell.'

'Oh God, I'm so sorry. Oh, Steve, how awful.' She leaped to her feet, numb with shock, reaching for his hand in an instinctive gesture of comfort.

They both turned at a shout from the orchard behind them. Peggy was hurrying after him. 'Steve, wait!'

'She killed him! She killed my dad!' Steve shouted wildly, snatching his hand away. He pointed at his mother.

Pat stared from one to the other in horror as he rushed on. 'I'm calling the police!' He ran to the house and went in through the kitchen door.

Peggy shook her head. She was panting hard as she ran after him. 'He doesn't understand.' She caught Pat's arm. 'Tell him! Tell him I had to do it. For the goddess!'

Steve had gone straight to the phone.

'No!' Peggy rushed after him. Wrenching it out of his hand, she pulled the cord out of the wall. 'No, you can't ring the police. Steve! Please! Don't be so stupid!'

Steve pushed her aside and headed to the front door. 'If I can't phone, then I'll go and fetch them.' Grabbing his car keys off the hall table, he disappeared outside.

Seconds later they heard the sound of a car engine. Peggy thumped her fist down on the table. 'Stupid! So stupid! He doesn't understand! Why didn't you stop him?'

'Peggy, I don't know what's going on.' Pat was immobile with shock.

'You do. Medb knows. Medb knows everything.' Peggy narrowed her eyes and suddenly she smiled. 'We need Medb now. She is a powerful woman; a Druidess. Trained in the arts. She can help me. Where is she? I need Medb!' She reached over and put her hand on Pat's forehead. Her fingers were ice cold.

Pat shrank back. 'Don't touch me!'

'Just relax, sweetheart, and let Medb in. I've told you before not to fight her. Let her come.' She was pushing Pat towards the wall. 'I can see her. She is there all over you. She knows I want her here.'

'Peggy –!' Pat was paralysed with horror.

'I need her.' Peggy didn't move. 'I need that brooch and I need that power.'

'Steve!' Suddenly Pat was screaming. Desperately she pushed at Peggy, her hands flat against the woman's chest. 'Viv! Where are you? Help me!'

There was no reply.

Medb was smiling.

The brooch was almost in sight.

VI

Shaking hands with James Oakley, Meryn stood for a second on the threshold of the cottage, then with a slight nod of satisfaction followed him inside. It felt good. Safe. Hugh was waiting in the snug and greeted Meryn with a handshake and a slap on the back. 'Am I glad to see you! I don't know why I ran. I'm sorry.'

Meryn scrutinised him briefly. 'I doubt if you had control of your actions.' The three men seated themselves in the three armchairs around the fire, then Meryn turned to James. 'There is a matter of protocol here, I feel. A clergyman could deal with these matters, surely.'

'I'm not sure I could,' James put in hastily. 'This would seem to be way beyond my competence. That's why I rang you. Quite apart from the fact that, should it be necessary, an old codger like me can't get up to the fort any more owing to my arthritis.' He liked the look of this man; he exuded warmth and humanity and a reassuring sense of calm confidence. 'I'll cheer from the sidelines, whatever needs to be done.'

Meryn smiled, his facing creasing into deep lines as he did so. 'I am sure I shall be very glad of your support. Venutios is a powerful adversary; and if he combines his efforts with Medb of the White Hands, it will probably take both of us to defeat them. This is a battle for people's souls. Something of which you have experience, I suspect.'

Hugh swallowed. He stared from one man to the other, trying to feel reassured and aware only of a deepening sense of panic. 'Wouldn't it be better if I just went away?'

Meryn shook his head. 'They would follow you, my friend. This has to be sorted out, once and for all.'

'And the brooch?'

'Is being used as a focus and a power source to fuel an ancient quarrel. It needs to be cleansed of the curses and charms and bitterness which have impregnated it. Where is it now?'

'Viv hid it somewhere up there.' Hugh nodded towards the window and all three men turned to stare up at the hill. From this far away they could see no sign of life up on the distant plateau which was once more bathed in sunshine, wisps of mist still clinging around some of the steeper ramparts. 'I don't dare go near her, Meryn,' Hugh said suddenly. 'I'm afraid of what he'll make me do.'

Meryn studied him. 'In the story, in your head, they are at war?'

Hugh nodded. 'And once the war started, there was – is – no going back.' He frowned.

Meryn stood up. 'I think we should go and see Cartimandua.'

Hugh blanched. 'We can't.'

'I shall be with you. Neither you nor Venutios are going to do anything with me there. And James, if he would accompany us.'

'No.' Hugh stood up agitatedly. 'No, I really don't want to. You two go, but not me. I've been thinking about this. I did go back to see her and thank God she wasn't there because Venutios is too strong for me!' Both men were watching him in silence. He paused, glancing from one to the other. 'You can see him, can't you! Shit!' He slammed his fist down on the table next to him. 'I will not risk hurting Viv! You have no idea how strong he is!'

Meryn and James stared after him as he strode out of the room, slamming the door behind him. In the silence that followed they heard his footsteps retreating up the stairs.

Meryn stood up. 'He is being forced to believe in the possession, but he still can't bring himself to believe there is a remedy.' He sighed. 'Poor Hugh.'

'What do we do?' James took off his spectacles and cleaned them anxiously.

'How far away is our Cartimandua?'

'Not far. A few miles.'

'Then maybe we should go there and assess the situation.' Meryn glanced up at the ceiling. 'My only hope is that Hugh stays put. We don't want him rampaging round the countryside without us.'

35

I

The farmhouse was silent as Viv walked down the stairs. She had no intention of looking for Pat or Peggy. They could draw their own conclusions about her departure. Pulling open the front door silently she carried her bag out to the car. There was one more thing to do before she could leave and that was to go and collect the brooch. Pushing the boot shut as silently as she could, she glanced over her shoulder. There was still no sign of anyone. Steve's car had gone.

Slipping out of the gate she carefully latched it behind her, then she hurried up the track.

For a long time she stood on the edge of the vast pavement of limestone looking out across the strange, lunar landscape, trying to orientate herself. There were several stunted thorns and junipers growing out of the stone, any one of which could have been the one she had thought so memorable. She turned round and round, feeling herself growing increasingly panicky, then walked towards one small tree and kneeling beside it, stared round, trying to locate a fissure where she might have pushed the box amongst the clusters of stonecrop. There was nothing there.

Scrambling to her feet, she moved a few yards on and tried again. The sun was beating down on her back and she could smell the honey scent of meadowsweet. Somewhere high up in the distance she heard the mew of a buzzard and staring up, she saw the tiny black speck circling against the intense blue of the sky.

'I thought I'd find you here.' Hugh's voice took her completely by surprise. She swung round in fright. 'So, this is where you hid the brooch.'

497

She stared at him, overwhelmed by conflicting emotions as fear and longing swept over her. 'Hugh?'

'This time I did follow you. I couldn't wait around while everyone else was out trying to sort out the vagaries of history! I saw you from right up there.' He pointed behind him. 'I could see you searching.'

'I can't find it.' She shook her head.

His eyes narrowed suspiciously, then abruptly he threw back his head and laughed. 'That, of all things, would be the final irony.'

'And no one would believe me.'

'No. They wouldn't.'

'Venutios?'

He grinned. 'I'm fighting him, Viv. Believe me, I'm fighting him. And I have allies. Meryn – I told you about him? My Druid friend – and James Oakley the local parson.'

Just for a second she felt her face twitch with amusement. 'A Druid and a parson?'

'I know. My street cred is all shot to pieces But this is their sort of thing. They've gone to the farm to look for you. I didn't want to go with them. I didn't dare. I was going to stay indoors, but I couldn't. I had to know what was happening!' His smile vanished suddenly. Something like pain flashed across his features. 'Did you hear that? Oh God! I should have turned back when I saw you. I should have gone back to the car and locked myself in!'

'What is it?'

'Hell and damnation! I can't cope with this! Not on my own. He wants the brooch back.'

'I can't find it, I told you! I can't give it to you.' His face had changed. She could see it – the mask overlaying his features. Terrified, she stepped back. 'Hugh?'

'Get away from me, Viv. Run!' Hugh was suddenly sweating. 'I can't fight him! I don't want to hurt you. I couldn't bear that! I love you, Viv, but he wants to kill Cartimandua!' His voice broke. 'Get away from me now!'

She stared at him in complete horror. 'Hugh?'

'Now!' He was gasping, his hands to his head. 'Can't you hear it? The carnyx! The beat of the drum! He's coming!'

And finally she registered what he was saying. She spun round in panic. Dodging past him she leaped across a crack in the rocks and headed down the hillside, jumping over stones onto the grass, dodging the larger outcrops, slipping and sliding on the loose scree.

Wiping the sweat away from his face with his forearm, Hugh shook his head desperately. He could sense Venutios's anger as the messengers cowered before him; feel every second of his helpless fury as they had told him how Cartimandua, his wife, had married Vellocatus! She had turned her back on him. She had married his shield bearer and his servant.

With a bellow of rage he had turned and hit the wall with his fists.

In the name of the great gods, Camulos and Lugh, he would be avenged! He would kill every man who fought for her and he would tear Vellocatus limb from limb if it was the last thing he did in this world. And then he would kill her.

'Viv!' Hugh's voice was lost in the roar of the wind behind her as she fled from him down the hill. 'Viv, I'm sorry. I didn't want it to be like this –'

She didn't hear him.

II

Pat groped for her watch and tried to focus. It was five. It must still be afternoon. She hadn't been asleep long. She lay staring at the ceiling. Her head was banging like a hammer and she felt violently sick. Medb had been there. She knew that much. And Peggy.

Aching in every limb, she climbed off the bed. She was beginning to remember in small intense flashes what had happened. They had been in the kitchen. Her head had been splitting; Peggy had given her something to drink from a bottle on the dresser, then helped her upstairs. What had happened next? She had felt Medb's hands on her face, the ice-cold fingers, then nothing. Sleep.

Quietly she opened her bedroom door and looked out into the passage. The house was silent. On tiptoe, her head still spinning, she crept along the corridor and at the top of the stairs she stopped and listened. There was a sound of rattling pans from the kitchen and water running from the tap. Peggy must be washing up. The normality of the sound reassured her.

Silently she tiptoed down and listened at the kitchen door. Peggy must have heard her for it opened suddenly. 'Are you feeling better, love?'

Pat nodded numbly.

'Good. Come with me and we'll fetch some more medicine for that headache.'

How did Peggy know she had a headache?

Pat could hardly walk. She felt Peggy take her arm and guide her down the passage towards the herb room where she reached for the light switch and they went inside, closing the door behind them. Peggy pushed her towards the bed. 'Sit there. I'll make up some more of that tisane. It will soothe you.' Pat put her hand to her forehead. Her head was splitting. Steve had come back. She could picture his face. His eyes had been wild. Someone had died. She frowned, watching as Peggy went over to the shelves where her store of herbs was kept in bottles and boxes and brown paper bags, each meticulously labelled. Carefully she mixed several tinctures. Before closing the little bottle she poured some into a glass.

'Steve,' Pat murmured. 'Steve was upset.'

'You forget Steve.' Peggy turned, the glass in her hand. She handed it to Pat. 'Drink that. It will make you feel better.'

Pat turned her head away, but Peggy was beside her, one hand behind her head, the other holding the glass to her lips. She had no strength to object. Swallowing, she groaned and retched. Peggy smiled. 'I know. It tastes disgusting, but in a few minutes you will feel wonderful. Look, I'll add some mead. That will sweeten it.' She screwed the lid on the bottle and slipped it into her pocket. 'We'll take this with us in case we want it again. Now, come with me and we'll go and look for Viv.'

III

The track was steep, the air close. After only twenty minutes Hugh's head began to pound. Groping in his daysack for his water bottle, he sat down on an outcrop of rock staring back the way he had come. Somewhere in the distance he could hear the cry of a buzzard as it circled below him. The occasional shout in the distance reminded him the re-enactors were up there somewhere. He had seen them with their tents and their costumes and their weapons. He thought he heard the clash of swords, then nothing. A breeze rustled through the grass and he heard the rattle of shifting shale as some loose scree settled nearby. He glanced over his shoulder, up towards the higher slopes. This would be a good place to rest for a while.

He shivered as a shadow fell across him. For a second he didn't dare open his eyes. There had been no sound. No sense that anyone was near, but suddenly he could feel him. Almost paralysed with terror, he forced his eyes open. There was no one in sight.

'So, my friend,' he said huskily. 'Are we going to talk about this, man to man, or am I going to tell you to go away, like Meryn said.'

He looked round. Nothing. The only sound was the wind in the short, sparse grasses around his feet. In the distance evening was coming.

'So, Venutios. You and I together on the hill where you defeated Cartimandua. How does it feel to be the winner?'

He shivered violently. The cold seemed to tiptoe over the hillside. Mist was drifting up across the limestone pavements below. Somehow the afternoon had slipped away without him noticing.

Venutios smiled. He had two priorities left. To find Medb.

And to kill the Roman who had rescued Cartimandua from his clutches.

IV

As Viv ran into the yard the front door opened and she found herself looking at Peggy, who was just coming out.

Peggy smiled. 'What's the hurry?' There was a game bag slung across her shoulders.

'Venutios! He wants the brooch!' Viv was gasping for breath. Behind her the track was empty. There was no sign of Hugh. Hugh, who had admitted he loved her before his whole being had been subsumed beneath that mask of hate.

Peggy smiled. 'We all want the brooch, Viv. Did you find it? No? Then we need to go back and look for it again.'

'Peggy! I told you! Hugh is up there. With Venutios. Now!' Viv was desperate. She doubled up, trying to regain her breath. 'He's going to kill me!'

Peggy smiled again before turning to call over her shoulder. 'Medb! Come out here. Viv is going to take us to her hiding place.'

Viv straightened abruptly. 'Medb?' Taking a deep breath to try and steady herself, Viv took in Peggy's face for the first time. It was shiny with sweat. Her eyes were hard and calculating, her expression set with a cold determination which made Viv's skin crawl. She glanced round at her car. It was only a few yards away.

Peggy shook her head and held up her hand. In it were Viv's car keys. 'I saw your room was empty. I didn't think it was very polite of you to leave without saying goodbye, Vivienne, my dear. And I didn't think it polite of you to come here masquerading as Steve's girlfriend, when you're in love with another man, so the least you can do is bring us the brooch as a gift for the goddess.'

Viv stared round frantically. 'Peggy, I'm sorry. I never said I was Steve's girlfriend. Why would you think that?' She glanced over her shoulder again. Any second Hugh was going to appear in the lane. She wasn't sure who she feared more, Venutios or Peggy. 'Where is Steve?'

'Steve's not here. He's gone.' Peggy smiled.

There was a movement in the doorway and Pat appeared out of the shadows behind her. She looked dazed and she was unsteady on her feet. 'Viv, you'd better give it to her.'

'I can't! I haven't got it!' Viv was panic-stricken. 'Look, Hugh is up there on the hillside! He wants it. Venutios wants it. And I couldn't find it. Perhaps Cartimandua hid it!' She gave a humourless laugh. 'You've got to help me. Please, Peggy, give me my car keys!' Holding out her hand, she walked up to Peggy who stared at her for a moment, then turned abruptly and went back into the farmhouse.

Viv turned desperately to Pat. 'What's wrong with her? What's wrong with you? Where's Steve?' His car had gone.

Pat shrugged. Her eyes weren't focussing. 'I'm fighting it, Viv. I'm sorry. Medb is too much for me. Help me!' She clutched at the doorpost, her words slurring, as Peggy reappeared behind her. She was carrying a shotgun. Viv stared at her in horror as she lifted it

502

waist high and pointed the barrel straight at her. 'Enough. If you want to live long enough to drive that car again, you'd better do as I say. Let's go and find Cartimandua's brooch. I need it. Now!'

V

'I can't go any further! I'm exhausted!' Viv stopped at last and turned to face Peggy.

Peggy lifted the gun a fraction higher. 'As soon as you find it, we'll go back.' She was tight-lipped. 'So, where is it?' The sun was sliding towards the north-west and a haze was forming below them. A transparent, three-quarter moon hung in the sky over the distant fells. Pat, who had stumbled up the hill in their wake, subsided onto a pile of stones. Ignoring her, Viv stared at Peggy. She was so frightened she was almost incapable of speech. 'I told you. I don't know where it is.'

'Ask her then. Ask Cartimandua.'

'I can't.'

'Oh, I think you can!'

'Come on, Viv,' Pat mumbled. 'This is not worth dying for.' Her speech was woolly. 'Just tell her where it is.'

'I told you, I couldn't find it. Perhaps someone else has picked it up!' Viv shook her head wearily. 'This is madness. What have you taken, Pat? What's wrong with you? Help me!' She was near to tears.

Pat shrugged. Her eyes were bleary. 'Peggy means it.'

Viv shook her head in despair. 'And Medb? She wants it as well, doesn't she. So which one of you gets it? Or are you going to shoot it out?'

'Let us worry about that.' Peggy gave a cold smile. She waved the gun barrel in Pat's direction and Pat shrank back. 'Come on, Vivienne. If you cannot find it, then Cartimandua will. Ask her!'

'Just go on with the story, Viv. You'll be safe there, in the past,' Pat whispered. 'Do it.'

Wearily Viv put her hands to her head. 'I can't.'

'You can. You must.' Pat stood up shakily and came to sit beside her, keeping a wary eye on Peggy. Below them the vast panorama of the countryside was silent and deserted as the sun began to sink into the haze.

'Come on! Cartimandua has hidden the brooch. She must have. She knows Medb is Venutios's mistress and his daemon!' Pat was growing increasingly incoherent. 'Go on. Close your eyes. She won't wait forever. She's going to kill us!' She gestured towards Peggy.

'Where is Steve? He'll follow us up here if he can't find us in the house.'

Peggy shook her head. She sat down on a rocky outcrop, the gun still pointing at Viv's chest. 'Steve has gone. I told you. He's not going to rescue you if that's what you imagine. Get on with it.'

Viv's mouth was dry. Where could Steve have gone? She could feel a clammy sweat on her back; the rocks were still radiating heat after the long day of sunshine. She had never been so frightened; around her the dry grasses rustled gently in the wind as she closed her eyes. Pat glanced at Peggy nervously. She was resting the gun on the rocks, pointing it at Viv. Her finger was still very near the trigger. The woman's gaze had not shifted from Viv's face.

Viv didn't notice. In her panic there was only one place to go. Within.

With a groan, she began to clutch her stomach.

Gruoch and Mairghread assisted at the birth. Gruoch, gentle and skilled, Mairghread resentful and angry. The Romans had gone, chasing Venutios northward, Vellocatus with them. Carta had been forced to remain behind by her condition. Until the last minute she had been there, at the head of her men, on the chariot, with Vellocatus at her side, but now at last she had acknowledged that she could go no further. Her pains had started during the night. By midday she was delivered of a small screaming daughter. She examined the child as Gruoch put her in her arms. 'She's perfect.' Gruoch smiled. 'And noisy. She'll be as determined as her mother.'

Behind her, Mairghread directed the servants to clear away the mess. Fresh herbs were thrown on the fire and the child was blessed. 'Will you give her a nursery name?' Gruoch fastened sacred beads round the child's tiny fist.

Cartimandua turned her head away. 'Vellocatus wanted a son. A warrior to succeed us as leader of our peoples.'

'That could not have happened, lady,' Gruoch replied as she touched her hand gently. 'Not without the blessing of the gods and the choice of the people. It is they who decide who will be king. Or queen.' She smiled reproachfully.

'Then I shall do as Artgenos advised.' Carta handed the baby back. 'See that she is fostered. She has my blessing.' Turning away, she lay back on the pillows and hid her face from the light.

Viv's eyes were full of tears. Blindly she wiped them with the back of her hand. 'So, that's that,' she said. She was very pale.

'No. No, it isn't.' Pat stood in front of her. It isn't by a long chalk! Go on.' Suddenly she was focussed, her voice angry and strong.

Peggy smiled. Medb had taken over. She could see the wispy form, the hard intense eyes concentrating on Viv's face.

'Not now, Pat.' Viv leaned back on the grass and closed her eyes. 'I'm too tired, I don't want to go on.'

'Now! We need to know what happened next. Did the child survive? Where did she go? What happened to the brooch?' There was a long pause. 'I'll tell you what happened, shall I? Venutios sent Medb away,' Pat went on. 'He said he never wanted to see her again but she didn't go far.' She laughed suddenly. 'Perhaps I'll tell you about that. But for now, we want to know what happened to Carta and Vellocatus. It's important.' She threw herself on her knees in front of Viv and thrust her face close to Viv's.

'Pat,' Peggy said quietly. 'Be quiet. Let her talk.' Her voice was hard.

Slowly Viv sat up. She sighed. 'I'm not sure I can.' Closing her eyes again, too tired to argue, she took a deep breath and listened. At once the sounds and the words and the memories so close around them flooded into her head.

'Where is she?' Carta was standing in the Druid's college facing Artgenos. In the distance they could hear the sound of the students reciting, chanting over and over the day's lesson. The old man was sitting by the fire in his comfortable wicker chair, wrapped in a thick white woollen mantle against the cold. There were cushions at his back and a flagon of mulled ale at his elbow.

'As you instructed, she was sent away. To be brought up as a fosterling.' On the table near him a basket of polished rock crystals sparkled in the firelight.

'And I want to know where.' Carta was furious. Her strength recovered, her figure slim and taut again she was, outwardly at least, as formidable and beautiful as ever.

With a sigh he levered himself to his feet, leaning heavily on his staff. 'She is well cared for, Carta. I have reports regularly. She is bright and alert and thriving. When she is six summers or so old, if she is as intelligent as I feel sure she is,' he smiled wryly, 'I will allow her into one of the Druid schools to be taught the craft. It is best she does not know who her parents are.'

For a moment Carta was too angry to speak. When at last she mastered her fury the look she gave him made even Artgenos quail. 'How dare you!'

'I have consulted the auguries, Carta,' he said mildly enough. He glanced at the door where the feathered cloak he wore when consulting the gods hung on an antler bracket. 'I have read her future. She will be no queen. Her presence here would only exacerbate the unrest in Brigantia.' He frowned. 'The Druids will need every talented new candidate possible, Carta. The Romans are bent on destroying us.' He paused sadly. 'Your allegiance with the governor of Rome is no longer tenable. And the new governor, Suetonius Paulinus is proving himself a fearsome soldier. Forget the child. She is safe and well and happy. Consider instead the gods and their needs. Ynys Môn itself, one of the most holy places in all these islands, is under threat. Paulinus is set on its destruction. I have spoken to Vellocatus. He is willing now to lead an army to cut off the legions –'

'No!' Carta tightened her lips. 'I forbid it. If the gods are threatened, they will protect their own.'

'The gods command you to fight for them, Carta. The omens are strong.'

'There are no such omens!' she contradicted furiously. 'I have spoken to the goddess, my goddess. I have sacrificed to her. She brought the Romans to save us and they threw out Venutios and chased him back to Caer Lugus.'

'And Venutios is one of the best chances we have as a people to vanquish Rome.' He glared at her sternly. 'It might still be possible to form an alliance with him again. You forget who you are, Cartimandua, and what you are sworn to do –'

'No! I remember who I am. I am Queen. I am supported by the legions, an ally of the Roman Governor and I am a woman of honour.' She narrowed her eyes. 'Everything I have done, I have done for my people, Artgenos!'

'Everything?' He raised an eyebrow. She didn't see the sad, quizzical smile.

'Everything!' She was pacing up and down the floor. 'I shall not change my mind!'

He bit back a curse. 'Why are you doing this? You are no longer an astute politician, Carta. You are a fool. You have lost your acumen. You have lost your brains!'

'That is enough!' She spoke so softly he thought for a moment he had misheard her. She turned and faced him. 'You have gone too far, Artgenos. Leave. Leave Brigantia today. You are no longer welcome in my kingdom. You defy me. You hide my baby from me and you support my enemies. If you are so worried about the fate of the Druids on Môn, I suggest you join them. Your prayers will be more useful there than here, Artgenos. And take Culann with you. I sense he disapproves of every breath I take. Let him support the Druids at your side at their most senior college.' She turned towards the doorway. 'Today!'

Could he not understand? If she changed her mind now, if she swapped her alliance with Rome for one with the rebels against the Empire it would be an acknowledgement that everything she had stood for had been a lie. That her betrayal of Caradoc had been pointless. That her stance for her people had been in vain. And she would have to surrender her leadership of her people to Venutios. She would rather die.

In the distance the hills rang to the roar of a stag. Further away a second answered it, the challenge echoing into silence.

'Peggy!' Pat whispered. She rubbed her eyes wearily. 'Look behind us. The weather is closing in. It will be getting dark soon.'

'Be quiet! Listen to her!' Peggy was very close to Viv, her eyes fixed on her face. 'The brooch. Where is the brooch?'

Viv was speaking more and more slowly, her voice growing steadily weaker.

'Mairghread! Bring me some wine. And something to eat. Have the Druids gone?' She shivered violently even as Carta shivered.

'They have, lady.' Mairghread pursed her lips. 'They have left Ban in charge of the college here.'

'And you haven't gone with them? I know you disapprove of what I'm doing. You've always secretly supported Venutios.'

'I am your friend,' Mairghread said stiffly. 'But I have always spoken my mind, so I'll speak now. I don't like the manner in which you dismissed Artgenos. It was not your place to do so. It was he who had the power to take your sovereignty from you! But he has chosen to go. To leave you to your fate. I don't like the way you grovel before the Romans but it is your decision to do so; for both reasons you need me more than ever, so I will stay.'

Carta didn't contradict. 'Thank you.' She shivered. 'Has Gruoch gone, too?'

'No. She will head the college with Ban. Brigantia needs the prayers and sacrifice of a senior Druid and she has Artgenos's blessing to continue here.'

Carta sighed. 'I see. It is all arranged.'

'As it must be.' Mairghread poured a goblet of wine and gave it to her.

'Does Gruoch know where my baby has gone?'

Mairghread shook her head. 'I heard her beg Artgenos to tell her. He had the child taken away in the night the same day she was born.'

'Do you think he had her killed?' Carta's eyes filled with tears.

Mairghread shook her head. 'He would never have done that, lady. Never. He is a good man as well as a great priest and Druid.'

Carta gave a wry smile. 'So. My supporters dwindle by the day. Where is Vellocatus?'

'He went hunting, lady. Remember?' She did not remind her that Vellocatus's disappointment at finding Carta had not borne him a son had been so acute he had drunk himself unconscious and stayed drunk for a week. After that he had ridden over the dales and into the forest with four companions. Two months had passed and he had not returned.

'Is there news from Môn?' Carta looked up at Mairghread as she tended the fire.

Mairghread shook her head.

'I will consult the goddess,' Carta said at last, uneasily. 'We should support the Druids. We could send warriors secretly. The Romans need not find out.'

Mairghread nodded. 'That would please your people.'

'And Vellocatus.'

'And Vellocatus.' Mairghread smiled sadly.

It was too late. As soon as the winter snows melted and the ground began to dry out, the Romans moved. Gruoch walked into Carta's private chamber and dismissed the queen's companions. 'The news over the last few days has been bad. Last night I looked into the waters of the sacred pool and they ran red with blood. I ordered my best young seer to sleep the sleep of true dreams and he has told me what is happening.' Her face was white.

Carta stood up and went to the side table. She poured mead from the jug there and pressed the goblet into Gruoch's hands. 'Tell me.' Her mouth was dry and with shaking hands she poured mead for herself as well.

'The Romans advanced into the land of the Deceangli. They made a base at Deva and another at Segontium so they could attack Môn by land and sea! They lined up on the shores of Afon Menai in formation and waited there, afraid to cross the strait.' She bit her lip. 'Our people were waiting on the far side of the water. They invoked the gods. They called out to the spirits of the sea and sky. The Romans were afraid. So very afraid. They would have fled but their leaders forced them on. And –' She paused, tears streaming down her face. 'They landed on the blessed island and put the community to the sword. Every one. Men, women and children. No one was spared. They have even burned the sacred groves – those ancient, blessed oaks!' She collapsed into a heap on the floor, weeping.

Carta swallowed. She felt a sheen of ice close over her body. 'Is there no one – nothing – left?'

'Nothing.' Gruoch shook her head. 'We could have helped them. We have known for months – years – what they intended.'

Slowly, Carta began to pace the floor. She entwined her fingers together in anguish. 'Artgenos?' She turned back to Gruoch in sudden horror. 'Was he in the vision?'

'He died fighting.' Gruoch stared up at her blindly. 'An old man in his eighties and he died fighting.'

There was a long silence. There were tears pouring down Viv's face.

'And the brooch?' Peggy whispered. 'Where is the brooch?' She spoke through clenched teeth.

Viv pushed her away, shaking her head. 'There is no one left to attend to the dead.' Her voice rang out across the darkening hillside, the voice of the goddess. 'Ravens. Kites. Wolves out of the forests. The gods are shamed. Look. The Romans are washing the blood of the Druids off their swords and their hands in our sacred pools. The creatures are weeping. The birds are crying. Their beaks are dripping with blood and gore. Sacrilege. Shame. Shame on you, Cartimandua. You could have stopped this happening.

'But that's not true!' Her voice changed. Her whole demeanour. She was Cartimandua again. 'They would have killed us, too. Our Druids would have died as well. Gruoch would have been slaughtered. As it is, she lives. She has recruited more men and women to the college and the mistletoe flourishes under her care. The Romans did not succeed. They left us alone. They went back south.' She frowned. 'News came, you know. Only days later. Of the rebellion of the Iceni. After Prasutagus died the Romans dishonoured their agreement. They violated his daughters. They whipped his queen and Boudica turned on them. She burned Camulodunum and Londinium and Verulamium. The whole of the south-east rose up in bloody revolt.'

Pat had risen unsteadily to her feet. Now she squatted down again. She put her hand on Viv's arm. 'So, why didn't you support her, Cartimandua?' Medb was back, now the drug was wearing off a little and her voice was heavy with sarcasm. 'You had it in your power to alter the whole course of history! If you had gone to her aid with your men, if you had allied with Venutios, you could have driven the Romans out of Britannia forever. You could have helped her win!' She laughed. The sound was harsh and cruel. Medb's laugh. 'But you didn't. Even then, you didn't. You couldn't bring yourself to fight the Romans, could you! You stayed at home with your lover!'

Vellocatus had come home. He rallied the men and sent them back to the training grounds and he came back to Carta's bed.

He drew her to him and kissed her forehead gently. 'I've been neglecting my wife. It is time we put that right.'

Nestling against him, she relaxed into his arms. 'I've missed you.'

He smiled, lifting her chin to kiss her mouth. 'I thought you no longer loved me.'

'How could you think that?' Indignantly she kissed him again.

'You are my life! My love! My world!' She wound her arms around his neck. 'And you will be the father of my sons.'

He smiled. 'We will have seven sons, my darling, and then seven more.' Sweeping her off her feet, he carried her to the bed and laid her gently on it. If she gave an anguished thought for her little lost daughter, she gave no sign.

They made love all night and rose only when a shaft of sunlight made its way through a chink in the roof thatch and strayed across her face. They didn't call the servants. He watched her dress, his eyes on her body, noting every movement, every languid shadow on breast and belly. She had changed since she had borne the child. She was more statuesque, her flesh richer, her hair thicker. She was if anything more desirable than ever.

Ready at last, she turned to him. 'Now I shall be your dresser. See, you may ask the Queen to comb your hair and your moustaches.' She picked up the carved comb from her table. 'And I shall help you on with your mantle and pin your cloak.'

She tipped the contents of her jewel casket onto the sheet and rummaged amongst her bangles and brooches.

'This one.' He bent and selected a pin from the tangle. 'I remember Venutios wearing this bird.' He smiled grimly. 'He swaggered with it on his cloak. It will give me great pleasure to sport it on mine.'

She paled as he held out the gold enamelled brooch on his palm. 'Not that one, Vellocatus. Any one but that.'

'Why not? A crane to bring me luck in battle.' He smiled and pulled her onto his knees. 'Venutios's luck changed when he ceased to wear it, remember? And surely, you would deny me nothing, sweetheart? You are not saving it to give to him again?'

She shook her head. 'I feared it was cursed. I've never worn it. Don't touch it. Please. It is through that brooch that Medb controlled Venutios.'

He threw back his head and laughed. 'What nonsense! It is beautiful. I shall wear it forever!'

He stifled her protests with a kiss and she was too besotted to argue further.

Within days he had left her side to hunt once more in the forests of the north. The moon waxed to the full and she knew she had not conceived.

In her dreams, she heard Medb's laughter echoing across the fells.

511

There was a long silence. Viv pushed her hair out of her eyes. They were still fixed on the distance.

'The Romans sent me reminders that I was their friend. That they had honoured our agreements. That they had saved me when I was in danger. That our Druids would not be harmed if I kept Brigantia out of the rebellion. Our people would not be put to the sword. Always I thought of our people. They were the children I never had. All that was left to me when my only baby was taken from me. I was their queen. The Romans never harmed them as long as I was there to stop them. Instead they sent me gold. They sent me Gaius.' She gave a low moan of unhappiness. 'They sent me Gaius, when all I wanted was Vellocatus.'

36

I

Suetonius Paulinus set off for the south from Anglesey the same day he heard of the outbreak of revolt of the Iceni. He sailed at once back to Deva and then rode south. One of his priorities was to send for Gaius Flavius Cerialis. He was to perform a secret and special, nay vital, mission. He was to ride north, at once, to the Queen of the Brigantes.

'Sir?' Gaius ground his teeth with frustration. 'You need me to fight the rebels.'

'I need you to ensure the Brigantians stay out of it.' The governor was curt. The table before him was littered with letters and plans. There was a line of officers waiting outside his tent for urgent meetings with him. He leaned forward and gazed hard into Gaius's face. 'This hell cat, Boudica, was the wife of a client king. She is a friend or a relative of Cartimandua – bound to be. I do not want Cartimandua unsettled. We cannot afford another rising on the northern front. It would be the end of us. Almost single-handed Cartimandua has kept her tribesmen out of our hair, even against Venutios. I do not intend to let her slip out of our clutches for the sake of a bit of diplomacy. And,' for a moment the governor's face slipped into something which could have been a leer, 'my informants tell me you are very good at diplomacy with the barbarian queen.'

Gaius felt his cheeks redden violently. 'I hoped for useful pillow talk, sir.'

'You do not have to explain, officer. I am assured of your loyalty.' Paulinus stood up. 'Take a small detachment of men and call at the treasury. Small rich gifts this time. Nothing that can't be taken in a saddlebag. Be careful; the roads are infested with British rebels. Do not get caught. Stay up north with her as long as you need to keep her occupied. Once we have defeated Boudica and sent her to her gods we can deal in whatever way is appropriate with Cartimandua.'

Gaius managed to school his features until he was out of the governor's sight. Then he let out a string of violent expletives. He wanted to fight. He did not want to go and crawl to that woman with her lustful thighs and her scornful eyes. He would have to grovel, ingratiate himself, win her over yet again and to hold her attention for as long as it took – attention which up until now had barely granted him one night in her bed before she had grown bored with him. On top of all that she was, so the report the governor had handed him recounted with much disgust, remarried to a young slave, her husband's shield bearer. A man she could not keep her hands off, she was so besotted with him.

He swore again.

But at the same time he was intrigued. There should be no competition, surely. He, battle-hardened, handsome – he tightened his jaw a fraction, aware of his own modest self-mockery – and charming, versus a barbarian peasant. No contest.

He took a hand-picked party of men, eight of them, on fast, well-trained horses. They travelled with the minimum of supplies and equipment, each man with a saddlebag of jewellery, gold coin and – Gaius's idea this – small packages of silk and brocade, ivory hair combs and rich face creams, that last the idea of his new wife, Augusta, a lady less than pleased at his assignment, as much as he had told her of it, but luckily preoccupied with their small new son.

The roads were swarming with British. They scattered at the sight of the Roman broadswords, but behind their backs there were jeers, thrown stones and vicious looks. These people had been violently and thoroughly disarmed by their conquerors and as long as they were scattered and without a leader they were no danger, but now they were all heading towards Camulodunum and they had found a leader. Boudica.

Gaius cursed yet again. He wanted to be there to fight the bastards face to face and beat them into submission. Pillow politics was not his idea of service. It would make him a laughing stock. No one ever won a commendation by bedding the enemy.

*

514

Cartimandua was now in Elmet. She had already received a series of messengers from Boudica – the first carrying pleas for aid against the governor's unjust treatment of a queen and a widow, in deliberate contradiction of her husband's will and his agreement with Rome, the second a shocked and angry account of what had happened to her and her daughters at the hands of Rome's hand-picked men and now a third demanding Cartimandua's support. Other messengers had ridden further north to Venutios. Boudica demanded that they make up their differences in order to help her defeat the enemy. The whole of Britain was about to rise. If they did not support her they would be the only two rulers who would not be a part of the insurrection.

It took four days for Gaius and his men to reach Brigantia, lightly laden as they were. They had to take frequent detours, to avoid the angry bands of Britons roaming the lands of the Trinovantes and the Iceni, and further north they faced disaffected men and women from the Catuvellauni and the Corieltauvi.

Gaius's party spent one brief night with the men of the IX legion, as they in their turn prepared to ride south to protect Camulodunum, then they rode on at dawn.

'I bring gifts yet again, great queen.' Gaius managed a gallant smile as he was ushered into her presence. He sensed hostility all around him in the township and it dawned on him for the first time that the Brigantians were well aware of what had happened on Môn and now in the south. If he had thought to reach her first and convince her before any word of what had happened to the Druids or to Boudica had reached her, he had been deluding himself. He decided on disarming honesty.

'I came to check you were all right. You've heard about the rebellions, of course?'

She was if anything more beautiful. Older, of course, as he was, and with the lines on her face now which came with experience of life, but still alluring, still powerful. Still undeniably attractive.

She raised an eyebrow at his comment. 'I have heard. The Queen of the Iceni is full of rage, quite rightly after the way she has been treated, and her people with her.'

'As you say, her rage is justifiable. The men who perpetrated this outrage have been punished.'

515

He had no idea what had happened to them. If they had been punished for anything, no doubt it would have been for stirring up such a cauldron of fury in an already unstable situation.

'The Governor sent me to speak to you. He is very grateful for your continuing support.'

She pursed her lips. The man must be a fool and take her for one as well. But she would play his game for now. 'How grateful?'

He met her eyes uncomfortably. 'I have brought gifts,' he said slowly.

'The same kind of gifts as before?' She looked straight at him. She was playing with him. He could see the intelligence in the woman's eyes and the cynicism – had that been there before? – as well as weary amusement.

'I have been told that you have a new husband, lady,' he said softly. 'I would not care to trespass on another man's territory.'

She smiled even more broadly. 'Not what I had heard about the Romans. Or about you, if I remember last time you came. I was married then, too.' She had seen in the scrying bowl Vellocatus and his men encamped by cold far-away northern lakes; they had killed bear and beaver and even in the chase he wore the golden crane. 'And you,' she narrowed her eyes, 'you have a new wife I'm told.'

He felt himself grow tense. How did she know that? 'I have indeed.'

'Your first wife died?' she went on.

'She did.'

He held her gaze boldly, almost daring her to ask about Portia who had died in childbirth. But she merely nodded imperceptibly and he realised that of course she knew. This woman was a Druid – he made the sign of protection secretly. They knew everything. Except how to save themselves from annihilation by the Roman army. The thought of the reports of what had happened on Môn comforted him. Her next words did not.

'I have read the omens. The seas around the lands of the Iceni run red with Roman blood. Boudica will not need my help.' Then, as though realising that that statement would release him from his charge of convincing her to stay out of the battle, she smiled again. 'You are lucky, Roman, that my new husband is away. He is hunting bear in the far mountains and will not return for another moon at least.' She put her head on one side coquettishly. 'His absence has made me lonely, I confess. We will talk this evening. I will order a feast for you and your men and you will tell me about your life in Camulodunum and about the new temple to Claudius they have built there.'

In his anxiety to distract her from the subject of the Roman action on Môn and what was happening in the south, news about which he suspected she probably actually knew more than he did, by one means or another, he told her far more than he intended. About the farm he had been given out on the coast on the edge of the marsh and the villa he was building there. About the Trinovantian slaves, the men who had owned the land and served their own royal prince before it had been confiscated and given to him and who now farmed it for him as slaves, about his wife and his new son, about working for Paulinus. About the temple of Claudius and the grandeur of the new great city which was the capital of the whole province of Britannia, with its council chamber and huge theatre, its circus, its houses and market place. He realised he had drunk too much wine and he saw the frown on the faces of one or two of his men, but he was telling her nothing secret. Nothing indiscreet. Nothing she didn't know already.

Obediently he followed her to her chamber later. She had new attendants, he noticed. Young. Pretty. Giggly. They peered at him nervously as they readied her for bed and trimmed the lamps and then they disappeared. It was a change after the sour-faced woman who used to look after her. As he fell naked into her bed he wondered briefly what had happened to her.

When Gaius slept at last, Carta had risen from her bed with a shiver. What she had done had been this time without enthusiasm. It was a betrayal of Vellocatus and their love, a sacrifice of her body for her people. With a sigh she wandered to the doorway. Mairghread was waiting in the darkness, wrapped in a black cloak. Seizing Carta's arm she dragged the queen down the passage between the two great round houses into the shadows, away from the leaping firelight.

'I have a knife. I will kill him. You go to the main feasting hall and listen to the bards. You cannot be blamed if you are not there when it happens.'

'No.' Carta pulled her own mantle closer. A thick white mist was drifting up from the stream threading its way between the houses.

517

She could hear the snort and stamp of the Roman horses from the stables at the edge of the camp. They were restless. Gaius's men were asleep by now in one of the guest lodges, discreetly watched and no doubt at least one of them discreetly watching. 'I forbid you to touch him.'

Mairghread stared at her. 'This man is a Roman soldier. For the Lady's sake, after what these people did on Ynys Môn you would protect him? Can you forget so soon what happened to Artgenos and the others?'

'Gaius was not on Môn'.

'That makes no difference. You can't – you cannot allow him to live!' Mairghread was hissing the words, spitting with fury.

'No. I forbid you, or anyone, to lay a hand on him or his men.'

'Then you betray everything that is sacred!' Mairghread whispered angrily. 'How can you? I can smell him on you! Have you no pride?'

'I have pride.' Carta was furious. 'Don't dare to question my actions. And don't dare to disobey me!' She stepped forward swiftly and wrenched the knife out of Mairghread's hand. 'If you touch him you will die.'

There was a moment's silence. 'Will Vellocatus be so tolerant when he hears what you have done?' Mairghread sneered suddenly. She was rubbing her wrist.

'You will tell him nothing.'

'I won't have to. The entire township knows you cannot keep your hands off this man. You seal your own destiny with this lust. If you need a man so desperately, take a warrior. Take a man of whom we can be proud.' Turning on her heel, she disappeared into the darkness.

Carta frowned. Mairghread was becoming a danger and a liability. Walking back into her chamber, she stood looking down at the drunken man sprawled across her bed and then at the knife in her hand. Why not? What had he done for her, save cause her confusion; make her hated within her own family, her own tribe, the whole of Brigantia. It was not as though she loved him. He had attracted her; he amused her and yes, in a way she lusted for his body, though not in the way she lusted after Vellocatus, her lover and her husband. No, it was that he was, in a real sense, her friend. Was it for that friendship she had betrayed her own people? Or was he an excuse? She sighed, unable to understand either herself

518

or her emotions. For a long moment she hesitated, looking down at him, then with a shiver of disgust at her own weakness, she turned away.

Through half-closed eyes he had seen the flash of the blade. He had seen her throw the knife down.

He also saw the look of disgust.

When it was clear she was not coming back he rose and dressed. Peering out of the entrance he saw there were no guards posted. Stupid woman. Straightening his shoulders he walked out of the house and strode towards the guest lodge. With his own man on guard, wide awake and standing to attention he exchanged a cheery, lewd greeting and a thumbs up sign. Then he went and threw himself down on one of the mattresses against the wall.

He was ready to ride by mid-morning, but his second in command, Lucius, shook his head. 'You don't know what she's going to do yet. You have to wait. You can't risk her calling out the Brigantes and heading south.' He stared round with a barely concealed shudder. 'This woman commands thousands of men. Your orders were to woo her. To keep her out of the fight, so,' the man grinned somewhat woodenly, 'woo her you must.'

That was not so easy. He did not see her that day or the following night. Nor the next although he and his men were made ostentatiously welcome, and entertained and fed as honoured guests. Where she was he didn't know. When at last she reappeared in the township, riding in at dusk on her chariot with Fergal at the reins, it was to summon him formally soon after to the great round house. Her warriors were there and her Druids, the leader of whom appeared, to his astonishment, to be a woman. It was then that Cartimandua broke the news to him of the sack of Camulodunum.

'The place is burned. The temple of Claudius utterly destroyed. The Romans murdered,' she said. Her face was impassive. He couldn't tell if she was pleased or sorry. 'I understand the IX legion was hurrying to their aid. They were ambushed. They too have been destroyed.'

Gaius could feel himself reeling with shock. He did not doubt for a minute the truth of what she told him. Her followers were staring at him impassively as she went on. 'I am sorry if your wife and child were involved –' For a moment he thought he saw a glimpse of real humanity in her eyes, then it had gone. 'If you wish to leave, I understand.'

519

He tried to think. For a long moment he was completely unable to throw off the shock. It was Lucius who answered for him. 'Gaius Flavius Cerialis thanks you, Great Queen, for your consideration, but our orders are to remain here at your service –' Was that the slightest hesitation? 'If his wife and child have died, they will be honoured as dying in the service of the Emperor.'

The man saw her frown slightly and glance at Gaius. He saw her face soften and he nodded, satisfied. She was only a woman. And as a woman Gaius would tame her.

Hugh groaned. How could she? How could she have betrayed the men she loved? Vellocatus. Venutios. But she was doing it for her people. Always for her people. Like Venutios, she was at heart a patriot. And she had never known how much Venutios had loved her.

It appeared she had sent messengers to enquire after his wife. Gaius listened incredulously as four days later she relayed the news. 'The lady Augusta was at your villa when Camulodunum was sacked. The slaves have gone, following Boudica, and are now freemen once again, but she is safe, as is your son.' She paused. 'You are blessed to have a son. I hope you realise it.' He saw the wistful regret in her eyes.

His relief was palpable as he bowed slightly. 'I am grateful for that news at least. Thank you.'

'Good.' She smiled. 'Then we will celebrate tonight.'

He had the feeling they were celebrating the sacking of his city, but he did not enquire into the reason for the feast too deeply. Instead he concentrated on his role. He was to distract the queen and distract her he did as the summer wore on and still her husband did not return.

Once again she played him like a fish and once again she pulled him in helpless before her wiles, perfectly aware that he thought himself the initiator of the distraction. Only when she permitted him finally to hear of the burning of Londinium and Verulamium did she allow him at last to leave.

'You have done your duty, Roman,' she said, eyebrow raised. 'Single-handed you have distracted me from supporting Queen

Boudica.' She was laughing at him as he stood before her. 'Don't worry. I won't tell of your role in upholding the frontiers of the Empire. It shall be our secret. But now I think your master would probably like you home. They must be running out of men.'

He felt his face grow hot. 'Rome will win in the end. They will quell this rebellion. Boudica will pay with her life and with the lives of thousands of her supporters.'

'You think so?' She stood for a moment, staring at him. 'We'll see.'

As he bowed and turned away he was left with the picture of her standing, arms folded, watching. She did not show any regret that he was leaving. Her face was like engraved stone.

II

Hugh leaned back against a rocky outcrop, exhausted, and surveyed the land falling away into the haze at his feet.

Venutios was sitting staring into the fire, exhausted with rage and grief at his defeat at the hands of Carta's Roman augmented army, when Medb found him at last. She stood, looking down at him, her clear eyes full of spite. 'So, now you know the full extent of their duplicity.'

He straightened with a frown. 'How did you get here? I thought I told you to go. I thought I told you never to come near me again!' He looked round for his servants, but the great house seemed strangely empty. The darkness was lit only by the licking flames.

She gave a small sneering smile. 'I have been watching you. Both of you. In the waters; in the clouds. I have seen it all. She has borne Vellocatus a child. The child you never allowed her to bear you.'

'I don't believe you!'

'It's true.' She smiled. 'Do you want me to show you in the fire? I'll conjure a vision for you.'

'And I'll still not believe it!'

'Then you'll believe this. You let her take the brooch I gave you. That has given her power.'

'Nonsense! That brooch was cursed.'

She smiled. 'That brooch tied us together, Venutios. When you gave it to her, you severed your ties to Brigantia. She gave it to Vellocatus.'

She smiled at the anguish on his face. 'If she did but know it, it binds them together. Through its magic, if she looks, she can follow his every move.'

'You did that to me?' Venutios turned on her.

She laughed. 'Did you not guess?'

'You bitch!' He said it almost fondly. 'So, now you will undo that magic.'

'Sadly I can't do that.' She shook her head. 'And why should I when through its power I can watch them.' She leaned towards him. 'Do you want to see them, Venutios? Do you want to see the woman who was your wife in bed with her new husband? Look into the flames! Let me show you!'

'No!' His shout echoed around the room.

'You should have kept me near you, Venutios!' She bared her small white teeth. 'I was a powerful ally. You do not want me as an enemy.'

'This is all your fault? This war with Cartimandua, her love for my charioteer is your fault?' He turned on her suddenly. 'You are telling me it could have been avoided?'

She laughed. 'Of yes, it could have been avoided. But that would have deprived me of so much pleasure. I wanted her to suffer. I wanted to see her weep and cry and scream her unhappiness and her agony. And I have succeeded. Her world has fallen apart. Her people will die and starve and watch their homes burn and they and she will know it is all her fault!'

'You evil hag!' Venutios lunged towards her.

She dodged out of his reach, laughing. 'And you, Venutios. You will know that I could have been your friend! I could have helped you!' She shook her head. 'She's slept with the Roman again as well, did you know that?' she taunted. 'She preferred even a Roman to you, Venutios!'

'You bitch!' There was no fondness in the term this time.

She laughed again. 'My magic could have saved you so much anguish, but you turned your back on me, and for that you will pay!' She ducked away from him but this time he was quicker than she was.

'Oh no.' He moved towards her, light-footed as a cat, and caught her wrist. 'Oh no, Medb, you will not escape me that easily.'

522

He dragged her close to him and held her, her face only inches from his own. 'I loved Cartimandua! She was the light of my soul. Because of you and your vicious jealousy and plotting you have torn apart our lives.' He was speaking through gritted teeth.

She laughed in his face. 'And will tear them some more!'

'I don't think so.' For several seconds he stared at her in silence until at last he saw a flicker of doubt in her eyes. She tried to wriggle free but he was far too strong. 'No.' He shook his head, almost sadly. 'No, Medb. Now you have overstepped the mark. I don't know why I was ever afraid of you. I thought you so powerful, so frightening, but you are nothing but a piece of dirt in the wind. You learned a few cheap tricks from the Druids at Dun Pelder who thought you were a promising student until they saw through you, and on those tricks you have relied all these years to work your vicious magic. No longer. You are going to pay for what you have done to Cartimandua with your life.'

'Not me.' She thrust her chin upwards in a last burst of courage. 'If you kill me, I shall haunt her and you forever!'

'Haunt away, lady.' He let go her wrists and grabbed her by the throat. 'Cartimandua and I will find a way of getting together again one day, I promise you, and we'll send you to the lands of the ever dead!'

She had such a slim throat.

He snapped her neck as if it were a twig and watched as she fell at his feet, a crumpled doll, her skirt folding gently around her like the petals of a flower trailing into the embers of the fire.

He stood for a long time looking down at her.

'I will fight Cartimandua because I have no option now; and I will probably kill her,' he said quietly to the lifeless woman. 'But one day, in another life, she and I will meet and love again. And this time you will not be there to push us apart. You and your cursed brooch and your filthy tricks.'

Only when a servant came in at last to build up the fire did he walk away, leaving the man staring in horror. 'Remove her and throw her body to the wolves,' he said shortly. 'She deserves no more.'

III

Peggy stood back 'That's enough.' She gestured with the gun barrel. 'We've wasted enough time.'

Pat had straightened. 'Why do you want the brooch so badly, Peggy?' she asked suddenly as she put her hand beneath Viv's elbow and pulled her to her feet.

'Because it contains all that is left of Medb's power.' Peggy smiled. 'Isn't that why you want it?' She laughed. 'Of course. You don't know, do you. You have no idea what you two have been playing with.'

'And you're planning to throw the brooch into the falls?' Pat's head was clearing slowly. Medb had gone.

'No!' Peggy shook her head. 'I shall use it. I shall use it the way Medb intended it to be used. The brooch is not a sacrifice! For sacrifice to the gods I shall use what the gods have always preferred. Human blood.' Her foot slipped on the loose stones and she lurched forward, waving the gun.

Pat ducked, her face white. 'For God's sake, be careful!' She took a deep breath. 'Viv, can't you remember where you put the brooch? It would be really good to find it, I think.'

Viv was standing, blinking around her, dazed. She nodded. 'I'm trying. Believe me, I'm trying. It's here. Somewhere. I tucked it deep into one of these cracks.'

'Grikes,' Peggy said, shaking her head. The gun wavered. 'We call them grikes. Grikes between the clints. Good hiding places.'

Pat reached for Viv's hand. 'Come on,' she said quietly. 'You lead the way.' She looked up and caught Viv's eye. It was only a glance but Viv saw Pat there. Not Medb. Her eyes had cleared.

IV

The farmhouse was deserted, the front door open when Meryn and James climbed out of the car. They were peering into the dark hall when a second car appeared in the distance, bumping down the track. They waited until the vehicle drew into the yard. It was a police car. Steve climbed out. 'Mr Oakley?' He was pale and drawn.

'Steve. This is one of my guests – Meryn Jones. We were looking for Viv Lloyd Rees.' James frowned. 'Is anything wrong?' He glanced from Steve to the two policemen who had followed him, putting on their caps.

'There's been an accident.' Steve bit his lip, his face heavy with misery. 'My father's dead.'

'Steve, I am so sorry.' Stepping forward in dismay, James squeezed his arm gently.

Steve was staring round, trying to distract himself; to hide his tears. 'Viv's put her bag in the car. Where is she?' He took a deep breath. 'My mother – 'he faltered. 'My mother hasn't been very well.' He shook his head. 'She's lost it, Mr Oakley. Completely.' Once again he took a deep breath and looked away. 'Are Pat and Viv not here? I'll call them . . .' He walked across to the front door and disappeared. Seconds later he was back. 'The .410 has gone. It was in the farm office.'

'Was it locked up? What about ammunition?' One of the policemen walked past Steve into the house. Steve shook his head. 'The gun was there, against the wall, behind the door. Dad had no time – ' he gave a wry smile '– for regulations.' He glanced past them at the hill. 'I don't know where they are.'

V

'I walked across here.' Exhausted, Viv stopped and looked round yet again. 'It looks different now the light's going. There were several little stunted trees. It's under one of them. I don't know which one.'

'That's enough!' The gun was heavy and Peggy was growing tired. The barrel wavered slightly as she kept it pointing at Viv, the stock once more tucked into her hip. 'You are trying to put me off. You have two more seconds!'

'Peggy!' Pat was frantic. Suddenly she was seeing everything clearly again. 'Don't be silly! Give her a chance. She's right. It all looks the same. And it's getting dark.'

'It's further over,' Viv said at last. 'Look. Over there, nearer the trees on the edge of the scree. The cracks in the rock are more pronounced there. I stuffed it down one of them.' She was beginning to panic again as Peggy, growing more and more impatient, shouldered the gun and began to line up the sights.

Pat moved towards the limestone outcrop, then she paused as she saw something move in the deep shadow behind it. There was someone there. Sagging with relief she scrambled towards the shadowy figure. 'Over here, Viv. Look.'

'Go on!' Peggy shouted. Her voice was growing hoarse. 'Go where she says!' She gripped the gun more firmly.

Viv stumbled towards the rocks. She was almost there when Hugh stood up from the shadows where he had been crouching watching them as they worked their way slowly towards him.

'I think I'll take that gun, Mrs Steadman, don't you?' He reached out to grab the barrel as Peggy let out a sharp cry and pulled the trigger.

As they wrestled the shot reverberated across the hillside. In the silence that followed the gun flew through the air to crash onto the stones. As shot pattered harmlessly around them, Peggy let out a scream of fury and broke free, turning to plunge behind the rocks and out of sight into the ravine beyond. Lunging after her, Hugh ran into the shadows and disappeared.

'Hugh!' Viv cried. 'Come back!'

'It's OK. She's dropped the gun!' Pat scrambled after them, leaving Viv standing alone on the edge of the stone outcrop.

'Wait!' Viv staggered forward. 'Pat, wait! What about Venutios!' The air was thick. Cartimandua was there.

The silence of the past was swirling all around her. Viv couldn't breathe.

Suddenly she was pitching forward into darkness.

37

I

Beside the farmhouse the five men stared up at the hill. 'That was a gunshot!' One of the policemen scanned the semi-darkness of the hillside, his hand shading his eyes. 'It seemed to come from beyond the Scars. We'll take the car and go round by road!' He turned to Steve. 'You go with these gentlemen. But be careful!' Already he was running. 'We need the armed response vehicle out here now!' he yelled, as his colleague threw himself into the driver's seat and gunning the engine, reached for his radio. 'Tell them the situation!' In seconds they had pulled out of the gate and disappeared up the track.

Steve and Meryn looked at James. He shrugged. 'My car is at your disposal, gentlemen.' It was an ancient four-wheel drive. 'Perhaps you'd better drive, Steve?' They piled in, with the two dogs sitting with James in the back as Steve put the car at the track and pressed his foot down hard.

Twice they stopped as the car left the rough stone track and cut across the grassland, scanning the horizon for a sign of life, then in the distance Meryn spotted two figures momentarily silhouetted on the skyline. 'There!' He pointed.

'We'll have to leave the car,' Steve said shortly. 'They're heading for the river.'

They stopped at the edge of the rock and scree. Steve leaped out and began to run, the dogs at his heels. There was no sign of the police.

James shook his head with a sigh. 'You go,' he said to Meryn, shrugging. 'I can't manage on this rough ground. I'm sorry.'

Climbing slowly out of the car, he stood staring after them. In the evening sky the moon was hanging over the shoulder of the hill. He could hear the crash and rattle of feet on stones from the deep ravine ahead. From the distance he could hear the roar of the waterfalls.

II

'Viv, are you listening?'

Pat gave up any hope of following Hugh and Peggy into the steep wild ravine and turned back. Kneeling, she put her hand on Viv's shoulder as Viv lay curled up on the ground, her head cushioned on her elbow, her eyes closed. 'You are there, aren't you? In Cartimandua's time? You must come back. I need you here. Now!'

Viv's eyelids fluttered. 'We have to find the brooch. Mairghread will tell Vellocatus I slept with the Roman. She will betray me.'

'The brooch doesn't matter any more. Peggy's gone mad. She's going to kill someone. Please, wake up!' Pat shook Viv by the arm. 'We don't need this now!' Her own head was clear. Whatever Peggy had given her earlier had worn off. 'I'm sorry about Medb. I'm sorry about everything. Please, Viv!'

Viv groaned. 'He is jealous. So jealous. The seers tell us he and his men have killed two bears. They have the meat and the pelts and they will be back before Samhain and he will be happy to see me until Mairghread spreads Medb's poison.'

Pat could feel the perspiration dripping down her face. 'Carta. Send Mairghread away. Send her to Venutios. Get rid of her. You don't need her any more. Do you hear me? Send Mairghread away. Then let Viv wake up.'

There was no reply.

'Viv, I need you here!' Pat was near to tears.

'The brooch is over there. Near the tree,' Viv whispered suddenly. 'Vivienne told me where to hide it. She knows it holds power.'

'God help us!' Pat stood up in despair. She froze suddenly. An elderly man was hobbling over the rough ground towards them.

'You must be Pat?' He smiled and held out his hand with

529

old-fashioned courtesy. 'I'm James Oakley. And is this Viv? Hugh was telling me about her.'

Pat stared at him, white to the lips.

'Can I help?' he went on, glancing over his shoulder towards the darkness of the ravine. 'We heard a shot.'

Pat turned and gestured towards Viv. 'Please.' Her voice was husky. 'Make her wake up.'

III

There was snow on the hills; months had passed, months of suspense while walls had been strengthened and watch towers built. There were more houses and more granaries and store rooms. Icicles hung from the broad eaves of the round house where Carta sat before the fire listening to her bard. Finlay had judged her mood to perfection as he always did. Starting his songs quietly, introspectively, gently, he built them surreptitiously in pace and humour, watching the queen in the firelight, lifting her mood. The house had been busy. Essylt was there with all her children. And her brother, Fintan, his wife and son and his family. They had come for the double winter festival of Brigantia and Imbolc and stayed, trapped by the weather. The compound had been noisy. Chaotic with children and dogs. Now they had gone. Finlay frowned as a figure appeared in the doorway, then relaxed as he recognised the king. Vellocatus stooped and kissed the top of the queen's head, then he threw himself down on the bench beside her. 'The thaw has set in at last. Spring will be here before we know it.' He glanced across at her. 'What is it?' He was wearing the golden bird on his mantle.

She shrugged. 'The flames speak of war. Soon. When the roads are passable.'

He swore under his breath. 'From which direction? Venutios again?'

'Always Venutios.' She sighed. 'One by one my warriors desert me. Fintan has gone now, with his wife and children.' Her voice broke. Her own brother's defection hurt more than she could bear.

'Through the snow?' He frowned.

'As you say, the thaw has set in. As soon as the wind changed he went silently in the night. And with him Diarmid, another of my best men, Vellocatus. I trusted them.'

Vellocatus, too, was staring into the flames. He sighed. 'You should not have married me. Your men cannot stomach me as their king. I have brought you nothing but misery.'

She gave a fond smile. 'I would never regret marrying you. Never. You are everything to me, my dear.'

The silence that followed was broken only by the gentle notes of the harp. There were no more songs.

In the distance a wolf howled.

Venutios invaded the northern territories under the first full moon of Cutios, in the time of wind, when the snows had gone but the ice had firmed and roughened the mud in the tracks enough to bear a horse and chariot at speed. His warriors swept down through the hills and took two of the Brigantian fortresses almost before Vellocatus had mobilised Cartimandua's army. The fighting was fierce, Venutios's men well-trained, his army large – far larger – than before.

The two armies faced one another along a broad stretch of moorland near the river beneath slate-grey skies. Vellocatus mounted his chariot – he had a driver of his own now – and saluted Carta with a jaunty wave of his spear. 'We'll send him packing, my queen, once and for all. Have no fear.'

As the horses thundered towards one another over ground which shook, Carta looked up. Kites and buzzards were circling, sensing the coming blood.

She had already seen disaster in the sky. *Neladoracht*. Divination by reading the clouds. It was something she was very good at.

They brought Vellocatus back on his chariot, a vicious spear wound in his chest. Gruoch was there even before he had arrived. She too had read the signs. She had a team of healers trained to deal with the worst of battle injuries, but Carta did not need to see their faces to know this one was mortal.

She spent a long time at his bedside, helping with their ministrations, then as dusk fell and he slipped into a feverish sleep she rose from his bedside and walked out into the cold night. Finding her way to the spring at the foot of the hill was second nature. She did not need a lamp. Silently and alone she walked over the rough ground, wrapped in a dark mantle, and threaded her way down through the trees, slipping on the pathway which led to the spring. In the moonlight the grass and the lichen-draped firs were silvered with moisture from the mist which had dropped away as the wind strengthened.

Quietly she sat down on the stone rim of the basin near the ancient head of the goddess, surrounded by the sound of water.

Vivienne!

She waited, staring down into the dark reflections.

Vivienne? I need you. Tell me what to do!

Viv frowned. She was aware of two figures near her, but they were of no interest; they were far away in time. They could not help.

Vivienne!

The voice had carried from far away, no more than a breath in the air.

Help me! A life for a life. Is that what you demand? Save him for me, great goddess. Spare him from this pain. I need him here. At my side.

Silence.

Viv strained her ears, not sure if she had heard the words aright.

Behind her in the distance a voice was calling her name. Turning her back, she closed her eyes.

Vivienne! You can make everything all right so Vellocatus can live. You can save him. You must save him!

The voice was insistent in her brain, calling her again and again.

In her dream, Viv glanced up at the moon. Tattered rags of cloud partly obscured it. Soon a larger, blacker swirl of cumulus would be drawn across it. Enough to bring darkness to the countryside. With a small whimper of fear, she forced herself back into the shadows. Carta was waiting beside the spring.

'Listen to the falls! After all this rain they are in full spate. Aren't they wonderful?'

Peggy had scrambled down the side of the steep valley, the game bag which was slung across her shoulders dragging behind her, catching on the undergrowth as she pushed and slid her way through dog's mercury and ramsons, ferns and tangled trees down towards the river. She stopped at last at the edge of the rock and turned to face Hugh with a smile of triumph. Deep in the ravine it was almost completely dark, the falls behind her deafening, glittering with silver foam as the light from the rising moon cut down over the hillside.

'So. We needed a man after all.' Peggy was still smiling at him. Her hair was tangled and wild, her face scratched. There was a tear across the front of her blouse. Groping blindly in the bag she drew out a large kitchen knife and brandished it in front of his face.

He backed away a little. 'Can we talk first?' He was still panting slightly, feeling the rock slippery under his feet.

She had scarcely any strength left, but she raised the knife and pointed it towards his chest. 'What have we to talk about?'

'We could talk about Medb. Venutios killed her, you know.'

'Which is why she's so angry.' Peggy smiled. 'You think I didn't know that?'

'She's angry because Venutios vowed that one day he and Cartimandua would be together again.' He paused. 'Be careful, Mrs Steadman. It's slippery from the spray.' Hugh edged backwards, still trying to catch his breath.

She shook her head. 'She was trying to use Pat. But Pat is weak. She is useless. She needed someone stronger.' She waved the knife again.

'Are you saying she needed you?' Hugh shook the spray off his face.

'Of course me! She has given me such power, even without the brooch! And all I have to do to please her is to kill Venutios! To make sure he never makes his peace with Cartimandua!' She laughed.

'And I walked into your trap.' Hugh sighed.

'Convenient, wasn't it!' She was beaming. 'One life. Two men. A professor and a king. How lucky can one get!'

Hugh glanced round in spite of himself. Was Venutios there? Venutios who had killed Medb with his bare hands. He was too frightened to feel anything save the cold damp from the spray seeping into his shirt. The woman's face was implacable as she watched him. 'Can you see him?' he asked. Engage her. Try to keep her talking.

She nodded.

He shuddered, resisting the urged to turn round and look where she was looking. 'Tell me what he looks like.' Somehow he had to distract her, see if he could get round beyond her to the safety of the cliff wall. He took a small side step and then another. The ground was shaking with the roar of the falls.

'He's tall; tattooed with war paint.' She narrowed her eyes. She was staring at a point just behind him. In spite of himself Hugh felt a shiver of pure terror. 'He is very close to you,' she went on. Her tone was conversational now. She shifted her grip on the knife.

'Because he doesn't want me to die, Mrs Steadman,' Hugh stated. 'On the contrary. He is anxious to keep me alive. He needs me.'

He could hear someone coming. A branch cracked further up the hillside and he heard footsteps slipping on the scree, tripping over tree roots, pushing through the curtains of wet leaves. 'Down here!' he shouted suddenly.

She smiled. 'No one can save you.'

'Ma?' Steve's voice reached them over the sound of the water. 'Where are you?'

She looked up at that, surprised. 'Steve?' she called. 'You've come back!'

Steve slid the last few feet down the wet rockface and landed a few feet from Hugh, the dogs after him. He saw the knife in her hands and recoiled. 'Ma? Is that one of your Sabatier set? What are you doing?'

'The gods need blood.' She shrugged. 'Medb needs blood.'

'What rubbish!' Steve stepped towards her. She swung the knife towards him and he stopped.

'We're going to have a party.' She brushed some spray off her face. 'Venutios has to drink our health before he jumps.'

'Shit!' Steve glanced at Hugh desperately. 'A party sounds like fun, Ma,' he said cautiously. He looked round. She and Hugh were so close to the edge, if either slipped they would plunge into the falls. She was holding the knife in front of her with both hands. 'Take my bag, Steve.' She slid the strap over her head and dropped it on the ground. 'I've brought mead.'

Steve reached over and hesitantly he took the bag as the dogs cowered behind him, staring at her. He had never seen them behave like that before. 'Go on.' She nodded towards it.

He opened it and withdrew the small brown bottle and two plastic mugs. 'We have to drink a toast in mead,' she went on casually. 'Unscrew the bottle.' She watched him do it. The sweetness of honey and herbs was so strong he could smell it over the scent of the river and the wet ferns and moss all around them. 'First a libation.' She gestured with the knife. 'An offering to the goddess.'

He poured a small drop out over the edge of the path into the falls.

'Now, for you and Venutios.'

Steve glanced at Hugh desperately. 'The police are coming,' he mouthed. He doubted if Hugh could hear him against the roar of the waters. Hugh was moving very carefully along the rock towards her now, as Steve poured mead into the two mugs. His hands were shaking.

'Give him one.' She swung the knife towards Hugh. He froze.

Steve sniffed at the mug cautiously. 'Bloody hell, this smells pretty potent, Ma.' He glanced back at his mother.

She smiled. 'It is. A drink fit for the gods. An ancient recipe.'

He took a sip and then another. After the initial bitterness it was extremely good.

'Why don't you sit down, Steve. Here, on the rocks where it's safe. Then you can watch.' She had found a flat place high above the water. 'This is perfect. A moonlit tryst.' She was watching them both carefully. 'Drink!' She waved the knife at Hugh.

Hastily he took the mug from Steve.

'Don't touch it, Hugh.' The voice suddenly so close behind her took Peggy by surprise. She swung round. Meryn was standing on the path. He raised his hands in a gesture of openness. 'Mrs Steadman. The gods do not need a sacrifice. It is the wrong time.' His voice was strong.

'You dare to tell me what the gods want?' Peggy sneered. 'I don't know who you are, but this is none of your business! Drink it!' She was pointing the knife at Hugh again.

Hugh raised the mug to his lips. It smelled sweet, but then mead always was, with behind it a bitter herbal undertone. Even the aroma made him feel unsteady. He lowered the mug without tasting it, staring out across the falls, mesmerised by the thunder of water on the rocks below.

Peggy smiled. 'It's good, isn't it.' She turned to Steve.

Nodding, he took another sip.

Meryn glanced at Hugh. Venutios was standing immediately behind him. As Meryn watched, the two figures blended into one.

'Hugh!' Meryn stepped closer. 'Move away from the falls.'

Hugh didn't hear him. It was Venutios who shook his head. 'This woman wants to perpetuate Medb's spite. She has to die. She can be a sacrifice to the gods.' His voice blended with the thundering of the waters behind him.

Meryn edged closer. 'The gods forbid this! The omens are wrong!'

'Sacrifice?' Steve looked up. He took another sip from the mug.

Behind them the moonlight swirled in the spray.

'Venutios! I forbid this!' Meryn moved closer. His voice was for-midable against the roar of the falls.

Venutios held his gaze. 'Medb died with a curse on her lips. She made promises which need to be broken!'

'No. Listen to me! This is forbidden!' Meryn was very close to him now. 'This woman is not a suitable messenger. She is tainted.'

Peggy looked round at him. She seemed confused. The knife wavered in her hand. The moonlight on the water was dazzling. The moment had come and she was ready. With a smile she stepped towards the edge of the path.

V

Carta kissed Vellocatus on the forehead as he lay unconscious on their bed, covered with furs to keep him warm, then she walked out through the great gates in the rampart walls. Vivienne would help Vellocatus. She would save him in exchange for a sacrifice. She would make everything all right again. She ignored the war-riors who ran after her and the flames that rent the night sky to the north. She ignored the distant steady beat of a deerskin drum. Her eyes were fixed on the path at her feet. She had to reach the place of sacrifice.

'Come back, now! We have to close the gates!' Someone caught her arm. Someone else was forcing her to turn, dragging her back inside as the huge oak gates were swung closed and barred.

She stood staring round, dazed. The whole tribe were there, huddling in the shelter of the ramparts, hundreds of people, wide-eyed, afraid. With their livestock and as many of their belongings as they could carry, they had been streaming in from their small-holdings and farms in the dales and on the moors and deep in the forest, up the hill towards the fort since Venutios's army had been spied marching inexorably southwards towards them.

'Come back to Vellocatus, lady. He needs you.' Gruoch and her Druids were there inside the stockade too, though the Carvetii would never harm the Druid college or any of its members.

'Venutios is here!' The words, laden with fear, were spreading like wildfire around the fort.

'Set up the ghost fence. The spirits of our ancestors will save us,' Carta implored Gruoch.

The woman shook her head. 'Not possible. Our ancestors will not guard us against our own brothers and our sons. These are our own people, Carta. Venutios is one of us!'

Slowly Carta climbed the steps to the top of the ramparts and stood looking out across the fells towards the forest. In her head she would transfer herself into the form of a bird, an owl to fly silently over the trees in the darkness so that she could still reach the great falls, the place of sacrifice. In her vision she would oversee it all. Vivienne was waiting. The priestess of the falls was ready.

In her dream she flew through the curtains of birch and yew and juniper and the tangle of undergrowth gliding downwards, until she could hear the roar of the water; smell it; sense its clean invigorating excitement. Her sacrifice would be to the goddess, Vivienne, but also this time to Camulos, the god of war. All was ready. The ceremony planned, the victim chosen and waiting by the great hungry falls. When at last she folded her wings and came to rest, feeling the rock tremble beneath her talons, she could see Peggy clearly. She was sitting with Steve on the rocks, right on the edge of the drop. In the moonlight the spray shone like silver, lighting the whole scene. Steve was lolling backwards; she could see his mouth open; was he laughing or screaming? She couldn't hear because of the thunder of the waters.

Venutios was watching, and with him a Druid priest.

Peggy! Stop! Don't!

That was what she wanted to say.

The goddess, cold and implacable, stopped her.

She could hear the sound of a horn, the deep note reverberating above the roar of the water. The note of the carnyx.

She felt herself grow cold.

Her voice, when she spoke again to Pat and James on the dark limestone slabs, was her own.

'Venutios was there. He arrived at Dun Righ before she witnessed the sacrifice and she knew this time he would kill her. If the gods would not help her she had no alternative but to send for Gaius again,' she whispered. 'In her despair, without Vellocatus to help her, she sent for Gaius and in the depths of the fire she watched her messenger ride south.'

The Brigantian, well aware of his mistress's watching eyes, demanded to see Gaius with such urgency that the legionnaire in the outer office bade the muddy, ragged, unshaven man wait and he sent word to Gaius at once. He was in attendance on the Governor.

'Cartimandua bade me find you. She needs you and your men, Roman. Venutios is at her gate again and this time he means to kill her.'

Gaius frowned, tempted to turn the man away. One glance at the man behind the desk told him otherwise.

'As always she is our last chance to hold the north at bay, Gaius. Without her the whole northern frontier will be at Venutios's mercy. We cannot afford the distraction now of all times.'

Even so, they could not spare a legion. A wing was mustered at once from the garrison at Deva and marched into the teeth of the wind.

Carta ordered her army to attack Venutios at dawn. It poured out of the gates, the men holding their banners before them to drive him from her walls.

She watched them go, then she withdrew to the royal house to sit with Vellocatus. His wound had turned black. The strongest herbs could not mask the smell of the putrid flesh as he lay tossing and turning with fever.

Gruoch and her Druidesses redressed the wound as best they could. Only the gods could save him now.

As the battle raged on the distant fells, only a handful of men remained to guard the fort and the women and children who remained there, and half of them secretly welcomed the coming of Venutios. Whilst Carta sat weeping at her husband's side the great gate opened a crack. Into the darkness of the compound a band of Carvetian warriors, a file of shadowy figures in the darkness, crept into the heart of the township. No one saw them come. No one opposed them until with shouts and yells of triumph they raced between the houses, brandishing their swords. Two of Carta's guards were cut down where they stood and the night sky flared as burning torches were tossed onto the heather roofs of the houses.

Carta did not move. If she heard anything she gave no sign, holding Vellocatus's hand. 'Soon you will be better, my love!' She sponged his forehead gently. 'I will make everything all right. Do not fear.'

The screams and shouts outside grew louder and now she could smell the burning as Gruoch ran into the room. 'My queen, the house is on fire. You must come. We'll move Vellocatus. You can't stay here.'

'You can't move him.' Carta stood up. 'It would kill him.'

'It will kill him if he stays!' Gruoch pursed her lips. 'You will die, my queen!' Gruoch was desperate.

'Leave me. The gods will protect us.' Wisps of burning heather blew in through the doorway. The roof was sodden from all the rain but in places the fire, fed by the pitch on the burning torches, was taking hold. They could hear the crackling above their heads.

'I will fetch men with a stretcher for him!' Gruoch whirled round and disappeared through the doorway.

'Such a fuss, sweetheart!' Carta knelt beside the bed.

Vellocatus reached up to her and touched her face. 'Go,' he whispered. 'Leave me. I'm dying anyway. Please go.'

'I would never leave you!' She bent to kiss him as Gruoch re-appeared in the doorway. Behind her strode three Roman soldiers. They had defied all the odds to reach Brigantia in time. 'There. He's there.' Gruoch gestured at the bed. 'Please save him.'

Two of the men carried a litter. The third was Gaius. 'Out, now.' He seized Carta's wrist. 'My men will bring your husband!'

He pulled her to her feet as a clump of burning heather dropped almost on top of them. There was a roar as the roof went up. 'Now!' Somehow he had her in his arms and ran with her out of the entrance, into the open air. Behind them the two men had thrown Vellocatus onto the litter. They had barely managed to emerge as the roof collapsed. All around them the Romans were fighting and the Carvetian warriors had fallen back. A few of them were running for the gate. Others were being hacked to pieces where they stood. The men with the litter ran with it towards the guest house near the wall, which was untouched by fire. As they carried Vellocatus inside, Gaius followed with Carta still in his arms. Only when they were inside did he set her down. Behind them two soldiers stood guard at the doorway.

'Vellocatus!' Carta flung herself down beside the litter which had been put down on the floor. 'Sweetheart, are you all right?' He did not answer. 'Vellocatus?' Her voice broke. The hand which had been hot with fever was ice cold. 'My love. My life.' She bent to kiss his forehead.

Gaius stood back with a sigh. He folded his arms. Behind him one of his men approached and saluted. 'They've gone. The fort is secure, sir. They thought there were more of us than there are.' He gave a grim smile.

Gaius nodded. 'You did well. Leave us now. I fear the king is dead.'

The man glanced at the man on the floor and the weeping woman and nodding, he withdrew.

'The goddess will save him.' Carta looked up at Gaius and smiled through her tears. 'He's only asleep.' She bent to Vellocatus again, her lips brushing his forehead. Suddenly she caught sight of the brooch on his mantle and with an exclamation of disgust she tore it off. Climbing to her feet, she ran outside and hurled it into the burning ruins of the round house. For a moment she stood watching as the walls of the building collapsed over it. When she returned she paused in the doorway as though seeing Gaius properly for the first time. 'Why are you here?'

'I came as you asked, Great Queen.' He frowned. Strangely she had never looked more beautiful to him in spite of her dishevelled gown, her soot-stained face, the tears. Great Queen. The words were ironic in the shambles of the burned-out fort with the roar of battle only some half-mile away.

'He will be all right?' 'She seemed completely disorientated as she stared down at the dead man on the litter at their feet. 'Look.' She put her hand into the fold of her cloak and pulled out a small golden knife. 'The sacrifice is being carried out as we speak.' She smiled again. 'A life for a life. The gods will spare Vellocatus if they receive another in his place.' She raised the knife as though about to stab the empty air.

Gaius found himself shuddering. Catching her wrist, he forced the knife out of her hand. 'Vellocatus is dead,' he said softly. 'It is too late.'

She stared at him. 'No. He sleeps. The goddess is going to spare him. She has promised . . .' She looked bewildered.

'Your goddess does not want more sacrifice.' He tucked the knife into his belt. 'Human sacrifice is banned under the Empire. Surely you know that?' He had seen no sign of the intended victim. 'Surely enough men have died today to satisfy even one of your blood-thirsty gods!'

'We are not part of the Empire.' She managed a reproof through the tears. 'Our gods are still strong, Gaius Flavius Cerialis, and I need to send them a messenger. Someone who will go willingly. You have my knife, but it doesn't matter. Someone else will sacrifice for me, tonight.'

Standing away from him, she raised her arms and threw back her head.

Vivienne!

Gaius quailed at her scream.

Vivienne, take the sacrifice I send you and give me back my love!

By the falls, Peggy stood up and held out the knife. The blade shone silver in the moonlight.

Steve was staring at her and he giggled. 'You look mag-nis-i-fent! Have some!' He waved the plastic mug towards her, spilling drops of mead across the rocks. None of them noticed the owl on the branch of the yew tree nearby, watching the scene with unblinking eyes.

Vivienne!

Did anyone else hear that desperate scream? Meryn frowned. He could see Venutios clearly; see him smiling. He was between the falls and Medb, silhouetted against the flash of white foam from the water below the path, and the moonlight on the spindrift.

Gaius touched Cartimandua's shoulder gently. 'You must collect any belongings that can be salvaged and summon your companions. It is not safe for you here. You are completely unprotected. There are other war bands in the area. We can't hold them off for long. Not this time.' He stepped back to allow her to leave the house in front of him. When she didn't move he put out a hand, and then an arm around her shoulder. 'Say goodbye to him, then come. We have to leave. We will send Vellocatus to the gods before we go.'

She shook her head. 'My warriors will return.'

'Your warriors have been wiped out, Carta.' His voice was gentle. 'There is nothing for you here. Venutios has won for now.'

'No. My people will support me.'

He grimaced. As far as he could see her people had gone. Even the Druidesses had fled as his soldiers searched the township for remnants of the Carvetian attackers. The Governor was going to be furious. The last bastion of the client kingdom had gone with her influence. Now there would be open war with Venutios all along the northern borders.

'I must take you somewhere safe, Carta. I'm sorry. You cannot stay.' He shook his head, desperately sorry for her. 'This is the end. You are no longer queen.'

VI

Viv stirred. She frowned. It was cold and dark. The moon had disappeared. Pat was sitting on the cold stone slabs near her; beside her stood an elderly man. 'What's happened? Why are we here?' Viv scrambled to her feet. 'I have to go! I have to stop her!' Someone had put a coat round her shoulders and she tore it off, throwing it onto the ground.

'Viv! Wait!' Pat grabbed at her but Viv had gone, scrambling over the rocks into the darkness. Not knowing where she was going she pushed through trees and shrubs, slid down through the mud and over rocks and stones, feeling brambles tearing at her arms and legs, drawn by the sound of water. As she reached the top of the falls the moon broke through the cloud and as the darkness drew back, she saw the figures on the path below her.

Steve was sitting on the edge of the path, one leg hanging over the edge of the rocks above the thundering water. He was swaying slightly, smiling, the empty beaker dangling from one hand.

'Peggy?' She heard the tall man standing near him call out. 'Can you hear me? Stay there. Don't move.' Peggy was standing on the very edge of the path, her arm outstretched. The blade of the knife in her hand caught the moonlight, a silver flash in the darkness. Viv gasped. This was her fault! She had created this scene in her dream. She looked desperately from one to the other as the stranger stepped closer to Peggy. 'Do you want your son to die, Peggy? Listen to me!' He was only a couple of feet from her now. 'Put down the knife and tell him to move away from the edge. This is not what the goddess wants!'

Hugh was there, not far from Steve, his clothes drenched by the spray. Except it wasn't Hugh. It was Venutios. She could see his tunic, the fur cloak, the necklace of bears' teeth around his neck. And suddenly she knew who this stranger was. This was Meryn. This was a Druid.

Moving forward, she stepped into the moonlight near them. 'Medb!' she screamed. 'Venutios! This man is a Druid! You have to obey him! He speaks with the gods!' She brushed the hair out of her eyes, leaving a streak of blood from the bramble scratches across her face.

Hugh stared at her. 'Cartimandua?' She couldn't hear him. The roar of the falls drowned out every sound.

Meryn moved another step towards Hugh. Viv could see his swirling cloak of sacred Druidic feathers, the staff in his fist as he raised both hands in a wild invocation and for a moment she quailed.

'The goddess does not want more blood!' he called. 'Venutios! Leave this man. Go now. I have battled with stronger men than you and won. You will obey me! Your people need you in another world. You have no place here. Medb has no place here. Nor Cartimandua.' He swung and faced Viv, holding her with his piercing

543

gaze. 'It is over. Your story is told! In the name of all the gods – go!' His words rang off the rocks around them. Viv felt the power of his gaze as a physical blow in her solar plexus. He was holding them all in the web of power between his upraised hands.

Viv gazed at Hugh. She was seeing double. She saw a shadow detach from his body. For a moment the figure of Venutios stood beside him, completely separate. She saw his face clearly, his tattoos, saw him lift his hand in her direction and with a sudden shock she felt her eyes fill with tears.

'Venutios!' It was Cartimandua who let out the wailing cry of farewell. Sadness and regret engulfed her. Then Venutios was gone.

Viv knew that Cartimandua too had left at last as she raised her head, aware that Hugh had put his arms around her. She stared at Meryn. 'You sent them away. I saw you! Your cloak of feathers! Your staff!' He was wearing an old checked shirt and jeans.

He smiled. 'What Hugh calls hocus pocus.'

Hugh gave a wry grin. 'I will never doubt you again.'

Viv glanced up at him. They were both in a state of shock. 'Venutios?'

'Has gone.'

'Are you sure?' She could see nothing for her tears. 'Will he come back?'

Hugh shook his head. His arms tightened around her as he glanced at Meryn for confirmation. 'We know his story now. We know what Medb did to him and we know he killed her for it. We know,' he paused, 'that he loved Cartimandua. He fought her, would perhaps have killed her too, but he loved her. He wanted the story known.'

'Just as she did.'

'Just as she did.' Hugh was still holding her tightly.

'So, it's all over?'

'It's all over.'

Behind them Medb laughed. 'So touching! And so pointless! Nothing will change history. Everyone will remember you as a traitor and a fool.' She was looking straight at Viv. Stepping closer to her, she raised her hand, pointing the knife straight at Viv's heart.

Pushing Viv behind him, Hugh threw himself forward, frantically trying to fend Peggy off, but Meryn was already between them. The Druid's staff once more in his hand, he pointed it straight at Peggy's chest. 'Cease your evil now!' His gaze made her recoil. 'In the name of the goddesses of these lands and by the power of these sacred waters I command you, Medb, to leave this woman, Peggy, and to return to the lands of the ever dead.'

Medb gasped. A silver wraith drifted for a moment around Peggy's shoulders. It was fading. Viv saw white fingers trail across the knife in Peggy's hand. Then Medb too was gone.

Bored, Steve shifted his position as he sat by the path. Completely unaware of what was happening around him, he leaned forward slightly to look down over the edge of the rocks and grinned up at the moonlight. 'It's beautiful, down there,' he said clearly. 'I'm going to fly down.'

'Steve. No!' Meryn's voice was a roar above the water.

Peggy turned and looked at her son. 'Steve? What are you doing? You're too near the edge!' She seemed aware for the first time of his danger. The knife was still in her hand.

'Throw the knife into the falls, Peggy. Give it to the goddess,' Meryn commanded.

There was a long silence. Peggy lowered her arm and stared at the knife.

'Throw it into the falls,' Meryn called again. 'Give it to the waters. Now!'

Peggy nodded. She hesitated for one more second, then raising it she held it for a moment in the moonlight. 'Blessed lady of the falls,' she called. 'To you I give the greatest sacrifice of all.'

For a fraction of a second the silvered blade hovered over Steve's head.

'Steve! No –!'

Viv was screaming as Meryn threw himself towards Peggy, reaching desperately for the knife, but it was too late. She plunged it into the side of Steve's throat as he sat gazing up at her in surprise.

'Ma?'

He was slipping outwards over the edge of the rock, a trail of scarlet droplets oozing down his shirt. As Meryn's hand snatched at Peggy's wrist, Steve half rose to his feet, his hand clasped to his neck as he lost his balance and began to fall.

'Steve!' Hugh lunged forward. With a supreme effort he managed to catch the young man's arm. For a moment the two men swayed to and fro on the edge of the ravine, then with a desperate heave Hugh dragged him back and half pushed, half threw him into the bushes behind them.

Peggy stared down at her son, puzzled, then staggered towards him as he lay sprawled at her feet in the wet grass.

'Leave him alone. You're insane –' Hugh tried to push her away, but he was off balance and she was too strong for him.

'Steve? You have to go, sweetheart!' Stooping, she snatched at the knife handle which protruded from Steve's shirt above his collar bone.

'Leave it! You'll kill him if you pull it out . . . !' Hugh's words faded helplessly on his lips as Peggy wrenched out the blade and blood fountained out of the wound, drenching the ground. With a little gasp, Steve fell back.

Peggy looked round soberly. 'I salute you, Professor. And you, great Druid!' She glanced at Meryn. She was herself again. 'But there was nothing to be done. The goddess needed her sacrifice as she still needs her messenger.' She raised her hand towards Steve's body and blew him a kiss, then turning, the knife still clutched in her hand, she leaped out into the falls.

VII

Hugh knelt down beside Steve and pressed two fingers gently to his neck, feeling for a pulse through the stickiness of the blood. He slumped beside the young man and took a deep breath, shaking his head. 'He's gone.'

'No!' Viv threw herself down beside him. 'No, please! Can't we try the kiss of life? Something?' Tears were pouring down her face as behind them the falls roared on, oblivious to the tragedy in which they had played such a part.

'I'm afraid it's no use,' Meryn answered her gently. 'I saw his spirit leave.' He stooped over Steve and closing the young man's eyes, carefully straightened his head, resting it gently on the mossy bank behind him as the two dogs crept closer, huddling against his body.

Hugh looked up at Meryn. He was white with shock. 'And Peggy?' His voice was husky.

Meryn shook his head. 'They are both gone.'

Sobbing, Viv flung herself into Hugh's arms, her face buried in his shoulder, her fingers clinging to his wet shirt. 'How could she? She loved him!'

Hugh closed his eyes, burying his face in her hair. She could feel him trembling as he held her. He seemed incapable of speech.

Wearily, Meryn moved across to the rock where Steve had been sitting only seconds before and he stood, staring down into the churning waters. There was no sign of Peggy in the darkness and the misted spray below him.

The blue plastic mug out of which Steve had been drinking had lodged in a crack of rock, half hidden by ferns. With a sigh he stooped and retrieved it. In this world of rules and law and forensics the sticky residue in the bottom would no doubt be evidence as so much of what had occurred here would not. As far as the police were concerned, this case would be straightforward. Peggy, pushed over the edge of sanity, had killed her husband and, unable to deal with what she had done, had murdered her son and then committed suicide. The coroner would not hear about Venutios or Medb or Cartimandua. He would never know that these deaths were part of a chain of events stretching back nearly two thousand years.

Turning with another deep sigh, he walked back to Hugh and Viv, glancing beyond them to see two figures appearing in the distance. Pat and James had come the long way round by the path. James had a torch in his hand.

'Are you all right?' James called as they approached. He hurried ahead of Pat. 'The police are on their way.' We saw their Land Rovers at the end of the track. They're on their way to take us all back to the farm.' He stopped abruptly, looking down at Steve. 'What's happened?'

'I'm afraid we've had a double tragedy,' Meryn said gently.

James held his gaze for a moment, then he moved forward and stiffly knelt at Steve's side. Putting his hand over Steve's cold fingers, he began to pray quietly as Pat hurried up behind him.

'Steve?'

Viv moved away from Hugh. She was still crying. 'Peggy stabbed him. He's dead!' Her voice broke in anguish.

Pat's mouth fell open. 'Jesus!' she breathed. 'Oh God! Poor Steve!'

'This is all my fault!' Viv cried suddenly. 'If I hadn't come to the farm! If I hadn't written the stupid book!' Her voice slid up hysterically.

'No.' Meryn put his hands on her shoulders and held her firmly, forcing her to look at him. 'You must never let yourself think that. Not for a moment. You three have been used. You were catalysts. If there is fault, and perhaps destiny is a better word, then it was the destiny of all of us, myself included, to be part of this drama tonight.'

Somewhere above them they could hear a helicopter in the distance, the beat of its rotors echoing from the rocks as it hovered above the hillside.

Help was on its way.

It was nearly four in the morning before the exhausted group of survivors sat down around the kitchen table at Winter Gill. Gordon's and Steve's bodies had been taken away and Peggy's retrieved from the river, and the police had gone at last. Meryn took the head of the table as Hugh threw himself into the chair next to Viv. Beyond them Pat and James sat glumly opposite one another, too tired even to speak. The two dogs were huddled together beside Meryn's chair.

Meryn gave them each a long steady look across the table. 'I want you all to understand that there were forces involved here tonight which no one could fight. Stories which had assumed such an impetus that nothing could stop them being told. These deaths have been the cataclysmic result of two millennia of emotions which had never been resolved. Nothing that we could do would have stopped them. We all have our weaknesses and maybe we need each of us to acknowledge that they may have played a part in all this, but it's done now. Finished.'

There was a long silence. Finally, Viv cleared her throat. 'I don't know about you, but I don't feel I could ever sleep again.' Tears spilled over suddenly and she dashed them away miserably. 'The police have gone away thinking this is all some sort of horrifying "domestic" which got out of hand. We know better. For Steve's sake we must make sure it's over.' Her voice cracked into a sob. 'Are we sure that the story has been told?'

'We can be sure.' Meryn nodded. 'We know the truth. The protagonists can rest in peace. The gods have had their last sacrifice.'

Pat was turning a cigarette packet round and round in her fingers. 'So, how does it finish? We know about Venutios and Medb's curse.

We know about Vellocatus. We know why Cartimandua supported the Romans. What else happened?'

'Gaius!' Viv whispered slowly. 'He was too late! Then he took Carta away from her people.' She fell silent. It was as though she could hear his voice in the distance.

'I saved Cartimandua! If Venutios had captured her, she would have died! My men and I took her over the pack horse trails to Deva after the king's dun fell to Venutios. As did all the other hill forts and townships one by one. He took back the whole of Brigantia.' He paused. 'Then he declared war on Rome.

'She had a good life, though. The governor at Deva took her into his own villa. She was given a suite of rooms, slaves, all the Roman luxuries she had loved so much and more she had never dreamed of: hot showers, central heating. The Romans were grateful for all she did for them over the years. They did not forget.'

But then nor did history. As the echo faded, Viv looked down at the table with a sigh. To historians Cartimandua would always be a quisling – the Celtic queen who sold out to the Romans.

Pat groped in the crumpled packet for her last cigarette and lit it with shaking hands. 'What happened to Venutios in the end?' she asked.

Viv gave a wry grimace. 'Somehow I know that too. He found the brooch in the smouldering ruins of Dun Righ and for a long time he thought Cartimandua was dead.' She shook her head. 'Mairghread told him the truth. She had gone with Cartimandua to Deva but she couldn't bring herself to stay in a Roman household and she went back to Brigantia. Venutios gave her a home.' She paused sadly. 'We know from history that the Romans defeated him in the end. In a great battle near Stanwick. Even the ghost fence didn't save him. It was all pointless.'

'Was he killed?'

Viv shrugged. 'I expect so.' She glanced up at Hugh. 'Perhaps the answer to that one will be in your book.'

'I doubt it. There won't be any guessing in my book.' He looked mortified as soon as the words were out of his mouth. 'I'm sorry. That came out wrong . . .'

'Did it?' She raised an eyebrow. 'I shall expect you to send me a copy, then I can read your conclusions.'

Hugh stared at her. 'I won't need to send it, Viv. I shall give it to you myself.'

'Not if I accept the post they've offered me in Ireland.'

There was a long silence. Viv was aware of everyone's eyes fixed on her face. 'Better money. Supportive team, so I'm assured. Far away from all this.' She shrugged miserably.

'Viv, please. We have to talk about this.' Hugh reached over and took her hands in his. 'You can't go. Not after everything that has happened. I need you. I can't live without you.'

She looked up at him and for a moment they held one another's gaze. Slowly she smiled. 'That's one I'll have to think about.'

Pat cleared her throat. 'Perhaps this is a good moment to change the subject.' She reached into her pocket and pulled out a small plastic box. 'I'd forgotten in all the awful mess of what's happened. What do you want to do with this?'

They all stared at it as she put it down in the middle of the table.

'Where did you find that?' Viv asked huskily.

'Where you told me to look.'

No one touched it.

'I wonder how it finally ended up at Stanwick,' Hugh said slowly at last.

Viv shrugged. 'Venutios took it there.' She wasn't sure how she knew this any more than all the other certainties which were in her head. 'He and Mairghread buried it there with all its evil and no one touched it for nearly two thousand years.'

'Till Wheeler and my father came along.' Hugh grimaced. He gave a wry, humourless laugh.

'Are we ever going to tell this story now? Or are we going to be the only ones who know what happened?' Pat asked at last. Her voice was flat.

'I think you should. Don't let the Steadmans have died in vain,' James put in. He glanced at Meryn. 'You owe it to them. Steve, I feel sure, would want the truth told. Perhaps you could dedicate your play to his memory.' He paused. 'As for this,' he reached forward and held his hand for a moment over the box, 'I think it should be destroyed.'

Meryn smiled enigmatically. Taking off the lid, he lifted the brooch out of its box and examined it closely. 'I will cleanse it of

Medb's curse and we will ask James to bless it. A double whammy like that should sort it out.' He nodded gravely. 'Then we will return it to its owner.' He looked at Hugh. 'Personally I agree with James. It should be disposed of. I would toss it into the falls, but I suspect the historian in you will want to see it put back behind glass. If so, I suggest it remains there for good.' He paused. 'We have seen terrible tragedy here tonight. Not because anyone was malicious or culpable or careless but because you were all involved in a tangled passionate story from long, long ago, all linked by one thing. You all touched this brooch. For all your sakes, that involvement must end now. Peggy and Gordon and Steve were drawn in by the land on which they lived; by the gods whom they encountered here. In my view, Viv, you and Pat should write your play to bring this all finally to an end. But no more consultations with the leading characters. Let them rest in peace. They have gone. Just use the material you have already.'

There was a long silence, broken at last as Hugh cleared his throat. 'So, no orthodox research at all, then,' he said wryly. 'Just what we in the trade call counter-factual speculation.' He sighed. 'Well, maybe in the long run it makes history just that bit more interesting!'

'There is one thing we don't know yet,' Pat interrupted. She was very pale with dark rings under her eyes, utterly exhausted. 'What happened to Carta in the end?'

'I don't think I want to know,' Viv put in hastily. 'Let's leave it there. Please. I agree with Meryn. Enough is enough. No more research.'

'Until the next book,' Hugh put in.

'And the play. We're still a team, right?' Pat added quietly. 'The Daughters of Fire will write again. Won't they?'

VIII

A week later Viv had another dream.

Cartimandua, white-haired now, was sitting by a fountain in a small courtyard. There were pots of lavender and rosemary near her and a brace of puppies were playing in the sun. A slave had brought her a letter and carefully she broke the seal and unrolled it. It was written in the secret script of the Druids. She frowned. It was a long time since she had deciphered such letters.

> To the Lady Cartimandua
> Extensive enquiries have been made as to the whereabouts of your daughter and at last she has been found. She was taken as a babe to Iou, the island of Druids, off the lands of the Caledones in the ocean where the sun sets, and is now a senior student in the college there, far beyond the reach of Rome. She is well and content and much praised for her skills as a poet and a healer. And she has her mother's way with horses.
> from Gruoch the Druidess
> Hail, blessing and farewell

Carta put down the letter and smiled.

Thank you, Vivienne, she whispered. Blessed goddess, thank you!

Postscript

Heather had finished watering her cheese plant and was turning towards the gurgling coffee machine when the door opened and Viv came into the office, her hair on end from the wind.

'Hi, Viv. Coffee? Your students haven't arrived yet. You've got time.' Heather reached for a couple of mugs from the tray as Viv dropped her bag of books on the floor in a patch of sunlight, unwound her scarf and pulled off her jacket. 'The Prof's already in,' Heather added. 'Just a few minutes ago, in fact.' She raised an eyebrow.

Viv smiled. 'All right, so we drove in together.' She knew it had been pointless hanging back so they would arrive separately. Heather's eagle eye missed nothing.

'From Aberlady?'

'Yes, from Aberlady.'

'You spent the weekend there?'

'If it's any of your business.'

'Of course it's my business.' Heather handed over the mug – a reward for honesty so far. 'So?'

Viv shrugged. 'So. We were working on the timetables.'

'Rubbish. I did the timetables.'

Viv shrugged again. 'You got me there!'

'So, what did you do?'

'If you must know we drove out to see Hugh's friend, Meryn.' Viv paused. 'He took the Steadmans' dogs home with him, Heather. They attached themselves to him, wouldn't let him out of their sight and Steve's brother has said he can keep them. As working dogs they might have been put down otherwise. It was fantastic to see them racing around on the mountain. They seemed so happy.'

Both women were silent for a moment, thinking of the horrors of the past three months: the police and then the coroner's enquiries, the publicity, the anger and disbelief of Steve's brother and sister and finally, their painful decision to sell the farm.

It hadn't been easy trying to put it all behind them. Of course it hadn't been easy. Looking back over these last months, Viv thought of the times she and Hugh had visited Meryn, listening to his patient gentle reassurance, both of them wearing always now the silver amulets he had given them.

She smiled at the memory of Hugh at first uncomfortably tucking his under his shirt, now used to it and displaying it in a distinctly rakish manner round his neck. In fact the new Hugh was distinctly rakish all round, a huge improvement, noticed and approved by the whole department.

They hadn't stopped quarrelling. In fact, the first time they had made love had been after yet another quarrel. She smiled to herself again, remembering the evening so clearly. They had been to the museum to look at the new display, in the centre of which, on a chunk of carved black bog oak, itself dating from the Iron Age, on a bed of clean, raked sand, lay the crane's head brooch. They had stood side by side, staring at it in silence.

'It's exquisite, isn't it,' she had said at last.

He nodded. 'Perhaps I'll borrow it again when *Venutios, Hero of the North* is published.'

Viv stared at him. 'You are joking!'

He shrugged. 'It's been disinfected and blessed. What harm could it do?'

'What harm?' Viv rounded on him. 'Have you learned nothing?'

He hadn't been serious, of course, but she hadn't seen it. Storming out of the gallery and out of the museum she had allowed her anger full rein.

He had followed her down Chambers Street. Followed her home. Followed her up the stone stair to her flat, by now as angry as she was, and following her inside had slammed the door behind them. Then he had taken her in his arms and shortly afterwards, to bed. One thing was for sure, life would never be boring with Hugh.

If there was going to be a life with Hugh. It was too early to tell yet.

He had taken such tender care of her after the tragedies at Winter Gill. Reassured her, comforted her, held her in his arms, and latterly since they had been together, cradled her when she woke screaming from the nightmares that still haunted her. Cathy had said they would get better. So had Meryn. Cathy and Pete had liked Meryn hugely when they met. Cathy and he had talked for hours and between them they had brought Viv back almost to her normal self.

Behind her, Heather had seated herself at her computer and was gazing at Viv's back as she stared out of the window, lost in thought. 'You OK?'

Viv turned, smiling. 'Sorry. Miles away.'

'Thinking about the play?'

Viv shook her head. 'The play's finished. Out of our hands now.'

Meryn had insisted on that, helped them and taken an unexpected interest in the technicalities and the studio production. It would be broadcast in the New Year and the Daughters of Fire Production Company had been asked to produce another. About Boudica. Maddie had commissioned a documentary about the making of the play, too, which would include a certain amount about its unorthodox research. Viv gave a wry smile. Facing their demons and admitting in public some of what had happened was something they were all learning to do slowly. Pat had gone back to London once the play was finished and almost at once had been cast in a TV series, but she would come back soon to start work with Viv again and in the meantime there had been a flood of requests for Viv to write articles, give talks, go on lecture tours from people who knew her through the book and its attendant publicity. Life was very full.

Donald Grant had taken up the position of Reader as planned. She didn't resent him for it. She didn't have time. She hadn't been sacked either, of course, and for now she was content to stay. Very content. The job offer in Ireland had been very tempting but she had turned it down. Maybe in the future there would be other opportunities and she would consider one of them, but for now she wasn't ready to make any decisions of that sort. For the immediate future her life would be here in Edinburgh.

A small group of students headed out of George Square Gardens and across the road towards the department. It was time to go back to work.

'Sounds as though your students have arrived, Viv,' Heather said quietly as they heard the outside door bang and a sudden burst of talk and laughter in the hallway outside. Viv nodded. Later, after her tutorials, Hugh and she were meeting Stephanie and Bill

Steadman for lunch to discuss the plan to set up a research fellowship in Steve's name. No doubt they would all shed more tears, but she knew Steve would be there in spirit. Meryn had reassured her about that. He had laughed and shaken his head when she accused him of being the reincarnation of Artgenos, but he had persuaded them all, even Hugh, of the possibility of a cycle and circle of events which would, with the strength of knowledge, always be essentially optimistic.

That meant that however bitter the tears, there would always be laughter as well.

Postscript Two

Why ghosts?
Part of an address given by Meryn Jones to the annual meeting
of the Celtic Society

As some of you know, I have studied many philosophies, many
histories, many religions in this lifetime and in many others. Those
of you who have read my books know that I have assimilated
much from these sources, and also from my own meditations. Many
scholars and churchmen disagree with me. That is of course their
privilege. But for those who seek answers may I put forward this
small contribution to the understanding of some of the more
unusual phenomena which sometimes puzzle those to whom they
occur.

Like Hamlet, I believe there are more things in heaven and earth
than are dreamed of in our philosophies.

Like many religions of the world, I believe the soul goes on many
journeys through many lifetimes, in many forms. It is given choices
and it makes them. And it never dies. The ideal destination of the
Celtic soul is of course Tir n'an Og, the land of the Ever Young. The
Isle of the Blessed.

But, like the Celt, I also believe in a form of reincarnation. Some
believe, and I agree with them, that the soul, on occasions, splits
into three parts on death, one part to reincarnate, one to go to the
Blessed Isle and one part to enter another life form – perhaps a bird
or a shooting star. Others believe, and I agree with them, that
sometimes the entire soul returns to this Earth in a new body.
Others again believe, and I agree with them also, that the soul can
choose to return to this Earth as a spirit. As a ghost. Indeed sometimes this occurs inadvertently and the soul finds itself trapped on
this Earth.

The Celts believed passionately that one's ancestors stayed in touch. They consulted them much in the way that many eastern religions still do. They are told all the news. They are available for consultation and advice and have strong views on everything. This implies of course that sometimes the soul just stays somewhere on another plane, ready to be of service in this way, and that too I believe.

On top of these strands of belief we have an assumption that everything has spirit. Not just animals, but plants – trees – rocks – everything. To the modern and to the Christian mind this has up to now been an anathema, but particle physics would appear to be bringing some interesting new angles on this. This is valuable for people who need scientific reassurance for everything they believe for fear they may be considered flaky and New Age. The Celt believes the evidence of his own eyes, his own inner or second sight and his intuition.

The choices the soul makes can leave it unhappy. The life it has led may not have been full of glory. It may have ended in anger, sorrow, unfulfilment. Some will go for another crack of the whip in a new lifetime. But others haunt the scenes of their last life. And in doing so they can grow frustrated and angry because they find that people on the whole cannot see or hear them. If they find people who can and who welcome them, they will make use of them.

Most souls, like most people, gossip inconsequentially. They seize on things to say which they feel will reassure or convince. Hence some of the less than world-shaking comments that mediums so frequently relay.

But some souls have a huge agenda. And this is where danger can lie. The men and women who inadvertently allow them into their lives can find themselves drawn into events over which they have no control and which can put their lives and their sanity in danger.

Beware, my friends. Think carefully before you let a passing stranger inside your head. I have seen what happens if you do.

558

Chronology of the story
(Historical dates in bold)

| 69/70 | Cartimandua rescued by Rome. The last mention of her in the historical record. Venutios succeeds as king in his own right. |
| 71–73/4 | Quintus Petillius Cerialis Governor of Britannia. At some point during his governorship Venutios is defeated and disappears from history. |

Within 10 years the conquest of Wales and much of Northern Britain had been accomplished. It didn't last.

Author's Note

With each book I write I realise I am more and more indebted to people who give their enthusiastic time and advice. This story is no different. Amongst the many who helped me I should especially like to thank, first and foremost, Annie McBrearty for our brainstorming sessions up in Wester Ross when I was first planning the story. I must reiterate my assurances, as I do in every book, that no one and nothing in this book bears any resemblance to anywhere or anyone real – especially in this case, not to any other Department of Celtic Studies at Edinburgh University! Thank you to Mandy Morton and Jon Hope-Lewis for their technical advice and to Jo and Ian McDonald for their wonderful hospitality and for showing me Traprain in all its stunning stark beauty. To Peter Buneman for geographical updates. To the members of the Order of Bards, Ovates and Druids who have given me their wisdom and their friendship over the last few years and guided me on my own spiritual journey. To Nick Kerr and AJ Hope-Lewis who, when my visits to Ingleborough failed, in spite of prayers and propitiation, to produce a single ray of sunshine went and explored on a day the sun did come out, triumphantly videoed for me and phoned me from the top (yes, their mobile did work!) to answer my questions about the view! They did a stirling, energetic and enthusiastic job. To Lis Redfearn who introduced me to the wonders of Shiatsu and rescued my creaking body from the horrors of RSI. To Rachel Hore for her immense patience and clear thinking, to Carole Blake for her support and enthusiasm and Lucy Ferguson for her eagle eye for detail. And above all thanks to Pat Taylor who showed me round her beloved Yorkshire and for her untiring companionship and humour as we explored the moors and the dales, hunted down the ghosts and sought out the glamorous and fascinating settings for this book.

Just as I have taken liberties, I'm afraid, with the geography of Yorkshire, so I have with names for my characters from the annals of Wales and Ireland and Scotland. But then, unlike Viv, I make no claims to be an academic. In the absence of written information one has to make do with imagination, dreams and deductive techniques of however dubious a nature! Sadly the star of the story did not appear to me save in one or two wild and wonderful dreams, but I trust even that much contact meant I have her approval. I have tried to be as accurate as possible with period detail and historical fact, but then this is, by and large, pre-history and above all, it is fiction. This is the place to confess that there is, as far as I know, no connection between Cartimandua and Ingleborough recorded. We don't know her tribe, or if she had children, and although far more is known about her life than that of her much more famous contemporary, Boudica, she is still an enigma.

So, for all that is known historically about Cartimandua I refer the reader to the Roman historians.

For the truth of her life we must consult archaeology and the oracles.

The rest is silence.